# Harry Potter
AND THE HALF-BLOOD PRINCE

# J.K. ROWLING

6

英汉对照版

# Harry Potter

哈利·波特与"混血王子"[下]

〔英〕J.K. 罗琳／著
马爱农 马爱新／译

人民文学出版社
PEOPLE'S LITERATURE PUBLISHING HOUSE

## CHAPTER SIXTEEN

# A Very Frosty Christmas

'So Snape was offering to help him? He was definitely *offering to help him*?'

'If you ask that once more,' said Harry, 'I'm going to stick this sprout –'

'I'm only checking!' said Ron. They were standing alone at The Burrow's kitchen sink, peeling a mountain of sprouts for Mrs Weasley. Snow was drifting past the window in front of them.

'*Yes, Snape was offering to help him!*' said Harry. 'He said he'd promised Malfoy's mother to protect him, that he'd made an Unbreakable Oath or something –'

'An Unbreakable Vow?' said Ron, looking stunned. 'Nah, he can't have ... are you sure?'

'Yes, I'm sure,' said Harry. 'Why, what does it mean?'

'Well, you can't break an Unbreakable Vow ...'

'I'd worked that much out for myself, funnily enough. What happens if you break it, then?'

'You die,' said Ron simply. 'Fred and George tried to get me to make one when I was about five. I nearly did, too, I was holding hands with Fred and everything when Dad found us. He went mental,' said Ron, with a reminiscent gleam in his eyes. 'Only time I've ever seen Dad as angry as Mum. Fred reckons his left buttock has never been the same since.'

'Yeah, well, passing over Fred's left buttock –'

'I beg your pardon?' said Fred's voice as the twins entered the kitchen. 'Aaah, George, look at this. They're using knives and everything. Bless them.'

'I'll be seventeen in two and a bit months' time,' said Ron grumpily, 'and then I'll be able to do it by magic!'

## 第 16 章

## 冰霜圣诞节

"斯内普说要帮他？他真的说要帮他？"

"如果你再问一遍，"哈利说，"我就把这甘蓝塞到——"

"我只是核实一下！"罗恩说。他们站在陋居厨房的水池前，为韦斯莱夫人削小山似的一堆球芽甘蓝。雪花在他们前面的窗户外飘飘地飞舞。

"是，斯内普说要帮他！"哈利说，"他说答应过马尔福的妈妈要保护他，而且还立过一个牢不可破的誓言什么的——"

"牢不可破的誓言？"罗恩目瞪口呆，"不，他不可能……你确定？"

"是啊，我确定。"哈利说，"但是这意味着什么呢？"

"牢不可破的誓言是不能违背的……"

"这一点我自己也估计出来了，不瞒你说。那么，要是违背了会怎么样呢？"

"死。"罗恩简单地说，"我五岁的时候，弗雷德和乔治想让我立一个，我差点儿就立了，已经在跟弗雷德握手什么的，被爸爸发现了，他气疯了，"罗恩眼里闪动着回忆的光芒，"这是我唯一一次看到爸爸像妈妈那样发火。弗雷德说他左半边屁股从此不一样了。"

"好了，先不说弗雷德的左半边屁股——"

"说什么哪？"弗雷德的声音说，双胞胎兄弟走进了厨房。

"啊，乔治，看看，他们在用小刀呢。上帝保佑他们。"

"我还有两个月多一点就十七岁了，"罗恩暴躁地说，"到时候就能用魔法了！"

# CHAPTER SIXTEEN   A Very Frosty Christmas

'But meanwhile,' said George, sitting down at the kitchen table and putting his feet up on it, 'we can enjoy watching you demonstrate the correct use of a – whoops-a-daisy.'

'You made me do that!' said Ron angrily, sucking his cut thumb. 'You wait, when I'm seventeen –'

'I'm sure you'll dazzle us all with hitherto unsuspected magical skills,' yawned Fred.

'And speaking of hitherto unsuspected skills, Ronald,' said George, 'what is this we hear from Ginny about you and a young lady called – unless our information is faulty – Lavender Brown?'

Ron turned a little pink, but did not look displeased as he turned back to the sprouts.

'Mind your own business.'

'What a snappy retort,' said Fred. 'I really don't know how you think of them. No, what we wanted to know was … how did it happen?'

'What d'you mean?'

'Did she have an accident or something?'

'What?'

'Well, how did she sustain such extensive brain damage? Careful, now!'

Mrs Weasley entered the room just in time to see Ron throw the sprouts knife at Fred, who turned it into a paper aeroplane with one lazy flick of his wand.

'*Ron!*' she said furiously. 'Don't you ever let me see you throwing knives again!'

'I won't,' said Ron, 'let you see,' he added under his breath, as he turned back to the sprout mountain.

'Fred, George, I'm sorry, dears, but Remus is arriving tonight, so Bill will have to squeeze in with you two!'

'No problem,' said George.

'Then, as Charlie isn't coming home, that just leaves Harry and Ron in the attic, and if Fleur shares with Ginny –'

'– that'll make Ginny's Christmas –' muttered Fred.

'– everyone should be comfortable. Well, they'll have a bed, anyway,' said Mrs Weasley, sounding slightly harassed.

496

## 第16章　冰霜圣诞节

"但在此之前，"乔治说着坐到厨房桌前，把脚跷到了桌上，"我们可以欣赏一下你示范怎样正确使用——哎哟。"

"都是你害的！"罗恩恼火地说，一边吮着割破的拇指，"你等着，我满了十七岁——"

"我相信你会用迄今没人想到的魔法把我们镇住。"弗雷德打着哈欠说。

"说到迄今没人想到的魔法，罗恩，"乔治说，"我们听金妮说，你和一个小姑娘有情况，如果我们的情报没错的话，那小姑娘叫拉文德·布朗。这是怎么回事？"

罗恩有点脸红，转身削起了甘蓝，但似乎并没有不高兴。

"别多管闲事。"

"好刺人的回答，"弗雷德说，"真不知道你是怎么想的，我们想知道的是……怎么会呢？"

"什么意思？"

"那女孩是不是出了车祸什么的？"

"什么？"

"她怎么会这样大面积脑损伤啊？小心！"

韦斯莱夫人走进来时，刚好看到罗恩把削甘蓝的小刀向弗雷德掷了过去。弗雷德懒洋洋地一挥魔杖，把小刀变成了一架纸飞机。

"罗恩！"韦斯莱夫人勃然大怒，"别让我再看见你扔刀子！"

"我不会，"罗恩说，他回身转向甘蓝山时，小声加了一句："——让你看见的。"

"弗雷德，乔治，对不起，莱姆斯今天晚上来，比尔只能跟你们两个挤一挤了！"

"没问题。"乔治说。

"查理不回来，所以哈利和罗恩正好可以住阁楼，如果芙蓉跟金妮住——"

"——那金妮的圣诞节就——"弗雷德嘟囔道。

"——每个人应该都挺舒服。好吧，至少都有张床。"韦斯莱夫人

## CHAPTER SIXTEEN   A Very Frosty Christmas

'Percy definitely not showing his ugly face, then?' asked Fred.

Mrs Weasley turned away before she answered.

'No, he's busy, I expect, at the Ministry.'

'Or he's the world's biggest prat,' said Fred, as Mrs Weasley left the kitchen. 'One of the two. Well, let's get going, then, George.'

'What are you two up to?' asked Ron. 'Can't you help us with these sprouts? You could just use your wand and then we'll be free, too!'

'No, I don't think we can do that,' said Fred seriously. 'It's very character-building stuff, learning to peel sprouts without magic, makes you appreciate how difficult it is for Muggles and Squibs –'

'– and if you want people to help you, Ron,' added George, throwing the paper aeroplane at him, 'I wouldn't chuck knives at them. Just a little hint. We're off to the village, there's a very pretty girl working in the paper shop who thinks my card tricks are something marvellous ... almost like real magic ...'

'Gits,' said Ron darkly, watching Fred and George setting off across the snowy yard. 'Would've only taken them ten seconds and then we could've gone, too.'

'I couldn't,' said Harry. 'I promised Dumbledore I wouldn't wander off while I'm staying here.'

'Oh, yeah,' said Ron. He peeled a few more sprouts and then said, 'Are you going to tell Dumbledore what you heard Snape and Malfoy saying to each other?'

'Yep,' said Harry. 'I'm going to tell anyone who can put a stop to it and Dumbledore's top of the list. I might have another word with your dad, too.'

'Pity you didn't hear what Malfoy's actually doing, though.'

'I couldn't have done, could I? That was the whole point, he was refusing to tell Snape.'

There was silence for a moment or two, then Ron said, 'Course, you know what they'll all say? Dad and Dumbledore and all of them? They'll say Snape isn't really trying to help Malfoy, he was just trying to find out what Malfoy's up to.'

'They didn't hear him,' said Harry flatly. 'No one's that good an actor, not even Snape.'

'Yeah ... I'm just saying, though,' said Ron.

## 第16章 冰霜圣诞节

的语气有些烦躁。

"珀西那张丑脸肯定不会出现吧？"弗雷德问。

韦斯莱夫人转过身去，然后答道：

"不会，我想他忙着呢，在部里。"

"或者他是世界上最大的蠢货，"韦斯莱夫人离开厨房时弗雷德说，"二者必居其一。我们走吧，乔治。"

"你们干什么去？"罗恩问，"不能帮我们削甘蓝吗？你们可以用一下魔杖，我们就解放了。"

"我想不能，"弗雷德一本正经地说，"这是非常磨炼性格的，学习不用魔法削甘蓝，能让你体会到麻瓜和哑炮是多么不容易——"

"——如果你想求人帮忙，罗恩，"乔治接着说，一边把纸飞机掷回给他，"就不会朝他们扔刀子。一点儿忠告。我们到村里去，那儿的纸店有个很漂亮的女孩，她觉得我的纸牌戏法神奇极了，简直像真正的魔法……"

"饭桶，"罗恩阴沉地说，看着弗雷德和乔治从落满积雪的院子里走了出去，"他们只要花十秒钟，我们俩就也能去了。"

"我不行，"哈利说，"我向邓布利多保证过在这儿不会跑出去。"

"哦，对了。"罗恩又削了几个甘蓝，然后说，"你要把斯内普和马尔福的对话告诉邓布利多吗？"

"嗯，我要告诉所有能制止他们的人，邓布利多是第一位。我也许还要跟你爸爸谈谈。"

"可惜你没听到马尔福到底在干什么。"

"我没法听到，是不是？这是最关键的，他都不肯告诉斯内普。"

沉默了一会儿，罗恩说："当然，你知道他们会怎么说。我爸爸、邓布利多和所有的人，他们会说斯内普不是真的想帮助马尔福，只是为了探出马尔福在干什么。"

"他们没听到他的口气，"哈利断然说道，"没人能演得那么像，即使是斯内普。"

"是啊……我只是说说。"罗恩说。

## CHAPTER SIXTEEN    A Very Frosty Christmas

Harry turned to face him, frowning.

'You think I'm right, though?'

'Yeah, I do!' said Ron hastily. 'Seriously, I do! But they're all convinced Snape's in the Order, aren't they?'

Harry said nothing. It had already occurred to him that this would be the most likely objection to his new evidence; he could hear Hermione now:

'*Obviously, Harry, he was pretending to offer help so he could trick Malfoy into telling him what he's doing ...*'

This was pure imagination, however, as he had had no opportunity to tell Hermione what he had overheard. She had disappeared from Slughorn's party before he returned to it, or so he had been informed by an irate McLaggen, and she had already gone to bed by the time he returned to the common room. As he and Ron had left for The Burrow early the next day, he had barely had time to wish her a Happy Christmas and to tell her that he had some very important news when they got back from the holidays. He was not entirely sure that she had heard him, though; Ron and Lavender had been saying a thoroughly non-verbal goodbye just behind him at the time.

Still, even Hermione would not be able to deny one thing: Malfoy was definitely up to something, and Snape knew it, so Harry felt fully justified in saying 'I told you so', which he had done several times to Ron already.

Harry did not get the chance to speak to Mr Weasley, who was working very long hours at the Ministry, until Christmas Eve night. The Weasleys and their guests were sitting in the living room, which Ginny had decorated so lavishly that it was rather like sitting in a paper-chain explosion. Fred, George, Harry and Ron were the only ones who knew that the angel on top of the tree was actually a garden gnome that had bitten Fred on the ankle as he pulled up carrots for Christmas dinner. Stupefied, painted gold, stuffed into a miniature tutu and with small wings glued to its back, it glowered down at them all, the ugliest angel Harry had ever seen, with a large bald head like a potato and rather hairy feet.

They were all supposed to be listening to a Christmas broadcast by Mrs Weasley's favourite singer, Celestina Warbeck, whose voice was warbling out of the large wooden wireless. Fleur, who seemed to find Celestina very dull, was talking so loudly in the corner that a scowling Mrs Weasley kept pointing her wand at the volume control, so that Celestina grew louder and louder. Under cover of a particularly jazzy number called 'A Cauldron Full

## 第16章 冰霜圣诞节

哈利转身看着他，皱起了眉头。

"你相信我吧？"

"我相信！"罗恩忙说，"真的，我相信！可是他们都相信斯内普是凤凰社的，对不对？"

哈利没说话，他已经想到这将是他的新证据最有可能遭到的反驳。他甚至都能听见赫敏在说：

"显然，哈利，他是在假装帮忙，骗马尔福对他说实话……"

但这只是想象，因为他还没找到机会跟赫敏说他听到的事情。他回去之前赫敏就从斯拉格霍恩的晚会上消失了，至少气愤的麦克拉根是这么说的。等哈利回到公共休息室，她已经睡觉去了。他第二天一大早就跟罗恩出发到陋居来了，只来得及祝她一句圣诞快乐，并说放假回来后有非常重要的消息告诉她。但他不太确定赫敏有没有听见，罗恩和拉文德正在他后面用不说话的方式进行告别。

但是，就连赫敏也无法否认一个事实：马尔福肯定在干着什么勾当，并且斯内普是知情的。所以哈利觉得有充分理由说"我告诉过你"，这句话他已经跟罗恩说了好几遍。

哈利没找到机会跟韦斯莱先生谈，他每天都在部里工作到很晚，直到圣诞节前一天。韦斯莱一家和客人们坐在客厅里，金妮把这间屋子装饰得五彩缤纷，花团锦簇，简直像发生过一场纸拉花的爆炸。只有弗雷德、乔治、哈利和罗恩知道圣诞树顶上的小天使其实是一个花园地精。弗雷德在拔圣诞晚餐用的胡萝卜时被这个地精咬了脚脖子，于是它被施了昏迷咒，涂成金色，塞进一件小芭蕾舞裙，背上粘了一对小翅膀，在树顶上对他们怒目而视。这是哈利见过的最丑的天使，长着土豆似的大秃脑袋，脚上还有很多毛。

他们都得听韦斯莱夫人最喜欢的歌手塞蒂娜·沃贝克的圣诞广播，她的歌声从大木头收音机中婉转流出。芙蓉似乎觉得塞蒂娜非常乏味，她在角落里大声说话，韦斯莱夫人皱着眉头，不停地用魔杖调整音量开关，使塞蒂娜唱得越来越响。在一首爵士味特别浓的曲子《一锅火热的爱》的掩护下，弗雷德、乔治跟金妮玩起了噼啪爆炸牌。罗恩的

## CHAPTER SIXTEEN    A Very Frosty Christmas

of Hot, Strong Love', Fred and George started a game of Exploding Snap with Ginny. Ron kept shooting Bill and Fleur covert looks, as though hoping to pick up tips. Meanwhile Remus Lupin, who was thinner and more ragged-looking than ever, was sitting beside the fire, staring into its depths as though he could not hear Celestina's voice.

> *'Oh, come and stir my cauldron,*
> *And if you do it right*
> *I'll boil you up some hot, strong love*
> *To keep you warm tonight.'*

'We danced to this when we were eighteen!' said Mrs Weasley, wiping her eyes on her knitting. 'Do you remember, Arthur?'

'Mphf?' said Mr Weasley, whose head had been nodding over the satsuma he was peeling. 'Oh yes ... marvellous tune ...'

With an effort he sat up a little straighter and looked round at Harry, who was sitting next to him.

'Sorry about this,' he said, jerking his head towards the wireless as Celestina broke into the chorus. 'Be over soon.'

'No problem,' said Harry, grinning. 'Has it been busy at the Ministry?'

'Very,' said Mr Weasley. 'I wouldn't mind if we were getting anywhere, but of the three arrests we've made in the last couple of months, I doubt that one of them is a genuine Death Eater – only don't repeat that, Harry,' he added quickly, looking much more awake all of a sudden.

'They're not still holding Stan Shunpike, are they?' asked Harry.

'I'm afraid so,' said Mr Weasley. 'I know Dumbledore's tried appealing directly to Scrimgeour about Stan ... I mean, anybody who has actually interviewed him agrees that he's about as much a Death Eater as this satsuma ... but the top levels want to look as though they're making some progress, and "three arrests" sounds better than "three mistaken arrests and releases" ... but again, this is all top secret ...'

'I won't say anything,' said Harry. He hesitated for a moment, wondering how best to embark on what he wanted to say; as he marshalled his thoughts, Celestina Warbeck began a ballad called 'You Charmed the Heart Right Out of Me'.

'Mr Weasley, you know what I told you at the station when we were setting off for school?'

## 第 16 章　冰霜圣诞节

眼睛老是偷瞟比尔和芙蓉，似乎想学点儿什么技巧。卢平更瘦了，也比以往显得更为憔悴，他坐在壁炉边，盯着炉火深处，仿佛听不见塞蒂娜的声音。

> 哦，来搅搅我的这锅汤，
> 如果你做得很恰当，
> 我会熬出火热的爱，
> 陪伴你今夜暖洋洋。

"我们十八岁时跟着这音乐跳过舞！"韦斯莱夫人用手里织的毛线擦了擦眼睛，"你还记得吗，亚瑟？"

"唔？"剥着小蜜橘打起了瞌睡的韦斯莱先生说，"哦，是啊……多棒的曲子……"

他努力坐直了一点儿，扭头看着坐在旁边的哈利。

"对不起啊，"他把脑袋朝收音机那边一摆，塞蒂娜已经唱起了副歌，"就快完了。"

"没事的。"哈利咧嘴一笑，说道，"部里忙吗？"

"非常忙，要是有进展也就罢了，可是我怀疑这两个月逮捕的三个人里，没有一个是真正的食死徒——不过别说出去，哈利。"他马上加了一句，看上去一下子清醒了许多。

"他们不会还关着桑帕克吧？"哈利问。

"恐怕还关着呢，我知道邓布利多曾经为桑帕克直接向斯克林杰进言……所有跟他谈过话的人都认为他像这小蜜橘一样不可能是食死徒……可是上面想显得有所进展，'逮捕三人'听起来比'误捕三人，后释放'好听多了……不过，这都是高度机密。"

"我不会说的。"哈利说。他犹豫了一下，不知道怎么切入他想讲的话题。当他整理思绪时，塞蒂娜已开始唱《你用魔法勾走了我的心》。

"韦斯莱先生，你还记得我去学校之前在车站告诉你的事吗？"

# CHAPTER SIXTEEN     A Very Frosty Christmas

'I checked, Harry,' said Mr Weasley at once. 'I went and searched the Malfoys' house. There was nothing, either broken or whole, that shouldn't have been there.'

'Yeah, I know, I saw in the *Prophet* that you'd looked ... but this is something different ... well, something more ...'

And he told Mr Weasley everything he had overheard between Malfoy and Snape. As Harry spoke, he saw Lupin's head turn a little towards him, taking in every word. When he had finished, there was silence, except for Celestina's crooning.

*'Oh, my poor heart, where has it gone?*
*It's left me for a spell ...'*

'Has it occurred to you, Harry,' said Mr Weasley, 'that Snape was simply pretending –'

'Pretending to offer help, so that he could find out what Malfoy's up to?' said Harry quickly. 'Yeah, I thought you'd say that. But how do we know?'

'It isn't our business to know,' said Lupin unexpectedly. He had turned his back on the fire now, and faced Harry across Mr Weasley. 'It's Dumbledore's business. Dumbledore trusts Severus, and that ought to be good enough for all of us.'

'But,' said Harry, 'just say – just say Dumbledore's wrong about Snape –'

'People have said it, many times. It comes down to whether or not you trust Dumbledore's judgement. I do; therefore, I trust Severus.'

'But Dumbledore can make mistakes,' argued Harry. 'He says it himself. And you –'

He looked Lupin straight in the eye.

'– do you honestly like Snape?'

'I neither like nor dislike Severus,' said Lupin. 'No, Harry, I am speaking the truth,' he added, as Harry pulled a sceptical expression. 'We shall never be bosom friends, perhaps; after all that happened between James and Sirius and Severus, there is too much bitterness there. But I do not forget that during the year I taught at Hogwarts, Severus made the Wolfsbane Potion for me every month, made it perfectly, so that I did not have to suffer as I usually do at the full moon.'

## 第16章　冰霜圣诞节

"我查过了，哈利。"韦斯莱先生马上说，"我去搜查了马尔福的家，没有发现不该有的东西，无论是碎的还是完整的。"

"嗯，我知道，我在《预言家日报》上看到你去搜查了……可这次不一样……更加……"

他对韦斯莱先生讲了马尔福与斯内普的密谈。在他们说话的时候，他看到卢平的脑袋稍稍偏向他们，聆听每一句话。他说完后一阵沉默，只听到塞蒂娜的低吟：

> 哦，我可怜的心，它去了哪里？
> 它离开了我，被魔法勾去……

"你有没有想过，哈利，"韦斯莱先生说，"斯内普只是假装——"

"假装要帮忙，以便发现马尔福在干什么？"哈利立刻说，"是啊，我想你会这么说的，可是我们怎么知道呢？"

"这不是我们的事。"卢平出人意料地说。他现在背对着炉火，隔着韦斯莱先生面对哈利。"是邓布利多的事。邓布利多信任西弗勒斯，对我们来说这应该就够了。"

"可是，"哈利说，"假如——假如邓布利多看错了斯内普——"

"有人这么说过，许多次了。说到底是你相不相信邓布利多的判断。我相信，所以，我信任西弗勒斯。"

"可是邓布利多也会犯错，"哈利争辩道，"他自己说过。你——"

他盯着卢平的眼睛。

"——你真喜欢斯内普？"

"我既不喜欢也不讨厌西弗勒斯。"卢平答道，见哈利显出怀疑的表情，他又说，"哈利，我说的是真话。也许我和他永远不会成为知心好友；在詹姆、小天狼星和西弗勒斯之间发生那些事情以后，积怨太多。但我不会忘记我在霍格沃茨任教的那年，斯内普每个月帮我配狼毒药剂，配得非常好，使我在满月时无须像过去那么痛苦。"

## CHAPTER SIXTEEN  A Very Frosty Christmas

'But he "accidentally" let it slip that you're a werewolf, so you had to leave!' said Harry angrily.

Lupin shrugged.

'The news would have leaked out anyway. We both know he wanted my job, but he could have wreaked much worse damage on me by tampering with the Potion. He kept me healthy. I must be grateful.'

'Maybe he didn't dare mess with the Potion with Dumbledore watching him!' said Harry.

'You are determined to hate him, Harry,' said Lupin with a faint smile. 'And I understand; with James as your father, with Sirius as your godfather, you have inherited an old prejudice. By all means tell Dumbledore what you have told Arthur and me, but do not expect him to share your view of the matter; do not even expect him to be surprised by what you tell him. It might have been on Dumbledore's orders that Severus questioned Draco.'

'*... and now you've torn it quite apart*
*I'll thank you to give back my heart!*'

Celestina ended her song on a very long, high-pitched note and loud applause issued out of the wireless, which Mrs Weasley joined in with enthusiastically.

'Eez eet over?' said Fleur loudly. 'Thank goodness, what an 'orrible –'

'Shall we have a nightcap, then?' asked Mr Weasley loudly, leaping to his feet. 'Who wants egg-nog?'

'What have you been up to lately?' Harry asked Lupin, as Mr Weasley bustled off to fetch the egg-nog and everybody else stretched and broke into conversation.

'Oh, I've been underground,' said Lupin. 'Almost literally. That's why I haven't been able to write, Harry; sending letters to you would have been something of a give-away.'

'What do you mean?'

'I've been living among my fellows, my equals,' said Lupin. 'Werewolves,' he added, at Harry's look of incomprehension. 'Nearly all of them are on Voldemort's side. Dumbledore wanted a spy and here I was ... ready-made.'

He sounded a little bitter, and perhaps realised it, for he smiled more warmly as he went on, 'I am not complaining; it is necessary work and who

"可是他'无意中'走漏了你是狼人的消息，结果你只好离开！"哈利愤然道。

卢平耸了耸肩膀。

"这件事总会泄漏的。我们都知道他想要得到我的职位，但他只需在药里做点手脚，就可以把我害得更惨。他让我保持健康，我应该心存感激。"

"也许有邓布利多监视，他不敢在药里下手？"

"你是决心要恨他，哈利，"卢平无力地一笑，"我理解，詹姆是你父亲，小天狼星是你教父，你继承了一种成见。你当然可以把你对亚瑟和我说的话告诉邓布利多，但别指望他跟你看法一致，甚至别指望他会吃惊。也许西弗勒斯是奉了邓布利多的命令去问德拉科的。"

……而今你已把它撕破
请把我的心还给我！

塞蒂娜以一个长长的高音结束了她的演唱，收音机里传出响亮的掌声，韦斯莱夫人也兴奋地鼓掌。

"完了？"芙蓉大声说，"谢天谢地，好难听——"

"睡觉前喝点饮料怎么样？"韦斯莱先生跳起来高声问道，"谁要蛋酒？"

"你最近在干什么？"哈利问卢平，韦斯莱先生跑去拿蛋酒，其他人都舒展着身体，聊起了天。

"哦，我在地下工作，"卢平说，"几乎真的是在地下。所以我没能写信，哈利，寄信给你会暴露的。"

"你说什么？"

"我生活在我那些人当中，我的同类。"卢平说，"狼人，"他见哈利有些不解，又补充道，"他们几乎全都是伏地魔一边的。邓布利多需要一个间谍，我正好是……现成的。"

听起来他有点像发牢骚，他自己可能也察觉了，便又笑得更热情

## CHAPTER SIXTEEN  A Very Frosty Christmas

can do it better than I? However, it has been difficult gaining their trust. I bear the unmistakeable signs of having tried to live among wizards, you see, whereas they have shunned normal society and live on the margins, stealing – and sometimes killing – to eat.'

'How come they like Voldemort?'

'They think that, under his rule, they will have a better life,' said Lupin. 'And it is hard to argue with Greyback out there ...'

'Who's Greyback?'

'You haven't heard of him?' Lupin's hands closed convulsively in his lap. 'Fenrir Greyback is, perhaps, the most savage werewolf alive today. He regards it as his mission in life to bite and to contaminate as many people as possible; he wants to create enough werewolves to overcome the wizards. Voldemort has promised him prey in return for his services. Greyback specialises in children ... bite them young, he says, and raise them away from their parents, raise them to hate normal wizards. Voldemort has threatened to unleash him upon people's sons and daughters; it is a threat that usually produces good results.'

Lupin paused and then said, 'It was Greyback who bit me.'

'What?' said Harry, astonished. 'When – when you were a kid, you mean?'

'Yes. My father had offended him. I did not know, for a very long time, the identity of the werewolf who had attacked me; I even felt pity for him, thinking that he had had no control, knowing by then how it felt to transform. But Greyback is not like that. At the full moon he positions himself close to victims, ensuring that he is near enough to strike. He plans it all. And this is the man Voldemort is using to marshal the werewolves. I cannot pretend that my particular brand of reasoned argument is making much headway against Greyback's insistence that we werewolves deserve blood, that we ought to revenge ourselves on normal people.'

'But you are normal!' said Harry fiercely. 'You've just got a – a problem –'

Lupin burst out laughing.

'Sometimes you remind me a lot of James. He called it my "furry little problem" in company. Many people were under the impression that I owned a badly behaved rabbit.'

He accepted a glass of egg-nog from Mr Weasley with a word of thanks, looking slightly more cheerful. Harry, meanwhile, felt a rush of excitement:

了一些,说道:"我不是抱怨,这是必要的工作,谁能比我更胜任这份工作呢?只不过,取得他们信任很难。我带着曾经在巫师中生活过的明显印记,而他们向来避开正常的社会,生活在边缘地带,偷东西吃——有时候还杀人。"

"他们怎么会喜欢伏地魔呢?"

"大概觉得在他的统治下,他们会过得更好。跟格雷伯克辩论是一件很困难……"

"格雷伯克是谁?"

"你没听说过他吗?"卢平的双手在膝上痉挛地握紧,"芬里尔·格雷伯克或许是当今世上最凶残的狼人。他以咬伤和传染尽可能多的人为己任,想造出大批狼人来打败巫师。伏地魔允诺给他一些猎物作为酬劳。格雷伯克专攻小孩……他说趁小时候咬,然后把孩子从父母身边带走,培养他们仇恨巫师。伏地魔威胁要把格雷伯克放出去咬人家的小孩,这威胁通常很有效。"

卢平停了一会儿,又说:"是格雷伯克咬的我。"

"什么?"哈利吃了一惊,"你是说在——在你小时候?"

"是的。我父亲冒犯了他。我有很长时间一直不知道袭击我的狼人是谁。我甚至怜悯他,以为他是控制不住,那时我已经知道一个人变成狼是什么滋味。但格雷伯克并不是那样,满月时他靠近猎物,确保袭击得手。他完全是有预谋的。伏地魔就是用他来召集狼人的。格雷伯克坚持认为我们狼人应该吸血,应该对正常人进行报复,我不敢说我那种理智的辩论对他有多少效果。"

"可你是正常的!"哈利激烈地说,"你只是有一个——一个问题——"

卢平笑了起来。

"有时你让我想起了詹姆的很多事。他当着人就说这是我的'毛茸茸的小问题'。许多人以为我养了一只不听话的兔子。"

他从韦斯莱先生手里接过一杯蛋酒,道了声谢,看上去稍稍快活了一些。哈利听卢平提到他父亲,感到一阵激动,想起了有件事一直

## CHAPTER SIXTEEN  A Very Frosty Christmas

this last mention of his father had reminded him that there was something he had been looking forward to asking Lupin.

'Have you ever heard of someone called the Half-Blood Prince?'

'The Half-Blood what?'

'Prince,' said Harry, watching him closely for signs of recognition.

'There are no wizarding princes,' said Lupin, now smiling. 'Is this a title you're thinking of adopting? I should have thought being the "Chosen One" would be enough.'

'It's nothing to do with me!' said Harry indignantly. 'The Half-Blood Prince is someone who used to go to Hogwarts, I've got his old Potions book. He wrote spells all over it, spells he invented. One of them was *Levicorpus* –'

'Oh, that one had a great vogue during my time at Hogwarts,' said Lupin reminiscently. 'There were a few months in my fifth year when you couldn't move for being hoisted into the air by your ankle.'

'My dad used it,' said Harry. 'I saw him in the Pensieve, he used it on Snape.'

He tried to sound casual, as though this was a throwaway comment of no real importance, but he was not sure he had achieved the right effect; Lupin's smile was a little too understanding.

'Yes,' he said, 'but he wasn't the only one. As I say, it was very popular ... you know how these spells come and go ...'

'But it sounds like it was invented while you were at school,' Harry persisted.

'Not necessarily,' said Lupin. 'Jinxes go in and out of fashion like everything else.' He looked into Harry's face and then said quietly, 'James was a pure-blood, Harry, and I promise you, he never asked us to call him "Prince".'

Abandoning pretence, Harry said, 'And it wasn't Sirius? Or you?'

'Definitely not.'

'Oh.' Harry stared into the fire. 'I just thought – well, he's helped me out a lot in Potions classes, the Prince has.'

'How old is this book, Harry?'

'I dunno, I've never checked.'

'Well, perhaps that will give you some clue as to when the Prince was at Hogwarts,' said Lupin.

Shortly after this, Fleur decided to imitate Celestina singing 'A Cauldron Full

打算问卢平。

"你听说过有个叫混血王子的人吗?"

"混血什么?"

"王子。"哈利密切观察卢平有没有想起来的迹象。

"巫师没有王子。"卢平微笑着说道,"你想用这个称号吗?我以为'救世之星'已经够了。"

"这跟我没关系!"哈利抗议道,"混血王子是以前在霍格沃茨待过的人。我拿了他用过的魔药课本。他在上面写满了咒语,他发明的咒语。有一个是倒挂金钟——"

"哦,这个咒语在我上霍格沃茨的时候很流行。"卢平怀旧地说,"我五年级时有几个月,经常有人被提着脚脖子倒吊在空中,没法动弹。"

"我爸爸用过它。"哈利说,"我在冥想盆里看到的,他对斯内普用过。"

他想用不经意的口气,好像只是随口提及,但不知是否达到了这种效果。卢平的笑容里包含着太多的理解。

"是啊,"他说,"但不只他一个人用过。就像我说的,它非常流行……你知道这些咒语都是一阵一阵的……"

"可听起来像是在你上学的那个时期发明的。"哈利坚持道。

"不一定。咒语和其他东西一样,都有流行和不流行的时候。"卢平注视着哈利的面孔,然后平静地说,"詹姆是纯血统,哈利,我向你保证,他从来没让我们叫过他'王子'。"

哈利放弃了掩饰,问道:"也不是小天狼星?或者你?"

"肯定不是。"

"哦,"哈利望着炉火,"我还以为——他在魔药课上帮了我很大的忙,那个王子。"

"那本书是什么时候的,哈利?"

"不知道,我从来没查过。"

"也许这能帮助你了解王子在霍格沃茨的时间。"卢平说。

没过多久,芙蓉决定模仿塞蒂娜唱《一埚火热的爱》,看到韦斯莱

## CHAPTER SIXTEEN    A Very Frosty Christmas

of Hot, Strong Love', which was taken by everyone, once they had glimpsed Mrs Weasley's expression, to be the cue to go to bed. Harry and Ron climbed all the way up to Ron's attic bedroom, where a camp bed had been added for Harry.

Ron fell asleep almost immediately, but Harry delved into his trunk and pulled out his copy of *Advanced Potion-Making* before getting into bed. There he turned its pages, searching, until he finally found, at the front of the book, the date that it had been published. It was nearly fifty years old. Neither his father, nor his father's friends, had been at Hogwarts fifty years ago. Feeling disappointed, Harry threw the book back into his trunk, turned off the lamp and rolled over, thinking of werewolves and Snape, Stan Shunpike and the Half-Blood Prince, and finally falling into an uneasy sleep full of creeping shadows and the cries of bitten children ...

'She's got to be joking ...'

Harry woke with a start to find a bulging stocking lying over the end of his bed. He put on his glasses and looked around; the tiny window was almost completely obscured with snow and in front of it Ron was sitting bolt upright in bed and examining what appeared to be a thick gold chain.

'What's that?' asked Harry.

'It's from Lavender,' said Ron, sounding revolted. 'She can't honestly think I'd wear ...'

Harry looked more closely and let out a shout of laughter. Dangling from the chain in large gold letters were the words *My Sweetheart*.

'Nice,' he said. 'Classy. You should definitely wear it in front of Fred and George.'

'If you tell them,' said Ron, shoving the necklace out of sight under his pillow, 'I – I – I'll –'

'Stutter at me?' said Harry, grinning. 'Come on, would I?'

'How could she think I'd like something like that, though?' Ron demanded of thin air, looking rather shocked.

'Well, think back,' said Harry. 'Have you ever let it slip that you'd like to go out in public with the words "My Sweetheart" round your neck?'

'Well ... we don't really talk much,' said Ron. 'It's mainly ...'

'Snogging,' said Harry.

'Well, yeah,' said Ron. He hesitated a moment, then said, 'Is Hermione really going out with McLaggen?'

'I dunno,' said Harry. 'They were at Slughorn's party together, but I don't think it went that well.'

## 第16章 冰霜圣诞节

夫人的表情之后,大家都把这当成了上床睡觉的信号。哈利和罗恩爬到阁楼上罗恩的卧室里,那儿为哈利搭了一张行军床。

罗恩几乎一沾枕头就睡着了。哈利上床前从旅行箱里找出《高级魔药制作》翻了翻,终于在前面找到了出版时间。将近五十年了。五十年前他父亲及其朋友们都不在霍格沃茨。哈利失望地把书扔回了箱子里,关上灯,翻了个身,想着狼人和斯内普、桑帕克和混血王子,终于迷迷糊糊地睡着了,梦里尽是鬼魅的阴影和被咬的孩子的哭声……

"她一定是在开玩笑……"

哈利一下子惊醒了,发现床脚放着一只鼓鼓囊囊的长袜。他戴上眼镜环顾四周,小窗几乎完全被雪遮住了,罗恩笔直地坐在窗前的床上,在看一个东西,好像是一条挺粗的金链子。

"那是什么?"哈利问。

"拉文德送的,"罗恩厌恶地说,"她不会真的以为我会戴吧……"

哈利凑近一看,哑然失笑,链子上挂着几个大大的金字:我的甜心。

"不错,漂亮。你一定要在弗雷德和乔治面前戴上。"

"如果你告诉他们,"罗恩说着把项链塞到了枕头底下,"我——我——我就——"

"跟我结巴上了?"哈利笑着说,"行了吧,我会说吗?"

"她怎么会以为我喜欢这种东西呢?"罗恩对着空气问,一副很震惊的样子。

"回想一下,"哈利说,"你有没有流露过喜欢脖子上挂着我的甜心出去招摇的想法?"

"嗯……我们没说多少话,"罗恩说,"主要是……"

"亲嘴。"

"是啊。"罗恩犹豫了一会儿,又说,"赫敏真的跟麦克拉根好上了?"

"不知道,斯拉格霍恩的晚会上他们在一起来着,可是我看并没有那么好。"

## CHAPTER SIXTEEN   A Very Frosty Christmas

Ron looked slightly more cheerful as he delved deeper into his stocking.

Harry's presents included a sweater with a large Golden Snitch worked on to the front, hand-knitted by Mrs Weasley, a large box of Weasleys' Wizard Wheezes products from the twins and a slightly damp, mouldy-smelling package which came with a label reading: *To Master, from Kreacher.*

Harry stared at it. 'D'you reckon this is safe to open?' he asked.

'Can't be anything dangerous, all our mail's still being searched at the Ministry,' replied Ron, though he was eyeing the parcel suspiciously.

'I didn't think of giving Kreacher anything! Do people usually give their house-elves Christmas presents?' asked Harry, prodding the parcel cautiously.

'Hermione would,' said Ron. 'But let's wait and see what it is before you start feeling guilty.'

A moment later, Harry had given a loud yell and leapt out of his camp bed; the package contained a large number of maggots.

'Nice,' said Ron, roaring with laughter. 'Very thoughtful.'

'I'd rather have them than that necklace,' said Harry, which sobered Ron up at once.

Everybody was wearing new sweaters when they all sat down for Christmas lunch, everyone except Fleur (on whom, it appeared, Mrs Weasley had not wanted to waste one) and Mrs Weasley herself, who was sporting a brand new midnight-blue witch's hat glittering with what looked like tiny starlike diamonds, and a spectacular golden necklace.

'Fred and George gave them to me! Aren't they beautiful?'

'Well, we find we appreciate you more and more, Mum, now we're washing our own socks,' said George, waving an airy hand. 'Parsnips, Remus?'

'Harry, you've got a maggot in your hair,' said Ginny cheerfully, leaning across the table to pick it out; Harry felt goosebumps erupt up his neck that had nothing to do with the maggot.

' 'Ow 'orrible,' said Fleur, with an affected little shudder.

'Yes, isn't it?' said Ron. 'Gravy, Fleur?'

In his eagerness to help her, he knocked the gravy boat flying; Bill waved his wand and the gravy soared up in the air and returned meekly to the boat.

'You are as bad as zat Tonks,' said Fleur to Ron, when she had finished kissing Bill in thanks. 'She is always knocking –'

## 第16章 冰霜圣诞节

罗恩心情似乎稍微好了些，又到袜子里头去掏礼物。

哈利的礼物包括一件胸前有金色飞贼的毛衣，是韦斯莱夫人亲手织的，双胞胎兄弟送的一大盒韦斯莱魔法把戏坊的产品，还有一个有点潮湿、带着霉味的包裹，标签上写着：致主人，克利切。

哈利瞪着它。"你说打开它安全吗？"

"不可能是危险品，我们的邮件仍然都经过魔法部的检查。"罗恩答道，不过他怀疑地打量着那个包裹。

"我没想到给克利切送东西！人们一般会给家养小精灵送圣诞礼物吗？"哈利问，一边小心地捅着包裹。

"赫敏会。还是先看看是什么再内疚吧。"

片刻之后，哈利大叫一声，从行军床上跳了下来，包裹里是一大堆蛆。

"不错，"罗恩哈哈大笑，"想得很周到。"

"我宁可要这个也不要那条项链。"哈利说，罗恩立刻冷静下来。

坐下吃圣诞午餐时，每个人都穿着新毛衣，除了芙蓉（韦斯莱夫人似乎不愿在她身上浪费一件）和韦斯莱夫人自己。韦斯莱夫人戴着一顶崭新的女巫帽，夜空一样的深蓝底色上闪烁着小星星般的钻石，还有一串夺目的金项链。

"弗雷德和乔治送给我的！漂亮吧？"

"我们越来越感激你了，妈妈，现在我们自己洗袜子了。"乔治说，一边潇洒地一挥手，"要防风草根吗，莱姆斯？"

"哈利，你头上有一条蛆。"金妮快活地说，隔着桌子欠身帮他拿掉了。哈利感到脖子上起了鸡皮疙瘩，但与那条蛆无关。

"哦，好恶心。"芙蓉说，做作地哆嗦了一下。

"可不。"罗恩说，"要肉卤吗，芙蓉？"

他急于献殷勤，把肉卤盘碰飞了。比尔一挥魔杖，肉卤升到空中，顺从地落回盘里。

"你跟那个唐克斯一样笨，"芙蓉亲了一下比尔之后对罗恩说，"她总是打翻——"

## CHAPTER SIXTEEN    A Very Frosty Christmas

'I invited *dear* Tonks to come along today,' said Mrs Weasley, setting down the carrots with unnecessary force and glaring at Fleur. 'But she wouldn't come. Have you spoken to her lately, Remus?'

'No, I haven't been in contact with anybody very much,' said Lupin. 'But Tonks has got her own family to go to, hasn't she?'

'Hmmm,' said Mrs Weasley. 'Maybe. I got the impression she was planning to spend Christmas alone, actually.'

She gave Lupin an annoyed look, as though it was all his fault she was getting Fleur for a daughter-in-law instead of Tonks, but Harry, glancing across at Fleur, who was now feeding Bill bits of turkey off her own fork, thought that Mrs Weasley was fighting a long-lost battle. He was, however, reminded of a question he had with regard to Tonks, and who better to ask than Lupin, the man who knew all about Patronuses?

'Tonks's Patronus has changed its form,' he told him. 'Snape said so, anyway. I didn't know that could happen. Why would your Patronus change?'

Lupin took his time chewing his turkey and swallowing before saying slowly, 'Sometimes ... a great shock ... an emotional upheaval ...'

'It looked big, and it had four legs,' said Harry, struck by a sudden thought and lowering his voice. 'Hey ... it couldn't be –?'

'Arthur!' said Mrs Weasley suddenly. She had risen from her chair; her hand was pressed over her heart and she was staring out of the kitchen window. 'Arthur – it's Percy!'

'*What?*'

Mr Weasley looked round. Everybody looked quickly at the window; Ginny stood up for a better view. There, sure enough, was Percy Weasley, striding across the snowy yard, his horn-rimmed glasses glinting in the sunlight. He was not, however, alone.

'Arthur, he's – he's with the Minister!'

And sure enough, the man Harry had seen in the *Daily Prophet* was following along in Percy's wake, limping slightly, his mane of greying hair and his black cloak flecked with snow. Before any of them could say anything, before Mr and Mrs Weasley could do more than exchange stunned looks, the back door opened and there stood Percy.

There was a moment's painful silence. Then Percy said rather stiffly, 'Merry Christmas, Mother.'

## 第16章 冰霜圣诞节

"我邀请了亲爱的唐克斯，"韦斯莱夫人重重地放下胡萝卜，瞪着芙蓉说，"可她不肯来。你最近跟她谈过吗，莱姆斯？"

"没有，我跟谁都没有多少联系。但唐克斯要回她自己的家，是不是？"

"嗯，"韦斯莱夫人说，"也许吧。我感觉她是打算一个人过圣诞节。"

她恼火地看了卢平一眼，好像她摊到芙蓉而不是唐克斯当儿媳全是卢平的错。哈利望望正用她自己的叉子喂比尔吃火鸡的芙蓉，感到韦斯莱夫人早就输定了。但他想起了关于唐克斯的一个问题，觉得问卢平是最合适的。卢平对守护神无所不知。

"唐克斯的守护神变了，斯内普说的。我不知道会有这种事。守护神为什么会变呢？"

卢平不慌不忙地嚼着火鸡，咽下之后缓缓地说道："有时……遭到大的打击……感情剧变……"

"它看上去很大，有四条腿，"哈利说，突然他闪过一个念头，压低声音说，"嘿……不会是——？"

"亚瑟！"韦斯莱夫人突然叫道。她从椅子上站起来，手捂着心口，瞪着厨房窗外。"亚瑟——是珀西！"

"什么？"

韦斯莱先生回过头，大家都立刻望着窗外，金妮站起来，以便看得更清楚。果然是珀西·韦斯莱，正踏着院中的积雪大步走来，粗框眼镜在阳光下一闪一闪。然而他并不是一个人。

"亚瑟，他——他是跟部长一起来的！"

果然如此，哈利在《预言家日报》上见过的那人正跟在珀西后面，他有一点儿跛，长而厚密的灰发和黑斗篷上落了片片白雪。大家谁也没来得及说话，韦斯莱夫妇刚交换了一个吃惊的眼神，后门就开了，珀西站在了门口。

一阵难堪的沉默，珀西生硬地说："圣诞快乐，妈妈。"

## CHAPTER SIXTEEN    A Very Frosty Christmas

'Oh, *Percy*!' said Mrs Weasley, and she threw herself into his arms.

Rufus Scrimgeour paused in the doorway, leaning on his walking stick and smiling as he observed this affecting scene.

'You must forgive this intrusion,' he said, when Mrs Weasley looked round at him, beaming and wiping her eyes. 'Percy and I were in the vicinity – working, you know – and he couldn't resist dropping in and seeing you all.'

But Percy showed no sign of wanting to greet any of the rest of the family. He stood, poker-straight and awkward-looking, and stared over everybody else's heads. Mr Weasley, Fred and George were all observing him, stony-faced.

'Please, come in, sit down, Minister!' fluttered Mrs Weasley, straightening her hat. 'Have a little purkey, or some tooding ... I mean –'

'No, no, my dear Molly,' said Scrimgeour. Harry guessed that he had checked on her name with Percy before they entered the house. 'I don't want to intrude, wouldn't be here at all if Percy hadn't wanted to see you all so badly ...'

'Oh, Perce!' said Mrs Weasley tearfully, reaching up to kiss him.

'... we've only looked in for five minutes, so I'll have a stroll around the yard while you catch up with Percy. No, no, I assure you I don't want to butt in! Well, if anybody cared to show me your charming garden ... ah, that young man's finished, why doesn't he take a stroll with me?'

The atmosphere around the table changed perceptibly. Everybody looked from Scrimgeour to Harry. Nobody seemed to find Scrimgeour's pretence that he did not know Harry's name convincing, or find it natural that he should be chosen to accompany the Minister around the garden when Ginny, Fleur and George also had clean plates.

'Yeah, all right,' said Harry into the silence.

He was not fooled; for all Scrimgeour's talk that they had just been in the area, that Percy wanted to look up his family, this must be the real reason that they had come, so that Scrimgeour could speak to Harry alone.

'It's fine,' he said quietly, as he passed Lupin, who had half risen from his chair. 'Fine,' he added, as Mr Weasley opened his mouth to speak.

'Wonderful!' said Scrimgeour, standing back to let Harry pass through the door ahead of him. 'We'll just take a turn around the garden and then Percy and I'll be off. Carry on, everyone!'

Harry walked across the yard towards the Weasleys' overgrown, snow-covered garden, Scrimgeour limping slightly at his side. He had, Harry knew,

## 第16章 冰霜圣诞节

"哦,珀西!"韦斯莱夫人叫着扑到了他怀里。

鲁弗斯·斯克林杰在门口停了下来,他拄着拐杖,微笑地看着这感人的一幕。

"打扰了,请原谅。"他说,这时韦斯莱夫人已转向他,笑吟吟地擦着眼睛,"珀西和我在附近——办事,您知道——他忍不住要来看看你们。"

但珀西并没有跟其他人打招呼的意思。他直挺挺地站在那儿,显得很不自然,目光越过众人的头顶。韦斯莱先生、弗雷德和乔治都板着面孔看着他。

"请进,坐吧,部长!"韦斯莱夫人慌乱地说,一边扶正自己的帽子,"吃一点窝鸡,或补丁……我是说——"

"不用,不用,亲爱的莫丽。"斯克林杰说。哈利猜想他在进屋前向珀西打听了韦斯莱夫人的名字。"我不想打扰,要不是珀西这么想见你们,我也不会来……"

"哦,珀西!"韦斯莱夫人含泪叫道,踮起脚尖去亲珀西。

"……我们只待五分钟,我到院子里走走,你们跟珀西多聊一会儿。不不,我真的不想打扰你们!嗯,如果有人愿意带我参观一下你们可爱的花园……啊,那个小伙子吃完了,你陪我散散步可以吗?"

餐桌旁的气氛明显变了,大家的目光从斯克林杰转移到了哈利身上。没人真的相信斯克林杰不知道哈利的名字,也没人觉得哈利被选中陪部长到花园散步很自然,因为金妮、芙蓉和乔治的盘子也都空了。

"好啊。"哈利打破沉默,说道。

他没有上当,斯克林杰说是在附近办事,珀西想来看看家人,但这才是他们来的真正原因:为了斯克林杰能跟哈利单独谈话。

"没事。"经过卢平身边时他小声说,因为他看到卢平正要从椅子上站起来。"没事。"看到韦斯莱先生张嘴要说话,他又加了一句。

"太好了!"斯克林杰向后退去,让哈利先走出门外,"我们就在花园里转转,然后我和珀西就走。继续吧,各位!"

哈利穿过院子朝杂草丛生、覆盖着白雪的韦斯莱家花园走去,斯

## CHAPTER SIXTEEN    A Very Frosty Christmas

been Head of the Auror Office; he looked tough and battle-scarred, very different from portly Fudge in his bowler hat.

'Charming,' said Scrimgeour, stopping at the garden fence and looking out over the snowy lawn and the indistinguishable plants. 'Charming.'

Harry said nothing. He could tell that Scrimgeour was watching him.

'I've wanted to meet you for a very long time,' said Scrimgeour, after a few moments. 'Did you know that?'

'No,' said Harry truthfully.

'Oh yes, for a very long time. But Dumbledore has been very protective of you,' said Scrimgeour. 'Natural, of course, natural, after what you've been through ... especially what happened at the Ministry ...'

He waited for Harry to say something, but Harry did not oblige, so he went on, 'I have been hoping for an occasion to talk to you ever since I gained office, but Dumbledore has – most understandably, as I say – prevented this.'

Still Harry said nothing, waiting.

'The rumours that have flown around!' said Scrimgeour. 'Well, of course, we both know how these stories get distorted ... all these whispers of a prophecy ... of you being the "Chosen One" ...'

They were getting near it now, Harry thought, the reason Scrimgeour was here.

'... I assume that Dumbledore has discussed these matters with you?'

Harry deliberated, wondering whether he ought to lie or not. He looked at the little gnome prints all around the flowerbeds, and the scuffed-up patch that marked the spot where Fred had caught the gnome now wearing the tutu at the top of the Christmas tree. Finally, he decided on the truth ... or a bit of it.

'Yeah, we've discussed it.'

'Have you, have you ...' said Scrimgeour. Harry could see, out of the corner of his eyes, Scrimgeour squinting at him, so pretended to be very interested in a gnome that had just poked its head out from underneath a frozen rhododendron. 'And what has Dumbledore told you, Harry?'

'Sorry, but that's between us,' said Harry.

He kept his voice as pleasant as he could, and Scrimgeour's tone, too, was light and friendly as he said, 'Oh, of course, if it's a question of confidences, I wouldn't want you to divulge ... no, no ... and in any case, does it really matter whether you are the Chosen One or not?'

## 第16章 冰霜圣诞节

克林杰一跛一跛地走在旁边。哈利知道他曾是傲罗办公室主任。他看上去很结实，身经百战，跟戴着圆礼帽、大腹便便的福吉大不一样。

"很漂亮，"斯克林杰说，他在花园篱笆前停下来，望着落满积雪的草坪和辨认不出的植物，"很漂亮。"

哈利没说话。他感觉到斯克林杰在观察他。

"我早就想见见你了，"过了一会儿斯克林杰说，"你知道吗？"

"不知道。"哈利诚实地说。

"哦，是的，早就想了。但邓布利多很护着你。"斯克林杰说，"当然，这很自然，很自然，在你经历了那些之后……尤其是部里发生的事……"

他想等哈利说些什么，但哈利没有理睬，于是他又说道："我上任之后一直希望有机会跟你谈谈，但是被邓布利多阻止了。我说过——这是完全可以理解的。"

哈利还是一言不发，等待着。

"传闻沸沸扬扬！"斯克林杰说，"当然，我们都知道这些故事传得多么走样……传说有一个预言……说你是'救世之星'……"

哈利想，话题现在接近斯克林杰的来意了。

"……我想邓布利多跟你谈过这些事情吧？"

哈利犹豫着，不知该不该说谎。他望着花坛四周的地精脚印，还有那块翻开的地皮，弗雷德就是在这里抓住了那个现在穿着芭蕾舞裙站在圣诞树顶的地精。最后他决定说实话……或说一点儿实话。

"对，我们谈过。"

"你们有没有，有没有……"哈利用眼角的余光看到斯克林杰正在注视着他，便假装对一个从结冰的杜鹃花丛下探出脑袋的地精很感兴趣，"邓布利多跟你说了什么，哈利？"

"对不起，这是我们之间的事。"哈利说。

他尽可能地让声音听上去很愉快，斯克林杰的语气也轻松而友好："哦，当然，如果是秘密，我不想让你泄漏……不，不……再说，你是不是救世之星真的要紧吗？"

## CHAPTER SIXTEEN  A Very Frosty Christmas

Harry had to mull that one over for a few seconds before responding.

'I don't really know what you mean, Minister.'

'Well, of course, to *you* it will matter enormously,' said Scrimgeour with a laugh. 'But to the wizarding community at large ... it's all perception, isn't it? It's what people believe that's important.'

Harry said nothing. He thought he saw, dimly, where they were heading, but he was not going to help Scrimgeour get there. The gnome under the rhododendron was now digging for worms at its roots and Harry kept his eyes fixed upon it.

'People believe you *are* the Chosen One, you see,' said Scrimgeour. 'They think you quite the hero – which, of course, you are, Harry, chosen or not! How many times have you faced He Who Must Not Be Named now? Well, anyway,' he pressed on, without waiting for a reply, 'the point is, you are a symbol of hope for many, Harry. The idea that there is somebody out there who might be able, who might even be *destined*, to destroy He Who Must Not Be Named – well, naturally, it gives people a lift. And I can't help but feel that, once you realise this, you might consider it, well, almost a duty, to stand alongside the Ministry, and give everyone a boost.'

The gnome had just managed to get hold of a worm. It was now tugging very hard on it, trying to get it out of the frozen ground. Harry was silent so long that Scrimgeour said, looking from Harry to the gnome, 'Funny little chaps, aren't they? But what say you, Harry?'

'I don't exactly understand what you want,' said Harry slowly. '"Stand alongside the Ministry" ... what does that mean?'

'Oh, well, nothing at all onerous, I assure you,' said Scrimgeour. 'If you were to be seen popping in and out of the Ministry from time to time, for instance, that would give the right impression. And of course, while you were there, you would have ample opportunity to speak to Gawain Robards, my successor as Head of the Auror Office. Dolores Umbridge has told me that you cherish an ambition to become an Auror. Well, that could be arranged very easily ...'

Harry felt anger bubbling in the pit of his stomach: so Dolores Umbridge was still at the Ministry, was she?

'So basically,' he said, as though he just wanted to clarify a few points, 'you'd like to give the impression that I'm working for the Ministry?'

'It would give everyone a lift to think you were more involved, Harry,' said

## 第 16 章 冰霜圣诞节

哈利琢磨了几秒钟后做出了回答。

"我不大懂您的意思,部长。"

"当然,对你来说非常要紧,"斯克林杰说着大笑起来,"然而对于巫师界……最要紧的是理念,是不是?人们相信的东西才是重要的。"

哈利没有搭腔。他觉得隐约看到了谈话会导向哪里,但他不想帮斯克林杰达到目的。杜鹃花丛底下的地精在树根附近挖起了虫子,哈利的眼睛一直盯着它。

"人们相信你是救世之星。你知道,"斯克林杰说,"他们认为你是英雄——你是英雄,哈利,不管是不是救世之星!你已多少次面对那个连名字都不能提的人了?总之,"他不等哈利回答,继续说了下去,"要紧的是,你在许多人的心目中是希望的象征,哈利。知道有人能,甚至注定能摧毁那个连名字都不能提的人——自然会让人们感到鼓舞。我不禁感到,一旦你认识到这一点,也许就会觉得你几乎有义务跟魔法部合作,给大家以信心。"

地精刚捉住一条虫子,正在使劲拉扯,想把虫子从冻硬的地里拽出来。哈利沉默了很久,斯克林杰看看他又看看地精,说道:"有趣的小家伙,是不是?可是你怎么想呢,哈利?"

"我不大明白你想要我做什么。"哈利缓缓地说,"'跟魔法部合作'……是什么意思?"

"哦,一点也不麻烦,我向你保证。比方说,如果你能时不时地出入魔法部,那就会给人一个有利的印象。当然,在部里的时候,你有许多机会和加德文·罗巴兹,也就是接替我的傲罗办公室主任多谈谈。多洛雷斯·乌姆里奇跟我说过你有志当一名傲罗。这很容易安排……"

哈利感到怒火中烧:这么说乌姆里奇还在魔法部?

"所以总的说来,"他说,好像只想澄清几点事实,"你想让大家以为我在为魔法部效力?"

"看到有你更多地参与,大家会受到鼓舞的,哈利,"斯克林杰说,

## CHAPTER SIXTEEN    A Very Frosty Christmas

Scrimgeour, sounding relieved that Harry had cottoned on so quickly. 'The "Chosen One", you know ... it's all about giving people hope, the feeling that exciting things are happening ...'

'But if I keep running in and out of the Ministry,' said Harry, still endeavouring to keep his voice friendly, 'won't that seem as though I approve of what the Ministry's up to?'

'Well,' said Scrimgeour, frowning slightly, 'well, yes, that's partly why we'd like –'

'No, I don't think that'll work,' said Harry pleasantly. 'You see, I don't like some of the things the Ministry's doing. Locking up Stan Shunpike, for instance.'

Scrimgeour did not speak for a moment, but his expression hardened instantly.

'I would not expect you to understand,' he said, and he was not as successful at keeping anger out of his voice as Harry had been. 'These are dangerous times, and certain measures need to be taken. You are sixteen years old –'

'Dumbledore's a lot older than sixteen, and he doesn't think Stan should be in Azkaban either,' said Harry. 'You're making Stan a scape-goat, just like you want to make me a mascot.'

They looked at each other, long and hard. Finally Scrimgeour said, with no pretence at warmth, 'I see. You prefer – like your hero Dumbledore – to disassociate yourself from the Ministry?'

'I don't want to be used,' said Harry.

'Some would say it's your duty to be used by the Ministry!'

'Yeah, and others might say it's your duty to check people really are Death Eaters before you chuck them in prison,' said Harry, his temper rising now. 'You're doing what Barty Crouch did. You never get it right, you people, do you? Either we've got Fudge, pretending everything's lovely while people get murdered right under his nose, or we've got you, chucking the wrong people into jail and trying to pretend you've got the Chosen One working for you!'

'So you're not the Chosen One?' said Scrimgeour.

'I thought you said it didn't matter either way?' said Harry, with a bitter laugh. 'Not to you, anyway.'

'I shouldn't have said that,' said Scrimgeour quickly. 'It was tactless –'

'No, it was honest,' said Harry. 'One of the only honest things you've

他似乎对哈利这么快就领悟了他的话感到很欣慰,"救世之星,你明白……就是要给人希望,让人感到激动人心的事情在发生……"

"可如果我出入魔法部,"哈利说,仍然努力保持友好的语气,"不会让人觉得我赞成部里的做法吗?"

"呃,"斯克林杰说道,微微皱了皱眉头,"是的,也正是因为这个,我们希望——"

"不,我想不行,"哈利彬彬有礼地说,"您知道,我不喜欢魔法部做的某些事情,比如关押斯坦·桑帕克。"

斯克林杰一时没说话,但脸色马上沉了下来。

"我不指望你理解,"他说,但没能像哈利那样做到话语中不流露怒气,"现在形势危险,某些措施是必要的。你才十六岁——"

"邓布利多可远远不止十六岁,他也不赞成把斯坦·桑帕克关在阿兹卡班。"哈利说,"你把斯坦·桑帕克当成替罪羊,同时又想把我当成福神。"

两人互相瞪视了许久,最后斯克林杰不再伪装友善了,说道:"我看得出,你希望——像你心目中的英雄邓布利多一样——脱离魔法部?"

"我不想被利用。"

"有人会说你有义务为魔法部效力!"

"是,有人会说你有义务在把人关进监牢前先查明他是不是食死徒。"哈利说,他的火气上来了,"你所做的跟巴蒂·克劳奇一样。你们这些人从来就没有做对过,是不是?要么是福吉,有人在他眼皮底下被杀了还假装天下太平;要么就是你,关押无辜,还假装有救世之星在为你工作!"

"你不是救世之星?"斯克林杰问。

"你不是说这不重要吗?"哈利说,讽刺地笑了一声,"至少对你不重要。"

"我不该那么说,"斯克林杰立刻说,"措辞不当——"

"不,这很诚实,"哈利说,"是你对我说过的少数实话之一。你不

## CHAPTER SIXTEEN    A Very Frosty Christmas

said to me. You don't care whether I live or die, but you do care that I help you convince everyone you're winning the war against Voldemort. I haven't forgotten, Minister ...'

He raised his right fist. There, shining white on the back of his cold hand, were the scars which Dolores Umbridge had forced him to carve into his own flesh: *I must not tell lies.*

'I don't remember you rushing to my defence when I was trying to tell everyone Voldemort was back. The Ministry wasn't so keen to be pals last year.'

They stood in silence as icy as the ground beneath their feet. The gnome had finally managed to extricate its worm and was now sucking on it happily, leaning against the bottom-most branches of the rhododendron bush.

'What is Dumbledore up to?' said Scrimgeour brusquely. 'Where does he go, when he is absent from Hogwarts?'

'No idea,' said Harry.

'And you wouldn't tell me if you knew,' said Scrimgeour, 'would you?'

'No, I wouldn't,' said Harry.

'Well, then, I shall have to see whether I can't find out by other means.'

'You can try,' said Harry indifferently. 'But you seem cleverer than Fudge, so I'd have thought you'd have learned from his mistakes. He tried interfering at Hogwarts. You might have noticed he's not Minister any more, but Dumbledore's still Headmaster. I'd leave Dumbledore alone, if I were you.'

There was a long pause.

'Well, it is clear to me that he has done a very good job on you,' said Scrimgeour, his eyes cold and hard behind his wire-rimmed glasses. 'Dumbledore's man through and through, aren't you, Potter?'

'Yeah, I am,' said Harry. 'Glad we straightened that out.'

And turning his back on the Minister for Magic, he strode back towards the house.

关心我的死活，你在意的是要我帮你使大家相信你在战胜伏地魔。我没忘记，部长……"

他举起右拳，冰冷的手背上那道伤痕发着白光，是乌姆里奇逼他刻下的字迹：我不可以说谎。

"当我告诉大家伏地魔回来了的时候，并没看见你冲出来帮助我，魔法部去年可没这么热心交朋友。"

两人僵立在那儿，气氛像他们脚下的土地一样冰冷。地精终于把虫子拽了出来，靠在杜鹃花丛最低的那几根枝条上开心地吮吸着。

"邓布利多在干什么？"斯克林杰唐突地问，"他不在霍格沃茨的时候会去哪儿？"

"不知道。"

"你就是知道也不会告诉我，是不是？"

"是的，不会。"

"好吧，我只有看看能不能用其他办法搞清楚了。"

"你可以试试，"哈利冷漠地说，"不过你看上去比福吉聪明，所以我认为你会吸取他的教训。他企图干涉霍格沃茨，你也许注意到他已经不是部长了，但邓布利多还是校长。如果我是你，就不去干涉邓布利多。"

一阵长时间的沉默。

"我看出他在你身上做得很成功，"斯克林杰说，金丝边眼镜后的眼睛冷漠而严厉，"你彻头彻尾是邓布利多的人，对不对，波特？"

"对，我是，"哈利说，"很高兴我们说清了这一点。"

他转身丢下魔法部部长，大步朝屋里走去。

## CHAPTER SEVENTEEN

# A Sluggish Memory

Late in the afternoon, a few days after New Year, Harry, Ron and Ginny lined up beside the kitchen fire to return to Hogwarts. The Ministry had arranged this one-off connection to the Floo Network to return students quickly and safely to the school. Only Mrs Weasley was there to say goodbye, as Mr Weasley, Fred, George, Bill and Fleur were all at work. Mrs Weasley dissolved into tears at the moment of parting. Admittedly, it took very little to set her off lately; she had been crying on and off ever since Percy had stormed from the house on Christmas Day with his glasses splattered with mashed parsnip (for which Fred, George and Ginny all claimed credit).

'Don't cry, Mum,' said Ginny, patting her on the back as Mrs Weasley sobbed into her shoulder. 'It's OK ...'

'Yeah, don't worry about us,' said Ron, permitting his mother to plant a very wet kiss on his cheek, 'or about Percy. He's such a prat, it's not really a loss, is it?'

Mrs Weasley sobbed harder than ever as she enfolded Harry in her arms.

'Promise me you'll look after yourself ... stay out of trouble ...'

'I always do, Mrs Weasley,' said Harry. 'I like a quiet life, you know me.'

She gave a watery chuckle and stood back.

'Be good, then, all of you ...'

Harry stepped into the emerald fire and shouted, 'Hogwarts!' He had one last fleeting view of the Weasleys' kitchen and Mrs Weasley's tearful face before the flames engulfed him; spinning very fast, he caught blurred glimpses of other wizarding rooms, which were whipped out of sight before he could get a proper look; then he was slowing down, finally stopping squarely in the fireplace in Professor McGonagall's office. She barely glanced up from her work as he clambered out over the grate.

## 第 17 章

## 混沌的记忆

过完新年几天后的一个傍晚,哈利、罗恩和金妮在厨房炉火边排队准备返回霍格沃茨。魔法部安排了这个一次性的飞路网连接,好让学生快速安全地返校。只有韦斯莱夫人为他们送行,韦斯莱先生、弗雷德、乔治、比尔和芙蓉都要上班。韦斯莱夫人在说再见时流泪了。不得不说,近来一丁点儿小事都会引起她的伤感。自从圣诞节那天珀西眼镜上被泼了防风草根酱(弗雷德、乔治和金妮都有功劳),冲出家门之后,她就时不时地会哭起来。

"别哭,妈妈,"金妮拍着她的背说,韦斯莱夫人这时正伏在她的肩头抽泣,"没事的……"

"就是,别为我们担心,"罗恩说,让母亲在他面颊上印下一个湿漉漉的吻,"也别为珀西担心,他是这么个傻瓜,没啥可惜的,是不是?"

韦斯莱夫人搂住哈利,抽泣得更厉害了。

"答应我要照顾好自己……别惹麻烦……"

"我一直是这样的,韦斯莱夫人,"哈利说,"我喜欢安静的生活,你知道。"

她含着眼泪笑了,退到了后面。

"那么,要好好的,你们每一个……"

哈利走进碧绿的炉火,喊了声"霍格沃茨!"最后瞥了一眼韦斯莱家的厨房和韦斯莱夫人的泪容,就被火焰包围了。在高速旋转中他模糊地看见一些巫师的房间,都是没等看清就一闪而过。然后他转得慢下来,端端正正地停在麦格教授办公室的壁炉里。他爬出来时,正在工作的教授几乎连头都没抬。

## CHAPTER SEVENTEEN  A Sluggish Memory

'Evening, Potter. Try not to get too much ash on the carpet.'

'No, Professor.'

Harry straightened his glasses and flattened his hair as Ron came spinning into view. When Ginny had arrived, all three of them trooped out of McGonagall's office and off towards Gryffindor Tower. Harry glanced out of the corridor windows as they passed; the sun was already sinking over grounds carpeted in deeper snow than had lain over The Burrow garden. In the distance, he could see Hagrid feeding Buckbeak in front of his cabin.

'Baubles,' said Ron confidently, when they reached the Fat Lady, who was looking rather paler than usual, and winced at his loud voice.

'No,' she said.

'What d'you mean, "no"?'

'There is a new password,' she said. 'And please don't shout.'

'But we've been away, how're we supposed to –?'

'Harry! Ginny!'

Hermione was hurrying towards them, very pink-faced and wearing a cloak, hat and gloves.

'I got back a couple of hours ago, I've just been down to visit Hagrid and Buck– I mean Witherwings,' she said breathlessly. 'Did you have a good Christmas?'

'Yeah,' said Ron at once, 'pretty eventful, Rufus Scrim–'

'I've got something for you, Harry,' said Hermione, neither looking at Ron nor giving any sign that she had heard him. 'Oh, hang on – password. *Abstinence*.'

'Precisely,' said the Fat Lady in a feeble voice, and swung forwards to reveal the portrait hole.

'What's up with her?' asked Harry.

'Overindulged over Christmas, apparently,' said Hermione, rolling her eyes as she led the way into the packed common room. 'She and her friend Violet drank their way through all the wine in that picture of drunk monks down by the Charms corridor. Anyway …'

She rummaged in her pocket for a moment, then pulled out a scroll of parchment with Dumbledore's writing on it.

'Great,' said Harry, unrolling it at once to discover that his next lesson with Dumbledore was scheduled for the following night. 'I've got loads to tell him – and you. Let's sit down –'

## 第17章 混沌的记忆

"晚上好，波特。别把地毯弄上太多的灰。"

"好的，教授。"

哈利戴正眼镜，抹平头发，罗恩也旋转着出现了。金妮到了之后，三人一起走出麦格教授的办公室，朝格兰芬多塔楼走去。哈利望了望走廊窗户外面，太阳已经落到地平线上，场地上的积雪比陋居花园里的还要深。远处可以看到海格在他的小屋前喂巴克比克。

"一文不值。"罗恩走到胖夫人跟前，自信地说。胖夫人看上去比平时更加苍白，听到他的大嗓门后畏缩了一下。

"不对。"她说。

"什么，'不对'？"

"换口令了。请不要嚷嚷。"

"可是我们离校了，怎么知道——"

"哈利！金妮！"

赫敏朝他们奔了过来，脸红通通的，穿着斗篷，戴着帽子和手套。

"我两小时前回来的。刚才去看了海格和巴克——我是说鹰翼。"她上气不接下气地说，"你们圣诞节过得好吗？"

"嗯，"罗恩马上说，"事儿挺多的，鲁弗斯·斯克林杰——"

"哈利，我有个东西要给你，"赫敏没看罗恩，好像根本没有听到他说话，"哦，等等——口令，戒酒。"

"正确。"胖夫人有气无力地说，旋开身体，露出了肖像洞口。

"她怎么了？"哈利问。

"显然是圣诞节玩得太疯了。"赫敏翻了翻眼睛，带头走进了拥挤的公共休息室，"她跟她的朋友维奥莱特，把魔咒课教室走廊旁那幅画着几个醉修士的图画里的酒全喝光了。总之……"

她在口袋里掏了一会儿，抽出一卷有邓布利多笔迹的羊皮纸。

"太好了，"哈利立刻展开它，发现他下一次跟邓布利多上课的时间就在明天晚上，"我有好多事要告诉他——还有你。我们坐下来吧——"

## CHAPTER SEVENTEEN    A Sluggish Memory

But at that moment there was a loud squeal of 'Won-Won!' and Lavender Brown came hurtling out of nowhere and flung herself into Ron's arms. Several onlookers sniggered; Hermione gave a tinkling laugh and said, 'There's a table over here ... coming, Ginny?'

'No, thanks, I said I'd meet Dean,' said Ginny, though Harry could not help noticing that she did not sound very enthusiastic. Leaving Ron and Lavender locked in a kind of vertical wrestling match, Harry led Hermione over to the spare table.

'So how was your Christmas?'

'Oh, fine,' she shrugged. 'Nothing special. How was it at Won-Won's?'

'I'll tell you in a minute,' said Harry. 'Look, Hermione, can't you –?'

'No, I can't,' she said flatly. 'So don't even ask.'

'I thought maybe, you know, over Christmas –'

'It was the Fat Lady who drank a vat of five-hundred-year-old wine, Harry, not me. So what was this important news you wanted to tell me?'

She looked too fierce to argue with at that moment, so Harry dropped the subject of Ron and recounted all that he had overheard between Malfoy and Snape.

When he had finished, Hermione sat in thought for a moment and then said, 'Don't you think –?'

'– he was pretending to offer help so that he could trick Malfoy into telling him what he's doing?'

'Well, yes,' said Hermione.

'Ron's dad and Lupin think so,' Harry said grudgingly. 'But this definitely proves Malfoy's planning something, you can't deny that.'

'No, I can't,' she answered slowly.

'And he's acting on Voldemort's orders, just like I said!'

'Hmm ... did either of them actually mention Voldemort's name?'

Harry frowned, trying to remember.

'I'm not sure ... Snape definitely said "your master", and who else would that be?'

'I don't know,' said Hermione, biting her lip. 'Maybe his father?'

She stared across the room, apparently lost in thought, not even noticing Lavender tickling Ron. 'How's Lupin?'

'Not great,' said Harry, and he told her all about Lupin's mission among

## 第17章 混沌的记忆

就在这时,他们忽然听见了一声响亮的尖叫:"罗－罗!"拉文德不知从哪儿冲了出来,扑进了罗恩怀里。旁边有几个人咻咻地笑着。赫敏银铃般地笑了一声,说道:"那边有张桌子……过去吗,金妮?"

"不,谢谢,我说好要去见迪安的。"金妮说。哈利不禁注意到她不是很有热情。罗恩和拉文德纠缠于一种直立式摔跤姿势,哈利就带着赫敏走到了那张空桌子前。

"你圣诞节过得怎么样?"

"哦,挺好的,"她耸了耸肩膀,"没什么特别的,罗－罗家呢?"

"待会儿告诉你。"哈利说,"喂,赫敏,你就不能——?"

"不能,"她坚决地说,"所以问都别问。"

"我想,也许过了圣诞节——"

"喝了一大桶五百年陈酒的是胖夫人,不是我,哈利。你要告诉我的重要消息是什么?"

这会儿她看上去脾气不好,没法跟她争,哈利丢开罗恩这个话题,讲了他听到的马尔福与斯内普的对话。

他说完后,赫敏坐在那儿沉思了片刻,说道:"你不觉得——?"

"——他是假装帮忙,骗马尔福跟他说实话?"

"嗯,是的。"赫敏说。

"罗恩的爸爸和卢平也这么想,"哈利不甘心地说,"但这肯定证明马尔福在密谋什么事情,你不能否认。"

"我不否认。"她缓缓地答道。

"他在执行伏地魔的命令,像我说的那样!"

"嗯……他们有谁提过伏地魔的名字吗?"

哈利皱起眉头,努力回忆。

"我不能确定……斯内普肯定说过'你的主人',那还能是谁?"

"我不知道,"赫敏咬着嘴唇说,"也许是他爸爸?"

她望着屋子那头,显然陷入了沉思,甚至没注意到拉文德在胳肢罗恩。"卢平好吗?"

"不大好,"哈利跟她讲了卢平在狼人中的使命以及他面临的困境,

## CHAPTER SEVENTEEN    A Sluggish Memory

the werewolves and the difficulties he was facing. 'Have you heard of this Fenrir Greyback?'

'Yes, I have!' said Hermione, sounding startled. 'And so have you, Harry!'

'When, History of Magic? You know full well I never listened ...'

'No, no, not History of Magic — Malfoy threatened Borgin with him!' said Hermione. 'Back in Knockturn Alley, don't you remember? He told Borgin that Greyback was an old family friend and that he'd be checking up on Borgin's progress!'

Harry gaped at her. 'I forgot! But this *proves* Malfoy's a Death Eater, how else could he be in contact with Greyback and telling him what to do?'

'It is pretty suspicious,' breathed Hermione. 'Unless ...'

'Oh, come on,' said Harry in exasperation, 'you can't get round this one!'

'Well ... there is the possibility it was an empty threat.'

'You're unbelievable, you are,' said Harry, shaking his head. 'We'll see who's right ... you'll be eating your words, Hermione, just like the Ministry. Oh yeah, I had a row with Rufus Scrimgeour as well ...'

And the rest of the evening passed amicably with both of them abusing the Minister for Magic, for Hermione, like Ron, thought that after all the Ministry had put Harry through the previous year, they had a great nerve asking him for help now.

The new term started next morning with a pleasant surprise for the sixth-years: a large sign had been pinned to the common-room notice-boards overnight.

> APPARITION LESSONS
>
> If you are seventeen years of age, or will turn seventeen on or before 31st August, you are eligible for a twelve-week course of Apparition Lessons from a Ministry of Magic Apparition Instructor. Please sign below if you would like to participate. Cost: 12 Galleons.

Harry and Ron joined the crowd that was jostling around the notice and taking it in turns to write their names underneath. Ron was just taking out his quill to sign after Hermione when Lavender crept up behind him, slipped her hands over his eyes and trilled, 'Guess who, Won-Won?' Harry turned

## 第17章 混沌的记忆

"你听说过芬里尔·格雷伯克吗？"

"听说过！"赫敏显得很吃惊，"你也听说过呀，哈利！"

"什么时候，魔法史课上？你明知道我从来不听……"

"不不，不是魔法史课上——马尔福用他威胁过博金！"赫敏说，"在翻倒巷，你不记得了？他对博金说格雷伯克是他家的老朋友，会来检查博金的进展！"

哈利愣愣地看着她。"我忘了！但这恰恰证明马尔福是食死徒，不然他怎么能接触格雷伯克，并吩咐他做事呢？"

"确实很可疑，"赫敏轻声道，"除非……"

"哦，得了吧，"哈利恼火地说，"你回避不了这个事实！"

"嗯……有可能只是空头威胁。"

"你的话真是让人难以置信。"哈利摇了摇头，说道，"我们以后会看到谁对谁错……你会收回你的话的，赫敏，像魔法部一样。哦，对了，我还跟鲁弗斯·斯克林杰吵了一架。"

晚上剩下的时间是在友好的气氛中度过的，两人共同批判了魔法部部长。赫敏跟罗恩一样认为，魔法部去年让哈利吃了那么多苦头，现在又来找他帮忙，脸皮真够厚的。

第二天早上新学期开始，六年级学生得到一个惊喜：公共休息室的布告栏上前一天晚上钉出了一张大告示。

### 幻影显形课

如果你已满十七岁或到八月三十一日年满十七岁，便可参加由魔法部幻影显形教员任教、为期十二周的幻影显形课程。

愿意参加者请在下面签名。

学费：十二加隆。

哈利和罗恩挤到告示前依次签名的学生中。罗恩刚拿出羽毛笔要在赫敏后面签名，拉文德悄悄走到他身后，用手蒙住了他的眼睛，嗲声嗲气地说："猜猜是谁，罗－罗？"哈利转身看到赫敏高傲地走开

## CHAPTER SEVENTEEN    A Sluggish Memory

to see Hermione stalking off; he caught up with her, having no wish to stay behind with Ron and Lavender, but to his surprise, Ron caught them up only a little way beyond the portrait hole, his ears bright red and his expression disgruntled. Without a word, Hermione sped up to walk with Neville.

'So – Apparition,' said Ron, his tone making it perfectly plain that Harry was not to mention what had just happened. 'Should be a laugh, eh?'

'I dunno,' said Harry. 'Maybe it's better when you do it yourself, I didn't enjoy it much when Dumbledore took me along for the ride.'

'I forgot you'd already done it ... I'd better pass my test first time,' said Ron, looking anxious. 'Fred and George did.'

'Charlie failed, though, didn't he?'

'Yeah, but Charlie's bigger than me,' Ron held his arms out from his body as though he were a gorilla, 'so Fred and George didn't go on about it much ... not to his face, anyway ...'

'When can we take the actual test?'

'Soon as we're seventeen. That's only March for me!'

'Yeah, but you wouldn't be able to Apparate in here, not in the castle ...'

'Not the point, is it? Everyone would know I *could* Apparate if I wanted.'

Ron was not the only one to be excited at the prospect of Apparition. All that day there was much talk about the forthcoming lessons; a great deal of store was set by being able to vanish and reappear at will.

'How cool will it be when we can just –' Seamus clicked his fingers to indicate disappearance. 'Me cousin Fergus does it just to annoy me, you wait till I can do it back ... he'll never have another peaceful moment ...'

Lost in visions of this happy prospect, he flicked his wand a little too enthusiastically, so that instead of producing the fountain of pure water that was the object of that day's Charms lesson, he let out a hose-like jet that ricocheted off the ceiling and knocked Professor Flitwick flat on his face.

'Harry's already Apparated,' Ron told a slightly abashed Seamus, after Professor Flitwick had dried himself off with a wave of his wand and set Seamus lines ('*I am a wizard, not a baboon brandishing a stick*'). 'Dum– er – someone took him. Side-Along-Apparition, you know.'

'Whoa!' whispered Seamus, and he, Dean and Neville put their heads a little closer to hear what Apparition felt like. For the rest of the day, Harry was besieged with requests from the other sixth-years to describe the sensation of

## 第 17 章 混沌的记忆

了,就追了上去,他也不想留在罗恩和拉文德旁边。但令他惊讶的是,罗恩在刚过肖像洞口不远处就追上了他们,耳朵通红,好像不大高兴。赫敏一句话没说,加快脚步跟纳威一起走了。

"这个——幻影显形,"罗恩的语气明显告诉哈利不许提刚才的事,"应该挺好玩的吧?"

"不知道,"哈利说,"也许自己做会好一点,邓布利多带我的那次可不大舒服。"

"我忘了你已经做过……我最好一次通过,"罗恩说,显得有点儿担心,"弗雷德和乔治都是一次就通过了。"

"但查理没有,是吧?"

"是的,可查理比我块头大,"罗恩伸长双臂,好像大猩猩那样,"所以弗雷德和乔治没有哪壶不开提哪壶……至少没有当着他的面……"

"我们什么时候可以参加考试?"

"满十七岁就行,我是三月!"

"噢,可你没法在这儿幻影显形,在这城堡里……"

"这不要紧,对不对?只要大家知道我能随意地幻影显形就够了。"

罗恩不是唯一一个为能学习幻影显形而兴奋的人。那一整天都有人在议论要开的这门课程,非常向往能够随意地消失和显形。

"多带劲啊,要是能——"西莫打了个响指代表消失,"我表哥菲戈故意用这招来气我,等我学会了……他就别想有一刻安生……"

他沉浸在憧憬中,挥魔杖的劲儿太足了点,把那天魔咒课作业要变的一股清泉变成了一道水柱,射到天花板上反弹下来,把弗立维教授打趴在地。

"哈利幻影显形过,"在弗立维教授挥动魔杖把自己弄干,并责罚西莫抄写句子我是个巫师,不是乱挥棍子的狒狒之后,罗恩对有点儿羞惭的西莫说,"邓——呃——有人带着他,随从显形过,知道吧。"

"哇!"西莫小声叫道,他、迪安和纳威把脑袋凑在一起,都想听听幻影显形是什么感觉。这一天剩下的时间里,哈利一直被缠着他讲述幻影显形的六年级学生包围。当他说那感觉很不舒服时,他们只是

## CHAPTER SEVENTEEN    A Sluggish Memory

Apparition. All of them seemed awed, rather than put off, when he told them how uncomfortable it was, and he was still answering detailed questions at ten to eight that evening, when he was forced to lie and say that he needed to return a book to the library, so as to escape in time for his lesson with Dumbledore.

The lamps in Dumbledore's office were lit, the portraits of previous headmasters were snoring gently in their frames and the Pensieve was ready upon the desk once more. Dumbledore's hands lay either side of it, the right one as blackened and burned-looking as ever. It did not seem to have healed at all and Harry wondered, for perhaps the hundredth time, what had caused such a distinctive injury, but did not ask; Dumbledore had said that he would know eventually and there was, in any case, another subject he wanted to discuss. But before Harry could say anything about Snape and Malfoy, Dumbledore spoke.

'I hear that you met the Minister for Magic over Christmas?'

'Yes,' said Harry. 'He's not very happy with me.'

'No,' sighed Dumbledore. 'He is not very happy with me, either. We must try not to sink beneath our anguish, Harry, but battle on.'

Harry grinned.

'He wanted me to tell the wizarding community that the Ministry's doing a wonderful job.'

Dumbledore smiled.

'It was Fudge's idea originally, you know. During his last days in office, when he was trying desperately to cling to his post, he sought a meeting with you, hoping that you would give him your support –'

'After everything Fudge did last year?' said Harry angrily. 'After *Umbridge*?'

'I told Cornelius there was no chance of it, but the idea did not die when he left office. Within hours of Scrimgeour's appointment we met and he demanded that I arrange a meeting with you –'

'So that's why you argued!' Harry blurted out. 'It was in the *Daily Prophet*.'

'The *Prophet* is bound to report the truth occasionally,' said Dumbledore, 'if only accidentally. Yes, that was why we argued. Well, it appears that Rufus found a way to corner you at last.'

'He accused me of being "Dumbledore's man through and through".'

'How very rude of him.'

'I told him I was.'

## 第17章 混沌的记忆

面露敬畏而不是失去兴趣。晚上八点差十分，他们还在要求他回答细节问题，哈利只好谎称要去图书馆还书，才抽身出来赶到邓布利多那儿去上课。

邓布利多办公室的灯亮着，历任校长的肖像在相框里轻轻打着鼾。冥想盆又摆在了桌上，邓布利多双手扶着盆沿，右手仍是焦黑色，似乎一点没有好转。哈利第一百次地纳闷是什么造成了这么特别的损伤，但他没有问。邓布利多说过他以后会知道的，况且他还有另一件事要说。但是没等哈利提起斯内普和马尔福，邓布利多就先开口了。

"我听说你圣诞节见过魔法部部长？"

"是的，他对我不大满意。"

"是啊，"邓布利多叹道，"他对我也不大满意。我们尽量不要因痛苦而消沉，哈利，继续奋斗。"

哈利笑了。

"他要我告诉巫师界，说魔法部干得很出色。"

邓布利多笑了起来。

"这原是福吉的主意。他在任的最后那些天，拼命要保住职位，曾经想要见你，希望你能支持他——"

"在福吉去年做了那些事之后？"哈利愤怒地问，"在乌姆里奇之后？"

"我告诉福吉不可能，但他离职后这个主意并没有消亡。斯克林杰被任命几小时后我们见了一面，他要求我安排和你面谈——"

"你们就为这个发生了争执？"哈利脱口而出，"《预言家日报》上登了。"

"《预言家日报》的确偶尔会报道一些真相，"邓布利多说，"虽然可能是无意的。对，我们就是为此发生了争执。看来鲁弗斯终于设法堵到了你。"

"他指责我'彻头彻尾是邓布利多的人'。"

"他真无礼。"

"我说我是的。"

## CHAPTER SEVENTEEN    A Sluggish Memory

Dumbledore opened his mouth to speak and then closed it again. Behind Harry, Fawkes the phoenix let out a low, soft, musical cry. To Harry's intense embarrassment, he suddenly realised that Dumbledore's bright blue eyes looked rather watery, and stared hastily at his own knees. When Dumbledore spoke, however, his voice was quite steady.

'I am very touched, Harry.'

'Scrimgeour wanted to know where you go when you're not at Hogwarts,' said Harry, still looking fixedly at his knees.

'Yes, he is very nosy about that,' said Dumbledore, now sounding cheerful, and Harry thought it safe to look up again. 'He has even attempted to have me followed. Amusing, really. He set Dawlish to tail me. It wasn't kind. I have already been forced to jinx Dawlish once; I did it again with the greatest regret.'

'So they still don't know where you go?' asked Harry, hoping for more information on this intriguing subject, but Dumbledore merely smiled over the top of his half-moon spectacles.

'No, they don't, and the time is not quite right for you to know, either. Now, I suggest we press on, unless there's anything else –?'

'There is, actually, sir,' said Harry. 'It's about Malfoy and Snape.'

'*Professor* Snape, Harry.'

'Yes, sir. I overheard them during Professor Slughorn's party ... well, I followed them, actually ...'

Dumbledore listened to Harry's story with an impassive face. When Harry had finished he did not speak for a few moments, then said, 'Thank you for telling me this, Harry, but I suggest that you put it out of your mind. I do not think that it is of great importance.'

'Not of great importance?' repeated Harry incredulously. 'Professor, did you understand –?'

'Yes, Harry, blessed as I am with extraordinary brainpower, I understood everything you told me,' said Dumbledore, a little sharply. 'I think you might even consider the possibility that I understood more than you did. Again, I am glad that you have confided in me, but let me reassure you that you have not told me anything that causes me disquiet.'

Harry sat in seething silence, glaring at Dumbledore. What was going on? Did this mean that Dumbledore had indeed ordered Snape to find out what Malfoy was doing, in which case he had already heard everything Harry had

## 第17章 混沌的记忆

邓布利多张嘴想说话,但又闭上了。在哈利身后,凤凰福克斯发出一声轻柔、悦耳的低鸣。哈利突然发现邓布利多那双明亮的蓝眼睛有些湿润,他大为窘迫,忙低头看着自己的膝盖。但邓布利多说话时,声音却相当平静。

"我很感动,哈利。"

"斯克林杰想知道你不在霍格沃茨的时候会去哪儿。"哈利仍然盯着膝盖。

"是啊,他很爱打听这个。"邓布利多的声音愉快起来,哈利感到可以抬头了,"他甚至企图盯我的梢,真是有趣。他派德力士跟踪我,这可不大好,我已经被迫对德力士用过恶咒,非常遗憾地又用了一次。"

"所以他们还不知道你去了哪儿?"哈利问,希望就这个他很好奇的问题获得更多信息,但邓布利多只是从半月形眼镜片上方望着他笑了笑。

"是啊,他们不知道,现在告诉你也还为时过早。现在,我建议我们继续上课,除非有别的事——?"

"有,先生,"哈利说,"是关于马尔福和斯内普的。"

"斯内普教授,哈利。"

"是的,先生。我听到他们在斯拉格霍恩教授的晚会上……嗯,实际上是我跟踪了他们……"

邓布利多不动声色地听着。哈利讲完后他沉默了一会儿,然后说道:"谢谢你告诉我,哈利,但我建议你别把这事放在心上。我认为这不是很重要。"

"不是很重要?"哈利不相信地说,"教授,你理解——?"

"是的,哈利,感谢上天赐予我非凡的智力,我理解你对我讲的一切。"邓布利多有点尖锐地说,"我想你甚至可以相信我比你更理解。我很高兴你能告诉我,但我向你保证,你没有说到令我不安的事情。"

哈利坐在那儿瞪着邓布利多,心里像开了锅。这到底是怎么回事?难道邓布利多真的授意斯内普去探明马尔福的动向,他已从斯内普口

## CHAPTER SEVENTEEN    A Sluggish Memory

just told him from Snape? Or was he really worried by what he had heard, but pretending not to be?

'So, sir,' said Harry, in what he hoped was a polite, calm voice, 'you definitely still trust –?'

'I have been tolerant enough to answer that question already,' said Dumbledore, but he did not sound very tolerant any more. 'My answer has not changed.'

'I should think not,' said a snide voice; Phineas Nigellus was evidently only pretending to be asleep. Dumbledore ignored him.

'And now, Harry, I must insist that we press on. I have more important things to discuss with you this evening.'

Harry sat there feeling mutinous. How would it be if he refused to permit the change of subject, if he insisted upon arguing the case against Malfoy? As though he had read Harry's mind, Dumbledore shook his head.

'Ah, Harry, how often this happens, even between the best of friends! Each of us believes that what he has to say is much more important than anything the other might have to contribute!'

'I don't think what you've got to say is unimportant, sir,' said Harry stiffly.

'Well, you are quite right, because it is not,' said Dumbledore briskly. 'I have two more memories to show you this evening, both obtained with enormous difficulty, and the second of them is, I think, the most important I have collected.'

Harry did not say anything to this; he still felt angry at the reception his confidences had received, but could not see what was to be gained by arguing further.

'So,' said Dumbledore, in a ringing voice, 'we meet this evening to continue the tale of Tom Riddle, whom we left last lesson poised on the threshold of his years at Hogwarts. You will remember how excited he was to hear that he was a wizard, that he refused my company on a trip to Diagon Alley and that I, in turn, warned him against continued thievery when he arrived at school.

'Well, the start of the school year arrived and with it came Tom Riddle, a quiet boy in his second-hand robes, who lined up with the other first-years to be Sorted. He was placed in Slytherin house almost the moment that the Sorting Hat touched his head,' continued Dumbledore, waving his blackened hand towards the shelf over his head where the Sorting Hat sat, ancient and unmoving. 'How soon Riddle learned that the famous founder of the house

## 第 17 章 混沌的记忆

中听过哈利所说的情况？抑或他实际上很担忧，只是装出一副若无其事的样子？

"那么，先生，"哈利用他希望是礼貌、平静的声音说，"你还是信任——"

"我已经够宽容地答复了这个问题，"邓布利多说，但语气不再宽容，"我的回答没有变。"

"我想也没有。"一个讥讽的声音说。菲尼亚斯·奈杰勒斯显然只是在装睡。邓布利多没有理他。

"现在，哈利，我必须坚持继续上课了。今晚我有更重要的事情跟你讨论。"

哈利不服气地坐在那儿，如果他拒绝转换话题呢，如果他坚持争论马尔福的问题呢？邓布利多摇了摇头，仿佛看透了哈利的心思。

"啊，哈利，这是多么常见的事情，即使在最好的朋友之间！都相信自己要说的比对方的重要得多！"

"我不认为你要说的不重要，先生。"哈利语气生硬地说。

"嗯，你说对了，它确实很重要。"邓布利多轻快地说，"我今晚要给你看两个回忆，它们都来之不易，我想第二个是我收集到的所有回忆中最重要的一个。"

哈利没有说话，还在为他的情报遭受冷遇而生气，但他也看出再争下去没有什么好处。

"所以，"邓布利多朗声说道，"我们今晚要继续汤姆·里德尔的故事，上节课讲到他正要跨入霍格沃茨的门槛。你大概还记得他听说自己是巫师时是多么兴奋，还有他拒绝让我陪他去对角巷，我也警告过他进校后不得继续偷窃。"

"新学年开始，汤姆·里德尔来了，一个穿着二手袍子的安静男孩，跟其他新生一起排队参加分院仪式。分院帽几乎是一碰到他的脑袋，就把他分到了斯莱特林学院。"邓布利多继续说着，焦黑的手朝身后一挥，指了指那顶待在他头顶架子上、一动不动的古老陈旧的分院帽，"我不知道里德尔什么时候了解到该学院著名的创始人会说蛇

## CHAPTER SEVENTEEN  A Sluggish Memory

could talk to snakes, I do not know — perhaps that very evening. The knowledge can only have excited him and increased his sense of self-importance.

'However, if he was frightening or impressing fellow Slytherins with displays of Parseltongue in their common room, no hint of it reached the staff. He showed no sign of outward arrogance or aggression at all. As an unusually talented and very good-looking orphan, he naturally drew attention and sympathy from the staff almost from the moment of his arrival. He seemed polite, quiet and thirsty for knowledge. Nearly all were most favourably impressed by him.'

'Didn't you tell them, sir, what he'd been like when you met him at the orphanage?' asked Harry.

'No, I did not. Though he had shown no hint of remorse, it was possible that he felt sorry for how he had behaved before and was resolved to turn over a fresh leaf. I chose to give him that chance.'

Dumbledore paused and looked enquiringly at Harry, who had opened his mouth to speak. Here, again, was Dumbledore's tendency to trust people in spite of overwhelming evidence that they did not deserve it! But then Harry remembered something ...

'But you didn't *really* trust him, sir, did you? He told me ... the Riddle who came out of that diary said "Dumbledore never seemed to like me as much as the other teachers did".'

'Let us say that I did not take it for granted that he was trustworthy,' said Dumbledore. 'I had, as I have already indicated, resolved to keep a close eye upon him, and so I did. I cannot pretend that I gleaned a great deal from my observations at first. He was very guarded with me; he felt, I am sure, that in the thrill of discovering his true identity he had told me a little too much. He was careful never to reveal as much again, but he could not take back what he had let slip in his excitement, nor what Mrs Cole had confided in me. However, he had the sense never to try and charm me as he charmed so many of my colleagues.

'As he moved up the school, he gathered about him a group of dedicated friends; I call them that, for want of a better term, although as I have already indicated, Riddle undoubtedly felt no affection for any of them. This group had a kind of dark glamour within the castle. They were a motley collection; a mixture of the weak seeking protection, the ambitious seeking some shared glory, and the thuggish, gravitating towards a leader who could show them more refined forms of cruelty. In other words, they were the forerunners of the Death Eaters, and indeed some of them became the first Death Eaters after leaving Hogwarts.

## 第 17 章  混沌的记忆

佬腔——也许就是当天晚上。这个消息想必令他十分兴奋，并增加了他的自负。

"或许他在公共休息室里用蛇佬腔吓唬过斯莱特林的同学，好让他们佩服他，然而，这些都没有传到教员们耳朵里。他外表没有露出丝毫的傲慢或侵略性。作为一个资质超常又十分英俊的孤儿，他自然是几乎一到校就吸引了教员们的注意和同情。他看上去有礼貌、安静、对知识如饥似渴。几乎所有的人都对他印象很好。"

"你没告诉他们吗，你在孤儿院见到他时他是什么样子？"

"没有。他尽管未曾表示过忏悔，但也许对以前的行为有所自责，决心重新做人，我选择了给他这个机会。"

邓布利多停了下来，询问地望着哈利。哈利张嘴想说话，因为这又一次证明邓布利多过于信任别人，尽管有确凿的证据表明那些人不值得信任。但哈利想起了什么……

"但是你并不真正相信他，是不是？他告诉我……那个从日记里出来的里德尔说：'邓布利多似乎从来不像其他教师那样喜欢我。'"

"这么说吧，我不是无条件地认为他值得信任。"邓布利多说，"前面已经提过，我决定密切观察他，我确实这么做了。我不能说从一开始的观察中就发现了很多问题。他对我很戒备。我相信他是感觉到了，他在发现自己真实身份时激动难耐，对我说得太多了一点。他小心地注意不再过多地暴露，但他无法收回那些他在兴奋中说漏的话，也无法收回科尔夫人对我吐露的那些。然而，他很明智，没有企图像迷惑我的那么多同事那样来迷惑我。

"在学校的几年里，他在身边笼络了一群死心塌地的朋友，我这么说是因为没有更好的词，但我已经提过，里德尔无疑对他们毫无感情。这帮人在城堡里形成一种黑暗势力，他们成分复杂，弱者为寻求庇护，野心家想沾些威风，还有生性残忍者，被一个能教会他们更高形式残忍的领袖所吸引。换句话说，他们是食死徒的前身，有的在离开霍格沃茨后真的成了第一批食死徒。

# CHAPTER SEVENTEEN — A Sluggish Memory

'Rigidly controlled by Riddle, they were never detected in open wrong-doing, although their seven years at Hogwarts were marked by a number of nasty incidents to which they were never satisfactorily linked, the most serious of which was, of course, the opening of the Chamber of Secrets, which resulted in the death of a girl. As you know, Hagrid was wrongly accused of that crime.

'I have not been able to find many memories of Riddle at Hogwarts,' said Dumbledore, placing his withered hand on the Pensieve. 'Few who knew him then are prepared to talk about him; they are too terrified. What I know, I found out after he had left Hogwarts, after much pains-taking effort, after tracing those few who could be tricked into speaking, after searching old records and questioning Muggle and wizard witnesses alike.

'Those whom I could persuade to talk told me that Riddle was obsessed with his parentage. This is understandable, of course; he had grown up in an orphanage and naturally wished to know how he came to be there. It seems that he searched in vain for some trace of Tom Riddle Senior on the shields in the trophy room, on the lists of prefects in the old school records, even in the books of wizarding history. Finally he was forced to accept that his father had never set foot in Hogwarts. I believe that it was then that he dropped the name for ever, assumed the identity of Lord Voldemort, and began his investigations into his previously despised mother's family – the woman whom, you will remember, he had thought could not be a witch if she had succumbed to the shameful human weakness of death.

'All he had to go upon was the single name "Marvolo", which he knew from those who ran the orphanage had been his mother's father's name. Finally, after painstaking research through old books of wizarding families, he discovered the existence of Slytherin's surviving line. In the summer of his sixteenth year, he left the orphanage to which he returned annually and set off to find his Gaunt relatives. And now, Harry, if you will stand ...'

Dumbledore rose, and Harry saw that he was again holding a small crystal bottle filled with swirling, pearly memory.

'I was very lucky to collect this,' he said, as he poured the gleaming mass into the Pensieve. 'As you will understand when we have experienced it. Shall we?'

Harry stepped up to the stone basin and bowed obediently until his face sank through the surface of the memory; he felt the familiar sensation of falling through nothingness and then landed upon a dirty stone floor into almost total darkness.

## 第17章 混沌的记忆

"里德尔对他们控制得很严,人们从未发现这帮人公开做坏事,虽然他们在校那七年霍格沃茨发生过多起恶性事件,但都未能确凿地与他们联系起来。最严重的一起当然是密室的开启,造成一名女生死亡。你知道,海格为此案受了冤枉。

"我在霍格沃茨没有找到多少关于里德尔的记忆,"邓布利多说着把他那只枯皱的手放在冥想盆上,"当时认识他的人没有几个愿意谈他,他们太害怕了。我现在所知道的,是在他离开霍格沃茨后,我费了许多的劲儿,寻访少数几个能够被引出话来的人,查找旧时的记录,询问麻瓜和巫师之后才了解到的。

"那些肯帮我回忆的人告诉我,里德尔对他的身世很着迷。当然这可以理解,他在孤儿院长大,自然想知道他是怎么到那儿去的。看来他曾在奖品陈列室、在学校历史记录的级长名单中,甚至在魔法史书里搜寻过老汤姆·里德尔的踪迹,但一无所获。最后他不得不承认他父亲从未进过霍格沃茨。我相信就是在那时他抛弃了这个名字,改称伏地魔的,并开始调查以前被他轻视的他母亲的家史——你应该记得,他曾认为那个女人既然屈从于死亡这一人类的可耻弱点,就不可能是巫师。

"他唯一的线索只有'马沃罗'这个名字,他从孤儿院管理人员那里得知这是他外祖父的名字。在巫师家族的故纸堆中进行了一番艰苦查询后,他终于发现了斯莱特林家族残存的一支。十六岁那年的夏天,他离开了每年要回去的孤儿院,去寻找他冈特家的亲戚。现在,哈利,请站起来……"

邓布利多站起身,哈利看到他又拿着一个小水晶瓶,里面盛满了打着旋的珍珠色的回忆。

"我能收集到这个非常幸运。"邓布利多一边说一边把那亮晶晶的东西倒进冥想盆,"等我们经历了之后,你就会理解了。可以了吗?"

哈利走近石盆,顺从地俯下身子,将面孔浸入了回忆中。他又体验到那种熟悉的在虚空中坠落的感觉,然后落在一处肮脏的石头地上,周围几乎一片漆黑。

## CHAPTER SEVENTEEN    A Sluggish Memory

It took him several seconds to recognise the place, by which time Dumbledore had landed beside him. The Gaunts' house was now more indescribably filthy than anywhere Harry had ever seen. The ceiling was thick with cobwebs, the floor coated in grime; mouldy and rotting food lay upon the table amidst a mass of crusted pots. The only light came from a single guttering candle placed at the feet of a man with hair and beard so overgrown Harry could see neither eyes nor mouth. He was slumped in an armchair by the fire, and Harry wondered for a moment whether he was dead. But then there came a loud knock on the door and the man jerked awake, raising a wand in his right hand, and a short knife in his left.

The door creaked open. There on the threshold, holding an old-fashioned lamp, stood a boy Harry recognised at once: tall, pale, dark-haired and handsome – the teenage Voldemort.

Voldemort's eyes moved slowly around the hovel and then found the man in the armchair. For a few seconds they looked at each other, then the man staggered upright, the many empty bottles at his feet clattering and tinkling across the floor.

'YOU!' he bellowed. 'YOU!'

And he hurtled drunkenly at Riddle, wand and knife held aloft.

'*Stop.*'

Riddle spoke in Parseltongue. The man skidded into the table, sending mouldy pots crashing to the floor. He stared at Riddle. There was a long silence while they contemplated each other. The man broke it.

'*You speak it?*'

'*Yes, I speak it,*' said Riddle. He moved forwards into the room, allowing the door to swing shut behind him. Harry could not help but feel a resentful admiration for Voldemort's complete lack of fear. His face merely expressed disgust and, perhaps, disappointment.

'*Where is Marvolo?*' he asked.

'*Dead,*' said the other. '*Died years ago, didn't he?*'

Riddle frowned.

'*Who are you, then?*'

'*I'm Morfin, ain't I?*'

'*Marvolo's son?*'

'*Course I am, then …*'

## 第 17 章 混沌的记忆

过了几秒钟他才认出了这个地方,这时邓布利多也落在了他身旁。冈特家污秽得无法形容,比哈利见过的任何地方都脏。天花板上结着厚厚的蛛网,地面黑乎乎的,桌上搁着霉烂的食物和一堆生锈的锅。唯一的光线来自一个男人脚边那根摇摇欲灭的蜡烛。男人的头发胡子已经长得遮住了眼睛和嘴巴。他瘫倒在烛火旁的一张扶手椅上,有那么一刻,哈利甚至猜测他是不是死了,但忽然响起的重重敲门声,使男人浑身一震,醒了过来,他右手举起魔杖,左手拿起一把短刀。

门吱呀一声开了,门口站着一个男孩,提着一盏老式的油灯。哈利立刻认了出来:高个儿,黑头发,脸色苍白,相貌英俊——少年伏地魔。

伏地魔的目光在脏屋子中缓缓移动,发现了扶手椅上的男人。他们对视了几秒钟,男人摇摇晃晃地站起来,脚边的许多酒瓶乒乒乓乓、叮叮当当地滚动着。

"你!"他吼道,"你!"

他醉醺醺地扑向里德尔,高举着魔杖和短刀。

"住手!"

里德尔用蛇佬腔说。那人刹不住脚撞到了桌子上,发了霉的锈锅摔落在地。他瞪着里德尔,两人久久地相互打量,男人先打破了沉默。

"你会说那种话?"

"对,我会说。"里德尔走进房间,门在他身后关上了。哈利不禁对伏地魔的毫无畏惧感到一种恼火的钦佩。伏地魔脸上显出厌恶,也许还有失望。

"马沃罗在哪儿?"他问。

"死了,"对方说,"死了好多年了,不是吗?"

里德尔皱了皱眉。

"那你是谁?"

"我是莫芬,不是吗?"

"马沃罗的儿子?"

"当然是了,那……"

## CHAPTER SEVENTEEN    A Sluggish Memory

Morfin pushed the hair out of his dirty face, the better to see Riddle, and Harry saw that he wore Marvolo's black-stoned ring on his right hand.

'*I thought you was that Muggle,*' whispered Morfin. '*You look mighty like that Muggle.*'

'*What Muggle?*' said Riddle sharply.

'*That Muggle what my sister took a fancy to, that Muggle what lives in the big house over the way,*' said Morfin, and he spat unexpectedly upon the floor between them. '*You look right like him. Riddle. But he's older now, i'n 'e? He's older'n you, now I think on it ...*'

Morfin looked slightly dazed and swayed a little, still clutching the edge of the table for support.

'*He come back, see,*' he added stupidly.

Voldemort was gazing at Morfin, as though appraising his possibilities. Now he moved a little closer and said, '*Riddle came back?*'

'*Ar, he left her, and serve her right, marrying filth!*' said Morfin, spitting on the floor again. '*Robbed us, mind, before she ran off! Where's the locket, eh, where's Slytherin's locket?*'

Voldemort did not answer. Morfin was working himself into a rage again; he brandished his knife and shouted, '*Dishonoured us, she did, that little slut! And who're you, coming here and asking questions about all that? It's over, innit ... it's over ...*'

He looked away, staggering slightly, and Voldemort moved forwards. As he did so, an unnatural darkness fell, extinguishing Voldemort's lamp and Morfin's candle, extinguishing everything ...

Dumbledore's fingers closed tightly around Harry's arm and they were soaring back into the present again. The soft golden light in Dumbledore's office seemed to dazzle Harry's eyes after that impenetrable darkness.

'Is that all?' said Harry at once. 'Why did it go dark, what happened?'

'Because Morfin could not remember anything from that point onwards,' said Dumbledore, gesturing Harry back into his seat. 'When he awoke next morning, he was lying on the floor, quite alone. Marvolo's ring had gone.

'Meanwhile, in the village of Little Hangleton, a maid was running along the high street, screaming that there were three bodies lying in the drawing room of the big house: Tom Riddle Senior, and his mother and father.

'The Muggle authorities were perplexed. As far as I am aware, they do not know to this day how the Riddles died, for the Avada Kedavra Curse does not usually leave any sign of damage ... the exception sits before me,' Dumbledore

## 第 17 章 混沌的记忆

莫芬拨开脏脸上的头发，好看清里德尔。哈利看出他右手上戴着马沃罗的黑宝石戒指。

"我以为你是那个麻瓜，"莫芬小声说，"你看上去特别像那个麻瓜。"

"哪个麻瓜？"里德尔厉声问。

"我妹妹迷上的那个麻瓜，住在对面大宅子里的那个麻瓜。"莫芬说着，出人意料地朝两人之间的地上啐了一口，"你看上去很像他。里德尔。但他现在年纪大了，是不是？他比你大，我想起来了……"

莫芬似乎有点儿晕，他摇晃了一下，但仍扶着桌边。

"他回来了，知道吧。"他傻乎乎地加了一句。

伏地魔盯着莫芬，好像在估计他的潜能。现在他走近了一些，说道："里德尔回来了？"

"啊，他抛弃了我妹妹，我妹妹活该，嫁给了垃圾！"莫芬又朝地上啐了一口，"还抢我们的东西，在她逃跑之前！挂坠盒呢，哼，斯莱特林的挂坠盒哪儿去了？"

伏地魔没有说话。莫芬又愤怒起来，挥舞着短刀大叫："丢了我们的脸，她，那个小荡妇！你是谁？到这儿来问这些问题？都过去了，不是吗……都过去了……"

他移开了目光，身子微微摇晃。伏地魔走上前。这时，一片异常的黑暗袭来，吞没了伏地魔的油灯和莫芬的蜡烛，吞没了一切……

邓布利多的手紧紧抓着哈利的胳膊，两人腾空飞回了现实。在经历了那穿不透的黑暗之后，邓布利多办公室柔和的金黄色灯光令哈利觉得有些刺眼。

"就这些？"哈利马上问，"为什么一下子黑了，发生了什么事？"

"因为莫芬想不起此后的事了。"邓布利多招手让哈利坐下，"他第二天早上醒来时是一个人躺在地上，马沃罗的戒指不见了。

"与此同时，在小汉格顿村，一个女仆在大街上尖叫狂奔，说大宅子的客厅里有三具尸体：老汤姆·里德尔和他的父母。

"麻瓜当局一筹莫展。据我所知，他们至今仍不知道里德尔一家是怎么死的，因为阿瓦达索命咒一般都不留任何伤痕……唯一的例外正

## CHAPTER SEVENTEEN    A Sluggish Memory

added, with a nod to Harry's scar. 'The Ministry, on the other hand, knew at once that this was a wizard's murder. They also knew that a convicted Muggle-hater lived across the valley from the Riddle house, a Muggle-hater who had already been imprisoned once for attacking one of the murdered people.

'So the Ministry called upon Morfin. They did not need to question him, to use Veritaserum or Legilimency. He admitted to the murder on the spot, giving details only the murderer could know. He was proud, he said, to have killed the Muggles, had been awaiting his chance all these years. He handed over his wand, which was proved at once to have been used to kill the Riddles. And he permitted himself to be led off to Azkaban without a fight. All that disturbed him was the fact that his father's ring had disappeared. "He'll kill me for losing it," he told his captors, over and over again. "He'll kill me for losing his ring." And that, apparently, was all he ever said again. He lived out the remainder of his life in Azkaban, lamenting the loss of Marvolo's last heirloom, and is buried beside the prison alongside the other poor souls who have expired within its walls.'

'So Voldemort stole Morfin's wand and used it?' said Harry, sitting up straight.

'That's right,' said Dumbledore. 'We have no memories to show us this, but I think we can be fairly sure what happened. Voldemort Stupefied his uncle, took his wand, and proceeded across the valley to "the big house over the way". There he murdered the Muggle man who had abandoned his witch mother, and, for good measure, his Muggle grandparents, thus obliterating the last of the unworthy Riddle line and revenging himself upon the father who never wanted him. Then he returned to the Gaunt hovel, performed the complex bit of magic that would implant a false memory in his uncle's mind, laid Morfin's wand beside its unconscious owner, pocketed the ancient ring he wore and departed.'

'And Morfin never realised he hadn't done it?'

'Never,' said Dumbledore. 'He gave, as I say, a full and boastful confession.'

'But he had this real memory in him all the time!'

'Yes, but it took a great deal of skilled Legilimency to coax it out of him,' said Dumbledore, 'and why should anybody delve further into Morfin's mind when he had already confessed to the crime? However, I was able to secure a visit to Morfin in the last weeks of his life, by which time I was attempting to discover as much as I could about Voldemort's past. I extracted this memory with difficulty. When I saw what it contained, I attempted to use it to secure Morfin's release from Azkaban. Before the Ministry reached their decision, however, Morfin had died.'

## 第 17 章 混沌的记忆

坐在我面前。"邓布利多朝哈利的伤疤点了一下头,接着说道,"但魔法部立刻就知道是巫师下的毒手。他们还知道一个素来憎恨麻瓜的人住在里德尔家对面,而且此人曾因袭击此案中的一名被害人而进过监狱。

"于是魔法部找到莫芬,都没用审问,也没用吐真剂或摄神取念,他当即供认不讳,提供了只有凶手才知道的细节,并说他为杀了那些麻瓜而自豪,说他多年来一直在等待这个机会。他交出的魔杖立刻被证明是杀害里德尔一家的凶器。他没有抵抗,乖乖地被带进了阿兹卡班。唯一令他不安的是他父亲的戒指不见了。'他会杀了我的。'他反复对逮捕他的人说,'我丢了他的戒指,他会杀了我的。'那似乎是他后来仅有的话。他在阿兹卡班度过余生,哀悼马沃罗最后一件传家宝的丢失,最后被葬在监狱旁边,与那些死在狱中的其他可怜人葬在一起。"

"伏地魔偷了莫芬的魔杖,用它杀了人?"哈利说着坐直了身体。

"不错,"邓布利多说,"没有回忆证明这一点,但我想应该是八九不离十。伏地魔击昏了他的舅舅,拿走了他的魔杖,穿过山谷到'对面的大宅子'去了,杀死了那个抛弃他那巫师母亲的麻瓜,顺带杀掉了他的麻瓜祖父母,抹去了不争气的里德尔家族,也报复了从来不想要他的那位生父。他回到冈特家,施了一点儿复杂的魔法,把假记忆植入他舅舅的脑子又将魔杖放在它昏迷的主人身旁,然后拿了那枚古老的戒指扬长而去。"

"莫芬从没想到不是他自己干的?"

"没有。我说过,他供认不讳,并且十分自豪。"

"但他一直保留着这段真实的记忆!"

"是的,但需要大量高技巧的摄神取念才能把它引出来。而且莫芬已经认罪,谁还会去挖他的思想呢?但我在他存世的最后几个星期里去探过监,那时我正努力设法了解伏地魔的过去。我好不容易提取了这段回忆,看到这些内容后,我试图争取把莫芬放出阿兹卡班。但魔法部还没有做出决定,莫芬就去世了。"

## CHAPTER SEVENTEEN    A Sluggish Memory

'But how come the Ministry didn't realise that Voldemort had done all that to Morfin?' Harry asked angrily. 'He was under age at the time, wasn't he? I thought they could detect under-age magic!'

'You are quite right – they can detect magic, but not the perpetrator: you will remember that you were blamed by the Ministry for the Hover Charm that was, in fact, cast by –'

'Dobby,' growled Harry; this injustice still rankled. 'So if you're under age and you do magic inside an adult witch or wizard's house, the Ministry won't know?'

'They will certainly be unable to tell who performed the magic,' said Dumbledore, smiling slightly at the look of great indignation on Harry's face. 'They rely on witch and wizard parents to enforce their offspring's obedience while within their walls.'

'Well, that's rubbish,' snapped Harry. 'Look what happened here, look what happened to Morfin!'

'I agree,' said Dumbledore. 'Whatever Morfin was, he did not deserve to die as he did, blamed for murders he had not committed. But it is getting late, and I want you to see this other memory before we part ...'

Dumbledore took from an inside pocket another crystal phial and Harry fell silent at once, remembering that Dumbledore had said it was the most important one he had collected. Harry noticed that the contents proved difficult to empty into the Pensieve, as though they had congealed slightly; did memories go off?

'This will not take long,' said Dumbledore, when he had finally emptied the phial. 'We shall be back before you know it. Once more into the Pensieve, then ...'

And Harry fell again through the silver surface, landing this time right in front of a man he recognised at once.

It was a much younger Horace Slughorn. Harry was so used to him bald that he found the sight of Slughorn with thick, shiny, straw-coloured hair quite disconcerting; it looked as though he had had his head thatched, though there was already a shiny Galleon-sized bald patch on his crown. His moustache, less massive than it was these days, was gingery-blond. He was not quite as rotund as the Slughorn Harry knew, though the golden buttons on his richly embroidered waistcoat were taking a fair amount of strain. His little feet resting upon a velvet pouffe, he was sitting well back in a comfortable winged armchair, one hand grasping a small glass of wine, the other searching through a box of crystallised pineapple.

## 第17章 混沌的记忆

"可魔法部怎么没想到伏地魔对莫芬做了什么呢？"哈利愤然道，"他当时还未成年，对吧？我以为他们能测出未成年人施的魔法呢！"

"你说得很对——他们能测出魔法，但测不出施魔法者：你还记得魔法部指控你施了悬停咒，而实际上是——"

"多比干的。"哈利低吼道，那次受冤枉依然让他愤愤不平，"所以如果你未成年，你在成年巫师的家里施魔法，魔法部不会知道？"

"他们肯定搞不清是谁施了魔法。"邓布利多说，对哈利大为愤慨的表情微微一笑，"他们靠巫师父母来监督孩子在家中的行为。"

"那是胡闹。"哈利激动地说，"看看发生了什么，看看莫芬！"

"我同意，"邓布利多说，"不管莫芬是什么人，他都不应该那样屈死在狱中，顶着一个他没有犯过的谋杀罪名。但时间已晚，我想在结束前再给你看一段记忆……"

邓布利多从衣服内侧的口袋里又摸出一个小水晶瓶，哈利顿时安静下来，想起邓布利多说这是他收集的记忆中最重要的一个。哈利注意到瓶里的东西不太容易倒进冥想盆，好像有点凝结，难道记忆也会变质吗？

"这个不长，"终于倒空小瓶后，邓布利多说，"我们一会儿就回来。好了，再次进入冥想盆吧……"

哈利又一次掉进了银色物质的表层，这次正落在一个人面前，他立刻认了出来。

这是年轻得多的霍拉斯·斯拉格霍恩，哈利习惯了他的秃顶，看到他此刻一头浓密光泽的淡黄色头发，觉得十分别扭，就好像他在头上盖了茅草，不过头顶已有一块亮亮的、金加隆那么大的秃斑。他的胡子没有现在多，是姜黄色的，身体也不像哈利认识的斯拉格霍恩那样滚圆，但那件绣花马甲的金纽扣已经绷得相当紧了。他一双小脚搁在天鹅绒大脚垫上，半躺在舒适的带翼扶手椅上，手里握着一小杯葡萄酒，另一只手在一盒菠萝蜜饯里挑拣着。

## CHAPTER SEVENTEEN — A Sluggish Memory

Harry looked around as Dumbledore appeared beside him and saw that they were standing in Slughorn's office. Half a dozen boys were sitting around Slughorn, all on harder or lower seats than his, and all in their mid-teens. Harry recognised Riddle at once. His was the most handsome face and he looked the most relaxed of all the boys. His right hand lay negligently upon the arm of his chair; with a jolt, Harry saw that he was wearing Marvolo's gold and black ring; he had already killed his father.

'Sir, is it true that Professor Merrythought is retiring?' Riddle asked.

'Tom, Tom, if I knew I couldn't tell you,' said Slughorn, wagging a reproving, sugar-covered finger at Riddle, though ruining the effect slightly by winking. 'I must say, I'd like to know where you get your information, boy; more knowledgeable than half the staff, you are.'

Riddle smiled; the other boys laughed and cast him admiring looks.

'What with your uncanny ability to know things you shouldn't, and your careful flattery of the people who matter – thank you for the pineapple, by the way, you're quite right, it is my favourite –'

As several of the boys tittered, something very odd happened. The whole room was suddenly filled with a thick white fog, so that Harry could see nothing but the face of Dumbledore, who was standing beside him. Then Slughorn's voice rang out through the mist, unnaturally loudly: '*– you'll go wrong, boy, mark my words.*'

The fog cleared as suddenly as it had appeared and yet nobody made any allusion to it, nor did anybody look as though anything unusual had just happened. Bewildered, Harry looked around as a small golden clock standing upon Slughorn's desk chimed eleven o'clock.

'Good gracious, is it that time already?' said Slughorn. 'You'd better get going, boys, or we'll all be in trouble. Lestrange, I want your essay by tomorrow or it's detention. Same goes for you, Avery.'

Slughorn pulled himself out of his armchair and carried his empty glass over to his desk as the boys filed out. Riddle, however, stayed behind. Harry could tell he had dawdled deliberately, wanting to be last in the room with Slughorn.

'Look sharp, Tom,' said Slughorn, turning round and finding him still present. 'You don't want to be caught out of bed out of hours, and you a prefect ...'

'Sir, I wanted to ask you something.'

'Ask away, then, m'boy, ask away ...'

## 第 17 章　混沌的记忆

邓布利多出现在身边，哈利环顾四周，发现他们站在斯拉格霍恩的办公室里。六个男孩围坐在斯拉格霍恩旁边，都是十五六岁，椅子都比他的硬或矮。哈利立刻认出了里德尔。他面容最英俊，也是看上去最放松的一个，右手漫不经心地搭在椅子扶手上。哈利心中一震，看到他戴着马沃罗的黑宝石金戒指，这么说这时他已经杀害了他的父亲。

"先生，梅乐思教授要退休了吗？"里德尔问。

"汤姆，汤姆，我知道也不能告诉你。"斯拉格霍恩责备地对他摇晃着一根沾满糖霜的手指，但又眨眨眼睛，使责备的效果略微受到了破坏，"我不得不说，我想知道你的消息是从哪儿得来的，孩子，你比一半的教员知道的都多。"

里德尔微微一笑，其他男孩也笑了起来，向他投去钦佩的目光。

"你这个鬼灵精，能知道不该知道的事，又会小心讨好重要的人——顺便谢谢你的菠萝，你猜中了，这是我最喜欢的——"

几个男孩窃笑时，一件怪事发生了。整个房间突然被白色的浓雾笼罩，哈利只能看到身边邓布利多的脸。斯拉格霍恩的声音在屋里响起，高亢得很不自然："——你会犯错误的，孩子，记住我的话。"

雾散了，跟来的时候一样突然，但是没人提到它，从那些人脸上也看不出刚刚发生过什么异常的事情。哈利困惑地环顾四周，斯拉格霍恩书桌上的金色小钟敲响了十一点。

"老天，已经这么晚了？"斯拉格霍恩说，"该走啦，孩子们，不然我们就麻烦了。莱斯特兰奇，明天交论文，不然就关禁闭。你也一样，埃弗里。"

斯拉格霍恩从椅子上站起身来，把空杯子拿到桌前，男孩们鱼贯而出。但里德尔落在后面。哈利看得出他在故意磨蹭，希望单独跟斯拉格霍恩留在屋里。

"快点儿，汤姆，"斯拉格霍恩转身发现他还在，说道，"你不想被人抓到你在熄灯时间还待在外面吧，你是级长……"

"先生，我想问您一点事儿。"

"那就快问，孩子，快问……"

## CHAPTER SEVENTEEN    A Sluggish Memory

'Sir, I wondered what you know about ... about Horcruxes?'

And it happened all over again: the dense fog filled the room so that Harry could not see Slughorn or Riddle at all; only Dumbledore, smiling serenely beside him. Then Slughorn's voice boomed out again, just as it had done before.

'*I don't know anything about Horcruxes and I wouldn't tell you if I did! Now get out of here at once and don't let me catch you mentioning them again!*'

'Well, that's that,' said Dumbledore placidly beside Harry. 'Time to go.'

And Harry's feet left the floor to fall, seconds later, back on to the rug in front of Dumbledore's desk.

'That's all there is?' said Harry blankly.

Dumbledore had said that this was the most important memory of all, but he could not see what was so significant about it. Admittedly the fog, and the fact that nobody seemed to have noticed it, was odd, but other than that nothing seemed to have happened except that Riddle had asked a question and failed to get an answer.

'As you might have noticed,' said Dumbledore, reseating himself behind his desk, 'that memory has been tampered with.'

'Tampered with?' repeated Harry, sitting back down too.

'Certainly,' said Dumbledore, 'Professor Slughorn has meddled with his own recollections.'

'But why would he do that?'

'Because, I think, he is ashamed of what he remembers,' said Dumbledore. 'He has tried to rework the memory to show himself in a better light, obliterating those parts which he does not wish me to see. It is, as you will have noticed, very crudely done, and that is all to the good, for it shows that the true memory is still there beneath the alterations.

'And so, for the first time, I am giving you homework, Harry. It will be your job to persuade Professor Slughorn to divulge the real memory, which will undoubtedly be our most crucial piece of information of all.'

Harry stared at him.

'But surely, sir,' he said, keeping his voice as respectful as possible, 'you don't need me – you could use Legilimency ... or Veritaserum ...'

'Professor Slughorn is an extremely able wizard who will be expecting both,' said Dumbledore. 'He is much more accomplished at Occlumency than poor Morfin Gaunt, and I would be astonished if he has not carried an

## 第17章 混沌的记忆

"先生,我想问您知不知道……魂器。"

又来了:屋里浓雾弥漫,哈利看不见斯拉格霍恩也看不见里德尔了,只有邓布利多在他身边安详地微笑着。然后斯拉格霍恩的声音再次洪亮地响起,跟刚才一样。

"我对魂器一无所知,即使知道也不会告诉你!马上出去,不要让我再听到你提这个!"

"嗯,就这样,"邓布利多在哈利旁边平静地说,"该走了。"

哈利双脚离开了地面,几秒钟后落回到邓布利多书桌前的地毯上。

"就这些?"哈利茫然地问道。

邓布利多说过这是最重要的记忆,可是哈利看不出重要在哪里。当然,那突如其来的白雾,而且竟然似乎没人注意到它,确实很奇怪,但除此之外好像并没发生什么,只是里德尔问了一个问题,没有得到回答。

"你可能注意到了,"邓布利多坐回桌子后面,说道,"这段记忆被篡改过了。"

"篡改过?"哈利重复道,也坐了下来。

"当然,"邓布利多说,"斯拉格霍恩教授篡改了他自己的记忆。"

"他为什么要那么做呢?"

"因为,我想,他对这段记忆感到羞愧,所以就把它篡改了,使自己体面一些,抹去了他不想让我看到的部分。你也看见了,篡改得很拙劣,这倒是好事,说明真实的记忆还在底下。

"所以,我第一次要给你布置作业了,哈利。你要设法使斯拉格霍恩教授透露真实的记忆,这无疑将成为我们最关键的资料。"

哈利瞪圆了眼望着他。

"可是,先生,"他说,尽量保持语气的恭敬,"您不需要我——您可以用摄神取念……或吐真剂……"

"斯拉格霍恩教授是个非常有能耐的巫师,会防到这两招的。他大脑封闭的功夫比可怜的莫芬高明多了。自从我逼他交给我这个失真的

## CHAPTER SEVENTEEN — A Sluggish Memory

antidote to Veritaserum with him ever since I coerced him into giving me this travesty of a recollection.

'No, I think it would be foolish to attempt to wrest the truth from Professor Slughorn by force, and might do much more harm than good; I do not wish him to leave Hogwarts. However, he has his weaknesses like the rest of us and I believe that you are the one person who might be able to penetrate his defences. It is most important that we secure the true memory, Harry ... how important, we will only know when we have seen the real thing. So, good luck ... and goodnight.'

A little taken aback by the abrupt dismissal, Harry got to his feet quickly.

'Goodnight, sir.'

As he closed the study door behind him, he distinctly heard Phineas Nigellus say, 'I can't see why the boy should be able to do it better than you, Dumbledore.'

'I wouldn't expect you to, Phineas,' replied Dumbledore, and Fawkes gave another low, musical cry.

## 第17章 混沌的记忆

记忆之后,他肯定随身带着吐真剂的解药。

"我想,企图强行从斯拉格霍恩教授那儿获取真相是愚蠢的,弊大于利。我不希望他离开霍格沃茨。不过,他像我们大家一样有自己的弱点,我相信你是能够突破他防线的人。拿到真实的记忆非常重要,哈利……具体有多重要,只有在看了真东西之后才知道。所以,祝你好运……晚安。"

哈利对自己突然被打发走有些吃惊,但还是马上站了起来。

"晚安,先生。"

带上书房的门时,他清楚地听到菲尼亚斯·奈杰勒斯说:"我看不出那男孩怎么能比你更合适,邓布利多。"

"我也不指望你能看出来,菲尼亚斯。"邓布利多答道。福克斯又发出一声悦耳的低鸣。

## CHAPTER EIGHTEEN

# Birthday Surprises

The next day Harry confided in both Ron and Hermione the task that Dumbledore had set him, though separately, for Hermione still refused to remain in Ron's presence longer than it took to give him a contemptuous look.

Ron thought that Harry was unlikely to have any trouble with Slughorn at all.

'He loves you,' he said over breakfast, waving an airy forkful of fried egg. 'Won't refuse you anything, will he? Not his little Potions Prince. Just hang back after class this afternoon and ask him.'

Hermione, however, took a gloomier view.

'He must be determined to hide what really happened if Dumbledore couldn't get it out of him,' she said in a low voice, as they stood in the deserted, snowy courtyard at break. 'Horcruxes ... *Horcruxes* ... I've never even heard of them ...'

'You haven't?'

Harry was disappointed; he had hoped that Hermione might have been able to give him a clue as to what Horcruxes were.

'They must be really advanced Dark Magic, or why would Voldemort have wanted to know about them? I think it's going to be difficult to get the information, Harry, you'll have to be very careful about how you approach Slughorn, think out a strategy ...'

'Ron reckons I should just hang back after Potions this afternoon ...'

'Oh, well, if *Won-Won* thinks that, you'd better do it,' she said, flaring up at once. 'After all, when has *Won-Won's* judgement ever been faulty?'

'Hermione, can't you –'

## 第 18 章

## 生日的意外

第二天，哈利把邓布利多给他布置的作业告诉了罗恩和赫敏，是分别告诉的，因为赫敏仍然不肯在罗恩面前久待，最多只是轻蔑地白他一眼。

罗恩认为哈利在斯拉格霍恩那里不可能会遇到什么麻烦。

"他喜欢你，"吃早饭时，罗恩漫不经心地挥着一叉子煎鸡蛋说，"什么都不会拒绝你的，是不是？你是他的魔药小王子。今天下午课后留下来问他好了。"

赫敏则悲观一些。

"如果连邓布利多都拿不到，他一定是决心隐瞒真相了。"她低声说，这时是课间休息，他们站在积满白雪、冷冷清清的院子里，"魂器……魂器……我都没听说过……"

"你没听说过？"

哈利很失望，他还指望赫敏能提供一些线索呢。

"准是很高级的黑魔法，不然伏地魔为什么想知道？我觉得要搞到这个情报很困难，哈利，你必须非常谨慎，要想个计策，怎么接近斯拉格霍恩。"

"罗恩说只要我今天魔药课后留下来……"

"哦，既然罗－罗说了，你最好照办，"她顿时火冒三丈，"罗－罗的判断什么时候错过啊？"

"赫敏，你就不能——"

## CHAPTER EIGHTEEN   Birthday Surprises

'*No!*' she said angrily, and stormed away, leaving Harry alone and ankle-deep in snow.

Potions lessons were uncomfortable enough these days, seeing as Harry, Ron and Hermione had to share a desk. Today, Hermione moved her cauldron around the table so that she was close to Ernie, and ignored both Harry and Ron.

'What've *you* done?' Ron muttered to Harry, looking at Hermione's haughty profile.

But before Harry could answer, Slughorn was calling for silence from the front of the room.

'Settle down, settle down, please! Quickly, now, lots of work to get through this afternoon! Golpalott's Third Law ... who can tell me –? But Miss Granger can, of course!'

Hermione recited at top speed: 'Golpalott's-Third-Law-states-that-the-antidote-for-a-blended-poison-will-be-equal-to-more-than-the-sum-of-the-antidotes-for-each-of-the-separate-components.'

'Precisely!' beamed Slughorn. 'Ten points for Gryffindor! Now, if we accept Golpalott's Third Law as true ...'

Harry was going to have to take Slughorn's word for it that Golpalott's Third Law was true, because he had not understood any of it. Nobody apart from Hermione seemed to be following what Slughorn said next, either.

'... which means, of course, that assuming we have achieved correct identification of the potion's ingredients by Scarpin's Revelaspell, our primary aim is not the relatively simple one of selecting antidotes to those ingredients in and of themselves, but to find that added component which will, by an almost alchemical process, transform these disparate elements –'

Ron was sitting beside Harry with his mouth half open, doodling absently on his new copy of *Advanced Potion-Making*. Ron kept forgetting that he could no longer rely on Hermione to help him out of trouble when he failed to grasp what was going on.

'... and so,' finished Slughorn, 'I want each of you to come and take one of these phials from my desk. You are to create an antidote for the poison within it before the end of the lesson. Good luck, and don't forget your protective gloves!'

Hermione had left her stool and was halfway towards Slughorn's desk

## 第18章 生日的意外

"不能！"她怒气冲冲地甩了一句，转身就走，把哈利一个人丢在齐踝深的雪地里。

这些天的魔药课已经让人够不自在的了，因为哈利、罗恩和赫敏不得不坐在一张桌子旁。今天赫敏把她的坩埚挪到一边，和厄尼挨着坐，对哈利和罗恩两个人都不理了。

"你怎么得罪她了？"罗恩看着赫敏高傲的侧影，小声问哈利。

哈利还没来得及答话，斯拉格霍恩就在前面叫大家安静了。

"请静一静，静一静！快点儿，今天下午有很多事要做！戈巴洛特第三定律……谁能给我讲讲——？当然是格兰杰小姐啦！"

赫敏用最快的速度背道："戈巴洛特第三定律称，混合毒药之解药大于等于每种单独成分之解药之总和。"

"完全正确！"斯拉格霍恩微笑道，"格兰芬多加十分！现在，如果我们承认戈巴洛特第三定律成立……"

哈利只能按斯拉格霍恩的话相信戈巴洛特第三定律成立，因为他压根儿没听懂。除了赫敏之外，似乎谁也没听懂斯拉格霍恩下面的话：

"……当然，这意味着，假使我们已用斯卡平的现形咒正确分析出魔药的成分，我们的首要目标不是简单地选择每种个体成分的解药，而是找到附加成分，它能通过近乎炼金术的程序，把各种互不相干的成分变形——"

罗恩半张着嘴坐在哈利旁边，心不在焉地在他那本崭新的《高级魔药制作》上乱画。罗恩总是忘记他现在听不懂课已经不能再靠赫敏救他了。

"……所以，"斯拉格霍恩最后说，"我要你们每人来我的讲台上拿一个小瓶子，在下课前必须配出瓶中毒药的解药。祝你们好运，别忘了戴防护手套！"

赫敏马上离开凳子朝讲台走去，她走到一半时，其他人才意识到

## CHAPTER EIGHTEEN    Birthday Surprises

before the rest of the class had realised it was time to move, and by the time Harry, Ron and Ernie returned to the table, she had already tipped the contents of her phial into her cauldron and was kindling a fire underneath it.

'It's a shame that the Prince won't be able to help you much with this, Harry,' she said brightly as she straightened up. 'You have to understand the principles involved this time. No short cuts or cheats!'

Annoyed, Harry uncorked the poison he had taken from Slughorn's desk, which was a garish shade of pink, tipped it into his cauldron and lit a fire underneath it. He did not have the faintest idea what he was supposed to do next. He glanced at Ron, who was now standing there looking rather gormless, having copied everything Harry had done.

'You sure the Prince hasn't got any tips?' Ron muttered to Harry.

Harry pulled out his trusty copy of *Advanced Potion-Making* and turned to the chapter on Antidotes. There was Golpalott's Third Law, stated word for word as Hermione had recited it, but not a single illuminating note in the Prince's hand to explain what it meant. Apparently the Prince, like Hermione, had had no difficulty understanding it.

'Nothing,' said Harry gloomily.

Hermione was now waving her wand enthusiastically over her cauldron. Unfortunately, they could not copy the spell she was doing because she was now so good at non-verbal incantations that she did not need to say the words aloud. Ernie Macmillan, however, was muttering, '*Specialis revelio!*' over his cauldron, which sounded impressive, so Harry and Ron hastened to imitate him.

It took Harry only five minutes to realise that his reputation as the best potion-maker in the class was crashing around his ears. Slughorn had peered hopefully into his cauldron on his first circuit of the dungeon, preparing to exclaim in delight as he usually did, and instead had withdrawn his head hastily, coughing, as the smell of bad eggs overwhelmed him. Hermione's expression could not have been any smugger; she had loathed being outperformed in every Potions class. She was now decanting the mysteriously separated ingredients of her poison into ten different crystal phials. More to avoid watching this irritating sight than anything else, Harry bent over the Half-Blood Prince's book and turned a few pages with unnecessary force.

And there it was, scrawled right across a long list of antidotes.

*Just shove a bezoar down their throats.*

## 第18章 生日的意外

要行动。等哈利、罗恩和厄尼回到桌前,她已经把瓶里的东西倒进了坩埚,在下面点起了火。

"可惜那个王子这次也帮不上你了,哈利,"她直起腰,愉快地说,"你必须理解其中的原理,没法儿投机取巧!"

哈利恼火地拔出瓶塞,把鲜艳的粉红色毒药倒进坩埚,点着了火,一点儿也不知道下面该干什么。他看看罗恩,罗恩傻头傻脑地站在那儿,只是依样做完了哈利所做的事。

"王子真的没有提示吗?"罗恩小声问哈利。

哈利抽出他那本宝贝的《高级魔药制作》,翻到解药那一章。有戈巴洛特第三定律,跟赫敏背的一字不差,但是没有王子写的注释。显然王子跟赫敏一样毫不费力就理解了。

"没有。"哈利沮丧地说。

赫敏劲头十足地在坩埚上方挥舞魔杖,可惜他们模仿不了她的魔咒,因为她现在已很擅长无声咒,不用把咒语念出来。这时厄尼正对着他的坩埚念叨"原形立现!"听起来挺像回事,哈利和罗恩赶紧效仿。

只过了五分钟,哈利就意识到他那班上第一魔药师的名声将要毁于一旦。斯拉格霍恩第一次巡视时朝他的坩埚里期待地看了看,正准备像往常那样兴奋地欢呼,却又立即缩回了头,被臭鸡蛋味熏得连连咳嗽。赫敏的表情得意到极点,她受够了每次魔药课上都被人超过。现在她正把那些神秘分离的成分小心地注入十个不同的小水晶瓶。哈利为了避免看到这恼人的情形,只好埋头去看混血王子的书,他猛地翻了几页。

有了,在那一长串解药名字的右边潦草地写着:

只需在嗓子里塞入一块粪石

## CHAPTER EIGHTEEN    Birthday Surprises

Harry stared at these words for a moment. Hadn't he once, long ago, heard of bezoars? Hadn't Snape mentioned them in their first ever Potions lesson? '*A stone taken from the stomach of a goat, which will protect from most poisons.*'

It was not an answer to the Golpalott problem, and had Snape still been their teacher, Harry would not have dared do it, but this was a moment for desperate measures. He hastened towards the store cupboard and rummaged within it, pushing aside unicorn horns and tangles of dried herbs until he found, at the very back, a small card box on which had been scribbled the word 'Bezoars'.

He opened the box just as Slughorn called, 'Two minutes left, everyone!' Inside were half a dozen shrivelled brown objects, looking more like dried-up kidneys than real stones. Harry seized one, put the box back in the cupboard and hurried back to his cauldron.

'Time's ... UP!' called Slughorn genially. 'Well, let's see how you've done! Blaise ... what have you got for me?'

Slowly, Slughorn moved around the room, examining the various antidotes. Nobody had finished the task, although Hermione was trying to cram a few more ingredients into her bottle before Slughorn reached her. Ron had given up completely, and was merely trying to avoid breathing in the putrid fumes issuing from his cauldron. Harry stood there waiting, the bezoar clutched in a slightly sweaty hand.

Slughorn reached their table last. He sniffed Ernie's potion and passed on to Ron's with a grimace. He did not linger over Ron's cauldron, but backed away swiftly, retching slightly.

'And you, Harry,' he said. 'What have you got to show me?'

Harry held out his hand, the bezoar sitting on his palm.

Slughorn looked down at it for a full ten seconds. Harry wondered, for a moment, whether he was going to shout at him. Then he threw back his head and roared with laughter.

'You've got a nerve, boy!' he boomed, taking the bezoar and holding it up so that the class could see it. 'Oh, you're like your mother ... well, I can't fault you ... a bezoar would certainly act as an antidote to all these potions!'

Hermione, who was sweaty-faced and had soot on her nose, looked livid. Her half-finished antidote, comprising fifty-two ingredients including a chunk of her own hair, bubbled sluggishly behind Slughorn, who had eyes for nobody but Harry.

## 第18章 生日的意外

哈利盯着这行字看了一会儿。粪石他不是听说过吗,很久以前,斯内普在第一堂魔药课上就提到:"山羊胃中的结石,可抵御多种毒药。"

这不是戈巴洛特问题的答案,如果这堂课还是斯内普教,哈利也不敢这么做,但此刻他顾不得了。他冲向储藏柜,推开独角兽角和一堆堆干草药,在里面胡乱地翻找,终于在最里面找到了一个小硬纸盒,上面潦草地写着粪石。

斯拉格霍恩叫道:"还有两分钟,各位!"哈利打开盒子,看见六块皱皱巴巴缩成一团的褐色物体,与其说像石头,不如说像干腰子。他拿了一块,把盒子放回柜中,快步走回坩埚旁。

"时间……到!"斯拉格霍恩愉快地说,"看看你们做得怎么样!布雷司……你的成果如何?"

斯拉格霍恩在教室中缓缓巡视,检查那些五花八门的解药。谁都没有做完,赫敏正争取在斯拉格霍恩过来之前往她的瓶里再塞入几样成分。罗恩彻底放弃了,只是努力避免吸入他坩埚里发出的腐臭气。哈利站在那儿等着,粪石攥在有点汗津津的手里。

斯拉格霍恩最后踱到了他们桌前,闻了闻厄尼的解药,皱着眉朝罗恩走去。他在罗恩的坩埚前没有多待,迅速退开了,有一点作呕。

"你呢,哈利,"他说,"你要给我看什么?"

哈利伸出手,掌心里躺着那块粪石。

斯拉格霍恩低头看了足足十秒钟,哈利都担心他要吼起来了,但他仰起头,放声大笑。

"你真有胆量,孩子!"他捏起粪石,高高地举起来让全班同学看,"哦,真像你母亲……我不能判你错……粪石当然能解所有这些魔药!"

赫敏满脸是汗,鼻子上沾着灰,面色铁青。她那没做完的解药在斯拉格霍恩身后慢吞吞地冒着泡,其中含有五十二种成分,包括一团她自己的头发。可是斯拉格霍恩眼中只有哈利。

## CHAPTER EIGHTEEN   Birthday Surprises

'And you thought of a bezoar all by yourself, did you, Harry?' she asked through gritted teeth.

'That's the individual spirit a real potion-maker needs!' said Slughorn happily, before Harry could reply. 'Just like his mother, she had the same intuitive grasp of potion-making, it's undoubtedly from Lily he gets it ... yes, Harry, yes, if you've got a bezoar to hand, of course that would do the trick ... although as they don't work on everything, and are pretty rare, it's still worth knowing how to mix antidotes ...'

The only person in the room looking angrier than Hermione was Malfoy, who, Harry was pleased to see, had spilled something that looked like cat sick over himself. Before either of them could express their fury that Harry had come top of the class by not doing any work, however, the bell rang.

'Time to pack up!' said Slughorn. 'And an extra ten points to Gryffindor for sheer cheek!'

Still chuckling, he waddled back to his desk at the front of the dungeon.

Harry dawdled behind, taking an inordinate amount of time to do up his bag. Neither Ron nor Hermione wished him luck as they left; both looked rather annoyed. At last Harry and Slughorn were the only two left in the room.

'Come on, now, Harry, you'll be late for your next lesson,' said Slughorn affably, snapping the gold clasps shut on his dragonskin briefcase.

'Sir,' said Harry, reminding himself irresistibly of Voldemort, 'I wanted to ask you something.'

'Ask away, then, my dear boy, ask away ...'

'Sir, I wondered what you know about ... about Horcruxes?'

Slughorn froze. His round face seemed to sink in upon itself. He licked his lips and said hoarsely, 'What did you say?'

'I asked whether you know anything about Horcruxes, sir. You see –'

'Dumbledore put you up to this,' whispered Slughorn.

His voice had changed completely. It was not genial any more, but shocked, terrified. He fumbled in his breast pocket and pulled out a handkerchief, mopping his sweating brow.

'Dumbledore's shown you that – that memory,' said Slughorn. 'Well? Hasn't he?'

'Yes,' said Harry, deciding on the spot that it was best not to lie.

'Yes, of course,' said Slughorn quietly, still dabbing at his white face. 'Of

## 第18章 生日的意外

"你是自己想到粪石的,是不是,哈利?"赫敏咬着牙问。

"这就是真正的魔药师需要的独立精神!"哈利还没答话,斯拉格霍恩高兴地说,"正像他的母亲,对魔药制作有着天生的悟性,他无疑是得了莉莉的遗传……对,哈利,对,如果你有粪石,那当然管用……不过,因为粪石不是什么毒都能解,而且它十分稀少,所以了解怎样配制解药还是有用的……"

全班唯一比赫敏更恼火的人是马尔福。哈利开心地看到他身上洒了猫的呕吐物似的东西。但他们还没来得及对哈利什么也没做就得了全班第一表示愤慨,下课铃就响了。

"收拾东西!"斯拉格霍恩说,"格兰芬多敢于冒险,加十分!"

他呵呵地笑着,摇摇摆摆地走回了讲台前。

哈利有意落后,磨磨蹭蹭地收拾书包。罗恩跟赫敏走时都没有祝他好运。两人都气鼓鼓的。最后教室里只剩下了哈利和斯拉格霍恩两个人。

"快点儿吧,哈利,你下节课要迟到了。"斯拉格霍恩亲切地说,一边扣上他那火龙皮公文包的金搭扣。

"先生,我想问你一点儿事。"哈利说,不禁想起了伏地魔。

"那就快问,亲爱的孩子,快问……"

"先生,我想问你知不知道……魂器。"

斯拉格霍恩僵住了,他的圆脸似乎凹陷下去。他舔舔嘴唇,沙哑地问:"你说什么?"

"我问你知不知道魂器,先生。"

"邓布利多让你来的?"斯拉格霍恩低声问。

他的语气完全变了,不再亲切,而是充满了震惊和恐惧。他在胸前的口袋里摸了一会儿,抽出一条手帕擦了擦冒汗的额头。

"邓布利多给你看了那个——那个记忆,是不是?"

"是的。"哈利临时决定最好不要撒谎。

"当然啦,"斯拉格霍恩轻声说,一边还在擦拭苍白的面孔,

CHAPTER EIGHTEEN    Birthday Surprises

course ... well, if you've seen that memory, Harry, you'll know that I don't know anything – *anything* –' he repeated the word forcefully '– about Horcruxes.'

He seized his dragonskin briefcase, stuffed his handkerchief back into his pocket and marched to the dungeon door.

'Sir,' said Harry desperately, 'I just thought there might be a bit more to the memory –'

'Did you?' said Slughorn. 'Then you were wrong, weren't you? WRONG!'

He bellowed the last word and, before Harry could say another word, slammed the dungeon door behind him.

Neither Ron nor Hermione was at all sympathetic when Harry told them of this disastrous interview. Hermione was still seething at the way Harry had triumphed without doing the work properly. Ron was resentful that Harry hadn't slipped him a bezoar, too.

'It would've just looked stupid if we'd both done it!' said Harry irritably. 'Look, I had to try and soften him up so I could ask him about Voldemort, didn't I? Oh, will you *get a grip*!' he added in exasperation, as Ron winced at the sound of the name.

Infuriated by his failure and by Ron and Hermione's attitudes, Harry brooded for the next few days over what to do next about Slughorn. He decided that, for the time being, he would let Slughorn think that he had forgotten all about Horcruxes; it was surely best to lull him into a false sense of security before returning to the attack.

When Harry did not question Slughorn again, the Potions master reverted to his usual affectionate treatment of him, and appeared to have put the matter from his mind. Harry awaited an invitation to one of his little evening parties, determined to accept this time, even if he had to reschedule Quidditch practice. Unfortunately, however, no such invitation arrived. Harry checked with Hermione and Ginny: neither of them had received an invitation and nor, as far as they knew, had anybody else. Harry could not help wondering whether this meant that Slughorn was not quite as forgetful as he appeared, simply determined to give Harry no additional opportunities to question him.

Meanwhile, the Hogwarts library had failed Hermione for the first time in living memory. She was so shocked, she even forgot that she was annoyed at Harry for his trick with the bezoar.

'I haven't found one single explanation of what Horcruxes do!' she told

## 第18章 生日的意外

"当然……如果你看了记忆,哈利,就会知道我对魂器一无所知——一无所知。"他用力重复着这几个字。

然后他抓起火龙皮公文包,把手帕塞回口袋里,朝地下教室外面走去。

"先生,"哈利急切地说,"我只是想,记忆里可能还有一点儿东西——"

"是吗?"斯拉格霍恩说,"那你就错了,是不是?**错了!**"

他吼出最后一个词,不等哈利说话,就砰地带上门走了。

听哈利讲述完这次灾难性的谈话,罗恩跟赫敏都毫不同情。赫敏还在为哈利没好好做功课就取胜而愤愤不平,罗恩则怨恨哈利没有塞给他一块粪石。

"如果我们两个人都那么做,只会显得很愚蠢!"哈利暴躁地说,"你看,我必须设法软化他,才能问他伏地魔的事,对吧?唉,你能不能振作点儿?"见罗恩听到那个名字畏缩了一下,哈利恼怒地说。

哈利对自己的失败以及罗恩、赫敏对自己的态度感到窝火,在后来的几天中,他一直在寻思下一步该拿斯拉格霍恩怎么办,最后决定暂时让斯拉格霍恩以为他已经忘掉了魂器。显然,最好先让对方产生一种安全感,再攻其不备。

哈利没有再去问斯拉格霍恩,魔药教师便对他又恢复了平日的宠爱,似乎把那件事忘到了脑后。哈利等着再接到他那种小聚会的邀请,打定主意这次聚会即使跟魁地奇训练冲突他也要参加。可是他没有等到。他问了赫敏和金妮,她们俩也没有接到邀请,并且据她们所知,别人也没有接到。哈利不禁想到也许斯拉格霍恩并非真的那么健忘,也许他是决意不让哈利有机会去问他了。

与此同时,霍格沃茨的图书馆破天荒第一次令赫敏失望了。她大为震惊,甚至忘了自己还在为哈利用粪石投机取巧而生气。

"我没有找到一条关于魂器用途的资料!"她对哈利说,"一条都

## CHAPTER EIGHTEEN     Birthday Surprises

him. 'Not a single one! I've been right through the restricted section and even in the most *horrible* books, where they tell you how to brew the most *gruesome* potions – nothing! All I could find was this, in the introduction to *Magick Moste Evile* – listen – "of the Horcrux, wickedest of magical inventions, we shall not speak nor give direction" ... I mean, why mention it, then?' she said impatiently, slamming the old book shut; it let out a ghostly wail. 'Oh, shut up,' she snapped, stuffing it back into her bag.

The snow melted around the school as February arrived, to be replaced by cold, dreary wetness. Purplish-grey clouds hung low over the castle and a constant fall of chilly rain made the lawns slippery and muddy. The upshot of this was that the sixth-years' first Apparition lesson, which was scheduled for a Saturday morning so that no normal lessons would be missed, took place in the Great Hall instead of in the grounds.

When Harry and Hermione arrived in the Hall (Ron had come down with Lavender) they found that the tables had disappeared. Rain lashed against the high windows and the enchanted ceiling swirled darkly above them as they assembled in front of Professors McGonagall, Snape, Flitwick and Sprout – the Heads of House – and a small wizard whom Harry took to be the Apparition Instructor from the Ministry. He was oddly colourless, with transparent eyelashes, wispy hair and an insubstantial air, as though a single gust of wind might blow him away. Harry wondered whether constant disappearances and reappearances had somehow diminished his substance, or whether this frail build was ideal for anyone wishing to vanish.

'Good morning,' said the Ministry wizard, when all the students had arrived and the Heads of House had called for quiet. 'My name is Wilkie Twycross and I shall be your Ministry Apparition Instructor for the next twelve weeks. I hope to be able to prepare you for your Apparition test in this time –'

'Malfoy, be quiet and pay attention!' barked Professor McGonagall.

Everybody looked round. Malfoy had flushed a dull pink; he looked furious as he stepped away from Crabbe, with whom he appeared to have been having a whispered argument. Harry glanced quickly at Snape, who also looked annoyed, though Harry strongly suspected that this was less because of Malfoy's rudeness than the fact that McGonagall had reprimanded one of his house.

'– by which time, many of you may be ready to take your test,' Twycross continued, as though there had been no interruption.

## 第18章 生日的意外

没有！我翻遍了禁书区，甚至看了最可怕的书，教你怎么熬制最恐怖的魔药的那些——都没有！我只在《至毒魔法》的序言中找到了这个，你听——关于魂器这一最邪恶的魔法发明，在此不加论述，亦不予指导……那干吗要提啊？"赫敏恼火地合上那本旧书，旧书发出幽灵般的哀号。"闭嘴！"她没好气地说，把书塞进了书包。

进入二月，学校周围的积雪融化了，取而代之的是凄冷的阴湿。灰紫色的云团低低地压在城堡上空，连绵的寒雨使得草坪变得湿滑、泥泞。结果六年级学生的第一节幻影显形课从场地移到了礼堂里，这门课被安排在星期六上午，以免耽误常规课程。

哈利和赫敏来到礼堂（罗恩和拉文德一起走了），发现桌子都不见了。雨水敲打着高高的窗户，施了魔法的天花板在头顶上昏暗地旋转着。他们在麦格、斯内普、弗立维和斯普劳特教授（四位院长）和一个小个子巫师的面前集合。哈利猜想这个巫师应该就是魔法部来的幻影显形课指导教师。他脸色苍白得出奇，睫毛透明，头发纤细，有一种不真实感，好像一阵风就会把他吹走。哈利想，或许是因为经常移形和显形削弱了他的体质，或是这种纤弱的体形最适于消失。

"上午好，"当学生们到齐、院长们叫大家安静下来之后，魔法部的巫师说，"我叫威基·泰克罗斯，在接下来的十二周中将担任你们的幻影显形课指导教师，希望能帮助你们为这次幻影显形考试做好准备——"

"马尔福，安静听讲！"麦格教授厉声说。

大家转过头，马尔福脸色暗红，满面怒容地从克拉布身边走开了，他们刚才似乎正在小声争吵。哈利瞥了一眼斯内普，他好像也很恼火，不过哈利怀疑这更多的是因为麦格教授批评了他学院的学生，而不是因为马尔福不守纪律。

"——到那时,许多同学也许已有能力参加考试。"泰克罗斯继续说，仿佛没有被打断似的。

## CHAPTER EIGHTEEN    Birthday Surprises

'As you may know, it is usually impossible to Apparate or Disapparate within Hogwarts. The Headmaster has lifted this enchantment, purely within the Great Hall, for one hour, so as to enable you to practise. May I emphasise that you will not be able to Apparate outside the walls of this Hall, and that you would be unwise to try.

'I would like each of you to place yourselves now so that you have a clear five feet of space in front of you.'

There was a great scrambling and jostling as people separated, banged into each other, and ordered others out of their space. The Heads of House moved among the students, marshalling them into position and breaking up arguments.

'Harry, where are you going?' demanded Hermione.

But Harry did not answer; he was moving quickly through the crowd, past the place where Professor Flitwick was making squeaky attempts to position a few Ravenclaws, all of whom wanted to be near the front, past Professor Sprout, who was chivvying the Hufflepuffs into line, until, by dodging around Ernie Macmillan, he managed to position himself right at the back of the crowd, directly behind Malfoy, who was taking advantage of the general upheaval to continue his argument with Crabbe, standing five feet away and looking mutinous.

'I don't know how much longer, all right?' Malfoy shot at him, oblivious to Harry standing right behind him. 'It's taking longer than I thought it would.'

Crabbe opened his mouth, but Malfoy appeared to second-guess what he was going to say.

'Look, it's none of your business what I'm doing, Crabbe, you and Goyle just do as you're told and keep a lookout!'

'I tell my friends what I'm up to, if I want them to keep a lookout for me,' Harry said, just loud enough for Malfoy to hear him.

Malfoy spun round on the spot, his hand flying to his wand, but at that precise moment the four Heads of House shouted, 'Quiet!' and silence fell again. Malfoy turned slowly to face the front.

'Thank you,' said Twycross. 'Now then ...'

He waved his wand. Old-fashioned wooden hoops instantly appeared on the floor in front of every student.

'The important things to remember when Apparating are the three Ds!' said Twycross. 'Destination, Determination, Deliberation!

'Step one: fix your mind firmly upon the desired *destination*,' said Twycross. 'In this case, the interior of your hoop. Kindly concentrate upon that destination now.'

## 第18章 生日的意外

"大家也许知道，在霍格沃茨校内一般无法幻影显形和移形。校长特地撤销了魔法，将这一限制暂时解除一小时，仅限于这个礼堂里，让大家可以练习。我强调一下，不可幻影显形到礼堂的墙外，谁要是尝试可就吃不了兜着走了。

"现在我希望大家各自站好，在身前留够五英尺的空间。"

礼堂里一片混乱，学生们纷纷散开，撞到一起，叫别人走出自己的范围。院长们在学生中走来走去，帮他们排好位置，调解纠纷。

"哈利，你去哪儿？"赫敏问。

哈利没有回答；他迅速穿过人群，从正尖叫着给几个都想靠前站的拉文克劳学生找位子的弗立维教授面前走了过去，又从正在轰赶赫奇帕奇学生站队的斯普劳特教授面前走了过去，随后躲开厄尼·麦克米兰，钻到了人群的末尾，站在正趁乱继续跟克拉布争吵的马尔福身后。克拉布站在五英尺外，看上去挺不服气。

"我不知道还要多久，明白吗？"马尔福凶狠地说，没注意哈利就在后面，"时间比我想的要长。"

克拉布张开嘴巴，但马尔福似乎猜到了他要说什么。

"听着，我在干什么不关你的事，克拉布，你和高尔只管执行命令和放哨！"

"我要是想让朋友为我放哨，就会告诉他们我在干什么。"哈利用刚好能让马尔福听见的声音说。

马尔福猛然转身，一只手疾速抓向魔杖，但此时四位院长正在高喊"安静！"礼堂里静了下来，他慢慢地转过身去，面朝前方。

"谢谢，"泰克罗斯说，"现在……"

他一挥魔杖。每个学生面前的地上立刻出现了一个老式的木圈。

"幻影显形时最重要的是记住三个D！"泰克罗斯说，"即目标，决心，从容！"

"第一步：把注意力集中到你的目标上，"泰克罗斯说，"当前，就是你们面前的这个木圈内。现在请把注意力集中到你们的目标上。"

## CHAPTER EIGHTEEN    Birthday Surprises

Everybody looked around furtively, to check that everyone else was staring into their hoop, then hastily did as they were told. Harry gazed at the circular patch of dusty floor enclosed by his hoop and tried hard to think of nothing else. This proved impossible, as he couldn't stop puzzling over what Malfoy was doing that needed lookouts.

'Step two,' said Twycross, 'focus your *determination* to occupy the visualised space! Let your yearning to enter it flood from your mind to every particle of your body!'

Harry glanced around surreptitiously. A little way to his left, Ernie Macmillan was contemplating his hoop so hard that his face had turned pink; it looked as though he was straining to lay a Quaffle-sized egg. Harry bit back a laugh and hastily returned his gaze to his own hoop.

'Step three,' called Twycross, 'and only when I give the command ... turn on the spot, feeling your way into nothingness, moving with *deliberation*! On my command, now ... one –'

Harry glanced around again; lots of people were looking positively alarmed at being asked to Apparate so quickly.

'– two –'

Harry tried to fix his thoughts on his hoop again; he had already forgotten what the three Ds stood for.

'– THREE!'

Harry spun on the spot, lost his balance and nearly fell over. He was not the only one. The whole Hall was suddenly full of staggering people; Neville was flat on his back; Ernie Macmillan, on the other hand, had done a kind of pirouetting leap into his hoop and looked momentarily thrilled, until he caught sight of Dean Thomas roaring with laughter at him.

'Never mind, never mind,' said Twycross dryly, who did not seem to have expected anything better. 'Adjust your hoops, please, and back to your original positions ...'

The second attempt was no better than the first. The third was just as bad. Not until the fourth did anything exciting happen. There was a horrible screech of pain and everybody looked around, terrified, to see Susan Bones of Hufflepuff wobbling in her hoop with her left leg still standing five feet away where she had started.

The Heads of House converged on her; there was a great bang and a puff

## 第18章 生日的意外

每个人都在偷偷打量周围，看大家是否都在盯着木圈，然后赶紧按要求做。哈利凝视着他的木圈里那块灰扑扑的圆形地面，努力不去想其他事情。结果发现这不可能，因为他忍不住琢磨马尔福到底在做什么事，会需要有人替他放哨。

"第二步：" 泰克罗斯说，"决心去占据你所想的那个空间！让想要进去的渴望淹没你们全身的每一个细胞！"

哈利偷眼看了看四周，左边稍远一点的地方，厄尼正铆足劲儿盯着他的木圈，脸都涨红了，仿佛正努力下一个鬼飞球大小的蛋。哈利咬住嘴唇没敢笑，赶紧把视线转回自己的木圈中。

"第三步：" 泰克罗斯喊道，"等我下令之后……原地旋转，让自己进入虚空状态，动作要从容！现在听我的口令……一——"

哈利又朝周围看了看；许多人似乎都对这么快就要他们幻影显形感到吃惊。

"——二——"

哈利努力重新把注意力集中到他的木圈上；他已经忘记了三个D是什么。

"——三！"

哈利原地旋转起来，一下子失去了平衡，差点儿摔倒。不只是他一个人这样，礼堂中突然到处都是摇摇晃晃的人。纳威仰面躺在地上，厄尼以芭蕾舞似的动作跳到了木圈里，兴奋了片刻，直到看见迪安在冲他哈哈大笑。

"没关系，没关系。" 泰克罗斯干巴巴地说，似乎他也没指望有更好的结果，"摆好木圈，站回原位……"

第二次尝试并不比第一次好，第三次也一样糟糕。直到第四次时才出现了一点刺激。有人发出一声可怕的尖叫，大家惊恐地转过身，只见赫奇帕奇的苏珊·博恩斯在木圈中摇摇晃晃，可左腿还留在五英尺外的原地。

院长们聚到她身边，砰的一声巨响，一阵紫色的烟雾散尽后，大

## CHAPTER EIGHTEEN  Birthday Surprises

of purple smoke, which cleared to reveal Susan sobbing, reunited with her leg but looking horrified.

'Splinching, or the separation of random body parts,' said Wilkie Twycross dispassionately, 'occurs when the mind is insufficiently *determined*. You must concentrate continually upon your *destination*, and move, without haste, but with *deliberation* ... thus.'

Twycross stepped forwards, turned gracefully on the spot with his arms outstretched and vanished in a swirl of robes, reappearing at the back of the Hall.

'Remember the three Ds,' he said, 'and try again ... one – two – three –'

But an hour later, Susan's Splinching was still the most interesting thing that had happened. Twycross did not seem discouraged. Fastening his cloak at his neck, he merely said, 'Until next Saturday, everybody, and do not forget: *Destination. Determination. Deliberation.*'

With that, he waved his wand, Vanishing the hoops, and walked out of the Hall accompanied by Professor McGonagall. Talk broke out at once as people began moving towards the Entrance Hall.

'How did you do?' asked Ron, hurrying towards Harry. 'I think I felt something the last time I tried – a kind of tingling in my feet.'

'I expect your trainers are too small, Won-Won,' said a voice behind them, and Hermione stalked past, smirking.

'I didn't feel anything,' said Harry, ignoring this interruption. 'But I don't care about that now –'

'What d'you mean, you don't care ... don't you want to learn to Apparate?' said Ron incredulously.

'I'm not fussed, really. I prefer flying,' said Harry, glancing over his shoulder to see where Malfoy was, and speeding up as they came into the Entrance Hall. 'Look, hurry up, will you, there's something I want to do ...'

Perplexed, Ron followed Harry back to Gryffindor Tower at a run. They were temporarily detained by Peeves, who had jammed a door on the fourth floor shut and was refusing to let anyone pass until they set fire to their own pants, but Harry and Ron simply turned back and took one of their trusted short cuts. Within five minutes, they were climbing through the portrait hole.

'Are you going to tell me what we're doing, then?' asked Ron, panting slightly.

'Up here,' said Harry, and he crossed the common room and led the way through the door to the boys' staircase.

家看到苏珊在抽泣,腿被安上了,但她仍是满脸恐惧。

"分体,即身体某部分的分离,"威基·泰克罗斯淡淡地说,"发生在决心不够坚定的时候。必须始终把注意力集中在目标上,然后移动,不要慌,要从容……像这样。"

泰克罗斯走向前,张开双臂,优雅地原地旋转起来,在袍子的飘旋中消失了,随后出现在礼堂的后面。

"记住三个D,"他说,"再来一次……一——二——三——"

可是一个小时过后,苏珊的分体还是这节课上最有趣的事件。泰克罗斯似乎并不气馁。他系上斗篷,说道:"下星期六再见,各位,不要忘记:目标,决心,从容。"

他一挥魔杖收去木圈,跟麦格教授一起走出了礼堂。学生们一边朝门厅走去,一边立刻议论纷纷起来。

"你做得怎么样?"罗恩急忙跑向哈利,问道,"我最后一次好像有点儿感觉了——脚底麻酥酥的。"

"我想是你的运动鞋太小了吧,罗-罗。"后面一个声音说,赫敏得意地笑着,大步从他们身边走过。

"我没有感觉,"哈利说,没理会赫敏的打岔,"但是现在我不关心了——"

"你说什么,不关心……你不想学幻影显形了?"罗恩不相信地问。

"我真的不大起劲,我更喜欢飞行。"哈利说,一边转头想看看马尔福在哪儿。走进门厅后,他加快了脚步。"快一些好吗,我有点事……"

罗恩纳闷地跟着哈利跑回格兰芬多塔楼,他们被皮皮鬼耽搁了一小会儿。皮皮鬼堵上了五楼的一扇门,非要每人把自己的裤子烧着才让过去,但哈利和罗恩掉头走了一条可靠的近道。五分钟内,两人爬进了肖像洞口。

"能说说我们去干什么吗?"罗恩问,微微有点气喘。

"上去。"哈利说着穿过公共休息室,走进通往男生宿舍楼梯的门。

## CHAPTER EIGHTEEN    Birthday Surprises

Their dormitory was, as Harry had hoped, empty. He flung open his trunk and began to rummage in it, while Ron watched impatiently.

'Harry ...'

'Malfoy's using Crabbe and Goyle as lookouts. He was arguing with Crabbe just now. I want to know ... aha.'

He had found it, a folded square of apparently blank parchment, which he now smoothed out and tapped with the tip of his wand.

'*I solemnly swear that I am up to no good* ... or Malfoy is, anyway.'

At once, the Marauder's Map appeared on the parchment's surface. Here was a detailed plan of every one of the castle's floors and, moving around it, the tiny, labelled black dots that signified each of the castle's occupants.

'Help me find Malfoy,' said Harry urgently.

He laid the map upon his bed and he and Ron leaned over it, searching.

'*There!*' said Ron, after a minute or so. 'He's in the Slytherin common room, look ... with Parkinson and Zabini and Crabbe and Goyle ...'

Harry looked down at the map, disappointed, but rallied almost at once.

'Well, I'm keeping an eye on him from now on,' he said firmly. 'And the moment I see him lurking somewhere with Crabbe and Goyle keeping watch outside, it'll be on with the old Invisibility Cloak and off to find out what he's –'

He broke off as Neville entered the dormitory, bringing with him a strong smell of singed material, and began rummaging in his trunk for a fresh pair of pants.

Despite his determination to catch Malfoy out, Harry had no luck at all over the next couple of weeks. Although he consulted the map as often as he could, sometimes making unnecessary visits to the bathroom between lessons to search it, he did not once see Malfoy anywhere suspicious. Admittedly, he spotted Crabbe and Goyle moving around the castle on their own more often than usual, sometimes remaining stationary in deserted corridors, but at these times Malfoy was not only nowhere near them, but impossible to locate on the map at all. This was most mysterious. Harry toyed with the possibility that Malfoy was actually leaving the school grounds, but could not see how he could be doing it, given the very high level of security now operating within the castle. He could only suppose that he was missing Malfoy amongst the hundreds of tiny black dots upon the map. As for the fact that Malfoy, Crabbe and Goyle appeared to be going their different ways when they were usually inseparable, these things happened as people got older – Ron and

## 第18章 生日的意外

正如他希望的那样，宿舍里没人。他打开箱子翻找起来，罗恩不耐烦地看着。

"哈利……"

"马尔福让克拉布和高尔放哨，他刚才和克拉布吵起来了。我想知道……啊哈！"

哈利找到了——一张折成方形、看似空白的羊皮纸。他把纸展开，用魔杖尖敲了敲。

"我庄严宣誓我不干好事……也许是马尔福不干好事。"

羊皮纸上立刻现出活点地图，绘着城堡每一层的详细平面图，许多带标记的小黑点正在上面移动，代表着城堡里的每个人。

"帮我找马尔福。"哈利急切地说。

他把地图摊在床上，两人俯身找了起来。

"这儿！"一两分钟后罗恩叫道，"他在斯莱特林的公共休息室里，看……跟帕金森、沙比尼、克拉布和高尔在一起……"

哈利看着地图，显得有点失望，但立刻又振作起来。

"从现在起我要监视他，"他坚决地说，"只要一看到他躲在什么地方，克拉布和高尔在外面放哨，我就披上隐形衣，去弄清他在——"

他突然打住了，纳威带着一股很重的焦煳味走了进来，径直到他箱子里找裤子。

虽然哈利决心要抓到马尔福在干什么，但之后的两个星期他运气实在不佳。他尽可能频繁地查看着活点地图，有时在课间不必要地去上盥洗室，可是一次都没在可疑地点发现马尔福。他倒是看到克拉布和高尔单独在城堡里活动的时间比平时多，有时停在空走廊里一动不动，但那时马尔福不仅不在附近，而且在活点地图上都找不到他。这太神秘了，哈利想马尔福会不会出了学校，但城堡中安全措施这么严密，他想不出马尔福怎么能出得去。他只能猜想马尔福是混在图上那几百个黑点之中了。原来形影不离的马尔福、克拉布和高尔分开了，也许人长大了就会这样吧——罗恩跟赫敏就是活生生的例子，哈利悲

## CHAPTER EIGHTEEN   Birthday Surprises

Hermione, Harry reflected sadly, were living proof.

February moved towards March with no change in the weather except that it became windy as well as wet. To general indignation, a sign went up on all common-room noticeboards that the next trip into Hogsmeade had been cancelled. Ron was furious.

'It was on my birthday!' he said. 'I was looking forward to that!'

'Not a big surprise, though, is it?' said Harry. 'Not after what happened to Katie.'

She had still not returned from St Mungo's. What was more, further disappearances had been reported in the *Daily Prophet*, including several relatives of students at Hogwarts.

'But now all I've got to look forward to is stupid Apparition!' said Ron grumpily. 'Big birthday treat ...'

Three lessons on, Apparition was proving as difficult as ever, though a few more people had managed to Splinch themselves. Frustration was running high and there was a certain amount of ill-feeling towards Wilkie Twycross and his three Ds, which had inspired a number of nick-names for him, the politest of which were Dog-breath and Dung-head.

'Happy birthday, Ron,' said Harry, when they were woken on the first of March by Seamus and Dean leaving noisily for breakfast. 'Have a present.'

He threw the package across on to Ron's bed, where it joined a small pile of them that must, Harry assumed, have been delivered by house-elves in the night.

'Cheers,' said Ron drowsily, and as he ripped off the paper Harry got out of bed, opened his own trunk and began rummaging in it for the Marauder's Map, which he hid after every use. He turfed out half the contents of his trunk before he found it hiding beneath the rolled-up socks in which he was still keeping his bottle of lucky potion, Felix Felicis.

'Right,' he murmured, taking it back to bed with him, tapping it quietly and murmuring, 'I solemnly swear that I am up to no good,' so that Neville, who was passing the foot of his bed at the time, would not hear.

'Nice one, Harry!' said Ron enthusiastically, waving the new pair of Quidditch Keeper's gloves Harry had given him.

'No problem,' said Harry absent-mindedly, as he searched the Slytherin dormitory closely for Malfoy. 'Hey ... I don't think he's in his bed ...'

Ron did not answer; he was too busy unwrapping presents, every now and then letting out an exclamation of pleasure.

## 第18章 生日的意外

哀地想。

由二月进入三月，天气没有什么变化，只是潮湿又加上了多风。公共休息室的所有布告栏上都贴出一张告示，说这次去霍格莫德的旅行取消了，大家都很不满，罗恩怨气冲天。

"是我的生日啊！我一直盼着呢！"

"并不特别意外，是不是？"哈利说，"在凯蒂出事之后。"

凯蒂还没有从圣芒戈魔法伤病医院回来。而且《预言家日报》又报道了新的失踪事件，其中有几位是霍格沃茨学生的亲戚。

"现在我能盼的只有无聊的幻影显形了！"罗恩没好气地说，"好一份生日大礼……"

三节课下来，幻影显形还是那么困难，只是又有几个人出现了分体。挫折感在增强，学生中对威基·泰克罗斯以及他那三个D有不少抵触情绪，给他起了好些绰号，最礼貌的是狗臭屁和粪脑袋。

"生日快乐，罗恩，"三月一日早上，他们被去吃早饭的西莫和迪安吵醒后，哈利说，"送你一件礼物。"

他把纸包扔到罗恩床上，落在一小堆包裹中间，哈利猜想那些包裹是家养小精灵夜里送来的。

"谢了。"罗恩迷迷糊糊地说。在罗恩撕开纸包时，哈利下了床，打开箱子找活点地图，他每次用完都把它藏在箱子里。哈利翻出了半箱东西，才在一堆卷好的袜子底下找到了地图，袜子里还藏着他那瓶幸运药水，福灵剂。

"好了，"他把活点地图拿到床上，轻轻敲了敲，小声念道，"我庄严宣誓我不干好事。"以免从床脚走过的纳威听见。

"太棒了，哈利！"罗恩兴奋地叫了起来，挥舞着哈利送给他的魁地奇守门员手套。

"小意思。"哈利心不在焉地说，一边在斯莱特林的宿舍里仔细寻找马尔福，"嘿……我想他不在床上……"

罗恩没有回答，他正忙着拆礼物，不时发出开心的大叫。

## CHAPTER EIGHTEEN  Birthday Surprises

'Seriously good haul this year!' he announced, holding up a heavy gold watch with odd symbols around the edge and tiny moving stars instead of hands. 'See what Mum and Dad got me? Blimey, I think I'll come of age next year too ...'

'Cool,' muttered Harry, sparing the watch a glance before peering more closely at the map. Where was Malfoy? He did not seem to be at the Slytherin table in the Great Hall, eating breakfast ... he was nowhere near Snape, who was sitting in his study ... he wasn't in any of the bathrooms or in the hospital wing ...

'Want one?' said Ron thickly, holding out a box of Chocolate Cauldrons.

'No thanks,' said Harry, looking up. 'Malfoy's gone again!'

'Can't have done,' said Ron, stuffing a second Cauldron into his mouth as he slid out of bed to get dressed. 'Come on, if you don't hurry up you'll have to Apparate on an empty stomach ... might make it easier, I suppose ...'

Ron looked thoughtfully at the box of Chocolate Cauldrons, then shrugged and helped himself to a third.

Harry tapped the map with his wand, muttered, 'Mischief managed,' though it hadn't been, and got dressed, thinking hard. There had to be an explanation for Malfoy's periodic disappearances, but he simply could not think what it could be. The best way of finding out would be to tail him, but even with the Invisibility Cloak this was an impractical idea; he had lessons, Quidditch practice, homework and Apparition; he could not follow Malfoy around school all day without his absence being remarked upon.

'Ready?' he said to Ron.

He was halfway to the dormitory door when he realised that Ron had not moved, but was leaning on his bedpost, staring out of the rain-washed window with a strangely unfocused look on his face.

'Ron? Breakfast.'

'I'm not hungry.'

Harry stared at him.

'I thought you just said –?'

'Well, all right, I'll come down with you,' sighed Ron, 'but I don't want to eat.'

Harry scrutinised him suspiciously.

'You've just eaten half a box of Chocolate Cauldrons, haven't you?'

586

## 第18章 生日的意外

"今年真是大丰收！"他宣布说，一边举起一块沉甸甸的金表，那表的边缘有奇特的符号，指针是用移动的小星星做的，"看，爸妈给我送了什么？嘿，我打算明年还要成年一次……"

"真酷。"哈利抬眼看了一下罗恩的手表，嘟囔了一声，又更加仔细地查看地图。马尔福在哪儿？他好像不在礼堂中斯莱特林的餐桌旁吃早饭……不在书房中坐着的斯内普旁边……也不在盥洗室和校医院……

"要吗？"罗恩举着一盒巧克力坩埚含混地问。

"不了，谢谢。"哈利抬头看了一眼，说道，"马尔福又不见了！"

"不可能。"罗恩把第二块巧克力坩埚塞进嘴里，从床上溜下来开始穿衣，"好啦，再不快点儿，你就只好空着肚子幻影显形了……也许倒容易些，我想……"

罗恩若有所思地看着那盒巧克力坩埚，然后耸耸肩，拿起了第三块。

哈利用魔杖敲了敲地图，念道："恶作剧完毕！"（其实并未完毕）。他一边穿衣一边苦苦思索：马尔福的不时失踪肯定有原因，但他就是想不出这原因是什么。最好的办法是盯他的梢，但即使有隐形衣这也是不切实际的，因为要上课，还有魁地奇训练、作业和幻影显形，若是整天在学校里跟踪马尔福，不可能不被人注意。

"好了吗？"他问罗恩。

快走到宿舍门口时，他发现罗恩还没有动身，而是倚在床柱上，凝视着被雨水洗刷的窗户，脸上带着一种古怪的茫然表情。

"罗恩，吃早饭。"

"我不饿。"

哈利瞪着他。

"你刚才不是说——？"

"唉，好吧，我跟你下去，"罗恩叹了口气，"可我不想吃。"

哈利怀疑地打量着他。

"你刚才吃了半盒巧克力坩埚，是不是？"

## CHAPTER EIGHTEEN  Birthday Surprises

'It's not that,' Ron sighed again. 'You ... you wouldn't understand.'

'Fair enough,' said Harry, albeit puzzled, as he turned to open the door.

'Harry!' said Ron suddenly.

'What?'

'Harry, I can't stand it!'

'You can't stand what?' asked Harry, now starting to feel definitely alarmed. Ron was rather pale and looked as though he was about to be sick.

'I can't stop thinking about her!' said Ron hoarsely.

Harry gaped at him. He had not expected this and was not sure he wanted to hear it. Friends they might be, but if Ron started calling Lavender 'Lav-Lav', he would have to put his foot down.

'Why does that stop you having breakfast?' Harry asked, trying to inject a note of common sense into the proceedings.

'I don't think she knows I exist,' said Ron with a desperate gesture.

'She definitely knows you exist,' said Harry, bewildered. 'She keeps snogging you, doesn't she?'

Ron blinked.

'Who are you talking about?'

'Who are *you* talking about?' said Harry, with an increasing sense that all reason had dropped out of the conversation.

'Romilda Vane,' said Ron softly, and his whole face seemed to illuminate as he said it, as though hit by a ray of purest sunlight.

They stared at each other for almost a whole minute, before Harry said, 'This is a joke, right? You're joking.'

'I think ... Harry, I think I love her,' said Ron in a strangled voice.

'OK,' said Harry, walking up to Ron to get a better look at the glazed eyes and the pallid complexion, 'OK ... say that again with a straight face.'

'I love her,' repeated Ron breathlessly. 'Have you seen her hair, it's all black and shiny and silky ... and her eyes? Her big dark eyes? And her –'

'This is really funny and everything,' said Harry impatiently, 'but joke's over, all right? Drop it.'

He turned to leave; he had got two steps towards the door when a crashing blow hit him on the right ear. Staggering, he looked round. Ron's fist was drawn right back, his face was contorted with rage; he was about to strike again.

## 第 18 章 生日的意外

"不是这回事,"罗恩又叹了口气,"你……你不懂。"

"好吧。"哈利说着转身去开门,心中仍是疑惑。

"哈利!"罗恩突然叫道。

"什么?"

"哈利,我受不了了!"

"你受不了什么?"哈利问,不禁吃了一惊,他看到罗恩脸色苍白,好像要生病的样子。

"我没法不想她!"罗恩声音沙哑地说。

哈利目瞪口呆,他没有料到会听到这个,也拿不准自己想不想听。虽然他们是朋友,但如果罗恩开始叫拉文德"拉-拉",他将不得不采取强硬立场。

"那也不妨碍你吃早饭吧?"哈利问,试图在这件事中注入一点正常思维。

"我想她不知道我的存在。"罗恩说着绝望地一摆手。

"她当然知道你的存在,"哈利被搞糊涂了,"她不是经常吻你吗?"

罗恩吃惊地眨了眨眼睛。

"你说的是谁啊?"

"你说的是谁啊?"哈利说,越来越感到这场谈话已经完全失去了理智。

"罗米达·万尼。"罗恩柔声道,整个面孔都亮了,好像被一道最纯净的阳光照透。

两人对视了近一分钟,哈利才说:"这是个玩笑,对吧?你在开玩笑。"

"我想……哈利,我想我爱她。"罗恩用哽咽的声音说。

"好,"哈利说着走近了罗恩,细细地打量他那呆滞的眼睛和苍白的脸色,"好……严肃地再说一遍。"

"我爱她,"罗恩屏息道,"你看到她的秀发了吗,又黑又亮,缎子似的……还有她的眼睛?她那双乌黑的大眼睛?还有她的——"

"真好笑,"哈利不耐烦地说,"可是玩笑结束了,好吗?别闹了。"

他转身离开,刚走出两步,他的右耳上重重挨了一击。他摇晃了两下,回过头去,罗恩刚把拳头收回去,脸都气歪了,正要再打。

## CHAPTER EIGHTEEN  Birthday Surprises

Harry reacted instinctively; his wand was out of his pocket and the incantation sprang to mind without conscious thought: *Levicorpus*!

Ron yelled as his heel was wrenched upwards once more; he dangled helplessly, upside-down, his robes hanging off him.

'*What was that for?*' Harry bellowed.

'You insulted her, Harry! You said it was a joke!' shouted Ron, who was slowly turning purple in the face as all the blood rushed to his head.

'This is insane!' said Harry. 'What's got into –?'

And then he saw the box lying open on Ron's bed and the truth hit him with the force of a stampeding troll.

'Where did you get those Chocolate Cauldrons?'

'They were a birthday present!' shouted Ron, revolving slowly in midair as he struggled to get free. 'I offered you one, didn't I?'

'You just picked them up off the floor, didn't you?'

'They'd fallen off my bed, all right? Let me go!'

'They didn't fall off your bed, you prat, don't you understand? They were mine, I chucked them out of my trunk when I was looking for the map. They're the Chocolate Cauldrons Romilda gave me before Christmas and they're all spiked with love potion!'

But only one word of this seemed to have registered with Ron.

'Romilda?' he repeated. 'Did you say Romilda? Harry – do you know her? Can you introduce me?'

Harry stared at the dangling Ron, whose face now looked tremendously hopeful, and fought a strong desire to laugh. A part of him – the part closest to his throbbing right ear – was quite keen on the idea of letting Ron down and watching him run amok until the effects of the potion wore off ... but on the other hand, they were supposed to be friends, Ron had not been himself when he had attacked, and Harry thought that he would deserve another punching if he permitted Ron to declare undying love for Romilda Vane.

'Yeah, I'll introduce you,' said Harry, thinking fast. 'I'm going to let you down now, OK?'

He sent Ron crashing back to the floor (his ear did hurt quite a lot), but Ron simply bounded to his feet again, grinning.

## 第 18 章　生日的意外

哈利本能地拔出魔杖，想都没想，一句咒语就跳入了脑中：倒挂金钟！

罗恩大叫一声，脚跟被猛然拽起。他无助地倒挂在空中，袍子翻垂下来。

"这是为什么？"哈利吼道。

"你侮辱了她，哈利！你说我在开玩笑！"罗恩大声说，他的血涌到了头部，脸渐渐地变紫了。

"真是荒唐！"哈利说，"你中了什么——"

他忽然注意到罗恩床上那个打开的盒子，心头像被狂奔的巨怪撞了一下，真相大白了。

"这巧克力坩埚是哪儿来的？"

"是生日礼物！"罗恩叫道。他吊在那儿缓缓转动着，竭力想挣脱。"我不是还给了你一块吗？"

"你从地上捡的，是不是？"

"是我床上掉下去的。好了吧？放我下来！"

"不是从你床上掉下去的，你这笨蛋，你不明白吗？这是我的，我找地图时从箱子里扔出来的。这是罗米达·万尼圣诞节前送给我的巧克力坩埚，里面加了迷情剂！"

但罗恩似乎只听进去了一个词。

"罗米达！你刚才说罗米达？哈利——你认识她？能给我介绍介绍吗？"

哈利瞪着倒挂的罗恩，瞪着那张现在带着无限渴望的面孔，忍住一阵强烈的笑意。他的一部分——最靠近灼痛的右耳的那部分——很想把罗恩放下来，由着他去发疯，一直到药力消失。然而另一方面，他们还是朋友，罗恩打他时是神志失常的。哈利想，如果他让罗恩去向罗米达·万尼表达不朽的爱意，他就真该再挨一拳。

"行,我给你介绍。"哈利脑筋一转,说道,"我这就放你下来,好吗？"

他让罗恩摔在地上（他的耳朵真的很疼），但罗恩马上跳了起来，眉开眼笑。

## CHAPTER EIGHTEEN    Birthday Surprises

'She'll be in Slughorn's office,' said Harry confidently, leading the way to the door.

'Why will she be in there?' asked Ron anxiously, hurrying to keep up.

'Oh, she has extra Potions lessons with him,' said Harry, inventing wildly.

'Maybe I could ask if I can have them with her?' said Ron eagerly.

'Great idea,' said Harry.

Lavender was waiting beside the portrait hole, a complication Harry had not foreseen.

'You're late, Won-Won!' she pouted. 'I've got you a birthday —'

'Leave me alone,' said Ron impatiently, 'Harry's going to introduce me to Romilda Vane.'

And without another word to her, he pushed his way out of the portrait hole. Harry tried to make an apologetic face to Lavender, but it might have turned out simply amused, because she looked more offended than ever as the Fat Lady swung shut behind them.

Harry had been slightly worried that Slughorn might be at breakfast, but he answered his office door at the first knock, wearing a green velvet dressing-gown and matching nightcap and looking rather bleary-eyed.

'Harry,' he mumbled. 'This is very early for a call ... I generally sleep late on a Saturday ...'

'Professor, I'm really sorry to disturb you,' said Harry as quietly as possible, while Ron stood on tiptoe, attempting to see past Slughorn into his room, 'but my friend Ron's swallowed a love potion by mistake. You couldn't make him an antidote, could you? I'd take him to Madam Pomfrey, but we're not supposed to have anything from Weasleys' Wizard Wheezes and, you know ... awkward questions ...'

'I'd have thought you could have whipped him up a remedy, Harry, an expert potioneer like you?' asked Slughorn.

'Er,' said Harry, somewhat distracted by the fact that Ron was now elbowing him in the ribs in an attempt to force his way into the room, 'well, I've never mixed an antidote for a love potion, sir, and by the time I get it right Ron might've done something serious —'

Helpfully, Ron chose this moment to moan, 'I can't see her, Harry — is he hiding her?'

'Was this potion within date?' asked Slughorn, now eyeing Ron with

## 第18章 生日的意外

"她在斯拉格霍恩的办公室。"哈利蛮有把握地说,一边带着他朝门口走去。

"她为什么在那儿?"罗恩赶紧跟上,着急地问。

"哦,她跟他补魔药课。"哈利信口胡诌。

"也许我可以申请跟她一起上?"罗恩热切地说。

"好主意。"哈利说道。

拉文德等在肖像洞口旁边,这是哈利没料到的。

"你迟到了,罗-罗!"她噘着嘴说,"我给你带了件生日——"

"走开,"罗恩不耐烦地说,"哈利要把我介绍给罗米达·万尼。"

他没再跟她说话,径自挤出了肖像洞口。哈利想对拉文德做个抱歉的表情,但可能显出的只是满脸愉快,因为当胖夫人在他们身后旋上时,拉文德看上去已经气急败坏了。

哈利担心斯拉格霍恩在吃早饭,但是只敲了一声门就开了。斯拉格霍恩穿着一件绿天鹅绒的晨衣,戴着一顶同样颜色的睡帽,还是睡眼惺忪的样子。

"哈利,"他嘟囔道,"太早了吧……我星期六一般起得晚……"

"教授,很抱歉打搅您,"哈利尽量轻声说,罗恩踮着脚尖,企图越过斯拉格霍恩朝房间里看,"可是我的朋友罗恩误服了迷情剂,您能不能给他配点解药?我本想带他去找庞弗雷女士,但是按理说我们不可以买韦斯莱魔法把戏坊的东西,所以,您知道……问起来会很尴尬……"

"我以为你已经给他弄出了解药呢,哈利,你不是个魔药专家吗?"斯拉格霍恩问。

"呃,"哈利有点分神,因为罗恩用胳膊肘捅他的肋骨,想要挤进屋去,"我从没配过迷情剂的解药,先生,等我配出来,罗恩可能已经做出了什么严重的——"

罗恩帮忙似的恰好在这时哀呼起来:"我看不到她,哈利——他把她藏起来了吗?"

"药水没过期吧?"斯拉格霍恩开始带着职业的兴趣打量罗恩,"你

### CHAPTER EIGHTEEN  Birthday Surprises

professional interest. 'They can strengthen, you know, the longer they're kept.'

'That would explain a lot,' panted Harry, now positively wrestling with Ron to keep him from knocking Slughorn over. 'It's his birthday, Professor,' he added imploringly.

'Oh, all right, come in, then, come in,' said Slughorn, relenting. 'I've got the necessary here in my bag, it's not a difficult antidote …'

Ron burst through the door into Slughorn's overheated, crowded study, tripped over a tasselled footstool, regained his balance by seizing Harry around the neck and muttered, 'She didn't see that, did she?'

'She's not here yet,' said Harry, watching Slughorn opening his potion kit and adding a few pinches of this and that to a small crystal bottle.

'That's good,' said Ron fervently. 'How do I look?'

'Very handsome,' said Slughorn smoothly, handing Ron a glass of clear liquid. 'Now drink that up, it's a tonic for the nerves, keep you calm when she arrives, you know.'

'Brilliant,' said Ron eagerly, and he gulped the antidote down noisily.

Harry and Slughorn watched him. For a moment, Ron beamed at them. Then, very slowly, his grin sagged and vanished, to be replaced by an expression of utmost horror.

'Back to normal, then?' said Harry, grinning. Slughorn chuckled. 'Thanks a lot, Professor.'

'Don't mention it, m'boy, don't mention it,' said Slughorn, as Ron collapsed into a nearby armchair, looking devastated. 'Pick-me-up, that's what he needs,' Slughorn continued, now bustling over to a table loaded with drinks. 'I've got Butterbeer, I've got wine, I've got one last bottle of this oak-matured mead … hmm … meant to give that to Dumbledore for Christmas … ah well …' he shrugged '… he can't miss what he's never had! Why don't we open it now and celebrate Mr Weasley's birthday? Nothing like a fine spirit to chase away the pangs of disappointed love …'

He chortled again and Harry joined in. This was the first time he had found himself almost alone with Slughorn since his disastrous first attempt to extract the true memory from him. Perhaps, if he could just keep Slughorn in a good mood … perhaps if they got through enough of the oak-matured mead …

## 第 18 章 生日的意外

知道，放的时间越长药劲会越强。"

"怪不得呢。"哈利气喘吁吁地说，他现在简直是在跟罗恩搏斗，以免他把斯拉格霍恩撞倒，"今天是他的生日，教授。"他哀求道。

"哦，好吧，进来吧，进来，"斯拉格霍恩发了慈悲，"我包里有必需品，这个解药不难……"

罗恩冲进斯拉格霍恩那间热烘烘的拥挤的书房，被一个带穗的脚凳绊了一下，赶紧抱住哈利的脖子才恢复了平衡。他小声说："她没看见，没看见吧？"

"她还没来呢。"哈利说，一边看着斯拉格霍恩打开配药箱，往一个小水晶瓶里加点儿这个又加点儿那个。

"那就好，"罗恩热切地说，"我看上去怎么样？"

"非常英俊。"斯拉格霍恩平静地说，他递给罗恩一杯澄清的液体，"把它喝了，这是滋补神经的，能让你在她来时保持镇静。"

"太棒了。"罗恩迫不及待地说，咕嘟一声喝下了解药。

哈利和斯拉格霍恩观察着他。有那么一刻，罗恩笑嘻嘻地望着他们，然后，他的笑容很慢很慢地消失了，变成了极度的恐惧。

"恢复正常了？"哈利笑着问，斯拉格霍恩呵呵地笑了。"非常感谢您，教授。"

"不客气，孩子，不客气。"斯拉格霍恩说，罗恩跌坐到旁边的扶手椅里，像被霜打了一般。"提提精神，这是他现在需要的。"斯拉格霍恩继续说，一边急忙走到一个摆满饮料的桌子前，"我有黄油啤酒、葡萄酒，还有最后一瓶橡木陈酿的蜂蜜酒……嗯……本想送给邓布利多做圣诞礼物的……算了……"他耸了耸肩膀，"他反正不知道！我们为什么不打开它，庆祝一下韦斯莱先生的生日呢？要驱散爱情幻灭的痛苦，莫过于一杯好酒……"

他又大笑起来，哈利也笑了。这是自上回灾难性的试探之后，他第一次单独跟斯拉格霍恩在一起。也许，只要让斯拉格霍恩保持好心情……让他喝够橡木陈酿的蜂蜜酒……

## CHAPTER EIGHTEEN   Birthday Surprises

'There you are, then,' said Slughorn, handing Harry and Ron a glass of mead each, before raising his own. 'Well, a very happy birthday, Ralph –'

'– Ron –' whispered Harry.

But Ron, who did not appear to be listening to the toast, had already thrown the mead into his mouth and swallowed it.

There was one second, hardly more than a heartbeat, in which Harry knew there was something terribly wrong and Slughorn, it seemed, did not.

'– and may you have many more –'

'*Ron!*'

Ron had dropped his glass; he half rose from his chair and then crumpled, his extremities jerking uncontrollably. Foam was dribbling from his mouth and his eyes were bulging from their sockets.

'Professor!' Harry bellowed. 'Do something!'

But Slughorn seemed paralysed by shock. Ron twitched and choked: his skin was turning blue.

'What – but –' spluttered Slughorn.

Harry leapt over a low table and sprinted towards Slughorn's open potion kit, pulling out jars and pouches, while the terrible sound of Ron's gargling breath filled the room. Then he found it – the shrivelled kidney-like stone Slughorn had taken from him in Potions.

He hurtled back to Ron's side, wrenched open his jaw and thrust the bezoar into his mouth. Ron gave a great shudder, a rattling gasp and his body became limp and still.

## 第18章 生日的意外

"来吧,"斯拉格霍恩递给哈利和罗恩每人一杯蜂蜜酒,举着杯子说,"生日快乐,拉尔弗——"

"——罗恩——"哈利小声说。

可是罗恩似乎没听到祝酒词,已经把酒倒进嘴里,咽了下去。

一秒钟之后,几乎只是一下心跳的时间,哈利感到出了可怕的问题,而斯拉格霍恩似乎没有发觉。

"——祝你有更多——"

"罗恩!"

罗恩丢掉杯子,想从椅子上站起来,但却倒了下去。他四肢剧烈地痉挛着,口吐白沫,眼珠凸了出来。

"教授!"哈利大叫,"快想想办法!"

可是斯拉格霍恩好像吓呆了。罗恩抽搐着,呼吸困难,皮肤开始变青。

"怎么——可是——"斯拉格霍恩结结巴巴地说。

哈利跃过一张矮桌,冲向斯拉格霍恩打开的配药箱,掏出瓶瓶罐罐和药包。罗恩那可怕的咕噜咕噜的呼吸声充满了房间。终于找到了——斯拉格霍恩在魔药课上收去的那块腰子状的石头。

他奔回罗恩身边,撬开他的嘴巴,把粪石塞进了他嘴里。罗恩剧烈地哆嗦了一下,咕噜噜倒吸了一口气,身体瘫软不动了。

## CHAPTER NINETEEN

# Elf Tails

'So, all in all, not one of Ron's better birthdays?' said Fred. It was evening; the hospital wing was quiet, the windows curtained, the lamps lit. Ron's was the only occupied bed. Harry, Hermione and Ginny were sitting around him; they had spent all day waiting outside the double doors, trying to see inside whenever somebody went in or out. Madam Pomfrey had only let them enter at eight o'clock. Fred and George had arrived at ten past.

'This isn't how we imagined handing over our present,' said George grimly, putting down a large wrapped gift on Ron's bedside cabinet and sitting beside Ginny.

'Yeah, when we pictured the scene, he was conscious,' said Fred.

'There we were in Hogsmeade, waiting to surprise him –' said George.

'You were in Hogsmeade?' asked Ginny, looking up.

'We were thinking of buying Zonko's,' said Fred gloomily. 'A Hogsmeade branch, you know, but a fat lot of good it'll do us if you lot aren't allowed out at weekends to buy our stuff any more … but never mind that now.'

He drew up a chair beside Harry and looked at Ron's pale face.

'How exactly did it happen, Harry?'

Harry retold the story he had already recounted what felt like a hundred times to Dumbledore, to McGonagall, to Madam Pomfrey, to Hermione and to Ginny.

'… and then I got the bezoar down his throat and his breathing eased up a bit, Slughorn ran for help, McGonagall and Madam Pomfrey turned up, and they brought Ron up here. They reckon he'll be all right. Madam Pomfrey says he'll have to stay here a week or so … keep taking Essence of Rue …'

第 19 章

小精灵尾巴

"**所**以,总而言之,罗恩这个生日过得不怎么样。"弗雷德说。

晚上,校医院很安静,拉着窗帘,亮着灯。只有罗恩这张病床上住了人。哈利、赫敏和金妮都坐在他身边。他们在门外等了一整天,每当有人进去或出来时便努力朝里面张望。庞弗雷女士八点钟才让他们进去。弗雷德和乔治是八点十分赶到的。

"我们没想到会是这样送礼物。"乔治阴郁地说着,把一个大礼包放在罗恩床头的柜子上,然后在金妮身边坐下来。

"就是,在我们想象的情景中,他是清醒的。"弗雷德说。

"我们还在霍格莫德,等着给他个惊喜——"乔治说。

"你们在霍格莫德?"金妮抬起头问。

"我们想买下佐科的店面,"弗雷德垂头丧气地说,"搞个霍格莫德分店。可是如果你们周末不能过去买东西,那个店还有个鬼用啊……不过现在不说它了。"

他拉了把椅子坐在哈利旁边,看着罗恩苍白的面孔。

"这事儿到底是怎么发生的,哈利?"

哈利又复述起他已经向邓布利多、麦格、庞弗雷女士、赫敏、金妮等人说了好像有一百遍的故事。

"……然后我把粪石塞进了他的嗓子里,他的呼吸通畅了一些,斯拉格霍恩跑去叫人,麦格和庞弗雷女士来了,把罗恩抬到了这里。他们认为他会好起来的。庞弗雷女士说他还要在这里待一两周……继续服用芸香精。"

## CHAPTER NINETEEN — Elf Tails

'Blimey, it was lucky you thought of a bezoar,' said George in a low voice.

'Lucky there was one in the room,' said Harry, who kept turning cold at the thought of what would have happened if he had not been able to lay hands on the little stone.

Hermione gave an almost inaudible sniff. She had been exceptionally quiet all day. Having hurtled, white-faced, up to Harry outside the hospital wing and demanded to know what had happened, she had taken almost no part in Harry and Ginny's obsessive discussion about how Ron had been poisoned, but merely stood beside them, clench-jawed and frightened-looking, until at last they had been allowed in to see him.

'Do Mum and Dad know?' Fred asked Ginny.

'They've already seen him, they arrived an hour ago – they're in Dumbledore's office now, but they'll be back soon ...'

There was a pause while they all watched Ron mumble a little in his sleep.

'So the poison was in the drink?' said Fred quietly.

'Yes,' said Harry at once; he could think of nothing else and was glad for the opportunity to start discussing it again. 'Slughorn poured it out –'

'Would he have been able to slip something into Ron's glass without you seeing?'

'Probably,' said Harry, 'but why would Slughorn want to poison Ron?'

'No idea,' said Fred, frowning. 'You don't think he could have mixed up the glasses by mistake? Meaning to get you?'

'Why would Slughorn want to poison Harry?' asked Ginny.

'I dunno,' said Fred, 'but there must be loads of people who'd like to poison Harry, mustn't there? The "Chosen One" and all that?'

'So you think Slughorn's a Death Eater?' said Ginny.

'Anything's possible,' said Fred darkly.

'He could be under the Imperius Curse,' said George.

'Or he could be innocent,' said Ginny. 'The poison could have been in the bottle, in which case it was probably meant for Slughorn himself.'

'Who'd want to kill Slughorn?'

'Dumbledore reckons Voldemort wanted Slughorn on his side,' said Harry. 'Slughorn was in hiding for a year before he came to Hogwarts. And ...' he thought of the memory Dumbledore had not yet been able to extract from

## 第19章 小精灵尾巴

"老天,多亏你想到了粪石。"乔治低声说。

"幸好屋里有一块。"哈利说,想到要是没找着那块小石头的后果,他不禁浑身发冷。

赫敏发出一声几乎听不见的抽泣。她这一整天特别安静。刚才她脸色煞白地冲到校医院门口,询问哈利是怎么回事,之后,她几乎没有参加哈利和金妮关于罗恩怎样中毒的反复讨论,只是咬着牙,神情恐惧地站在旁边,直到终于允许他们进去看他。

"爸爸妈妈知道吗?"弗雷德问金妮。

"他们已经看过他了,一小时前来的——这会儿在邓布利多的办公室呢,但很快就会回来……"

停了一会儿,大家看着罗恩在昏睡中小声嘟囔。

"毒药在酒里?"弗雷德轻声问。

"是的。"哈利马上说。他现在没法想别的,很高兴有机会重新讨论这个话题。"斯拉格霍恩把它从——"

"他会不会趁你不注意时往罗恩杯子里放了什么东西?"

"有可能,可斯拉格霍恩为什么要对罗恩下毒呢?"

"不知道,"弗雷德皱起眉头,"你觉得他有没有可能把杯子搞混了?本来是想害你的?"

"斯拉格霍恩为什么要对哈利下毒?"金妮问。

"我不知道,"弗雷德说,"不过肯定有好多人想对哈利下毒,是不是?'救世之星'嘛。"

"你认为斯拉格霍恩是食死徒?"金妮问。

"什么都有可能。"弗雷德阴沉地说。

"他可能中了夺魂咒。"乔治插嘴道。

"他也可能是无辜的。"金妮说,"毒药可能下在酒瓶里,这样对象就可能是斯拉格霍恩本人。"

"谁会想害斯拉格霍恩呢?"

"邓布利多认为伏地魔想把斯拉格霍恩拉过去,"哈利说,"斯拉格霍恩在来霍格沃茨之前已经躲了一年。而且……"他想到了邓布利多

## CHAPTER NINETEEN   Elf Tails

Slughorn, 'and maybe Voldemort wants him out of the way, maybe he thinks he could be valuable to Dumbledore.'

'But you said Slughorn had been planning to give that bottle to Dumbledore for Christmas,' Ginny reminded him. 'So the poisoner could just as easily have been after Dumbledore.'

'Then the poisoner didn't know Slughorn very well,' said Hermione, speaking for the first time in hours and sounding as though she had a bad head-cold. 'Anyone who knew Slughorn would have known there was a good chance he'd keep something that tasty for himself.'

'Er-my-nee,' croaked Ron unexpectedly from between them.

They all fell silent, watching him anxiously, but after muttering incomprehensibly for a moment he merely started snoring.

The dormitory doors flew open, making them all jump: Hagrid came striding towards them, his hair rain-flecked, his bearskin coat flapping behind him, a crossbow in his hand, leaving a trail of muddy dolphin-sized footprints all over the floor.

'Bin in the Forest all day!' he panted. 'Aragog's worse, I bin readin' to him – didn' get up ter dinner till jus' now an' then Professor Sprout told me abou' Ron! How is he?'

'Not bad,' said Harry. 'They say he'll be OK.'

'No more than six visitors at a time!' said Madam Pomfrey, hurrying out of her office.

'Hagrid makes six,' George pointed out.

'Oh ... yes ...' said Madam Pomfrey, who seemed to have been counting Hagrid as several people due to his vastness. To cover her confusion she hurried off to clear up his muddy footprints with her wand.

'I don' believe this,' said Hagrid hoarsely, shaking his great shaggy head as he stared down at Ron. 'Jus' don' believe it ... look at him lyin' there ... who'd want ter hurt him, eh?'

'That's just what we were discussing,' said Harry. 'We don't know.'

'Someone couldn' have a grudge against the Gryffindor Quidditch team, could they?' said Hagrid anxiously. 'Firs' Katie, now Ron ...'

'I can't see anyone trying to bump off a Quidditch team,' said George.

'Wood might've done the Slytherins if he could've got away with it,' said Fred fairly.

## 第 19 章 小精灵尾巴

还没从斯拉格霍恩那里获得的那段回忆,"也许伏地魔想除掉他,觉得他可能会对邓布利多很有价值。"

"可你说斯拉格霍恩打算把那瓶酒送给邓布利多做圣诞礼物的,"金妮提醒他,"所以投毒者也可能是针对邓布利多的。"

"那么投毒者是不大了解斯拉格霍恩。"赫敏这么多小时里第一次开口,听上去像得了重伤风,"了解斯拉格霍恩的人都知道,他很可能把好吃的东西都自己留着。"

"呃——敏——恩。"罗恩突然嘶哑地叫道。

大家沉默下来,担心地看着他,但他嘟囔了几声人们听不懂的话之后又打起鼾来。

病房门猛然打开了,他们都吓了一跳,海格大步走进来,头发上带着雨水,熊皮大衣在身后摆动着,手里拿着弩弓,在地上踏出海豚一般大的泥脚印。

"一天都在林子里!"他喘着气说,"阿拉戈克病得更重了,我念东西给他听——刚刚才上来吃晚饭,斯普劳特教授跟我讲了罗恩的事!他怎么样?"

"还好,"哈利说,"他们说他会好的。"

"一次探视不能超过六人!"庞弗雷女士急忙从办公室里跑了过来。

"加上海格是六个。"乔治指出。

"哦……对……"庞弗雷女士似乎把庞大的海格当成了好几个人,为了掩饰她的错误,她赶紧去用魔杖清除他的泥脚印。

"我不相信,"海格俯视着罗恩,摇摇他那乱蓬蓬的大脑袋,粗声粗气地说,"就是不相信……看他躺在那儿……谁会想伤害他呢?"

"这正是我们在讨论的问题,"哈利说,"我们也不知道。"

"不会是有人跟格兰芬多魁地奇球队过不去吧?"海格担心地说,"先是凯蒂,现在是罗恩……"

"我看不出有谁想干掉一支魁地奇球队。"乔治说。

"如果不会受处罚的话,伍德可能会对斯莱特林这么干。"弗雷德比较公正。

## CHAPTER NINETEEN   Elf Tails

'Well, I don't think it's Quidditch, but I think there's a connection between the attacks,' said Hermione quietly.

'How d'you work that out?' asked Fred.

'Well, for one thing, they both ought to have been fatal and weren't, although that was pure luck. And for another, neither the poison nor the necklace seems to have reached the person who was supposed to be killed. Of course,' she added broodingly, 'that makes the person behind this even more dangerous in a way, because they don't seem to care how many people they finish off before they actually reach their victim.'

Before anybody could respond to this ominous pronouncement, the dormitory doors opened again and Mr and Mrs Weasley hurried up the ward. They had done no more than satisfy themselves that Ron would make a full recovery on their last visit to the ward: now Mrs Weasley seized hold of Harry and hugged him very tightly.

'Dumbledore's told us how you saved him with the bezoar,' she sobbed. 'Oh, Harry, what can we say? You saved Ginny ... you saved Arthur ... now you've saved Ron ...'

'Don't be ... I didn't ...' muttered Harry awkwardly.

'Half our family does seem to owe you their lives, now I stop and think about it,' Mr Weasley said in a constricted voice. 'Well, all I can say is that it was a lucky day for the Weasleys when Ron decided to sit in your compartment on the Hogwarts Express, Harry.'

Harry could not think of any reply to this and was almost glad when Madam Pomfrey reminded them again that there were only supposed to be six visitors around Ron's bed; he and Hermione rose at once to leave and Hagrid decided to go with them, leaving Ron with his family.

'It's terrible,' growled Hagrid into his beard, as the three of them walked back along the corridor to the marble staircase. 'All this new security, an' kids are still gettin' hurt ... Dumbledore's worried sick ... he don' say much, but I can tell ...'

'Hasn't he got any ideas, Hagrid?' asked Hermione desperately.

'I 'spect he's got hundreds of ideas, brain like his,' said Hagrid staunchly. 'But he doesn' know who sent that necklace nor who put poison in that wine, or they'd've bin caught, wouldn' they? Wha' worries me,' said Hagrid, lowering his voice and glancing over his shoulder (Harry, for good measure, checked the ceiling for Peeves), 'is how long Hogwarts can stay open if kids are bein' attacked. Chamber o' Secrets all over again, isn' it? There'll be panic, more parents takin' their kids outta school, an' nex' thing yeh know the board o' governors ...'

604

## 第19章 小精灵尾巴

"我想不是为了魁地奇，但这两次事件之间有联系。"赫敏轻声说。

"何以见得？"弗雷德问。

"第一，两次本来都该致命的，却都没有致命，尽管这纯粹是运气。第二，毒药和项链似乎都没有害到原定要害的人。当然，"她沉吟地说，"这样看来幕后那个人更加阴险，因为他们为了袭击真正的目标似乎不在乎干掉多少人。"

还没有人对这个不祥的预言做出回答，病房的门又开了，韦斯莱夫妇匆匆走向病床。他们上次探视只是确定罗恩能完全康复。现在韦斯莱夫人抓住哈利，紧紧地拥抱他。

"邓布利多告诉我们你用粪石救了他。"她抽泣道，"哦，哈利，我们说什么好呢？你救过金妮……救过亚瑟……现在又救了罗恩……"

"不用……我没有……"哈利局促地说。

"还真是，现在想起来，我们家好像有一半人的命都是你救的。"韦斯莱先生说，他的嗓子眼有些发紧，"我只能说，罗恩在霍格沃茨特快列车上决定坐在你的包厢里，那真是幸运的一天，哈利。"

哈利不知道该怎么回答，当庞弗雷女士又提醒他们罗恩床边只能有六位探视者时，他几乎有些庆幸。哈利和赫敏立刻起身离去，海格决定跟他们一起走，让罗恩跟他的家人待在一起。

"真可怕，"海格吹着他的大胡子咆哮道，三人沿着走廊往大理石台阶走去，"采取了这么多新的安保措施，还是不断有孩子受伤……邓布利多担心坏了……他不大说，但我看得出……"

"他没有什么主意吗，海格？"赫敏急切地问。

"我想他有几百个主意，他那样的脑子，"海格忠诚地说，"可他不知道是谁送的项链，谁在酒里下的毒，要不然早就抓住他们了，是不是？我担心的是，"海格压低嗓门，回头看了看（哈利则帮着看天花板上有没有皮皮鬼），"像这样接连有孩子出事，霍格沃茨还能办多久。这不又像密室事件了吗？会搞得人心惶惶，家长把孩子接出学校，然后董事会……"

## CHAPTER NINETEEN  Elf Tails

Hagrid stopped talking as the ghost of a long-haired woman drifted serenely past, then resumed in a hoarse whisper, '... the board o' governors'll be talkin' about shuttin' us up fer good.'

'Surely not?' said Hermione, looking worried.

'Gotta see it from their point o' view,' said Hagrid heavily. 'I mean, it's always bin a bit of a risk sendin' a kid ter Hogwarts, hasn' it? Yer expect accidents, don' yeh, with hundreds of underage wizards all locked up tergether, but attempted murder, tha's diff'rent. 'S no wonder Dumbledore's angry with Sn—'

Hagrid stopped in his tracks, a familiar, guilty expression on what was visible of his face above his tangled black beard.

'What?' said Harry quickly. 'Dumbledore's angry with Snape?'

'I never said tha',' said Hagrid, though his look of panic could not have been a bigger give-away. 'Look at the time, it's gettin' on fer midnight, I need ter —'

'Hagrid, why is Dumbledore angry with Snape?' Harry asked loudly.

'Shhhh!' said Hagrid, looking both nervous and angry. 'Don' shout stuff like that, Harry, d'you wan' me ter lose me job? Mind, I don' suppose you'd care, would yeh, not now you've given up Care of Mag—'

'Don't try and make me feel guilty, it won't work!' said Harry forcefully. 'What's Snape done?'

'I dunno, Harry, I shouldn'ta heard it at all! I — well, I was comin' outta the Forest the other evenin' an' I overheard 'em talkin' — well, arguin'. Didn't like ter draw attention to meself, so I sorta skulked an' tried not ter listen, but it was a — well, a heated discussion, an' it wasn' easy ter block it out.'

'Well?' Harry urged him, as Hagrid shuffled his enormous feet uneasily.

'Well — I jus' heard Snape sayin' Dumbledore took too much fer granted an' maybe he — Snape — didn' wan' ter do it any more —'

'Do what?'

'I dunno, Harry, it sounded like Snape was feelin' a bit overworked, tha's all — anyway, Dumbledore told him flat out he'd agreed ter do it an' that was all there was to it. Pretty firm with him. An' then he said summat abou' Snape makin' investigations in his house, in Slytherin. Well, there's nothin' strange abou' that!' Hagrid added hastily, as Harry and Hermione exchanged looks full of meaning. 'All the Heads o' House were asked ter look inter that

## 第19章 小精灵尾巴

一个长发女郎的幽灵恬静地飘过,海格停了下来,然后沙哑地小声说:"……董事会就会讨论把我们永远关掉。"

"不会的吧?"赫敏担心地问。

"你得从他们的观点来看。"海格语气沉重地说,"把孩子送进霍格沃茨总会有一些风险,是不是?几百个未成年的巫师关在一起,难免会有事故,是不是?可是谋杀未遂事件性质不同啊,难怪邓布利多那么生斯内——"

海格突然刹住了,蓬乱的黑胡子间露出的那块面孔带着熟悉的心虚表情。

"什么?"哈利马上问,"邓布利多生斯内普的气?"

"我没那么说。"海格否认道,但那副惶恐的样子是对他最有力的揭发,"看看时间,快十二点了,我得——"

"海格,邓布利多为什么生斯内普的气?"哈利大声问。

"嘘——"海格说,看上去既紧张又恼火,"别嚷嚷那种话,你想让我丢掉工作吗?哦,我想你不在乎,是不是?反正你已经放弃了保护神奇——"

"别想让我觉得内疚,那没用!"哈利激烈地说,"斯内普干了什么?"

"我不知道,哈利,我根本不该听到的!我——唉,那天晚上我从林子里出来,听到他们在说话——在吵架。我不想被他们发现,就偷偷走在后面,努力不听,可那是一场——激烈的讨论,想不听也不容易。"

"说呀?"哈利催促道,海格那双大脚不安地动了动。

"嗯——我听到斯内普说邓布利多太想当然,也许他——斯内普——不想再干了——"

"再干什么?"

"我不知道,哈利,听起来好像斯内普觉得工作太重了,就是这样——但是,邓布利多直截了当地说是斯内普同意干的,没什么可说的。对他态度挺强硬的。然后又说到要斯内普调查他的学院,斯莱特林。咳,这没什么奇怪的!"海格见哈利和赫敏意味深长地对视了一下,急忙说,

necklace business –'

'Yeah, but Dumbledore's not having rows with the rest of them, is he?' said Harry.

'Look,' Hagrid twisted his crossbow uncomfortably in his hands; there was a loud splintering sound and it snapped in two, 'I know what yeh're like abou' Snape, Harry, an' I don' want yeh ter go readin' more inter this than there is.'

'Look out,' said Hermione tersely.

They turned just in time to see the shadow of Argus Filch looming over the wall behind them before the man himself turned the corner, hunchbacked, his jowls aquiver.

'Oho!' he wheezed. 'Out of bed so late, this'll mean detention!'

'No it won', Filch,' said Hagrid shortly. 'They're with me, aren' they?'

'And what difference does that make?' asked Filch obnoxiously.

'I'm a ruddy teacher, aren' I, yeh sneakin' Squib!' said Hagrid, firing up at once.

There was a nasty hissing noise as Filch swelled with fury; Mrs Norris had arrived, unseen, and was twisting herself sinuously around Filch's skinny ankles.

'Get goin',' said Hagrid out of the corner of his mouth.

Harry did not need telling twice; he and Hermione both hurried off, Hagrid and Filch's raised voices echoing behind them as they ran. They passed Peeves near the turning into Gryffindor Tower, but he was streaking happily towards the source of the yelling, cackling and calling,

> *'When there's strife and when there's trouble*
> *Call on Peevsie, he'll make double!'*

The Fat Lady was snoozing and not pleased to be awoken, but swung forwards grumpily to allow them to clamber into the mercifully peaceful and empty common room. It did not seem that people knew about Ron yet; Harry was very relieved, he had been interrogated enough that day. Hermione bade him goodnight and set off for the girls' dormitory. Harry, however, remained behind, taking a seat beside the fire and looking down into the dying embers.

So Dumbledore had argued with Snape. In spite of all he had told Harry, in spite of his insistence that he trusted Snape completely, he had lost his temper

## 第19章 小精灵尾巴

"所有学院的院长都要调查项链的事——"

"对,可是邓布利多没跟其他人争吵,是不是?"哈利说。

"听着,"海格说,一边局促地扳着弩弓,嘎嘣一声,弩弓折成了两半,"我知道你对斯内普是怎么想的,哈利,我不希望你去猜疑本来没有的事情。"

"小心!"赫敏急促地说。

他们回过头,看见阿格斯·费尔奇的阴影正投到他们身后的墙上,然后他本人从一个拐角走了出来,他佝偻着背,下巴的垂肉抖动着。

"哦嗬!"他呼哧呼哧地说,"这么晚了还不睡觉,关禁闭!"

"不,费尔奇,"海格马上说,"他们跟我在一起,是吧?"

"那有什么区别?"费尔奇可憎地问。

"我是教师,不是吗?你这鬼鬼祟祟的哑炮!"海格登时火了。

费尔奇勃然大怒,发出可怕的嘶嘶声,洛丽丝夫人不知什么时候来了,蛇一样绕在费尔奇的瘦脚脖子上。

"走。"海格从牙缝中挤出声音说。

哈利不需要再提醒,跟赫敏一起匆匆逃走了,海格和费尔奇的高嗓门在身后回响。在即将拐进格兰芬多塔楼时,他们碰到了皮皮鬼,他正快活地朝着吵嚷声的方向冲去,咯咯地笑着叫道:

哪儿有打架,哪儿有麻烦,
就叫皮皮鬼,他会去添乱!

胖夫人正在打瞌睡,被吵醒了不大高兴,拉长了脸,但还是旋开了,让他们爬了进去。幸好公共休息室里一片清静,空无一人。大家似乎还不知道罗恩的事,哈利大大地松了口气,他今天已经被问得够多了。赫敏跟他道了晚安,回女生宿舍了。哈利留了下来,坐在壁炉旁凝视着即将燃尽的余火。

邓布利多跟斯内普吵架了,尽管他对哈利口口声声说他完全信任

609

## CHAPTER NINETEEN   Elf Tails

with him ... he did not think that Snape had tried hard enough to investigate the Slytherins ... or, perhaps, to investigate a single Slytherin: Malfoy?

Was it because Dumbledore did not want Harry to do anything foolish, to take matters into his own hands, that he had pretended there was nothing in Harry's suspicions? That seemed likely. It might even be that Dumbledore did not want anything to distract Harry from their lessons, or from procuring that memory from Slughorn. Perhaps Dumbledore did not think it right to confide suspicions about his staff to sixteen-year-olds ...

'There you are, Potter!'

Harry jumped to his feet in shock, his wand at the ready. He had been quite convinced that the common room was empty; he had not been at all prepared for a hulking figure to rise, suddenly, out of a distant chair. A closer look showed him that it was Cormac McLaggen.

'I've been waiting for you to come back,' said McLaggen, disregarding Harry's drawn wand. 'Must've fallen asleep. Look, I saw them taking Weasley up to the hospital wing earlier. Didn't look like he'll be fit for next week's match.'

It took Harry a few moments to realise what McLaggen was talking about.

'Oh ... right ... Quidditch,' he said, putting his wand back into the belt of his jeans and running a hand wearily through his hair. 'Yeah ... he might not make it.'

'Well, then, I'll be playing Keeper, won't I?' said McLaggen.

'Yeah,' said Harry. 'Yeah, I suppose so ...'

He could not think of an argument against it; after all, McLaggen had certainly performed second best in the trials.

'Excellent,' said McLaggen in a satisfied voice. 'So when's practice?'

'What? Oh ... there's one tomorrow evening.'

'Good. Listen, Potter, we should have a talk beforehand. I've got some ideas on strategy you might find useful.'

'Right,' said Harry unenthusiastically. 'Well, I'll hear them tomorrow, then. I'm pretty tired now ... see you ...'

The news that Ron had been poisoned spread quickly next day, but it did not cause the sensation that Katie's attack had done. People seemed to think that it might have been an accident, given that he had been in the Potion master's room at the time, and that as he had been given an antidote immediately there was no real harm done. In fact, the Gryffindors were

## 第19章 小精灵尾巴

斯内普,他还是跟斯内普发脾气了……觉得斯内普没有尽力调查斯莱特林……或调查某一个斯莱特林的学生——马尔福?

邓布利多是否因为不希望哈利做傻事,害怕哈利自己插手去管,才假装说哈利怀疑的事情是无中生有?有可能。甚至他可能是不希望哈利上课分心或耽误了从斯拉格霍恩那里搞到真实的记忆。也可能邓布利多觉得不该对一个十六岁学生袒露他对教员的怀疑……

"你在这儿,波特!"

哈利惊得跳了起来,拿起魔杖。他本来以为休息室里没人,完全没想到远处座位上会突然冒出一个庞大的身影。哈利定睛一看,是考迈克·麦克拉根。

"我一直在等你回来,"麦克拉根说,没理会哈利拔出的魔杖,"准是打了个盹儿。早些时候,我看到他们把韦斯莱抬到校医院去了。看样子他不能参加下星期的比赛了。"

哈利过了一会儿才明白他在说什么。

"哦……对了……魁地奇,"他把魔杖插回牛仔裤的腰带中,疲惫地捋了一下头发,"是啊……他可能去不了啦。"

"那就该我当守门员了,是不是?"麦克拉根问。

"啊,"哈利说,"啊,我想是……"

哈利想不出反驳的理由,毕竟,麦克拉根在选拔中名列第二。

"太好了,"麦克拉根用满意的口气说,"什么时候训练?"

"什么?哦……明天晚上有一次。"

"好,听我说,波特,我们应该事先谈一谈。我有一些战略想法,可能对你有用。"

"行,"哈利不太热情地说,"我明天再听吧,现在挺累的……再见……"

罗恩中毒的事第二天就迅速传开了,但没有像凯蒂受伤那么轰动,大家似乎认为这也许是个意外,因为他当时在魔药老师的屋里,而且立刻服了解药,没什么大碍。实际上,格兰芬多的学生普遍更关心

generally much more interested in the upcoming Quidditch match against Hufflepuff, for many of them wanted to see Zacharias Smith, who played Chaser on the Hufflepuff team, punished soundly for his commentary during the opening match against Slytherin.

Harry, however, had never been less interested in Quidditch; he was rapidly becoming obsessed with Draco Malfoy. Still checking the Marauder's Map whenever he got a chance, he sometimes made detours to wherever Malfoy happened to be, but had not yet detected him doing anything out of the ordinary. And still there were those inexplicable times when Malfoy simply vanished from the map ...

But Harry did not get a lot of time to consider the problem, what with Quidditch practice, homework, and the fact that he was now being dogged wherever he went by Cormac McLaggen and Lavender Brown.

He could not decide which of them was more annoying. McLaggen kept up a constant stream of hints that he would make a better permanent Keeper for the team than Ron, and that now Harry was seeing him play regularly he would surely come around to this way of thinking, too; he was also keen to criticise the other players and provide Harry with detailed training schemes, so that more than once Harry was forced to remind him who was Captain.

Meanwhile, Lavender kept sidling up to Harry to discuss Ron, which Harry found almost more wearing than McLaggen's Quidditch lectures. At first, Lavender had been very annoyed that nobody had thought to tell her that Ron was in the hospital wing – 'I mean, I *am* his girlfriend!' – but unfortunately she had now decided to forgive Harry this lapse of memory and was keen to have lots of in-depth chats with him about Ron's feelings, a most uncomfortable experience that Harry would have happily forgone.

'Look, why don't you talk to Ron about all this?' Harry asked, after a particularly long interrogation from Lavender that took in everything from precisely what Ron had said about her new dress robes to whether or not Harry thought that Ron considered his relationship with Lavender to be 'serious'.

'Well, I would, but he's always asleep when I go and see him!' said Lavender fretfully.

'Is he?' said Harry, surprised, for he had found Ron perfectly alert every time he had been up to the hospital wing, both highly interested in the news of Dumbledore and Snape's row and keen to abuse McLaggen as much as possible.

'Is Hermione Granger still visiting him?' Lavender demanded suddenly.

## 第19章 小精灵尾巴

的是对赫奇帕奇的魁地奇比赛,很多人都想看到对方的追球手扎卡赖斯·史密斯受到惩罚,因为他在格兰芬多对斯莱特林的开场赛中解说得那么恶劣。

哈利对魁地奇的兴趣却从未像现在这样低过,他的心思已迅速被德拉科·马尔福占满,除了一有机会就查看活点地图,有时还会绕到马尔福所在的地方,但仍未发现他有异常行为。不过还是有些神秘的时刻,马尔福会完全从地图上消失……

但哈利没有很多时间想这个问题,要参加魁地奇训练,要做作业,而且走到哪儿都会遭到麦克拉根和拉文德的纠缠。

哈利不能确定这两个人哪个更讨厌。麦克拉根不断暗示他当守门员会比罗恩更好,认为现在哈利经常看到他的训练,一定会得出同样的结论。他还喜欢批评其他球员,向哈利提供详细的训练方案,哈利好几次不得不提醒他谁是队长。

与此同时,拉文德经常凑上来讨论罗恩,哈利觉得这几乎比麦克拉根的魁地奇讲座更令人厌烦。一开始,拉文德很生气没人想到告诉她罗恩进了校医院——"我是他的女朋友!"不幸的是,她现在决定原谅哈利的失忆,很喜欢跟他就罗恩的感情做一次次深谈,这种极不舒服的经历哈利宁可没有。

"听我说,你为什么不跟罗恩谈这些呢?"哈利问。

在一次特别长的问话里,拉文德问东问西,从罗恩对她的新袍子到底发表了什么评论,一直问到哈利是否觉得罗恩对她是"认真的"。

"唉,我是想问啊,可我去看他的时候,他总是在睡觉。"拉文德烦恼地说。

"是吗?"哈利很惊讶,因为每次他去校医院,罗恩都很清醒,对邓布利多和斯内普吵架的消息很感兴趣,骂起麦克拉根来也积极起劲。

"赫敏·格兰杰还去看他吗?"拉文德突然问。

## CHAPTER NINETEEN   Elf Tails

'Yeah, I think so. Well, they're friends, aren't they?' said Harry uncomfortably.

'Friends, don't make me laugh,' said Lavender scornfully. 'She didn't talk to him for weeks after he started going out with me! But I suppose she wants to make up with him now he's all *interesting* ...'

'Would you call getting poisoned being interesting?' asked Harry. 'Anyway – sorry, got to go – there's McLaggen coming for a talk about Quidditch,' said Harry hurriedly, and he dashed sideways through a door pretending to be solid wall and sprinted down the short cut that would take him off to Potions where, thankfully, neither Lavender nor McLaggen could follow him.

On the morning of the Quidditch match against Hufflepuff Harry dropped in on the hospital wing before heading down to the pitch. Ron was very agitated; Madam Pomfrey would not let him go down to watch the match, feeling it would overexcite him.

'So how's McLaggen shaping up?' he asked Harry nervously, apparently forgetting that he had already asked the same question twice.

'I've told you,' said Harry patiently, 'he could be world class and I wouldn't want to keep him. He keeps trying to tell everyone what to do, he thinks he could play every position better than the rest of us. I can't wait to be shot of him. And speaking of getting shot of people,' Harry added, getting to his feet and picking up his Firebolt, 'will you stop pretending to be asleep when Lavender comes to see you? She's driving me mad as well.'

'Oh,' said Ron, looking sheepish. 'Yeah. All right.'

'If you don't want to go out with her any more, just tell her,' said Harry.

'Yeah ... well ... it's not that easy, is it?' said Ron. He paused. 'Hermione going to look in before the match?' he added casually.

'No, she's already gone down to the pitch with Ginny.'

'Oh,' said Ron, looking rather glum. 'Right. Well, good luck. Hope you hammer McLag– I mean, Smith.'

'I'll try,' said Harry, shouldering his broom. 'See you after the match.'

He hurried down through the deserted corridors; the whole school was outside, either already seated in the stadium or heading down towards it. He was looking out of the windows he passed, trying to gauge how much wind they were facing, when a noise ahead made him glance up and he saw Malfoy walking towards him, accompanied by two girls, both of whom looked sulky and resentful.

## 第19章 小精灵尾巴

"嗯，我想是的。他们是朋友嘛，是不是？"哈利尴尬地答道。

"朋友？别逗我了。"拉文德轻蔑地说，"罗恩跟我好了之后，赫敏几星期都没跟他说话！可是我估计她想跟罗恩和好，因为现在罗恩那么有趣……"

"你是说中毒有趣？算了——对不起，我该走了——麦克拉根要过来谈魁地奇了。"哈利急忙说，然后冲进旁边一扇伪装成墙壁的门里，抄近路逃去上魔药课了，幸好拉文德和麦克拉根不能跟去。

在对赫奇帕奇比赛的那天早上，哈利去球场前到校医院看了看。罗恩焦躁不安，庞弗雷女士不让他去观看比赛，怕他兴奋过度。

"麦克拉根表现得怎么样？"他紧张地问哈利，好像不记得他已经问过两遍了。

"我跟你说了，"哈利耐心地说，"他就是世界一流我也不想留他。他老是教训别人，觉得他在哪个位置都能比我们其他人更好。我巴不得早点儿摆脱他。说到摆脱，"哈利站起来，拿起他的火弩箭，"你能不能在拉文德来看你时不要假装睡觉？她也要把我逼疯了。"

"哦，"罗恩难为情地说，"是，好的。"

"如果你不想再跟她处下去，就告诉她。"哈利说。

"嗯……这……不那么容易，是不是？"罗恩停了一会儿，又不经意地加了一句，"赫敏比赛前会来吗？"

"不，她已经跟金妮去球场了。"

"哦，"罗恩显得有些沮丧，"好吧，祝你们好运，希望你痛揍麦克拉——我是说史密斯。"

"我尽量。"哈利说着扛起飞天扫帚，"赛后再见。"

他匆匆穿过无人的走廊。全校人都出去了，不是已坐在体育场里就是正往那儿走。哈利边走边看窗外，判断风力多大。听到前方有响动，他抬起目光，只见马尔福朝他走来，旁边有两个女孩，都面有愠色。

## CHAPTER NINETEEN   Elf Tails

Malfoy stopped short at the sight of Harry, then gave a short, humourless laugh and continued walking.

'Where're you going?' Harry demanded.

'Yeah, I'm really going to tell you, because it's your business, Potter,' sneered Malfoy. 'You'd better hurry up, they'll be waiting for the Chosen Captain – the Boy Who Scored – whatever they call you these days.'

One of the girls gave an unwilling giggle. Harry stared at her. She blushed. Malfoy pushed past Harry and she and her friend followed at a trot, turning the corner and vanishing from view.

Harry stood rooted on the spot and watched them disappear. This was infuriating; he was already cutting it fine to get to the match on time and yet there was Malfoy, skulking off while the rest of the school was absent: Harry's best chance yet of discovering what Malfoy was up to. The silent seconds trickled past, and Harry remained where he was, frozen, gazing at the place where Malfoy had vanished ...

'Where have you been?' demanded Ginny, as Harry sprinted into the changing room. The whole team was changed and ready; Coote and Peakes, the Beaters, were both hitting their clubs nervously against their legs.

'I met Malfoy,' Harry told her quietly, as he pulled his scarlet robes over his head.

'So?'

'So I wanted to know how come he's up at the castle with a couple of girlfriends while everyone else is down here ...'

'Does it matter right now?'

'Well, I'm not likely to find out, am I?' said Harry, seizing his Firebolt and pushing his glasses straight. 'Come on, then!'

And without another word, he marched out on to the pitch to deafening cheers and boos. There was little wind; the clouds were patchy; every now and then there were dazzling flashes of bright sunlight.

'Tricky conditions!' McLaggen said bracingly to the team. 'Coote, Peakes, you'll want to fly out of the sun, so they don't see you coming –'

'I'm the Captain, McLaggen, shut up giving them instructions,' said Harry angrily. 'Just get up by the goalposts!'

Once McLaggen had marched off, Harry turned to Coote and Peakes.

'Make sure you *do* fly out of the sun,' he told them grudgingly.

## 第19章 小精灵尾巴

看到哈利，马尔福突然停住了，然后短促地干笑一声，继续往前走。

"你去哪儿？"哈利问。

"啊，我正要告诉你呢，因为这是你的事，波特，"马尔福讥笑道，"你最好快点儿，他们在等'救世队长'——'得分之星'——谁知道他们现在叫你什么呢。"

一个女孩勉强地笑了一声，哈利盯着她，她脸红了。马尔福从哈利身旁挤了过去，女孩跟她的朋友小跑着跟上，转过拐角不见了。

哈利定在原地，眼睁睁地看着他们消失。真够气人的，他已经是掐着时间去赛场，却发现马尔福趁全校人都去看球赛的时候在偷偷行动：到现在为止，这是搞清马尔福在干什么的最好机会。时间一秒一秒无声地过去，哈利还站在那儿，望着马尔福消失的地方……

"你去哪儿了？"哈利冲进更衣室时金妮问。全队都已换好衣服，准备上场了。击球手古特和珀克斯紧张地用球棍敲着腿。

"我碰到马尔福了。"哈利小声告诉她，一边把红色的球袍套到头上。

"然后呢？"

"我想知道，所有的人都在这儿，他怎么会带着两个女孩在城堡里……"

"这个时候这件事很要紧吗？"

"咳，现在也不可能搞清楚了，是不是？"哈利抓起火弩箭，戴好眼镜，"走吧！"

他没再说话，大步走到球场上，迎来了震耳欲聋的欢呼和嘘声。没有什么风，天上白云朵朵，时而有耀眼的阳光射出。

"麻烦的天气！"麦克拉根给队员们打气说，"古特，珀克斯，你们要在阳光照不到的地方飞，让对方看不到你们过来——"

"我是队长，麦克拉根，不要再指导他们了，"哈利恼火地说，"到球门那儿去。"

麦克拉根走了之后，哈利转向了古特和珀克斯。

"记着要在阳光照不到的地方飞。"他不情愿地叮嘱道。

## CHAPTER NINETEEN  Elf Tails

He shook hands with the Hufflepuff Captain, and then, on Madam Hooch's whistle, kicked off and rose into the air, higher than the rest of his team, streaking around the pitch in search of the Snitch. If he could catch it good and early, there might be a chance he could get back up to the castle, seize the Marauder's Map and find out what Malfoy was doing ...

'And that's Smith of Hufflepuff with the Quaffle,' said a dreamy voice, echoing over the grounds. 'He did the commentary last time, of course, and Ginny Weasley flew into him, I think probably on purpose – it looked like it. Smith was being quite rude about Gryffindor, I expect he regrets that now he's playing them – oh, look, he's lost the Quaffle, Ginny took it from him, I do like her, she's very nice ...'

Harry stared down at the commentator's podium. Surely, nobody in their right mind would have let Luna Lovegood commentate? But even from above there was no mistaking that long, dirty-blonde hair, or the necklace of Butterbeer corks ... Beside Luna, Professor McGonagall was looking slightly uncomfortable, as though she was indeed having second thoughts about this appointment.

'... but now that big Hufflepuff player's got the Quaffle from her, I can't remember his name, it's something like Bibble – no, Buggins –'

'It's Cadwallader!' said Professor McGonagall loudly from beside Luna. The crowd laughed.

Harry stared around for the Snitch; there was no sign of it. Moments later, Cadwallader scored. McLaggen had been shouting criticism at Ginny for allowing the Quaffle out of her possession, with the result that he had not noticed the large red ball soaring past his right ear.

'McLaggen, will you pay attention to what you're supposed to be doing and leave everyone else alone!' bellowed Harry, wheeling round to face his Keeper.

'You're not setting a great example!' McLaggen shouted back, red-faced and furious.

'And Harry Potter's now having an argument with his Keeper,' said Luna serenely, while both Hufflepuffs and Slytherins below in the crowd cheered and jeered. 'I don't think that'll help him find the Snitch, but maybe it's a clever ruse ...'

Swearing angrily, Harry spun round and set off around the pitch again, scanning the skies for some sign of the tiny winged golden ball.

## 第19章 小精灵尾巴

哈利跟赫奇帕奇的队长握了手,然后在霍琦女士的哨声中腾空而起,升得比其他队员都高,围绕球场疾驰,寻找飞贼。如果能早点儿抓到它,也许还有机会返回城堡拿上活点地图,去弄清马尔福在干什么……

"赫奇帕奇的史密斯拿到了鬼飞球,"一个梦幻般的声音在球场上空回响,"当然,上次是他做的解说。金妮·韦斯莱撞到了他,我想可能是故意的——看上去很像。史密斯上次对格兰芬多出言不逊。我想他现在后悔了——哦,快看,他丢掉了鬼飞球,金妮抢了过去,我喜欢她,她人很好……"

哈利朝解说台看去,哪个头脑正常的人会让卢娜做解说呢?可就是在高空也不会看错,那暗金色的长发,黄油啤酒瓶塞做的项链……她旁边的麦格教授显得有点不自在,好像确实对这一任命感到有些后悔。

"……可现在那个赫奇帕奇的大个子球员把鬼飞球从金妮手里夺走了,我不记得他的名字,好像是毕勃——不,巴金思——"

"是卡德瓦拉德!"麦格教授在卢娜旁边高声说道,观众哄堂大笑。

哈利举目四望寻找飞贼,却不见它的踪影。过了一会儿,卡德瓦拉德进了一球。麦克拉根在那儿大声指责金妮丢掉了鬼飞球,结果没注意大红球从他右耳边飞了过去。

"麦克拉根,请专心做你该做的事,不要干涉别人!"哈利转过身冲着他的守门员吼道。

"你也没做个好榜样!"麦克拉根也吼道,面孔通红,怒气冲冲。

"哈利·波特在和他的守门员争吵,"卢娜平静地说,下面赫奇帕奇和斯莱特林的观众都喝起了倒彩,"我不认为那有助于他找到飞贼,但这也许是个巧妙的幌子……"

哈利愤怒地诅咒了一声,转身继续绕场疾驰,在天空中搜寻那个带翅膀的小金球的影子。

## CHAPTER NINETEEN    Elf Tails

Ginny and Demelza scored a goal apiece, giving the red-and-gold-clad supporters below something to cheer about. Then Cadwallader scored again, making things level, but Luna did not seem to have noticed; she appeared singularly uninterested in such mundane things as the score, and kept attempting to draw the crowd's attention to such things as interestingly shaped clouds and the possibility that Zacharias Smith, who had so far failed to maintain possession of the Quaffle for longer than a minute, was suffering from something called 'Loser's Lurgy'.

'Seventy–forty to Hufflepuff!' barked Professor McGonagall into Luna's megaphone.

'Is it, already?' said Luna vaguely. 'Oh, look! The Gryffindor Keeper's got hold of one of the Beater's bats.'

Harry spun round in midair. Sure enough, McLaggen, for reasons best known to himself, had pulled Peakes's bat from him and appeared to be demonstrating how to hit a Bludger towards an oncoming cadwallader.

'*Will you give him back his bat and get back to the goalposts!*' roared Harry, pelting towards McLaggen just as McLaggen took a ferocious swipe at the Bludger and mis-hit it.

A blinding, sickening pain … a flash of light … distant screams … and the sensation of falling down a long tunnel …

And the next thing Harry knew, he was lying in a remarkably warm and comfortable bed and looking up at a lamp that was throwing a circle of golden light on to a shadowy ceiling. He raised his head awkwardly. There on his left was a familiar-looking, freckly, red-haired person.

'Nice of you to drop in,' said Ron, grinning.

Harry blinked and looked around. Of course: he was in the hospital wing. The sky outside was indigo streaked with crimson. The match must have finished hours ago … as had any hope of cornering Malfoy. Harry's head felt strangely heavy; he raised a hand and felt a stiff turban of bandages.

'What happened?'

'Cracked skull,' said Madam Pomfrey, bustling up and pushing him back against his pillows. 'Nothing to worry about, I mended it at once, but I'm keeping you in overnight. You shouldn't overexert yourself for a few hours.'

'I don't want to stay here overnight,' said Harry angrily, sitting up and throwing back his covers, 'I want to find McLaggen and kill him.'

## 第19章 小精灵尾巴

金妮和德米尔扎各进一球,让下面穿着红金双色服装的观众有了一点可以欢呼的理由。然后卡德瓦拉德又进了一球,把比分扳平,但卢娜好像没注意到。她似乎对比分这种庸俗的东西特别不感兴趣,总是把观众的注意力引到别处,如奇形怪状的云彩,还有扎卡赖斯·史密斯开场后把鬼飞球拿在手里都没超过一分钟,是不是得了"丢球症",等等。

"赫奇帕奇队七十比四十领先!"麦格教授朝卢娜的麦克风中喊道。

"是吗,已经这样了?"卢娜茫然地说,"哦,看哪!格兰芬多的守门员抓住了一个击球手的球棍。"

哈利在空中急忙转过身,果然,麦克拉根出于只有他自己才知道的原因,从珀克斯手里夺过了球棍,好像在示范怎么把游走球击向飞来的卡德瓦拉德。

"把球棍还给他,回球门里去!"哈利咆哮着朝麦克拉根冲了过去,麦克拉根朝游走球狠抽一棍,但没击中球。

一阵头晕目眩的剧痛……一道亮光……远处的尖叫声……然后像在长长的隧道里坠落……

哈利知道的下一件事,就是发现自己躺在异常温暖舒适的床上,头上是一盏在朦胧的天花板上投下金色光圈的吊灯。他艰难地抬起头,看见左边有一个很眼熟的雀斑脸、红头发的人。

"谢谢你来陪我。"罗恩笑嘻嘻地说。

哈利眨眨眼睛,环顾四周。没错,他在校医院里。外面的天空靛蓝中夹着深红的条纹。比赛一定早结束了……抓住马尔福的希望也落空了。哈利觉得脑袋沉得出奇,他举起手,摸到了一大圈硬硬的绷带,像阿拉伯人的缠头巾。

"怎么回事?"

"头骨碎裂,"庞弗雷女士急忙走来,把他按回枕头上,"不用担心,我立刻就能让它愈合,但你要住一晚上,几小时之内不可用力过度。"

"我不想在这儿过夜,"哈利愤怒地说,一边掀开被单坐了起来,"我想找到麦克拉根,把他杀了。"

## CHAPTER NINETEEN    Elf Tails

'I'm afraid that would come under the heading of "overexertion",' said Madam Pomfrey, pushing him firmly back on to the bed and raising her wand in a threatening manner. 'You will stay here until I discharge you, Potter, or I shall call the Headmaster.'

She bustled back into her office and Harry sank back into his pillows, fuming.

'D'you know how much we lost by?' he asked Ron through clenched teeth.

'Well, yeah I do,' said Ron apologetically. 'Final score was three hundred and twenty to sixty.'

'Brilliant,' said Harry savagely. 'Really brilliant! When I get hold of McLaggen –'

'You don't want to get hold of him, he's the size of a troll,' said Ron reasonably. 'Personally I think there's a lot to be said for hexing him with that toenail thing of the Prince's. Anyway, the rest of the team might've dealt with him before you get out of here, they're not happy ...'

There was a note of badly suppressed glee in Ron's voice; Harry could tell he was nothing short of thrilled that McLaggen had messed up so badly. Harry lay there, staring up at the patch of light on the ceiling, his recently mended skull not hurting, precisely, but feeling slightly tender underneath all the bandaging.

'I could hear the match commentary from here,' said Ron, his voice now shaking with laughter. 'I hope Luna always commentates from now on ... *Loser's Lurgy* ...'

But Harry was still too angry to see much humour in the situation, and after a while Ron's snorts subsided.

'Ginny came in to visit while you were unconscious,' he said, after a long pause, and Harry's imagination zoomed into overdrive, rapidly constructing a scene in which Ginny, weeping over his lifeless form, confessed her feelings of deep attraction to him while Ron gave them his blessing ... 'She reckons you only just arrived in time for the match. How come? You left here early enough.'

'Oh ...' said Harry, as the scene in his mind's eye imploded. 'Yeah ... well, I saw Malfoy sneaking off with a couple of girls who didn't look like they wanted to be with him, and that's the second time he's made sure he isn't down on the Quidditch pitch with the rest of the school. He skipped the last match too, remember?' Harry sighed. 'Wish I'd followed him now, the match was such a fiasco ...'

'Don't be stupid,' said Ron sharply. 'You couldn't have missed a Quidditch match just to follow Malfoy, you're the Captain!'

## 第 19 章 小精灵尾巴

"这恐怕属于'用力过度'。"庞弗雷女士坚决地把他推回床上，威胁地举起魔杖，"你要住到我让你出院为止，波特，不然我就叫校长了。"

她匆匆走回办公室，哈利倒回枕头上，怒不可遏。

"你知道我们输了多少？"他咬着牙问罗恩。

"嗯，我知道，"罗恩抱歉地说，"最后比分是三百二十比六十。"

"精彩，"哈利说，气得眼睛都红了，"真精彩！等我抓住麦克拉根——"

"别抓他，他的块头像巨怪。"罗恩理智地说，"我个人认为完全可以用王子那个让脚趾疯长的咒语教训他一下。不过，在你出院前可能其他队员已经整过他了，他们都不痛快……"

罗恩的语气中有抑制不住的开心。哈利看得出他为麦克拉根捅了这么大的娄子而暗暗高兴。哈利躺在那儿，盯着天花板上的光斑，新愈合的头骨疼得并不厉害，只是在绷带下隐隐作痛。

"在这儿能听到解说，"罗恩说，他笑得声音都抖了，"我希望以后都由卢娜解说……丢球症！……"

但哈利还在盛怒中，看不出这里面有多少幽默。过了一会儿，罗恩的笑声低了下去。

"你昏迷的时候金妮来过。"停了好长时间，他说。哈利的想象立刻超速运转起来，飞快地构思出一幕画面：金妮对着他没有知觉的身体抽泣，表白着对他深深的爱恋，罗恩为他们俩祝福……"她说你去的时候刚刚赶上比赛，怎么会呢？你走得挺早的啊。"

"哦……"哈利说，脑海中幻想的那一幕坍塌了，"是……我看到马尔福跟两个女孩偷偷溜走了，她们好像不想跟他走，这是他第二次没跟全校师生一起待在魁地奇球场。他上次比赛也溜了，记得吗？"哈利叹了口气，"当时要跟踪他就好了，比赛输得这么惨……"

"别傻了，"罗恩劈头说，"你不能为跟踪马尔福而错过魁地奇比赛，你是队长！"

## CHAPTER NINETEEN    Elf Tails

'I want to know what he's up to,' said Harry. 'And don't tell me it's all in my head, not after what I overheard between him and Snape –'

'I never said it was all in your head,' said Ron, hoisting himself up on an elbow in turn and frowning at Harry, 'but there's no rule saying only one person at a time can be plotting anything in this place! You're getting a bit obsessed with Malfoy, Harry. I mean, thinking about missing a match just to follow him ...'

'I want to catch him at it!' said Harry in frustration. 'I mean, where's he going when he disappears off the map?'

'I dunno ... Hogsmeade?' suggested Ron, yawning.

'I've never seen him going along any of the secret passageways on the map. I thought they were being watched now, anyway?'

'Well, then, I dunno,' said Ron.

Silence fell between them. Harry stared up at the circle of lamplight above him, thinking ...

If only he had Rufus Scrimgeour's power, he would have been able to set a tail upon Malfoy, but unfortunately Harry did not have an office full of Aurors at his command ... he thought fleetingly of trying to set something up with the DA, but there again was the problem that people would be missed from lessons; most of them, after all, still had full timetables ...

There was a low, rumbling snore from Ron's bed. After a while Madam Pomfrey came out of her office, this time wearing a thick dressing-gown. It was easiest to feign sleep; Harry rolled over on to his side and listened to all the curtains closing themselves as she waved her wand. The lamps dimmed, and she returned to her office; he heard the door click behind her, and knew that she was off to bed.

This was, Harry reflected in the darkness, the third time that he had been brought to the hospital wing because of a Quidditch injury. Last time he had fallen off his broom due to the presence of Dementors around the pitch, and the time before that, all the bones had been removed from his arm by the incurably inept Professor Lockhart ... that had been his most painful injury by far ... he remembered the agony of regrowing an armful of bones in one night, a discomfort not eased by the arrival of an unexpected visitor in the middle of the –

Harry sat bolt upright, his heart pounding, his bandage turban askew. He had the solution at last: there *was* a way to have Malfoy followed – how could he have forgotten, why hadn't he thought of it before?

## 第19章 小精灵尾巴

"我想知道他在干什么。别跟我说这都是我的想象,我听到他和斯内普——"

"我从来没说这都是你的想象,"罗恩用胳膊肘支起身子,皱着眉头对哈利说道,"可是没有哪条规定说这地方每次只能有一个人搞阴谋啊!你对马尔福有点着魔了,哈利,竟然想为了跟踪他而放弃比赛……"

"我想抓住他!"哈利沮丧地说,"我的意思是,他从活点地图上消失的时候都到哪儿去了?"

"不知道……霍格莫德?"罗恩打着哈欠说。

"我在地图上没见他走过秘密通道。再说我想通道也受到监视了,是不是?"

"那我就不知道了。"罗恩说。

两人沉默下来。哈利盯着天花板上的光圈,思索着……

要是他有鲁弗斯·斯克林杰的权力,就可以派人盯马尔福的梢。可惜哈利没有一批傲罗听他调遣……他想到利用D.A.,可仍然有缺课的问题,大部分人的日程还是挺满的……

罗恩的床上响起了低沉的呼噜声。稍后庞弗雷女士走了进来,这次她穿了件厚厚的睡衣。装睡最容易不过了,哈利翻了个身,听到她挥动魔杖拉上了所有的窗帘。灯暗下来,她走回办公室,只听门咔嗒一声关上,哈利知道她去睡觉了。

哈利在黑暗中回忆,这是他第三次在魁地奇赛场上受伤而被送进校医院。上次是因为球场周围有摄魂怪,他从扫帚上摔了下来。再上次是因为不可救药的洛哈特教授把他手臂内的骨头变没了……那是他最痛的一次……他想起了一夜间长出手臂里全部骨头的那种剧痛,即使是意外的午夜访客也没能减轻——

哈利腾地坐了起来,心嗵嗵地跳着,绷带歪到了一边。他终于有一个可以跟踪马尔福的办法了——他怎么会忘了呢?为什么先前没有想起来呢?

## CHAPTER NINETEEN   Elf Tails

But the question was, how to call him? What did you do?

Quietly, tentatively, Harry spoke into the darkness.

'Kreacher?'

There was a very loud *crack* and the sounds of scuffling and squeaks filled the silent room. Ron awoke with a yelp.

'What's going –?'

Harry pointed his wand hastily at the door of Madam Pomfrey's office and muttered '*Muffliato!* ' so that she would not come running. Then he scrambled to the end of his bed for a better look at what was going on.

Two house-elves were rolling around on the floor in the middle of the dormitory, one wearing a shrunken maroon jumper and several woolly hats, the other, a filthy old rag strung over his hips like a loincloth. Then there was another loud bang, and Peeves the poltergeist appeared in midair above the wrestling elves.

'I was watching that, Potty!' he told Harry indignantly, pointing at the fight below, before letting out a loud cackle. 'Look at the ickle creatures squabbling, bitey bitey, punchy punchy –'

'Kreacher will not insult Harry Potter in front of Dobby, no he won't, or Dobby will shut Kreacher's mouth for him!' cried Dobby in a high-pitched voice.

'– kicky, scratchy!' cried Peeves happily, now pelting bits of chalk at the elves to enrage them further. 'Tweaky, pokey!'

'Kreacher will say what he likes about his master, oh yes, and what a master he is, filthy friend of Mudbloods, oh, what would poor Kreacher's mistress say –?'

Exactly what Kreacher's mistress would have said they did not find out, for at that moment Dobby sank his knobbly little fist into Kreacher's mouth and knocked out half of his teeth. Harry and Ron both leapt out of their beds and wrenched the two elves apart, though they continued to try to kick and punch each other, egged on by Peeves, who swooped around the lamp squealing, 'Stick your fingers up his nosey, draw his cork and pull his earsies –'

Harry aimed his wand at Peeves and said, '*Langlock!* ' Peeves clutched at his throat, gulped, then swooped from the room making obscene gestures but unable to speak, owing to the fact that his tongue had just glued itself to the roof of his mouth.

## 第19章 小精灵尾巴

问题是，怎么去叫他？怎么做呢？

哈利轻声试探着向黑暗中呼唤。

"克利切？"

噼啪一声巨响，扭打声和尖叫声随即充满了原本寂静的病房。

罗恩惊醒了，叫道："出了什么——"

哈利急忙用魔杖指着庞弗雷女士的房门念道："闭耳塞听！"免得她冲过来。然后他爬到床脚，细看发生了什么。

两个家养小精灵在病房中央的地板上打滚，一个穿着件缩水的栗色套头衫，戴着几顶绒线帽，另一个屁股上裹着块脏兮兮的破布。然后又是一声巨响，恶作剧精灵皮皮鬼出现在扭成一团的小精灵上空。

"我正在看好戏呢，傻宝宝波特！"皮皮鬼愤愤不平地指着下面打架的小精灵告诉哈利，然后高声尖笑道，"看那两个小东西互相掐架，咬呀咬，打呀打。"

"不许克利切在多比面前侮辱哈利·波特，不许！不然多比就帮克利切闭上嘴巴！"多比尖叫道。

"——踢呀踢，抓呀抓！"皮皮鬼兴奋地喊道，一边朝小精灵扔粉笔头，给他们火上浇油，"掐呀掐，戳呀戳！"

"克利切对他主人想说什么就说什么，没错。什么主人呀，龌龊的泥巴种的朋友，哦，克利切的女主人会怎么说——？"

克利切的女主人到底会说什么，他们没听到，因为这时多比把他那疙疙瘩瘩的小拳头杵进了克利切的嘴里，打掉了他的半口牙齿。哈利和罗恩一齐从床上跳了起来，拉开了两个小精灵，但他们还在企图踢打对方。皮皮鬼在旁边煽风点火，一边绕着吊灯飞舞，一边尖叫道："用手指捅他鼻孔，打他的鼻子，揪他的耳朵——"

哈利用魔杖朝皮皮鬼一指，"锁舌封喉！"皮皮鬼抓着喉咙，噎住了，从窗口飞了出去，一边做着下流的手势，但说不出话来，因为他的舌头跟上腭粘到了一起。

## CHAPTER NINETEEN  Elf Tails

'Nice one,' said Ron appreciatively, lifting Dobby into the air so that his flailing limbs no longer made contact with Kreacher. 'That was another Prince hex, wasn't it?'

'Yeah,' said Harry, twisting Kreacher's wizened arm into a half-nelson. 'Right – I'm forbidding you to fight each other! Well, Kreacher, you're forbidden to fight Dobby. Dobby, I know I'm not allowed to give you orders –'

'Dobby is a free house-elf and he can obey anyone he likes and Dobby will do whatever Harry Potter wants him to do!' said Dobby, tears now streaming down his shrivelled little face on to his jumper.

'OK, then,' said Harry and he and Ron both released the elves, who fell to the floor, but did not continue fighting.

'Master called me?' croaked Kreacher, sinking into a bow even as he gave Harry a look that plainly wished him a painful death.

'Yeah, I did,' said Harry, glancing towards Madam Pomfrey's office door to check that the *Muffliato* spell was still working; there was no sign that she had heard any of the commotion. 'I've got a job for you.'

'Kreacher will do whatever Master wants,' said Kreacher, sinking so low that his lips almost touched his gnarled toes, 'because Kreacher has no choice, but Kreacher is ashamed to have such a Master, yes –'

'Dobby will do it, Harry Potter!' squeaked Dobby, his tennis-ball-sized eyes still swimming with tears. 'Dobby would be honoured to help Harry Potter!'

'Come to think of it, it would be good to have both of you,' said Harry. 'OK, then ... I want you to tail Draco Malfoy.'

Ignoring the look of mingled surprise and exasperation on Ron's face, Harry went on, 'I want to know where he's going, who he's meeting and what he's doing. I want you to follow him around the clock.'

'Yes, Harry Potter!' said Dobby at once, his great eyes shining with excitement. 'And if Dobby does it wrong, Dobby will throw himself off the topmost tower, Harry Potter!'

'There won't be any need for that,' said Harry hastily.

'Master wants me to follow the youngest of the Malfoys?' croaked Kreacher. 'Master wants me to spy upon the pure-blood great-nephew of my old mistress?'

'That's the one,' said Harry, foreseeing a great danger and determining to prevent it immediately. 'And you're forbidden to tip him off, Kreacher, or to

## 第19章 小精灵尾巴

"漂亮，"罗恩欣赏地说着，把多比举到空中，使他乱舞的四肢再也碰不到克利切，"又是王子的魔法吧？"

"对。"哈利扭着克利切枯瘦的胳膊，扼住他的脖子，"——我禁止你们再打架！噢，克利切，禁止你再打多比。多比，我知道我不能命令你——"

"多比是自由的家养小精灵，可以服从他喜欢的任何人，多比会做哈利·波特要他做的任何事情！"多比说，泪水顺着他皱巴巴的小脸淌到套头衫上。

"那好。"哈利说。他和罗恩放开小精灵，他们落到地上，没有再打架。

"主人叫我？"克利切嘶哑地问，鞠了一躬，尽管他那眼神显然希望哈利不得好死。

"是的，我叫你。"哈利看看庞弗雷女士的房门，确定闭耳塞听咒还有效，因为看不出她有听到吵闹声的迹象，"我要给你一个任务。"

"克利切听凭主人吩咐，"克利切腰弯得那么深，嘴几乎碰到了他那疙疙瘩瘩的脚趾，"因为克利切别无选择，但克利切为有这样一个主人而羞耻，没错——"

"多比愿意做，哈利·波特！"多比尖叫道，他那网球大的眼睛里仍盈满泪水，"能为哈利·波特效劳是多比的荣幸！"

"细想起来，有你们两个在一起倒不错。"哈利说，"好吧，那么……我希望你们跟踪德拉科·马尔福。"

他不顾罗恩脸上又惊又恼的表情，接着说："我想知道他去哪儿，见谁，干什么。我要你们全天盯着他。"

"是，哈利·波特！"多比马上说，大圆眼睛闪着兴奋的光芒，"要是多比做错了，多比就从最高的塔楼跳下去，哈利·波特！"

"那可不必。"哈利忙说。

"主人要我跟踪马尔福家最小的公子？"克利切嘶声道，"主人要我监视我旧主人的纯血统侄孙？"

"正是他，"哈利看到一个很大的危险，决定立刻防止，"禁止你向

show him what you're up to, or to talk to him at all, or to write him messages, or ... or to contact him in any way. Got it?'

He thought he could see Kreacher struggling to see a loophole in the instructions he had just been given, and waited. Ater a moment or two, and to Harry's great satisfaction, Kreacher bowed deeply again and said, with bitter resentment, 'Master thinks of everything and Kreacher must obey him even though Kreacher would much rather be the servant of the Malfoy boy, oh yes ...'

'That's settled, then,' said Harry. 'I'll want regular reports, but make sure I'm not surrounded by people when you turn up. Ron and Hermione are OK. And don't tell anyone what you're doing. Just stick to Malfoy like a couple of wart plasters.'

## 第 19 章 小精灵尾巴

他告密，克利切，禁止让他知道你在干什么，禁止跟他说话、给他写信，或……或用任何方式跟他联系。听到了吗？"

他看出克利切正努力在刚才的命令里寻找漏洞，就停在那儿等待着。过了一会儿，哈利很满意地看到克利切又深鞠一躬，恨恨地说："主人把一切都想到了，克利切必须服从他，尽管克利切宁可当马尔福少爷的仆人，没错……"

"那就这么定了。"哈利说，"我要你们定期汇报，但是要看准我周围没人时再来，罗恩和赫敏在场没关系。别告诉其他任何人你们在干什么。只要像两张膏药一样粘着马尔福。"

## CHAPTER TWENTY

## Lord Voldemort's Request

Harry and Ron left the hospital wing first thing on Monday morning, restored to full health by the ministrations of Madam Pomfrey and now able to enjoy the benefits of having been knocked out and poisoned, the best of which was that Hermione was friends with Ron again. Hermione even escorted them down to breakfast, bringing with her the news that Ginny had argued with Dean. The drowsing creature in Harry's chest suddenly raised its head, sniffing the air hopefully.

'What did they row about?' he asked, trying to sound casual as they turned into a seventh-floor corridor which was deserted but for a very small girl who had been examining a tapestry of trolls in tutus. She looked terrified at the sight of the approaching sixth-years and dropped the heavy brass scales she was carrying.

'It's all right!' said Hermione kindly, hurrying forwards to help her. 'Here ...' She tapped the broken scales with her wand and said, '*Reparo.*'

The girl did not say thank you, but remained rooted to the spot as they passed and watched them out of sight; Ron glanced back at her.

'I swear they're getting smaller,' he said.

'Never mind her,' said Harry, a little impatiently. 'What did Ginny and Dean row about, Hermione?'

'Oh, Dean was laughing about McLaggen hitting that Bludger at you,' said Hermione.

'It must've looked funny,' said Ron reasonably.

'It didn't look funny at all!' said Hermione hotly. 'It looked terrible, and if Coote and Peakes hadn't caught Harry he could have been very badly hurt!'

'Yeah, well, there was no need for Ginny and Dean to split up over it,' said Harry, still trying to sound casual. 'Or are they still together?'

## 第 20 章

## 伏地魔的请求

哈利和罗恩星期一一早就出院了,在庞弗雷女士的照料下,他们已完全康复,正享受着被打晕和中毒的好处,最好的一点就是赫敏跟罗恩和好了。她甚至领着他们去吃早饭,还带来了金妮跟迪安吵架的消息。哈利胸中那头昏睡的野兽突然抬起头,满怀希望地嗅着空气。

"他们吵什么?"他努力装出随便的口气问。三人拐进八楼的一条走廊,只有一个很小的女孩在看一幅巨怪穿芭蕾舞裙的挂毯。看到这几个六年级学生走过来,她好像很害怕,把拿在手里的一个很沉的铜天平掉在了地上。

"没事!"赫敏温和地说,一边快步走过去帮她。"来……"她说,用魔杖敲了敲摔坏的天平,"恢复如初。"

小女孩没有道谢,木头似的立在原地,看着他们走过去。罗恩回头望了望她。

"我真觉得新生越来越小了。"他说。

"别管她。"哈利有点不耐烦地说,"金妮和迪安吵什么呢,赫敏?"

"哦,迪安觉得麦克拉根用游走球打你很好笑。"赫敏说。

"看起来一定是挺滑稽的。"罗恩公平地说。

"一点儿都不滑稽!"赫敏激烈地反驳道,"可吓人了,要不是古特和珀克斯抓住了哈利,他可能会伤得非常重!"

"嗯,不过,金妮和迪安没有理由为这个闹崩啊。"哈利说,仍努力装出一副不经意的口气,"他们还在一起吗?"

## CHAPTER TWENTY — Lord Voldemort's Request

'Yes, they are – but why are you so interested?' asked Hermione, giving Harry a sharp look.

'I just don't want my Quidditch team messed up again!' he said hastily, but Hermione continued to look suspicious, and he was most relieved when a voice behind them called, 'Harry!', giving him an excuse to turn his back on her.

'Oh, hi, Luna.'

'I went to the hospital wing to find you,' said Luna, rummaging in her bag. 'But they said you'd left ...'

She thrust what appeared to be a green onion, a large spotted toad-stool and a considerable amount of what looked like cat litter into Ron's hands, finally pulling out a rather grubby scroll of parchment that she handed to Harry.

'... I've been told to give you this.'

It was a small roll of parchment, which Harry recognised at once as another invitation to a lesson with Dumbledore.

'Tonight,' he told Ron and Hermione, once he had unrolled it.

'Nice commentary last match!' said Ron to Luna, as she took back the green onion, the toadstool and the cat litter. Luna smiled vaguely.

'You're making fun of me, aren't you?' she said. 'Everyone says I was dreadful.'

'No, I'm serious!' said Ron earnestly. 'I can't remember enjoying commentary more! What is this, by the way?' he added, holding the onionlike object up to eye-level.

'Oh, it's a Gurdyroot,' she said, stuffing the cat litter and the toad-stool back into her bag. 'You can keep it if you like, I've got a few of them. They're really excellent for warding off Gulping Plimpies.'

And she walked away, leaving Ron chortling, still clutching the Gurdyroot.

'You know, she's grown on me, Luna,' he said, as they set off again for the Great Hall. 'I know she's insane, but it's in a good –'

He stopped talking very suddenly. Lavender Brown was standing at the foot of the marble staircase looking thunderous.

'Hi,' said Ron nervously.

'C'mon,' Harry muttered to Hermione, and they sped past, though not before they had heard Lavender say, 'Why didn't you tell me you were getting out today? And why was *she* with you?'

Ron looked both sulky and annoyed when he appeared at breakfast half an hour later, and though he sat with Lavender, Harry did not see them

## 第20章 伏地魔的请求

"在一起——你为什么这么感兴趣？"赫敏问道，尖锐地看了哈利一眼。

"我只是不想球队再出乱子！"哈利赶忙说，但赫敏仍然面带怀疑，这时后面一个声音叫道："哈利！"他如释重负地转过身，背对赫敏。

"哦，你好，卢娜。"

"我去校医院找你，"卢娜一边说一边在包里翻着，"他们说你出院了……"

她把一头绿洋葱似的玩意儿、一个花斑大伞菌和一大堆类似猫褥草的东西塞在罗恩手里，最后抽出一卷脏兮兮的羊皮纸递给了哈利。

"……这是让我带给你的。"

是个小纸卷，哈利立刻看出又是邓布利多让他去上课的邀请。

"今天晚上。"他一打开羊皮纸卷就对罗恩和赫敏说。

"你上次解说得很不错！"卢娜拿回绿洋葱、伞菌和猫褥草时，罗恩对她说。卢娜不置可否地笑了笑。

"你在笑话我，是不是？"她说，"人人都说我很糟糕。"

"不，我是说正经的，"罗恩真诚地说，"我不记得有哪次解说让我听得这么开心！哎，这是什么呀？"他把那洋葱一样的玩意儿举到了眼前。

"哦，是戈迪根。"卢娜说着把猫褥草和伞菌塞回包里，"你要喜欢就留下吧，我有好几个呢。这个能挡住大嘴彩球鱼，很有效。"

她走了，罗恩哈哈大笑，手里还抓着戈迪根。

"嘿嘿，我对她印象好起来了，对卢娜。"三人继续向礼堂走去时，罗恩说，"我知道她神经有问题，但是是一种好的——"

他突然住了口，拉文德·布朗气势汹汹地站在大理石台阶下面。

"嘿。"罗恩不安地说。

"快走。"哈利小声提醒赫敏，两人匆匆溜走，但是已经听到拉文德说："你为什么不跟我说你今天出院？为什么跟她在一起？"

半小时后罗恩来吃早饭时，显得很恼火。虽然他和拉文德坐在一

635

## CHAPTER TWENTY  Lord Voldemort's Request

exchange a word all the time they were together. Hermione was acting as though she was quite oblivious to all of this, but once or twice Harry saw an inexplicable smirk cross her face. All that day she seemed to be in a particularly good mood, and that evening in the common room she even consented to look over (in other words, finish writing) Harry's Herbology essay, something she had been resolutely refusing to do up to that point, because she had known that Harry would then let Ron copy his work.

'Thanks a lot, Hermione,' said Harry, giving her a hasty pat on the back as he checked his watch and saw that it was nearly eight o'clock. 'Listen, I've got to hurry or I'll be late for Dumbledore ...'

She did not answer, but merely crossed out a few of his feebler sentences in a weary sort of way. Grinning, Harry hurried out through the portrait hole and off to the Headmaster's office. The gargoyle leapt aside at the mention of toffee eclairs and Harry took the spiral staircase two steps at a time, knocking on the door just as a clock within chimed eight.

'Enter,' called Dumbledore, but as Harry put out a hand to push the door, it was wrenched open from inside. There stood Professor Trelawney.

'Aha!' she cried, pointing dramatically at Harry as she blinked at him through her magnifying spectacles. 'So this is the reason I am to be thrown unceremoniously from your office, Dumbledore!'

'My dear Sybill,' said Dumbledore in a slightly exasperated voice, 'there is no question of throwing you unceremoniously from anywhere, but Harry does have an appointment and I really don't think there is any more to be said –'

'Very well,' said Professor Trelawney, in a deeply wounded voice. 'If you will not banish the usurping nag, so be it ... perhaps I shall find a school where my talents are better appreciated ...'

She pushed past Harry and disappeared down the spiral staircase; they heard her stumble halfway down and Harry guessed that she had tripped over one of her trailing shawls.

'Please close the door and sit down, Harry,' said Dumbledore, sounding rather tired.

Harry obeyed, noticing as he took his usual seat in front of Dumbledore's desk that the Pensieve lay between them once more, as did two more tiny crystal bottles full of swirling memory.

'Professor Trelawney still isn't happy Firenze is teaching, then?' Harry asked.

## 第20章 伏地魔的请求

起，但哈利没见他们说一句话。赫敏好像对这一切浑然不觉，但有一两次哈利看到她脸上掠过一丝令人不解的笑意。一整天她心情似乎特别好，晚上在公共休息室甚至答应看看（也就是帮着写完）哈利的草药课论文。在此之前她是坚决不肯的，因为她知道哈利会借给罗恩去抄。

"多谢了，赫敏。"哈利说着匆匆拍了拍她的后背，又看了看表，发现已经快八点了，"哟，我得快点儿，不然去邓布利多那儿就要迟到了。"

赫敏没有回答，只是没精打采地划掉了他的几个差劲的句子。哈利咧嘴一笑，赶紧爬出肖像洞口，朝校长办公室跑去。滴水嘴石兽听到"太妃手指饼"后跳到一边。哈利一步两级地登上螺旋形楼梯，他敲门时里面的钟正好打响八点。

"进来。"邓布利多叫道。哈利伸手去推门，门却从里面被猛地拽开了，特里劳尼教授站在那儿。

"啊哈！"她戏剧性地指着哈利，从放大镜一样的镜片后面眨着眼睛看着他，"这就是我被粗暴地赶出你办公室的原因，邓布利多！"

"亲爱的西比尔，"邓布利多说，语气有点恼火，"没有谁想把你粗暴地赶出去，但是哈利预约了，而且我确实觉得已经没什么可说——"

"很好，"特里劳尼教授用受了很大伤害的口气说，"如果你不肯赶走那匹驽马，也罢……也许我会找到一所更能欣赏我才华的学校……"

她推开哈利，消失在螺旋形楼梯上。听到她在半道绊了一下，哈利猜她可能是踩到了她的哪一条长披肩。

"请关上门，坐下，哈利。"邓布利多的声音很疲惫。

哈利照办了，坐在邓布利多桌前那个老位子上，他注意到冥想盆又摆在那里，还有两个小水晶瓶，里面是打着旋儿的记忆。

"特里劳尼教授还在为费伦泽教课的事不高兴？"哈利问。

## CHAPTER TWENTY  Lord Voldemort's Request

'No,' said Dumbledore. 'Divination is turning out to be much more trouble than I could have foreseen, never having studied the subject myself. I cannot ask Firenze to return to the forest, where he is now an outcast, nor can I ask Sybill Trelawney to leave. Between ourselves, she has no idea of the danger she would be in outside the castle. She does not know – and I think it would be unwise to enlighten her – that she made the prophecy about you and Voldemort, you see.'

Dumbledore heaved a deep sigh, then said, 'But never mind my staff problems. We have much more important matters to discuss. Firstly – have you managed the task I set you at the end of our previous lesson?'

'Ah,' said Harry, brought up short. What with Apparition lessons and Quidditch and Ron being poisoned and getting his skull cracked and his determination to find out what Draco Malfoy was up to, Harry had almost forgotten about the memory Dumbledore had asked him to extract from Professor Slughorn ... 'Well, I asked Professor Slughorn about it at the end of Potions, sir, but, er, he wouldn't give it to me.'

There was a little silence.

'I see,' said Dumbledore eventually, peering at Harry over the top of his half-moon spectacles and giving Harry the usual sensation that he was being X-rayed. 'And you feel that you have exerted your very best efforts in this matter, do you? That you have exercised all of your considerable ingenuity? That you have left no depth of cunning unplumbed in your quest to retrieve the memory?'

'Well,' Harry stalled, at a loss for what to say next. His single attempt to get hold of the memory suddenly seemed embarrassingly feeble. 'Well ... the day Ron swallowed love potion by mistake I took him to Professor Slughorn. I thought maybe if I got Professor Slughorn in a good enough mood –'

'And did that work?' asked Dumbledore.

'Well, no, sir, because Ron got poisoned –'

'– which, naturally, made you forget all about trying to retrieve the memory; I would have expected nothing else, while your best friend was in danger. Once it became clear that Mr Weasley was going to make a full recovery, however, I would have hoped that you returned to the task I set you. I thought I made it clear to you how very important that memory is. Indeed, I did my best to impress upon you that it is the most crucial memory of all and that we will be wasting our time without it.'

A hot, prickly feeling of shame spread from the top of Harry's head all

## 第20章 伏地魔的请求

"不高兴。"邓布利多说,"占卜课比我想象的麻烦得多,我本人从没上过这个课。我不能让费伦泽返回禁林,因为他被驱逐出来了。我也不能让西比尔·特里劳尼离开。我们私下说说:她没意识到城堡外有多么危险。她还不知道——我觉得告诉她这个也是不明智的——她做过关于你和伏地魔的预言。"

邓布利多深深叹了口气,说道:"不过,别管我的教员的事了。我们有更重要的事情要谈。首先——我上节课布置的作业你做了吗?"

"啊,"哈利猛然想起,因为幻影显形课、魁地奇比赛、罗恩中毒、自己头骨碎裂,还有一心要搞清马尔福在干什么,他几乎忘了邓布利多要他弄到斯拉格霍恩教授的记忆……"嗯,魔药课后我问了一下斯拉格霍恩教授,可是,呃,他不肯给我。"

片刻的沉默。

"噢,"邓布利多终于开口,他从半月形眼镜片的上方盯着哈利,哈利又有一种被 X 光照射的感觉,"你觉得已经尽了最大努力,是吗?已经充分发挥了你的聪明才智?想尽了一切点子来拿到这段记忆?"

"呃。"哈利语塞了,不知该说什么。他的那一次尝试突然显得那么微不足道。"呃……罗恩误服迷情剂的那天,我把他带到斯拉格霍恩教授那里,我想如果能让斯拉格霍恩教授心情好些,也许——"

"成功了吗?"邓布利多问。

"嗯,没有,先生。罗恩中毒了——"

"——自然,于是你就忘了找寻记忆的事,我没指望会有别的反应,因为你的好朋友有危险。但是,一旦确定韦斯莱先生会彻底康复,我以为你会回头完成我布置的作业。我觉得我已经对你说明那个记忆多么重要了。实际上,我曾竭力让你认识到那是最关键的一段记忆,没有它,我们只会浪费时间。"

一阵火辣辣的、针扎般的羞耻感从哈利的头顶传遍全身。邓布利

## CHAPTER TWENTY    Lord Voldemort's Request

the way down his body. Dumbledore had not raised his voice, he did not even sound angry, but Harry would have preferred him to yell; this cold disappointment was worse than anything.

'Sir,' he said, a little desperately, 'it isn't that I wasn't bothered or anything, I've just had other – other things ...'

'Other things on your mind,' Dumbledore finished the sentence for him. 'I see.'

Silence fell between them again, the most uncomfortable silence Harry had ever experienced with Dumbledore; it seemed to go on and on, punctuated only by the little grunting snores of the portrait of Armando Dippet over Dumbledore's head. Harry felt strangely diminished, as though he had shrunk a little since he had entered the room.

When he could stand it no longer he said, 'Professor Dumbledore, I'm really sorry. I should have done more ... I should have realised you wouldn't have asked me to do it if it wasn't really important.'

'Thank you for saying that, Harry,' said Dumbledore quietly. 'May I hope, then, that you will give this matter higher priority from now on? There will be little point our meeting after tonight unless we have that memory.'

'I'll do it, sir, I'll get it from him,' Harry said earnestly.

'Then we shall say no more about it just now,' said Dumbledore more kindly, 'but continue with our story where we left off. You remember where that was?'

'Yes, sir,' said Harry quickly. 'Voldemort killed his father and his grandparents and made it look as though his uncle Morfin did it. Then he went back to Hogwarts and he asked ... he asked Professor Slughorn about Horcruxes,' he mumbled shamefacedly.

'Very good,' said Dumbledore. 'Now, you will remember, I hope, that I told you at the very outset of these meetings of ours that we would be entering the realms of guesswork and speculation?'

'Yes, sir.'

'Thus far, as I hope you agree, I have shown you reasonably firm sources of fact for my deductions as to what Voldemort did until the age of seventeen?'

Harry nodded.

'But now, Harry,' said Dumbledore, 'now things become murkier and stranger. If it was difficult to find evidence about the boy Riddle, it has been almost impossible to find anyone prepared to reminisce about the man Voldemort. In fact, I doubt whether there is a soul alive, apart from himself, who

## 第 20 章 伏地魔的请求

多没有提高嗓门,甚至话语中也没带怒气,但哈利宁愿他大吼大叫,这种冰冷的失望比什么都令人难受。

"先生,"他有点绝望地说,"不是我不上心,我只是有其他——其他事情……"

"其他事情让你惦记着,"邓布利多帮他把话说完,"我知道了。"

两人又沉默了,这是哈利在邓布利多身边经历过的最难堪的沉默,它似乎无休无止,只是时而被邓布利多头顶上阿芒多·迪佩特哼哼哧哧的鼾声打断。哈利有一种奇怪的渺小感,好像自己进屋后缩小了。

他再也忍受不住,于是说道:"邓布利多教授,我真的很抱歉。我应该做得更多……我应该想到如果不是真的重要,你也不会叫我去做。"

"谢谢你这么说,"邓布利多平静地说,"那我可否希望,你从此能把这件事往前提一提?如果没有那个记忆,我们之后再上课也就没有什么意义了。"

"我会的,先生,我会弄到它的。"哈利热切地说。

"那么现在就不再谈它了,"邓布利多语气亲切了一些,"接着讲上次的故事。你记得讲到哪儿了吗?"

"记得,先生,"哈利马上说,"伏地魔杀了他的爸爸和爷爷奶奶,让人以为是他舅舅莫芬干的。然后他回到霍格沃茨,向……向斯拉格霍恩教授打听魂器。"他惭愧地喃喃道。

"很好。"邓布利多说道,"现在,我希望你还记得,我在一开始给你单独授课时就告诉过你,我们会进入猜测和臆想的领域。"

"记得,先生。"

"我希望你也同意,到目前为止,我给你看的都是相当可靠的事实,我凭这些推想出了伏地魔十七岁前的情况。"

哈利点了点头。

"但是,哈利,现在情况更加迷离而诡异,如果说找到关于少年里德尔的证据已很困难,那找到愿意回忆成年伏地魔的人则几乎不可能。事实上,我怀疑除了他自己之外,是否还有一个活人能向我们详细讲

CHAPTER TWENTY    Lord Voldemort's Request

could give us a full account of his life since he left Hogwarts. However, I have two last memories that I would like to share with you.' Dumbledore indicated the two little crystal bottles gleaming beside the Pensieve. 'I shall then be glad of your opinion as to whether the conclusions I have drawn from them seem likely.'

The idea that Dumbledore valued his opinion this highly made Harry feel even more deeply ashamed that he had failed in the task of retrieving the Horcrux memory, and he shifted guiltily in his seat as Dumbledore raised the first of the two bottles to the light and examined it.

'I hope you are not tired of diving into other people's memories, for they are curious recollections, these two,' he said. 'This first one came from a very old house-elf by the name of Hokey. Before we see what Hokey witnessed, I must quickly recount how Lord Voldemort left Hogwarts.

'He reached the seventh year of his schooling with, as you might have expected, top grades in every examination he had taken. All around him, his classmates were deciding which jobs they were to pursue once they had left Hogwarts. Nearly everybody expected spectacular things from Tom Riddle, prefect, Head Boy, winner of the Special Award for Services to the School. I know that several teachers, Professor Slughorn amongst them, suggested that he join the Ministry of Magic, offered to set up appointments, put him in touch with useful contacts. He refused all offers. The next thing the staff knew, Voldemort was working at Borgin and Burkes.'

'At Borgin and Burkes?' Harry repeated, stunned.

'At Borgin and Burkes,' repeated Dumbledore calmly. 'I think you will see what attractions the place held for him when we have entered Hokey's memory. But this was not Voldemort's first choice of job. Hardly anyone knew of it at the time – I was one of the few in whom the then Headmaster confided – but Voldemort first approached Professor Dippet and asked whether he could remain at Hogwarts as a teacher.'

'He wanted to stay here? Why?' asked Harry, more amazed still.

'I believe he had several reasons, though he confided none of them to Professor Dippet,' said Dumbledore. 'Firstly, and very importantly, Voldemort was, I believe, more attached to this school than he has ever been to a person. Hogwarts was where he had been happiest; the first and only place he had felt at home.'

Harry felt slightly uncomfortable at these words, for this was exactly how he felt about Hogwarts, too.

述他离开霍格沃茨后的生活。然而,我有最后两个记忆要跟你分享。"邓布利多说着指了指冥想盆旁边两个闪闪发亮的小水晶瓶,"之后,我将很高兴听你判断我所得出的结论是否合理。"

邓布利多这样重视他的判断,使哈利对没能弄到关于魂器的记忆更加羞愧。他内疚地在椅子上动了动,邓布利多把第一个瓶子举到光线下细细端详。

"我希望你没有对潜进别人的记忆感到厌倦,因为这两个记忆是很奇特的。"他说,"第一个来自一个很老的家养小精灵,她叫郝琪。在目睹郝琪的见证之前,我必须简单说一下伏地魔是怎么离开霍格沃茨的。

"你可能已经猜到,他以门门考试最优的成绩升到了七年级。周围的同学都在考虑毕业后从事什么职业。几乎所有的人都认为汤姆·里德尔会有惊人的建树,他是级长,男生学生会主席,得到过学校的特别嘉奖。我知道有几位教师,包括斯拉格霍恩教授,建议他进魔法部,并愿意主动为他引见,但他一概予以拒绝。后来教员们得知,他去博金-博克工作了。"

"博金-博克?"哈利愕然地重复道。

"博金-博克。"邓布利多平静地说,"我想,等进入了郝琪的记忆,你就会看到那个地方对他有什么吸引力了。但这不是伏地魔的第一选择。当时没有什么人知道——我是听老校长说过此事的少数人之———伏地魔先找了迪佩特教授,询问是否可以留在霍格沃茨执教。"

"他想留在这儿?为什么?"哈利更惊诧了。

"我相信他有好几条理由,尽管他一条也没有告诉迪佩特教授。"邓布利多说,"首先,很重要的一条是,我相信伏地魔对这所学校比他对任何一个人更有感情。霍格沃茨是他最开心的地方,是他感到像家的第一个地方,也是唯一的地方。"

哈利听到这些话有点儿不舒服,因为这也正是他对霍格沃茨的感受。

### CHAPTER TWENTY    Lord Voldemort's Request

'Secondly, the castle is a stronghold of ancient magic. Undoubtedly Voldemort had penetrated many more of its secrets than most of the students who pass through the place, but he may have felt that there were still mysteries to unravel, stores of magic to tap.

'And thirdly, as a teacher, he would have had great power and influence over young witches and wizards. Perhaps he had gained the idea from Professor Slughorn, the teacher with whom he was on best terms, who had demonstrated how influential a role a teacher can play. I do not imagine for an instant that Voldemort envisaged spending the rest of his life at Hogwarts, but I do think that he saw it as a useful recruiting ground, and a place where he might begin to build himself an army.'

'But he didn't get the job, sir?'

'No, he did not. Professor Dippet told him that he was too young at eighteen, but invited him to reapply in a few years, if he still wished to teach.'

'How did you feel about that, sir?' asked Harry hesitantly.

'Deeply uneasy,' said Dumbledore. 'I had advised Armando against the appointment – I did not give the reasons I have given you, for Professor Dippet was very fond of Voldemort and convinced of his honesty – but I did not want Lord Voldemort back at this school, and especially not in a position of power.'

'Which job did he want, sir? What subject did he want to teach?'

Somehow, Harry knew the answer even before Dumbledore gave it.

'Defence Against the Dark Arts. It was being taught at the time by an old Professor by the name of Galatea Merrythought, who had been at Hogwarts for nearly fifty years.

'So Voldemort went off to Borgin and Burkes, and all the staff who had admired him said what a waste it was, a brilliant young wizard like that, working in a shop. However, Voldemort was no mere assistant. Polite and handsome and clever, he was soon given particular jobs of the type that only exist in a place like Borgin and Burkes, which specialises, as you know, Harry, in objects with unusual and powerful properties. Voldemort was sent to persuade people to part with their treasures for sale by the partners, and he was, by all accounts, unusually gifted at doing this.'

'I'll bet he was,' said Harry, unable to contain himself.

'Well, quite,' said Dumbledore, with a faint smile. 'And now it is time to hear from Hokey the house-elf, who worked for a very old, very rich witch by

## 第20章 伏地魔的请求

"第二，这座城堡是古老魔法的据点，伏地魔无疑比该校的大多数学生探知了这里更多的秘密，但他可能觉得还有不少未解之谜，还有不少魔法的宝藏可以发掘。

"第三，当了教师，他可以对少年巫师有很大的影响力。这个思想或许来自斯拉格霍恩教授，那是跟他关系最好的一位教授。斯拉格霍恩使他看到教师能发挥多么大的影响。我从来不认为伏地魔打算在霍格沃茨待一辈子，我想他是把这里看成一个招兵买马的好地方，他可以给自己拉起一支队伍。"

"可他没有得到这份工作，先生？"

"没有。迪佩特教授说他才十八岁，太年轻了，但欢迎他过两年再来申请，如果那时候他还想教书的话。"

"你对此事是怎么想的，先生？"哈利迟疑地问。

"非常不安。"邓布利多说，"我建议阿芒多不要聘他——我没有摆出刚才说的这些理由，因为迪佩特教授很喜欢伏地魔，对他的诚实深信不疑——但我不希望伏地魔回到这所学校，尤其是得到有权力的职位。"

"他想要什么职位？想教什么课？"

不知为何，邓布利多还没回答，哈利就知道了答案。

"黑魔法防御术，当时授课的是一位名叫加拉提亚·梅乐思的老教授，他在霍格沃茨已有将近五十年了。

"伏地魔去了博金-博克，所有欣赏他的教员都说可惜，那样一个才华出众的年轻巫师去当了店员。但伏地魔不只是店员。他因为彬彬有礼、英俊聪明，很快就得到了只有博金-博克这种地方才有的特殊工作。你知道，哈利，这家商店专销有强大特异性能的物品。伏地魔被派去说服别人将宝物交给店里出售，据说，他对此事特别擅长。"

"我相信他很擅长。"哈利忍不住说。

"是啊，"邓布利多说着无力地微微一笑，"现在该听听家养小精灵郝琪的记忆了，她的主人是一位年纪很大、非常富有的女巫，名叫赫

## CHAPTER TWENTY   Lord Voldemort's Request

the name of Hepzibah Smith.'

Dumbledore tapped a bottle with his wand, the cork flew out and he tipped the swirling memory into the Pensieve, saying as he did so, 'After you, Harry.'

Harry got to his feet and bent once more over the rippling silver contents of the stone basin until his face touched them. He tumbled through dark nothingness and landed in a sitting room in front of an immensely fat old lady wearing an elaborate ginger wig and a brilliant pink set of robes that flowed all around her, giving her the look of a melting iced cake. She was looking into a small jewelled mirror and dabbing rouge on to her already scarlet cheeks with a large powder puff, while the tiniest and oldest house-elf Harry had ever seen laced her fleshy feet into tight satin slippers.

'Hurry up, Hokey!' said Hepzibah imperiously. 'He said he'd come at four, it's only a couple of minutes to and he's never been late yet!'

She tucked away her powder puff as the house-elf straightened up. The top of the elf's head barely reached the seat of Hepzibah's chair and her papery skin hung off her frame just like the crisp linen sheet she wore draped like a toga.

'How do I look?' said Hepzibah, turning her head to admire the various angles of her face in the mirror.

'Lovely, madam,' squeaked Hokey.

Harry could only assume that it was down in Hokey's contract that she must lie through her teeth when asked this question, because Hepzibah Smith looked a long way from lovely in his opinion.

A tinkling doorbell rang and both mistress and elf jumped.

'Quick, quick, he's here, Hokey!' cried Hepzibah and the elf scurried out of the room, which was so crammed with objects that it was difficult to see how anybody could navigate their way across it without knocking over at least a dozen things: there were cabinets full of little lacquered boxes, cases full of gold-embossed books, shelves of orbs and celestial globes and many flourishing pot plants in brass containers: in fact, the room looked like a cross between a magical antique shop and a conservatory.

The house-elf returned within minutes, followed by a tall young man Harry had no difficulty whatsoever in recognising as Voldemort. He was plainly dressed in a black suit; his hair was a little longer than it had been at school and his cheeks were hollowed, but all of this suited him: he looked more handsome than ever. He picked his way through the cramped room

## 第20章 伏地魔的请求

普兹巴·史密斯。"

邓布利多用魔杖敲了敲一个小瓶,瓶塞飞了出去,他把打着旋儿的记忆倒进了冥想盆,说道:"你先来,哈利。"

哈利站了起来,再次俯身凑近石盆中荡着涟漪的银色物质,直到面孔接触到它。他翻着跟头在黑暗的虚空中坠落,落到了一间起居室里,看见一个很胖很胖的老太太,戴着一顶精致的姜黄色假发,艳丽的粉红色长袍在她四周铺散开来,使她看上去像一块融化的冰淇淋蛋糕。她正对着一面镶嵌着珠宝的小镜子,用一块大粉扑往已经鲜红的面颊上涂胭脂。一个哈利所见过的最瘦小、最苍老的家养小精灵,正在给老太太的胖脚上穿的一双紧绷绷的缎子鞋系鞋带。

"快点儿,郝琪!"赫普兹巴专横地说,"他说四点来,只有两分钟了,他还从没迟到过呢。"

她收起粉扑。家养小精灵直起腰,脑袋才齐到赫普兹巴的椅垫,纸一般的皮肤挂在骨架上,像她身上当成长袍披的那块破亚麻布一样。

"我怎么样?"赫普兹巴问,一边转动脑袋,从各个角度欣赏她镜中的面孔。

"很美丽,夫人。"郝琪尖声说。

哈利只能推测郝琪的契约里要求她在回答这个问题时必须咬牙说谎,因为在他看来赫普兹巴·史密斯离美丽差远了。

门铃叮叮当当地响了,女主人和小精灵都跳起来。

"快,快,他来了,郝琪!"赫普兹巴叫道,小精灵奔出屋去。屋里非常拥挤,简直想象不出有人能在房间里走动而不撞倒至少一打东西。陈列描漆小盒的橱柜,排满烫金书籍的书架,摆着大小水晶球和星象仪的架子,还有许多长在铜器皿中的茂盛植物。这间屋子看上去像是魔法古玩店和温室拼凑而成的。

小精灵一会儿就回来了,后面跟着一个高个子青年,哈利一下就认出是伏地魔。他穿着一套黑西服,头发比上学时长了一些,面颊凹了下去,但这些都很适合他,他看上去更英俊了。他小心地穿过拥挤

## CHAPTER TWENTY  Lord Voldemort's Request

with an air that showed he had visited many times before and bowed low over Hepzibah's fat little hand, brushing it with his lips.

'I brought you flowers,' he said quietly, producing a bunch of roses from nowhere.

'You naughty boy, you shouldn't have!' squealed old Hepzibah, though Harry noticed that she had an empty vase standing ready on the nearest little table. 'You do spoil this old lady, Tom ... sit down, sit down ... where's Hokey ... ah ...'

The house-elf had come dashing back into the room carrying a tray of little cakes, which she set at her mistress's elbow.

'Help yourself, Tom,' said Hepzibah, 'I know how you love my cakes. Now, how are you? You look pale. They overwork you at that shop, I've said it a hundred times ...'

Voldemort smiled mechanically and Hepzibah simpered.

'Well, what's your excuse for visiting this time?' she asked, batting her lashes.

'Mr Burke would like to make an improved offer for the goblin-made armour,' said Voldemort. 'Five hundred Galleons, he feels it is a more than fair –'

'Now, now, not so fast, or I'll think you're only here for my trinkets!' pouted Hepzibah.

'I am ordered here because of them,' said Voldemort quietly. 'I am only a poor assistant, madam, who must do as he is told. Mr Burke wishes me to enquire –'

'Oh, Mr Burke, phooey!' said Hepzibah, waving a little hand. 'I've something to show you that I've never shown Mr Burke! Can you keep a secret, Tom? Will you promise you won't tell Mr Burke I've got it? He'd never let me rest if he knew I'd shown it to you, and I'm not selling, not to Burke, not to anyone! But you, Tom, you'll appreciate it for its history, not how many Galleons you can get for it ...'

'I'd be glad to see anything Miss Hepzibah shows me,' said Voldemort quietly, and Hepzibah gave another girlish giggle.

'I had Hokey bring it out for me ... Hokey, where are you? I want to show Mr Riddle our *finest* treasure ... in fact, bring both, while you're at it ...'

'Here, madam,' squeaked the house-elf, and Harry saw two leather boxes, one on top of the other, moving across the room as if of their own volition, though he knew the tiny elf was holding them over her head as she wended her way between tables, pouffes and footstools.

的房间,看样子已来过许多次,然后低低地弯下腰,嘴唇轻轻碰了一下赫普兹巴的小胖手。

"我给你带了花。"他小声说,手里变出了一束玫瑰。

"你这个淘气的孩子,你不该这样!"老赫普兹巴尖叫道,不过哈利注意到她已在旁边一张小桌上准备了一个空花瓶,"你把我这个老太太宠坏了,汤姆……坐下,坐下……郝琪在哪儿……啊……"

家养小精灵端着一盘小糕点冲进屋来,把盘子摆在女主人肘边。

"随便吃吧,汤姆,"赫普兹巴说,"我知道你很喜欢我的糕点。你怎么样?脸色有点苍白。店里把你用得太狠了,我说过一百回了……"

赫普兹巴扭怩作态,伏地魔机械地微笑着。

"哎,这次来看我的借口是什么?"她扑扇着眼睫毛问。

"那副妖精做的盔甲,博克先生想出个更高点的价钱,五百加隆,他觉得这够公道的了——"

"哎呀,哎呀,不要这么急嘛,不然我会以为你只是为了我的玩意儿才来的!"赫普兹巴噘着嘴说道。

"我是为了它们才被派来的。"伏地魔轻声说,"我只是个小小的店员,夫人,只能听人吩咐。博克先生要我问——"

"哦,博克先生,呸!"赫普兹巴说着小手一摆,"我要给你看一样博克先生从来没见过的东西!你能保密吗,汤姆?你能保证不告诉博克先生我有这个吗?他要是知道我给你看过,永远都不会让我安生的。这个我不卖,不会卖给博克,不会卖给任何人!可是你,汤姆,你会欣赏它的历史,而不是只想着能赚多少加隆……"

"我很乐意看赫普兹巴小姐给我看的任何东西。"伏地魔轻声说,赫普兹巴又像小姑娘似的咯咯笑了起来。

"我让郝琪拿出来了……郝琪,你在哪儿?我要让里德尔先生看看我们最好的宝贝……干脆两样都拿来吧……"

"在这儿呢,夫人。"家养小精灵尖声说,哈利看到两个摆在一起的皮盒子穿过房间,好像自动飘过来似的,他知道是那个一丁点儿大的小精灵举着它们,在桌子、躺椅和脚凳中间穿行。

## CHAPTER TWENTY   Lord Voldemort's Request

'Now,' said Hepzibah happily, taking the boxes from the elf, laying them in her lap and preparing to open the topmost one, 'I think you'll like this, Tom ... oh, if my family knew I was showing you ... they can't wait to get their hands on this!'

She opened the lid. Harry edged forwards a little to get a better view and saw what looked like a small golden cup with two finely wrought handles.

'I wonder whether you know what it is, Tom? Pick it up, have a good look!' whispered Hepzibah, and Voldemort stretched out a long-fingered hand and lifted the cup by one handle out of its snug silken wrappings. Harry thought he saw a red gleam in his dark eyes. His greedy expression was curiously mirrored on Hepzibah's face, except that her tiny eyes were fixed upon Voldemort's handsome features.

'A badger,' murmured Voldemort, examining the engraving upon the cup. 'Then this was ...?'

'Helga Hufflepuff's, as you very well know, you clever boy!' said Hepzibah, leaning forwards with a loud creaking of corsets and actually pinching his hollow cheek. 'Didn't I tell you I was distantly descended? This has been handed down in the family for years and years. Lovely, isn't it? And all sorts of powers it's supposed to possess, too, but I haven't tested them thoroughly, I just keep it nice and safe in here ...'

She hooked the cup back off Voldemort's long forefinger and restored it gently to its box, too intent upon settling it carefully back into position to notice the shadow that crossed Voldemort's face as the cup was taken away.

'Now then,' said Hepzibah happily, 'where's Hokey? Oh yes, there you are – take that away now, Hokey –'

The elf obediently took the boxed cup, and Hepzibah turned her attention to the much flatter box in her lap.

'I think you'll like this even more, Tom,' she whispered. 'Lean in a little, dear boy, so you can see ... of course, Burke knows I've got this one, I bought it from him, and I daresay he'd love to get it back when I'm gone ...'

She slid back the fine, filigree clasp and flipped open the box. There upon the smooth crimson velvet lay a heavy golden locket.

Voldemort reached out his hand without invitation this time and held it up to the light, staring at it.

'Slytherin's mark,' he said quietly, as the light played upon an ornate, serpentine S.

## 第 20 章 伏地魔的请求

"好,"赫普兹巴愉快地说,从小精灵手里接过盒子,搁在膝上,准备打开上面的那个,"我想你会喜欢的,汤姆……哦,如果我家的亲戚知道我让你看了……他们马上就会来抢走的!"

她打开了盖子。哈利朝前凑了凑,好看得更清楚,里面像是一个小金杯,有两个精致的耳柄。

"你知道这是什么吗,汤姆?拿起来好好看看!"赫普兹巴轻声说。伏地魔伸出细长的手指,捏住一边的耳柄,把杯子从柔软的缎子衬垫上拿起来。哈利看到他的黑眼睛里似乎闪过一丝红光。他贪婪的表情也奇异地出现在赫普兹巴的脸上,只不过她的小眼睛盯着的是伏地魔英俊的面庞。

"獾。"伏地魔辨认着杯子上的雕饰,喃喃地说道,"这是……"

"赫尔加·赫奇帕奇的,你很在行,聪明的孩子!"赫普兹巴说着倾身捏了捏他凹陷的面颊,胸衣发出响亮的嘎吱一声,"我没跟你说过我是赫奇帕奇的远房后代吗?这东西在我家传了好多好多年。很漂亮,是不是?据说还有各种魔力,但我没怎么试过,我只是把它好好地收在这儿……"

她把杯子从伏地魔瘦长的食指上钩了回来,轻轻地放回盒子里,专心致志地把它嵌回原处,没有注意到杯子被拿回时伏地魔脸上掠过的一丝阴影。

"好啦,"赫普兹巴愉快地说,"郝琪在哪儿?哦,在这儿——把它拿走吧,郝琪——"

小精灵顺从地接过装杯子的盒子。赫普兹巴的注意力转向了她膝上那个扁一些的盒子。

"我想这个你会更喜欢的,汤姆。"她轻声说,"凑近一点儿,亲爱的孩子,看清楚……当然,博克知道我有这个,我从他那儿买来的。我敢说等我死后他一定想把它拿回去……"

她拨开精致的金丝扣,打开了盒盖。光滑的深红色天鹅绒衬垫上躺着一个沉甸甸的金色小挂坠盒。

伏地魔这次没等邀请就伸手把小挂坠盒拿了起来,举到光下细看。

"斯莱特林的记号。"他轻声说,光中闪耀着一个华丽的蛇形的"S"。

## CHAPTER TWENTY    Lord Voldemort's Request

'That's right!' said Hepzibah, delighted, apparently, at the sight of Voldemort gazing at her locket, transfixed. 'I had to pay an arm and a leg for it, but I couldn't let it pass, not a real treasure like that, had to have it for my collection. Burke bought it, apparently, from a ragged-looking woman who seemed to have stolen it, but had no idea of its true value –'

There was no mistaking it this time: Voldemort's eyes flashed scarlet at her words and Harry saw his knuckles whiten on the locket's chain.

'– I daresay Burke paid her a pittance, but there you are ... pretty, isn't it? And again, all kinds of powers attributed to it, though I just keep it nice and safe ...'

She reached out to take the locket back. For a moment Harry thought Voldemort was not going to let go of it, but then it had slid through his fingers and was back on its red velvet cushion.

'So there you are, Tom, dear, and I hope you enjoyed that!'

She looked him full in the face and, for the first time, Harry saw her foolish smile falter.

'Are you all right, dear?'

'Oh yes,' said Voldemort quietly. 'Yes, I'm very well ...'

'I thought – but a trick of the light, I suppose –' said Hepzibah, looking unnerved, and Harry guessed that she, too, had seen the momentary red gleam in Voldemort's eyes. 'Here, Hokey, take these away and lock them up again ... the usual enchantments ...'

'Time to leave, Harry,' said Dumbledore quietly, and as the little elf bobbed away bearing the boxes, Dumbledore grasped Harry once again above the elbow and together they rose up through oblivion and back to Dumbledore's office.

'Hepzibah Smith died two days after that little scene,' said Dumbledore, resuming his seat and indicating that Harry should do the same. 'Hokey the house-elf was convicted by the Ministry of poisoning her mistress's evening cocoa by accident.'

'No way!' said Harry angrily.

'I see we are of one mind,' said Dumbledore. 'Certainly, there are many similarities between this death and that of the Riddles. In both cases, somebody else took the blame, someone who had a clear memory of having caused the death –'

'Hokey confessed?'

## 第20章 伏地魔的请求

"对啦!"看到伏地魔出神地盯着她的小金盒,赫普兹巴显然很高兴,"为这个我可花了大价钱,可是我不能错过这样一件珍宝,一定要把它纳入我的收藏。博克是从一个寒酸的女人那儿买来的,那女人大概是偷的,不知道它的真实价值——"

这次错不了:她说话时伏地魔的眼睛里闪烁着红光,哈利看见他攥着小金盒链子的手指关节都变白了。

"——我敢说博克没付给她几个钱,可是你看……多漂亮,是不是?还有各种魔力,虽然我只是把它安全地收着……"

她伸手想拿回小金盒。有那么一刻,哈利以为伏地魔不会放手,但小金盒从他指间滑下,落到了红天鹅绒垫子上。

"好了,汤姆,亲爱的,我希望你喜欢!"

她端详着他的面孔,哈利第一次看到她脸上的傻笑变得犹豫了。

"你没事吧,亲爱的?"

"没事,"伏地魔安静地说,"没事,我很好……"

"我以为——可能是光线吧——"赫普兹巴说,好像有点慌乱。哈利猜她可能也看到了伏地魔眼中那瞬间闪过的红光。"来,郝琪,把它们拿走,重新锁起来……用老魔法……"

"该走了,哈利。"邓布利多轻声说。小精灵举着盒子摇摇摆摆地走开时,邓布利多抓住哈利的胳膊,一起穿过一片虚空,升回到邓布利多的办公室。

"赫普兹巴·史密斯在这之后两天就去世了。"邓布利多坐了下来,示意哈利也坐下,"魔法部判定,是家养小精灵郝琪在她女主人的晚饮可可中误放了毒药。"

"不可能!"哈利气愤地说。

"看来我们意见一致。"邓布利多答道,"当然,这起死亡案与里德尔家的命案有许多相似点。两起案子中都有替罪羊,替罪羊对杀人经过都有清楚的记忆——"

"郝琪承认了?"

## CHAPTER TWENTY    Lord Voldemort's Request

'She remembered putting something in her mistress's cocoa that turned out not to be sugar, but a lethal and little-known poison,' said Dumbledore. 'It was concluded that she had not meant to do it, but being old and confused –'

'Voldemort modified her memory, just like he did with Morfin!'

'Yes, that is my conclusion, too,' said Dumbledore. 'And, just as with Morfin, the Ministry was predisposed to suspect Hokey –'

'– because she was a house-elf,' said Harry. He had rarely felt more in sympathy with the society Hermione had set up, S.P.E.W.

'Precisely,' said Dumbledore. 'She was old, she admitted to having tampered with the drink and nobody at the Ministry bothered to enquire further. As in the case of Morfin, by the time I traced her and managed to extract this memory, her life was almost over – but her memory, of course, proves nothing except that Voldemort knew of the existence of the cup and the locket.

'By the time Hokey was convicted, Hepzibah's family had realised that two of her greatest treasures were missing. It took them a while to be sure of this, for she had many hiding places, having always guarded her collection most jealously. But before they were sure beyond doubt that the cup and the locket were both gone, the assistant who had worked at Borgin and Burkes, the young man who had visited Hepzibah so regularly and charmed her so well, had resigned his post and vanished. His superiors had no idea where he had gone; they were as surprised as anyone at his disappearance. And that was the last that was seen or heard of Tom Riddle for a very long time.

'Now,' said Dumbledore, 'if you don't mind, Harry, I want to pause once more to draw your attention to certain points of our story. Voldemort had committed another murder; whether it was his first since he killed the Riddles, I do not know, but I think it was. This time, as you will have seen, he killed not for revenge, but for gain. He wanted the two fabulous trophies that poor, besotted old woman showed him. Just as he had once robbed the other children at his orphanage, just as he had stolen his uncle Morfin's ring, so he ran off now with Hepzibah's cup and locket.'

'But,' said Harry, frowning, 'it seems mad ... risking everything, throwing away his job, just for those ...'

'Mad to you, perhaps, but not to Voldemort,' said Dumbledore. 'I hope you will understand in due course exactly what those objects meant to him, Harry, but you must admit that it is not difficult to imagine that he saw the

## 第20章 伏地魔的请求

"她记得在女主人的可可茶里放了点儿东西，后来发现那不是糖，而是一种罕见而致命的毒药。判决说她不是蓄意谋杀，而是老眼昏花——"

"伏地魔篡改了她的记忆，就像对莫芬那样！"

"对，这也是我的结论。而且，也像对莫芬那样，魔法部本来就倾向于怀疑郝琪——"

"——因为她是家养小精灵。"哈利说，他从没像现在这样赞同赫敏组织的社团：家养小精灵权益促进会。

"正是，而且她老了，她承认在饮料里放了东西之后，魔法部就没人想到再去调查。跟莫芬的情况一样，等我找到郝琪，取得她的记忆时，她几乎已经走到生命的尽头。当然，她的记忆只能证明伏地魔知道杯子和挂坠盒的存在。

"郝琪被定罪时，赫普兹巴家族发现老太太的两件最贵重的宝物不翼而飞。他们花了一段时间才确定了这件事，因为她有很多秘密的藏宝地点，总是把她的收藏看得特别严。而在他们认定杯子和挂坠盒都不见了之前，博金-博克的那个店员，那个经常去看赫普兹巴并且那样会讨她欢心的青年，已经辞职消失了。他的老板也不知道他的去向，对他消失也像别人一样感到意外。汤姆·里德尔在很长一段时间里销声匿迹。

"现在，"邓布利多说，"如果你不介意，哈利，我想再提醒你注意一下故事中的某些细节。伏地魔又犯下了一桩谋杀案。不知道这是不是继里德尔家命案之后的第一桩，我想是的。想必你也看到了，这一次他不是为了报复，而是为了利益。他想得到那可怜的糊涂老太太给他看的两件奇宝。就像他抢孤儿院其他孩子的东西一样，就像他偷他舅舅的戒指一样，这次他盗走了赫普兹巴的杯子和挂坠盒。"

"可是，"哈利皱着眉头说道，"这看起来很疯狂……冒那么大的风险，丢掉工作，就为了……"

"也许对你来说是疯狂，但对伏地魔不是。"邓布利多说，"我希望你将来能理解这些东西对他的意义，哈利。但是你必须承认，我们至

CHAPTER TWENTY   Lord Voldemort's Request

locket, at least, as rightfully his.'

'The locket maybe,' said Harry, 'but why take the cup as well?'

'It had belonged to another of Hogwarts' founders,' said Dumbledore. 'I think he still felt a great pull towards the school and that he could not resist an object so steeped in Hogwarts' history. There were other reasons, I think ... I hope to be able to demonstrate them to you, in due course.

'And now for the very last recollection I have to show you, at least until you manage to retrieve Professor Slughorn's memory for us. Ten years separate Hokey's memory and this one, ten years during which we can only guess at what Lord Voldemort was doing ...'

Harry got to his feet once more as Dumbledore emptied the last memory into the Pensieve.

'Whose memory is it?' he asked.

'Mine,' said Dumbledore.

And Harry dived after Dumbledore through the shifting silver mass, landing in the very office he had just left. There was Fawkes, slumbering happily on his perch, and there, behind the desk, was Dumbledore, who looked very similar to the Dumbledore standing beside Harry, though both hands were whole and undamaged and his face was, perhaps, a little less lined. The one difference between the present-day office and this one was that it was snowing in the past; bluish flecks were drifting past the window in the dark and building up on the outside ledge.

The younger Dumbledore seemed to be waiting for something, and sure enough, moments after their arrival, there was a knock on the door and he said, 'Enter.'

Harry let out a hastily stifled gasp. Voldemort had entered the room. His features were not those Harry had seen emerge from the great stone cauldron almost two years before; they were not as snake-like, the eyes were not yet scarlet, the face not yet masklike, and yet he was no longer handsome Tom Riddle. It was as though his features had been burned and blurred; they were waxy and oddly distorted, and the whites of the eyes now had a permanently bloody look, though the pupils were not yet the slits that Harry knew they would become. He was wearing a long black cloak and his face was as pale as the snow glistening on his shoulders.

The Dumbledore behind the desk showed no sign of surprise. Evidently this visit had been made by appointment.

## 第 20 章 伏地魔的请求

少不难想象他认为挂坠盒理所当然是属于他的。"

"挂坠盒也许吧,"哈利说,"可是他为什么把杯子也拿走呢?"

"那只杯子曾属于霍格沃茨的另一位创始人。我想这所学校对伏地魔仍有很大的吸引力,他无法抗拒一个浸透着霍格沃茨历史的东西。我想还有其他原因……我希望将来合适的时候能向你证明。

"接下来我要向你展示的是我收集的最后一段记忆,至少,在你能帮我们弄到斯拉格霍恩教授的记忆之前,这是最后一件记忆藏品。郝琪的记忆和这段记忆之间隔了十年,我们只能猜测伏地魔在这十年里做了什么……"

邓布利多把最后一瓶记忆倒入冥想盆,哈利再次站了起来。

"这是谁的记忆?"

"我的。"邓布利多说。

哈利跟着邓布利多潜入流动的银色物质,落到他刚刚离开的办公室里。福克斯在栖木上酣睡。书桌后是邓布利多,看上去跟站在哈利身边的邓布利多很像,不过两只手是完好无损的,脸上皱纹或许略少一些。这间办公室与现在的唯一区别是外面在下雪,淡青色的雪片在黑暗中飘过窗前,堆积在外面的窗台上。

年轻一些的邓布利多似乎在等待什么,果然,不一会儿便响起了敲门声,他说:"进来。"

哈利倒吸了一口气,但赶紧忍住了。伏地魔走了进来,他的面孔不是哈利两年前看到从大石头坩埚里升起的那样,不那么像蛇,眼睛还不是通红,脸也不像面具,但已经不是当年那个英俊帅气的汤姆·里德尔了。他的面孔似乎被烧过,五官模糊,像蜡一样,古怪地扭曲着。眼白现在似乎永久性地充血,但瞳孔还不是哈利后来所看到的那两条缝。他身上披着一件长长的黑斗篷,脸色像肩头的雪花一样白。

桌后的邓布利多没有显出吃惊之色,这次来访显然是有预约的。

## CHAPTER TWENTY  Lord Voldemort's Request

'Good evening, Tom,' said Dumbledore easily. 'Won't you sit down?'

'Thank you,' said Voldemort, and he took the seat to which Dumbledore had gestured – the very seat, by the looks of it, that Harry had just vacated in the present. 'I heard that you had become Headmaster,' he said, and his voice was slightly higher and colder than it had been. 'A worthy choice.'

'I am glad you approve,' said Dumbledore, smiling. 'May I offer you a drink?'

'That would be welcome,' said Voldemort. 'I have come a long way.'

Dumbledore stood and swept over to the cabinet where he now kept the Pensieve, but which then was full of bottles. Having handed Voldemort a goblet of wine and poured one for himself, he returned to the seat behind his desk.

'So, Tom ... to what do I owe the pleasure?'

Voldemort did not answer at once, but merely sipped his wine.

'They do not call me "Tom" any more,' he said. 'These days, I am known as –'

'I know what you are known as,' said Dumbledore, smiling pleasantly. 'But to me, I'm afraid, you will always be Tom Riddle. It is one of the irritating things about old teachers, I am afraid, that they never quite forget their charges' youthful beginnings.'

He raised his glass as though toasting Voldemort, whose face remained expressionless. Nevertheless, Harry felt the atmosphere in the room change subtly: Dumbledore's refusal to use Voldemort's chosen name was a refusal to allow Voldemort to dictate the terms of the meeting, and Harry could tell that Voldemort took it as such.

'I am surprised you have remained here so long,' said Voldemort after a short pause. 'I always wondered why a wizard such as yourself never wished to leave school.'

'Well,' said Dumbledore, still smiling, 'to a wizard such as myself, there can be nothing more important than passing on ancient skills, helping hone young minds. If I remember correctly, you once saw the attraction of teaching, too.'

'I see it still,' said Voldemort. 'I merely wondered why you – who is so often asked for advice by the Ministry, and who has twice, I think, been offered the post of Minister –'

'Three times at the last count, actually,' said Dumbledore. 'But the Ministry never attracted me as a career. Again, something we have in common, I think.'

## 第20章 伏地魔的请求

"晚上好，汤姆，"邓布利多轻松地说，"坐吧。"

"谢谢。"伏地魔坐到邓布利多指的椅子上——看上去就是哈利刚刚离开的那张，"我听说你当了校长，"他的声音比先前要高一些、冷一些，"可敬的选择。"

"我很高兴你赞成。"邓布利多微笑道，"可以请你喝杯饮料吗？"

"那太感谢了，"伏地魔说，"我走了很远的路。"

邓布利多站了起来，快步走到现在放冥想盆的柜子前，但那时里面摆满了酒瓶。他递给伏地魔一杯葡萄酒，给自己也倒了一杯，然后回到书桌后面坐着。

"那么，汤姆……是什么风把你吹来的？"

伏地魔没有马上回答，只是呷着酒。

"他们不再叫我'汤姆'了，如今我被称为——"

"我知道你被称为什么，"邓布利多愉快地微笑道，"但是对我，你恐怕永远都将是汤姆·里德尔。这或许就是当老师的让人讨厌的地方之一，他们从来不会完全忘记学生当初的情形。"

他举起杯子，像要跟伏地魔干杯。伏地魔还是面无表情。但哈利感觉到屋里的气氛发生了微妙的变化：邓布利多拒绝用伏地魔选定的称呼，是拒绝让伏地魔支配这场谈话。哈利看得出伏地魔也感觉到了。

"我惊讶你在这儿待了这么久，"伏地魔停了一会儿说，"我一直奇怪，你这样一位巫师怎么从来不想离开学校。"

"哦，"邓布利多说，依旧面带笑容，"对于我这样的巫师来说，没有什么比传授古老技艺和训练年轻头脑更重要了。如果我记得不错，你也曾经看到过教师职业的吸引力。"

"我现在仍然能看到，"伏地魔说，"我只是奇怪为什么你——经常被魔法部请教，并且好像两次被提名为魔法部部长的人——"

"实际上有三次了，但魔法部的职业对我从来没有吸引力。这是你我的共同之处，我想。"

## CHAPTER TWENTY  Lord Voldemort's Request

Voldemort inclined his head, unsmiling, and took another sip of wine. Dumbledore did not break the silence that stretched between them now, but waited, with a look of pleasant expectancy, for Voldemort to talk first.

'I have returned,' he said, after a little while, 'later, perhaps, than Professor Dippet expected ... but I have returned, nevertheless, to request again what he once told me I was too young to have. I have come to you to ask that you permit me to return to this castle, to teach. I think you must know that I have seen and done much since I left this place. I could show and tell your students things they can gain from no other wizard.'

Dumbledore considered Voldemort over the top of his own goblet for a while before speaking.

'Yes, I certainly do know that you have seen and done much since leaving us,' he said quietly. 'Rumours of your doings have reached your old school, Tom. I should be sorry to believe half of them.'

Voldemort's expression remained impassive as he said, 'Greatness inspires envy, envy engenders spite, spite spawns lies. You must know this, Dumbledore.'

'You call it "greatness", what you have been doing, do you?' asked Dumbledore delicately.

'Certainly,' said Voldemort, and his eyes seemed to burn red. 'I have experimented; I have pushed the boundaries of magic further, perhaps, than they have ever been pushed —'

'Of some kinds of magic,' Dumbledore corrected him quietly. 'Of some. Of others, you remain ... forgive me ... woefully ignorant.'

For the first time, Voldemort smiled. It was a taut leer, an evil thing, more threatening than a look of rage.

'The old argument,' he said softly. 'But nothing I have seen in the world has supported your famous pronouncements that love is more powerful than my kind of magic, Dumbledore.'

'Perhaps you have been looking in the wrong places,' suggested Dumbledore.

'Well, then, what better place to start my fresh researches than here, at Hogwarts?' said Voldemort. 'Will you let me return? Will you let me share my knowledge with your students? I place myself and my talents at your disposal. I am yours to command.'

Dumbledore raised his eyebrows.

## 第20章 伏地魔的请求

伏地魔不带笑容地低下头，又呷了口酒。邓布利多没有打破两人之间的沉默，而是带着愉快的表情期待伏地魔先开口。

"我回来了，"过了片刻伏地魔说，"可能比迪佩特教授期望的晚了一点……但是回来了，为的是再次申请他那时说我太年轻而不适合担任的职位。我来请求你允许我回到这座城堡执教，你想必知道我离开这里后见识了很多，也做了很多，我可以教授你的学生从其他巫师那里学不到的东西。"

邓布利多从他的杯子上面打量了伏地魔一会儿才开口。

"是的，我知道你离开我们之后见识了很多，也做了很多。"他平静地说，"关于你所作所为的传闻也传到了你的母校，汤姆。如果它们有一半可信，我将感到非常遗憾。"

伏地魔依然面无表情，说道："伟大引起嫉妒，嫉妒导致怨毒，怨毒滋生谎言。这你一定了解，邓布利多。"

"你把你的所作所为说成'伟大'，是吗？"邓布利多优雅地问。

"当然，"伏地魔说，他的眼睛好像烧红了，"我做了实验，可能已把魔法推进到前所未有的——"

"是某些魔法，"邓布利多平静地纠正他说，"某些。但在另一些魔法上，你还是……恕我直言……无知得可悲。"

伏地魔第一次笑了，那是一种睥睨的讥笑，邪恶的表情，比暴怒更加可怕。

"又是老一套。"他轻声说，"可是，邓布利多，我在世上所见没有一样能证明你那著名的观点：爱比我那种魔法更加强大。"

"也许你找的地方不对。"邓布利多提醒道。

"那么，还有哪里比这儿——霍格沃茨——更适合我开始新的研究呢？"伏地魔说，"你愿意让我回来吗？你能让我与你的学生分享我学到的东西吗？我将我自己和我的才能交给你，听你指挥。"

邓布利多扬起了眉毛。

## CHAPTER TWENTY    Lord Voldemort's Request

'And what will become of those whom *you* command? What will happen to those who call themselves – or so rumour has it – the Death Eaters?'

Harry could tell that Voldemort had not expected Dumbledore to know this name; he saw Voldemort's eyes flash red again and the slitlike nostrils flare.

'My friends,' he said, after a moment's pause, 'will carry on without me, I am sure.'

'I am glad to hear that you consider them friends,' said Dumbledore. 'I was under the impression that they are more in the order of servants.'

'You are mistaken,' said Voldemort.

'Then if I were to go to the Hog's Head tonight, I would not find a group of them – Nott, Rosier, Mulciber, Dolohov – awaiting your return? Devoted friends indeed, to travel this far with you on a snowy night, merely to wish you luck as you attempted to secure a teaching post.'

There could be no doubt that Dumbledore's detailed knowledge of those with whom he was travelling was even less welcome to Voldemort; however, he rallied almost at once.

'You are omniscient as ever, Dumbledore.'

'Oh, no, merely friendly with the local barmen,' said Dumbledore lightly. 'Now, Tom ...'

Dumbledore set down his empty glass and drew himself up in his seat, the tips of his fingers together in a very characteristic gesture.

'... let us speak openly. Why have you come here tonight, surrounded by henchmen, to request a job we both know you do not want?'

Voldemort looked coldly surprised.

'A job I do not want? On the contrary, Dumbledore, I want it very much.'

'Oh, you want to come back to Hogwarts, but you do not want to teach any more than you wanted to when you were eighteen. What is it you're after, Tom? Why not try an open request for once?'

Voldemort sneered.

'If you do not want to give me a job –'

'Of course I don't,' said Dumbledore. 'And I don't think for a moment you expected me to. Nevertheless, you came here, you asked, you must have had a purpose.'

## 第20章 伏地魔的请求

"听你指挥的那些人呢？那些自称——或据说自称食死徒的人怎么办？"

哈利看出伏地魔没想到邓布利多知道这个名字；他看到伏地魔的眼睛又闪着红光，两道缝隙般的鼻孔张大了。

"我的朋友们，"他停了一刻说，"他们没有我也会继续干下去，我相信。"

"我很高兴听到你把他们称作朋友，"邓布利多说，"我以为他们更像是仆人。"

"你错了。"伏地魔说。

"那么，如果我今晚去猪头酒吧，不会看到那群人——诺特、罗齐尔、穆尔塞伯、多洛霍夫——在等你回去吧？真是忠诚的朋友啊，跟你在雪夜里跋涉了这么远，只是为了祝你谋到一个教职。"

邓布利多对伏地魔的随行者如此了解，无疑使伏地魔更加不快，但他几乎立刻镇定下来。

"你还是无所不知，邓布利多。"

"哦，哪里，只是跟当地酒吧服务员的关系不错而已。"邓布利多轻松地说，"现在，汤姆……"

邓布利多放下空酒杯，坐直身子，双手指尖碰在一起，这是他惯有的姿势。

"……我们把话说开吧，你今晚为什么带着手下到这里来，申请一份你我都知道你并不想要的工作？"

伏地魔显出冷冷的惊讶。

"我不想要的工作？恰恰相反，邓布利多，我非常想要。"

"哦，你想回到霍格沃茨，但你其实并不比十八岁时更想教书。你究竟想要什么，汤姆？为什么不能坦率一次呢？"

伏地魔冷笑了一声。

"如果你不想给我一份工作——"

"当然不想，"邓布利多说，"而且我看你也没有指望我会给你。但你还是来了，提出了申请，你一定有所企图。"

### CHAPTER TWENTY — Lord Voldemort's Request

Voldemort stood up. He looked less like Tom Riddle than ever, his features thick with rage.

'This is your final word?'

'It is,' said Dumbledore, also standing.

'Then we have nothing more to say to each other.'

'No, nothing,' said Dumbledore, and a great sadness filled his face. 'The time is long gone when I could frighten you with a burning wardrobe and force you to make repayment for your crimes. But I wish I could, Tom ... I wish I could ...'

For a second, Harry was on the verge of shouting a pointless warning: he was sure that Voldemort's hand had twitched towards his pocket and his wand; but then the moment had passed, Voldemort had turned away, the door was closing and he was gone.

Harry felt Dumbledore's hand close over his arm again, and moments later, they were standing together on almost the same spot, but there was no snow building on the window-ledge, and Dumbledore's hand was blackened and dead-looking once more.

'Why?' said Harry at once, looking up into Dumbledore's face. 'Why did he come back? Did you ever find out?'

'I have ideas,' said Dumbledore, 'but no more than that.'

'What ideas, sir?'

'I shall tell you, Harry, when you have retrieved that memory from Professor Slughorn,' said Dumbledore. 'When you have that last piece of the jigsaw, everything will, I hope, be clear ... to both of us.'

Harry was still burning with curiosity, and even though Dumbledore had walked to the door and was holding it open for him, he did not move at once.

'Was he after the Defence Against the Dark Arts job again, sir? He didn't say ...'

'Oh, he definitely wanted the Defence Against the Dark Arts job,' said Dumbledore. 'The aftermath of our little meeting proved that. You see, we have never been able to keep a Defence Against the Dark Arts teacher for longer than a year since I refused the post to Lord Voldemort.'

## 第20章 伏地魔的请求

伏地魔站了起来,满面怒容,看上去比以前任何时候都不像汤姆·里德尔。

"这是你的最后决定?"

"是的。"邓布利多也站了起来。

"那我们就没有什么可谈的了。"

"没有了。"邓布利多说,脸上露出深深的悲哀,"我能用燃烧的衣柜吓住你,迫使你赎罪的时间早已过去。可是我希望能,汤姆……我希望能……"

有那么一瞬间,哈利差点喊出一声无用的警告,他确信伏地魔的手突然移向了口袋里的魔杖……但那一瞬间过去了,伏地魔已转身走开,门在关上,他不见了。

哈利感到邓布利多的手又抓住了他的胳膊,过了一会儿,他们站到了几乎相同的地方,但外面没有雪花飘落到窗台上,邓布利多的手又变得焦枯了。

"为什么?"哈利马上问,仰望着邓布利多的面孔,"他为什么回来?你搞清楚了吗?"

"我有些想法,但只是想法而已。"

"什么想法,先生?"

"等你拿到斯拉格霍恩教授的那段记忆,我就会告诉你,哈利。"邓布利多说,"当你找到那最后一块拼图,我希望,一切都会明白的……对我们两人都是。"

哈利仍是满肚子好奇,当邓布利多走到门口、为他打开门时,他并没有马上动身。

"他还是想教黑魔法防御术吗,先生?他没说……"

"哦,他肯定是想教黑魔法防御术。我们那次短暂会面的后果证明了这一点。自从我拒绝伏地魔之后,就没有一个黑魔法防御术教师能教满一年以上。"

## CHAPTER TWENTY-ONE

# The Unknowable Room

Harry racked his brains over the next week as to how he was to persuade Slughorn to hand over the true memory, but nothing in the nature of a brainwave occurred and he was reduced to doing what he did increasingly these days when at a loss: poring over his Potions book, hoping that the Prince would have scribbled something useful in a margin, as he had done so many times before.

'You won't find anything in there,' said Hermione firmly, late on Sunday evening.

'Don't start, Hermione,' said Harry. 'If it hadn't been for the Prince, Ron wouldn't be sitting here now.'

'He would if you'd just listened to Snape in our first year,' said Hermione dismissively.

Harry ignored her. He had just found an incantation (*Sectumsempra!*) scrawled in a margin above the intriguing words 'For Enemies', and was itching to try it out, but thought it best not to in front of Hermione. Instead, he surreptitiously folded down the corner of the page.

They were sitting beside the fire in the common room; the only other people still up were fellow sixth-years. There had been a certain amount of excitement earlier when they had come back from dinner to find a new sign on the noticeboard that announced the date for their Apparition test. Those who would be seventeen on or before the first test date, the twenty-first of April, had the option of signing up for additional practice sessions, which would take place (heavily supervised) in Hogsmeade.

Ron had panicked on reading this notice; he had still not managed to Apparate and feared he would not be ready for the test. Hermione, who had now achieved Apparition twice, was a little more confident, but Harry, who would not be seventeen for another four months, could not take the test whether ready or not.

第 21 章

神秘的房间

在接下来的一个星期里,哈利绞尽脑汁考虑怎么能让斯拉格霍恩交出真实的记忆,可是没有一点儿灵感,他只好做起如今他在无计可施时做得越来越多的事情:翻他的魔药课本,希望王子在空白处写了点高招,就像之前的很多次那样。

"你找不到的。"星期天的晚上,赫敏断言道。

"别说了,赫敏,"哈利说,"要不是王子,罗恩现在不会坐在这儿了。"

"他会的,只要你在一年级时认真听斯内普讲课。"赫敏不以为然地说。

哈利不理她,他刚发现空白处写了个咒语(神锋无影!),下面还有对敌人三个令人蠢蠢欲动的字。哈利心里痒痒的很想试一下,但觉得最好不要在赫敏跟前试,便偷偷把页角折了起来。

他们坐在公共休息室的炉边,还没睡觉的都是六年级学生,今天大家有些兴奋:吃过晚饭回来时,发现布告栏上贴出了一张新告示,通知幻影显形考试的日期。第一场考试(四月二十一日)之前或当天年满十七岁的同学可报名到霍格莫德参加额外训练(有严格监督)。

罗恩看了告示后惊慌起来,他还不会幻影显形,担心考试通不过。已经成功两次的赫敏要自信一些。哈利还有四个月才满十七岁,不管练没练好都不能参加考试。

## CHAPTER TWENTY-ONE  The Unknowable Room

'At least you can Apparate, though!' said Ron tensely. 'You'll have no trouble come July!'

'I've only done it once,' Harry reminded him; he had finally managed to disappear and rematerialise inside his hoop during their previous lesson.

Having wasted a lot of time worrying aloud about Apparition, Ron was now struggling to finish a viciously difficult essay for Snape that Harry and Hermione had already completed. Harry fully expected to receive low marks on his, because he had disagreed with Snape on the best way to tackle Dementors, but he did not care: Slughorn's memory was the most important thing to him now.

'I'm telling you, the stupid Prince isn't going to be able to help you with this, Harry!' said Hermione, more loudly. 'There's only one way to force someone to do what you want, and that's the Imperius Curse, which is illegal –'

'Yeah, I know that, thanks,' said Harry, not looking up from the book. 'That's why I'm looking for something different. Dumbledore says Veritaserum won't do it, but there might be something else, a potion or a spell ...'

'You're going about it the wrong way,' said Hermione. 'Only you can get the memory, Dumbledore says. That must mean you can persuade Slughorn where other people can't. It's not a question of slipping him a potion, anyone could do that –'

'How d'you spell "belligerent"?' said Ron, shaking his quill very hard while staring at his parchment. 'It can't be B – U – M –'

'No, it isn't,' said Hermione, pulling Ron's essay towards her. 'And "augury" doesn't begin O – R – G either. What kind of quill are you using?'

'It's one of Fred and George's Spell-Checking ones ... but I think the charm must be wearing off ...'

'Yes, it must,' said Hermione, pointing at the title of his essay, 'because we were asked how we'd deal with Dementors, not "Dugbogs", and I don't remember you changing your name to "Roonil Wazlib", either.'

'Ah, no!' said Ron, staring horror-struck at the parchment. 'Don't say I'll have to write the whole thing out again!'

'It's OK, we can fix it,' said Hermione, pulling the essay towards her and taking out her wand.

'I love you, Hermione,' said Ron, sinking back in his chair, rubbing his eyes wearily.

## 第 21 章 神秘的房间

"可你至少会幻影显形了!"罗恩紧张地说,"你到了七月份不会有问题的。"

"我才成功了一次。"哈利提醒道。他上节课终于做到了消失后在木圈里现身。

罗恩浪费了很多时间唠叨对幻影显形的担心,然后痛苦地给斯内普写一篇特别难的论文。哈利和赫敏都已经写完了。哈利等着拿一个低分,因为他在对付摄魂怪的最佳办法上与斯内普观点不一致。但哈利不在乎,现在对他来说,拿到斯拉格霍恩的记忆才是最重要的。

"我告诉你,那个蠢王子帮不到你的,哈利!"赫敏说,她的声音更响了,"只有一个办法可以强迫别人做你想让他们做的事,那就是夺魂咒,但那是违法的——"

"嗯,我知道,谢谢,"哈利看着书,头也不抬地说,"所以我才另外寻找办法。邓布利多说吐真剂没用,但可能有别的东西,魔药或魔咒……"

"你的方法不对,"赫敏说,"邓布利多说只有你才能搞到那段记忆,他肯定是说你能说服斯拉格霍恩而别人不能。这不是给他下魔药的问题,那个谁都会——"

"'挑衅'怎么写?"罗恩问,一边盯着羊皮纸使劲摇羽毛笔,"不可能是'桃畔'——"

"不是,"赫敏说着拉过罗恩的论文,"'占卜'也不是'古十'。你用的什么笔呀?"

"是弗雷德和乔治的拼写检查笔……但我想魔法开始失灵了……"

"一定是的,"赫敏指着他的论文题目说,"我们要写的是如何对付摄魂怪,不是对付'挖泥泽',我也不记得你什么时候改名叫'罗鸟·卫其利'了。"

"啊?!"罗恩惊恐地瞪着羊皮纸说,"可别叫我重写啊!"

"没事,可以改好。"赫敏说着把论文拉过去,抽出了魔杖。

"我爱你,赫敏。"罗恩说着倒回椅子里,困乏地揉着眼睛。

## CHAPTER TWENTY-ONE  The Unknowable Room

Hermione turned faintly pink, but merely said, 'Don't let Lavender hear you saying that.'

'I won't,' said Ron into his hands. 'Or maybe I will ... then she'll ditch me ...'

'Why don't you ditch her if you want to finish it?' asked Harry.

'You haven't ever chucked anyone, have you?' said Ron. 'You and Cho just –'

'Sort of fell apart, yeah,' said Harry.

'Wish that would happen with me and Lavender,' said Ron gloomily, watching Hermione silently tapping each of his misspelled words with the end of her wand, so that they corrected themselves on the page. 'But the more I hint I want to finish it, the tighter she holds on. It's like going out with the Giant Squid.'

'There,' said Hermione, some twenty minutes later, handing back Ron's essay.

'Thanks a million,' said Ron. 'Can I borrow your quill for the conclusion?'

Harry, who had found nothing useful in the Half-Blood Prince's notes so far, looked around; the three of them were now the only ones left in the common room, Seamus having just gone up to bed cursing Snape and his essay. The only sounds were the crackling of the fire and Ron scratching out one last paragraph on Dementors using Hermione's quill. Harry had just closed the Half-Blood Prince's book, yawning, when –

*Crack.*

Hermione let out a little shriek; Ron spilled ink all over his essay and Harry said, 'Kreacher!'

The house-elf bowed low and addressed his own gnarled toes.

'Master said he wanted regular reports on what the Malfoy boy is doing so Kreacher has come to give –'

*Crack.*

Dobby appeared alongside Kreacher, his tea-cosy hat askew.

'Dobby has been helping too, Harry Potter!' he squeaked, casting Kreacher a resentful look. 'And Kreacher ought to tell Dobby when he is coming to see Harry Potter so they can make their reports together!'

'What is this?' asked Hermione, still looking shocked by these sudden appearances. 'What's going on, Harry?'

Harry hesitated before answering, because he had not told Hermione about setting Kreacher and Dobby to tail Malfoy; house-elves were always such a touchy subject with her.

## 第21章 神秘的房间

赫敏脸微微一红，但只说了句："可别让拉文德听见。"

"不会的，"罗恩捂着嘴说，"也许会的……这样她就会甩掉我了……"

"如果你想结束，为什么不甩掉她呢？"哈利问。

"你从来没有甩过人，是不是？"罗恩说，"你和秋只是——"

"分开了。"哈利说。

"希望我跟拉文德也能那样，"罗恩阴郁地说，一边看着赫敏默默地用魔杖尖轻叩他的每个错别字，把它们改正过来，"可是我越暗示想结束，她就缠得越厉害，跟巨乌贼似的。"

"好了。"大约二十分钟后，赫敏把论文还给了罗恩。

"多谢多谢，"罗恩说，"我能借你的笔写结论吗？"

哈利在混血王子的笔记中没有找到什么帮助，他环顾四周，休息室内只剩下他们三个人，西莫刚刚上楼睡觉去了，边走边诅咒着斯内普和他布置的论文。这里唯有炉火的噼啪声和罗恩用赫敏的笔写最后一段摄魂怪论文的沙沙声。哈利刚打着哈欠合上混血王子的书，忽然——

噼啪。

赫敏发出一声短促的尖叫，罗恩把墨水洒到了论文上，哈利叫道："克利切！"

家养小精灵低低地弯下腰，对着自己疙疙瘩瘩的脚趾说：

"主人说要经常向他汇报马尔福少爷的动向，所以克利切来——"

噼啪。

多比出现在克利切身旁，茶壶保暖套做的帽子歪在一边。

"多比也在帮忙，哈利·波特！"他尖声说，又怨恨地看了克利切一眼，"克利切应该告诉多比他什么时候来见哈利·波特，这样可以一起汇报！"

"什么呀？"赫敏问，似乎还在为他们的突然出现而吃惊，"怎么回事，哈利？"

哈利犹豫着，他还没有把让克利切和多比跟踪马尔福的事告诉赫敏，因为家养小精灵对于她总是一个敏感的话题。

'Well ... they've been following Malfoy for me,' he said.

'Night and day,' croaked Kreacher.

'Dobby has not slept for a week, Harry Potter!' said Dobby proudly, swaying where he stood.

Hermione looked indignant.

'You haven't slept, Dobby? But surely, Harry, you didn't tell him not to –'

'No, of course I didn't,' said Harry quickly. 'Dobby, you can sleep, all right? But has either of you found out anything?' he hastened to ask, before Hermione could intervene again.

'Master Malfoy moves with a nobility that befits his pure blood,' croaked Kreacher at once. 'His features recall the fine bones of my mistress and his manners are those of –'

'Draco Malfoy is a bad boy!' squeaked Dobby angrily. 'A bad boy who – who –'

He shuddered from the tassel of his tea cosy to the toes of his socks and then ran at the fire, as though about to dive into it; Harry, to whom this was not entirely unexpected, caught him around the middle and held him fast. For a few seconds Dobby struggled, then went limp.

'Thank you, Harry Potter,' he panted. 'Dobby still finds it difficult to speak ill of his old masters ...'

Harry released him; Dobby straightened his tea cosy and said defiantly to Kreacher, 'But Kreacher should know that Draco Malfoy is not a good master to a house-elf!'

'Yeah, we don't need to hear about you being in love with Malfoy,' Harry told Kreacher. 'Let's fast forward to where he's actually been going.'

Kreacher bowed again, looking furious, and then said, 'Master Malfoy eats in the Great Hall, he sleeps in a dormitory in the dungeons, he attends his classes in a variety of –'

'Dobby, you tell me,' said Harry, cutting across Kreacher. 'Has he been going anywhere he shouldn't have?'

'Harry Potter, sir,' squeaked Dobby, his great orblike eyes shining in the firelight, 'the Malfoy boy is breaking no rules that Dobby can discover, but he is still keen to avoid detection. He has been making regular visits to the seventh floor with a variety of other students, who keep watch for him while he enters –'

'The Room of Requirement!' said Harry, smacking himself hard on the forehead with *Advanced Potion-Making*. Hermione and Ron stared at him.

## 第21章 神秘的房间

"嗯……他们在为我跟踪马尔福。"

"日日夜夜。"克利切声音沙哑地说。

"多比一星期没睡觉了,哈利·波特!"多比自豪地说,身体摇晃着。赫敏立刻变得愤然。

"你没睡觉,多比?可是哈利,你没跟他说不许——"

"当然没有,"哈利忙说,"多比,你可以睡觉的,对不对?可你们发现什么了吗?"他趁赫敏插嘴之前赶紧问道。

"马尔福少爷举止高贵,不愧是纯血统,"克利切立刻又嗓音沙哑地说道,"他的外貌让人想起我女主人那精致的轮廓,他的风度是——"

"德拉科·马尔福是个坏男孩!"多比气愤地尖叫道,"一个坏男孩,他——他——"

他浑身上下都哆嗦起来,从茶壶保暖套的流苏到袜子头,然后他冲向炉火,好像要跳进去。哈利不是完全没有料到,连忙紧紧抱住他的腰,多比挣扎几秒钟后软了下来。

"谢谢你,哈利·波特,"他喘着气说,"多比还是很难说旧主人的坏话……"

哈利放开了他。多比把茶壶保暖套戴好,挑战似的对克利切说:"但克利切应该知道德拉科·马尔福不是家养小精灵的好主人!"

"是啊,我们不需要听你说有多爱马尔福,"哈利说,"还是快说说他到哪儿去了吧。"

克利切又怒冲冲地鞠了个躬,说道:"马尔福少爷在礼堂吃饭,睡在地下教室的一间宿舍里,他到许多教室上课——"

"多比,你来说,"哈利打断了克利切,"他有没有去不该去的地方?"

"哈利·波特,先生,"多比尖声说,大大的圆眼睛在火光中闪亮,"多比没有发现马尔福少爷违反任何规定,但他仍然小心防止被人发现。他经常带着不同的学生去八楼,他们给他放哨,他走进——"

"有求必应屋!"哈利把《高级魔药制作》在头上重重一拍。赫敏和罗恩都瞪着他。"他就是溜到那儿去了!那儿就是他干那个……鬼知

673

## CHAPTER TWENTY-ONE  The Unknowable Room

'That's where he's been sneaking off to! That's where he's doing ... whatever he's doing! And I bet that's why he's been disappearing off the map – come to think of it, I've never seen the Room of Requirement on there!'

'Maybe the Marauders never knew the Room was there,' said Ron.

'I think it'll be part of the magic of the Room,' said Hermione. 'If you need it to be unplottable, it will be.'

'Dobby, have you managed to get in to have a look at what Malfoy's doing?' said Harry eagerly.

'No, Harry Potter, that is impossible,' said Dobby.

'No, it's not,' said Harry at once. 'Malfoy got into our Headquarters there last year, so I'll be able to get in and spy on him, no problem.'

'But I don't think you will, Harry,' said Hermione slowly. 'Malfoy already knew exactly how we were using the Room, didn't he, because that stupid Marietta had blabbed. He needed the Room to become the Headquarters of the DA, so it did. But you don't know what the Room becomes when Malfoy goes in there, so you don't know what to ask it to transform into.'

'There'll be a way around that,' said Harry dismissively. 'You've done brilliantly, Dobby.'

'Kreacher's done well, too,' said Hermione kindly; but far from looking grateful, Kreacher averted his huge, bloodshot eyes and croaked at the ceiling, 'The Mudblood is speaking to Kreacher, Kreacher will pretend he cannot hear –'

'Get out of it,' Harry snapped at him, and Kreacher made one last deep bow and Disapparated. 'You'd better go and get some sleep too, Dobby.'

'Thank you, Harry Potter, sir!' squeaked Dobby happily, and he, too, vanished.

'How good's this?' said Harry enthusiastically, turning to Ron and Hermione the moment the room was elf-free again. 'We know where Malfoy's going! We've got him cornered now!'

'Yeah, it's great,' said Ron glumly, who was attempting to mop up the sodden mass of ink that had recently been an almost completed essay. Hermione pulled it towards her and began siphoning the ink off with her wand.

'But what's all this about him going up there with a "variety of students"?' said Hermione. 'How many people are in on it? You wouldn't think he'd trust lots of them to know what he's doing ...'

674

## 第21章 神秘的房间

道什么事的地方！我打赌这就是他从地图上消失的原因——现在想起来，我从没在地图上看到过有求必应屋！"

"说不定制作活点地图的人根本不知道有那间屋子。"罗恩说。

"我想这是那间屋子魔法的一部分，"赫敏说，"如果你需要它在地图上显示不出来，它就显示不出来。"

"多比，你进去看见马尔福在干什么了吗？"哈利急切地问。

"没有，哈利·波特，这不可能。"多比说。

"没有什么不可能，"哈利马上说，"马尔福去年闯进了我们总部，所以我也能进去偷看他，没问题。"

"我想不行，哈利。"赫敏慢慢地说，"那次是因为玛丽埃塔那个笨蛋走漏了消息，马尔福已经知道我们怎么使用那间屋子，他要那间屋子变成 D.A. 总部，它就变成了那样。可是现在，你不清楚马尔福进去时那间屋子是什么样子，所以你不知道让它变成什么样子。"

"会有办法的。"哈利不以为然地说，"你干得很好，多比。"

"克利切也干得不错。"赫敏好心地补了一句，但克利切不仅没有显出感激，反而把充血的大眼睛一翻，对着天花板沙哑地说："泥巴种跟克利切说话，克利切假装听不见——"

"走开！"哈利厉声说，克利切最后深鞠一躬，幻影移形了，"你也去睡一觉吧，多比。"

"谢谢，哈利·波特，先生！"多比快乐地尖声说，也消失不见了。

"太好了！"小精灵刚一离开，哈利马上转向罗恩和赫敏，兴奋地说，"我们知道马尔福到哪儿去了！现在可以堵到他了！"

"是的，好极了。"罗恩阴沉地说，他正试图擦去纸上那一大片墨水，那儿刚才是一篇快写完的论文。赫敏把纸拖了过去，开始用魔杖把墨水吸走。

"可是带着'不同的学生'是怎么回事？"赫敏问，"有多少人参与？按说他不会让很多人知道他在干什么……"

'Yeah, that is weird,' said Harry, frowning. 'I heard him telling Crabbe it wasn't Crabbe's business what he was doing ... so what's he telling all these ... all these ...'

Harry's voice tailed away; he was staring at the fire.

'God, I've been stupid,' he said quietly. 'It's obvious, isn't it? There was a great vat of it down in the dungeon ... he could've nicked some any time during that lesson ...'

'Nicked what?' said Ron.

'Polyjuice Potion. He stole some of the Polyjuice Potion Slughorn showed us in our first Potions lesson ... there aren't a whole variety of students standing guard for Malfoy ... it's just Crabbe and Goyle as usual ... yeah, it all fits!' said Harry, jumping up and starting to pace in front of the fire. 'They're stupid enough to do what they're told even if he won't tell them what he's up to ... but he doesn't want them to be seen lurking around outside the Room of Requirement, so he's got them taking Polyjuice to make them look like other people ... those two girls I saw him with when he missed Quidditch – ha! Crabbe and Goyle!'

'Do you mean to say,' said Hermione in a hushed voice, 'that that little girl whose scales I repaired –?'

'Yeah, of course!' said Harry loudly, staring at her. 'Of course! Malfoy must've been inside the Room at the time, so she – what am I talking about? – *he* dropped the scales to tell Malfoy not to come out, because there was someone there! And there was that girl who dropped the toad-spawn, too! We've been walking past him all the time and not realising it!'

'He's got Crabbe and Goyle transforming into girls?' guffawed Ron. 'Blimey ... no wonder they don't look too happy these days ... I'm surprised they don't tell him to stuff it ...'

'Well, they wouldn't, would they, if he's shown them his Dark Mark,' said Harry.

'Hmmm ... the Dark Mark we don't know exists,' said Hermione sceptically, rolling up Ron's dried essay before it could come to any more harm and handing it to him.

'We'll see,' said Harry confidently.

'Yes, we will,' Hermione said, getting to her feet and stretching. 'But, Harry, before you get all excited, I still don't think you'll be able to get into the Room of Requirement without knowing what's there first. And I don't

"是啊，这很蹊跷，"哈利皱着眉道，"我听到他叫克拉布别管他在干什么……现在怎么又告诉这么多……这么多……"

哈利的声音低了下去，眼睛望着炉火。

"天哪，我真笨，"他轻声说，"很明显，是不是？地下教室里有一大缸呢……他在那节课上随时都可能偷到……"

"偷到什么？"罗恩问。

"复方汤剂。他偷了斯拉格霍恩在第一堂魔药课上给我们看的复方汤剂……根本没有什么不同的学生给马尔福放哨……就是克拉布和高尔……对，这下都对上了！"哈利跳了起来，在火炉前踱着步，"因为只有这两个人才会蠢到即使马尔福不说他在干什么，也能听他吩咐……但他不想让人看到这两个人总守在有求必应屋外面，所以就让他们喝了复方汤剂，变成别人的样子……他没去魁地奇比赛那天我看到的两个女孩——哈！就是克拉布和高尔！"

"你是说，"赫敏屏着气说，"我帮助修天平的那个小女生——？"

"对，当然！"哈利望着她大声说，"当然！马尔福当时一定在有求必应屋，所以那个女生——我说错了——那个男生丢掉天平，告诉马尔福不要出来，外面有人！还有，那个把癞蛤蟆卵掉到地上的女生！我们一直在他旁边走来走去，却不知道！"

"他把克拉布和高尔变成了女生？"罗恩说着大笑起来，"老天……难怪他们最近不大开心……我奇怪他们怎么不对他说'见鬼去吧'……"

"他们不会的，是不是？如果他给他们看过他的黑魔标记。"哈利说。

"哦……那个不知是否存在的黑魔标记。"赫敏怀疑地说，一边卷起擦干的论文还给罗恩，免得它再遭不测。

"看着吧。"哈利自信地说。

"好，那就看着吧。"赫敏说着站起来伸了伸懒腰，"可是哈利，你先别太兴奋了，我还是觉得，你如果不知道屋里有什么，是进不了有

## CHAPTER TWENTY-ONE    The Unknowable Room

think you should forget,' she heaved her bag on to her shoulder and gave him a very serious look, 'that what you're *supposed* to be concentrating on is getting that memory from Slughorn. Goodnight.'

Harry watched her go, feeling slightly disgruntled. Once the door to the girls' dormitories had closed behind her he rounded on Ron.

'What d'you think?'

'Wish I could Disapparate like a house-elf,' said Ron, staring at the spot where Dobby had vanished. 'I'd have that Apparition test in the bag.'

Harry did not sleep well that night. He lay awake for what felt like hours, wondering how Malfoy was using the Room of Requirement and what he, Harry, would see when he went in there the following day, for whatever Hermione said, Harry was sure that if Malfoy had been able to see the Headquarters of the DA, he would be able to see Malfoy's ... what could it be? A meeting place? A hideout? A storeroom? A workshop? Harry's mind worked feverishly and his dreams, when he finally fell asleep, were broken and disturbed by images of Malfoy, who turned into Slughorn, who turned into Snape ...

Harry was in a state of great anticipation over breakfast the following morning; he had a free period before Defence Against the Dark Arts and was determined to spend it trying to get into the Room of Requirement. Hermione was rather ostentatiously showing no interest in his whispered plans for forcing entry into the Room, which irritated Harry, because he thought she might be a lot of help if she wanted to.

'Look,' he said quietly, leaning forwards and putting a hand on the *Daily Prophet*, which she had just removed from a post owl, to stop her opening it and vanishing behind it. 'I haven't forgotten about Slughorn, but I haven't got a clue how to get that memory off him, and until I get a brainwave why shouldn't I find out what Malfoy's doing?'

'I've already told you, you need to *persuade* Slughorn,' said Hermione. 'It's not a question of tricking him or bewitching him, or Dumbledore could have done it in a second. Instead of messing around outside the Room of Requirement,' she jerked the *Prophet* out from under Harry's hand and unfolded it to look at the front page, 'you should go and find Slughorn and start appealing to his better nature.'

'Anyone we know –?' asked Ron, as Hermione scanned the headlines.

'Yes!' said Hermione, causing both Harry and Ron to gag on their breakfast,

## 第 21 章 神秘的房间

求必应屋的。而且我认为你不应该忘记，"她把书包甩到肩上，十分严肃地看了他一眼，"你应该集中精力搞到斯拉格霍恩的记忆。晚安。"

哈利看着她走开，感觉有点儿不悦。通往女生宿舍的门在她身后一关上，他就转向了罗恩。

"你是怎么想的？"

"我希望能像家养小精灵一样幻影移形，"罗恩盯着多比消失的地方说，"那么幻影显形考试就十拿九稳了。"

哈利这一夜没睡好，感觉自己醒着躺了好几个小时，一直在猜测马尔福用有求必应屋干什么，想象着自己明天进去后会看到什么。尽管赫敏泼了凉水，哈利还是相信既然马尔福能看到 D.A. 总部，他就能看到马尔福的……什么呢？集会地点？藏身处？储藏室？工作间？哈利的脑子飞快地转动着，后来终于睡着了，但睡得很不安稳，梦中仍受到马尔福形象的侵扰，马尔福一会儿变成斯拉格霍恩，一会儿变成斯内普……

第二天吃早饭时，哈利满怀期待。黑魔法防御术课前有一段空闲，他决定设法进入有求必应屋。对他悄声说出闯进屋子的方案，赫敏夸张地表示不感兴趣。哈利有些恼火，因为他觉得赫敏如果愿意是可以帮上大忙的。

"喂，"他凑向前悄悄地说，一只手按住赫敏刚从送信的猫头鹰身上解下的《预言家日报》，不让赫敏躲到报纸后面去，"我没忘记斯拉格霍恩，可我不知道怎么搞到他的记忆，在灵感来临之前我为什么不能去看看马尔福在干什么呢？"

"我已经告诉过你了，"赫敏说，"你得说服斯拉格霍恩，而不是对他下药或者施魔法。否则邓布利多一下子就办到了。你不要在有求必应屋外面浪费时间了。"她把《预言家日报》从哈利手底下抽出，打开来看着第一版，"你应该去找斯拉格霍恩，努力感化他。"

"有没有我们认识的——？"赫敏浏览报纸标题时，罗恩问道。

"有！"赫敏说，哈利和罗恩一听都噎着了，"不过还好，他没死——

## CHAPTER TWENTY-ONE    The Unknowable Room

'but it's all right, he's not dead – it's Mundungus, he's been arrested and sent to Azkaban! Something to do with impersonating an Inferius during an attempted burglary ... and someone called Octavius Pepper has vanished ... oh, and how horrible, a nine-year-old boy has been arrested for trying to kill his grandparents, they think he was under the Imperius Curse ...'

They finished their breakfast in silence. Hermione set off immediately for Ancient Runes, Ron for the common room, where he still had to finish his conclusion on Snape's Dementor essay, and Harry for the corridor on the seventh floor and the stretch of wall opposite the tapestry of Barnabas the Barmy teaching trolls to do ballet.

Harry slipped on his Invisibility Cloak once he had found an empty passage, but he need not have bothered. When he reached his destination he found it deserted. Harry was not sure whether his chances of getting inside the Room were better with Malfoy inside it or out, but at least his first attempt was not going to be complicated by the presence of Crabbe or Goyle pretending to be an eleven-year-old girl.

He closed his eyes as he approached the place where the Room of Requirement's door was concealed. He knew what he had to do; he had become most accomplished at it last year. Concentrating with all his might he thought, *I need to see what Malfoy's doing in here ... I need to see what Malfoy's doing in here ... I need to see what Malfoy's doing in here ...*

Three times he walked past the door, then, his heart pounding with excitement, he opened his eyes and faced it – but he was still looking at a stretch of mundanely blank wall.

He moved forwards and gave it an experimental push. The stone remained solid and unyielding.

'OK,' said Harry aloud. 'OK ... I thought the wrong thing ...'

He pondered for a moment, then set off again, eyes closed, concentrating as hard as he could.

*I need to see the place where Malfoy keeps coming secretly ... I need to see the place where Malfoy keeps coming secretly ...*

After three walks past, he opened his eyes expectantly.

There was no door.

'Oh, come off it,' he told the wall irritably. 'That was a clear instruction ... fine ...'

He thought hard for several minutes before striding off once more.

*I need you to become the place you become for Draco Malfoy ...*

He did not immediately open his eyes when he had finished his patrolling; he

## 第21章 神秘的房间

是蒙顿格斯,给抓起来送进阿兹卡班了!说是扮成阴尸入室行窃……有一个叫奥塔维·佩珀的失踪了……哎呀,多可怕,一名九岁男孩企图杀死祖父母而被逮捕,据说是中了夺魂咒……"

他们默默吃完早饭,赫敏马上赶去上古代如尼文课,罗恩去了公共休息室,准备把斯内普要的摄魂怪论文写完。哈利直奔八楼走廊,目标是傻巴拿巴教巨怪跳芭蕾舞的挂毯对面的那段空墙。

一到僻静地段,哈利就披上了隐形衣。其实没有必要。他发现目的地根本没人。哈利不知道马尔福在里面还是在外面时自己进去的机会更大,但至少他的初次尝试不会被扮成十一岁女生的克拉布或高尔打搅了。

哈利走近隐藏着有求必应屋的地方,他闭上眼睛。他知道该做什么,去年已经练得很熟了。他专心致志地想:我需要看看马尔福在这儿干什么……我需要看看马尔福在这儿干什么……我需要看看马尔福在这儿干什么……

他三次走过那个地方,激动得心咚咚地跳,然后,他睁开眼睛转向它——可眼前仍是一段普通的白墙。

他走上前推了推,石头还是硬邦邦的,一动不动。

"好吧,"哈利大声说,"好吧……我想得不对……"

他想了一会儿,又走了起来,闭着眼睛,集中意念。

*我需要看到马尔福经常偷偷来的地方……我需要看到马尔福经常偷偷来的地方……*

走过三次之后,他期待地睁开眼睛。

门没有出现。

"哦,别这样,"他烦躁地对着墙壁说,"要求已经提得很清楚了呀……好吧……"

他使劲想了几分钟,又大步走了起来。

*我需要你变成你为德拉科·马尔福变成的地方……*

走完后,他没有马上睁开眼睛,而是侧耳聆听,似乎希望听见门

## CHAPTER TWENTY-ONE  The Unknowable Room

was listening hard, as though he might hear the door pop into existence. He heard nothing, however, except the distant twittering of birds outside. He opened his eyes.

There was still no door.

Harry swore. Someone screamed. He looked around to see a gaggle of first-years running back round the corner, apparently under the impression that they had just encountered a particularly foul-mouthed ghost.

Harry tried every variation of 'I need to see what Draco Malfoy is doing inside you' that he could think of for a whole hour, at the end of which he was forced to concede that Hermione might have had a point: the Room simply did not want to open for him. Frustrated and annoyed, he set off for Defence Against the Dark Arts, pulling off his Invisibility Cloak and stuffing it into his bag as he went.

'Late again, Potter,' said Snape coldly, as Harry hurried into the candlelit classroom. 'Ten points from Gryffindor.'

Harry scowled at Snape as he flung himself into the seat beside Ron; half the class was still on its feet, taking out books and organising its things; he could not be much later than any of them.

'Before we start, I want your Dementor essays,' said Snape, waving his wand carelessly, so that twenty-five scrolls of parchment soared into the air and landed in a neat pile on his desk. 'And I hope for your sakes they are better than the tripe I had to endure on resisting the Imperius Curse. Now, if you will all open your books at page – what is it, Mr Finnigan?'

'Sir,' said Seamus, 'I've been wondering, how do you tell the difference between an Inferius and a ghost? Because there was something in the *Prophet* about an Inferius –'

'No, there wasn't,' said Snape in a bored voice.

'But sir, I heard people talking –'

'If you had actually read the article in question, Mr Finnigan, you would have known that the so-called Inferius was nothing but a smelly sneak-thief by the name of Mundungus Fletcher.'

'I thought Snape and Mundungus were on the same side?' muttered Harry to Ron and Hermione. 'Shouldn't he be upset Mundungus has been arrest–?'

'But Potter seems to have a lot to say on the subject,' said Snape, pointing suddenly at the back of the room, his black eyes fixed on Harry. 'Let us ask Potter how we would tell the difference between an Inferius and a ghost.'

## 第21章 神秘的房间

突然出现的声音。可是没有听见,只有远处小鸟的啁啾。他睁开了眼睛。

还是没有出现门。

哈利诅咒了一声,听到有人尖叫。他转过头,看到一群一年级新生逃回了拐角,显然是以为碰到了一个满嘴粗话的幽灵。

哈利花了一个小时尝试"我需要看看德拉科·马尔福在里面做什么"的各种变化形式,最后不得不承认赫敏可能说得有道理,那间屋子就是不想让他进去。他沮丧而恼火地赶去上黑魔法防御术课,在路上脱下隐形衣,塞进了书包。

"又迟到了,波特,"哈利匆匆跑进点着蜡烛的教室时,斯内普冷冷地说,"格兰芬多扣十分。"

哈利对斯内普怒目而视,冲到罗恩旁边的椅子上坐下。班上半数人都还站着,正在拿书和整理东西,他并没有晚多少。

"开始上课之前,我想看到你们的摄魂怪论文。"斯内普说着漫不经心地一挥魔杖,二十五卷羊皮纸升到空中,在他桌上整齐地落成一堆,"为了你们考虑,我希望这次比那篇抵御夺魂咒的狗屁不通的东西好些。现在,请打开书,翻到——什么事,斐尼甘先生?"

"先生,"西莫说,"我有个问题,怎么区分阴尸和幽灵呢?因为《预言家日报》中提到了阴尸——"

"没有,没有这回事。"斯内普用厌倦的语气说。

"可是先生,我听到人们说——"

"如果你好好读了那篇文章,斐尼甘先生,就会知道所谓的阴尸只是一个臭烘烘的小偷,蒙顿格斯·弗莱奇。"

"斯内普跟蒙顿格斯不是一边的吗?"哈利小声问罗恩和赫敏,"蒙顿格斯被抓起来了,他不应该感到难受吗?"

"波特似乎对这个问题有很多话要说,"斯内普说着突然朝教室后面一指,黑眼睛盯着哈利,"让我们问问波特,如何区分阴尸和幽灵。"

## CHAPTER TWENTY-ONE   The Unknowable Room

The whole class looked round at Harry, who hastily tried to recall what Dumbledore had told him the night that they had gone to visit Slughorn.

'Er – well – ghosts are transparent –' he said.

'Oh, very good,' interrupted Snape, his lip curling. 'Yes, it is easy to see that nearly six years of magical education have not been wasted on you, Potter. *Ghosts are transparent.*'

Pansy Parkinson let out a high-pitched giggle. Several other people were smirking. Harry took a deep breath and continued calmly, though his insides were boiling, 'Yeah, ghosts are transparent, but Inferi are dead bodies, aren't they? So they'd be solid –'

'A five-year-old could have told us as much,' sneered Snape. 'The Inferius is a corpse that has been reanimated by a Dark wizard's spells. It is not alive, it is merely used like a puppet to do the wizard's bidding. A ghost, as I trust that you are all aware by now, is the imprint of a departed soul left upon the earth ... and of course, as Potter so wisely tells us, *transparent.*'

'Well, what Harry said is the most useful if we're trying to tell them apart!' said Ron. 'When we come face to face with one down a dark alley we're going to be having a shufti to see if it's solid, aren't we, we're not going to be asking, "Excuse me, are you the imprint of a departed soul?"'

There was a ripple of laughter, instantly quelled by the look Snape gave the class.

'Another ten points from Gryffindor,' said Snape. 'I would expect nothing more sophisticated from you, Ronald Weasley, the boy so solid he cannot Apparate half an inch across a room.'

'*No!*' whispered Hermione, grabbing Harry's arm as he opened his mouth furiously. 'There's no point, you'll just end up in detention again, leave it!'

'Now open your books at page two hundred and thirteen,' said Snape, smirking a little, 'and read the first two paragraphs on the Cruciatus Curse ...'

Ron was very subdued all through the class. When the bell sounded at the end of the lesson, Lavender caught up with Ron and Harry (Hermione mysteriously melted out of sight as she approached) and abused Snape hotly for his jibe about Ron's Apparition, but this seemed merely to irritate Ron, and he shook her off by making a detour into the boys' bathroom with Harry.

'Snape's right, though, isn't he?' said Ron, after staring into a cracked

## 第21章 神秘的房间

全班都回头看着哈利，他急忙回忆那天晚上去拜访斯拉格霍恩时邓布利多说的话。

"呃——这个——幽灵是透明的——"

"哦，很好，"斯内普撇着嘴打断了他，"对，显而易见，近六年的魔法教育在你身上没有白费，波特。幽灵是透明的。"

潘西·帕金森发出高声尖笑。还有几个人也傻笑起来。尽管怒火中烧，哈利还是深深吸了口气，镇静地说了下去："幽灵是透明的，但阴尸是死尸，是吧？所以它们应该是实心的——"

"五岁小孩也能讲出这些。"斯内普讥笑道，"阴尸是被黑巫师的魔咒唤起的死尸。它没有生命，只是像木偶一样被用来执行巫师的命令。而幽灵，我相信大家现在都已知道，是离去的灵魂留在世间的印记……当然，正如波特英明指出的那样，它是透明的。"

"哈利说的是最实用的区分方法！"罗恩说，"假使在黑巷子里迎面碰到一个，我们会赶快看一看它是不是实心的，而不会问：'对不起，你是不是一个离去的灵魂留在世间的印记？'"

教室里发出一片笑声，但立刻被斯内普的眼色压了下去。

"格兰芬多再扣十分。我不指望你能说出更高明的话，罗恩·韦斯莱——你真是个实心的男生，在这间屋子里连幻影显形半英寸都做不到。"

"不要！"赫敏见哈利愤怒地张嘴要说话，忙抓住他的胳膊小声说，"没有意义，只会又被关禁闭，算了吧。"

"现在打开书，翻到二百一十三页。"斯内普得意地微笑道，"读一读关于钻心咒的前两段……"

罗恩整堂课都特别蔫，下课铃响了，拉文德追上罗恩和哈利（她走近时赫敏神秘蒸发了），痛骂斯内普在课堂上嘲笑罗恩幻影显形的事。可这似乎只能更加激怒罗恩，他跟哈利拐进男生盥洗室，把拉文德甩掉了。

"斯内普说得对,是不是？"罗恩盯着破镜子看了一两分钟后说，"我

## CHAPTER TWENTY-ONE  The Unknowable Room

mirror for a minute or two. 'I dunno whether it's worth me taking the test. I just can't get the hang of Apparition.'

'You might as well do the extra practice sessions in Hogsmeade and see where they get you,' said Harry reasonably. 'It'll be more interesting than trying to get into a stupid hoop, anyway. Then, if you're still not – you know – as good as you'd like to be, you can postpone the test, do it with me over the summ– Myrtle, this is the boys' bathroom!'

The ghost of a girl had risen out of the toilet in a cubicle behind them and was now floating in midair, staring at them through thick, white, round glasses.

'Oh,' she said glumly. 'It's you two.'

'Who were you expecting?' said Ron, looking at her in the mirror.

'Nobody,' said Myrtle, picking moodily at a spot on her chin. 'He said he'd come back and see me, but then *you* said you'd pop in and visit me, too ...' she gave Harry a reproachful look '... and I haven't seen you for months and months. I've learned not to expect too much from boys.'

'I thought you lived in that girls' bathroom?' said Harry, who had been careful to give the place a wide berth for some years now.

'I do,' she said, with a sulky little shrug, 'but that doesn't mean I can't *visit* other places. I came and saw you in your bath once, remember?'

'Vividly,' said Harry.

'But I thought he liked me,' she said plaintively. 'Maybe if you two left, he'd come back again ... we had lots in common ... I'm sure he felt it ...'

And she looked hopefully towards the door.

'When you say you had lots in common,' said Ron, sounding rather amused now, 'd'you mean he lives in an S-bend, too?'

'No,' said Myrtle defiantly, her voice echoing loudly around the old tiled bathroom. 'I mean he's sensitive, people bully him, too, and he feels lonely and hasn't got anybody to talk to, and he's not afraid to show his feelings and cry!'

'There's been a boy in here crying?' said Harry curiously. 'A young boy?'

'Never you mind!' said Myrtle, her small, leaky eyes fixed on Ron, who was now definitely grinning. 'I promised I wouldn't tell anyone and I'll take his secret to the –'

## 第21章 神秘的房间

不知道去考试有没有意义,我就是学不会幻影显形。"

"你可以参加霍格莫德的额外训练,看看会怎么样,"哈利理智地说,"至少,那会比显形到一个愚蠢的木圈里有趣一些。然后,如果你还是不能——嗯——做到像你希望的那样好,还可以推迟考试,到夏天跟我一起——桃金娘,这是男生盥洗室!"

一个女孩的幽灵从他们后面的一个抽水马桶里升了起来,在半空中飘浮,一双眼睛从厚厚的白色圆形眼镜后面瞪着他们。

"哦,"她闷闷不乐地说,"是你们两个。"

"你在等谁?"罗恩问,一边从镜子里看着她。

"没有等谁。"桃金娘忧郁地抠着下巴上一个小点说,"他说他会回来看我,后来你又说会来看我……"她嗔怪地看了哈利一眼……"好多个月都没看到你们,我已经学会对男孩不抱太多期望了。"

"我以为你住在女生盥洗室呢。"哈利说,那个地方他已经避开好几年了。

"是啊,"桃金娘说着气呼呼地耸了耸肩膀,"可那并不意味着我不能访问别的地方。有一次我来看过你洗澡,记得吗?"

"记忆犹新。"哈利说。

"可我以为他喜欢我。"她哀怨地说,"也许等你们走了,他还会回来的……我们有很多共同点……我相信他感觉到了……"

她期待地望着门口。

"你说你们有很多共同点,"罗恩说,现在似乎被逗乐了,"是指他也住在下水管里吗?"

"不是,"桃金娘抗议道,声音在老式的瓷砖盥洗室中回响,"我是说他很敏感,他也被人欺负,觉得孤单,没人说话,他不怕暴露自己的感情,想哭就哭!"

"有个男生在这儿哭过?"哈利好奇地问,"小男生?"

"不要你管!"桃金娘说,那双泪汪汪的小眼睛盯着已在咧嘴发笑的罗恩,"我保证过不告诉任何人,我要把他的秘密带进——"

687

## CHAPTER TWENTY-ONE  The Unknowable Room

'– not the grave, surely?' said Ron with a snort. 'The sewers, maybe ...'

Myrtle gave a howl of rage and dived back into the toilet, causing water to slop over the sides and on to the floor. Goading Myrtle seemed to have put fresh heart into Ron.

'You're right,' he said, swinging his schoolbag back over his shoulder, 'I'll do the practice sessions in Hogsmeade before I decide about taking the test.'

And so the following weekend, Ron joined Hermione and the rest of the sixth-years who would turn seventeen in time to take the test in a fortnight. Harry felt rather jealous watching them all get ready to go into the village; he missed making trips there, and it was a particularly fine spring day, one of the first clear skies they had seen in a long time. However, he had decided to use the time to attempt another assault on the Room of Requirement.

'You'd do better,' said Hermione, when he confided this plan to Ron and her in the Entrance Hall, 'to go straight to Slughorn's office and try and get that memory from him.'

'I've been trying!' said Harry crossly, which was perfectly true. He had lagged behind after every Potions lesson that week in an attempt to corner Slughorn, but the Potions master always left the dungeon so fast that Harry had not been able to catch him. Twice, Harry had gone to his office and knocked, but received no reply, though on the second occasion he was sure he had heard the quickly stifled sounds of an old gramophone.

'He doesn't want to talk to me, Hermione! He can tell I've been trying to get him on his own again and he's not going to let it happen!'

'Well, you've just got to keep at it, haven't you?'

The short queue of people waiting to file past Filch, who was doing his usual prodding act with the Secrecy Sensor, moved forwards a few steps and Harry did not answer in case he was overheard by the care-taker. He wished Ron and Hermione luck, then turned and climbed the marble staircase again, determined, whatever Hermione said, to devote an hour or two to the Room of Requirement.

Once out of sight of the Entrance Hall, Harry pulled out the Marauder's Map and his Invisibility Cloak from his bag. Having concealed himself, he tapped the map, murmured, 'I solemnly swear that I am up to no good,' and scanned it carefully.

As it was Sunday morning, nearly all the students were inside their various common rooms, the Gryffindors in one tower, the Ravenclaws in another, the Slytherins in the dungeons and the Hufflepuffs in the basement near the

## 第21章 神秘的房间

"——不是坟墓吧?"罗恩笑道,"也许是下水道……"

桃金娘发出一声愤怒的号叫,钻回了抽水马桶,水溅在马桶的周围和地板上。刺激桃金娘似乎让罗恩重新获得了勇气。

"你说得对,"他说着把书包甩回肩上,"我要参加霍格莫德的额外训练,然后再决定去不去考试。"

到了周末,罗恩加入了赫敏和另一些两星期后满十七岁要参加考试的六年级学生当中。哈利看着他们都准备去村子里,感到有些嫉妒。他很想念霍格莫德。天气又特别好,春意融融,是很久以来难得一见的大晴天。不过,他已经决定利用这个时间再去偷袭一下有求必应屋。

"你还不如直接去斯拉格霍恩的办公室,把他的记忆搞到手呢。"当他在门厅那儿对罗恩和赫敏透露这一计划时,赫敏说。

"我一直在努力啊!"哈利烦躁地说,这倒是真的,那个星期的每节魔药课后他都留下来,想堵住斯拉格霍恩,可是魔药教师总是溜得很快,他一次都没有堵到。哈利两次去敲他办公室的门,可是敲不开,其实第二次他确信听到了被迅速掐断的留声机声。

"他不想跟我说话,赫敏!他看出我又想跟他单独交谈,不肯给我这个机会!"

"可你必须锲而不舍,是不是?"

排在费尔奇面前的一小队人往前走了几步,哈利怕被这个照例拿着探密器捣捣戳戳的管理员听到,就没有回答。他祝罗恩和赫敏好运,然后转身爬上大理石台阶,决心不管赫敏怎么说,他都要花一两个小时去对付有求必应屋。

等到门厅的人看不见他了,哈利从包里抽出活点地图和隐形衣。隐形之后,他敲敲地图念道:"我庄严宣誓我不干好事。"然后仔细查看起来。

因为是星期天上午,几乎所有的学生都在各自的公共休息室里,格兰芬多的在一座塔楼,拉文克劳的在另一座,斯莱特林的在地下室,

## CHAPTER TWENTY-ONE  The Unknowable Room

kitchens. Here and there a stray person meandered around the library or up a corridor ... there were a few people out in the grounds ... and there, alone in the seventh-floor corridor, was Gregory Goyle. There was no sign of the Room of Requirement, but Harry was not worried about that; if Goyle was standing guard outside it, the Room was open, whether the map was aware of it or not. He therefore sprinted up the stairs, slowing down only when he reached the corner into the corridor, when he began to creep, very slowly, towards the very same little girl, clutching her heavy brass scales, that Hermione had so kindly helped a fortnight before. He waited until he was right behind her before bending very low and whispering, 'Hello ... you're very pretty, aren't you?'

Goyle gave a high-pitched scream of terror, threw the scales up into the air and sprinted away, vanishing from sight long before the sound of the scales smashing had stopped echoing around the corridor. Laughing, Harry turned to contemplate the blank wall behind which, he was sure, Draco Malfoy was now standing frozen, aware that someone unwelcome was out there, but not daring to make an appearance. It gave Harry a most agreeable feeling of power as he tried to remember what form of words he had not yet tried.

Yet this hopeful mood did not last long. Half an hour later, having tried many more variations of his request to see what Malfoy was up to, the wall was just as doorless as ever. Harry felt frustrated beyond belief; Malfoy might be just feet away from him, and there was still not the tiniest shred of evidence as to what he was doing in there. Losing his patience completely, Harry ran at the wall and kicked it.

'OUCH!'

He thought he might have broken his toe; as he clutched it and hopped on one foot, the Invisibility Cloak slipped off him.

'Harry?'

He spun round, one-legged, and toppled over. There, to his utter astonishment, was Tonks, walking towards him as though she frequently strolled up this corridor.

'What're you doing here?' he said, scrambling to his feet again; why did she always have to find him lying on the floor?

'I came to see Dumbledore,' said Tonks.

Harry thought she looked terrible; thinner than usual, her mouse-coloured hair lank.

'His office isn't here,' said Harry, 'it's round the other side of the castle, behind the gargoyle –'

## 第21章 神秘的房间

赫奇帕奇的在厨房附近的地下室。有零零星星的人在图书馆或走廊闲逛……还有几个人在场地上……看到了，高尔一个人在八楼走廊里。地图上看不到有求必应屋，但哈利不担心这一点。既然高尔在外面放哨，那么屋子就是开着的，无论地图是否知道。他箭步冲上楼梯，到了走廊口的拐角处才放慢脚步。他蹑手蹑脚地向赫敏两星期前好心帮过的那个端着铜天平的小女孩走去，一直走到她身后，才弯下腰小声说："你好……你很漂亮，是不是？"

高尔惊恐地尖叫了一声，把天平扔向空中，撒腿就跑，在天平摔到地上的回响散去前早就跑得无踪无影。哈利大笑着转身面对那段空墙，他相信德拉科·马尔福正僵立在后面，知道外面有不受欢迎的人却不敢出来。这给了哈利一种非常痛快的感觉，他开始思索还有哪种说法没有试过。

可是乐观的情绪没有维持多久。他花了半个小时，又试了很多说法想探出马尔福在做什么，墙上还是没有出现门。哈利感到遭受了难以置信的挫折，马尔福近在咫尺，却半点也看不出他在干什么。哈利彻底失去了耐心，冲过去朝墙上踢了一脚。

"哎哟！"

他觉得脚指头可能折断了，抱着脚单腿跳，隐形衣滑落了。

"哈利？"

他金鸡独立来了个急转身，结果摔倒了。他十分吃惊地看到唐克斯正迎面走来，好像她经常来这条走廊散步似的。

"你来这儿干什么？"他问，一边急忙爬起来，为什么唐克斯总是看到他躺在地上呢？

"我来见邓布利多。"唐克斯说。

哈利觉得她的样子很糟糕，比平常更瘦，灰褐色的头发很稀疏。

"他的办公室不在这儿，"哈利说，"在城堡的那一边，滴水嘴石兽后面——"

## CHAPTER TWENTY-ONE    The Unknowable Room

'I know,' said Tonks. 'He's not there. Apparently he's gone away again.'

'Has he?' said Harry, putting his bruised foot gingerly back on the floor. 'Hey – you don't know where he goes, I suppose?'

'No,' said Tonks.

'What did you want to see him about?'

'Nothing in particular,' said Tonks, picking, apparently unconsciously, at the sleeve of her robe. 'I just thought he might know what's going on ... I've heard rumours ... people getting hurt ...'

'Yeah, I know, it's all been in the papers,' said Harry. 'That little kid trying to kill his –'

'The *Prophet's* often behind the times,' said Tonks, who didn't seem to be listening to him. 'You haven't had any letters from anyone in the Order recently?'

'No one from the Order writes to me any more,' said Harry, 'not since Sirius –'

He saw that her eyes had filled with tears.

'I'm sorry,' he muttered awkwardly. 'I mean ... I miss him, as well ...'

'What?' said Tonks blankly, as though she had not heard him. 'Well ... I'll see you around, Harry ...'

And she turned abruptly and walked back down the corridor, leaving Harry to stare after her. After a minute or so, he pulled the Invisibility Cloak on again and resumed his efforts to get into the Room of Requirement, but his heart was not in it. Finally, a hollow feeling in his stomach and the knowledge that Ron and Hermione would soon be back for lunch made him abandon the attempt and leave the corridor to Malfoy who, hopefully, would be too afraid to leave for some hours to come.

He found Ron and Hermione in the Great Hall, already halfway through an early lunch.

'I did it – well, kind of!' Ron told Harry enthusiastically when he caught sight of him. 'I was supposed to be Apparating to outside Madam Puddifoot's teashop and I overshot it a bit, ended up near Scrivenshaft's, but at least I moved!'

'Good one,' said Harry. 'How'd you do, Hermione?'

'Oh, she was perfect, obviously,' said Ron, before Hermione could answer. 'Perfect deliberation, divination and desperation, or whatever the hell it is – we all went for a quick drink in the Three Broomsticks after and you should've heard Twycross going on about her – I'll be surprised if he doesn't pop the question soon –'

## 第21章 神秘的房间

"我知道，"唐克斯说，"他不在那儿，显然又走了。"

"是吗？"哈利说着把踢伤的脚轻轻放回地面，"嘿——你不知道他去哪儿了吧？"

"不知道。"

"你找他有什么事吗？"

"没什么，"唐克斯说，仿佛是在无心地扯着她衣袍的袖子，"我只是想他可能了解情况……我听到传闻……有人受伤……"

"是啊，我知道，都见报了，"哈利说，"那个小孩企图杀死他的……"

"《预言家日报》的报道经常滞后。"唐克斯说，似乎没有听他说话，"你最近没收到凤凰社成员的信吧？"

"凤凰社没人给我写信了，自从小天狼星——"

他看到唐克斯眼中已泪水涟涟。

"对不起，"他不安地说，"我……我也很怀念他……"

"什么？"唐克斯茫然问道，仿佛没有听到他的话，"……回头见吧，哈利……"

她突然转身往回走，留下哈利呆呆地望着她。约莫一分钟后，哈利又披上隐形衣，继续设法进入有求必应屋，但心思已经不在这上头。终于，腹中空空的感觉和罗恩、赫敏就要回来吃午饭的事实使他放弃了尝试，把走廊让给了马尔福，希望他吓得再待上几小时也不敢出来。

他在大礼堂里找到罗恩和赫敏，他们都已经吃了一半。

"我成功了——差不多吧！"罗恩一看到哈利就兴奋地说，"应该幻影显形到帕笛芙夫人茶馆的外面，我超过了一点儿，到了文人居旁边，但至少我移动了！"

"太棒了。"哈利说，"你怎么样，赫敏？"

"哦，她显然是完美的，"罗恩抢先回答说，"完美的目光、决绝和从容——管它是哪几点呢。结束后我们一起在三把扫帚喝了一杯，你没听到泰克罗斯怎么不停地夸她呢。他要是过两天不求婚才怪——"

## CHAPTER TWENTY-ONE   The Unknowable Room

'And what about you?' asked Hermione, ignoring Ron. 'Have you been up at the Room of Requirement all this time?'

'Yep,' said Harry. 'and guess who I ran into up there? Tonks!'

'Tonks?' repeated Ron and Hermione together, looking surprised.

'Yeah, she said she'd come to visit Dumbledore ...'

'If you ask me,' said Ron once Harry had finished describing his conversation with Tonks, 'she's cracking up a bit. Losing her nerve after what happened at the Ministry.'

'It's a bit odd,' said Hermione, who for some reason looked very concerned. 'She's supposed to be guarding the school, why's she suddenly abandoning her post to come and see Dumbledore when he's not even here?'

'I had a thought,' said Harry tentatively. He felt strange about voicing it; this was much more Hermione's territory than his. 'You don't think she can have been ... you know ... in love with Sirius?'

Hermione stared at him.

'What on earth makes you say that?'

'I dunno,' said Harry, shrugging, 'but she was nearly crying when I mentioned his name ... and her Patronus is a big four-legged thing now ... I wondered whether it hadn't become ... you know ... him.'

'It's a thought,' said Hermione slowly. 'But I still don't know why she'd be bursting into the castle to see Dumbledore, if that's really why she was here ...'

'Goes back to what I said, doesn't it?' said Ron, who was now shovelling mashed potato into his mouth. 'She's gone a bit funny. Lost her nerve. Women,' he said wisely to Harry. 'They're easily upset.'

'And yet,' said Hermione, coming out of her reverie, 'I doubt you'd find a *woman* who sulked for half an hour because Madam Rosmerta didn't laugh at their joke about the hag, the Healer and the *Mimbulus mimbletonia*.'

Ron scowled.

## 第21章 神秘的房间

"你呢?"赫敏问道,没去理睬罗恩,"一直在有求必应屋那儿?"

"是的,"哈利说,"猜猜我在那儿碰到谁了?唐克斯!"

"唐克斯?"罗恩和赫敏一齐惊讶地说。

"对,她说是来找邓布利多……"

"依我看,"哈利说完他和唐克斯的对话后,罗恩立刻说,"她有点崩溃了,在魔法部发生了那些事之后六神无主。"

"这有点奇怪,"赫敏说,显得很担心,"她应该守护学校,为什么突然擅离职守来找邓布利多呢,何况他还不在?"

"我有个想法,"哈利试探地说,他觉得说这个有点怪,这似乎更像是赫敏的领域,"你觉得她会不会……会不会……爱着小天狼星?"

赫敏瞪着他。

"你怎么会这么说?"

"我不知道,"哈利耸了耸肩膀,"可我提到小天狼星的名字时,她差点哭出来……她的守护神现在是个四条腿的庞然大物……我想会不会是变成……变成……他了。"

"这倒是个想法,"赫敏慢吞吞地说,"可我还是不明白她为什么要冲进城堡找邓布利多,如果这真是她来的原因……"

"还是我说的吧?"罗恩说,他正在把土豆泥舀进嘴里,"她有点儿反常,六神无主,女人嘛,"他煞有介事地对哈利说,"就是容易沉不住气。"

"可是,"赫敏说,她已从沉思中回过神来,"我怀疑没有哪个女人会为罗斯默塔女士听了女妖、治疗师和米布米宝的笑话没有笑而生半小时闷气。"

罗恩瞪起了眼睛。

## CHAPTER TWENTY-TWO

## After the Burial

Patches of bright blue sky were beginning to appear over the castle turrets, but these signs of approaching summer did not lift Harry's mood. He had been thwarted, both in his attempts to find out what Malfoy was doing, and in his efforts to start a conversation with Slughorn that might lead, somehow, to Slughorn handing over the memory he had apparently suppressed for decades.

'For the last time, just forget about Malfoy,' Hermione told Harry firmly.

They were sitting with Ron in a sunny corner of the courtyard after lunch. Hermione and Ron were both clutching a Ministry of Magic leaflet: *Common Apparition Mistakes and How to Avoid Them*, for they were taking their tests that very afternoon, but by and large the leaflets had not proved soothing to the nerves. Ron gave a start and tried to hide behind Hermione as a girl came round the corner.

'It isn't Lavender,' said Hermione wearily.

'Oh, good,' said Ron, relaxing.

'Harry Potter?' said the girl. 'I was asked to give you this.'

'Thanks ...'

Harry's heart sank as he took the small scroll of parchment. Once the girl was out of earshot he said, 'Dumbledore said we wouldn't be having any more lessons until I got the memory!'

'Maybe he wants to check on how you're doing?' suggested Hermione, as Harry unrolled the parchment; but rather than finding Dumbledore's long, narrow, slanting writing he saw an untidy sprawl, very difficult to read due to the presence of large blotches on the parchment where the ink had run.

DEAR HARRY, RON AND HERMIONE,
ARAGOG DIED LAST NIGHT. HARRY AND RON,

# 第 22 章

# 葬礼之后

片片明朗的蓝天开始出现在城堡塔楼上空,但是夏天来临的这些迹象并未让哈利心情好起来。他既没能侦查出马尔福在干什么,也没能跟斯拉格霍恩单独谈上话,让他交出看样子已经隐藏数十年的记忆。

"说最后一遍,忘掉马尔福吧。"赫敏果断地对哈利说。

这是午饭后,他们和罗恩坐在院中一个阳光明媚的角落里。赫敏和罗恩都捏着一份魔法部的小册子:《幻影显形常见错误及避免方法》,今天下午就要考试了,但小册子基本上没能镇定他们紧张的神经。一个女孩从拐角走了出来,罗恩一惊,忙躲到赫敏身后。

"不是拉文德。"赫敏厌倦地说。

"哦,还好。"罗恩说着放松下来。

"哈利·波特?"那女孩说,"有人让我把这个带给你。"

"谢谢……"

哈利接过那小卷羊皮纸,心猛地往下一沉。那女孩走开后他说:"邓布利多说过在我搞到记忆之前不上课的呀!"

"也许他想问问你进展如何。"赫敏猜测道,哈利打开纸卷。上面不是邓布利多那细长的斜体字,而是凌乱潦草的字迹,纸上还有大团墨渍,字迹很难辨认。

亲爱的哈利、罗恩、赫敏:

阿拉戈克昨天夜里死了。哈利和罗恩,你们见过他,知道他

## CHAPTER TWENTY-TWO  After the Burial

> YOU MET HIM, AND YOU KNOW HOW SPECIAL HE WAS. HERMIONE, I KNOW YOU'D HAVE LIKED HIM. IT WOULD MEAN A LOT TO ME IF YOU'D NIP DOWN FOR THE BURIAL LATER THIS EVENING. I'M PLANNING ON DOING IT ROUND DUSK, THAT WAS HIS FAVOURITE TIME OF DAY. I KNOW YOU'RE NOT SUPPOSED TO BE OUT THAT LATE, BUT YOU CAN USE THE CLOAK. WOULDN'T ASK BUT I CAN'T FACE IT ALONE.
> HAGRID

'Look at this,' said Harry, handing the note to Hermione.

'Oh, for heaven's sake,' she said, scanning it quickly and passing it to Ron, who read it through looking increasingly incredulous.

'He's *mental*!' he said furiously. 'That thing told its mates to eat Harry and me! Told them to help themselves! And now Hagrid expects us to go down there and cry over its horrible hairy body!'

'It's not just that,' said Hermione. 'He's asking us to leave the castle at night, and he knows security's a million times tighter and how much trouble we'd be in if we were caught.'

'We've been down to see him by night before,' said Harry.

'Yes, but for something like this?' said Hermione. 'We've risked a lot to help Hagrid out, but after all – Aragog's dead. If it were a question of saving him –'

'– I'd want to go even less,' said Ron firmly. 'You didn't meet him, Hermione. Believe me, being dead will have improved him a lot.'

Harry took the note back and stared down at the inky blotches all over it. Tears had clearly fallen thick and fast upon the parchment ...

'Harry, you *can't* be thinking of going,' said Hermione. 'It's such a pointless thing to get detention for.'

Harry sighed.

'Yeah, I know,' he said. 'I s'pose Hagrid'll have to bury Aragog without us.'

'Yes, he will,' said Hermione, looking relieved. 'Look, Potions will be almost empty this afternoon, with us all off doing our tests ... try and soften Slughorn up a bit then!'

'Fifty-seventh time lucky, you think?' said Harry bitterly.

'Lucky,' said Ron suddenly. 'Harry, that's it – get lucky!'

'What d'you mean?'

## 第22章 葬礼之后

多么特殊。赫敏，我知道你也会喜欢他的。如果你们今晚能来参加葬礼，对我意义很大。我打算黄昏时分举行葬礼，这是一天中他最喜欢的时间。我知道你们不允许那么晚出来，但可以用隐形衣。我本来不想提这个要求，可是我无法独自面对。

海　格

"你看。"哈利把纸条递给了赫敏。

"哦，上帝。"她迅速扫了一遍后递给罗恩，罗恩也读了一遍，脸上露出越来越不敢相信的表情。

"他疯了！"罗恩激烈地说，"那畜生叫它的同伴把哈利和我吃掉！说是随便吃！现在海格却要我们去对着它那恐怖的、毛森森的尸体痛哭！"

"不仅如此，"赫敏说，"他还要我们晚上离开城堡，明知道安保措施已经严了一百万倍，被抓到会有多大的麻烦！"

"我们以前也在夜里去看过他。"哈利说。

"去过，可是为这种事值吗？"赫敏说，"我们为海格冒过很多风险，可是毕竟——阿拉戈克已经死了。如果是为了救它——"

"——我更不想去，"罗恩坚决地说，"你没见过它，赫敏。相信我，它死了还可爱得多。"

哈利拿回纸条，盯着那满纸的墨渍，显然曾有大滴大滴的泪水不断掉在羊皮纸上。

"哈利，你不会打算去吧？"赫敏问，"为这个关禁闭太不值了。"

哈利叹了口气。

"是，我知道，我想海格只能自己安葬阿拉戈克了。"

"就是。"赫敏看上去松了口气，"哎，今天下午魔药课没什么人了，我们都去考试……想办法说服一下斯拉格霍恩吧！"

"你觉得第五十七次会幸运吗？"哈利苦涩地说。

"幸运，"罗恩突然说，"哈利，对了——幸运！"

"你说什么呀？"

## CHAPTER TWENTY-TWO    After the Burial

'Use your lucky potion!'

'Ron, that's – that's it!' said Hermione, sounding stunned. 'Of course! Why didn't I think of it?'

Harry stared at them both. 'Felix Felicis?' he said. 'I dunno ... I was sort of saving it ...'

'What for?' demanded Ron incredulously.

'What on earth is more important than this memory, Harry?' asked Hermione.

Harry did not answer. The thought of that little golden bottle had hovered on the edges of his imagination for some time; vague and unformulated plans that involved Ginny splitting up with Dean, and Ron somehow being happy to see her with a new boyfriend, had been fermenting in the depths of his brain, unacknowledged except during dreams or the twilight time between sleeping and waking ...

'Harry? Are you still with us?' asked Hermione.

'Wha–? Yeah, of course,' he said, pulling himself together. 'Well ... OK. If I can't get Slughorn to talk this afternoon, I'll take some Felix and have another go this evening.'

'That's decided, then,' said Hermione briskly, getting to her feet and performing a graceful pirouette. 'Destination ... determination ... deliberation ...' she murmured.

'Oh, stop that,' Ron begged her, 'I feel sick enough as it is – quick, hide me!'

'It isn't Lavender!' said Hermione impatiently, as another couple of girls appeared in the courtyard and Ron dived behind her.

'Cool,' said Ron, peering over Hermione's shoulder to check. 'Blimey, they don't look happy, do they?'

'They're the Montgomery sisters and of course they don't look happy, didn't you hear what happened to their little brother?' said Hermione.

'I'm losing track of what's happening to everyone's relatives, to be honest,' said Ron.

'Well, their brother was attacked by a werewolf. The rumour is that their mother refused to help the Death Eaters. Anyway, the boy was only five and he died in St Mungo's, they couldn't save him.'

'He died?' repeated Harry, shocked. 'But surely werewolves don't kill, they just turn you into one of them?'

'They sometimes kill,' said Ron, who looked unusually grave now. 'I've heard of it happening when the werewolf gets carried away.'

## 第22章 葬礼之后

"用幸运药水!"

"罗恩,对——对啊!"赫敏似乎惊呆了,"当然!我怎么没想到呢?"

哈利瞪着他们俩。"福灵剂?我不知道……我还想留着呢……"

"留着干什么?"罗恩不解地问。

"哈利,还有什么比这个记忆更重要的吗?"赫敏问。

哈利没有回答。那个小金瓶已在他脑际萦绕了一段时间,一些模糊而不成形的想法(金妮和迪安分手,罗恩高兴地看到她有新男友)在他的脑海深处酝酿,只有在梦中或半梦半醒的蒙眬时刻才会意识到……

"哈利?你在听吗?"赫敏问。

"什——?是,当然,"他回过神来,"嗯……好吧。如果今天下午还不能让斯拉格霍恩开口,我晚上就喝一些福灵剂去再试一次。"

"那就这么定了。"赫敏轻快地说,她站了起来,踮起脚尖做了个优雅的旋转动作,一边念念有词,"目标……决心……从容……"

"哦,停止,"罗恩央求道,"我已经够晕的了——快,掩护我!"

"不是拉文德!"赫敏不耐烦地说,这时又有一对女孩出现在院子里,罗恩急忙躲到她身后。

"太好了。"罗恩说着从赫敏肩头偷偷看了一眼,"嘿,她们好像不大开心,是不是?"

"她们是蒙哥马利姐妹,当然不开心了,你没听说她们小弟弟的事吗?"赫敏说。

"说实话,我已经不了解别人家的情况了。"罗恩说。

"她们的弟弟被狼人咬了,据说是因为她们的母亲拒绝帮助食死徒。总之,那男孩才五岁,死在圣芒戈医院了,他们救不了他。"

"死了?"哈利震惊地问,"可狼人不杀人的啊,他们不是只会把你变成狼人吗?"

"有时也杀人,"罗恩表情异常严峻,"我听说过狼人失去控制的时候就会。"

## CHAPTER TWENTY-TWO  After the Burial

'What was the werewolf's name?' said Harry quickly.

'Well, the rumour is that it was that Fenrir Greyback,' said Hermione.

'I knew it – the maniac who likes attacking kids, the one Lupin told me about!' said Harry angrily.

Hermione looked at him bleakly.

'Harry, you've got to get that memory,' she said. 'It's all about stopping Voldemort, isn't it? These dreadful things that are happening are all down to him ...'

The bell rang overhead in the castle and both Hermione and Ron jumped to their feet, looking terrified.

'You'll do fine,' Harry told them both, as they headed towards the Entrance Hall to meet the rest of the people taking their Apparition test. 'Good luck.'

'And you too!' said Hermione with a significant look, as Harry headed off to the dungeons.

There were only three of them in Potions that afternoon: Harry, Ernie and Draco Malfoy.

'All too young to Apparate just yet?' said Slughorn genially. 'Not turned seventeen yet?'

They shook their heads.

'Ah well,' said Slughorn cheerily, 'as we're so few, we'll do something *fun*. I want you all to brew me up something amusing!'

'That sounds good, sir,' said Ernie sycophantically, rubbing his hands together. Malfoy, on the other hand, did not crack a smile.

'What do you mean, something "amusing"?' he said irritably.

'Oh, surprise me,' said Slughorn airily.

Malfoy opened his copy of *Advanced Potion-Making* with a sulky expression. It could not have been plainer that he thought this lesson was a waste of time. Undoubtedly, Harry thought, watching him over the top of his own book, Malfoy was begrudging the time he could otherwise be spending in the Room of Requirement.

Was it his imagination, or did Malfoy, like Tonks, look thinner? Certainly he looked paler; his skin still had that greyish tinge, probably because he so rarely saw daylight these days. But there was no air of smugness, or excitement, or superiority; none of the swagger that he had had on the Hogwarts Express, when he had boasted openly of the mission he had been given by Voldemort ... there could be only one conclusion, in Harry's opinion: the mission, whatever it was, was going badly.

## 第22章 葬礼之后

"那狼人叫什么?"哈利忙问。

"听说是那个芬里尔·格雷伯克。"赫敏说。

"我知道——那个喜欢袭击小孩的疯子。卢平跟我说过!"哈利愤怒地说。

赫敏黯然地看着他。

"哈利,你必须搞到那段记忆。"赫敏说,"这都是为了阻止伏地魔,是不是?现在发生的这些可怕的事都要归到他头上……"

城堡里的钟声响了,赫敏和罗恩跳了起来,显得很害怕。

"你们没问题,"他们俩走向门厅,去跟其他参加幻影显形考试的学生会合时,哈利说,"祝你们好运!"

"你也是!"赫敏意味深长地看了他一眼,哈利朝地下教室走去。

那天下午魔药课上只有三个学生:哈利、厄尼和德拉科·马尔福。

"你们都不到幻影显形的年龄?"斯拉格霍恩和蔼可亲地问,"还没有满十七岁?"

三人点了点头。

"那好,"斯拉格霍恩快活地说,"既然人数这么少,我们来做点儿好玩的,我要你们每人给我配一点有趣的东西!"

"听起来很棒,先生。"厄尼搓着手奉承道。马尔福却没有一丝笑容。

"什么意思,'有趣'的东西?"他烦躁地问。

"哦,给我一个惊喜。"斯拉格霍恩轻松地答道。

马尔福沉着脸打开了他的《高级魔药制作》,他显然认为这门课是白耽误工夫。哈利越过自己的课本偷偷地看着他,想道,马尔福无疑是不愿意浪费本来可以去有求必应屋的时间。

是幻觉吗,马尔福怎么似乎像唐克斯一样变瘦了?他无疑是更加苍白了,皮肤仍带着那种淡灰色,也许是由于他这些天很少见阳光。他没有了得意、兴奋或高傲的神气,也全无在霍格沃茨列车上公开吹嘘伏地魔给他的任务时那种趾高气扬,在哈利想来,这只能有一个结论:那个任务不管是什么,都进行得不顺利。

## CHAPTER TWENTY-TWO    After the Burial

Cheered by this thought, Harry skimmed through his copy of *Advanced Potion-Making* and found a heavily corrected Half-Blood Prince's version of An Elixir to Induce Euphoria, which seemed not only to meet Slughorn's instructions, but which might (Harry's heart leapt as the thought struck him) put Slughorn into such a good mood that he would be prepared to hand over that memory if Harry could persuade him to taste some …

'Well, now, this looks absolutely wonderful,' said Slughorn clapping his hands together an hour and a half later, as he stared down into the sunshine-yellow contents of Harry's cauldron. 'Euphoria, I take it? And what's that I smell? Mmmm … you've added just a sprig of peppermint, haven't you? Unorthodox, but what a stroke of inspiration, Harry. Of course, that would tend to counterbalance the occasional side-effects of excessive singing and nose-tweaking … I really don't know where you get these brainwaves, my boy … unless –'

Harry pushed the Half-Blood Prince's book deeper into his bag with his foot.

'– it's just your mother's genes coming out in you!'

'Oh … yeah, maybe,' said Harry, relieved.

Ernie was looking rather grumpy; determined to outshine Harry for once, he had most rashly invented his own potion, which had curdled and formed a kind of purple dumpling at the bottom of his cauldron. Malfoy was already packing up, sour-faced; Slughorn had pronounced his Hiccoughing Solution merely 'passable'.

The bell rang and both Ernie and Malfoy left at once.

'Sir,' Harry began, but Slughorn immediately glanced over his shoulder; when he saw that the room was empty but for himself and Harry he hurried away as fast as he could.

'Professor – Professor, don't you want to taste my po–?' called Harry desperately.

But Slughorn had gone. Disappointed, Harry emptied the cauldron, packed up his things, left the dungeon and walked slowly back upstairs to the common room.

Ron and Hermione returned in the late afternoon.

'Harry!' cried Hermione as she climbed through the portrait hole. 'Harry, I passed!'

'Well done!' he said. 'And Ron?'

'He – he *just* failed,' whispered Hermione, as Ron came slouching into the room looking most morose. 'It was really unlucky, a tiny thing, the examiner just spotted that he'd left half an eyebrow behind … how did it go with Slughorn?'

## 第22章 葬礼之后

受了这个念头的鼓舞,哈利翻看他的《高级魔药制作》,找到一个被混血王子改动了很多的名为欢欣剂的魔药,它似乎不仅符合斯拉格霍恩的要求,而且(想到这儿,哈利的心狂跳起来)如果能让他尝上一点的话,或许可以使他心花怒放,交出记忆……

"啊,看上去妙极了。"一个半小时后,斯拉格霍恩盯着哈利坩埚中阳光般金黄的液体拍手叫道,"欢欣剂,是不是?那是什么味道?嗯……你加了小小一枝椒薄荷,是不是?不大正统,然而这是多么天才的灵感,哈利。当然啦,这可以抵消偶尔引起的唱歌太多和拧鼻子等副作用。我真不知道你从哪儿得到的这些奇思妙想,我的孩子……除非——"

哈利用脚把混血王子的课本往书包深处塞了塞。

"——是你母亲的基因在你身上显出来了!"

"哦……也许吧。"哈利松了口气。

厄尼一脸怨气,他决心要胜过哈利一次,急急忙忙发明了自己的魔药,可它却在坩埚底凝结为紫色的汤团。马尔福已经板着脸收拾好书包,斯拉格霍恩说他的打嗝药水只是"还过得去"。

下课铃一响,厄尼和马尔福立刻就走了。

"先生,"哈利开口道,但斯拉格霍恩左右望望,看到屋里只剩下了他和哈利,赶紧用最快的速度溜掉了。

"教授——教授,你不想尝尝我的魔——?"哈利绝望地问。

但斯拉格霍恩已经走了。哈利失望地倒空坩埚,收拾好东西,离开了地下教室,慢慢地上楼回公共休息室了。

罗恩和赫敏下午很晚才回来。

"哈利!"赫敏钻过肖像洞口时叫道,"哈利,我考过了!"

"好样的!罗恩呢?"

"他——他只差一点儿。"赫敏小声说。罗恩无精打采地钻了过来,看上去颓丧极了。"真是倒霉,因为一丁点大的事——考官刚好看到他落下了半根眉毛……斯拉格霍恩怎么样?"

## CHAPTER TWENTY-TWO    After the Burial

'No joy,' said Harry, as Ron joined them. 'Bad luck, mate, but you'll pass next time – we can take it together.'

'Yeah, I s'pose,' said Ron grumpily. 'But *half an eyebrow*! Like that matters!'

'I know,' said Hermione soothingly, 'it does seem really harsh ...'

They spent most of their dinner roundly abusing the Apparition examiner and Ron looked fractionally more cheerful by the time they set off back to the common room, now discussing the continuing problem of Slughorn and the memory.

'So, Harry – you going to use the Felix Felicis or what?' Ron demanded.

'Yeah, I s'pose I'd better,' said Harry. 'I don't reckon I'll need all of it, not twelve hours' worth, it can't take all night ... I'll just take a mouthful. Two or three hours should do it.'

'It's a great feeling when you take it,' said Ron reminiscently. 'Like you can't do anything wrong.'

'What are you talking about?' said Hermione, laughing. 'You've never taken any!'

'Yeah, but I *thought* I had, didn't I?' said Ron, as though explaining the obvious. 'Same difference really ...'

As they had only just seen Slughorn enter the Great Hall and knew that he liked to take time over meals, they lingered for a while in the common room, the plan being that Harry should go to Slughorn's office once the teacher had had time to get back there. When the sun had sunk to the level of the treetops in the Forbidden Forest they decided the moment had come, and, after checking carefully that Neville, Dean and Seamus were all in the common room, sneaked up to the boys' dormitory.

Harry took out the rolled-up socks at the bottom of his trunk and extracted the tiny, gleaming bottle.

'Well, here goes,' said Harry, and he raised the little bottle and took a carefully measured gulp.

'What does it feel like?' whispered Hermione.

Harry did not answer for a moment. Then, slowly but surely, an exhilarating sense of infinite opportunity stole through him; he felt as though he could have done anything, anything at all ... and getting the memory from Slughorn seemed suddenly not only possible, but positively easy ...

He got to his feet smiling, brimful of confidence.

## 第22章 葬礼之后

"没戏。"这时罗恩走了过来,哈利说,"不走运啊,伙计。但你下次一定能通过——我们俩可以一起考。"

"我想是吧。"罗恩郁闷地说,"就半根眉毛!好像多要紧似的!"

"我理解,"赫敏安慰道,"是很苛刻……"

他们吃晚饭的大部分时间都在骂幻影显形考官,后来走回公共休息室时,罗恩的心情似乎略微好了一点儿,话题又转到了斯拉格霍恩和他的记忆这个老问题上。

"那,哈利——你要不要用福灵剂?"罗恩问。

"嗯,我想最好用一下。"哈利说,"我觉得不需要全用掉,因为要不了十二个小时,要不了一个通宵……我只要喝一口,两三小时应该就够了。"

"那种感觉美妙极了,"罗恩怀念地说,"好像你干什么都不会出错。"

"你说什么呀?"赫敏笑道,"你又没喝过!"

"是啊,可我以为自己喝过,是不是?"罗恩煞有介事地说,"其实差不多……"

他们刚才看到斯拉格霍恩进了礼堂,知道他喜欢慢慢用餐,就在公共休息室等了一会儿,计划是等斯拉格霍恩回去之后哈利就立刻去他的办公室。

太阳落到禁林的树梢上时,他们判断时间到了,看准纳威、迪安和西莫都在休息室里,便偷偷溜进了男生宿舍。

哈利拿出箱底的袜子,抽出了一个闪闪发光的小瓶子。

"找到了。"哈利举起小瓶,掐好量喝了一口。

"感觉如何?"赫敏小声问。

哈利一时没有回答,接着,慢慢地但是确确实实地,一种无比振奋的感觉流向全身,仿佛有无限的机会摆在面前。他感到自己能做任何事,什么都不在话下……从斯拉格霍恩那里搞到记忆突然好像不仅可能,而且简直是轻而易举……

他微笑着站了起来,充满自信。

## CHAPTER TWENTY-TWO  After the Burial

'Excellent,' he said. 'Really excellent. Right ... I'm going down to Hagrid's.'

'What?' said Ron and Hermione together, looking aghast.

'No, Harry – you've got to go and see Slughorn, remember?' said Hermione.

'No,' said Harry confidently. 'I'm going to Hagrid's, I've got a good feeling about going to Hagrid's.'

'You've got a good feeling about burying a giant spider?' asked Ron, looking stunned.

'Yeah,' said Harry, pulling his Invisibility Cloak out of his bag. 'I feel like it's the place to be tonight, you know what I mean?'

'No,' said Ron and Hermione together, both looking positively alarmed now.

'This *is* Felix Felicis, I suppose?' said Hermione anxiously, holding up the bottle to the light. 'You haven't got another little bottle full of – I don't know –'

'Essence of Insanity?' suggested Ron, as Harry swung his Cloak over his shoulders.

Harry laughed and Ron and Hermione looked even more alarmed.

'Trust me,' he said. 'I know what I'm doing ... or at least ...' he strolled confidently to the door, 'Felix does.'

He pulled the Invisibility Cloak over his head and set off down the stairs, Ron and Hermione hurrying along behind him. At the foot of the stairs Harry slid through the open door.

'What were you doing up there with *her*?' shrieked Lavender Brown, staring right through Harry at Ron and Hermione emerging together from the boys' dormitories. Harry heard Ron spluttering behind him as he darted across the room away from them.

Getting through the portrait hole was simple; as he approached it, Ginny and Dean came through it and Harry was able to slip between them. As he did so, he brushed accidentally against Ginny.

'*Don't* push me, please, Dean,' she said, sounding annoyed. 'You're always doing that, I can get through perfectly well on my own ...'

The portrait swung closed behind Harry, but not before he had heard Dean make an angry retort ... his feeling of elation increasing, Harry strode off through the castle. He did not have to creep along, for he met nobody on his way, but this did not surprise him in the slightest: this evening, he was the luckiest person at Hogwarts.

Why he knew that going to Hagrid's was the right thing to do, he had no

## 第22章 葬礼之后

"妙极了,真是妙极了。好……我要去海格那儿。"

"什么?"罗恩和赫敏大吃一惊。

"不,哈利——你要去见斯拉格霍恩,还记得吗?"赫敏说。

"不,"哈利自信地说,"我要去海格那儿,我对这件事感觉很好。"

"你对埋葬一只巨蜘蛛感觉很好?"罗恩惊愕地问。

"对,"哈利从包里抽出隐形衣,"我感觉今天晚上应该去那儿,你懂我的意思吗?"

"不懂。"罗恩和赫敏一起说,两人现在都很惊恐。

"这是福灵剂吗?"赫敏担心地问,一边把瓶子举到亮光前,"你不会还有一瓶——什么——"

"疯狂素?"罗恩猜测道,这时哈利已经把隐形衣披到了肩上。

哈利哈哈大笑,他们俩好像更害怕了。

"相信我,我知道自己在干什么……或至少……"他自信地走向门口,"福灵剂知道。"

他把隐形衣拉到头上,往楼下走去,罗恩、赫敏紧跟在后面。下了楼梯,哈利从敞开的门里溜了出去。

"你跟她在上面干什么?"拉文德·布朗尖叫道,目光越过哈利盯着从男生宿舍下来的罗恩和赫敏。哈利听到罗恩结结巴巴地分辩着,他快步穿过房间,甩掉了他们。

过肖像洞口很简单,他走近时,金妮和迪安正好爬进来。哈利从他们两人之间钻了过去,不小心碰了金妮一下。

"请别碰我,迪安,"金妮说,语气有些恼火,"你老是这样,我自己能爬进去……"

肖像在哈利身后旋上,但他听到迪安在生气地反驳……他的快感在增强。哈利在城堡里大步流星地走着,不需要蹑手蹑脚,因为路上没有碰到一个人,但这一点也不令他奇怪。今晚他是霍格沃茨最幸运的人。

为什么相信自己该去海格那儿,他也不知道,仿佛魔药一次只能

## CHAPTER TWENTY-TWO    After the Burial

idea. It was as though the potion was illuminating a few steps of the path at a time: he could not see the final destination, he could not see where Slughorn came in, but he knew that he was going the right way to get that memory. When he reached the Entrance Hall he saw that Filch had forgotten to lock the front door. Beaming, Harry threw it open and breathed in the smell of clean air and grass for a moment before walking down the steps into the dusk.

It was when he reached the bottom step that it occurred to him how very pleasant it would be to pass the vegetable patch on his walk to Hagrid's. It was not strictly on the way, but it seemed clear to Harry that this was a whim on which he should act, so he directed his feet immediately towards the vegetable patch where he was pleased, but not altogether surprised, to find Professor Slughorn in conversation with Professor Sprout. Harry lurked behind a low stone wall, feeling at peace with the world and listening to their conversation.

'... I do thank you for taking the time, Pomona,' Slughorn was saying courteously. 'Most authorities agree that they are at their most efficacious if picked at twilight.'

'Oh, I quite agree,' said Professor Sprout warmly. 'That enough for you?'

'Plenty, plenty,' said Slughorn, who, Harry saw, was carrying an armful of leafy plants. 'This should allow for a few leaves for each of my third-years, and some to spare if anybody overstews them ... well, good evening to you, and many thanks again!'

Professor Sprout headed off into the gathering darkness in the direction of her greenhouses and Slughorn directed his steps to the spot where Harry stood, invisible.

Seized with an immediate desire to reveal himself, Harry pulled off the Cloak with a flourish.

'Good evening, Professor.'

'Merlin's beard, Harry, you made me jump,' said Slughorn, stopping dead in his tracks and looking wary. 'How did you get out of the castle?'

'I think Filch must've forgotten to lock the doors,' said Harry cheerfully, and was delighted to see Slughorn scowl.

'I'll be reporting that man, he's more concerned about litter than proper security if you ask me ... but why are you out here, Harry?'

'Well, sir, it's Hagrid,' said Harry, who knew that the right thing to do just now was to tell the truth. 'He's pretty upset ... but you won't tell anyone, Professor? I don't want trouble for him ...'

## 第22章 葬礼之后

照亮几步,他看不到最后会通向哪里,看不到斯拉格霍恩会在哪儿出现,但他知道自己是在能搞到记忆的正确道路上。到了门厅,哈利看到费尔奇忘了锁大门,他微笑着打开门,呼吸着清新的空气和青草的气味,然后下台阶走入了暮色中。

到了台阶最底下,他才想起途中到菜地里走走会是多么惬意。虽然不完全顺路,但哈利清楚地感到他应该听从这一冲动。于是他立刻迈动双脚朝菜地方向走去。到了那里,他高兴但并不十分惊讶地发现斯拉格霍恩教授在跟斯普劳特教授说话。哈利躲在低矮的石墙后面,心境平和地聆听着他们的对话。

"……真是谢谢你费心了,波莫娜,"斯拉格霍恩客气地说,"多数权威认为此药在黄昏时采摘药效最佳。"

"哦,我同意,"斯普劳特热情地说,"够了吗?"

"足够,足够,"斯拉格霍恩连声道谢,哈利看见他抱了一大捧多叶植物,"我的三年级学生每人都可分到几片,还能余下一些,防止有人煮过头……好,祝你晚安,再次感谢!"

斯普劳特教授在渐浓的暮色中朝温室的方向走去,斯拉格霍恩迈步朝哈利隐身的地方踱了过来。

哈利突然感到一种想要现身的冲动,一把扯下了隐形衣。

"晚上好,教授。"

"梅林的胡子啊,哈利,你吓了我一跳。"斯拉格霍恩猛然止步,警惕地看着他,"你怎么从城堡里出来了?"

"我想费尔奇忘记锁门了。"哈利愉快地说,他高兴地看到斯拉格霍恩皱起了眉头。

"我要揭发那个人,依我看他更关心垃圾而不是师生的安全……可你为什么在这儿呢,哈利?"

"哦,先生,是海格,"哈利知道现在应该实话实说,"他很难过……你不会告诉别人吧,教授?我不想给他惹麻烦……"

## CHAPTER TWENTY-TWO · After the Burial

Slughorn's curiosity was evidently aroused.

'Well, I can't promise that,' he said gruffly. 'But I know that Dumbledore trusts Hagrid to the hilt, so I'm sure he can't be up to anything very dreadful ...'

'Well, it's this giant spider, he's had it for years ... it lived in the Forest ... it could talk and everything –'

'I heard rumours there were Acromantula in the Forest,' said Slughorn softly, looking over at the mass of black trees. 'It's true, then?'

'Yes,' said Harry. 'But this one, Aragog, the first one Hagrid ever got, it died last night. He's devastated. He wants company while he buries it and I said I'd go.'

'Touching, touching,' said Slughorn absent-mindedly, his large droopy eyes fixed upon the distant lights of Hagrid's cabin. 'But Acromantula venom is very valuable ... if the beast has only just died it might not yet have dried out ... of course, I wouldn't want to do anything insensitive if Hagrid is upset ... but if there were any way to procure some ... I mean, it's almost impossible to get venom from an Acromantula while it's alive ...'

Slughorn seemed to be talking more to himself than Harry now.

'... seems an awful waste not to collect it ... might get a hundred Galleons a pint ... to be frank, my salary is not large ...'

And now Harry saw clearly what was to be done.

'Well,' he said, with a most convincing hesitancy, 'well, if you wanted to come, Professor, Hagrid would probably be really pleased ... give Aragog a better send-off, you know ...'

'Yes, of course,' said Slughorn, his eyes now gleaming with enthusiasm. 'I tell you what, Harry, I'll meet you down there with a bottle or two ... we'll drink the poor beast's – well – not health – but we'll send it off in style, anyway, once it's buried. And I'll change my tie, this one is a little exuberant for the occasion ...'

He bustled back into the castle, and Harry sped off to Hagrid's, delighted with himself.

'Yeh came,' croaked Hagrid, when he opened the door and saw Harry emerging from the Invisibility Cloak in front of him.

'Yeah – Ron and Hermione couldn't, though,' said Harry. 'They're really sorry.'

'Don' – don' matter ... he'd've bin touched yeh're here, though, Harry ...'

## 第22章 葬礼之后

斯拉格霍恩的好奇心显然被勾起来了。

"这个，我不能保证，"他粗声说，"但我知道邓布利多对海格深信不疑，所以我相信海格不会做太可怕的……"

"哦，是那只巨蜘蛛，海格养了好多年的……它住在林子里……会说话，会做好多事——"

"我也曾听说林子里有八眼巨蛛。"斯拉格霍恩望着黑森森的树林，轻声说，"这么说是真的？"

"对。"哈利说，"这一只，阿拉戈克，是海格养的第一只，它昨天夜里死了。海格非常难过，他希望有人陪他埋葬阿拉戈克，我说我去。"

"令人感动，很感人。"斯拉格霍恩心不在焉地说，那双眼皮向下耷拉的大眼睛盯着远处海格小屋的灯光，"八眼巨蛛的毒汁是非常珍贵的……如果那畜生刚死，毒汁可能还没干……当然，如果海格不高兴，我不想冒昧。但如果有办法搞到一些……要知道，从活的八眼巨蛛身上搞到毒汁几乎是不可能的……"

斯拉格霍恩更像是在自言自语。

"……不采集它似乎太浪费了……也许一品脱能值一百加隆呢……老实说，我的薪水不高……"

现在哈利看清该做什么了。

"嗯，"他装得很像地犹豫了一会儿，说道，"教授，如果你想去，海格可能会很高兴的……可以更隆重地给阿拉戈克送行……"

"是的，当然，"斯拉格霍恩说，他的眼睛现在闪着热切的光，"好吧，哈利，我带上一两瓶酒到那里跟你会合……我们为那可怜的畜生——不是祝寿——而是在下葬之后好好为它送行。我去换一下领带，这条太花哨了点儿……"

他匆匆跑回城堡。哈利加快脚步往海格那儿走去，对自己很满意。

"你来了。"海格打开门，看到哈利掀开隐形衣出现在他面前，他声音沙哑地说。

"是啊——罗恩和赫敏来不了，他们很抱歉。"

"不——不要紧……但你来了他会很感动的，哈利……"

## CHAPTER TWENTY-TWO  After the Burial

Hagrid gave a great sob. He had made himself a black armband out of what looked like a rag dipped in boot polish and his eyes were puffy, red and swollen. Harry patted him consolingly on the elbow, which was the highest point of Hagrid he could easily reach.

'Where are we burying him?' he asked. 'The Forest?'

'Blimey, no,' said Hagrid, wiping his streaming eyes on the bottom of his shirt. 'The other spiders won' let me anywhere near their webs now Aragog's gone. Turns out it was on'y on his orders they didn' eat me! Can yeh believe that, Harry?'

The honest answer was 'yes'; Harry recalled with painful ease the scene when he and Ron had come face to face with the Acromantula: they had been quite clear that Aragog was the only thing that stopped them eating Hagrid.

'Never bin an area o' the Forest I couldn' go before!' said Hagrid, shaking his head. 'It wasn' easy, gettin' Aragog's body out o' there, I can tell yeh – they usually eat their dead, see ... but I wanted ter give 'im a nice burial ... a proper send-off ...'

He broke into sobs again and Harry resumed the patting of his elbow, saying as he did so (for the potion seemed to indicate that it was the right thing to do), 'Professor Slughorn met me coming down here, Hagrid.'

'Not in trouble, are yeh?' said Hagrid, looking up, alarmed. 'Yeh shouldn' be outta the castle in the evenin', I know it, it's my fault –'

'No, no, when he heard what I was doing he said he'd like to come and pay his last respects to Aragog too,' said Harry. 'He's gone to change into something more suitable, I think ... and he said he'd bring some bottles so we can drink to Aragog's memory ...'

'Did he?' said Hagrid, looking both astonished and touched. 'Tha's – tha's righ' nice of him, tha' is, an' not turnin' you in, either. I've never really had a lot ter do with Horace Slughorn before ... comin' ter see old Aragog off, though, eh? Well ... he'd've liked that, Aragog would ...'

Harry thought privately that what Aragog would have liked most about Slughorn was the ample amount of edible flesh he provided, but he merely moved to the rear window of Hagrid's hut where he saw the rather horrible sight of the enormous dead spider lying on its back outside, its legs curled and tangled.

'Are we going to bury him here, Hagrid, in your garden?'

'Jus' beyond the pumpkin patch, I thought,' said Hagrid in a choked voice. 'I've already dug the – you know – grave. Jus' thought we'd say a few nice things over him – happy memories, yeh know –'

## 第22章 葬礼之后

海格大声抽泣了一下。他给自己做了个黑袖套，好像是用破布条蘸了鞋油做的。他眼睛又红又肿。哈利安慰地拍拍海格的胳膊肘，这是他不用费劲可以够到的最高部位。

"在哪儿安葬他？"哈利问，"林子里？"

"老天，不行。"海格说着用衬衫角擦了擦泪眼，"阿拉戈克一死，其他蜘蛛就不肯让我靠近他们的网。看来他们只是因为他的命令才没有吃掉我！你能相信吗，哈利？"

诚实的回答是"相信"，哈利还痛苦而清晰地记得他和罗恩遭遇那只八眼巨蛛的情景，他们很清楚阿拉戈克是阻止那些巨蛛吃掉海格的唯一原因。

"以前林子里从来没有我不能去的地方！"海格摇头道，"不容易啊，把阿拉戈克的尸体搬出来。跟你说吧——他们一般会把尸体吃掉……可是我想给他一个体面的葬礼……好好送行……"

他又抽泣起来，哈利一边拍着他的胳膊肘一边说（魔药似乎暗示正该这么做）："海格，我在路上碰到斯拉格霍恩教授了。"

"没有麻烦吧？"海格说着惊恐地抬起头，"我知道你不该晚上离开城堡，是我的错——"

"不，不，他听了我来做什么之后，说他也想来跟阿拉戈克告个别。他去换衣服了，我想……他还说要带点酒来祭奠阿拉戈克……"

"是吗？"海格说，又是惊讶又是感动，"那——那他真好，而且没有告发你。我跟霍拉斯·斯拉格霍恩从来没多少交情……但他要来送老阿拉戈克？嗯……阿拉戈克会喜欢的……"

哈利暗想，阿拉戈克最喜欢的可能是斯拉格霍恩的一身肥肉。他走到后窗口，看到了一幕相当恐怖的情景，外面朝天躺着一只巨大的死蜘蛛，蛛腿弯曲纠结。

"就葬在这儿吗，海格，在你的花园里？"

"南瓜地后面，我想。"海格哽噎道，"我已经挖了——坟墓。只是觉得我们应该说点什么——美好的回忆……"

## CHAPTER TWENTY-TWO   After the Burial

His voice quivered and broke. There was a knock on the door and he turned to answer it, blowing his nose on his great spotted handkerchief as he did so. Slughorn hurried over the threshold, several bottles in his arms, and wearing a sombre black cravat.

'Hagrid,' he said, in a deep, grave voice. 'So very sorry to hear of your loss.'

'Tha's very nice of yeh,' said Hagrid. 'Thanks a lot. An' thanks fer not givin' Harry detention, neither ...'

'Wouldn't have dreamed of it,' said Slughorn. 'Sad night, sad night ... where is the poor creature?'

'Out here,' said Hagrid in a shaky voice. 'Shall we – shall we do it, then?'

The three of them stepped out into the back garden. The moon was glistening palely through the trees and its rays mingled with the light spilling from Hagrid's window to illuminate Aragog's body lying on the edge of a massive pit, beside a ten-foot-high mound of freshly dug earth.

'Magnificent,' said Slughorn, approaching the spider's head, where eight milky eyes stared blankly at the sky and two huge, curved pincers shone, motionless, in the moonlight. Harry thought he heard the tinkle of bottles as Slughorn bent over the pincers, apparently examining the enormous hairy head.

'It's not ev'ryone appreciates how beau'iful they are,' said Hagrid to Slughorn's back, tears leaking from the corners of his crinkled eyes. 'I didn' know yeh were int'rested in creatures like Aragog, Horace.'

'Interested? My dear Hagrid, I revere them,' said Slughorn, stepping back from the body. Harry saw the glint of a bottle disappear beneath his cloak, though Hagrid, mopping his eyes once more, noticed nothing. 'Now ... shall we proceed to the burial?'

Hagrid nodded and moved forwards. He heaved the gigantic spider into his arms and, with an enormous grunt, rolled it into the dark pit. It hit the bottom with a rather horrible, crunchy thud. Hagrid started to cry again.

'Of course, it's difficult for you, who knew him best,' said Slughorn, who, like Harry, could reach no higher than Hagrid's elbow, but patted it all the same. 'Why don't I say a few words?'

He must have got a lot of good-quality venom from Aragog, Harry thought, for Slughorn wore a satisfied smirk as he stepped up to the rim of the pit and said, in a slow, impressive voice, 'Farewell, Aragog, king of arachnids, whose long and faithful friendship those who knew you won't

## 第22章 葬礼之后

他的声音颤抖着中断了。敲门声响起，他转身去开门，一边用斑点图案的大手帕擤着鼻子。斯拉格霍恩匆匆跨进门，怀里抱着几个酒瓶，脖子上戴了一条肃穆的黑色领巾。

"海格，"他用低沉庄重的语气说，"我很难过。"

"你太好了，"海格说，"非常感谢，也谢谢你不关哈利的禁闭……"

"绝不会那么做的。"斯拉格霍恩说，"悲哀的夜晚，悲哀的夜晚……那可怜的动物在哪儿？"

"外面，"海格用颤抖的声音说，"我们——我们开始吗？"

三人走进了后花园，月亮在树缝间发出惨淡的光，与海格窗口的灯光混合在一起，照着躺在一个大坑边上的阿拉戈克的尸体，旁边是一堆十英尺高的新土。

"真漂亮。"斯拉格霍恩说着走近蜘蛛的脑袋，那上面八只乳白色的眼睛茫然地盯着苍穹，两只弯曲的大螯在月光中一动不动。斯拉格霍恩在大螯前弯下腰，似乎在察看那毛森森的大脑袋，哈利仿佛听到了瓶子的叮当声。

"不是所有的人都能欣赏他们的美。"海格对着斯拉格霍恩的后背说，眼泪从布满皱纹的眼角流了下来，"我不知道你对阿拉戈克这样的动物感兴趣，霍拉斯。"

"感兴趣？亲爱的海格，我敬畏他们。"斯拉格霍恩从尸体前退回来，哈利看见瓶子的反光一闪，隐没在他的斗篷里，海格又在那里擦眼睛，对此全未察觉，"现在……开始葬礼吧？"

海格点点头，走上前去，拖起巨蜘蛛，大吼一声，把它滚进了黑坑。尸体撞到坑底时发出一声可怕的嘎吱吱的巨响，海格又哭了起来。

"当然，你受不了，因为你最了解他。"斯拉格霍恩说，他像哈利一样，也只够得到海格的胳膊肘，但还是拍了拍他，"我说两句吧。"

哈利想，斯拉格霍恩一定从阿拉戈克身上搞到了很多优质毒汁，因为他往坑边走去时脸上带着满意的微笑。斯拉格霍恩用缓慢、庄严的语调说："别了，阿拉戈克，蜘蛛之王，认识你的人不会忘记你长久忠诚的友谊！虽然你的肉体会腐烂，你的精神将留在你森林之家那片

### CHAPTER TWENTY-TWO    After the Burial

forget! Though your body will decay, your spirit lingers on in the quiet, web-spun places of your Forest home. May your many-eyed descendants ever flourish and your human friends find solace for the loss they have sustained.'

'Tha' was ... tha' was ... beau'iful!' howled Hagrid and he collapsed on to the compost heap, crying harder than ever.

'There, there,' said Slughorn, waving his wand so that the huge pile of earth rose up and then fell, with a muffled sort of crash, on to the dead spider, forming a smooth mound. 'Let's get inside and have a drink. Get on his other side, Harry ... that's it ... up you come, Hagrid ... well done ...'

They deposited Hagrid in a chair at the table. Fang, who had been skulking in his basket during the burial, now came padding softly across to them and put his heavy head into Harry's lap as usual. Slughorn uncorked one of the bottles of wine he had brought.

'I have had it *all* tested for poison,' he assured Harry, pouring most of the first bottle into one of Hagrid's bucket-sized mugs and handing it to Hagrid. 'Had a house-elf taste every bottle after what happened to your poor friend Rupert.'

Harry saw, in his mind's eye, the expression on Hermione's face if she ever heard about this abuse of house-elves, and decided never to mention it to her.

'One for Harry ...' said Slughorn, dividing a second bottle between two mugs, '... and one for me. Well,' he raised his mug high, 'to Aragog.'

'Aragog,' said Harry and Hagrid together.

Both Slughorn and Hagrid drank deeply. Harry, however, with the way ahead illuminated for him by Felix Felicis, knew that he must not drink, so he merely pretended to take a gulp and then set the mug back on the table before him.

'I had him from an egg, yeh know,' said Hagrid morosely. 'Tiny little thing he was when he hatched. 'Bout the size of a Pekinese.'

'Sweet,' said Slughorn.

'Used ter keep him in a cupboard up at the school until ... well ...'

Hagrid's face darkened and Harry knew why: Tom Riddle had contrived to have Hagrid thrown out of school, blamed for opening the Chamber of Secrets. Slughorn, however, did not seem to be listening; he was looking up at the ceiling, from which a number of brass pots hung, and also a long, silky skein of bright white hair.

'That's never unicorn hair, Hagrid?'

## 第22章 葬礼之后

静谧的、蛛网交织的所在。愿你多眼的后代繁衍不息，也愿你的人类朋友在哀痛中得到慰藉。"

"说得……说得……太美了！"海格号叫一声，倒在肥料堆上，哭得更凶了。

"好了，好了，"斯拉格霍恩说着一挥魔杖，那一大堆泥土升了起来，沉闷地压在死蜘蛛身上，形成了一个光滑的土丘，"我们进去喝一杯吧。哈利，扶着他那一边……对了……起来，海格……好……"

他们把海格扶到桌前的一把椅子上，葬礼中一直躲在篮筐里的牙牙现在轻轻走过来，像平时那样把沉重的脑袋搁到哈利的腿上。斯拉格霍恩打开了一瓶他带来的酒。

"我全都检查过了，没有毒药。"他向哈利保证说，一边把大半瓶酒倒进海格那水桶大小的杯子里，"在你可怜的朋友鲁伯特出事后，我让一个家养小精灵尝了每一瓶酒。"

哈利想象着赫敏听了这种虐待家养小精灵的做法后会是什么表情，暗自决定永远不对她提起。

"一杯给哈利……"斯拉格霍恩说着把第二瓶酒分别倒进两只杯子，"……一杯给我。好，"他高高举起杯子，"为了阿拉戈克。"

"阿拉戈克。"哈利和海格一起说。

斯拉格霍恩和海格都痛饮了一大口，但哈利得了福灵剂的启示，知道他不能喝，便假装喝了一口，把杯子放回到桌上。

"我把他从一个卵养大的，"海格悲伤地说，"刚孵出来时多小啊，才哈巴狗那么大。"

"真可爱。"斯拉格霍恩说。

"以前把他养在学校的碗柜里，直到……唉……"

海格的脸色阴沉下来，哈利知道为什么：由汤姆·里德尔主使，将密室事件嫁祸于海格，结果海格被赶出学校。但斯拉格霍恩似乎没在听，他只是望着天花板，那儿挂着几只铜壶，还有一束长长的柔顺光洁的白毛。

"这不会是独角兽的毛吧，海格？"

719

## CHAPTER TWENTY-TWO   After the Burial

'Oh, yeah,' said Hagrid indifferently. 'Gets pulled out of their tails, they catch it on branches an' stuff in the forest, yeh know ...'

'But my dear chap, do you know how much that's *worth*?'

'I use it fer bindin' on bandages an' stuff if a creature gets injured,' said Hagrid, shrugging. 'It's dead useful ... very strong, see.'

Slughorn took another deep draught from his mug, his eyes moving carefully around the cabin now, looking, Harry knew, for more treasures that he might be able to convert into a plentiful supply of oak-matured mead, crystallised pineapple and velvet smoking jackets. He refilled Hagrid's mug and his own, and questioned him about the creatures that lived in the Forest these days and how Hagrid was able to look after them all. Hagrid, becoming expansive under the influence of the drink and Slughorn's flattering interest, stopped mopping his eyes and entered happily into a long explanation of Bowtruckle husbandry.

The Felix Felicis gave Harry a little nudge at this point and he noticed that the supply of drink that Slughorn had brought was running out fast. Harry had not yet managed to bring off the Refilling Charm without saying the incantation aloud, but the idea that he might not be able to do it tonight was laughable: indeed, Harry grinned to himself as, unnoticed by either Hagrid or Slughorn (now swapping tales of the illegal trade in dragon eggs), he pointed his wand under the table at the emptying bottles and they immediately began to refill.

After an hour or so, Hagrid and Slughorn began making extravagant toasts: to Hogwarts, to Dumbledore, to elf-made wine and to –

'Harry Potter!' bellowed Hagrid, slopping some of his fourteenth bucket of wine down his chin as he drained it.

'Yes, indeed,' cried Slughorn a little thickly, 'Parry Otter, the Chosen Boy Who – well – something of that sort,' he mumbled, and drained his mug, too.

Not long after this, Hagrid became tearful again and pressed the whole unicorn tail upon Slughorn, who pocketed it with cries of, 'To friendship! To generosity! To ten Galleons a hair!'

And for a while after that, Hagrid and Slughorn were sitting side by side, arms around each other, singing a slow sad song about a dying wizard called Odo.

'Aaargh, the good die young,' muttered Hagrid, slumping low on to the table, a little cross-eyed, while Slughorn continued to warble the refrain. 'Me

## 第22章 葬礼之后

"哦，是独角兽的毛，"海格不在意地说，"从尾巴上扯下来的，它在林子里挂到了树枝上……"

"可是亲爱的朋友，你知道那得值多少钱？"

"动物受伤的时候，我用它绑绷带，"海格说着耸了耸肩膀，"特别好使……特别结实，你瞧。"

斯拉格霍恩又痛饮了一口，目光仔细地在小屋里搜寻，哈利知道他是在找更多的宝物，可以给他换来大量橡木陈酿的蜂蜜酒、菠萝蜜饯和天鹅绒的吸烟衫。斯拉格霍恩把海格和自己的杯子又斟满了，问到现在林子里住着的生物，又问海格怎么能照看得过来。海格在酒精的作用和斯拉格霍恩的奉承之下开朗起来，停止了擦眼睛，开始兴致勃勃地大讲起护树罗锅的饲养。

此时福灵剂轻轻推了哈利一下，他注意到斯拉格霍恩带来的酒很快要喝光了。哈利还不会不出声地施续满咒，但今晚不可能的念头是可笑的。果然，哈利拿魔杖在桌子下朝快空了的瓶子一指，瓶子里的酒立即就增加了，海格和斯拉格霍恩都没有察觉（他们正在交流非法交易火龙蛋的故事），哈利自己咧嘴一笑。

约一小时后，海格和斯拉格霍恩开始放纵地祝酒：为霍格沃茨，为邓布利多，为小精灵酿的酒，为——

"哈利·波特！"海格吼道，把第十四桶葡萄酒一饮而尽，流了一下巴。

"对啊，"斯拉格霍恩有些口齿不清地叫道，"巴利·沃特，救世少年——嗯——差不多那个意思。"他嘟囔道，也跟着一饮而尽。

没过多久，海格泪汪汪地把整条独角兽的尾巴塞到了斯拉格霍恩手中，后者高喊着"为友谊！为慷慨！为十加隆一根！"把它揣进了衣服口袋里。

接下来有一会儿，海格和斯拉格霍恩并排坐着，搂住对方，唱起了一首舒缓忧伤的歌。唱的是一个垂死的巫师奥多。

"啊，好人不长命，"海格嘟囔着趴到桌子上，有一点儿对眼，斯拉格霍恩还在颤声歌唱，"我爸爸那么年轻就走了……你爸爸妈妈也是，

## CHAPTER TWENTY-TWO   After the Burial

dad was no age ter go ... nor were your mum an' dad, Harry ...'

Great fat tears oozed out of the corners of Hagrid's crinkled eyes again; he grasped Harry's arm and shook it.

'... bes' wiz and witchard o' their age I never knew ... terrible thing ... terrible thing ...'

Slughorn sang plaintively:

> *And Odo the hero, they bore him back home*
> *To the place that he'd known as a lad,*
> *They laid him to rest with his hat inside out*
> *And his wand snapped in two, which was sad.'*

'... terrible,' Hagrid grunted and his great shaggy head rolled sideways on to his arms and he fell asleep, snoring deeply.

'Sorry,' said Slughorn with a hiccough. 'Can't carry a tune to save my life.'

'Hagrid wasn't talking about your singing,' said Harry quietly. 'He was talking about my mum and dad dying.'

'Oh,' said Slughorn, repressing a large belch. 'Oh, dear. Yes, that was – was terrible indeed. Terrible ... terrible ...'

He looked quite at a loss for what to say, and resorted to refilling their mugs.

'I don't – don't suppose you remember it, Harry?' he asked awkwardly.

'No – well, I was only one when they died,' said Harry, his eyes on the flame of the candle flickering in Hagrid's heavy snores. 'But I've found out pretty much what happened since. My dad died first. Did you know that?'

'I – I didn't,' said Slughorn in a hushed voice.

'Yeah ... Voldemort murdered him and then stepped over his body towards my mum,' said Harry.

Slughorn gave a great shudder, but he did not seem able to tear his horrified gaze away from Harry's face.

'He told her to get out of the way,' said Harry remorselessly. 'He told me she needn't have died. He only wanted me. She could have run.'

## 第22章 葬礼之后

哈利……"

硕大的泪珠又从海格爬满皱纹的眼角涌出，他抓住哈利的胳膊摇晃着。

"……他们那个年纪的巫师里面，我见过的最好的一对……可怕……可怕……"

斯拉格霍恩伤感地唱着：

> 英雄奥多被抬回故乡，
> 抬到他儿时熟悉的地方，
> 帽子翻过来，入土安葬，
> 魔杖折两段，多么悲伤。

"……可怕。"海格哼哼道，蓬乱的大脑袋滚到了臂弯里，低沉地打起鼾来。

"对不起，"斯拉格霍恩打了个嗝说，"我从来唱不准调子。"

"海格不是说你唱歌，"哈利轻声说，"他说的是我爸爸妈妈的死。"

"哦，"斯拉格霍恩抑制住一个大嗝说，"哦，是啊，那真是——非常可怕。可怕……可怕……"

他似乎不知说什么好，又去往杯里添酒。

"我想——你不记得了吧，哈利？"他笨拙地问。

"不记得——他们死的时候我才一岁。"哈利说，一边盯着烛火在海格粗重的呼噜中摇曳，"但我后来了解到不少。我爸爸先死的，你知道吗？"

"我——我不知道。"斯拉格霍恩声音微弱地说。

"是……伏地魔杀死了他，然后跨过他的尸体朝我妈妈走了过去。"哈利说。

斯拉格霍恩猛地哆嗦一下，但好像无法将恐惧的目光从哈利脸上移开。

"他叫我妈妈走开。"哈利无情地说，"伏地魔告诉我，我妈妈本来可以不死的，他只想杀我，她本来可以逃走的。"

## CHAPTER TWENTY-TWO    After the Burial

'Oh dear,' breathed Slughorn. 'She could have ... she needn't ... that's awful ...'

'It is, isn't it?' said Harry, in a voice barely more than a whisper. 'But she didn't move. Dad was already dead, but she didn't want me to go too. She tried to plead with Voldemort ... but he just laughed ...'

'That's enough!' said Slughorn suddenly, raising a shaking hand. 'Really, my dear boy, enough ... I'm an old man ... I don't need to hear ... I don't want to hear ...'

'I forgot,' lied Harry, Felix Felicis leading him on. 'You liked her, didn't you?'

'Liked her?' said Slughorn, his eyes brimming with tears once more. 'I don't imagine anyone who met her wouldn't have liked her ... very brave ... very funny ... it was the most horrible thing ...'

'But you won't help her son,' said Harry. 'She gave me her life, but you won't give me a memory.'

Hagrid's rumbling snores filled the cabin. Harry looked steadily into Slughorn's tear-filled eyes. The Potions master seemed unable to look away.

'Don't say that,' he whispered. 'It isn't a question ... if it were to help you, of course ... but no purpose can be served ...'

'It can,' said Harry clearly. 'Dumbledore needs information. I need information.'

He knew he was safe: Felix was telling him that Slughorn would remember nothing of this in the morning. Looking Slughorn straight in the eye, Harry leant forwards a little.

'I am the Chosen One. I have to kill him. I need that memory.'

Slughorn turned paler than ever; his shiny forehead gleamed with sweat.

'You *are* the Chosen One?'

'Of course I am,' said Harry calmly.

'But then ... my dear boy ... you're asking a great deal ... you're asking me, in fact, to aid you in your attempt to destroy –'

'You don't want to get rid of the wizard who killed Lily Evans?'

'Harry, Harry, of course I do, but –'

'You're scared he'll find out you helped me?'

Slughorn said nothing; he looked terrified.

## 第22章 葬礼之后

"哦，天哪，"斯拉格霍恩轻声说，"她本来可以……她不用……太可怕了……"

"是啊，"哈利的声音近乎耳语，"可是我妈妈没有动。我爸爸已经死了，她不想我也死掉。她试图向伏地魔求情……可他只是大笑……"

"够了！"斯拉格霍恩突然叫道，举起颤抖的手，"真的，亲爱的孩子，够了……我是个老人……我不需要听……我不想听……"

"我忘了，"哈利撒了个谎，福灵剂引导着他，"你喜欢她，是不是？"

"喜欢她？"斯拉格霍恩说，眼里又汪满了泪水，"我不能想象有哪个见过她的人会不喜欢她……非常勇敢……非常活泼……啊，最可怕的事……"

"可是你不肯帮助她的儿子。她把她的生命给了我，你却连一段记忆都不肯给我。"

海格如雷的鼾声充满了小屋。哈利牢牢地盯着斯拉格霍恩泪汪汪的眼睛。魔药教师似乎无法转移视线。

"别那么说，"他小声说，"如果能帮助你的话……当然不成问题……可是那东西又没有用处……"

"有用，"哈利清楚地说，"邓布利多需要了解，我需要了解。"

他知道自己是安全的：福灵剂告诉他，斯拉格霍恩明天早上什么也不会记得。哈利直视着斯拉格霍恩的眼睛，身子微微前倾。

"我是救世之星，我必须杀死他，我需要那段记忆。"

斯拉格霍恩脸色更加苍白，脑门上亮晶晶的全是汗。

"你是救世之星？"

"当然。"哈利镇静地说。

"可是……亲爱的孩子……你要求得太多了……实际上，你在要我帮你摧毁——"

"你不想除掉杀死莉莉·伊万斯的巫师？"

"哈利，哈利，我当然想，可是——"

"你害怕他会发现你帮了我？"

斯拉格霍恩没说话，但神色恐惧。

## CHAPTER TWENTY-TWO    After the Burial

'Be brave like my mother, Professor ...'

Slughorn raised a pudgy hand and pressed his shaking fingers to his mouth; he looked for a moment like an enormously overgrown baby.

'I am not proud ...' he whispered through his fingers. 'I am ashamed of what – of what that memory shows ... I think I may have done great damage that day ...'

'You'd cancel out anything you did by giving me the memory,' said Harry. 'It would be a very brave and noble thing to do.'

Hagrid twitched in his sleep and snored on. Slughorn and Harry stared at each other over the guttering candle. There was a long, long silence, but Felix Felicis told Harry not to break it, to wait.

Then, very slowly, Slughorn put his hand in his pocket and pulled out his wand. He put his other hand inside his cloak and took out a small, empty bottle. Still looking into Harry's eyes, Slughorn touched the tip of his wand to his temple and withdrew it, so that a long, silver thread of memory came away too, clinging to the wand-tip. Longer and longer the memory stretched until it broke and swung, silvery bright, from the wand. Slughorn lowered it into the bottle where it coiled, then spread, swirling like gas. He corked the bottle with a trembling hand and then passed it across the table to Harry.

'Thank you very much, Professor.'

'You're a good boy,' said Professor Slughorn, tears trickling down his fat cheeks into his walrus moustache. 'And you've got her eyes ... just don't think too badly of me once you've seen it ...'

And he, too, put his head on his arms, gave a deep sigh, and fell asleep.

## 第22章 葬礼之后

"希望你像我妈妈一样勇敢,教授……"

斯拉格霍恩举起胖手,把颤抖的手指按在嘴上,他一时看上去像个庞大的婴儿。

"我觉得不光彩……"他从指缝间小声喃喃道,"我为——为那段记忆显示的事情而感到羞耻……我想我那天可能造成了很大危害……"

"你把记忆交给我,就一切都抵消了,"哈利说,"这是非常勇敢和高尚的事。"

海格在梦中抽搐了一下,继续打着呼噜。斯拉格霍恩和哈利隔着烛光摇曳的蜡烛对视,沉默持续了很久,福灵剂告诉哈利不要打破这份沉默,再等一等。

最后,斯拉格霍恩很慢很慢地把手伸进兜里,抽出了魔杖,另一只手从斗篷里摸出一个小小的空瓶子。他仍然盯着哈利的眼睛,将魔杖尖抵在太阳穴上,然后拿开。杖尖带出一缕长长的银丝般的记忆。它越拉越长,终于断了,银光闪闪地在杖尖上飘荡。斯拉格霍恩把它放进瓶中,银丝卷了起来,继而展开了,像气体一样盘旋着。他用颤抖的手塞紧瓶盖,隔着桌子递给了哈利。

"非常感谢您,教授。"

"你是个好孩子,"斯拉格霍恩说,泪水顺着肥胖的面颊流进了他的海象胡须中,"你有她那样的眼睛……看了这个之后别把我想得太坏……"

他也把脑袋搁到臂弯里,长叹一声,睡着了。

## CHAPTER TWENTY-THREE

# Horcruxes

Harry could feel the Felix Felicis wearing off as he crept back into the castle. The front door had remained unlocked for him, but on the third floor he met Peeves and only narrowly avoided detection by diving sideways through one of his short cuts. By the time he got up to the portrait of the Fat Lady and pulled off his Invisibility Cloak, he was not surprised to find her in a most unhelpful mood.

'What sort of time do you call this?'

'I'm really sorry – I had to go out for something important –'

'Well, the password changed at midnight, so you'll just have to sleep in the corridor, won't you?'

'You're joking!' said Harry. 'Why did it have to change at midnight?'

'That's the way it is,' said the Fat Lady. 'If you're angry, go and take it up with the Headmaster, he's the one who's tightened security.'

'Fantastic,' said Harry bitterly, looking around at the hard floor. 'Really brilliant. Yeah, I would go and take it up with Dumbledore if he was here, because he's the one who wanted me to –'

'He is here,' said a voice behind Harry. 'Professor Dumbledore returned to the school an hour ago.'

Nearly Headless Nick was gliding towards Harry, his head wobbling as usual upon his ruff.

'I had it from the Bloody Baron, who saw him arrive,' said Nick. 'He appeared, according to the Baron, to be in good spirits, though a little tired, of course.'

'Where is he?' said Harry, his heart leaping.

'Oh, groaning and clanking up on the Astronomy Tower, it's a favourite pastime of his –'

'Not the Bloody Baron, Dumbledore!'

# 第 23 章

# 魂　器

悄悄走回城堡时，哈利能感觉到福灵剂的效力在渐渐消失。大门还没锁，但在四楼他碰到了皮皮鬼，急忙钻进旁边一条近道，才没被发现。他走到胖夫人肖像前扯下隐形衣时，发现她的情绪对他非常不利，但他并不觉得意外。

"你知道现在是什么时间吗？"

"非常抱歉——我有重要的事情必须出去——"

"半夜里改了口令，你只能睡走廊了。"

"开玩笑！"哈利说，"为什么要半夜改口令？"

"就是这样的，"胖夫人说，"你要是有气就跟校长说去，是他让加强安保措施的。"

"好啊，"哈利看看坚硬的地面，怨恨地说，"真是妙极了。对，如果邓布利多在学校，我确实要去跟他说说，因为是他要我——"

"他在，"哈利身后一个声音说，"邓布利多教授一小时前就回学校了。"

差点没头的尼克朝哈利飘了过来，脑袋依旧在皱领上摇摇晃晃。

"我听血人巴罗说的，他看到了。巴罗说邓布利多看上去心情很好，就是有点累，那是当然的。"

"他在哪儿？"哈利问，他的心怦怦跳了起来。

"哦，在天文塔上哼哼唧唧，丁零当啷。这是他最喜欢的消遣——"

"不是血人巴罗，我问的是邓布利多！"

## CHAPTER TWENTY-THREE   Horcruxes

'Oh – in his office,' said Nick. 'I believe, from what the Baron said, that he had business to attend to before turning in –'

'Yeah, he has,' said Harry, excitement blazing in his chest at the prospect of telling Dumbledore he had secured the memory. He wheeled about and sprinted off again, ignoring the Fat Lady who was calling after him.

'Come back! All right, I lied! I was annoyed you woke me up! The password's still "tapeworm"!'

But Harry was already hurtling back along the corridor, and, within minutes, he was saying 'toffee eclairs' to Dumbledore's gargoyle, which leapt aside, permitting Harry entrance on to the spiral staircase.

'Enter,' said Dumbledore when Harry knocked. He sounded exhausted.

Harry pushed open the door. There was Dumbledore's office, looking the same as ever, but with black, star-strewn skies beyond the windows.

'Good gracious, Harry,' said Dumbledore in surprise. 'To what do I owe this very late pleasure?'

'Sir – I've got it. I've got the memory from Slughorn.'

Harry pulled out the tiny glass bottle and showed it to Dumbledore. For a moment or two, the Headmaster looked stunned. Then his face split in a wide smile.

'Harry, this is spectacular news! Very well done indeed! I knew you could do it!'

All thought of the lateness of the hour apparently forgotten, he hurried around his desk, took the bottle with Slughorn's memory in his uninjured hand and strode over to the cabinet where he kept the Pensieve.

'And now,' said Dumbledore, placing the stone basin upon his desk and emptying the contents of the bottle into it, 'now, at last, we shall see. Harry, quickly ...'

Harry bowed obediently over the Pensieve and felt his feet leave the office floor ... once again he fell through darkness and landed in Horace Slughorn's office many years before.

There was the much younger Horace Slughorn, with his thick, shiny, straw-coloured hair and his gingery-blond moustache, sitting again in the comfortable winged armchair in his office, his feet resting upon a velvet pouffe, a small glass of wine in one hand, the other rummaging in a box of crystallised pineapple. And there were the half a dozen teenage boys sitting around Slughorn with Tom Riddle in the midst of them, Marvolo's gold and black ring gleaming on his finger.

## 第23章 魂器

"哦——在他的办公室,"尼克说,"据巴罗说,他睡觉前还有点事要办——"

"是,没错。"一想到可以告诉邓布利多他搞到了记忆,哈利满心兴奋,掉头就跑。胖夫人在后面叫了起来。

"回来!我骗你的!我是生气你把我吵醒了!口令还是'绦虫'!"

但哈利早就跑远了,几分钟后,他已经在对邓布利多的滴水嘴石兽说"太妃手指饼"了。石兽跳到一旁,让哈利走上了螺旋形楼梯。

"进来。"哈利敲门后听到邓布利多说,声音似乎疲惫不堪。

哈利推开门。邓布利多的办公室还是老样子,但窗外换成了缀满星斗的黑色夜空。

"哎呀,哈利,"邓布利多惊讶地说,"这么晚来有什么事吗?"

"先生——我搞到了,我搞到了斯拉格霍恩的记忆。"

哈利掏出小玻璃瓶给邓布利多看。校长似乎愣了片刻,然后脸上绽开了笑容。

"哈利,这是激动人心的消息!真是太棒了!我就知道你能办到!"

他显然完全忘记了已是深夜,急忙从桌后出来,用那只好手接过斯拉格霍恩的记忆,大步走到摆着冥想盆的柜子前。

"现在,"邓布利多把石盆搁在桌上,把瓶里的东西倒了进去,"现在,我们终于要看到了。哈利,快……"

哈利顺从地探身俯在冥想盆上,感到双脚离开了地面……他再次在黑暗中坠落,掉到多年前斯拉格霍恩的办公室里。

还是那个年轻得多的斯拉格霍恩,一头浓密光泽的草黄色头发,姜黄色的小胡子,坐在一把舒适的带翼扶手椅里,脚搁在天鹅绒大脚垫上,一手端着一小杯葡萄酒,另一只手在一盒菠萝蜜饯里挑挑拣拣。六个十多岁的男孩围坐在斯拉格霍恩旁边,其中有汤姆·里德尔。马沃罗的黑宝石金戒指在里德尔的手上闪烁。

## CHAPTER TWENTY-THREE  Horcruxes

Dumbledore landed beside Harry just as Riddle asked, 'Sir, is it true that Professor Merrythought is retiring?'

'Tom, Tom, if I knew I couldn't tell you,' said Slughorn, wagging his finger reprovingly at Riddle, though winking at the same time. 'I must say, I'd like to know where you get your information, boy; more knowledgeable than half the staff, you are.'

Riddle smiled; the other boys laughed and cast him admiring looks.

'What with your uncanny ability to know things you shouldn't, and your careful flattery of the people who matter – thank you for the pineapple, by the way, you're quite right, it is my favourite –'

Several of the boys tittered again.

'– I confidently expect you to rise to Minister for Magic within twenty years. Fifteen, if you keep sending me pineapple. I have *excellent* contacts at the Ministry.'

Tom Riddle merely smiled as the others laughed again. Harry noticed that he was by no means the eldest of the group of boys, but that they all seemed to look to him as their leader.

'I don't know that politics would suit me, sir,' he said when the laughter had died away. 'I don't have the right kind of background, for one thing.'

A couple of the boys around him smirked at each other. Harry was sure they were enjoying a private joke: undoubtedly about what they knew, or suspected, regarding their gang leader's famous ancestor.

'Nonsense,' said Slughorn briskly, 'couldn't be plainer you come from decent wizarding stock, abilities like yours. No, you'll go far, Tom, I've never been wrong about a student yet.'

The small golden clock standing upon Slughorn's desk chimed eleven o'clock behind him and he looked round.

'Good gracious, is it that time already? You'd better get going, boys, or we'll all be in trouble. Lestrange, I want your essay by tomorrow or it's detention. Same goes for you, Avery.'

One by one the boys filed out of the room. Slughorn heaved himself out of his armchair and carried his empty glass over to his desk. A movement behind him made him look round; Riddle was still standing there.

'Look sharp, Tom, you don't want to be caught out of bed out of hours, and you a prefect ...'

## 第23章 魂器

邓布利多落到哈利身边时，里德尔正问："先生，梅乐思教授要退休了吗？"

"汤姆，汤姆，我知道也不能告诉你。"斯拉格霍恩责备地对他摇着一根手指，但又眨眨眼睛，"我不得不说，我想知道你的消息是从哪儿得来的，孩子。你比一半的教员知道得都多。"

里德尔微微一笑，其他男孩也笑起来，向他投去钦佩的目光。

"你这个鬼灵精，能知道不该知道的事，又会小心讨好重要的人——顺便谢谢你的菠萝，你猜中了，这是我最喜欢的——"

几个男孩窃笑起来。

"——我相信你二十年内就会升为魔法部部长。也许只要十五年，如果你经常给我送菠萝蜜饯的话。我在部里有很硬的关系。"

其他男孩又笑起来，汤姆·里德尔只是微露笑容。哈利注意到在这些男孩中他绝不是年龄最大的，但他们似乎都把他看作领袖。

"我不知道政界是否适合我，先生，"笑声渐止后汤姆·里德尔说，"首先我没有背景。"

旁边两个男孩相视而笑。哈利相信他们是想到了一个私下流传的笑话，无疑是他们知道或猜测的，与他们头儿的显赫祖先有关。

"什么话，"斯拉格霍恩爽朗地说，"你那样的才能，一定出自体面的巫师世家，这一点再清楚不过了。你前途无量，汤姆，我还从来没看错过一个学生。"

斯拉格霍恩书桌上的金色小钟打响了十一点，斯拉格霍恩回头看了看。

"老天，已经这么晚了？该走啦，孩子们，不然我们就麻烦了。莱斯特兰奇，明天交论文，交不出就关禁闭。你也一样，埃弗里。"

男孩们鱼贯而出。斯拉格霍恩从椅子上站起身来，把空杯子拿到桌前。身后的动静使他回过头来，里德尔还站在那儿。

"快点儿，汤姆，你不想被人抓到熄灯时间还在外面吧，你是级长……"

## CHAPTER TWENTY-THREE — Horcruxes

'Sir, I wanted to ask you something.'

'Ask away, then, m'boy, ask away ...'

'Sir, I wondered what you know about ... about Horcruxes?'

Slughorn stared at him, his thick fingers absent-mindedly caressing the stem of his wine glass.

'Project for Defence Against the Dark Arts, is it?'

But Harry could tell that Slughorn knew perfectly well that this was not schoolwork.

'Not exactly, sir,' said Riddle. 'I came across the term while reading and I didn't fully understand it.'

'No ... well ... you'd be hard-pushed to find a book at Hogwarts that'll give you details on Horcruxes, Tom. That's very Dark stuff, very Dark indeed,' said Slughorn.

'But you obviously know all about them, sir? I mean, a wizard like you – sorry, I mean, if you can't tell me, obviously – I just knew if anyone could tell me, you could – so I just thought I'd ask –'

It was very well done, thought Harry, the hesitancy, the casual tone, the careful flattery, none of it overdone. He, Harry, had had too much experience of trying to wheedle information out of reluctant people not to recognise a master at work. He could tell that Riddle wanted the information very, very much; perhaps had been working towards this moment for weeks.

'Well,' said Slughorn, not looking at Riddle, but fiddling with the ribbon on top of his box of crystallised pineapple, 'well, it can't hurt to give you an overview, of course. Just so that you understand the term. A Horcrux is the word used for an object in which a person has concealed part of their soul.'

'I don't quite understand how that works, though, sir,' said Riddle.

His voice was carefully controlled, but Harry could sense his excitement.

'Well, you split your soul, you see,' said Slughorn, 'and hide part of it in an object outside the body. Then, even if one's body is attacked or destroyed, one cannot die, for part of the soul remains earthbound and undamaged. But, of course, existence in such a form ...'

Slughorn's face crumpled and Harry found himself remembering words he had heard nearly two years before.

*'I was ripped from my body, I was less than spirit, less than the meanest ghost ... but still, I was alive.'*

## 第 23 章 魂 器

"先生，我想问你点事。"

"那就快问，孩子，快问……"

"先生，我想问你知不知道……魂器。"

斯拉格霍恩瞪着他，心不在焉地用胖手指抚摸着杯脚。

"黑魔法防御术的课题，是吗？"

但是哈利看出斯拉格霍恩明知这不是学校的功课。

"不是，先生，我在书上看到的，不大理解。"

"嗯……是啊……在霍格沃茨很难找到一本详细介绍魂器的书，汤姆。那是非常邪恶的东西，非常邪恶。"斯拉格霍恩说。

"但你显然很了解，是不是，先生？我是说，像你这样的巫师——对不起，我的意思是，也许你不能告诉我，看得出来——我只知道如果有人能告诉我，那就是你——所以我就想问一问——"

恰到好处，哈利想，那种犹豫的、不经意的语气，巧妙的恭维，一点儿都没有过火。哈利自己有过太多从不情愿的人嘴里套取信息的经历，不会认不出一个行家。他看得出里德尔非常非常想得到这个信息，也许为这一刻已经筹划了好几个星期。

"嗯，"斯拉格霍恩说，他没看里德尔，而是玩弄着菠萝蜜饯盒子上的缎带，"当然，给你简单介绍一下不会有什么坏处，只是让你理解这个名词。魂器是指藏有一个人的部分灵魂的物体。"

"可我不大明白那是怎么回事，先生。"里德尔说。

他的声音是小心控制的，但哈利能感觉到他的激动。

"就是说，你把你的灵魂分裂开，"斯拉格霍恩说，"将一部分藏在身体外的某个物体中。这样，即使你的身体遭到袭击或摧毁，你也死不了，因为还有一部分灵魂留在世间，未受损害。但是，当然，以这种形式存在……"

斯拉格霍恩的脸皱了起来，哈利想起他大概在两年前听到的话。

"我被剥离了肉体，比幽灵还不如，比最卑微的游魂还不如……但我还活着。"

## CHAPTER TWENTY-THREE    Horcruxes

'... few would want it, Tom, very few. Death would be preferable.'

But Riddle's hunger was now apparent; his expression was greedy, he could no longer hide his longing.

'How do you split your soul?'

'Well,' said Slughorn uncomfortably, 'you must understand that the soul is supposed to remain intact and whole. Splitting it is an act of violation, it is against nature.'

'But how do you do it?'

'By an act of evil – the supreme act of evil. By committing murder. Killing rips the soul apart. The wizard intent upon creating a Horcrux would use the damage to his advantage: he would encase the torn portion –'

'Encase? But how –?'

'There is a spell, do not ask me, I don't know!' said Slughorn, shaking his head like an old elephant bothered by mosquitoes. 'Do I look as though I have tried it – do I look like a killer?'

'No, sir, of course not,' said Riddle quickly. 'I'm sorry ... I didn't mean to offend ...'

'Not at all, not at all, not offended,' said Slughorn gruffly. 'It's natural to feel some curiosity about these things ... wizards of a certain calibre have always been drawn to that aspect of magic ...'

'Yes, sir,' said Riddle. 'What I don't understand, though – just out of curiosity – I mean, would one Horcrux be much use? Can you only split your soul once? Wouldn't it be better, make you stronger, to have your soul in more pieces? I mean, for instance, isn't seven the most powerfully magical number, wouldn't seven –?'

'Merlin's beard, Tom!' yelped Slughorn. 'Seven! Isn't it bad enough to think of killing one person? And in any case ... bad enough to divide the soul ... but to rip it into seven pieces ...'

Slughorn looked deeply troubled now: he was gazing at Riddle as though he had never seen him plainly before and Harry could tell that he was regretting entering into the conversation at all.

'Of course,' he muttered, 'this is all hypothetical, what we're discussing, isn't it? All academic ...'

'Yes, sir, of course,' said Riddle quickly.

'But all the same, Tom ... keep it quiet, what I've told – that's to say, what

## 第23章 魂 器

"……很少有人想那样,汤姆,少而又少。死去还痛快些。"

但是此刻里德尔的饥渴十分明显,他表情贪婪,已经隐藏不住他的欲望。

"怎么分裂灵魂呢?"

"哦,"斯拉格霍恩不安地说,"你必须明白,灵魂应该保持完整无缺。分裂灵魂是一种违逆,是反自然的。"

"可是怎么分裂呢?"

"通过邪恶的行为——最邪恶的行为,通过谋杀。杀人会使灵魂分裂,想要制造魂器的巫师就利用这种裂变:把分裂出的灵魂碎片封存——"

"封存?可是怎么——?"

"有一个咒语,不要问我,我不知道!"斯拉格霍恩像被蚊子叮烦的老象一样摇着脑袋,"我看上去像是试过的吗——我像杀人犯吗?"

"不,先生,当然不是,"里德尔忙说,"对不起……我不是有意冒犯……"

"哪里,哪里,没有冒犯,"斯拉格霍恩粗声粗气地说,"对这些事情感到好奇是正常的……有才能的巫师总会被魔法的那一面所吸引……"

"是的,先生,"里德尔说,"可我不明白的是——我仅仅是出于好奇,想问的问题是,一个魂器用处大吗?灵魂是不是只能分裂一次?多分几片是不是更好,能让你更强大?比如说,七不是最有魔力的数字吗,七个——?"

"梅林的胡子啊,汤姆!"斯拉格霍恩叫道,"七个!想杀一个人还不够邪恶吗?无论如何……分裂灵魂已经够邪恶了……而分成七片……"

斯拉格霍恩此时显得非常不安:他瞪着里德尔,好像以前没看清他,哈利看得出他在后悔参与了这场谈话。

"当然,"他小声说,"我们谈的这些都是假设,是不是?只是学术性的……"

"是的,先生,当然。"里德尔马上说。

"不过,汤姆……我所讲的——我们所讨论的这些,还是别说出

CHAPTER TWENTY-THREE   Horcruxes

we've discussed. People wouldn't like to think we've been chatting about Horcruxes. It's a banned subject at Hogwarts, you know ... Dumbledore's particularly fierce about it ...'

'I won't say a word, sir,' said Riddle and he left, but not before Harry had glimpsed his face, which was full of that same wild happiness it had worn when he had first found out that he was a wizard, the sort of happiness that did not enhance his handsome features, but made them, somehow, less human ...

'Thank you, Harry,' said Dumbledore quietly. 'Let us go ...'

When Harry landed back on the office floor, Dumbledore was already sitting down behind his desk. Harry sat too, and waited for Dumbledore to speak.

'I have been hoping for this piece of evidence for a very long time,' said Dumbledore at last. 'It confirms the theory on which I have been working, it tells me that I am right, and also how very far there is still to go ...'

Harry suddenly noticed that every single one of the old headmasters and headmistresses in the portraits around the walls was awake and listening in on their conversation. A corpulent, red-nosed wizard had actually taken out an ear-trumpet.

'Well, Harry,' said Dumbledore, 'I am sure you understood the significance of what we just heard. At the same age as you are now, give or take a few months, Tom Riddle was doing all he could to find out how to make himself immortal.'

'You think he succeeded then, sir?' asked Harry. 'He made a Horcrux? And that's why he didn't die when he attacked me? He had a Horcrux hidden somewhere? A bit of his soul was safe?'

'A bit ... or more,' said Dumbledore. 'You heard Voldemort: what he particularly wanted from Horace was an opinion on what would happen to the wizard who created more than one Horcrux, what would happen to the wizard so determined to evade death that he would be prepared to murder many times, rip his soul repeatedly, so as to store it in many, separately concealed Horcruxes. No book would have given him that information. As far as I know – as far, I am sure, as Voldemort knew – no wizard had ever done more than tear his soul in two.'

Dumbledore paused for a moment, marshalling his thoughts, and then said, 'Four years ago, I received what I considered certain proof that Voldemort had split his soul.'

'Where?' asked Harry. 'How?'

'You handed it to me, Harry,' said Dumbledore. 'The diary, Riddle's diary,

## 第23章 魂器

去。人们知道我们聊过魂器会不高兴的。这在霍格沃茨是禁止的，你知道……邓布利多尤其激烈……"

"我不会说出去的，先生。"里德尔说完就离开了。但哈利瞥见了他的面孔，上面充满了狂喜，就像他刚发现自己是巫师时一样，那种喜悦没有令他的面庞更显英俊，反而显得有些狰狞……

"谢谢你，哈利，"邓布利多低声说，"我们走吧……"

哈利落回到办公室的地上，邓布利多已经坐在书桌后。哈利也坐了下来，等着邓布利多开口。

"我等这个证据已经有很久了，"邓布利多终于说，"它证实了我的推测，证明我是对的，也告诉我前面的道路还很长……"

哈利突然发现墙上肖像中的老校长们全都醒了，在偷听他们的谈话。一个红鼻子的肥胖巫师还拿出了助听器。

"哈利，"邓布利多说，"我相信你了解刚才那段对话的重要性。就在差不多你这样的年龄，汤姆·里德尔正千方百计打听怎样能让他永远不死。"

"那么你认为他成功了，先生？"哈利问，"他做成了魂器？所以他袭击我之后没有死？他在某个地方藏有一个魂器？他的一小片灵魂是完好的？"

"一小片……或者更多。"邓布利多说，"你听到了伏地魔的话：他特别想从霍拉斯口中知道的是，如果一个巫师制造多个魂器会怎么样，如果一个巫师为了逃避死亡而不惜多次杀人，多次分裂他的灵魂，存放在多个单独储藏的魂器中，会有什么后果。没有书本能给他这个知识。据我所知——我想伏地魔也知道——没有一个巫师曾把他的灵魂分裂为两片以上。"

邓布利多停了停，整理着思绪，然后说："四年前，我得到了一个确凿的证据，表明伏地魔分裂了他的灵魂。"

"在哪儿？"哈利问，"怎么知道的？"

"是你交给我的，哈利。"邓布利多说，"那本日记，里德尔的日记，

## CHAPTER TWENTY-THREE  Horcruxes

the one giving instructions on how to reopen the Chamber of Secrets.'

'I don't understand, sir,' said Harry.

'Well, although I did not see the Riddle who came out of the diary, what you described to me was a phenomenon I had never witnessed. A mere memory starting to act and think for itself? A mere memory, sapping the life out of the girl into whose hands it had fallen? No, something much more sinister had lived inside that book ... a fragment of soul, I was almost sure of it. The diary had been a Horcrux. But this raised as many questions as it answered. What intrigued and alarmed me most was that that diary had been intended as a weapon as much as a safeguard.'

'I still don't understand,' said Harry.

'Well, it worked as a Horcrux is supposed to work – in other words, the fragment of soul concealed inside it was kept safe and had undoubtedly played its part in preventing the death of its owner. But there could be no doubt that Riddle really wanted that diary read, wanted the piece of his soul to inhabit or possess somebody else, so that Slytherin's monster would be unleashed again.'

'Well, he didn't want his hard work to be wasted,' said Harry. 'He wanted people to know he was Slytherin's heir, because he couldn't take credit at the time.'

'Quite correct,' said Dumbledore, nodding. 'But don't you see, Harry, that if he intended the diary to be passed to, or planted on, some future Hogwarts student, he was being remarkably blasé about that precious fragment of his soul concealed within it. The point of a Horcrux is, as Professor Slughorn explained, to keep part of the self hidden and safe, not to fling it into somebody else's path and run the risk that they might destroy it – as indeed happened: that particular fragment of soul is no more; you saw to that.

'The careless way in which Voldemort regarded this Horcrux seemed most ominous to me. It suggested that he must have made – or been planning to make – more Horcruxes, so that the loss of his first would not be so detrimental. I did not wish to believe it, but nothing else seemed to make sense.

'Then you told me, two years later, that on the night that Voldemort returned to his body, he made a most illuminating and alarming statement to his Death Eaters. "*I, who have gone further than anybody along the path that leads to immortality.*" That was what you told me he said. "*Further than anybody.*" and I thought I knew what that meant, though the Death Eaters did not. He was referring to his Horcruxes, Horcruxes in the plural, Harry, which I do not believe any other wizard has ever had. Yet it fitted: Lord Voldemort had

## 第23章 魂器

教人怎样重新打开密室的那本。"

"我不明白,先生。"哈利说。

"哦,虽然我没有看到从日记中现身的里德尔,但你向我描述的是我从未见过的现象。仅仅一个记忆,会有自己的行动和思想?仅仅一个记忆,竟会吸取拿到它的那个女孩的生命?不,那本日记里还有邪恶得多的东西……一片灵魂。我几乎可以确信,那日记本是一个魂器。可是这又提出了更多的问题。令我最感兴趣也最为震惊的是那本日记曾经既被当作防护器,又被当作武器。"

"我还是不明白。"哈利说。

"它起到了魂器的作用——换句话说,藏在里面的那片灵魂是安全的,并且的确起着帮助主人避免死亡的作用。但里德尔无疑希望有人读到那本日记,希望他的那片灵魂附到别人身上,以便将斯莱特林的怪物重新释放出来。"

"嗯,他不想让他的辛苦白费,"哈利说,"他希望人们知道他是斯莱特林的继承人,因为他当时没有这个名分。"

"很对,"邓布利多点点头说,"但你有没有想到,哈利,如果他希望某个未来的霍格沃茨学生拿到日记本,并且被它操控的话,那他对里面宝贵的灵魂碎片可就太不当心了。正如斯拉格霍恩教授所说,魂器的用途,是把自己的一部分灵魂安全地封存起来,而不是扔到别人的路上,去冒被消灭的危险——这实际上发生了:那一片灵魂已不复存在,这你也看到了。

"伏地魔对这个魂器如此不当回事,让我感到十分不祥。这意味着他很可能已经做成——或计划要做更多的魂器,所以失去一个不会构成多大危险。我不愿相信这一点,但似乎没有其他解释可以说得通。

"两年后你告诉我,在伏地魔恢复肉身的那个夜里,他对食死徒说了一句最令人警醒的话:'我,在长生的路上比谁走得都远。'你告诉我这就是他说的话:'比谁走得都远。'食死徒不清楚,但是我想我知道它的含义。他是在指他的魂器,多个魂器,哈利。我相信这是其他

## CHAPTER TWENTY-THREE    Horcruxes

seemed to grow less human with the passing years, and the transformation he had undergone seemed to me to be only explicable if his soul was mutilated beyond the realms of what we might call usual evil ...'

'So he's made himself impossible to kill by murdering other people?' said Harry. 'Why couldn't he make a Philosopher's Stone, or steal one, if he was so interested in immortality?'

'Well, we know that he tried to do just that, five years ago,' said Dumbledore. 'But there are several reasons why, I think, a Philosopher's Stone would appeal less than Horcruxes to Lord Voldemort.

'While the Elixir of Life does indeed extend life, it must be drunk regularly, for all eternity, if the drinker is to maintain his immortality. Therefore, Voldemort would be entirely dependent on the Elixir, and if it ran out, or was contaminated, or if the Stone was stolen, he would die just like any other man. Voldemort likes to operate alone, remember. I believe that he would have found the thought of being dependent, even on the Elixir, intolerable. Of course he was prepared to drink it if it would take him out of the horrible part-life to which he was condemned after attacking you, but only to regain a body. Thereafter, I am convinced, he intended to continue to rely on his Horcruxes: he would need nothing more, if only he could regain a human form. He was already immortal, you see ... or as close to immortal as any man can be.

'But now, Harry, armed with this information, the crucial memory you have succeeded in procuring for us, we are closer to the secret of finishing Lord Voldemort than anyone has ever been before. You heard him, Harry: "Wouldn't it be better, make you stronger, to have your soul in more pieces ... isn't seven the most powerfully magical number ..." *Isn't seven the most powerfully magical number.* Yes, I think the idea of a seven-part soul would greatly appeal to Lord Voldemort.'

'He made *seven* Horcruxes?' said Harry, horror-struck, while several of the portraits on the walls made similar noises of shock and outrage. 'But they could be anywhere in the world – hidden – buried or invisible –'

'I am glad to see you appreciate the magnitude of the problem,' said Dumbledore calmly. 'But firstly, no, Harry, not seven Horcruxes: six. The seventh part of his soul, however maimed, resides inside his regenerated body. That was the part of him that lived a spectral existence for so many years during his exile; without that, he has no self at all. That seventh piece of soul will be the last that anybody wishing to kill Voldemort must attack – the piece that lives in his body.'

## 第23章 魂 器

任何巫师都不曾有过的。但是种种迹象都很吻合：这些年来伏地魔似乎变得越来越不像人，我想那种变形只能解释为，他的灵魂受到的破坏超出了我们所说的一般邪恶的范围……"

"他靠杀人使自己不死？"哈利说，"如果他那么想长生不死，为什么不造一块魔法石，或者偷一块呢？"

"我们知道，他五年前正是那么做的。但我想魔法石不如魂器对伏地魔的胃口，原因有这么几点。

"长生不老药确实能延长生命，但必须经常喝，永远喝下去，才能保持不死。那样，伏地魔将完全依赖此药。如果药用完了或受到污染，或是魔法石被盗，他就会像其他人一样死去。伏地魔喜欢单独行动，记得吗？我相信他会觉得依赖是不可容忍的，哪怕是依赖长生不老药。当然，为了摆脱他在袭击你之后那种半生半死的可怕状态，他愿意喝它，但只是为了重获肉身。之后，我相信他还是打算继续依靠他的魂器：他不再需要别的，只要能重获一个人身。他已经长生不死了……或者说比任何人都更接近长生不死。

"但是现在，哈利，有了你为我们搞到的这个关键的记忆，我们比任何人都更接近如何将伏地魔消灭的秘密。哈利，你听见他说了：'多分几块是不是更好，能让你更强大……七不是最有魔力的数字吗……'七不是最有魔力的数字吗。对，我认为把灵魂分成七片对伏地魔很有吸引力。"

"他做了七个魂器？"哈利惊恐地问，墙上几个肖像也发出震惊和愤慨之声，"但它们可能在世界上任何地方——隐藏——埋着或隐形——"

"我很高兴你能看到问题的严重程度，"邓布利多镇静地说，"但是首先，哈利，不是七个魂器，是六个。第七部分灵魂，无论怎样残破，仍在他复活的身体里，就是这一部分的他在多年流亡中以幽灵般的形式存在着，没有了它，他就没有了自己。这第七部分灵魂，将是想要杀死伏地魔的人最后必须攻击的对象——他体内的那一片。"

## CHAPTER TWENTY-THREE   Horcruxes

'But the six Horcruxes, then,' said Harry, a little desperately, 'how are we supposed to find them?'

'You are forgetting ... you have already destroyed one of them. And I have destroyed another.'

'You have?' said Harry eagerly.

'Yes indeed,' said Dumbledore, and he raised his blackened, burned-looking hand. 'The ring, Harry. Marvolo's ring. And a terrible curse there was upon it too. Had it not been – forgive me the lack of seemly modesty – for my own prodigious skill, and for Professor Snape's timely action when I returned to Hogwarts, desperately injured, I might not have lived to tell the tale. However, a withered hand does not seem an unreasonable exchange for a seventh of Voldemort's soul. The ring is no longer a Horcrux.'

'But how did you find it?'

'Well, as you now know, I have made it my business for many years to discover as much as I can about Voldemort's past life. I have travelled widely, visiting those places he once knew. I stumbled across the ring hidden in the ruin of the Gaunts' house. It seems that once Voldemort had succeeded in sealing a piece of his soul inside it, he did not want to wear it any more. He hid it, protected by many powerful enchantments, in the shack where his ancestors had once lived (Morfin having been carted off to Azkaban, of course), never guessing that I might one day take the trouble to visit the ruin, or that I might be keeping an eye open for traces of magical concealment.

'However, we should not congratulate ourselves too heartily. You destroyed the diary and I the ring, but if we are right in our theory of a seven-part soul, four Horcruxes remain.'

'And they could be anything?' said Harry. 'They could be old tin cans, or, I dunno, empty potion bottles ...?'

'You are thinking of Portkeys, Harry, which must be ordinary objects, easy to overlook. But Lord Voldemort use tin cans or old potion bottles to guard his own precious soul? You are forgetting what I have shown you. Lord Voldemort liked to collect trophies, and he preferred objects with a powerful magical history. His pride, his belief in his own superiority, his determination to carve for himself a startling place in magical history; these things suggest to me that Voldemort would have chosen his Horcruxes with some care, favouring objects worthy of the honour.'

'The diary wasn't that special.'

## 第23章 魂 器

"可是那六个魂器,"哈利有些急不可耐地说,"怎么才能找到它们呢?"

"你忘了……你已经摧毁了一个,我又摧毁了一个。"

"你摧毁了一个?"哈利忙问。

"是的,"邓布利多举起他那只焦黑的手说,"那个戒指,哈利,马沃罗的戒指。那上面有一个可怕的咒语。要不是——请原谅我的不谦虚——要不是我本领高强,还有斯内普教授在我重伤回到霍格沃茨后及时相助,我可能就不会活着讲这个故事了。不过,一只枯手换取伏地魔七分之一的灵魂似乎不算太贵。戒指已不再是魂器了。"

"可你是怎么找到它的?"

"你知道,我多年来想方设法了解伏地魔过去的生活,跑了很多地方,寻访他的踪迹。我发现这个戒指藏在冈特家的废墟中。似乎伏地魔把他的一片灵魂藏在里面之后,就不想再戴它了。他把戒指藏在他祖先住过的小屋里(莫芬当然已被押往阿兹卡班),用许多强大的魔法保护着它。但是伏地魔没想到我有一天会去踏访那个废墟,并留意寻找魔法隐藏的痕迹。

"然而,我们不要庆祝得太早。你消灭了日记,我消灭了戒指,如果关于七片灵魂的猜测是正确的,那就还有四个魂器。"

"它们可能是任何东西?"哈利说,"可能是旧铁罐,或者,空药瓶……?"

"你想的是门钥匙,哈利,那是容易被忽略的普通物件。但是伏地魔会用旧铁罐或空药瓶来保存他自己宝贵的灵魂吗?你忘了我曾告诉过你,伏地魔喜欢收集纪念品,喜欢具有强大魔法且有历史意义的物品。他的骄傲、他的优越感、他为自己在魔法史上占取惊人地位的决心,这些都让我觉得伏地魔会精心挑选他的魂器,偏爱配得上这份荣誉的物品。"

"日记没那么特殊。"

## CHAPTER TWENTY-THREE    Horcruxes

'The diary, as you have said yourself, was proof that he was the heir of Slytherin; I am sure that Voldemort considered it of stupendous importance.'

'So, the other Horcruxes?' said Harry. 'Do you think you know what they are, sir?'

'I can only guess,' said Dumbledore. 'For the reasons I have already given, I believe that Lord Voldemort would prefer objects that, in themselves, have a certain grandeur. I have therefore trawled back through Voldemort's past to see if I can find evidence that such artefacts have disappeared around him.'

'The locket!' said Harry loudly. 'Hufflepuff's cup!'

'Yes,' said Dumbledore, smiling, 'I would be prepared to bet – perhaps not my other hand – but a couple of fingers, that they became Horcruxes three and four. The remaining two, assuming again that he created a total of six, are more of a problem, but I will hazard a guess that, having secured objects from Hufflepuff and Slytherin, he set out to track down objects owned by Gryffindor or Ravenclaw. Four objects from the four founders would, I am sure, have exerted a powerful pull over Voldemort's imagination. I cannot answer for whether he ever managed to find anything of Ravenclaw's. I am confident, however, that the only known relic of Gryffindor remains safe.'

Dumbledore pointed his blackened fingers to the wall behind him, where a ruby-encrusted sword reposed within a glass case.

'Do you think that's why he really wanted to come back to Hogwarts, sir?' said Harry. 'To try and find something from one of the other founders?'

'My thoughts precisely,' said Dumbledore. 'But unfortunately, that does not advance us much further, for he was turned away, or so I believe, without the chance to search the school. I am forced to conclude that he never fulfilled his ambition of collecting four founders' objects. He definitely had two – he may have found three – that is the best we can do for now.'

'Even if he got something of Ravenclaw's or of Gryffindor's, that leaves a sixth Horcrux,' said Harry, counting on his fingers. 'Unless he got both?'

'I don't think so,' said Dumbledore. 'I think I know what the sixth Horcrux is. I wonder what you will say when I confess that I have been curious for a while about the behaviour of the snake, Nagini?'

'The snake?' said Harry, startled. 'You can use animals as Horcruxes?'

## 第23章 魂器

"你自己说过，日记能证明他是斯莱特林的继承人，我相信伏地魔认为它意义重大。"

"那么，其他魂器呢？"哈利问，"你知道它们都是什么吗，先生？"

"我只能猜测。"邓布利多说，"由于已经说过的原因，我相信伏地魔会偏爱本身品质高贵的物品。因此我仔细搜索伏地魔的过去，看能否找到这种物品在他周围消失的痕迹。"

"金挂坠盒！"哈利大声说，"赫奇帕奇的杯子！"

"对，"邓布利多微笑道，"我可以打赌——也许不能用我这只好手，但可以用两根手指打赌，它们就是第三和第四个魂器。另外两个要难猜一点——假设他一共做了六个，但我试着猜一下吧，他得到赫奇帕奇和斯莱特林的宝物之后，就会去寻找格兰芬多或拉文克劳的遗物。我想，四位创始人的四件宝物一定对伏地魔有着极大的吸引力。我无法回答他是否找到了拉文克劳的东西，但我确信，格兰芬多唯一已知的遗物安然无恙。"

邓布利多用焦黑的手朝他身后的墙上一指，那儿的玻璃匣子里躺着一把镶着红宝石的宝剑。

"你认为这是他想回霍格沃茨的真正原因吗，先生？"哈利说，"为了找到其他创始人的遗物？"

"这正是我的猜测。可惜并未给我们多少帮助，因为他还没有来得及在校内搜索就被赶走了，至少我相信如此。我只能推断，他未能实现收集四位创始人遗物的野心。他肯定有了两个，也许找到了三个——我们目前就只能推知这么多。"

"就算他得到了拉文克劳或格兰芬多的东西，那还剩下第六个魂器，"哈利扳着手指说，"除非他两样都搞到了？"

"我认为没有，"邓布利多说，"我想我知道第六个魂器是什么。如果我坦白地告诉你，我对那条蛇——纳吉尼的行为已经关注了一段时间，不知你会说什么。"

"蛇？"哈利很吃惊，"可以用动物做魂器？"

## CHAPTER TWENTY-THREE    Horcruxes

'Well, it is inadvisable to do so,' said Dumbledore, 'because to confide a part of your soul to something that can think and move for itself is obviously a very risky business. However, if my calculations are correct, Voldemort was still at least one Horcrux short of his goal of six when he entered your parents' house with the intention of killing you.

'He seems to have reserved the process of making Horcruxes for particularly significant deaths. You would certainly have been that. He believed that in killing you, he was destroying the danger the prophecy had outlined. He believed he was making himself invincible. I am sure that he was intending to make his final Horcrux with your death.

'As we know, he failed. After an interval of some years, however, he used Nagini to kill an old Muggle man, and it might then have occurred to him to turn her into his last Horcrux. She underlines the Slytherin connection, which enhances Lord Voldemort's mystique. I think he is perhaps as fond of her as he can be of anything; he certainly likes to keep her close and he seems to have an unusual amount of control over her, even for a Parselmouth.'

'So,' said Harry, 'the diary's gone, the ring's gone. The cup, the locket and the snake are still intact and you think there might be a Horcrux that was once Ravenclaw's or Gryffindor's?'

'An admirably succinct and accurate summary, yes,' said Dumbledore, bowing his head.

'So ... are you still looking for them, sir? Is that where you've been going when you've been leaving the school?'

'Correct,' said Dumbledore. 'I have been looking for a very long time. I think ... perhaps ... I may be close to finding another one. There are hopeful signs.'

'And if you do,' said Harry quickly, 'can I come with you and help get rid of it?'

Dumbledore looked at Harry very intently for a moment before saying, 'Yes, I think so.'

'I can?' said Harry, thoroughly taken aback.

'Oh yes,' said Dumbledore, smiling slightly. 'I think you have earned that right.'

Harry felt his heart lift. It was very good not to hear words of caution and protection for once. The headmasters and headmistresses around the walls seemed less impressed by Dumbledore's decision; Harry saw a few of them shaking their heads and Phineas Nigellus actually snorted.

'Does Voldemort know when a Horcrux is destroyed, sir? Can he feel it?'

## 第23章 魂器

"不大可取,因为把你灵魂的一部分托付给一个自己能行动、有思维的东西是非常冒险的。但是,如果我估计正确,伏地魔在进你父母家想杀你的时候,至少还缺少一个魂器,尚未达到他要做成六个的目标。

"他似乎在利用特别重要的谋杀来制作魂器,你当然是这样一个目标。他相信如果杀了你,就消灭了预言所提示的危险。他相信这样他就天下无敌了。我想他一定是打算用你的死来做他的最后一个魂器。

"我们知道,他失败了。但时隔几年之后,他用纳吉尼杀死了一个麻瓜老头,也许他就是那时想到了把这条蛇变成他的最后一个魂器。纳吉尼可以突出斯莱特林的家世,增加伏地魔的神秘性。我想这可能是他最喜欢的东西了。他无疑喜欢把纳吉尼带在身边,而且似乎对它有着异乎寻常的支配力,这即使在蛇佬腔中也是罕见的。"

"这么说来,日记毁了,戒指毁了,杯子、挂坠盒和蛇还在,你认为还有一个魂器可能是拉文克劳或格兰芬多的遗物?"

"很好,总结得简练而准确,是的。"邓布利多点头赞许道。

"那么……你还在寻找它们吗,先生?你离开学校就是去做这件事吗?"

"对,我找了很长时间。我想……也许……我快要找到另一个了,有了一些蛛丝马迹。"

"如果你找到了,"哈利马上说,"我能跟你去帮忙消灭它吗?"

邓布利多非常认真地看了哈利一会儿,然后说:"我想可以。"

"我可以?"哈利说,吃了一惊。

"哦,是的,"邓布利多说着微微一笑,"我想你赢得了这个权利。"

哈利的心飞了起来。终于有一次听到不是谨慎和保护之类的话了,感觉真好。墙上的校长们似乎不那么赞赏邓布利多的决定。哈利看到有几个人在摇头,菲尼亚斯·奈杰勒斯哼了一声。

"魂器被毁的时候,伏地魔会知道吗,先生?他能感觉到吗?"哈

## CHAPTER TWENTY-THREE    Horcruxes

Harry asked, ignoring the portraits.

'A very interesting question, Harry. I believe not. I believe that Voldemort is now so immersed in evil, and these crucial parts of himself have been detached for so long, he does not feel as we do. Perhaps, at the point of death, he might be aware of his loss ... but he was not aware, for instance, that the diary had been destroyed until he forced the truth out of Lucius Malfoy. When Voldemort discovered that the diary had been mutilated and robbed of all its powers, I am told that his anger was terrible to behold.'

'But I thought he meant Lucius Malfoy to smuggle it into Hogwarts?'

'Yes he did, years ago, when he was sure he would be able to create more Horcruxes, but still Lucius was supposed to wait for Voldemort's say-so, and he never received it, for Voldemort vanished shortly after giving him the diary. No doubt he thought that Lucius would not dare do anything with the Horcrux other than guard it carefully, but he was counting too much upon Lucius's fear of a master who had been gone for years and whom Lucius believed dead. Of course, Lucius did not know what the diary really was. I understand that Voldemort had told him the diary would cause the Chamber of Secrets to reopen, because it was cleverly enchanted. Had Lucius known he held a portion of his master's soul in his hands he would undoubtedly have treated it with more reverence – but instead he went ahead and carried out the old plan for his own ends: by planting the diary upon Arthur Weasley's daughter, he hoped to discredit Arthur, have me thrown out of Hogwarts and get rid of a highly incriminating object in one stroke. Ah, poor Lucius ... what with Voldemort's fury about the fact that he threw away the Horcrux for his own gain, and the fiasco at the Ministry last year, I would not be surprised if he is secretly glad to be safe in Azkaban at the moment.'

Harry sat in thought for a moment, then asked, 'So if all of his Horcruxes are destroyed, Voldemort *could* be killed?'

'Yes, I think so,' said Dumbledore. 'Without his Horcruxes, Voldemort will be a mortal man with a maimed and diminished soul. Never forget, though, that while his soul may be damaged beyond repair, his brain and his magical power remain intact. It will take uncommon skill and power to kill a wizard like Voldemort, even without his Horcruxes.'

'But I haven't got uncommon skill and power,' said Harry, before he could stop himself.

## 第23章 魂器

利问道，没去理睬那些肖像。

"非常有趣的问题，哈利。我想不会。因为伏地魔现在罪恶太深，而他的这些重要部分又分离得太久，我相信他的感觉已经不如我们。也许在临死时，他才会感觉到损失……比如那本日记被毁的时候他就没有察觉，后来才从卢修斯·马尔福口中逼问出来。我听说，当伏地魔发现日记被摧毁并失去了所有魔力之后，曾经大发雷霆，非常可怕。"

"可我以为是他要卢修斯·马尔福把日记偷偷带进霍格沃茨的。"

"是的，那是多年以前，伏地魔确信自己可以制造多个魂器的时候。但是卢修斯仍要等待伏地魔的许可才能行动，他没有等到，因为伏地魔交托日记后不久便消失了。他无疑认为卢修斯对魂器除了小心看护之外不敢做任何事。他是过于依靠卢修斯对主人的畏惧了——要知道这个主人已失踪多年并被卢修斯认为已经死亡。当然，卢修斯不知道那本日记实际上是什么。我想伏地魔只会跟他说日记被施了巧妙的魔法，能使密室重新打开。如果卢修斯知道他手里捧了主人的一片灵魂，一定会对它更加敬重一些——但事实是，卢修斯为了自己的目的执行了老计划：把日记安置在亚瑟·韦斯莱的女儿身上。他希望以此败坏亚瑟的名声，把我赶出霍格沃茨，同时除掉一件非常容易惹祸的物证。啊，可怜的卢修斯……出于私心丢掉魂器而触怒了伏地魔，去年又在魔法部遭遇那样的惨败，如果他此刻暗自庆幸能在阿兹卡班苟且偷安，我不会奇怪。"

哈利坐在那里沉思了一会儿，问道："如果魂器全部给销毁了，伏地魔就能被杀死吗？"

"我想是的，"邓布利多说，"没有了魂器，伏地魔就是个灵魂已经残损的凡人。但不要忘记，尽管灵魂残破得无法修复，他的脑子和魔力仍完好无损。伏地魔这样的巫师即使已经没有魂器，杀死他还是需要超常的能力与本领。"

"可我没有超常的能力与本领。"哈利脱口而出。

## CHAPTER TWENTY-THREE    Horcruxes

'Yes, you have,' said Dumbledore firmly. 'You have a power that Voldemort has never had. You can –'

'I know!' said Harry impatiently. 'I can love!' It was only with difficulty that he stopped himself adding, 'Big deal!'

'Yes, Harry, you can love,' said Dumbledore, who looked as though he knew perfectly well what Harry had just refrained from saying. 'Which, given everything that has happened to you, is a great and remarkable thing. You are still too young to understand how unusual you are, Harry.'

'So, when the prophecy says that I'll have "power the Dark Lord knows not", it just means – love?' asked Harry, feeling a little let down.

'Yes – just love,' said Dumbledore. 'But Harry, never forget that what the prophecy says is only significant because Voldemort made it so. I told you this at the end of last year. Voldemort singled you out as the person who would be most dangerous to him – and in doing so, he *made* you the person who would be most dangerous to him!'

'But it comes to the same –'

'No, it doesn't!' said Dumbledore, sounding impatient now. Pointing at Harry with his black, withered hand, he said, 'You are setting too much store by the prophecy!'

'But,' spluttered Harry, 'but you said the prophecy means –'

'If Voldemort had never heard of the prophecy, would it have been fulfilled? Would it have meant anything? Of course not! Do you think every prophecy in the Hall of Prophecy has been fulfilled?'

'But,' said Harry, bewildered, 'but last year, you said one of us would have to kill the other –'

'Harry, Harry, only because Voldemort made a grave error, and acted on Professor Trelawney's words! If Voldemort had never murdered your father, would he have imparted in you a furious desire for revenge? Of course not! If he had not forced your mother to die for you, would he have given you a magical protection he could not penetrate? Of course not, Harry! Don't you see? Voldemort himself created his worst enemy, just as tyrants everywhere do! Have you any idea how much tyrants fear the people they oppress? All of them realise that, one day, amongst their many victims, there is sure to be one who rises against them and strikes back! Voldemort is no different! Always he was on the lookout for the one who would challenge him. He

## 第23章 魂器

"你有,"邓布利多坚定地说,"你有伏地魔从未有过的能力。你有——"

"我知道!"哈利不耐烦地说,"我有爱!"他好容易才没有加上:"有什么了不起!"

"是的,哈利,你有爱。"邓布利多好像很了解哈利舌头底下压着的话,"想想你经历的一切,那是非常了不起的。你还太年轻,不知道你是多么特殊,哈利。"

"那么,预言说我有'黑魔头所不了解的力量',指的就是——爱?"哈利问,他感到有点失望。

"对——就是爱。"邓布利多说,"但是哈利,永远不要忘记,预言的意义其实都是伏地魔制造的。我去年年底跟你讲过这一点。伏地魔把你当成对他最危险的人——这样一来,他就使你变成了对他最危险的人!"

"可这是一回事——"

"不是一回事!"邓布利多语气有些不耐烦了。他用枯黑的手指着哈利说:"你太把那个预言当回事了!"

"可是,"哈利结结巴巴地说,"你说过那个预言意味着——"

"如果伏地魔从未听说过那个预言,它还会应验吗?它还会有意义吗?当然不会!你认为预言厅中的每个预言都应验了吗?"

"可是,"哈利糊涂了,"可是去年,你说过我们中间必有一个要把对方杀死——"

"哈利呀,哈利,那只是因为伏地魔犯了个大错,他按特里劳尼教授的预言采取了行动!如果伏地魔没有杀死你的父亲,你还会产生强烈的复仇欲望吗?当然不会!如果他没有逼你母亲为你而死,你还会得到他无法穿透的魔法保护吗?当然不会!哈利。你不明白吗?伏地魔自己制造了他最可怕的敌人,就像普天下的暴君一样!你知道暴君多么害怕被压迫的人民吗?他们都知道总有一天,在众多受害者中会有一个起来奋起反击!伏地魔也一样。他总是在寻找那个会向他挑战

## CHAPTER TWENTY-THREE    Horcruxes

heard the prophecy and he leapt into action, with the result that he not only handpicked the man most likely to finish him, he handed him uniquely deadly weapons!'

'But –'

'It is essential that you understand this!' said Dumbledore, standing up and striding about the room, his glittering robes swooshing in his wake; Harry had never seen him so agitated. 'By attempting to kill you, Voldemort himself singled out the remarkable person who sits here in front of me, and gave him the tools for the job! It is Voldemort's fault that you were able to see into his thoughts, his ambitions, that you even understand the snakelike language in which he gives orders, and yet, Harry, despite your privileged insight into Voldemort's world (which, incidentally, is a gift any Death Eater would kill to have), you have never been seduced by the Dark Arts, never, even for a second, shown the slightest desire to become one of Voldemort's followers!'

'Of course I haven't!' said Harry indignantly. 'He killed my mum and dad!'

'You are protected, in short, by your ability to love!' said Dumbledore loudly. 'The only protection that can possibly work against the lure of power like Voldemort's! In spite of all the temptation you have endured, all the suffering, you remain pure of heart, just as pure as you were at the age of eleven, when you stared into a mirror that reflected your heart's desire, and it showed you only the way to thwart Lord Voldemort, and not immortality or riches. Harry, have you any idea how few wizards could have seen what you saw in that mirror? Voldemort should have known then what he was dealing with, but he did not!

'But he knows it now. You have flitted into Lord Voldemort's mind without damage to yourself, but he cannot possess you without enduring mortal agony, as he discovered in the Ministry. I do not think he understands why, Harry, but he was in such a hurry to mutilate his own soul, he never paused to understand the incomparable power of a soul that is untarnished and whole.'

'But, sir,' said Harry, making valiant efforts not to sound argumentative, 'it all comes to the same thing, doesn't it? I've got to try and kill him, or –'

'Got to?' said Dumbledore. 'Of course you've got to! But not because of the prophecy! Because you, yourself, will never rest until you've tried! We both know it! Imagine, please, just for a moment, that you had never heard that prophecy! How would you feel about Voldemort now? Think!'

## 第23章 魂器

的人,听到预言后就马上行动,结果他不仅亲手选出了那个最有可能除掉他的人,而且给了那个人特别致命的武器!"

"可是——"

"你必须明白这一点!"邓布利多站了起来,在屋子里大步地走来走去,闪亮的袍子在身后呼呼飘动。哈利还从没见他这么激动过,"因为企图杀死你,伏地魔亲自选出了坐在我面前的这位卓越人物,并为其提供了工具!你能看到伏地魔的思想、野心,甚至能听懂他发令时那蛇语般的语言,这都只能怪他自己。可是,哈利,尽管你能洞察伏地魔的世界——要知道,这是任何食死徒不惜用杀人来换取的能力,但是你却从未接受黑魔法的诱惑,从未显露过丝毫想要追随伏地魔的欲望,一秒钟都没有!"

"当然不会!"哈利愤怒地说,"他杀了我的父母!"

"简而言之,是你的爱保护了你!"邓布利多大声说,"唯有这一种保护,才有可能抵御伏地魔那样的权力的诱惑!虽然经历了那么多诱惑、那么多痛苦,你依然心地纯洁,还像十一岁时那样。当时你向那面能照出你内心愿望的镜子中望去,看到的只有怎样挫败伏地魔,而没有对长生和财富的渴望。哈利,你知不知道,世上没有几个巫师能看到你在镜中看到的东西?伏地魔那时就该知道他要对付的是什么,可惜他没有!

"但他现在知道了。你侵入了伏地魔的思想而未受任何损害,他想附在你身上时却不能不忍受剧烈的痛苦,他在部里已经发现了这一点。但我认为他不了解这是为什么,哈利。但他那样急于破坏自己的灵魂,从来无暇去了解一个纯洁健全的灵魂拥有何等无与伦比的力量。"

"可是,先生,"哈利说,竭力不想显得像是在争辩,"说到底还是一样,是不是?我必须设法杀死他,否则——"

"必须?"邓布利多说,"你当然必须!但不是因为预言!而是因为你自己,你不这样做就不会安心!我们都知道这一点!请想象一下,如果你从未听过那个预言!你对伏地魔会有什么想法呢?想一想!"

## CHAPTER TWENTY-THREE  Horcruxes

Harry watched Dumbledore striding up and down in front of him, and thought. He thought of his mother, his father and Sirius. He thought of Cedric Diggory. He thought of all the terrible deeds he knew Lord Voldemort had done. A flame seemed to leap inside his chest, searing his throat.

'I'd want him finished,' said Harry quietly. 'and I'd want to do it.'

'Of course you would!' cried Dumbledore. 'You see, the prophecy does not mean you *have* to do anything! But the prophecy caused Lord Voldemort to *mark you as his equal* ... in other words, you are free to choose your way, quite free to turn your back on the prophecy! But Voldemort continues to set store by the prophecy. He will continue to hunt you ... which makes it certain, really, that –'

'That one of us is going to end up killing the other,' said Harry. 'Yes.'

But he understood at last what Dumbledore had been trying to tell him. It was, he thought, the difference between being dragged into the arena to face a battle to the death and walking into the arena with your head held high. Some people, perhaps, would say that there was little to choose between the two ways, but Dumbledore knew – and so do I, thought Harry, with a rush of fierce pride, and so did my parents – that there was all the difference in the world.

## 第23章 魂器

看着面前踱来踱去的邓布利多,哈利沉思起来。他想到了他的母亲、他的父亲和小天狼星,想到了塞德里克,想到了伏地魔的种种罪行。他的胸中腾起一股烈焰,直烧到喉咙口。

"我想除掉他,"哈利轻声说,"我想去做这件事。"

"你当然会!"邓布利多叫道,"你看,预言并没表示你必须做什么!但预言使伏地魔认定你是他的对手……换句话说,你有权选择自己的道路,有权不理睬那个预言!但伏地魔还是会对它念念不忘,他会继续追杀你……这就必然使得——"

"我们中有一个会把对方杀死,"哈利说,"是的。"

他终于明白了邓布利多要告诉他的意思,那就是:被拽进角斗场去面对一场殊死搏斗和自己昂首走进去是不一样的。也许有人会说这二者之间并无多少不同,但邓布利多知道——我也知道,哈利带着强烈的自豪感想道,我的父母也知道——这是世界上所有的不同。

## CHAPTER TWENTY-FOUR

# Sectumsempra

Exhausted but delighted with his night's work, Harry told Ron and Hermione everything that had happened during next morning's Charms lesson (having first cast the *Muffliato* spell upon those nearest them). They were both satisfyingly impressed by the way he had wheedled the memory out of Slughorn and positively awed when he told them about Voldemort's Horcruxes and Dumbledore's promise to take Harry along, should he find another one.

'Wow,' said Ron, when Harry had finally finished telling them everything; Ron was waving his wand very vaguely in the direction of the ceiling without paying the slightest bit of attention to what he was doing. 'Wow. You're actually going to go with Dumbledore ... and try and destroy ... wow.'

'Ron, you're making it snow,' said Hermione patiently, grabbing his wrist and redirecting his wand away from the ceiling from which, sure enough, large white flakes had started to fall. Lavender Brown, Harry noticed, glared at Hermione from a neighbouring table through very red eyes and Hermione immediately let go of Ron's arm.

'Oh yeah,' said Ron, looking down at his shoulders in vague surprise. 'Sorry ... looks like we've all got horrible dandruff now ...'

He brushed some of the fake snow off Hermione's shoulder.

Lavender burst into tears. Ron looked immensely guilty and turned his back on her.

'We split up,' he told Harry out of the corner of his mouth. 'Last night. When she saw me coming out of the dormitory with Hermione. Obviously she couldn't see you, so she thought it had just been the two of us.'

'Ah,' said Harry. 'Well – you don't mind it's over, do you?'

'No,' Ron admitted. 'It was pretty bad while she was yelling, but at least I

# 第 24 章

# 神锋无影

晚上的活动累得哈利精疲力竭,但心情很愉快。第二天上午的魔咒课上,他把事情的经过一五一十都告诉了罗恩和赫敏(先对附近同学施了闭耳塞听咒)。他们俩都对他诱使斯拉格霍恩交出记忆颇为满意。当他说到伏地魔的魂器,又说到邓布利多答应发现另一个魂器后会带他一起去时,他们都显得十分敬畏。

"哇,"哈利终于说完时,罗恩叫道,手里的魔杖对着天花板乱晃,根本没意识到自己在干什么,"哇,你真要跟邓布利多一起去……去消灭……哇。"

"罗恩,你在造雪啊。"赫敏和颜悦色地说,一边抓住他的手腕不让魔杖指向天花板,那儿已经有大片白色的雪花飘下。哈利发现旁边座位上的拉文德·布朗用红红的眼睛瞪着赫敏,赫敏立刻放开了罗恩的胳膊。

"哦,对了,"罗恩看看自己的肩头,有点儿惊讶地说,"对不起……我们都好像沾上了讨厌的头皮屑……"

他掸掉赫敏肩上的一些假雪花,拉文德哭了起来。罗恩显得很内疚,转身背对她。

"我们分手了,"他悄悄地告诉哈利,"昨天晚上。她看到我跟赫敏从宿舍里出来。她显然看不到你,以为只有我们俩。"

"啊,"哈利说,"那么——你不介意吹了吧?"

"不介意,"罗恩承认道,"她大吵大闹的时候确实挺难受,但至少

## CHAPTER TWENTY-FOUR  Sectumsempra

didn't have to finish it.'

'Coward,' said Hermione, though she looked amused. 'Well, it was a bad night for romance all round. Ginny and Dean split up too, Harry.'

Harry thought there was a rather knowing look in her eye as she told him that, but she could not possibly know that his insides were suddenly dancing the conga: keeping his face as immobile and his voice as indifferent as he could, he asked, 'How come?'

'Oh, something really silly ... she said he was always trying to help her through the portrait hole, like she couldn't climb in herself ... but they've been a bit rocky for ages.'

Harry glanced over at Dean on the other side of the classroom. He certainly looked unhappy.

'Of course, this puts you in a bit of a dilemma, doesn't it?' said Hermione.

'What d'you mean?' said Harry quickly.

'The Quidditch team,' said Hermione. 'If Ginny and Dean aren't speaking ...'

'Oh – oh yeah,' said Harry.

'Flitwick,' said Ron in a warning tone. The tiny little Charms master was bobbing his way towards them and Hermione was the only one who had managed to turn vinegar into wine; her glass flask was full of deep crimson liquid, whereas the contents of Harry's and Ron's were still murky brown.

'Now, now, boys,' squeaked Professor Flitwick reproachfully. 'A little less talk, a little more action ... let me see you try ...'

Together they raised their wands, concentrating with all their might, and pointed them at their flasks. Harry's vinegar turned to ice; Ron's flask exploded.

'Yes ... for homework ...' said Professor Flitwick, re-emerging from under the table and pulling shards of glass out of the top of his hat, *'practise.'*

They had one of their rare joint free periods after Charms and walked back to the common room together. Ron seemed to be positively light-hearted about the end of his relationship with Lavender and Hermione seemed cheery, too, though when asked what she was grinning about she simply said, 'It's a nice day.' Neither of them seemed to have noticed that a fierce battle was raging inside Harry's brain:

*She's Ron's sister.*

But she's ditched Dean!

*She's still Ron's sister.*

## 第24章 神锋无影

不用我提出分手了。"

"懦夫。"赫敏说,不过看上去挺愉快的,"哎,昨晚好像情场普遍失利,金妮和迪安也分手了,哈利。"

哈利觉得赫敏对他说这话时带着一种意味深长的眼神,但她不可能知道他内心突然跳起了康茄舞。他尽量不动声色地问:"怎么搞的?"

"哦,很可笑的事……金妮说钻肖像洞口时迪安总想帮她一把,好像她自己爬不进来似的……但他们磕磕绊绊已经很久了。"

哈利看了看教室另一头的迪安,他看上去显然很不开心。

"当然,这让你左右为难了,是不是?"赫敏问。

"什么意思?"哈利赶紧问。

"魁地奇球队,如果金妮和迪安不说话了……"

"哦——是啊。"哈利说。

"弗立维。"罗恩警告道。小个子魔咒课教师正朝他们快速走过来,只有赫敏已经把醋变成了酒,她的玻璃烧瓶里盛满了深红色的液体,而哈利和罗恩的瓶里还是浑浊的棕黄色。

"好了,好了,男孩子们,"弗立维教授尖声责备地说,"少说点话,多干点活……让我看你们做一次……"

哈利和罗恩一起举起魔杖,竭力聚精会神,将魔杖指向烧瓶。哈利的醋变成了冰,罗恩的烧瓶炸了。

"好……家庭作业……"弗立维教授说着从桌子底下钻出来,择去帽顶上的玻璃片,"练习。"

魔咒课后,难得三个人都是空闲时间,他们一起走回公共休息室。罗恩似乎对跟拉文德分手感到很愉快。赫敏也兴致不错,虽然问她笑什么时她只是说"天气好"。他们似乎都没注意到哈利内心正在进行激烈的斗争:

她是罗恩的妹妹。

可她甩掉了迪安!

她还是罗恩的妹妹。

## CHAPTER TWENTY-FOUR   Sectumsempra

I'm his best mate!
*That'll make it worse.*
If I talked to him first –
*He'd hit you.*
What if I don't care?
*He's your best mate!*

Harry barely noticed that they were climbing through the portrait hole into the sunny common room, and only vaguely registered the small group of seventh-years clustered together there, until Hermione cried, 'Katie! You're back! Are you OK?'

Harry stared: it was indeed Katie Bell, looking completely healthy and surrounded by her jubilant friends.

'I'm really well!' she said happily. 'They let me out of St Mungo's on Monday, I had a couple of days at home with Mum and Dad and then came back here this morning. Leanne was just telling me about McLaggen and the last match, Harry ...'

'Yeah,' said Harry, 'well, now you're back and Ron's fit, we'll have a decent chance of thrashing Ravenclaw, which means we could still be in the running for the Cup. Listen, Katie ...'

He had to put the question to her at once; his curiosity even drove Ginny temporarily from his brain. He dropped his voice as Katie's friends started gathering up their things; apparently they were late for Transfiguration.

'... that necklace ... can you remember who gave it to you now?'

'No,' said Katie, shaking her head ruefully. 'Everyone's been asking me, but I haven't got a clue. The last thing I remember was walking into the ladies' in the Three Broomsticks.'

'You definitely went into the bathroom, then?' said Hermione.

'Well, I know I pushed open the door,' said Katie, 'so I suppose whoever Imperiused me was standing just behind it. After that, my memory's a blank until about two weeks ago in St Mungo's. Listen, I'd better go, I wouldn't put it past McGonagall to give me lines even if it is my first day back ...'

She caught up her bag and books and hurried after her friends, leaving Harry, Ron and Hermione to sit down at a window table and ponder what she had told them.

我是罗恩的好朋友！

那只会更难办。

如果我先跟罗恩说——

他会打你的。

如果我不在乎呢？

他是你的好朋友！

哈利几乎没注意到他们是怎样从肖像洞口爬进洒满阳光的公共休息室的，他只是模糊地意识到屋里聚集了一小群七年级学生，这时赫敏叫了起来："凯蒂！你回来啦！好了吗？"

哈利瞪大了眼睛：果然是凯蒂·贝尔，看上去完全康复了，被欢乐的朋友们围在中间。

"我真的好了！"她快活地说，"星期一出的院，在家跟爸爸妈妈待了两天，今天早上回来的。利妮跟我讲了麦克拉根和上次比赛的事，哈利……"

"是啊，"哈利说，"不过，现在你回来了，罗恩也好了，我们有希望打败拉文克劳，也就是说还有夺杯的机会。哎，凯蒂……"

他必须马上问她，他的好奇心甚至把金妮暂时挤到了脑后。凯蒂的朋友们开始收拾东西，显然变形课要迟到了。他压低嗓门问道："……那条项链……你想起来是谁给你的了吗？"

"没有。"凯蒂懊恼地摇摇头，"每个人都问我，可我一点儿都想不起来。我记得的最后一件事是走进三把扫帚的厕所。"

"你确定你进了厕所？"赫敏说。

"嗯，我记得我当时推开了门，因此我认为，对我施夺魂咒的家伙肯定就在门后。之后我的记忆就是一片空白，直到两星期前在圣芒戈医院醒来。对不起，我该走了，我想麦格教授不见得会因为这是我第一天回学校就不罚我抄写。"

她抓起书包和书，匆匆去追赶同伴，哈利、罗恩和赫敏坐到一张靠窗的桌子前，思考刚才她说的情况。

## CHAPTER TWENTY-FOUR  Sectumsempra

'So it must have been a girl or a woman who gave Katie the necklace,' said Hermione, 'to be in the ladies' bathroom.'

'Or someone who looked like a girl or a woman,' said Harry. 'Don't forget, there was a cauldronful of Polyjuice Potion at Hogwarts. We know some of it got stolen ...'

In his mind's eye he watched a parade of Crabbes and Goyles prance past, all transformed into girls.

'I think I'm going to take another swig of Felix,' said Harry, 'and have a go at the Room of Requirement again.'

'That would be a complete waste of potion,' said Hermione flatly, putting down the copy of *Spellman's Syllabary* she had just taken out of her bag. 'Luck can only get you so far, Harry. The situation with Slughorn was different; you always had the ability to persuade him, you just needed to tweak the circumstances a bit. Luck isn't enough to get you through a powerful enchantment, though. Don't go wasting the rest of that potion! You'll need all the luck you can get if Dumbledore takes you along with him ...' She dropped her voice to a whisper.

'Couldn't we make some more?' Ron asked Harry, ignoring Hermione. 'It'd be great to have a stock of it ... have a look in the book ...'

Harry pulled his copy of *Advanced Potion-Making* out of his bag and looked up Felix Felicis.

'Blimey, it's seriously complicated,' he said, running an eye down the list of ingredients. 'And it takes six months ... you've got to let it stew ...'

'Typical,' said Ron.

Harry was about to put his book away again when he noticed the corner of a page folded down; turning to it, he saw the *Sectumsempra* spell, captioned 'For Enemies', that he had marked a few weeks previously. He had still not found out what it did, mainly because he did not want to test it around Hermione, but he was considering trying it out on McLaggen next time he came up behind him unawares.

The only person who was not particularly pleased to see Katie Bell back at school was Dean Thomas, because he would no longer be required to fill her place as Chaser. He took the blow stoically enough when Harry told him, merely grunting and shrugging, but Harry had the distinct feeling as he walked away that Dean and Seamus were muttering mutinously behind his back.

## 第24章 神锋无影

"那么,把项链给凯蒂的一定是个女人,"赫敏说,"因为是在女厕所。"

"或者看上去像女人,"哈利说,"别忘了,霍格沃茨有一大锅复方汤剂,我们知道被偷掉了一些……"

他在想象中看到克拉布和高尔神气活现地走过,都变成了女孩模样。

"我想再喝一口福灵剂,到有求必应屋去看看。"哈利说。

"那纯粹是浪费魔药,"赫敏放下刚从书包里拿出来的《魔法字音表》,断然说道,"运气只能帮你这么多了,哈利。斯拉格霍恩的情况不一样,你一向有说服他的能力,只需要调整一下环境。但运气不足以帮你穿透强大的魔法。别浪费剩下的魔药了!如果邓布利多带你去行动的话,你会需要你能得到的所有运气……"她压低声音说。

"不能再配点吗?"罗恩问哈利,没有理会赫敏,"要能备上一些就好了……看看书……"

哈利从书包里抽出《高级魔药制作》,查找福灵剂。

"天哪,太复杂了,"他扫视着那一长串的配料说,"要六个月……得慢慢熬……"

"都是这一套。"罗恩说。

哈利正要把书收起来,忽然发现有一页折着,他翻到那里,是神锋无影咒,注有对敌人,是自己几星期前做的记号。他还没有试过它是什么样,主要是不想在赫敏的周围尝试。他想下次悄悄走近麦克拉根时试它一下。

只有迪安一个人不是特别高兴看到凯蒂回来,因为这意味着不需要他当追球手了。哈利跟他谈这件事时,迪安对这个打击的反应还算平静,只是耸耸肩哼了一声。但哈利走开时,还是真切地感到迪安和西莫在背后不服气地嘟囔着。

765

## CHAPTER TWENTY-FOUR — Sectumsempra

The following fortnight saw the best Quidditch practices Harry had known as Captain. His team was so pleased to be rid of McLaggen, so glad to have Katie back at last, that they were flying extremely well.

Ginny did not seem at all upset about the break-up with Dean; on the contrary, she was the life and soul of the team. Her imitations of Ron anxiously bobbing up and down in front of the goalposts as the Quaffle sped towards him, or of Harry bellowing orders at McLaggen before being knocked out cold, kept them all highly amused. Harry, laughing with the others, was glad to have an innocent reason to look at Ginny; he had received several more Bludger injuries during practice because he had not been keeping his eyes on the Snitch.

The battle still raged inside his head: Ginny or Ron? Sometimes he thought that the post-Lavender Ron might not mind too much if he asked Ginny out, but then he remembered Ron's expression when he had seen her kissing Dean, and was sure that Ron would consider it base treachery if Harry so much as held her hand ...

Yet Harry could not help himself talking to Ginny, laughing with her, walking back from practice with her; however much his conscience ached, he found himself wondering how best to get her on her own: it would have been ideal if Slughorn had given another of his little parties, for Ron would not be around – but unfortunately, Slughorn seemed to have given them up. Once or twice Harry considered asking for Hermione's help, but he did not think he could stand seeing the smug look on her face; he thought he caught it sometimes when Hermione spotted him staring at Ginny, or laughing at her jokes. And to complicate matters, he had the nagging worry that if he didn't do it, somebody else was sure to ask Ginny out soon: he and Ron were at least agreed on the fact that she was too popular for her own good.

All in all, the temptation to take another gulp of Felix Felicis was becoming stronger by the day, for surely this was a case for, as Hermione put it, 'tweaking the circumstances'? The balmy days slid gently through May, and Ron seemed to be there at Harry's shoulder every time he saw Ginny. Harry found himself longing for a stroke of luck that would somehow cause Ron to realise that nothing would make him happier than his best friend and his sister falling for each other and to leave them alone together for longer than a few seconds. There seemed no chance of either while the final Quidditch game of the season was looming; Ron wanted to talk tactics with Harry all the time and had little thought for anything else.

## 第24章 神锋无影

接下来的两个星期,哈利看到了他当队长以来最好的魁地奇训练。他的队员们为赶走了麦克拉根和终于迎回了凯蒂而欢欣鼓舞,飞得异常出色。

金妮似乎一点都不为跟迪安分手而难过,相反,她成了全队的灵魂人物。她模仿罗恩看到鬼飞球过来时紧张地在球门柱前忽上忽下,模仿哈利被撞晕前朝麦克拉根大吼,把大家逗得很开心。哈利跟队员们一起大笑,很高兴自己有正当理由盯着金妮看。因为眼睛没有一直注意看飞贼,他被游走球额外多撞了几次。

他脑子里仍在激烈地斗争着:金妮还是罗恩?有时他想,经过了同拉文德的恋爱,罗恩可能不会太介意他与金妮约会。但他又想起金妮亲吻迪安时罗恩的表情,断定自己就是拉拉金妮的手都会被罗恩看作卑鄙的背叛……

但哈利忍不住要跟金妮说话,跟她一起笑,训练完跟她一起走回去。不管良心怎样不安,他还是不禁幻想着怎么能跟她单独相处:最好斯拉格霍恩再召集一个小聚会,那样罗恩就不会在场——不幸的是,斯拉格霍恩似乎不会再举办聚会了。哈利有一两次想到找赫敏帮忙,但觉得自己会受不了她脸上的得意表情。有时候,赫敏看到他盯着金妮或被金妮逗得大笑时,他好像就发现过这种表情。更麻烦的是,他焦虑地想到如果自己不采取行动,肯定很快就会有别人约会金妮。他和罗恩至少在这一点上看法是一致的:金妮太招人喜欢了,这对她本人没好处。

总之,再喝一口福灵剂的诱惑日益增强,因为这种情况应当算是赫敏所说的需要"调整一下环境"吧?和煦的五月天轻轻溜走,好像他每次看到金妮的时候罗恩都在旁边。哈利发现自己渴望有一个好运,能让罗恩觉得没有什么比好朋友哈利和妹妹金妮倾心相爱更令他开心了,并且能让他和金妮单独相处几秒钟以上。但这两条似乎都没机会实现,因为本赛季最后一场魁地奇比赛在即,罗恩总想跟哈利讨论战术,无暇顾及其他。

CHAPTER TWENTY-FOUR  Sectumsempra

Ron was not unique in this respect; interest in the Gryffindor-Ravenclaw game was running extremely high throughout the school, for the match would decide the championship, which was still wide open. If Gryffindor beat Ravenclaw by a margin of three hundred points (a tall order, and yet Harry had never known his team fly better) then they would win the championship. If they won by less than three hundred points, they would come second to Ravenclaw; if they lost by a hundred points they would be third behind Hufflepuff and if they lost by more than a hundred, they would be in fourth place and nobody, Harry thought, would ever, ever let him forget that it had been he who had captained Gryffindor to their first bottom-of-the-table defeat in two centuries.

The run-up to this crucial match had all the usual features: members of rival houses attempting to intimidate opposing teams in the corridors; unpleasant chants about individual players being rehearsed loudly as they passed; the team members themselves either swaggering around enjoying all the attention or else dashing into bathrooms between classes to throw up. Somehow, the game had become inextricably linked in Harry's mind with success or failure in his plans for Ginny. He could not help feeling that if they won by more than three hundred points, the scenes of euphoria and a nice loud after-match party might be just as good as a hearty swig of Felix Felicis.

In the midst of all his preoccupations Harry had not forgotten his other ambition: finding out what Malfoy was up to in the Room of Requirement. He was still checking the Marauder's Map and, as he was often unable to locate Malfoy on it, deduced that Malfoy was still spending plenty of time within the Room. Although Harry was losing hope that he would ever succeed in getting inside the Room, he attempted it whenever he was in the vicinity, but no matter how he reworded his request, the wall remained firmly doorless.

A few days before the match against Ravenclaw, Harry found himself walking down to dinner alone from the common room, Ron having rushed off into a nearby bathroom to throw up yet again, and Hermione having dashed off to see Professor Vector about a mistake she thought she might have made in her last Arithmancy essay. More out of habit than anything, Harry made his usual detour along the seventh-floor corridor, checking the Marauder's Map as he went. For a moment he could not find Malfoy anywhere, and assumed he must indeed be inside the Room of Requirement again, but then he saw Malfoy's tiny, labelled dot standing in a boys' bathroom on the floor below, accompanied, not by Crabbe or Goyle, but by Moaning Myrtle.

## 第24章 神锋无影

在这方面罗恩并不特殊，全校同学都对格兰芬多—拉文克劳球赛的兴趣极为高涨。因为这场比赛将决出尚难料定的冠军杯名次。如果格兰芬多领先拉文克劳三百分（难度很大，但哈利从没见他的球队飞得像现在这么出色），他们就能夺杯；如果领先不到三百分，就要排在拉文克劳后面，屈居第二；如果落后一百分，就会排到赫奇帕奇后面，名列第三；如果落后一百分以上，就会掉到第四。那样的话，哈利想，就永远没有人会让他忘记，是他率领格兰芬多球队拿了两百年来的第一个倒数第一。

这场关键性的比赛的前奏仍旧是那些内容：两个学院的学生在走廊上威吓对方的球队；在个别球员走过时大声排练针对他们的口号；球员们则要么大摇大摆地享受关注，要么在课间冲进盥洗室呕吐。不知为何，在哈利的脑子里，这场比赛与他对金妮的计划的成败密切联系在一起。他忍不住想，如果他们领先三百分以上，热烈的庆祝场面和赛后的联欢也许能赶得上一大口福灵剂的效果。

在所有这些烦琐的事情中，哈利始终没有忘记他的另一个目标：搞清马尔福在有求必应屋干什么。他仍然查看活点地图，在图上经常找不到马尔福，他推测马尔福很多时间都待在那间屋里。哈利正在对进入有求必应屋失去希望，但只要在附近他还是会去试试，然而无论他怎么变换说法，墙上还是没有出现门。

在同拉文克劳比赛的几天之前，哈利独自从公共休息室走去吃晚饭，因为罗恩又冲进旁边的盥洗室呕吐去了，赫敏则跑去找维克多教授，因为她想起上次交的算术占卜课论文可能有个错误。哈利多半是出于习惯，又拐到八楼走廊上，边走边看活点地图。一开始他找不到马尔福，猜想那小子又去有求必应屋了，然后他看到标着马尔福的小点站在楼下一个男盥洗室里，旁边不是克拉布和高尔，而是哭泣的桃金娘。

## CHAPTER TWENTY-FOUR    Sectumsempra

Harry only stopped staring at this unlikely coupling when he walked right into a suit of armour. The loud crash brought him out of his reverie; hurrying from the scene lest Filch should turn up, he dashed down the marble staircase and along the passageway below. Outside the bathroom, he pressed his ear against the door. He couldn't hear anything. He very quietly pushed the door open.

Draco Malfoy was standing with his back to the door, his hands clutching either side of the sink, his white-blond head bowed.

'Don't,' crooned Moaning Myrtle's voice from one of the cubicles. 'Don't ... tell me what's wrong ... I can help you ...'

'No one can help me,' said Malfoy. His whole body was shaking. 'I can't do it ... I can't ... it won't work ... and unless I do it soon ... he says he'll kill me ...'

And Harry realised, with a shock so huge it seemed to root him to the spot, that Malfoy was crying – actually crying – tears streaming down his pale face into the grimy basin. Malfoy gasped and gulped and then, with a great shudder, looked up into the cracked mirror and saw Harry staring at him over his shoulder.

Malfoy wheeled round, drawing his wand. Instinctively, Harry pulled out his own. Malfoy's hex missed Harry by inches, shattering the lamp on the wall beside him; Harry threw himself sideways, thought *Levicorpus!* and flicked his wand, but Malfoy blocked the jinx and raised his wand for another –

'No! No! Stop it!' squealed Moaning Myrtle, her voice echoing loudly around the tiled room. 'Stop! STOP!'

There was a loud bang and the bin behind Harry exploded; Harry attempted a Leg-Locker Curse that backfired off the wall behind Malfoy's ear and smashed the cistern beneath Moaning Myrtle, who screamed loudly; water poured everywhere and Harry slipped over as Malfoy, his face contorted, cried, 'Cruci–'

'SECTUMSEMPRA!' bellowed Harry from the floor, waving his wand wildly.

Blood spurted from Malfoy's face and chest as though he had been slashed with an invisible sword. He staggered backwards and collapsed on to the waterlogged floor with a great splash, his wand falling from his limp right hand.

'No –' gasped Harry.

Slipping and staggering, Harry got to his feet and plunged towards Malfoy, whose face was now shining scarlet, his white hands scrabbling at his blood-soaked chest.

## 第24章 神锋无影

哈利盯着这不太可能的组合，没留神撞到了一副盔甲上。稀里哗啦的响声把他从沉思中唤醒。他怕费尔奇出现，赶快冲向大理石楼梯，跑到下一层走廊上。他把耳朵贴到盥洗室的门上，但什么也听不见。他轻轻地推开了门。

德拉科·马尔福背对门站着，手扶着水池边，淡金色的脑袋低垂着。

"别这样，"哭泣的桃金娘温柔的声音从一个隔间传了出来，"别这样……告诉我是什么事……我可以帮你……"

"谁也帮不了我，"马尔福说，全身都在发抖，"我干不了……干不了……办不成……如果不快点办成……他说他会杀了我……"

哈利心中猛然一震，脚像被钉在了那儿，他发现马尔福在哭——真的在哭，眼泪从他苍白的脸上流到肮脏的池子里。马尔福抽噎着抬起头，不由得打了一个寒战，从破镜子里看到哈利正在身后瞪着他。

马尔福急忙转身抽出魔杖，哈利也本能地拔杖自卫。马尔福的魔咒稍稍打偏了一点儿，击碎了哈利身旁的壁灯。哈利闪到一旁，默念倒挂金钟！魔杖点出，但马尔福挡住了这个咒语，又举起了魔杖——

"别打了！别打了！"哭泣的桃金娘尖叫着，声音在瓷砖盥洗室里回响，"**别打了！别打了！**"

砰的一声，哈利身后的垃圾箱爆炸了。哈利试了个锁腿咒，却从马尔福耳后的墙上弹回，把哭泣的桃金娘身下那个抽水马桶的水箱打得粉碎。桃金娘高声尖叫，水漫了一地，哈利滑倒了，马尔福扭歪了面孔叫道："钻心剜——"

"**神锋无影！**"哈利在地上大吼一声，疯狂地挥舞着魔杖。

马尔福的脸上和胸口血如泉涌，好像被无形的宝剑劈过一般。他踉跄着向后退去，扑通一声倒在积水的地上，溅起大片水花，魔杖从他软绵绵的右手里滑了出去。

"不——"哈利大惊。

哈利脚下打着滑，摇摇晃晃地爬起来，奔向马尔福，只见他的面孔已经变得殷红，苍白的手抓着浸透鲜血的胸膛。

## CHAPTER TWENTY-FOUR  Sectumsempra

'No – I didn't –'

Harry did not know what he was saying; he fell to his knees beside Malfoy, who was shaking uncontrollably in a pool of his own blood. Moaning Myrtle let out a deafening scream.

'MURDER! MURDER IN THE BATHROOM! MURDER!'

The door banged open behind Harry and he looked up, terrified: Snape had burst into the room, his face livid. Pushing Harry roughly aside, he knelt over Malfoy, drew his wand and traced it over the deep wounds Harry's curse had made, muttering an incantation that sounded almost like song. The flow of blood seemed to ease; Snape wiped the residue from Malfoy's face and repeated his spell. Now the wounds seemed to be knitting.

Harry was still watching, horrified by what he had done, barely aware that he too was soaked in blood and water. Moaning Myrtle was still sobbing and wailing overhead. When Snape had performed his counter-curse for the third time, he half lifted Malfoy into a standing position.

'You need the hospital wing. There may be a certain amount of scarring, but if you take dittany immediately we might avoid even that ... come ...'

He supported Malfoy across the bathroom, turning at the door to say in a voice of cold fury, 'And you, Potter ... you wait here for me.'

It did not occur to Harry for a second to disobey. He stood up slowly, shaking, and looked down at the wet floor. There were blood-stains floating like crimson flowers across its surface. He could not even find it in himself to tell Moaning Myrtle to be quiet, as she continued to wail and sob with increasingly evident enjoyment.

Snape returned ten minutes later. He stepped into the bathroom and closed the door behind him.

'Go,' he said to Myrtle and she swooped back into her toilet at once, leaving a ringing silence behind her.

'I didn't mean it to happen,' said Harry at once. His voice echoed in the cold, watery space. 'I didn't know what that spell did.'

But Snape ignored this.

'Apparently I underestimated you, Potter,' he said quietly. 'Who would have thought you knew such Dark Magic? Who taught you that spell?'

## 第24章 神锋无影

"不——我没有——"

哈利不知道自己在说什么,他在马尔福身边跪了下来。马尔福倒在血泊中控制不住地哆嗦着,哭泣的桃金娘发出一声震耳欲聋的尖叫。

"杀人啦!盥洗室里杀人啦!杀人啦!"

门在哈利身后砰地打开,他惊恐地抬起头:斯内普冲了进来,脸色铁青。他粗暴地把哈利推到一边,跪在马尔福跟前,抽出魔杖,沿着哈利咒语造成的那些深深的口子移动,嘴里念着一种唱歌似的咒语。出血似乎减轻了。斯内普擦去马尔福脸上的污物,又念了一遍咒语,现在伤口好像正在愈合。

哈利还在旁边看着,被自己做的事吓傻了,几乎没意识到他也浸在鲜血和污水里。哭泣的桃金娘还在他们头顶上抽泣和哀号。斯内普第三次施完破解咒后,半拖半抱地把马尔福扶了起来。

"你需要去校医院,可能会留下一些伤疤,但如果及时用白鲜的话,也许连伤疤都可以避免……走吧……"

斯内普搀着马尔福走出去时,在门口回过头来,用冰冷而愤怒的语气说道:"你,波特……在这儿等我。"

哈利丝毫都没有想到不服从,他慢慢站起来,浑身战栗,低头看着积水的地面,那上面浮着一朵朵红花般的血迹。他甚至没有勇气叫哭泣的桃金娘停止吵闹,她还在继续哭哭啼啼,但已越来越明显地带有享受的味道。

斯内普十分钟后回来了,他走进盥洗室,关上了门。

"走开。"他对桃金娘说,她倏地钻回抽水马桶,留下一片令人耳鸣的寂静。

"我不是有意的,"哈利马上说,他的声音在冰冷、潮湿的空间回响,"我不知道那个魔咒是干什么的。"

但斯内普没有理睬。

"我显然低估了你,波特,"他平静地说,"谁想得到你竟然会这种黑魔法呢?那个魔咒是谁教你的?"

'I – read about it somewhere.'

'Where?'

'It was – a library book,' Harry invented wildly. 'I can't remember what it was call–'

'Liar,' said Snape. Harry's throat went dry. He knew what Snape was going to do and he had never been able to prevent it ...

The bathroom seemed to shimmer before his eyes; he struggled to block out all thought, but try as he might, the Half-Blood Prince's copy of *Advanced Potion-Making* swam hazily to the forefront of his mind ...

And then he was staring at Snape again, in the midst of this wrecked, soaked bathroom. He stared into Snape's black eyes, hoping against hope that Snape had not seen what he feared, but –

'Bring me your schoolbag,' said Snape softly, 'and all of your school books. *All* of them. Bring them to me here. Now!'

There was no point arguing. Harry turned at once and splashed out of the bathroom. Once in the corridor, he broke into a run towards Gryffindor Tower. Most people were walking the other way; they gaped at him drenched in water and blood, but he answered none of the questions fired at him as he ran past.

He felt stunned; it was as though a beloved pet had turned suddenly savage. What had the Prince been thinking to copy such a spell into his book? And what would happen when Snape saw it? Would he tell Slughorn – Harry's stomach churned – how Harry had been achieving such good results in Potions all year? Would he confiscate or destroy the book that had taught Harry so much ... the book that had become a kind of guide and friend? Harry could not let it happen ... he could not ...

'Where've you –? Why are you soaking –? Is that *blood*?'

Ron was standing at the top of the stairs, looking bewildered at the sight of Harry.

'I need your book,' Harry panted. 'Your Potions book. Quick ... give it to me ...'

'But what about the Half-Blood –?'

'I'll explain later!'

Ron pulled his copy of *Advanced Potion-Making* out of his bag and handed it over; Harry sprinted off past him and back to the common room. Here, he seized his schoolbag, ignoring the amazed looks of several people who had already finished their dinner, threw himself back out of the portrait hole and

## 第24章 神锋无影

"我——我看来的。"

"在哪儿？"

"是——图书馆的一本书里，"哈利临时乱编道，"我想不起书名——"

"撒谎。"斯内普说。哈利喉咙发干，他知道斯内普要做什么，而自己从来不能阻止……

盥洗室在他眼前晃动起来，他努力摒除所有的思想，但不管怎么努力，混血王子的《高级魔药制作》还是模糊地浮到了眼前……

然后他又看见了斯内普，在这一片狼藉的浸水的盥洗室中央。他望着那双深不可测的黑眼睛，侥幸地希望斯内普没有看到，然而——

"把你的书包拿给我，"斯内普轻声说，"还有你所有的课本。所有的。拿到这儿来。快！"

争辩已经没用，哈利马上转身踩着水跑出盥洗室。一到走廊里，他便拔腿朝格兰芬多塔楼奔去。大部分人都在朝相反的方向走，见到他一身血水都很惊诧，但他只顾往前跑，没有回答向他投来的一个个问题。

他感到惊愕不解，好像一个可爱的宠物突然变得凶残起来。王子把这样一个魔咒抄到书上时是怎么想的呢？斯内普看到了又会怎样？他会不会告诉斯拉格霍恩（哈利的胃里翻腾起来）——哈利这一学年魔药课的好成绩是怎么来的？他会不会把那本教了哈利这么多知识的书没收或撕毁……那本已经变得像导师和朋友的书？哈利不能让这种事发生……他不能……

"你去哪儿了——怎么湿淋淋的——那是血吗？"

罗恩站在楼梯顶上，困惑地望着哈利。

"我需要你的书，"哈利气喘吁吁地说，"你的魔药课本。快……快拿给我……"

"可是混血王子——？"

"以后再解释！"

罗恩从包里抽出《高级魔药制作》递给了他。哈利冲进公共休息室，抓起书包，不顾几个已经吃完晚饭的人惊讶的目光，钻出肖像洞口，

## CHAPTER TWENTY-FOUR    Sectumsempra

hurtled off along the seventh-floor corridor.

He skidded to a halt beside the tapestry of dancing trolls, closed his eyes and began to walk.

*I need a place to hide my book ... I need a place to hide my book ... I need a place to hide my book ...*

Three times he walked up and down in front of the stretch of blank wall. When he opened his eyes, there it was at last: the door to the Room of Requirement. Harry wrenched it open, flung himself inside and slammed it shut.

He gasped. Despite his haste, his panic, his fear of what awaited him back in the bathroom, he could not help but be overawed by what he was looking at. He was standing in a room the size of a large cathedral, whose high windows were sending shafts of light down upon what looked like a city with towering walls, built of what Harry knew must be objects hidden by generations of Hogwarts inhabitants. There were alleyways and roads bordered by teetering piles of broken and damaged furniture, stowed away, perhaps, to hide the evidence of mis-handled magic, or else hidden by castle-proud house-elves. There were thousands and thousands of books, no doubt banned or graffitied or stolen. There were winged catapults and Fanged Frisbees, some still with enough life in them to hover half-heartedly over the mountains of other forbidden items; there were chipped bottles of congealed potions, hats, jewels, cloaks; there were what looked like dragon-egg shells, corked bottles whose contents still shimmered evilly, several rusting swords and a heavy, bloodstained axe.

Harry hurried forwards into one of the many alleyways between all this hidden treasure. He turned right past an enormous stuffed troll, ran on a short way, took a left at the broken Vanishing Cabinet in which Montague had got lost the previous year, finally pausing beside a large cupboard which seemed to have had acid thrown at its blistered surface. He opened one of the cupboard's creaking doors: it had already been used as a hiding place for something in a cage that had long-since died; its skeleton had five legs. He stuffed the Half-Blood Prince's book behind the cage and slammed the door. He paused for a moment, his heart thumping horribly, gazing around at the clutter ... would he be able to find this spot again, amidst all this junk? Seizing the chipped bust of an ugly old warlock from on top of a nearby crate, he stood it on the cupboard where the book was now hidden, perched a dusty old wig and a tarnished tiara on the statue's head to make it more distinctive, then sprinted back through the alleyways of hidden junk as fast as he could go, back to the door, back out on to the corridor, where he slammed the door behind him and it turned at once back into stone.

## 第24章 神锋无影

沿八楼走廊疾奔。

他在巨怪跳舞的挂毯前突然刹住脚步，闭上眼睛开始来回踱步。

我需要一个地方让我藏书……我需要一个地方让我藏书……我需要一个地方让我藏书……

他在那段空墙前来回走了三次，当他睁开眼睛时，终于看到了有求必应屋的门。哈利拽开它冲了进去，把门撞上了。

他倒吸了一口气。尽管着急、恐惧，害怕盥洗室里等着他的事情，他还是不禁对眼前的景象惊叹不已。他站在一间大教堂那么大的屋子里，高窗投下的光柱照出的像是一座高墙林立的城市，哈利看出那都是由历代霍格沃茨人藏进来的物品堆砌而成的。那一条条巷道边是堆得摇摇欲坠的破家具，可能是为了掩藏误施魔法的证据而被塞到了这里，或是由那些维护城堡体面的家养小精灵藏起来的。这里有成千上万本书籍，无疑都是禁书、被乱涂过的书或偷来的书；有带翼弹弓和狼牙飞碟，其中有几个仍然有气无力地在堆积如山的禁物上盘旋；一些破瓶子里盛着已经凝固的魔药；还有帽子，珠宝，斗篷，像是火龙蛋壳的东西；几个塞住口的瓶子里仍在闪着邪恶的光；还有几柄生锈的剑和一把血迹斑斑的大斧。

哈利匆匆走进这宝藏堆中的一条小巷，向右一拐，经过一个巨怪标本，又跑了一小段，在破裂的消失柜（就是去年蒙太在里面消失的那个）旁边向左一拐，最后停在一个表面起泡、像被泼过强酸的大柜子前。他打开吱吱嘎嘎的柜门，那里面已经藏了一个笼子，笼子里的东西早就死了，从骨骼看有五条腿。他把混血王子的书塞到笼子后面，用力关上门。他停了一会儿，心脏剧烈地跳着，环顾着杂物堆……在这么多破烂中间，他能找得到这个地方吗？他从旁边的板条箱顶上抓下一个丑陋的老男巫的破半身像，搁在藏有那本书的柜子上面，为了更显眼，又在老男巫的头上盖了一顶灰扑扑的旧发套和一顶锈暗的冠冕。然后他飞快地冲过藏满杂物的巷道，一直跑到走廊上，砰地带上门。门立刻又变成了石墙。

## CHAPTER TWENTY-FOUR    Sectumsempra

Harry ran flat out towards the bathroom on the floor below, cramming Ron's copy of *Advanced Potion-Making* into his bag as he did so. A minute later, he was back in front of Snape, who held out his hand wordlessly for Harry's schoolbag. Harry handed it over, panting, a searing pain in his chest, and waited.

One by one Snape extracted Harry's books and examined them. Finally the only book left was the Potions book, which he looked at very carefully before speaking.

'This is your copy of *Advanced Potion-Making*, is it, Potter?'

'Yes,' said Harry, still breathing hard.

'You're quite sure of that, are you, Potter?'

'Yes,' said Harry, with a touch more defiance.

'This is the copy of *Advanced Potion-Making* that you purchased from Flourish and Blotts?'

'Yes,' said Harry firmly.

'Then why,' asked Snape, 'does it have the name "Roonil Wazlib" written inside the front cover?'

Harry's heart missed a beat.

'That's my nickname,' he said.

'Your nickname,' repeated Snape.

'Yeah ... that's what my friends call me,' said Harry.

'I understand what a nickname is,' said Snape. The cold, black eyes were boring once more into Harry's; he tried not to look into them. *Close your mind ... close your mind ...* but he had never learned how to do it properly ...

'Do you know what I think, Potter?' said Snape, very quietly. 'I think that you are a liar and a cheat and that you deserve detention with me every Saturday until the end of term. What do you think, Potter?'

'I – I don't agree, sir,' said Harry, still refusing to look into Snape's eyes.

'Well, we shall see how you feel after your detentions,' said Snape. 'Ten o'clock Saturday morning, Potter. My office.'

'But, sir ...' said Harry, looking up desperately. 'Quidditch ... the last match of the –'

'Ten o'clock,' whispered Snape, with a smile that showed his yellow teeth. 'Poor Gryffindor ... fourth place this year, I fear ...'

## 第24章 神锋无影

哈利全速奔向楼下的盥洗室,边跑边把罗恩的《高级魔药制作》塞进自己的书包。一分钟后,他上气不接下气地回到斯内普面前,胸口火烧一般地痛。斯内普一言不发地伸出手来,哈利把书包递过去。

斯内普把哈利的书一本本拿出来检查。最后只剩下那本魔药课本了,他非常仔细地盯着它看了一会儿。

"这是你的《高级魔药制作》吗,波特?"

"是的。"哈利仍在喘着粗气。

"你很确定,是不是,波特?"

"是。"哈利语气中多了一点叛逆。

"这是你从丽痕书店买的《高级魔药制作》?"

"是。"哈利一口咬定。

"那封面背后怎么写着罗鸟·卫其利呢?"

哈利的心跳停了一下。

"那是我的绰号。"他说。

"你的绰号?"

"对……就是朋友给我起的名字。"

"我知道绰号是什么意思。"斯内普说,冷酷的黑眼睛又钻子般地盯住哈利的双眼。哈利努力不去看那眼睛。封闭你的大脑……封闭你的大脑……但他还没有学会……

"你知道我是怎么想的吗,波特?"斯内普轻轻地说,"我认为你是个撒谎的人,骗子。应该罚你每星期六都给我关禁闭,直至学期结束。你觉得怎么样,波特?"

"我——我不能同意,先生。"哈利说,依然拒绝看斯内普的眼睛。

"好,等关禁闭之后看你会有什么感觉。"斯内普说,"星期六上午十点,波特,到我的办公室。"

"可是,先生……"哈利说着绝望地抬起头,"魁地奇……最后一场——"

"十点钟,"斯内普小声说,脸上浮起微笑,露出了黄牙,"可怜的格兰芬多……恐怕今年要拿第四了……"

## CHAPTER TWENTY-FOUR    Sectumsempra

And he left the bathroom without another word, leaving Harry to stare into the cracked mirror, feeling sicker, he was sure, than Ron had ever felt in his life.

'I won't say "I told you so",' said Hermione, an hour later in the common room.

'Leave it, Hermione,' said Ron angrily.

Harry had never made it to dinner; he had no appetite at all. He had just finished telling Ron, Hermione and Ginny what had happened, not that there seemed to have been much need. The news had travelled very fast: apparently Moaning Myrtle had taken it upon herself to pop up in every bathroom in the castle to tell the story; Malfoy had already been visited in the hospital wing by Pansy Parkinson, who had lost no time in vilifying Harry far and wide, and Snape had told the staff precisely what had happened: Harry had already been called out of the common room to endure fifteen highly unpleasant minutes in the company of Professor McGonagall, who had told him he was lucky not to have been expelled and that she supported whole-heartedly Snape's punishment of detention every Saturday until the end of term.

'I told you there was something wrong with that Prince person,' Hermione said, evidently unable to stop herself. 'And I was right, wasn't I?'

'No, I don't think you were,' said Harry stubbornly.

He was having a bad enough time without Hermione lecturing him; the looks on the Gryffindor team's faces when he had told them he would not be able to play on Saturday had been the worst punishment of all. He could feel Ginny's eyes on him now, but did not meet them; he did not want to see disappointment or anger there. He had just told her that she would be playing Seeker on Saturday and that Dean would be rejoining the team as Chaser in her place. Perhaps, if they won, Ginny and Dean would make up during the post-match euphoria ... the thought went through Harry like an icy knife ...

'Harry,' said Hermione, 'how can you still stick up for that book when that spell –'

'Will you stop harping on about the book!' snapped Harry. 'The Prince only copied it out! It's not like he was advising anyone to use it! For all we know, he was making a note of something that had been used against him!'

'I don't believe this,' said Hermione. 'You're actually defending –'

'I'm not defending what I did!' said Harry quickly. 'I wish I hadn't done it, and not just because I've got about a dozen detentions. You know I wouldn't've used a spell like that, not even on Malfoy, but you can't blame the Prince, he hadn't written "Try this out, it's really good" – he was just making

## 第24章 神锋无影

他扬长而去,留下哈利望着破镜子,他相信罗恩这辈子都没有像他此刻这么难受过。

"我不想说'我跟你说过'了。"一小时后,赫敏在公共休息室里说。

"行了,赫敏。"罗恩恼火地说。

哈利没有去吃晚饭,他一点胃口也没有。他刚刚给罗恩、赫敏和金妮说完他的遭遇,这其实似乎没什么必要,消息已不胫而走。哭泣的桃金娘显然在城堡里的每个盥洗室都冒出来讲过这个故事;潘西·帕金森已经去校医院看过马尔福,立刻到处说哈利的坏话;斯内普对教员们宣传了此事。哈利被叫出公共休息室,在麦格教授跟前熬过了极其难堪的十五分钟。麦格说他没被开除已经很幸运了,并说她完全支持斯内普做出的处分:每星期六关禁闭,直到学期结束。

"我跟你说过那个什么王子有问题,"赫敏说,显然还是忍不住要表示,"我说对了吧?"

"我想不是。"哈利固执地说。

即使赫敏不在这里唠唠叨叨地给他上课,哈利也已经够受的了。听说他星期六不能参加比赛,格兰芬多球员脸上的表情是对哈利最严酷的惩罚。他能感到金妮的目光在盯着他,但他不敢面对,不想看到失望或愤怒。他刚刚告诉金妮,星期六由她当找球手,迪安回来顶替她当追球手。如果他们赢了,也许金妮和迪安会在赛后的兴奋中重归于好……这个念头像一把冰刀刺入了哈利的心房。

"哈利,"赫敏说,"你怎么还护着那本书呢,那个魔咒——"

"你能不能别再唠叨那本书了?"哈利没好气地说,"王子只是把它抄在那儿!并没有建议别人使用!说不定,他只是记录了一个别人对他用过的咒语!"

"我不信。你其实是在为你做的事辩护——"

"我不是在为我做的事辩护!"哈利马上说,"我希望没有做,不只是因为要关那么多次禁闭。你知道我不会去用那样的魔咒,哪怕是对马尔福。但你不能怪王子,他并没有写'这个真不错,试试吧'——

## CHAPTER TWENTY-FOUR  Sectumsempra

notes for himself, wasn't he, not for anyone else ...'

'Are you telling me,' said Hermione, 'that you're going to go back –?'

'And get the book? Yeah, I am,' said Harry forcefully. 'Listen, without the Prince I'd never have won the Felix Felicis. I'd never have known how to save Ron from poisoning, I'd never have –'

'– got a reputation for Potions brilliance you don't deserve,' said Hermione nastily.

'Give it a rest, Hermione!' said Ginny, and Harry was so amazed, so grateful, he looked up. 'By the sound of it Malfoy was trying to use an Unforgivable Curse, you should be glad Harry had something good up his sleeve!'

'Well, of course I'm glad Harry wasn't cursed!' said Hermione, clearly stung, 'but you can't call that *Sectumsempra* spell good, Ginny, look where it's landed him! And I'd have thought, seeing what this has done to your chances in the match –'

'Oh, don't start acting as though you understand Quidditch,' snapped Ginny, 'you'll only embarrass yourself.'

Harry and Ron stared: Hermione and Ginny, who had always got on together very well, were now sitting with their arms folded, glaring in opposite directions. Ron looked nervously at Harry, then snatched up a book at random and hid behind it. Harry, however, though he knew he little deserved it, felt unbelievably cheerful all of a sudden, even though none of them spoke again for the rest of the evening.

His light-heartedness was short-lived. There were Slytherin taunts to be endured next day, not to mention much anger from fellow Gryffindors, who were most unhappy that their Captain had got himself banned from the final match of the season. By Saturday morning, whatever he might have told Hermione, Harry would have gladly exchanged all the Felix Felicis in the world to be walking down to the Quidditch pitch with Ron, Ginny and the others. It was almost unbearable to turn away from the mass of students streaming out into the sunshine, all of them wearing rosettes and hats and brandishing banners and scarves, to descend the stone steps into the dungeons and walk until the distant sounds of the crowd were quite obliterated, knowing that he would not be able to hear a word of commentary, or a cheer or groan.

'Ah, Potter,' said Snape, when Harry had knocked on his door and entered the unpleasantly familiar office that Snape, despite teaching floors above now, had not vacated; it was as dimly lit as ever and the same slimy dead objects

## 第24章 神锋无影

他只是自己做了个记录，对吧，不是给别人……"

"你是不是要告诉我，"赫敏说，"你还要回去——"

"拿那本书？没错，我会的。"哈利坚决地说，"听我说，没有王子我就不会赢到福灵剂，也不会知道怎么给罗恩解毒，也不会——"

"——得到你不配得的'魔药奇才'的美名。"赫敏尖刻地说。

"行了，赫敏！"金妮说，哈利又是惊讶又是感激地抬起头来，"听起来马尔福是想用一个不可饶恕咒，你应该庆幸哈利有一个好招数对付他！"

"我当然很庆幸哈利没有中咒！"赫敏说，显然是被刺痛了，"但你不能说那个神锋无影咒好吧，金妮。看它把哈利害到了什么田地！想到你们比赛的前景，我本来以为——"

"哦，别开始假装你懂魁地奇，"金妮抢白道，"那只会自找尴尬。"

哈利和罗恩目瞪口呆：向来关系很好的赫敏和金妮此刻都抱着胳膊坐在那里，眼睛瞪着相反的方向。罗恩不安地看看哈利，然后随手抓起一本书，躲到书后面去了。哈利知道自己受之有愧，却还是突然感到难以置信的快乐，尽管他们一晚上都没有再说话。

哈利的好心情没有保持多久，第二天他要忍受斯莱特林学生的奚落，更不用提格兰芬多学生的怒气，因为他们的队长闯了祸被禁止参加本赛季的最后一场比赛。到了星期六上午，不管他嘴上对赫敏怎么说，哈利内心都甘愿用世上所有的福灵剂来换取跟罗恩、金妮他们一同走向魁地奇球场。这种惩罚简直是无法忍受的：离开那一群群戴着玫瑰形徽章和帽子、挥着旗子和围巾拥进阳光中的同学，独自走下石阶，进入地下教室，一直走到远处的喧闹声再也听不见了。他知道自己在这里听不到一句解说，也听不到一声喝彩或叹息。

"啊，波特。"哈利敲门走进那间熟悉而讨厌的办公室时，斯内普说。他虽然已经到楼上教课，却还没有腾出这个房间。屋里还是那么昏暗，沿墙的架子上还是摆着许多颜色各异的魔药罐，罐里浮

## CHAPTER TWENTY-FOUR    Sectumsempra

were suspended in coloured potions all around the walls. Ominously, there were many cobwebbed boxes piled on a table where Harry was clearly supposed to sit; they had an aura of tedious, hard and pointless work about them.

'Mr Filch has been looking for someone to clear out these old files,' said Snape softly. 'They are the records of other Hogwarts wrongdoers and their punishments. Where the ink has grown faint, or the cards have suffered damage from mice, we would like you to copy out the crimes and punishments afresh and, making sure that they are in alphabetical order, replace them in the boxes. You will not use magic.'

'Right, Professor,' said Harry, with as much contempt as he could put into the last three syllables.

'I thought you could start,' said Snape, a malicious smile on his lips, 'with boxes one thousand and twelve to one thousand and fifty-six. You will find some familiar names in there, which should add interest to the task. Here, you see ...'

He pulled out a card from one of the topmost boxes with a flourish and read, '"*James Potter and Sirius Black. Apprehended using an illegal hex upon Bertram Aubrey. Aubrey's head twice normal size. Double detention.*"' Snape sneered. 'It must be such a comfort to think that, though they are gone, a record of their great achievements remains ...'

Harry felt the familiar boiling sensation in the pit of his stomach. Biting his tongue to prevent himself retaliating, he sat down in front of the boxes and pulled one towards him.

It was, as Harry had anticipated, useless, boring work, punctuated (as Snape had clearly planned) with the regular jolt in the stomach that meant he had just read his father or Sirius's names, usually coupled together in various petty misdeeds, occasionally accompanied by those of Remus Lupin and Peter Pettigrew. And while he copied out all their various offences and punishments, he wondered what was going on outside, where the match would have just started ... Ginny playing Seeker against Cho ...

Harry glanced again and again at the large clock ticking on the wall. It seemed to be moving half as fast as a regular clock; perhaps Snape had bewitched it to go extra slowly? He could not have been here for only half an hour ... an hour ... an hour and a half ...

Harry's stomach started rumbling when the clock showed half past twelve. Snape, who had not spoken at all since setting Harry his task, finally looked up at ten past one.

## 第24章 神锋无影

着各种令人恶心的东西。不祥的是，一张显然是给哈利坐的桌子上堆着许多结了蛛网的盒子，散发着一种枯燥、艰苦而毫无意义的工作所特有的气息。

"费尔奇先生想找人清理这些旧档案，"斯内普轻声说，"是霍格沃茨犯错的人及其惩罚的记录。在墨水变淡或是卡片被老鼠破坏的地方，我们希望你把不清楚的字迹誊写清楚，并按字母顺序排列，放回盒子里。不许使用魔法。"

"是，教授。"哈利说，尽量在后两个字中加入深深的蔑视。

"我想你可以开始了，"斯内普嘴角浮现出恶意的微笑，"在1012到1056号盒子里，你会看到一些熟悉的名字，这会增加工作的乐趣。这儿，你看……"

他夸张地扬手从顶上一个盒子里抽出一张卡片，念道："詹姆·波特和小天狼星布莱克，对伯特伦·奥布里使用非法恶咒，奥布里的头变成两倍大。两人都关禁闭。"斯内普冷笑一声，"想起来一定很欣慰吧，他们虽然不在了，但他们伟大事迹的记录还在……"

哈利又感到怒火中烧，他咬着牙不让自己反击，在文件盒前面坐了下来，把一个盒子拖到面前。

正如哈利预料的那样，这个工作枯燥乏味，毫无意义，时而还会让他心中一揪（显然是斯内普安排的），因为他读到了父亲或小天狼星的名字，通常是两人一起犯了各种各样的小错误，有时还加上莱姆斯·卢平和小矮星彼得。他一边抄写他们的种种过错和对他们的惩罚，一边想象着外面的情形，比赛大概刚刚开始……找球手是金妮对秋……

哈利一次次地去瞄墙上嘀嗒嘀嗒的大钟，它好像走得只有普通的钟一半快，也许斯内普施了魔法故意让它走得特别慢？他不可能才来了半小时……一小时……一个半小时……

时针指到十二点半的时候，哈利的肚子开始咕咕叫了。一点十分，给哈利分配过任务后就没再说话的斯内普终于抬起头来。

## CHAPTER TWENTY-FOUR    Sectumsempra

'I think that will do,' he said coldly. 'Mark the place you have reached. You will continue at ten o'clock next Saturday.'

'Yes, sir.'

Harry stuffed a bent card into the box at random and hurried out of the door before Snape could change his mind, racing back up the stone steps, straining his ears to hear a sound from the pitch, but all was quiet ... it was over, then ...

He hesitated outside the crowded Great Hall, then ran up the marble staircase; whether Gryffindor had won or lost, the team usually celebrated or commiserated in their own common room.

'*Quid agis?*' he said tentatively to the Fat Lady, wondering what he would find inside.

Her expression was unreadable as she replied, 'You'll see.'

And she swung forwards.

A roar of celebration erupted from the hole behind her. Harry gaped as people began to scream at the sight of him; several hands pulled him into the room.

'We won!' yelled Ron, bounding into sight and brandishing the silver Cup at Harry. 'We won! Four hundred and fifty to a hundred and forty! We won!'

Harry looked around; there was Ginny running towards him; she had a hard, blazing look in her face as she threw her arms around him. And without thinking, without planning it, without worrying about the fact that fifty people were watching, Harry kissed her.

After several long moments – or it might have been half an hour – or possibly several sunlit days – they broke apart. The room had gone very quiet. Then several people wolf-whistled and there was an outbreak of nervous giggling. Harry looked over the top of Ginny's head to see Dean Thomas holding a shattered glass in his hand and Romilda Vane looking as though she might throw something. Hermione was beaming, but Harry's eyes sought Ron. At last he found him, still clutching the Cup and wearing an expression appropriate to having been clubbed over the head. For a fraction of a second they looked at each other, then Ron gave a tiny jerk of the head that Harry understood to mean, 'Well – if you must.'

The creature in his chest roaring in triumph, Harry grinned down at Ginny and gestured wordlessly out of the portrait hole. a long walk in the grounds seemed indicated, during which – if they had time – they might discuss the match.

## 第24章 神锋无影

"我想可以了,"他冷冷地说,"弄到哪里做个记号,下星期六上午十点继续。"

"是,先生。"

哈利把一张折起的卡片胡乱塞进盒子里,在斯内普改变主意之前赶紧溜出门,冲上石阶,竖起耳朵捕捉球场传来的声音,可是那边静悄悄的……这么说,已经结束了……

他在拥挤的大礼堂外犹豫了一会儿,然后跑上大理石台阶。无论格兰芬多输了还是赢了,球队通常都在公共休息室里庆祝或悲伤。

"如何?"他试探性地问胖夫人,不知里面会是什么情况。

胖夫人带着不可捉摸的表情答道:"你会知道的。"

她向前旋开了。

她身后的洞口里爆发出喧闹的欢呼声,哈利呆住了,人们看到他都高喊起来,几只手把他拽进了房间。

"我们赢了!"罗恩大声叫着跳过来,朝哈利挥舞着银杯,"我们赢了!四百五比一百四!我们赢了!"

哈利看看周围,金妮向他奔来,张开双臂抱住了他,脸上是一种炽烈的表情。于是,没有想,没有准备,没有担心有五十个人在看着,哈利吻了她。

过了长长的几分钟——也可能有半个小时——或阳光灿烂的几天——他们才分开。屋里变得非常安静。然后有几个人吹起了口哨,有人不自然地咻咻笑了起来。哈利越过金妮的头顶,看到迪安手里举着一个破杯子,罗米达·万尼好像要摔东西,赫敏在笑,但哈利的眼睛在寻找罗恩,终于找到了,他还攥着奖杯,看上去像当头挨了一棍似的。两人对视了片刻,罗恩的脑袋微微动了一下,哈利知道那意思是:"好吧——如果你一定要。"

他胸中的野兽在胜利地咆哮,哈利看着金妮咧嘴一笑,指了指肖像洞口。他的意思似乎是要在校园里散步很久,如果有时间的话,两人可以谈谈球赛。

## CHAPTER TWENTY-FIVE

## The Seer Overheard

The fact that Harry Potter was going out with Ginny Weasley seemed to interest a great number of people, most of them girls, yet Harry found himself newly and happily impervious to gossip over the next few weeks. After all, it made a very nice change to be talked about because of something that was making him happier than he could remember being for a very long time, rather than because he had been involved in horrific scenes of Dark Magic.

'You'd think people had better things to gossip about,' said Ginny, as she sat on the common-room floor, leaning against Harry's legs and reading the *Daily Prophet*. 'Three Dementor attacks in a week, and all Romilda Vane does is ask me if it's true you've got a Hippogriff tattooed across your chest.'

Ron and Hermione both roared with laughter. Harry ignored them.

'What did you tell her?'

'I told her it's a Hungarian Horntail,' said Ginny, turning a page of the newspaper idly. 'Much more macho.'

'Thanks,' said Harry, grinning. 'And what did you tell her Ron's got?'

'A Pygmy Puff, but I didn't say where.'

Ron scowled as Hermione rolled around laughing.

'Watch it,' he said, pointing warningly at Harry and Ginny. 'Just because I've given my permission doesn't mean I can't withdraw it –'

'"*Your permission*",' scoffed Ginny. 'Since when did you give me permission to do anything? Anyway, you said yourself you'd rather it was Harry than Michael or Dean.'

'Yeah, I would,' said Ron grudgingly. 'And just as long as you don't start snogging each other in public –'

# 第25章

# 被窃听的预言

哈利·波特和金妮·韦斯莱好上的事好像引起了很多人的兴趣，大多数是女孩子，但哈利觉得自己这几个星期丝毫没有受这些闲言碎语的影响，心情十分愉快。毕竟，这是一个很不错的改变，人们谈论的是一件让他感到久违了的乐事，而不是他又亲历了哪个黑魔法的恐怖场面。

"我还以为别人会有更有趣的事情来闲谈呢。"金妮说，她坐在公共休息室的地板上，靠着哈利的腿，在读《预言家日报》，"摄魂怪一星期内发动了三次袭击，罗米达·万尼却只想让我问问你胸口上是不是文了一只鹰头马身有翼兽。"

罗恩和赫敏两个哈哈大笑。哈利没有睬他们。

"那你对她说了什么呢？"

"我告诉她是一头匈牙利树蜂，"金妮说，懒懒地翻了一页报纸，"更有男子气。"

"谢谢，"哈利露齿一笑，"那你对她说罗恩的是什么？"

"一只侏儒蒲，但我没说在哪儿。"

赫敏笑得前仰后合，罗恩皱起了眉头。

"小心点儿，"他警告地指着哈利和金妮说，"不要因为我允许你们交往，就以为我不能收回——"

"'你允许'，"金妮嘲笑道，"从什么时候开始我做事要你允许了？不管怎样，你自己说过，宁可他是哈利，也不要是迈克尔或迪安。"

"那是，"罗恩勉强地说，"只要你们不在公共场所接吻——"

## CHAPTER TWENTY-FIVE   The Seer Overheard

'You filthy hypocrite! What about you and Lavender, thrashing around like a pair of eels all over the place?' demanded Ginny.

But Ron's tolerance was not to be tested much as they moved into June, for Harry and Ginny's time together was becoming increasingly restricted. Ginny's O.W.L.s were approaching and she was therefore forced to revise for hours into the night. On one such evening, when Ginny had retired to the library and Harry was sitting beside the window in the common room, supposedly finishing his Herbology homework but in reality reliving a particularly happy hour he had spent down by the lake with Ginny at lunchtime, Hermione dropped into the seat between him and Ron with an unpleasantly purposeful look on her face.

'I want to talk to you, Harry.'

'What about?' said Harry suspiciously. Only the previous day, Hermione had told him off for distracting Ginny when she ought to be working hard for her examinations.

'The so-called Half-Blood Prince.'

'Oh, not again,' he groaned. 'Will you please drop it?'

He had not dared to return to the Room of Requirement to retrieve his book, and his performance in Potions was suffering accordingly (though Slughorn, who approved of Ginny, had jocularly attributed this to Harry being lovesick). But Harry was sure that Snape had not yet given up hope of laying hands on the Prince's book, and was determined to leave it where it was while Snape remained on the lookout.

'I'm not dropping it,' said Hermione firmly, 'until you've heard me out. Now, I've been trying to find out a bit about who might make a hobby of inventing Dark spells –'

'He didn't make a hobby of it –'

'He, he – who says it's a he?'

'We've been through this,' said Harry crossly. '*Prince*, Hermione, *Prince*!'

'Right!' said Hermione, red patches blazing in her cheeks as she pulled a very old piece of newsprint out of her pocket and slammed it down on the table in front of Harry. 'Look at that! Look at the picture!'

Harry picked up the crumbling piece of paper and stared at the moving photograph, yellowed with age; Ron leaned over for a look, too. The picture showed a skinny girl of around fifteen. She was not pretty; she looked simultaneously cross and sullen, with heavy brows and a long, pallid face.

# 第 25 章 被窃听的预言

"你这个卑鄙的伪君子！你和拉文德当时是怎么回事？到处亲热，就像一对鳗鱼黏在一起！"金妮质问道。

进入六月，罗恩的忍耐没有受到多少考验，因为哈利和金妮在一起的时间越来越有限。金妮的 O.W.L. 考试日渐临近，她每晚不得不花好几个小时复习功课。在这样一个晚上，金妮去了图书馆，哈利坐在公共休息室的窗边，本想完成他的草药课家庭作业，但事实上他正在重温午饭时与金妮在湖边度过的一段非常愉快的时光。这时赫敏挤进了他和罗恩之间的座位，脸上是一种很坚决的表情，让人看了很不舒服。

"我想和你谈谈，哈利。"

"谈什么？"哈利疑惑地问。赫敏昨天刚数落过他，怪他打扰了应该努力复习迎考的金妮。

"那个所谓的混血王子。"

"哦，又来了，"他嘟囔道，"你能不能换个话题？"

他还没敢返回有求必应屋去拿他的那本书，他的魔药课成绩也因此掉了下来（不过，斯拉格霍恩对金妮很有好感，他诙谐地将哈利的成绩下降归于相思病）。哈利觉得斯内普一定还没有放弃搜查王子的课本，由于斯内普一直在监视他，他决定暂时不去碰那本书。

"我不换话题，"赫敏坚定地说，"直到你听我说完。我一直想找出是谁把发明黑魔咒当成了嗜好——"

"此兄没有把这当成嗜好——"

"此兄，此兄——你说他是男的？"

"我们已经说过了，"哈利不耐烦地说，"王子，赫敏，王子！"

"好吧！"赫敏说着脸颊上泛起红晕，从口袋里掏出一张很旧的报纸，朝哈利的桌子上猛地一扔，"看这个！看看上面的照片！"

哈利拿起那张破报纸，盯着上面年久发黄的活动照片；罗恩也凑过来看。照片上是个大约十五岁的瘦瘦女孩。她并不漂亮，看起来既有点乖戾，又有点闷闷不乐。她眉毛粗重，一张脸长长的，面色苍白。

## CHAPTER TWENTY-FIVE  The Seer Overheard

Underneath the photograph was the caption: *Eileen Prince, Captain of the Hogwarts Gobstones Team.*

'So?' said Harry, scanning the short news item to which the picture belonged; it was a rather dull story about interschool competitions.

'Her name was Eileen Prince. *Prince*, Harry.'

They looked at each other and Harry realised what Hermione was trying to say. He burst out laughing.

'No way.'

'What?'

'You think she was the Half-Blood …? Oh, come on.'

'Well, why not? Harry, there aren't any real princes in the wizarding world! It's either a nickname, a made-up title somebody's given themselves, or it could be their actual name, couldn't it? No, listen! If, say, her father was a wizard whose surname was "Prince", and her mother was a Muggle, then that would make her a "half-blood Prince"!'

'Yeah, very ingenious, Hermione …'

'But it would! Maybe she was proud of being half a Prince!'

'Listen, Hermione, I can tell it's not a girl. I can just tell.'

'The truth is that you don't think a girl would have been clever enough,' said Hermione angrily.

'How can I have hung round with you for five years and not think girls are clever?' said Harry, stung by this. 'It's the way he writes. I just know the Prince was a bloke, I can tell. This girl hasn't got anything to do with it. Where did you get this, anyway?'

'The library,' said Hermione, predictably. 'There's a whole collection of old *Prophets* up there. Well, I'm going to find out more about Eileen Prince if I can.'

'Enjoy yourself,' said Harry irritably.

'I will,' said Hermione. 'And the first place I'll look,' she shot at him, as she reached the portrait hole, 'is records of old Potions awards!'

Harry scowled after her for a moment, then continued his contemplation of the darkening sky.

'She's just never got over you outperforming her in Potions,' said Ron, returning to his copy of *One Thousand Magical Herbs and Fungi*.

'You don't think I'm mad, wanting that book back, do you?'

照片下面的说明是：艾琳·普林斯，霍格沃茨高布石队队长。

"怎么了？"哈利说着扫了一眼相关的短文，那不过是一条校际比赛的平淡新闻。

"她的名字叫作艾琳·普林斯。普林斯，哈利。"

他们互相对视了一眼，哈利意识到赫敏要说什么。他突然大笑起来。

"不可能。"

"什么？"

"你认为她是混血……？哦，别逗了。"

"为什么不可能？哈利，在巫师界没有真正的王子！这个词要么是昵称，要么是某个人自封的头衔，也有可能就是真名，不可能吗？听我说！如果她有一个姓'普林斯'的巫师爸爸，并且她的妈妈是麻瓜，那么她就可能是'混血王子'啊！"

"对，真是天才，赫敏……"

"但这很有可能！也许她就以自己是'混血王子'为荣呢！"

"听着，赫敏，我知道这人不是女的，我能感觉出来。"

"你就是认为女孩子不可能有这么聪明。"赫敏生气地说。

"我和你相处五年了，怎么可能还认为女孩子不聪明呢？"哈利说，觉得被刺痛了，"我是从他写字的方式知道这个'王子'是男的，我判断得出来。跟这女孩子一点儿关系也没有，你是从哪儿弄到这张照片的？"

"图书馆，"赫敏不出所料地说，"那里有全部的旧《预言家日报》。我会尽量找到有关艾琳·普林斯的更多材料。"

"祝你找得愉快。"哈利烦躁地说。

"我会的。"赫敏说，走到肖像洞口时，又冲他扔下一句，"我首先要找的，就是所有魔药课的奖励记录！"

哈利冲她皱了皱眉头，然后继续凝视逐渐黑下来的夜空。

"她还没有原谅你在魔药课上超过她。"罗恩说完，继续看起他的《千种神奇草药及蕈类》。

"我想把那本书拿回来，你不认为我有点发疯吧？"

## CHAPTER TWENTY-FIVE  The Seer Overheard

'Course not,' said Ron robustly. 'He was a genius, the Prince. Anyway ... without his bezoar tip ...' he drew his finger significantly across his own throat, 'I wouldn't be here to discuss it, would I? I mean, I'm not saying that spell you used on Malfoy was great –'

'Nor am I,' said Harry quickly.

'But he healed all right, didn't he? Back on his feet in no time.'

'Yeah,' said Harry; this was perfectly true, although his conscience squirmed slightly all the same. 'Thanks to Snape ...'

'You still got detention with Snape this Saturday?' Ron continued.

'Yeah, and the Saturday after that, and the Saturday after that,' sighed Harry. 'And he's hinting now that if I don't get all the boxes done by the end of term, we'll carry on next year.'

He was finding these detentions particularly irksome because they cut into the already limited time he could have been spending with Ginny. Indeed, he had frequently wondered lately whether Snape did not know this, for he was keeping Harry later and later every time, while making pointed asides about Harry having to miss the good weather and the varied opportunities it offered.

Harry was shaken from these bitter reflections by the appearance at his side of Jimmy Peakes, who was holding out a scroll of parchment.

'Thanks, Jimmy ... hey, it's from Dumbledore!' said Harry excitedly, unrolling the parchment and scanning it. 'He wants me to go to his office as quick as I can!'

They stared at each other.

'Blimey,' whispered Ron. 'You don't reckon ... he hasn't found ...?'

'Better go and see, hadn't I?' said Harry, jumping to his feet.

He hurried out of the common room and along the seventh floor as fast as he could, passing nobody but Peeves, who swooped past in the opposite direction, throwing bits of chalk at Harry in a routine sort of way and cackling loudly as he dodged Harry's defensive jinx. Once Peeves had vanished, there was silence in the corridors; with only fifteen minutes left until curfew, most people had already returned to their common rooms.

And then Harry heard a scream and a crash. He stopped in his tracks, listening.

'How – *dare* – you – aaaaargh!'

## 第25章 被窃听的预言

"当然不,"罗恩毫不含糊地说,"王子,他是一个天才。不管怎样……没有他的粪石秘诀……"他意味深长地摸着自己的喉咙,"我就不可能在这儿和你讨论这个了,是吧?当然,我不是说你对马尔福施的那个魔咒很棒——"

"我也不认为。"哈利迅速地说。

"但他伤口愈合得挺好,是吧?很快就恢复了。"

"是,"哈利说,这确是事实,但他的良心一直隐隐不安,"多亏斯内普……"

"这个星期六你还要到斯内普那儿关禁闭?"罗恩接着问。

"是啊,还有下个星期六,下下个星期六。"哈利叹着气说,"他还暗示说,如果我这学期结束前不把所有的文件盒整理完,明年还要继续。"

他发现这些禁闭特别讨厌,占用了本来就很少的和金妮在一起的时间。事实上,他最近常常怀疑斯内普是不是知道这一点,因为他把哈利关得越来越久,并且有意提及哈利错过了美好的天气及其带来的各种机会。

吉米·珀克斯手拿一卷羊皮纸出现在哈利身旁,把他从痛苦的沉思中唤醒了。

"谢谢你,吉米……嘿,是邓布利多的!"哈利激动地说,连忙展开羊皮纸看了起来,"他要我去他的办公室,越快越好!"

哈利和罗恩对视着。

"哎呀,"罗恩小声道,"你认为……他会不会找到了……?"

"最好去看看,不是吗?"哈利说着一跃而起。

他赶忙走出公共休息室,顺着八楼向前急奔,一个人都没遇到,只碰到皮皮鬼迎面飞来,像往常一样朝哈利扔粉笔头,一边咯咯笑着躲避哈利的防御咒。皮皮鬼消失后,走廊里一片寂静,还有十五分钟就到宵禁时间了,大部分人已经回到公共休息室。

这时,哈利听到一声尖叫和一声撞击。他停下脚步,侧耳细听。

"你——竟——敢——啊——!"

## CHAPTER TWENTY-FIVE    The Seer Overheard

The noise was coming from a corridor nearby; Harry sprinted towards it, his wand at the ready, hurtled round another corner and saw Professor Trelawney sprawled upon the floor, her head covered in one of her many shawls, several sherry bottles lying beside her, one broken.

'Professor —'

Harry hurried forwards and helped Professor Trelawney to her feet. Some of her glittering beads had become entangled with her glasses. She hiccoughed loudly, patted her hair and pulled herself up on Harry's helping arm.

'What happened, Professor?'

'You may well ask!' she said shrilly. 'I was strolling along, brooding upon certain Dark portents I happen to have glimpsed …'

But Harry was not paying much attention. He had just noticed where they were standing: there on the right was the tapestry of dancing trolls and, on the left, that smoothly impenetrable stretch of stone wall that concealed –

'Professor, were you trying to get into the Room of Requirement?'

'… omens I have been vouchsafed – what?'

She looked suddenly shifty.

'The Room of Requirement,' repeated Harry. 'Were you trying to get in there?'

'I – well – I didn't know students knew about –'

'Not all of them do,' said Harry. 'But what happened? You screamed … it sounded as though you were hurt …'

'I – well,' said Professor Trelawney, drawing her shawls around her defensively and staring down at him with her vastly magnified eyes. 'I wished to – ah – deposit certain – um – personal items in the Room …' And she muttered something about 'nasty accusations'.

'Right,' said Harry, glancing down at the sherry bottles. 'But you couldn't get in and hide them?'

He found this very odd; the Room had opened for him, after all, when he had wanted to hide the Half-Blood Prince's book.

'Oh, I got in all right,' said Professor Trelawney, glaring at the wall. 'But there was somebody already in there.'

'Somebody in –? Who?' demanded Harry. 'Who was in there?'

## 第25章 被窃听的预言

声音是从旁边一个走廊里传出来的,哈利握紧魔杖冲了过去,又转过一个拐弯,看见特里劳尼教授倒在地板上,脑袋被她那许多披肩中的一条盖住了,几个雪利酒瓶散落在一边,有一个已经碎了。

"教授——"

哈利急忙跑上前去扶她。她的一些闪亮的珠子和她的眼镜缠在了一起。她大声地打了个嗝,拍了拍头发,在哈利的搀扶下站了起来。

"这是怎么了,教授?"

"你问得好!"她刺耳地说,"我刚才一个人在散步,一边想着某些我碰巧瞥见的不祥征兆……"

哈利没太注意她在说什么。他刚注意到他们站在什么地方:右边是巨怪跳舞的挂毯,左边是光滑坚硬的石墙,后面藏着——

"教授,你刚才是不是想进有求必应屋?"

"……天赐我的征兆——你说什么?"

她的目光突然变得有点躲躲闪闪。

"有求必应屋,"哈利重复道,"你是想要进去吗?"

"我——嗯——我不知道学生们也知道——"

"不是所有的人都知道。"哈利说,"出了什么事?你尖叫了……听起来好像受了伤……"

"我——嗯,"特里劳尼教授说,一边警惕地用披肩围住自己,低头用她那双放大了好几倍的眼睛盯着哈利,"我本来希望——啊——存放一些——呃——个人用品在有求必应屋里……"她嘟哝了句什么"恶毒的指控"。

"噢,"哈利说着扫了一眼地上的雪利酒瓶,"但你没能进去藏它们?"

他觉得这很奇怪,当初他想藏起混血王子的课本时,有求必应屋为他开过门。

"哦,我可以进去,"特里劳尼教授瞪着那堵墙说,"但是里面已经有人了。"

"有人在里面——?谁?"哈利问道,"谁在里面?"

### CHAPTER TWENTY-FIVE    The Seer Overheard

'I have no idea,' said Professor Trelawney, looking slightly taken aback at the urgency in Harry's voice. 'I walked into the Room and I heard a voice, which has never happened before in all my years of hiding – of using the Room, I mean.'

'A voice? Saying what?'

'I don't know that it was saying anything,' said Professor Trelawney. 'It was ... whooping.'

'*Whooping?*'

'Gleefully,' she said, nodding.

Harry stared at her.

'Was it male or female?'

'I would hazard a guess at male,' said Professor Trelawney.

'And it sounded happy?'

'Very happy,' said Professor Trelawney sniffily.

'As though it was celebrating?'

'Most definitely.'

'And then –?'

'And then I called out, "Who's there?"'

'You couldn't have found out who it was without asking?' Harry asked her, slightly frustrated.

'The Inner Eye,' said Professor Trelawney with dignity, straightening her shawls and many strands of glittering beads, 'was fixed upon matters well outside the mundane realms of whooping voices.'

'Right,' said Harry hastily; he had heard about Professor Trelawney's Inner Eye all too often before. 'And did the voice say who was there?'

'No, it did not,' she said. 'Everything went pitch black and the next thing I knew, I was being hurled head first out of the Room!'

'And you didn't see that coming?' said Harry, unable to help himself.

'No, I did not, as I say, it was pitch –' She stopped and glared at him suspiciously.

'I think you'd better tell Professor Dumbledore,' said Harry. 'He ought to know Malfoy's celebrating – I mean, that someone threw you out of the Room.'

To his surprise, Professor Trelawney drew herself up at this suggestion, looking haughty.

## 第25章 被窃听的预言

"我也不知道。"特里劳尼教授说,看上去有点被哈利急切的问话吓着了,"我进了屋里,听到有人的声音,这是我这些年隐藏——使用这个屋子时从未碰到过的。"

"有人的声音?说些什么?"

"我不知道是不是在说什么,"特里劳尼教授说,"那是……叫喊声。"

"叫喊声?"

"愉快的叫喊声。"她点着头说道。

哈利盯着她。

"是男的还是女的?"

"我猜是男的。"特里劳尼教授说。

"听起来有点高兴?"

"很高兴。"特里劳尼教授轻蔑地说。

"好像是在庆祝什么?"

"肯定。"

"后来呢——?"

"后来我叫了一声'谁在那里?'"

"你不问就没法知道是谁吗?"哈利有点失望地问她。

"天目,"特里劳尼教授端着架子说,一边拉拉她的披肩以及那许多串闪亮的珠子,"不是用来关注喊叫这种尘世间的俗事的。"

"没错,"哈利连忙说,他已经太多次地听说特里劳尼教授的天目了,"那个声音回答是谁了吗?"

"不,没有,"她说,"一切变得漆黑,接着我就知道我头朝前被扔了出来!"

"你没有看到这事会发生?"哈利忍不住问道。

"没有看到,我刚才说了,当时一片漆黑——"她停住话,怀疑地瞪着他。

"我认为你最好告诉邓布利多教授,"哈利说,"应当让他知道马尔福在庆祝——我是说,那个把你从屋里扔出来的人。"

令他惊讶的是,特里劳尼教授听到这个建议后挺直了身体,一副很傲慢的样子。

## CHAPTER TWENTY-FIVE    The Seer Overheard

'The Headmaster has intimated that he would prefer fewer visits from me,' she said coldly. 'I am not one to press my company upon those who do not value it. If Dumbledore chooses to ignore the warnings the cards show –'

Her bony hand closed suddenly around Harry's wrist.

'Again and again, no matter how I lay them out –'

And she pulled a card dramatically from underneath her shawls.

'– the lightning-struck tower,' she whispered. 'Calamity. Disaster. Coming nearer all the time ...'

'Right,' said Harry again. 'Well ... I still think you should tell Dumbledore about this voice and everything going dark and being thrown out of the Room ...'

'You think so?' Professor Trelawney seemed to consider the matter for a moment, but Harry could tell that she liked the idea of retelling her little adventure.

'I'm going to see him right now,' said Harry. 'I've got a meeting with him. We could go together.'

'Oh, well, in that case,' said Professor Trelawney with a smile. She bent down, scooped up her sherry bottles and dumped them unceremoniously in a large blue and white vase standing in a nearby niche.

'I miss having you in my classes, Harry,' she said soulfully, as they set off together. 'You were never much of a Seer ... but you were a wonderful Object ...'

Harry did not reply; he had loathed being the Object of Professor Trelawney's continual predictions of doom.

'I am afraid,' she went on, 'that the nag – I'm sorry, the centaur – knows nothing of cartomancy. I asked him – one Seer to another – had he not, too, sensed the distant vibrations of coming catastrophe? But he seemed to find me almost comical. Yes, comical!'

Her voice rose rather hysterically and Harry caught a powerful whiff of sherry even though the bottles had been left behind.

'Perhaps the horse has heard people say that I have not inherited my great-great-grandmother's gift. Those rumours have been bandied about by the jealous for years. You know what I say to such people, Harry? Would Dumbledore have let me teach at this great school, put so much trust in me all these years, had I not proved myself to him?'

Harry mumbled something indistinct.

## 第25章 被窃听的预言

"校长暗示过希望我最好少去拜访他,"她冷淡地说,"我不会死乞白赖地缠着不尊重我的人。如果邓布利多决定不理会纸牌的警示——"

她那瘦骨嶙峋的手突然一把抓住了哈利的手腕。

"一次又一次,无论我怎么摆——"

她戏剧性地从层层披肩下拿出一张纸牌。

"——闪电击中的塔楼,"她喃喃道,"灾难,不幸,越来越近……"

"没错,"哈利又说,"嗯……我还是认为你应该告诉邓布利多,关于这个声音,后来的漆黑一片,以及你被扔出有求必应屋……"

"你这么认为?"特里劳尼教授似乎考虑了一会儿,但是哈利看得出来,她喜欢再讲述一遍她这段小小的历险。

"我正要去见他,"哈利说,"我和他约好的,我们可以一起去。"

"哦,那好吧。"特里劳尼教授笑着说。她弯下腰,抱起她的雪利酒瓶,随手扔进了旁边壁龛上的一个蓝白色大花瓶里。

"我真怀念你在班上的时光,哈利,"他们一起往邓布利多的办公室走去时,她深情地说道,"你从来没有多少先知的天分……但你是一个很理想的对象……"

哈利没有回答,他一直不愿意成为特里劳尼教授连续预测厄运的对象。

"我担心,"特里劳尼教授接着道,"那匹驽马——对不起,是马人——对纸牌占卜一窍不通。我问过他——先知之间的对话——难道他没有感觉到灾难来临前那隐隐的震动吗?但他似乎觉得我很滑稽。对,是滑稽!"

她的声音歇斯底里地提高了很多,尽管瓶子已经在身后很远的地方,但哈利突然闻到一股非常浓烈的雪利酒的气味。

"那匹马大概听别人说过我没有继承我高祖母的天赋。这些谣言已经由嫉妒的人传播好几年了。哈利,你知道我对这些人是怎么说的吗?如果我没有向邓布利多证明我的能力,他会让我在这所优秀的学校里教书,这些年来会对我如此信任吗?"

哈利嘟囔了一声。

# CHAPTER TWENTY-FIVE   The Seer Overheard

'I well remember my first interview with Dumbledore,' went on Professor Trelawney, in throaty tones. 'He was deeply impressed, of course, deeply impressed ... I was staying at the Hog's Head, which I do not advise, incidentally – bed bugs, dear boy – but funds were low. Dumbledore did me the courtesy of calling upon me in my room at the inn. He questioned me ... I must confess that, at first, I thought he seemed ill-disposed towards Divination ... and I remember I was starting to feel a little odd, I had not eaten much that day ... but then ...'

And now Harry was paying attention properly for the first time, for he knew what had happened then: Professor Trelawney had made the prophecy that had altered the course of his whole life, the prophecy about him and Voldemort.

'... but then we were rudely interrupted by Severus Snape!'

'What?'

'Yes, there was a commotion outside the door and it flew open, and there was that rather uncouth barman standing with Snape, who was waffling about having come the wrong way up the stairs, although I'm afraid that I myself rather thought he had been apprehended eaves-dropping on my interview with Dumbledore – you see, he himself was seeking a job at the time, and no doubt hoped to pick up tips! Well, after that, you know, Dumbledore seemed much more disposed to give me a job, and I could not help thinking, Harry, that it was because he appreciated the stark contrast between my own unassuming manners and quiet talent, compared to the pushing, thrusting young man who was prepared to listen at keyholes – Harry, dear?'

She looked back over her shoulder, having only just realised that Harry was no longer with her; he had stopped walking and they were now ten feet from each other.

'Harry?' she repeated uncertainly.

Perhaps his face was white, to make her look so concerned and frightened. Harry was standing stock-still as waves of shock crashed over him, wave after wave, obliterating everything except the information that had been kept from him for so long ...

It was Snape who had overheard the prophecy. It was Snape who had carried the news of the prophecy to Voldemort. Snape and Peter Pettigrew together had sent Voldemort hunting after Lily and James and their son ...

## 第25章 被窃听的预言

"我清楚地记得邓布利多对我的第一次面试,"特里劳尼教授用沙哑的声音接着说,"他深深地被我打动了,没错,深深地打动了……我住的是猪头酒吧,那地方我不推荐给别人——有臭虫,亲爱的孩子——但是当时经费紧张。邓布利多很客气,亲自到旅馆里来拜访我。他问我……我必须承认,一开始我觉得他对占卜似乎没什么好感……我记得我开始感到有点奇怪,我那天没吃多少东西……但是后来……"

现在哈利才开始真正注意听了,因为他知道当时发生了什么:特里劳尼教授做出了那个改变他一生经历的预言,那个关于他和伏地魔的预言。

"……但是后来我们被西弗勒斯·斯内普粗暴地打断了!"

"什么?"

"是这样,当时门外一阵骚动,随即门被撞开了,那个十分粗俗的酒吧招待和斯内普站在外面,斯内普胡扯说是上错了楼梯,但我疑心他是在偷听邓布利多对我的面试时被抓到了——你瞧,他自己当时也在找工作,无疑想学到一些经验。嗯,在那之后,你是知道的,邓布利多似乎很愿意给我一份工作,哈利,我不禁想到那是因为他欣赏我不装腔作势的风格和从容的天赋,与那个藏起来从钥匙孔偷听、自以为是、咄咄逼人的男青年形成了鲜明的对照——哈利,亲爱的?"

她这才意识到哈利已经不在身边,回过头看了看,哈利站在那里,离她已有十步之遥。

"哈利?"她疑惑地又叫了一声。

可能是因为哈利脸色苍白,所以她才显得这么担心和害怕。哈利一动不动地站在那里,一波又一波的震惊向他袭来,一波接着一波,淹没了一切,只剩下那个他以前一直不知道的情况……

是斯内普偷听了预言。是斯内普把预言的消息告诉了伏地魔。是斯内普和小矮星彼得两个人让伏地魔去追杀莉莉、詹姆和他们的儿子……

## CHAPTER TWENTY-FIVE    The Seer Overheard

Nothing else mattered to Harry just now.

'Harry?' said Professor Trelawney again. 'Harry – I thought we were going to see the Headmaster together?'

'You stay here,' said Harry through numb lips.

'But, dear ... I was going to tell him how I was assaulted in the Room of –'

'You stay here!' Harry repeated angrily.

She looked alarmed as he ran past her, round the corner into Dumbledore's corridor, where the lone gargoyle stood sentry. Harry shouted the password at the gargoyle and ran up the moving spiral staircase three steps at a time. He did not knock upon Dumbledore's door, he hammered; and the calm voice answered 'Enter' after Harry had already flung himself into the room.

Fawkes the phoenix looked round, his bright black eyes gleaming with reflected gold from the sunset beyond the window. Dumbledore was standing at the window looking out at the grounds, a long, black travelling cloak in his arms.

'Well, Harry, I promised that you could come with me.'

For a moment or two, Harry did not understand; the conversation with Trelawney had driven everything else out of his head and his brain seemed to be moving very slowly.

'Come ... with you ...?'

'Only if you wish it, of course.'

'If I ...'

And then Harry remembered why he had been eager to come to Dumbledore's office in the first place.

'You've found one? You've found a Horcrux?'

'I believe so.'

Rage and resentment fought shock and excitement: for several moments, Harry could not speak.

'It is natural to be afraid,' said Dumbledore.

'I'm not scared!' said Harry at once, and it was perfectly true; fear was one emotion he was not feeling at all. 'Which Horcrux is it? Where is it?'

## 第 25 章 被窃听的预言

现在哈利再也不关心其他事情了。

"哈利?"特里劳尼教授又喊了一遍,"哈利——我想我们是要一起去见校长的吧?"

"你待在这里。"哈利用麻木的嘴唇说道。

"但是,亲爱的……我还想告诉他,我是怎么在有求必应屋受到攻击的——"

"你待在这里!"哈利生气地又说了一遍。

特里劳尼教授看起来有点惊慌。哈利从她身边跑过,拐入通往邓布利多办公室的走廊,那尊孤零零的滴水嘴石兽守卫在那里。哈利冲着石兽大声喊出口令,然后一步三级地冲上移动的螺旋形楼梯。他不是轻轻地敲响邓布利多的门,而是咚咚地捶门。哈利已经冲进了门内,那个镇静的声音才回答说:"进来。"

凤凰福克斯转身看了一眼,明亮的黑眼睛里映着窗外金色的落日,闪闪发光。邓布利多正站在窗前看着校园,臂上搭着一条长长的黑色旅行斗篷。

"嗯,哈利,我答应过你可以跟我一道去。"

哈利愣了一下,与特里劳尼教授的交谈似乎使他忘记了所有的事情,他的头脑也好像反应迟钝了。

"跟……你一起去……?"

"当然啦,如果你愿意的话。"

"如果我……"

这时,哈利才想起他最初迫切想赶到邓布利多办公室来的原因。

"你找到一个了?你找到一个魂器了?"

"我想是的。"

愤怒和憎恨在他心中与震惊和激动斗争着。有好一会儿,哈利几乎一句话也说不出来。

"感到害怕是很自然的。"邓布利多说。

"我不害怕!"哈利马上说,这话是绝对真实的,害怕是他此刻完全没有的感觉,"哪一个魂器?在哪儿?"

## CHAPTER TWENTY-FIVE   The Seer Overheard

'I am not sure which it is – though I think we can rule out the snake – but I believe it to be hidden in a cave on the coast many miles from here, a cave I have been trying to locate for a very long time: the cave in which Tom Riddle once terrorised two children from his orphanage on their annual trip; you remember?'

'Yes,' said Harry. 'How is it protected?'

'I do not know; I have suspicions that may be entirely wrong.' Dumbledore hesitated, then said, 'Harry, I promised you that you could come with me, and I stand by that promise, but it would be very wrong of me not to warn you that this will be exceedingly dangerous.'

'I'm coming,' said Harry, almost before Dumbledore had finished speaking. Boiling with anger at Snape, his desire to do something desperate and risky had increased tenfold in the last few minutes. This seemed to show on Harry's face, for Dumbledore moved away from the window, and looked more closely at Harry, a slight crease between his silver eyebrows.

'What has happened to you?'

'Nothing,' lied Harry promptly.

'What has upset you?'

'I'm not upset.'

'Harry, you were never a good Occlumens –'

The word was the spark that ignited Harry's fury.

'Snape!' he said, very loudly, and Fawkes gave a soft squawk behind them. 'Snape's what's happened! He told Voldemort about the prophecy, it was *him*, *he* listened outside the door, Trelawney told me!'

Dumbledore's expression did not change, but Harry thought his face whitened under the bloody tinge cast by the setting sun. For a long moment, Dumbledore said nothing.

'When did you find out about this?' he asked at last.

'Just now!' said Harry, who was refraining from yelling with enormous difficulty. And then, suddenly, he could not stop himself. 'AND YOU LET HIM TEACH HERE AND HE TOLD VOLDEMORT TO GO AFTER MY MUM AND DAD!'

Breathing hard as though he were fighting, Harry turned away from Dumbledore, who still had not moved a muscle, and paced up and down the study, rubbing his knuckles in his hand and exercising every last bit of

## 第25章 被窃听的预言

"我也不能确定是哪一个——不过我认为可以排除那条蛇——我相信魂器藏在遥远的海边的一个山洞里,一个我努力寻找了很久的山洞里。汤姆·里德尔在孤儿院每年一次的旅行中曾经恐吓过两个孤儿的那个山洞,你记得吗?"

"记得,"哈利说,"它有些什么防御机关呢?"

"我不知道,只有一些猜测,也可能完全不对。"邓布利多犹豫了一下说道,"哈利,我答应过你可以跟着我一起去,我遵守那个诺言,但是如果我不事先警告你这会有超乎寻常的危险,可就太不应该了。"

"我去。"几乎还没等邓布利多说完,哈利就抢着说。他内心充满了对斯内普的憎恨,想不顾一切地去冒险做点什么的欲望在这几分钟里陡增了十倍。这一切似乎都写在哈利的脸上,邓布利多把目光从窗前移开,更仔细地看着哈利,他银色的双眉紧锁着,中间形成一条浅浅的竖纹。

"你怎么了?"

"没什么。"哈利赶紧撒谎道。

"什么让你这么不高兴?"

"我没有不高兴。"

"哈利,你大脑封闭术从来就不高——"

这句话像火星一样点燃了哈利的愤怒。

"斯内普!"哈利极其大声地说,他们身后的福克斯轻轻地尖叫了一声,"原来都是斯内普!是他把预言告诉了伏地魔,就是他,他在房间外偷听了,特里劳尼告诉我的!"

邓布利多的表情毫无变化,但哈利似乎觉得,在鲜红的落日映衬下,邓布利多的脸色还是变白了。过了好一会儿,邓布利多一句话也没说。

"你是什么时候知道这些的?"他最终问道。

"刚刚知道!"哈利说,竭力控制着自己不要吼出来。然后,他突然不能自已,"你还让他在这里教书,是他告诉伏地魔去追杀我的父母的!"

哈利喘着粗气,像在搏斗一样,转过身背朝着仍然一动不动的邓布利多,在书房里来回踱步,搓着手指的关节,尽力克制着要摔东西

## CHAPTER TWENTY-FIVE  The Seer Overheard

restraint to prevent himself knocking things over. He wanted to rage and storm at Dumbledore, but he also wanted to go with him to try and destroy the Horcrux; he wanted to tell him that he was a foolish old man for trusting Snape, but he was terrified that Dumbledore would not take him along unless he mastered his anger ...

'Harry,' said Dumbledore quietly. 'Please listen to me.'

It was as difficult to stop his relentless pacing as to refrain from shouting. Harry paused, biting his lip, and looked into Dumbledore's lined face.

'Professor Snape made a terrible –'

'Don't tell me it was a mistake, sir, he was listening at the door!'

'Please let me finish.' Dumbledore waited until Harry had nodded curtly, then went on. 'Professor Snape made a terrible mistake. He was still in Lord Voldemort's employ on the night he heard the first half of Professor Trelawney's prophecy. Naturally, he hastened to tell his master what he had heard, for it concerned his master most deeply. But he did not know – he had no possible way of knowing – which boy Voldemort would hunt from then onwards, or that the parents he would destroy in his murderous quest were people that Professor Snape knew, that they were your mother and father –'

Harry let out a yell of mirthless laughter.

'He hated my dad like he hated Sirius! Haven't you noticed, Professor, how the people Snape hates tend to end up dead?'

'You have no idea of the remorse Professor Snape felt when he realised how Lord Voldemort had interpreted the prophecy, Harry. I believe it to be the greatest regret of his life and the reason that he returned –'

'But *he's* a very good Occlumens, isn't he, sir?' said Harry, whose voice was shaking with the effort of keeping it steady. 'And isn't Voldemort convinced that Snape's on his side, even now? Professor ... how can you be *sure* Snape's on our side?'

Dumbledore did not speak for a moment; he looked as though he was trying to make up his mind about something. At last he said, 'I am sure. I trust Severus Snape completely.'

Harry breathed deeply for a few moments in an effort to steady himself. It did not work.

'Well, I don't!' he said, as loudly as before. 'He's up to something with Draco Malfoy right now, right under your nose, and you still –'

# 第25章 被窃听的预言

的冲动。他想冲邓布利多发火和咆哮,同时又想跟着他去摧毁魂器;他想说邓布利多是老糊涂了,居然相信斯内普,但又害怕如果自己控制不住愤怒,邓布利多就不会带他一起去……

"哈利,"邓布利多平静地说,"请听我说。"

哈利想停下脚步,但这竟和控制自己的怒吼一样困难。他顿了一下,咬着嘴唇,看着邓布利多满是皱纹的脸。

"斯内普教授犯了一个严重的——"

"别告诉我是一个错误,先生,他当时在房间外偷听!"

"请让我说完。"邓布利多等哈利草草地点了点头,接着说道,"斯内普教授犯了一个严重的错误。他在听到特里劳妮教授上半部分预言的时候,仍然听命于伏地魔。因为这件事跟他的主人密切相关,他自然就急急忙忙地把他所听到的告诉了他的主人。但他当时不知道——他也不可能知道——从那以后伏地魔会追杀哪个男孩,也不知道被屠戮的父母会是斯内普教授认识的人,也就是你的母亲和父亲——"

哈利大声地冷笑着。

"他恨我爸爸,也恨小天狼星!你没注意到吗,教授,为什么斯内普恨的人最后都以死亡而告终呢?"

"哈利,当斯内普教授意识到伏地魔会那样去理解预言时,你不知道他有多么懊悔。我相信这是他一生中最大的遗憾,也是他回来的理由——"

"但他是一个很厉害的大脑封闭大师,不是吗,先生?"哈利说,他尽力保持镇静,但声音还是有点颤抖,"伏地魔不是很相信斯内普站在他那一边吗?即使现在也是?教授……你怎么能确定斯内普是站在我们这一边的呢?"

邓布利多有一会儿没有说话,他似乎正在下一个决心。最后他说道:"我确定。我完全信任西弗勒斯·斯内普。"

哈利做了几个深呼吸,想努力稳定一下自己的情绪,但没有效果。

"哼,我不信任他!"他和刚才一样大声地说,"他现在同德拉科·马尔福在一些事情上勾勾搭搭,就在你的鼻子底下,你仍然——"

## CHAPTER TWENTY-FIVE    The Seer Overheard

'We have discussed this, Harry,' said Dumbledore, and now he sounded stern again. 'I have told you my views.'

'You're leaving the school tonight and I'll bet you haven't even considered that Snape and Malfoy might decide to –'

'To what?' asked Dumbledore, his eyebrows raised. 'What is it that you suspect them of doing, precisely?'

'I ... they're up to something!' said Harry and his hands curled into fists as he said it. 'Professor Trelawney was just in the Room of Requirement, trying to hide her sherry bottles, and she heard Malfoy whooping, celebrating! He's trying to mend something dangerous in there and if you ask me he's fixed it at last and you're about to just walk out of school without –'

'Enough,' said Dumbledore. He said it quite calmly, and yet Harry fell silent at once; he knew that he had finally crossed some invisible line. 'Do you think that I have once left the school unprotected during my absences this year? I have not. Tonight, when I leave, there will again be additional protection in place. Please do not suggest that I do not take the safety of my students seriously, Harry.'

'I didn't –' mumbled Harry, a little abashed, but Dumbledore cut across him.

'I do not wish to discuss the matter any further.'

Harry bit back his retort, scared that he had gone too far, that he had ruined his chance of accompanying Dumbledore, but Dumbledore went on, 'Do you wish to come with me tonight?'

'Yes,' said Harry at once.

'Very well, then: listen.'

Dumbledore drew himself up to his full height.

'I take you with me on one condition: that you obey any command I might give you at once, and without question.'

'Of course.'

'Be sure to understand me, Harry. I mean that you must follow even such orders as "run", "hide" or "go back". Do I have your word?'

'I – yes, of course.'

'If I tell you to hide, you will do so?'

'Yes.'

## 第25章 被窃听的预言

"我们已经讨论过这些了,哈利,"邓布利多说,声音又显得严厉了,"我已经把我的观点告诉过你。"

"你今天晚上要离开学校,我敢打赌你肯定没有考虑过斯内普和马尔福可能会决定——"

"什么?"邓布利多扬起眉毛问,"你怀疑他们会做什么?说明确一点儿。"

"我——他们有阴谋!"哈利说着,双手攥成了拳头,"特里劳尼教授刚才在有求必应屋里,准备藏她的雪利酒瓶,结果听到了马尔福的叫喊声、庆贺声!他在那里面试图修复什么危险的东西,据我看,他已经终于修好了。而你却要离开学校,不去——"

"够了。"邓布利多说。虽然他说得极其平静,但是哈利马上沉默下来,因为他知道自己最终越过了一道看不见的底线,"你以为今年我有哪次是不采取保护措施就离开学校的吗?从来没有过。今晚,当我离开时,各处将会增加额外的防御措施。请不要认为我没有认真对待我的学生们的安全,哈利。"

"我没有——"哈利喃喃道,有点惭愧,但邓布利多打断了他。

"我不想就这个问题再深入讨论下去了。"

哈利忍住反驳的话,他害怕自己说得太多,丧失了陪同邓布利多的机会。但邓布利多接着问道:"你愿意今晚跟我一道去吗?"

"愿意。"哈利马上答道。

"很好,那么听着。"

邓布利多挺直了腰。

"我带你去有一个条件:你必须毫无疑问地立刻服从我的任何命令。"

"当然。"

"你要听明白,哈利。我是说你甚至必须服从像'快跑''藏起来'或'回去'这样的命令。你答应吗?"

"我——答应,当然。"

"如果我叫你藏起来,你会吗?"

"会。"

## CHAPTER TWENTY-FIVE    The Seer Overheard

'If I tell you to flee, you will obey?'

'Yes.'

'If I tell you to leave me, and save yourself, you will do as I tell you?'

'I –'

'Harry?'

They looked at each other for a moment.

'Yes, sir.'

'Very good. Then I wish you to go and fetch your Cloak and meet me in the Entrance Hall in five minutes' time.'

Dumbledore turned back to look out of the fiery window; the sun was now a ruby-red glare along the horizon. Harry walked quickly from the office and down the spiral staircase. His mind was oddly clear all of a sudden. He knew what to do.

Ron and Hermione were sitting together in the common room when he came back. 'What does Dumbledore want?' Hermione said at once. 'Harry, are you OK?' she added anxiously.

'I'm fine,' said Harry shortly, racing past them. He dashed up the stairs and into his dormitory, where he flung open his trunk and pulled out the Marauder's Map and a pair of balled-up socks. Then he sped back down the stairs and into the common room, skidding to a halt where Ron and Hermione sat, looking stunned.

'I haven't got much time,' Harry panted, 'Dumbledore thinks I'm getting my Invisibility Cloak. Listen ...'

Quickly he told them where he was going, and why. He did not pause either for Hermione's gasps of horror or for Ron's hasty questions; they could work out the finer details for themselves later.

'... so you see what this means?' Harry finished at a gallop. 'Dumbledore won't be here tonight, so Malfoy's going to have another clear shot at whatever he's up to. *No, listen to me!*' he hissed angrily, as both Ron and Hermione showed every sign of interrupting. 'I know it was Malfoy celebrating in the Room of Requirement. Here –' He shoved the Marauder's Map into Hermione's hand. 'You've got to watch him and you've got to watch Snape, too. Use anyone else who you can rustle up from the DA. Hermione, those contact Galleons will still work, right? Dumbledore says he's

## 第 25 章 被窃听的预言

"如果我叫你逃走,你会服从吗?"

"会。"

"如果我叫你离开我,保全自己,你会照我说的做吗?"

"我——"

"哈利?"

他们对视了一会儿。

"会,先生。"

"很好。那么我希望你去拿你的隐形衣,五分钟后我们在门厅见面。"

邓布利多转过身,看着火红的窗户外面,现在太阳正在天边闪耀着红宝石一般的光芒。哈利快速地走出办公室,走下螺旋形楼梯。他的思维很奇怪地突然变得很清晰,他知道要做什么了。

哈利回来时,罗恩和赫敏正一起坐在公共休息室里。"邓布利多想要什么?"赫敏马上问道。"哈利,你没事吧?"她又担心地说。

"我没事。"哈利简单地回答,他从他们身边跑过,冲上楼梯进了宿舍,猛地打开衣箱,拿出活点地图和一双卷好的袜子,然后又快速冲下楼梯,进了公共休息室,在罗恩和赫敏坐的地方刹住脚。他们俩满脸惊讶。

"我没有多少时间,"哈利喘着气说道,"邓布利多要我来拿隐形衣。听着……"

他很快讲了他要去哪里和为什么要去。赫敏惊恐地抽了一口冷气,罗恩匆忙地提出问题,但是哈利没有做任何停顿,待会儿他们自己可以弄清更详尽的细节。

"……你们明白吗?"哈利飞快地讲完了,"邓布利多今天晚上不在,所以马尔福可以放手去干他的阴谋。不,听我说!"因为罗恩和赫敏都显出要打断他的迹象,哈利生气地压低声音说,"我知道那是马尔福在有求必应屋里庆贺。喏——"他猛地把活点地图塞进赫敏手里,"你们必须盯着他,也必须盯着斯内普。调用你们能找到的每一个 D.A. 成员。赫敏,那些联络用的加隆硬币仍然能用,对吗?邓布利多说他已经加强了学校的保卫,但如果斯内普掺和进来,他会知道邓布利多的保护

## CHAPTER TWENTY-FIVE     The Seer Overheard

put extra protection in the school, but if Snape's involved, he'll know what Dumbledore's protection is, and how to avoid it – but he won't be expecting you lot to be on the watch, will he?'

'Harry –' began Hermione, her eyes huge with fear.

'I haven't got time to argue,' said Harry curtly. 'Take this as well –' He thrust the socks into Ron's hands.

'Thanks,' said Ron. 'Er – why do I need socks?'

'You need what's wrapped in them, it's the Felix Felicis. Share it between yourselves and Ginny too. Say goodbye to her from me. I'd better go, Dumbledore's waiting –'

'No!' said Hermione, as Ron unwrapped the tiny little bottle of golden potion, looking awestruck. 'We don't want it, you take it, who knows what you're going to be facing?'

'I'll be fine, I'll be with Dumbledore,' said Harry. 'I want to know you lot are OK ... don't look like that, Hermione, I'll see you later ...'

And he was off, hurrying back through the portrait hole towards the Entrance Hall.

Dumbledore was waiting beside the oaken front doors. He turned as Harry came skidding out on to the topmost stone step, panting hard, a searing stitch in his side.

'I would like you to wear your Cloak, please,' said Dumbledore, and he waited until Harry had thrown it on before saying, 'Very good. Shall we go?'

Dumbledore set off at once down the stone steps, his own travelling cloak barely stirring in the still summer air. Harry hurried alongside him under the Invisibility Cloak, still panting and sweating rather a lot.

'But what will people think when they see you leaving, Professor?' Harry asked, his mind on Malfoy and Snape.

'That I am off into Hogsmeade for a drink,' said Dumbledore lightly. 'I sometimes offer Rosmerta my custom, or else visit the Hog's Head ... or I appear to. It is as good a way as any of disguising one's true destination.'

They made their way down the drive in the gathering twilight. The air was full of the smells of warm grass, lake water and wood smoke from Hagrid's cabin. It was difficult to believe that they were heading for anything dangerous or frightening.

措施是什么，知道怎么去避免——但他不会知道你们俩也被分配了监视的任务，不是吗？"

"哈利——"赫敏开始发问，她由于害怕而瞪大了双眼。

"我没有时间和你们争辩，"哈利急忙说，"把这个也拿上——"他把袜子扔进罗恩的手里。

"谢谢。"罗恩说，"呃——为什么要给我袜子？"

"你们需要袜子里面裹的东西，那是福灵剂。也分一点给金妮。替我向她说声再见。我得走了，邓布利多在等着呢——"

"不！"赫敏说，这时罗恩拿出了那个装有金色药水的小瓶子，满脸敬畏的表情，"我们不需要这个，你带着它，谁知道你会遇上什么情况？"

"我没事的，我和邓布利多在一起，"哈利说，"我想确保你们没问题……别那样，赫敏，再见……"

然后他就走了，匆匆钻过肖像洞口朝门厅赶去。

邓布利多正在橡木大门口等着。他转过身，哈利正好刹住脚，站在最上面的石头台阶上，喘着粗气，两肋间火辣辣地刺痛。

"我希望你穿上隐形衣，"邓布利多说，等哈利穿上后，他又说，"很好。我们走吧？"

邓布利多立刻下了石头台阶，他的旅行斗篷在夏日静止的空气里几乎纹丝不动。哈利穿着隐形衣匆匆地跟着他，仍在喘气，身上出了很多汗。

"可是别人看到你出去会怎么想呢，教授？"哈利问，脑子里想着马尔福和斯内普。

"我去霍格莫德喝一杯。"邓布利多轻松地说，"我有时候去罗斯默塔那儿坐坐，或者去猪头酒吧……或者假装去那里，这是一个掩饰真实目的地的好方法。"

他们在渐浓的暮色中沿着车道走去。空气中充满温暖的青草气息、湖水的味道，以及从海格的小屋飘来的烧木头的烟味。很难相信他们要去做危险的、令人恐惧的事情。

# CHAPTER TWENTY-FIVE  The Seer Overheard

'Professor,' said Harry quietly, as the gates at the bottom of the drive came into view, 'will we be Apparating?'

'Yes,' said Dumbledore. 'You can Apparate now, I believe?'

'Yes,' said Harry, 'but I haven't got a licence.'

He felt it best to be honest; what if he spoiled everything by turning up a hundred miles from where he was supposed to go?

'No matter,' said Dumbledore, 'I can assist you again.'

They turned out of the gates into the twilit, deserted lane to Hogsmeade. Darkness descended fast as they walked and by the time they reached the High Street night was falling in earnest. Lights twinkled from windows over shops and as they neared the Three Broomsticks they heard raucous shouting.

'– and stay out!' shouted Madam Rosmerta, forcibly ejecting a grubby-looking wizard. 'Oh, hello, Albus ... you're out late ...'

'Good evening, Rosmerta, good evening ... forgive me, I'm off to the Hog's Head ... no offence, but I feel like a quieter atmosphere tonight ...'

A minute later they turned the corner into the side street where the Hog's Head's sign creaked a little, though there was no breeze. In contrast to the Three Broomsticks, the pub appeared to be completely empty.

'It will not be necessary for us to enter,' muttered Dumbledore, glancing around. 'As long as nobody sees us go ... now place your hand upon my arm, Harry. There is no need to grip too hard, I am merely guiding you. On the count of three – one ... two ... three ...'

Harry turned. At once, there was that horrible sensation that he was being squeezed through a thick rubber tube; he could not draw breath, every part of him was being compressed almost past endurance and then, just when he thought he must suffocate, the invisible bands seemed to burst open, and he was standing in cool darkness, breathing in lungfuls of fresh, salty air.

## 第25章 被窃听的预言

"教授,"当车道尽头处的大门映入眼帘时,哈利轻轻地问,"我们要幻影显形吗?"

"是的,"邓布利多说,"你现在已经能够幻影显形了,是吧?"

"是的,"哈利说,"但我还没有证书。"

他觉得最好实话实说,不然显形后离他要去的地方还有一百英里,那不就坏了事吗?

"没关系,"邓布利多说,"我可以再帮助你一次。"

他们出了大门,走上了暮色笼罩的通往霍格莫德的荒凉小路。随着他们行进,夜幕迅速降临,当他们来到大街上时天已经完全黑了。店铺的窗户里闪着灯光,他们走近三把扫帚酒吧时,听到了刺耳的叫喊声。

"——不许进来!"罗斯默塔女士大喊道,强行撵出一个看起来很邋遢的巫师,"哦,你好,阿不思……这么晚出来……"

"晚上好,罗斯默塔,晚上好……原谅我,我要去猪头酒吧……别见怪,只是我今晚想有一个更安静的氛围……"

过了一小会儿,他们拐进了一条小街,猪头酒吧的标记在吱吱地发出轻响,尽管并没有风。与三把扫帚相比,这间酒吧里显得空空荡荡。

"我们没有必要进去,"邓布利多扫视了一圈,喃喃地说,"但愿没有人看见我们离开……现在你把手放在我的胳膊上,哈利。不用抓得太紧,我只是引着你。我数三声——一……二……三……"

哈利旋转起来。立刻又是那种恐怖的感觉,像是被挤在一个厚厚的橡皮管子里,他不能呼吸,身体的每个部位都遭受着挤压,简直要超过他忍耐的极限了。然后,就在他认为自己肯定要窒息时,无形的管子突然迸裂开来,他站在凉爽的黑暗中,大口大口地呼吸着新鲜的、咸丝丝的空气。

## CHAPTER TWENTY-SIX

# The Cave

Harry could smell salt and hear rushing waves; a light, chilly breeze ruffled his hair as he looked out at moonlit sea and star-strewn sky. He was standing upon a high outcrop of dark rock, water foaming and churning below him. He glanced over his shoulder. a towering cliff stood behind, a sheer drop, black and faceless. a few large chunks of rock, such as the one upon which Harry and Dumbledore were standing, looked as though they had broken away from the cliff face at some point in the past. It was a bleak, harsh view; the sea and the rock unrelieved by any tree or sweep of grass or sand.

'What do you think?' asked Dumbledore. He might have been asking Harry's opinion on whether it was a good site for a picnic.

'They brought the kids from the orphanage here?' asked Harry, who could not imagine a less cosy spot for a daytrip.

'Not here, precisely,' said Dumbledore. 'There is a village of sorts about halfway along the cliffs behind us. I believe the orphans were taken there for a little sea air and a view of the waves. No, I think it was only ever Tom Riddle and his youthful victims who visited this spot. No Muggle could reach this rock unless they were uncommonly good mountaineers, and boats cannot approach the cliffs; the waters around them are too dangerous. I imagine that Riddle climbed down; magic would have served better than ropes. And he brought two small children with him, probably for the pleasure of terrorising them. I think the journey alone would have done it, don't you?'

Harry looked up at the cliff again and felt goosebumps.

'But his final destination – and ours – lies a little further on. Come.'

# 第 26 章

# 岩　洞

哈利可以闻到大海的气味，听见波涛汹涌的声音。他望着月光下的大海和繁星点点的夜空，一阵寒冷的微风吹拂着他的头发。他站在一块露出海面的高高的黑色岩石上，海浪在他脚下翻滚，泛起泡沫。他扭头朝后望去。身后耸立着一座悬崖，陡峭的岩壁直落而下，黑乎乎的看不清面目。几块很大的岩石，如哈利和邓布利多站着的这块，似乎是过去某个时候从悬崖的正面脱落下来的。四下里光秃秃的，满目荒凉，除了苍茫的大海和岩石，看不见一棵树，也没有草地和沙滩。

"你觉得怎么样？"邓布利多问。听他那口气，仿佛他在问哈利这里是不是一个理想的野餐地点。

"他们把孤儿院的孩子带到这儿来了？"哈利问，他想象不出比这儿更不舒服的旅游地了。

"确切地说，不是这儿。"邓布利多说，"在我们后面那些悬崖的半腰上，有一个勉强称得上村庄的地方。我相信他们把孤儿们带到了那儿，让他们呼呼吸吸大海的空气，看看海浪。不，我认为只有汤姆·里德尔和那几个被他欺负的孩子曾经到过这个地方。麻瓜不可能爬上这块岩石，除非他们特别擅长攀岩；船也没法靠近悬崖，周围的水域太危险了。我可以想象里德尔是怎么爬下来的，魔法肯定比绳索更管用。他还带了两个小孩子，大概是为了享受恐吓他们的乐趣吧。我想其实这趟旅途本身就够吓唬他们了，你说呢？"

哈利又抬头看了看那道悬崖，身上起了一层鸡皮疙瘩。

"可是他的——还有我们的——目的地还在更远一点的地方。走吧。"

## CHAPTER TWENTY-SIX    The Cave

Dumbledore beckoned Harry to the very edge of the rock, where a series of jagged niches that made footholds led down to boulders that lay half submerged in water and closer to the cliff. It was a treacherous descent and Dumbledore, hampered slightly by his withered hand, moved slowly. The lower rocks were slippery with sea water. Harry could feel flecks of cold salt spray hitting his face.

'*Lumos*,' said Dumbledore, as he reached the boulder closest to the cliff face. A thousand flecks of golden light sparkled upon the dark surface of the water a few feet below where he crouched; the black wall of rock beside him was illuminated too.

'You see?' said Dumbledore quietly, holding his wand a little higher. Harry saw a fissure in the cliff into which dark water was swirling.

'You will not object to getting a little wet?'

'No,' said Harry.

'Then take off your Invisibility Cloak – there is no need for it now – and let us take the plunge.'

And with the sudden agility of a much younger man, Dumbledore slid from the boulder, landed in the sea and began to swim, with a perfect breaststroke, towards the dark slit in the rock face, his lit wand held in his teeth. Harry pulled off his Cloak, stuffed it into his pocket and followed.

The water was icy; Harry's waterlogged clothes billowed around him and weighed him down. Taking deep breaths that filled his nostrils with the tang of salt and seaweed, he struck out for the shimmering, shrinking light now moving deeper into the cliff.

The fissure soon opened into a dark tunnel that Harry could tell would be filled with water at high tide. The slimy walls were barely three feet apart and glimmered like wet tar in the passing light of Dumbledore's wand. A little way in, the passageway curved to the left and Harry saw that it extended far into the cliff. He continued to swim in Dumbledore's wake, the tips of his benumbed fingers brushing the rough, wet rock.

Then he saw Dumbledore rising out of the water ahead, his silver hair and dark robes gleaming. When Harry reached the spot he found steps that led into a large cave. He clambered up them, water streaming from his soaking

# 第26章 岩洞

邓布利多示意哈利走到岩石边缘，岩石上有许多参差不齐的凹缝可供踩脚，通向下面那些在悬崖周围、半露出海面的巨型卵石。从这里攀岩而下非常危险，邓布利多那只焦枯的手不听使唤，行动比较迟缓。低处的岩石被海水冲刷得滑溜溜的。哈利感觉到散发着海腥味儿的冰冷水花溅在他脸上。

"荧光闪烁！"邓布利多下到最靠近悬崖正面的那块巨型卵石上，蹲下身念了句咒语。星星点点的金光在他身下几英尺处的黝黑海面上闪烁。他身边那道漆黑的岩壁也被照亮了。

"看见了吗？"邓布利多轻声问，一边把魔杖举得更高一些。哈利看见悬崖上有一道裂缝，黑黢黢的海水在里面打着旋儿。

"你不介意把身上弄湿吧？"

"没关系。"哈利说。

"那就把你的隐形衣脱掉——现在没必要穿着它了——然后让我们冒险试一试吧。"

邓布利多突然变得像年轻人一样身手敏捷，他从那块卵石上轻轻地滑进海水里，朝岩石表面那道漆黑的裂缝游去。他把点亮的魔杖叼在嘴里，采用的是完美的蛙泳姿势。哈利脱下隐形衣塞进口袋，也跟了上去。

海水冷极了。哈利的衣服被水浸透之后，变得涨鼓鼓沉甸甸的，拽着他直往下沉。他深深吸了几口气，闻到刺鼻的盐腥味儿和海藻味儿，他游向那道正往悬崖深处移动、变得越来越小的闪烁的亮光。

很快，裂缝变成了一条漆黑的暗道，哈利看得出来，涨潮的时候暗道肯定会被海水灌满。两边粘满黏泥的岩壁只间隔三英尺宽，在邓布利多魔杖一闪而过的亮光照耀下，像柏油一样闪着湿漉漉的光。再往里去一点，暗道向左一拐，哈利看见它一直伸向悬崖的最深处。他继续跟着邓布利多往前游，冻得麻木的指尖在粗糙、潮湿的岩石上擦过。

然后，他看见前面的邓布利多从水里站了起来，银白色的头发和黑色长袍都闪烁着水光。哈利游过去，发现有台阶通向一个很大的岩洞。他费力地登上台阶，水从湿透的衣服里哗哗地往下流。他终于走出了

## CHAPTER TWENTY-SIX — The Cave

clothes, and emerged, shivering uncontrollably, into the still and freezing air.

Dumbledore was standing in the middle of the cave, his wand held high as he turned slowly on the spot, examining the walls and ceiling.

'Yes, this is the place,' said Dumbledore.

'How can you tell?' Harry spoke in a whisper.

'It has known magic,' said Dumbledore simply.

Harry could not tell whether the shivers he was experiencing were due to his spine-deep coldness or to the same awareness of enchantments. He watched as Dumbledore continued to revolve on the spot, evidently concentrating on things Harry could not see.

'This is merely the ante-chamber, the entrance hall,' said Dumbledore after a moment or two. 'We need to penetrate the inner place ... now it is Lord Voldemort's obstacles that stand in our way, rather than those nature made ...'

Dumbledore approached the wall of the cave and caressed it with his blackened fingertips, murmuring words in a strange tongue that Harry did not understand. Twice Dumbledore walked right around the cave, touching as much of the rough rock as he could, occasionally pausing, running his fingers backwards and forwards over a particular spot, until finally he stopped, his hand pressed flat against the wall.

'Here,' he said. 'We go on through here. The entrance is concealed.'

Harry did not ask how Dumbledore knew. He had never seen a wizard work things out like this, simply by looking and touching; but Harry had long since learned that bangs and smoke were more often the marks of ineptitude than expertise.

Dumbledore stepped back from the cave wall and pointed his wand at the rock. For a moment, an arched outline appeared there, blazing white as though there was a powerful light behind the crack.

'You've d-done it!' said Harry through chattering teeth, but before the words had left his lips the outline had gone, leaving the rock as bare and solid as ever. Dumbledore looked round.

'Harry, I'm so sorry, I forgot,' he said; he pointed his wand at Harry and at once Harry's clothes were as warm and dry as if they had been hanging in front of a blazing fire.

## 第26章 岩洞

海水，周围的空气寂静而寒冷，他控制不住地瑟瑟发抖。

邓布利多已经站在了岩洞中央，魔杖高高地举在手里，他原地缓缓地转着圈，仔细查看着岩壁和洞顶。

"没错，就是这个地方。"邓布利多说。

"你怎么知道的？"哈利小声问。

"它见识过魔法。"邓布利多简短地说。

哈利不知道他这样浑身发抖，是因为寒冷侵入了骨髓呢，还是因为他也意识到了魔咒的存在。他注视着邓布利多继续在原地慢慢旋转，显然是在专注地研究某些哈利看不见的东西。

"这只是前厅，是入口大厅，"邓布利多过了片刻说道，"我们需要进到里面去……现在挡住我们的是伏地魔布下的机关，而不是大自然设置的障碍……"

邓布利多走近洞壁，用焦黑的指尖抚摸着它，又用一种奇怪的、哈利听不懂的语言轻声说着什么。邓布利多紧绕着岩洞走了两圈，边走边尽可能地触摸粗糙的洞壁，偶尔停下来用手指在某个地方上上下下地摸索一番。最后，他终于停住脚步，把手掌平按在洞壁上。

"这儿，"他说，"我们从这儿进去。入口是隐蔽的。"

哈利没有问邓布利多是怎么知道的。他从没见过哪个巫师这样解决难题：只用眼睛看，用手摸。不过哈利早就知道，弄得乒乒乓乓、烟雾大作的，通常是菜鸟的特点，而不是高手的做派。

邓布利多从洞壁前往后退了几步，用魔杖指向岩石。片刻后，那里出现了一道拱门的轮廓，放射出耀眼的白光，似乎裂缝后面有强烈的灯光照着。

"你成——成功了！"哈利说，牙齿嘚嘚地打着战，但他的话音未落，那道轮廓就不见了，岩石还跟刚才一样坚硬厚实，上面什么也没有。邓布利多扭头看了看。

"哈利，真对不起，我忘记了。"他说。他用魔杖一指哈利，哈利的衣服立刻变得干爽、暖和，就像挂在熊熊的炉火前烘过一样。

# CHAPTER TWENTY-SIX  The Cave

'Thank you,' said Harry gratefully, but Dumbledore had already turned his attention back to the solid cave wall. He did not try any more magic, but simply stood there staring at it intently, as though something extremely interesting was written on it. Harry stayed quite still; he did not want to break Dumbledore's concentration.

Then, after two solid minutes, Dumbledore said quietly, 'Oh, surely not. So crude.'

'What is it, Professor?'

'I rather think,' said Dumbledore, putting his uninjured hand inside his robes and drawing out a short silver knife of the kind Harry used to chop potion ingredients, 'that we are required to make payment to pass.'

'Payment?' said Harry. 'You've got to give the door something?'

'Yes,' said Dumbledore. 'Blood, if I am not much mistaken.'

'*Blood?*'

'I said it was crude,' said Dumbledore, who sounded disdainful, even disappointed, as though Voldemort had fallen short of the standards Dumbledore expected. 'The idea, as I am sure you will have gathered, is that your enemy must weaken him or herself to enter. Once again, Lord Voldemort fails to grasp that there are much more terrible things than physical injury.'

'Yeah, but still, if you can avoid it …' said Harry, who had experienced enough pain not to be keen for more.

'Sometimes, however, it is unavoidable,' said Dumbledore, shaking back the sleeve of his robes and exposing the forearm of his injured hand.

'Professor!' protested Harry, hurrying forwards as Dumbledore raised his knife. 'I'll do it, I'm —'

He did not know what he was going to say — younger, fitter? But Dumbledore merely smiled. There was a flash of silver, and a spurt of scarlet; the rock face was peppered with dark, glistening drops.

'You are very kind, Harry,' said Dumbledore, now passing the tip of his wand over the deep cut he had made in his own arm, so that it healed instantly, just as Snape had healed Malfoy's wounds. 'But your blood is worth more than mine. Ah, that seems to have done the trick, doesn't it?'

## 第26章 岩洞

"谢谢。"哈利感激地说，可是邓布利多已经又把注意力转向了坚实的洞壁。他没有再尝试别的魔法，只是站在那里，全神贯注地盯着洞壁，似乎那上面写着什么极为有趣的东西。哈利一动不动地站在那儿，他不想打断邓布利多的思路。

足足过了两分钟，邓布利多轻声说："哦，当然不会。太低级了。"

"你说什么，教授？"

"我认为，"邓布利多说着用那只没有受伤的手从长袍里掏出一把银质的短刀，就是哈利用来切魔药配料的那种，"我们需要付出代价才能通过。"

"代价？"哈利说，"你必须给这道门一些东西？"

"是的，"邓布利多说，"如果我没有弄错的话，是血。"

"血？"

"所以我说太低级了。"邓布利多说，口气里透着轻蔑，甚至失望，似乎伏地魔没能达到邓布利多预期的标准，"我相信你也明白，其道理是想让对手削弱自己方能进入。伏地魔又一次没能理解，有许多东西比肉体的伤害可怕得多。"

"是啊，但如果能够避免……"哈利说，他遭受过的痛苦太多了，不愿意再经历更多。

"有时候是无法避免的。"邓布利多说着把长袍袖子往上抖了抖，露出了那只受伤的手的小臂。

"教授！"哈利看见邓布利多举起了短刀，赶紧走上前去阻止道，"让我来，我——"

他不知道自己要说什么——更年轻，更结实？然而邓布利多只是微微笑了笑。一道银光闪过，喷出一股殷红，岩石表面顿时洒满了闪亮的、暗红色的血珠。

"你很善良，哈利。"邓布利多说，一边用魔杖尖划过他在自己手臂上割开的那道深深的伤口，伤口立刻就愈合了，就像斯内普给马尔福疗伤的情景一样，"可是你的血比我的更有价值。啊，看来真的有效，是不是？"

## CHAPTER TWENTY-SIX  The Cave

The blazing silver outline of an arch had appeared in the wall once more, and this time it did not fade away: the blood-spattered rock within it simply vanished, leaving an opening into what seemed total darkness.

'After me, I think,' said Dumbledore, and he walked through the archway with Harry on his heels, lighting his own wand hastily as he went.

An eerie sight met their eyes: they were standing on the edge of a great black lake, so vast that Harry could not make out the distant banks, in a cavern so high that the ceiling, too, was out of sight. A misty greenish light shone far away in what looked like the middle of the lake; it was reflected in the completely still water below. The greenish glow and the light from the two wands were the only things that broke the otherwise velvety blackness, though their rays did not penetrate as far as Harry would have expected. The darkness was somehow denser than normal darkness.

'Let us walk,' said Dumbledore quietly. 'Be very careful not to step into the water. Stay close to me.'

He set off around the edge of the lake and Harry followed close behind him. Their footsteps made echoing, slapping sounds on the narrow rim of rock that surrounded the water. On and on they walked, but the view did not vary: on one side of them, the rough cavern wall; on the other, the boundless expanse of smooth, glassy blackness, in the very middle of which was that mysterious greenish glow. Harry found the place and the silence oppressive, unnerving.

'Professor?' he said finally. 'Do you think the Horcrux is here?'

'Oh yes,' said Dumbledore. 'Yes, I'm sure it is. The question is, how do we get to it?'

'We couldn't ... we couldn't just try a Summoning Charm?' Harry said, sure that it was a stupid suggestion, but much keener than he was prepared to admit on getting out of this place as soon as possible.

'Certainly we could,' said Dumbledore, stopping so suddenly that Harry almost walked into him. 'Why don't you do it?'

'Me? Oh ... OK ...'

Harry had not expected this, but cleared his throat and said loudly, wand aloft, '*Accio Horcrux!*'

## 第26章 岩洞

洞壁上又一次出现了那道白得耀眼的拱门轮廓，这次它没有隐去。拱门里那块洒满鲜血的岩石突然消失了，露出一个门洞，里面似乎是无尽的黑暗。

"跟我来吧。"邓布利多说着走过了门洞，哈利跟在他后面走了进去，一边匆匆点亮自己的魔杖。

眼前是一幅十分怪异的景象。他们站在一片黑色的大湖岸边，湖面无比宽阔，一望无际，哈利看不见远处的对岸。他们所处的山洞很高，抬头望去也看不见洞顶。远远地，像是在湖的中央，闪烁着一道朦胧的、绿莹莹的光，倒映在下面死寂的湖水中。除了那道绿光和两根魔杖发出的亮光，四下里完全是浓得化不开的黑暗，而这几道亮光的穿透性也不像哈利预想的那么强，这里的黑暗似乎比普通的黑暗更稠密、更厚重。

"我们往前走吧，"邓布利多轻声说，"千万小心，不要踩进水里。紧紧地跟着我。"

他绕着湖岸往前走，哈利紧跟在他后面。他们的脚步踏在湖边狭窄的岩石上，发出啪啪的回声。他们一直往前走，可是四周的景象没有丝毫改变：一边是粗糙的岩洞壁，另一边是无边无际、光滑如镜的黑色湖面，湖的正中央闪烁着那道神秘的绿光。哈利感觉这个地方以及这种寂静令人压抑，令人心神不安。

"教授？"他忍不住问道，"你认为魂器藏在这里？"

"哦，是的，"邓布利多说，"是的，我相信是藏在这里。问题是，我们怎么才能找到它。"

"我们不能……我们不能试一试召唤咒吗？"哈利说，他知道这肯定是一个愚蠢的建议，他虽然嘴上不愿意承认，心里却巴不得赶紧离开这个鬼地方。

"当然可以，"邓布利多说着突然停住脚步，哈利差点儿撞到他身上，"你为什么不试一试呢？"

"我？噢……好吧……"

哈利没有料到这点，他清了清嗓子，举起魔杖，大声说道："魂器飞来！"

## CHAPTER TWENTY-SIX   The Cave

With a noise like an explosion, something very large and pale erupted out of the dark water some twenty feet away; before Harry could see what it was, it had vanished again with a crashing splash that made great, deep ripples on the mirrored surface. Harry leapt backwards in shock and hit the wall; his heart was still thundering as he turned to Dumbledore.

'What was that?'

'Something, I think, that is ready to respond should we attempt to seize the Horcrux.'

Harry looked back at the water. The surface of the lake was once more shining black glass: the ripples had vanished unnaturally fast; Harry's heart, however, was still pounding.

'Did you think that would happen, sir?'

'I thought *something* would happen if we made an obvious attempt to get our hands on the Horcrux. That was a very good idea, Harry; much the simplest way of finding out what we are facing.'

'But we don't know what the thing was,' said Harry, looking at the sinisterly smooth water.

'What the things *are*, you mean,' said Dumbledore. 'I doubt very much that there is only one of them. Shall we walk on?'

'Professor?'

'Yes, Harry?'

'Do you think we're going to have to go into the lake?'

'Into it? Only if we are very unfortunate.'

'You don't think the Horcrux is at the bottom?'

'Oh no ... I think the Horcrux is in the *middle*.'

And Dumbledore pointed towards the misty green light in the centre of the lake.

'So we're going to have to cross the lake to get to it?'

'Yes, I think so.'

Harry did not say anything. His thoughts were all of water-monsters, of giant serpents, of demons, kelpies and sprites ...

'Aha,' said Dumbledore and he stopped again; this time, Harry really did walk into him; for a moment he toppled on the edge of the dark water and Dumbledore's uninjured hand closed tightly around his upper arm, pulling

## 第26章 岩洞

随着爆炸般的一声巨响,一个白森森的大家伙从二十英尺开外的漆黑湖面蹿了上来。哈利还没来得及看清那是什么,哗啦一声,它又消失了,在平静的水面溅起大片很深的波纹。哈利惊得往后一跳,撞在了岩壁上。他转向邓布利多,心脏仍在咚咚地狂跳。

"那是什么?"

"我想,如果我们试图夺取魂器,它就会做出反应。"

哈利转脸又看了看湖水。湖面又变得像黑色的玻璃一样,明亮而光滑了。那些波纹消失的速度快得离奇,但哈利的心仍跳得像打鼓一样。

"你早就知道会发生那样的事吗,先生?"

"我早就知道如果我们明目张胆地想拿到那个魂器,肯定会遭遇一些什么。哈利,你的主意很不错,用最简便的方法弄清了我们面对的是什么。"

"但是我们并不知道那个东西是什么。"哈利说,眼睛望着平静而凶险的湖面。

"你应该说那些东西,"邓布利多说,"我不相信它们只有一个。我们继续往前走好吗?"

"教授?"

"怎么了,哈利?"

"你认为我们需要下到湖里去吗?"

"下湖?除非我们的运气特别不好。"

"你不认为魂器在湖底下吗?"

"哦,不……我认为魂器在湖的中央。"

邓布利多指了指湖中央那道朦胧的绿光。

"那么我们必须到湖中央才能拿到它了?"

"是的,我认为是这样。"

哈利没再说什么。他脑子里想的净是水怪、水妖、水鬼、巨蟒和幽灵……

"啊哈!"邓布利多说着又停住了脚步,这次哈利真的撞到了他身上。哈利在黑黢黢的湖水边踉跄着眼看快要栽倒,邓布利多用那只没

## CHAPTER TWENTY-SIX   The Cave

him back. 'So sorry, Harry, I should have given warning. Stand back against the wall, please; I think I have found the place.'

Harry had no idea what Dumbledore meant; this patch of dark bank was exactly like every other bit as far as he could tell, but Dumbledore seemed to have detected something special about it. This time he was running his hand not over the rocky wall, but through the thin air, as though expecting to find and grip something invisible.

'Oho,' said Dumbledore happily, seconds later. His hand had closed in midair upon something Harry could not see. Dumbledore moved closer to the water; Harry watched nervously as the tips of Dumbledore's buckled shoes found the utmost edge of the rock rim. Keeping his hand clenched in midair, Dumbledore raised his wand with the other and tapped his fist with the point.

Immediately a thick coppery green chain appeared out of thin air, extending from the depths of the water into Dumbledore's clenched hand. Dumbledore tapped the chain, which began to slide through his fist like a snake, coiling itself on the ground with a clinking sound that echoed noisily off the rocky walls, pulling something from the depths of the black water. Harry gasped as the ghostly prow of a tiny boat broke the surface, glowing as green as the chain, and floated, with barely a ripple, towards the place on the bank where Harry and Dumbledore stood.

'How did you know that was there?' Harry asked in astonishment.

'Magic always leaves traces,' said Dumbledore, as the boat hit the bank with a gentle bump, 'sometimes very distinctive traces. I taught Tom Riddle. I know his style.'

'Is ... is this boat safe?'

'Oh yes, I think so. Voldemort needed to create a means to cross the lake without attracting the wrath of those creatures he had placed within it, in case he ever wanted to visit or remove his Horcrux.'

'So the things in the water won't do anything to us if we cross in Voldemort's boat?'

'I think we must resign ourselves to the fact that they will, at some point, realise we are not Lord Voldemort. Thus far, however, we have done well. They have allowed us to raise the boat.'

## 第26章 岩 洞

有受伤的手紧紧抓住他的手臂，把他拉了回来。"真抱歉，哈利，我应该打个招呼的。请往后站，贴在岩壁上，我认为我已经找着地方了。"

哈利不明白邓布利多的意思。在他看来，这一片漆黑的湖岸跟别处没有什么不同，然而邓布利多像是觉察到了某些特殊之处。这次，他的手不是在岩壁上抚摸，而是在空气中慢慢划动，似乎想找到并抓住某个无形的东西。

"嗬嗬！"几秒钟后，邓布利多高兴地说。他把手一合，抓住了空气中哈利看不见的某个东西。邓布利多挪向湖边，哈利紧张地注视着邓布利多带搭扣的鞋尖挪到了岩石边缘的最外面。邓布利多仍然悬空攥着那只手，另一只手举着魔杖，用杖尖敲了敲他的拳头。

立刻，一条粗粗的绿色铜链突然从湖水深处冒了出来，蹿向邓布利多紧攥的拳头。邓布利多用魔杖敲了敲链条，链条便开始像蛇一样从他的拳头里滑过，在地上盘成一堆，叮叮当当的声音撞在岩壁上，发出响亮的回声。链条把某个东西从漆黑的湖底拽了上来。一条小船的船头如幽灵一般突然冒出湖面，哈利倒吸了一口气，小船像链条一样发出绿莹莹的光，朝哈利和邓布利多站着的湖岸漂浮过来，几乎没有带起一丝涟漪。

"你怎么知道它在那儿？"哈利惊诧地问。

"魔法总会留下痕迹的，"邓布利多说，随着砰的一声轻响，小船撞上了湖岸，"有时候是非常明显的痕迹。我教过汤姆·里德尔，知道他的风格。"

"这……这只小船安全吗？"

"哦，我认为是安全的。伏地魔需要有一种办法，在他万一需要探望或取走他的魂器时，可以顺利地穿过湖面，以免激怒他安置在湖里的那些家伙。"

"那么，如果我们乘伏地魔的船过湖，水里那些家伙就不会对我们下手了，是吗？"

"我认为我们必须做好心理准备，一旦它们发现我们不是伏地魔，肯定还是会对我们下手的。不过，到目前为止，我们进行得还算顺利。它们允许我们把小船从湖里弄了上来。"

## CHAPTER TWENTY-SIX    The Cave

'But why have they let us?' asked Harry, who could not shake off the vision of tentacles rising out of the dark water the moment they were out of sight of the bank.

'Voldemort would have been reasonably confident that none but a very great wizard would have been able to find the boat,' said Dumbledore. 'I think he would have been prepared to risk what was, to his mind, the most unlikely possibility that somebody else would find it, knowing that he had set other obstacles ahead that only he would be able to penetrate. We shall see whether he is right.'

Harry looked down into the boat. It really was very small.

'It doesn't look like it was built for two people. Will it hold both of us? Will we be too heavy together?'

Dumbledore chuckled.

'Voldemort will not have cared about the weight, but about the amount of magical power that crossed his lake. I rather think an enchantment will have been placed upon this boat so that only one wizard at a time will be able to sail in it.'

'But then –?'

'I do not think you will count, Harry: you are under age and unqualified. Voldemort would never have expected a sixteen-year-old to reach this place: I think it unlikely that your powers will register compared to mine.'

These words did nothing to raise Harry's morale; perhaps Dumbledore knew it, for he added, 'Voldemort's mistake, Harry, Voldemort's mistake ... age is foolish and forgetful when it underestimates youth ... now, you first this time, and be careful not to touch the water.'

Dumbledore stood aside and Harry climbed carefully into the boat. Dumbledore stepped in, too, coiling the chain on to the floor. They were crammed in together; Harry could not comfortably sit, but crouched, his knees jutting over the edge of the boat, which began to move at once. There was no sound other than the silken rustle of the boat's prow cleaving the water; it moved without their help, as though an invisible rope were pulling it onwards towards the light in the centre. Soon they could no longer see the walls of the cavern; they might have been at sea except that there were no waves.

Harry looked down and saw the reflected gold of his wand-light sparkling

## 第26章 岩 洞

"可是它们为什么要让我们这么做呢?"哈利问,他无法摆脱脑海里浮现的可怕画面:当他们远远离开湖岸时,便会有许多触手从漆黑的湖水里伸出来。

"伏地魔坚信只有技艺十分高超的巫师才能发现那条小船,他的自信是有道理的。"邓布利多说,"我认为,他准备好了冒险让别人发现小船——在他看来这几乎是不可能的,因为他在前面还设置了一些只有他自己能够穿越的障碍。待会儿我们能看到他的判断是否正确。"

哈利低头看看小船。确实是一条很小的船。

"它好像不是给两个人坐的,能吃得住我们俩的重量吗?我们俩加在一起会不会太重了?"

邓布利多轻声笑了。

"伏地魔不会考虑到重量,他只考虑有多少魔法力量穿越了他的湖。我倒认为这条船可能被施了一个魔咒,一次只能乘坐一位巫师。"

"那——?"

"我认为你不能算在内,哈利,你不够年龄,还没有资格。伏地魔怎么也不会想到一个十六岁的少年会来到这个地方。我认为,跟我的力量相比,你的力量恐怕可以忽略不计。"

这番话听得哈利垂头丧气,邓布利多大概也意识到了这点,他又补充道:"伏地魔错了,哈利,伏地魔错了……上了年纪的人低估年轻人,是愚蠢和健忘的……好了,这次你先上,留神别碰到水。"

邓布利多让到一边,哈利小心翼翼地爬上船。邓布利多也跨了进来,把链条盘起来堆在船底。他们紧紧地挤在一起,哈利没法舒舒服服地坐着,只能蹲下来,膝盖顶在船帮上。小船立刻就出发了,四下里一片寂静,只有船头破水前进发出柔和的沙沙声。小船在自动行驶,不用他们动手,似乎有一根看不见的绳索把它拉向湖中央的那道绿光。很快,山洞的岩壁看不见了,他们感觉就像在大海上一样,只是周围没有海浪。

哈利低头看去,随着小船的行进,只见魔杖的光亮映在黑乎乎的

## CHAPTER TWENTY-SIX  The Cave

and glittering on the black water as they passed. The boat was carving deep ripples upon the glassy surface, grooves in the dark mirror ...

And then Harry saw it, marble-white, floating inches below the surface.

'Professor!' he said, and his startled voice echoed loudly over the silent water.

'Harry?'

'I think I saw a hand in the water – a human hand!'

'Yes, I am sure you did,' said Dumbledore calmly.

Harry stared down into the water, looking for the vanished hand, and a sick feeling rose in his throat.

'So that thing that jumped out of the water –?'

But Harry had his answer before Dumbledore could reply; the wand-light had slid over a fresh patch of water and showed him, this time, a dead man lying face up inches beneath the surface: his open eyes misted as though with cobwebs, his hair and his robes swirling around him like smoke.

'There are bodies in here!' said Harry, and his voice sounded much higher than usual and most unlike his own.

'Yes,' said Dumbledore placidly, 'but we do not need to worry about them at the moment.'

'At the moment?' Harry repeated, tearing his gaze from the water to look at Dumbledore.

'Not while they are merely drifting peacefully below us,' said Dumbledore. 'There is nothing to be feared from a body, Harry, any more than there is anything to be feared from the darkness. Lord Voldemort, who of course secretly fears both, disagrees. But once again he reveals his own lack of wisdom. It is the unknown we fear when we look upon death and darkness, nothing more.'

Harry said nothing; he did not want to argue, but he found the idea that there were bodies floating around them and beneath them horrible, and what was more, he did not believe that they were not dangerous.

'But one of them jumped,' he said, trying to make his voice as level and calm as Dumbledore's. 'When I tried to Summon the Horcrux, a body leapt out of the lake.'

'Yes,' said Dumbledore. 'I am sure that once we take the Horcrux, we shall

## 第26章 岩洞

水面上,闪烁着点点金光。小船在玻璃一般光滑的湖面切开深深的波纹,像黑色镜面上的沟槽……

就在这时,哈利看见了它——白得像大理石一样,在水面下几英寸的地方漂浮。

"教授!"他说,惊恐的声音在寂静的水面上发出响亮的回音。

"哈利?"

"我好像看见水里有一只手———只人的手!"

"是的,我相信你看见了。"邓布利多平静地说。

哈利低头望着湖水深处,寻找那只消失了的手,嗓子眼里涌起一种想吐的感觉。

"那么,刚才从水里蹿出来的那个东西——?"

没等邓布利多回答,哈利就自己找到了答案。魔杖的亮光又掠过一片水面,这次哈利看见离水面几英寸的地方仰面躺着一个死人:那双睁着的眼睛迷迷蒙蒙,好像里面结着蛛网,头发和长袍像烟雾一样在他身体周围打着旋儿飘荡。

"这里面有死尸!"哈利说,声音听上去比平常尖厉得多,简直不像是他自己的。

"是的,"邓布利多心平气和地说,"但是我们暂时还用不着担心它们。"

"暂时?"哈利重复了一遍这个词,把目光从湖水里收了回来,望着邓布利多。

"只要它们仅仅在我们船底下静静地漂浮,"邓布利多说,"一具死尸没有什么可害怕的,哈利,就像黑暗没有什么可害怕的一样。可伏地魔不这样认为,他肯定暗暗地害怕这两样东西。他又一次暴露了他缺乏智慧。当面对死亡和黑暗时,我们害怕的只是未知,除此之外没有别的。"

哈利什么也没说。他不想争辩,但一想到他们周围和他们船底下漂浮着死尸,就觉得特别恐怖,而且,他不相信那些死尸没有危险。

"可是刚才就有一具跳了出来。"他说,努力想使声音像邓布利多的那样平静自然,"我试着用召唤咒唤来魂器时,一具死尸蹿出了湖面。"

"是啊,"邓布利多说,"我相信当我们去拿魂器时,就会发现它

## CHAPTER TWENTY-SIX  The Cave

find them less peaceable. However, like many creatures that dwell in cold and darkness, they fear light and warmth, which we shall therefore call to our aid should the need arise. Fire, Harry,' Dumbledore added with a smile, in response to Harry's bewildered expression.

'Oh ... right ...' said Harry quickly. He turned his head to look at the greenish glow towards which the boat was still inexorably sailing. He could not pretend, now, that he was not scared. The great black lake, teeming with the dead ... it seemed hours and hours ago that he had met Professor Trelawney, that he had given Ron and Hermione the Felix Felicis ... he suddenly wished he had said a better goodbye to them ... and he hadn't seen Ginny at all ...

'Nearly there,' said Dumbledore cheerfully.

Sure enough, the greenish light seemed to be growing larger at last, and within minutes, the boat had come to a halt, bumping gently into something that Harry could not see at first, but when he raised his illuminated wand he saw that they had reached a small island of smooth rock in the centre of the lake.

'Careful not to touch the water,' said Dumbledore again as Harry climbed out of the boat.

The island was no larger than Dumbledore's office: an expanse of flat dark stone on which stood nothing but the source of that greenish light, which looked much brighter when viewed close to. Harry squinted at it; at first he thought it was a lamp of some kind, but then he saw that the light was coming from a stone basin rather like the Pensieve, which was set on top of a pedestal.

Dumbledore approached the basin and Harry followed. Side by side they looked down into it. The basin was full of an emerald liquid emitting that phosphorescent glow.

'What is it?' asked Harry quietly.

'I am not sure,' said Dumbledore. 'Something more worrisome than blood and bodies, however.'

Dumbledore pushed back the sleeve of his robe over his blackened hand, and stretched out the tips of his burned fingers towards the surface of the potion.

'Sir, no, don't touch –!'

'I cannot touch,' said Dumbledore, smiling faintly. 'See? I cannot approach any nearer than this. You try.'

Staring, Harry put his hand into the basin and attempted to touch the

## 第26章 岩洞

们不那么安静了。不过，就像居住在寒冷和黑暗中的许多生物一样，它们害怕光明和温暖，到时候如果需要，我们可以求助于这些——就是火呀，哈利。"邓布利多看到哈利脸上困惑的表情，又微笑着补充道。

"噢……是啊……"哈利急忙说。他转过脸去望着那道绿光，小船仍然不可阻挡地朝那里驶去。现在，他再也无法假装自己不害怕了。一望无际的黑湖，里面漂浮着死尸……他觉得他碰见特里劳尼教授，把福灵剂交给罗恩和赫敏，已经是很久很久以前的事了……他突然希望自己当时好好地跟他们告一个别……而且，他甚至没有见金妮一面……

"快要到了。"邓布利多欢快地说。

果然，绿光似乎终于变得更大更亮了，几分钟后，小船轻轻地撞在一个什么东西上，停住了。哈利起先没有看清，等他举起点亮的魔杖，便看见他们来到了湖中央一座光滑的岩石小岛上。

"小心别碰到湖水。"哈利从船上下来时，邓布利多再次警告道。

小岛跟邓布利多的办公室差不多大：一大块平坦的黑色石板，上面空荡荡的，只有发出那道绿光的光源。现在离近了看，绿光显得明亮多了。哈利眯起眼睛看着它，起初以为是一盏什么灯，接着看到绿光是从一个类似冥想盆的石盆里发出来的，石盆下面有个底座。

邓布利多走近石盆，哈利也跟了过去。他们并排站在那里，望着石盆里面。满满一盆翠绿色的液体，发出闪闪的磷光。

"这是什么？"哈利轻声问。

"我不能肯定，"邓布利多说，"应该是比鲜血和死尸更令人担心的东西。"

邓布利多把遮住那只黑手的长袍袖子朝上抖了抖，枯焦的手指尖伸向了液体表面。

"先生，不，别碰它——！"

"我碰不到它。"邓布利多淡淡地笑了笑，"看见了吗？我的手没办法再往前伸了。你试试看。"

哈利瞪着眼睛把手伸向石盆，想去触摸那些液体。可是遇到了一

## CHAPTER TWENTY-SIX  The Cave

potion. He met an invisible barrier that prevented him coming within an inch of it. No matter how hard he pushed, his fingers encountered nothing but what seemed to be solid and inflexible air.

'Out of the way, please, Harry,' said Dumbledore.

He raised his wand and made complicated movements over the surface of the potion, murmuring soundlessly. Nothing happened, except perhaps that the potion glowed a little brighter. Harry remained silent while Dumbledore worked, but after a while Dumbledore withdrew his wand and Harry felt it was safe to talk again.

'You think the Horcrux is in there, sir?'

'Oh, yes.' Dumbledore peered more closely into the basin. Harry saw his face reflected, upside-down, in the smooth surface of the green potion. 'But how to reach it? This potion cannot be penetrated by hand, Vanished, parted, scooped up or siphoned away, nor can it be Transfigured, Charmed or otherwise made to change its nature.'

Almost absent-mindedly, Dumbledore raised his wand again, twirled it once in midair and then caught the crystal goblet that he had conjured out of nowhere.

'I can only conclude that this potion is supposed to be drunk.'

'What?' said Harry. 'No!'

'Yes, I think so: only by drinking it can I empty the basin and see what lies in its depths.'

'But what if – what if it kills you?'

'Oh, I doubt that it would work like that,' said Dumbledore easily. 'Lord Voldemort would not want to kill the person who reached this island.'

Harry couldn't believe it. Was this more of Dumbledore's insane determination to see good in everyone?

'Sir,' said Harry, trying to keep his voice reasonable, 'sir, this is *Voldemort* we're –'

'I'm sorry, Harry; I should have said, he would not want *immediately* to kill the person who reached this island,' Dumbledore corrected himself. 'He would want to keep them alive long enough to find out how they managed to penetrate so far through his defences and, most importantly of all, why they were so intent upon emptying the basin. Do not forget that Lord Voldemort believes that he alone knows about his Horcruxes.'

## 第26章 岩洞

股无形的阻力，他的手无法接近液体。不管手怎么使劲往下伸，手指碰到的似乎都是坚硬无比、牢不可摧的空气。

"哈利，请你让开。"邓布利多说。

他举起魔杖，在液体表面做出一些复杂的动作，嘴里无声地念叨着什么。什么动静也没有，只是液体发出的光似乎更明亮了一些。哈利默默地看着邓布利多作法，直到邓布利多收回魔杖，他才觉得又可以说话了。

"你认为魂器就藏在这里面吗，先生？"

"哦，是的。"邓布利多更专注地凝视着石盆。哈利看见他的脸倒映在平滑的绿色液面上。"可是怎么才能拿到它呢？这种液体，手伸不进去，不能使它分开、把它舀干或者抽光，也不能用消失咒使它消失、用魔法使它变形或用其他方式改变它的性质。"

邓布利多似乎是心不在焉地又举起魔杖，在空中旋转了一下，变出一只高脚水晶酒杯抓在手里。

"我只能得出这样的结论：这种液体需要喝掉。"

"什么？"哈利说，"不行！"

"我认为是这样：只有把它喝掉，我才能让石盆变空，看清底下藏着什么。"

"可是如果——如果它把你毒死了呢？"

"哦，我相信它不会有那样的作用。"邓布利多轻松地说，"伏地魔不会愿意毒死来到这座小岛上的人。"

哈利无法相信。难道邓布利多又是那样荒唐地一味把人往好处想吗？

"先生，"哈利说，努力使自己的声音听上去显得通情达理，"先生，我们面对的是伏地魔——"

"对不起，哈利。我应该这么说：他不会愿意立即害死来到这座小岛的人，"邓布利多自己纠正道，"他会让他们再活一段时间，弄清他们怎么能够穿越他的那些防御机关，最重要的是，弄清他们为什么如此渴望清空石盆。你别忘了，伏地魔相信只有他一个人知道他的魂器。"

## CHAPTER TWENTY-SIX  The Cave

Harry made to speak again, but this time Dumbledore raised his hand for silence, frowning slightly at the emerald liquid, evidently thinking hard.

'Undoubtedly,' he said finally, 'this potion must act in a way that will prevent me taking the Horcrux. It might paralyse me, cause me to forget what I am here for, create so much pain I am distracted, or render me incapable in some other way. This being the case, Harry, it will be your job to make sure I keep drinking, even if you have to tip the potion into my protesting mouth. You understand?'

Their eyes met over the basin; each pale face lit with that strange, green light. Harry did not speak. Was this why he had been invited along – so that he could force-feed Dumbledore a potion that might cause him unendurable pain?

'You remember,' said Dumbledore, 'the condition on which I brought you with me?'

Harry hesitated, looking into the blue eyes that had turned green in the reflected light of the basin.

'But what if –?'

'You swore, did you not, to follow any command I gave you?'

'Yes, but –'

'I warned you, did I not, that there might be danger?'

'Yes,' said Harry, 'but –'

'Well, then,' said Dumbledore, shaking back his sleeves once more and raising the empty goblet, 'you have my orders.'

'Why can't I drink the potion instead?' asked Harry desperately.

'Because I am much older, much cleverer, and much less valuable,' said Dumbledore. 'Once and for all, Harry, do I have your word that you will do all in your power to make me keep drinking?'

'Couldn't –?'

'Do I have it?'

'But –'

'*Your word, Harry.*'

'I – all right, but –'

## 第26章 岩洞

哈利还想说话,但邓布利多举起一只手让他别出声。邓布利多对着翠绿色的液体微微皱起眉头,显然在费力地思索着什么。

"毫无疑问,"他最后说道,"这种药剂肯定会阻止我获取魂器。它大概会使我瘫痪,使我忘记我到这里来的目的,使我感到极度痛苦,无法集中意念,或者以其他方式使我丧失能力。如果出现这种情况,哈利,就需要你来确保我不停地喝下去,哪怕必须把药水灌进我紧闭的嘴巴里。明白吗?"

他们的目光在石盆上方相遇了。两张惨白的脸都被那种古怪的、绿莹莹的光映照着。哈利没有回答。难道,就是为了这个才邀请他一起来的——就是为了他能强迫邓布利多喝下一种或许会带来无法忍受的痛苦的药水?

"你还记得我带你一起来的条件吗?"邓布利多问。

哈利迟疑着,望着那双被石盆的光映得发绿的蓝眼睛。

"可是,万一——?"

"你发誓要听从我的命令的,是不是?"

"是的,可是——"

"我提醒过你可能会有危险,是不是?"

"是的,"哈利说,"可是——"

"那就好,"邓布利多说着又把袖子往上抖了抖,举起空的高脚酒杯,"这就是我的命令。"

"为什么不能让我来喝药水呢?"哈利绝望地问。

"因为我比你老得多、聪明得多,而我的价值比你小得多。"邓布利多说,"我最后再问一遍,哈利,你能不能向我发誓,你会尽全部的力量让我继续喝下去?"

"难道不可以——?"

"你能不能发誓?"

"可是——"

"发誓,哈利!"

"我——好吧,可是——"

## CHAPTER TWENTY-SIX  The Cave

Before Harry could make any further protest, Dumbledore lowered the crystal goblet into the potion. For a split second Harry hoped that he would not be able to touch the potion with the goblet, but the crystal sank into the surface as nothing else had; when the glass was full to the brim, Dumbledore lifted it to his mouth.

'Your good health, Harry.'

And he drained the goblet. Harry watched, terrified, his hands gripping the rim of the basin so hard that his fingertips were numb.

'Professor?' he said anxiously, as Dumbledore lowered the empty glass. 'How do you feel?'

Dumbledore shook his head, his eyes closed. Harry wondered whether he was in pain. Dumbledore plunged the glass blindly back into the basin, refilled it, and drank once more.

In silence, Dumbledore drank three gobletfuls of the potion. Then, halfway through the fourth goblet, he staggered and fell forwards against the basin. His eyes were still closed, his breathing heavy.

'Professor Dumbledore?' said Harry, his voice strained. 'Can you hear me?'

Dumbledore did not answer. His face was twitching as though he were deeply asleep, but dreaming a horrible dream. His grip on the goblet was slackening; the potion was about to spill from it. Harry reached forwards and grasped the crystal cup, holding it steady.

'Professor, can you hear me?' he repeated loudly, his voice echoing around the cavern.

Dumbledore panted and then spoke in a voice Harry did not recognise, for he had never heard Dumbledore frightened like this.

'I don't want ... don't make me ...'

Harry stared into the whitened face he knew so well, at the crooked nose and half-moon spectacles, and did not know what to do.

'... don't like ... want to stop ...' moaned Dumbledore.

'You ... you can't stop, Professor,' said Harry. 'You've got to keep drinking, remember? You told me you had to keep drinking. Here ...'

Hating himself, repulsed by what he was doing, Harry forced the goblet back towards Dumbledore's mouth and tipped it, so that Dumbledore drank the remainder of the potion inside.

# 第26章 岩洞

不等哈利再提出异议,邓布利多就把水晶杯放进了液体。那一瞬间,哈利真希望邓布利多不能用酒杯接触到药水,然而,水晶杯一下子就沉了下去。杯子满了,邓布利多把它举到了嘴边。

"祝你健康,哈利。"

他一饮而尽。哈利惊恐地注视着,两只手紧紧地攥着石盆的边缘,攥得指尖都发麻了。

"教授?"他看到邓布利多放下了空杯子,便担忧地问,"你感觉怎么样?"

邓布利多摇了摇头,他的眼睛是闭着的。哈利不知道他是不是很痛苦。邓布利多闭着眼睛再一次把杯子伸进石盆,舀起满满的一杯,又喝了下去。

邓布利多默默地喝了三杯。喝到第四杯时,他踉踉跄跄地往前扑倒在石盆上。他的眼睛仍然闭着,呼吸很沉重。

"邓布利多教授?"哈利说,他的嗓子眼发紧,"你能听见我说话吗?"

邓布利多没有回答。他的脸在抽搐,似乎他正在沉睡,正在做一个可怕的噩梦。他攥着杯子的手松弛下来,药水眼看就要洒了,哈利上前一步抓住水晶杯,把它端得稳稳的。

"教授,你能听见我说话吗?"他又大声问了一遍,声音在山洞里回荡。

邓布利多喘着粗气说话了,哈利简直听不出那是他的声音,因为他从未见过邓布利多这样害怕。

"我不想……别逼我……"

哈利望着他如此熟悉的这张苍白的面孔,望着那个歪鼻子和那副半月形眼镜,不知道自己该怎么办。

"……不喜欢……想停止……"邓布利多呻吟着说。

"你……你不能停止,教授,"哈利说,"你必须不停地喝下去,记得吗?你告诉过我,你必须不停地喝下去。来……"

哈利把杯子硬塞到邓布利多的嘴边往里灌,邓布利多把杯子里剩下的药水喝了下去。哈利真讨厌自己,从心底里反感自己的行为。

## CHAPTER TWENTY-SIX  The Cave

'No ...' he groaned, as Harry lowered the goblet back into the basin and refilled it for him. 'I don't want to ... I don't want to ... let me go ...'

'It's all right, Professor,' said Harry, his hand shaking. 'It's all right, I'm here –'

'Make it stop, make it stop,' moaned Dumbledore.

'Yes ... yes, this'll make it stop,' lied Harry. He tipped the contents of the goblet into Dumbledore's open mouth.

Dumbledore screamed; the noise echoed all around the vast chamber, across the dead black water.

'No, no, no ... no ... I can't ... I can't, don't make me, I don't want to ...'

'It's all right, Professor, it's all right!' said Harry loudly, his hands shaking so badly he could hardly scoop up the sixth gobletful of potion; the basin was now half empty. 'Nothing's happening to you, you're safe, it isn't real, I swear it isn't real – take this, now, take this ...'

And obediently, Dumbledore drank, as though it was an antidote Harry offered him, but upon draining the goblet, he sank to his knees, shaking uncontrollably.

'It's all my fault, all my fault,' he sobbed, 'please make it stop, I know I did wrong, oh, please make it stop and I'll never, never again ...'

'This will make it stop, Professor,' Harry said, his voice cracking as he tipped the seventh glass of potion into Dumbledore's mouth.

Dumbledore began to cower as though invisible torturers surrounded him; his flailing hand almost knocked the refilled goblet from Harry's trembling hands as he moaned, 'Don't hurt them, don't hurt them, please, please, it's my fault, hurt me instead ...'

'Here, drink this, drink this, you'll be all right,' said Harry desperately, and once again Dumbledore obeyed him, opening his mouth even as he kept his eyes tight shut and shook from head to foot.

And now he fell forwards, screaming again, hammering his fists upon the ground, while Harry filled the ninth goblet.

'Please, please, please, no ... not that, not that, I'll do anything ...'

'Just drink, Professor, just drink ...'

## 第 26 章 岩 洞

"不……"邓布利多呻吟着,哈利重新把酒杯放进石盆,为他舀起满满一杯,"我不想……我不想……放开我……"

"没事的,教授,"哈利说,他的手在颤抖,"没事的,有我呢……"

"让它停止,让它停止。"邓布利多呻吟道。

"好的……好的,这就让它停止。"哈利哄骗他说。又把酒杯里的液体灌进了邓布利多张开的嘴巴里。

邓布利多失声尖叫,凄厉的声音越过沉寂的黑湖,在大山洞里回荡。

"不,不,不……不……我不能……我不能,别逼我,我不想……"

"没事的,教授,没事的!"哈利大声说,他的手抖得太厉害了,几乎舀不起第六杯药水。石盆已经空了一半。"你什么事也没有,你是安全的,这不是真的,我发誓这不是真的——来,把这个喝了,把这个喝了……"

邓布利多听话地喝了下去,就好像哈利递给他的是一种解药,可是,他刚喝光杯里的药水,就扑通跪倒在地上,全身无法控制地颤抖起来。

"都是我的错,都是我的错,"他哭泣着说,"请让它停止吧,我知道我做错了,哦,请让它停止吧,我再也、再也不会了……"

"这就让它停止,教授。"哈利说,他的声音变得又粗又哑,他把第七杯药水灌进了邓布利多的嘴里。

邓布利多蜷缩成一团,似乎周围有一些看不见的人在折磨他。他的手胡乱挥动着,差点把哈利颤抖的手里那只重新舀满的杯子打翻,嘴里呻吟道:"别伤害他们,别伤害他们,求求你,求求你,都是我的错,冲我来吧……"

"来,把这个喝了,把这个喝了,你很快就没事了。"哈利不顾一切地说,邓布利多又一次听话地张开嘴巴,尽管他的眼睛闭得紧紧的,从头到脚抖个不停。

然后,他向前一扑,再一次大声惨叫,并用拳头捶打着地面,哈利满满地舀起了第九杯药水。

"求求你,求求你,求求你,不要……不要那个,不要那个,让我做什么都行……"

"喝吧,教授,喝吧……"

## CHAPTER TWENTY-SIX  The Cave

Dumbledore drank like a child dying of thirst, but when he had finished, he yelled again as though his insides were on fire.

'No more, please, no more ...'

Harry scooped up a tenth gobletful of potion and felt the crystal scrape the bottom of the basin.

'We're nearly there, Professor, drink this, drink it ...'

He supported Dumbledore's shoulders and again, Dumbledore drained the glass; Harry was on his feet once more, refilling the goblet as Dumbledore began to scream in more anguish than ever, 'I want to die! I want to die! Make it stop, make it stop, I want to die!'

'Drink this, Professor, drink this ...'

Dumbledore drank, and no sooner had he finished than he yelled, 'KILL ME!'

'This – this one will!' gasped Harry. 'Just drink this ... it'll be over ... all over!'

Dumbledore gulped at the goblet, drained every last drop and then, with a great, rattling gasp, rolled over on to his face.

'No!' shouted Harry, who had stood to refill the goblet again; instead he dropped the cup into the basin, flung himself down beside Dumbledore and heaved him over on to his back; Dumbledore's glasses were askew, his mouth agape, his eyes closed. 'No,' said Harry, shaking Dumbledore, 'no, you're not dead, you said it wasn't poison, wake up, wake up – *Rennervate*!' he cried, his wand pointing at Dumbledore's chest; there was a flash of red light but nothing happened. '*Rennervate* – sir – please –'

Dumbledore's eyelids flickered; Harry's heart leapt.

'Sir, are you –?'

'Water,' croaked Dumbledore.

'Water,' panted Harry, '– yes –'

He leapt to his feet and seized the goblet he had dropped in the basin; he barely registered the golden locket lying curled beneath it.

'*Aguamenti!*' he shouted, jabbing the goblet with his wand.

The goblet filled with clear water; Harry dropped to his knees beside Dumbledore, raised his head and brought the glass to his lips – but it was empty. Dumbledore groaned and began to pant.

## 第26章 岩洞

邓布利多像个渴极了的孩子一样喝着，可是刚一喝完又惨叫起来，好像他的五脏六腑都着了火似的。

"不要了，求求你，不要了……"

哈利舀起第十杯药水，觉得水晶杯已经擦着盆底了。

"我们就要成功了，教授，把这个喝了，把这个喝了吧……"

他支起邓布利多的肩膀，邓布利多又一次喝干了杯里的液体。哈利重新站起来舀了满满一杯，邓布利多突然喊叫起来，声音比任何时候都要痛苦："我想死！我想死！让它停止，让它停止吧，我想死！"

"把这个喝了，教授，把这个喝了吧……"

邓布利多又喝了，可是刚一喝完，他就喊道："**让我死吧！**"

"喝完——喝完这一杯就行！"哈利喘着气说，"就喝这一杯……快要结束了……一切都结束了！"

邓布利多大口喝光了杯子里的最后一滴药水，然后，他呼噜呼噜地喘着粗气，脸朝下翻滚在地上。

"不！"站起来重新用酒杯舀药水的哈利喊道，他把杯子扔进石盆，冲过来扑在邓布利多身边，把他翻过来仰面躺着。邓布利多的眼镜歪了，嘴巴张得大大的，双眼紧闭。"不，"哈利一边摇晃着邓布利多一边说，"不，你没有死，你说过这不是毒药，醒醒，快醒醒——快快复苏！"他用魔杖指着邓布利多的胸口喊道，一道红光一闪，可是什么反应也没有。"快快复苏——先生——求求你——"

邓布利多的眼皮在抖动，哈利的心欢跳起来。

"先生，你——？"

"水。"邓布利多声音嘶哑地说。

"水，"哈利喘着粗气说，"——好的——"

他一跃而起，抓起刚才丢在石盆里的杯子。他没有注意到那个金挂坠盒就盘绕在杯子下面。

"清水如泉！"他用魔杖指着酒杯大喊一声。

杯里立刻出现了满满的清水。哈利跪在邓布利多身边，扶起他的头，把杯子端到他的唇边——可是杯子已经空了。邓布利多呻吟了一声，又开始重重地喘着粗气。

847

## CHAPTER TWENTY-SIX   The Cave

'But I had some – wait – *Aguamenti*!' said Harry again, pointing his wand at the goblet. Once more, for a second, clear water gleamed within it, but as he approached Dumbledore's mouth, the water vanished again.

'Sir, I'm trying, I'm trying!' said Harry desperately, but he did not think that Dumbledore could hear him; he had rolled on to his side and was drawing great, rattling breaths that sounded agonising. '*Aguamenti – Aguamenti – AGUAMENTI!*'

The goblet filled and emptied once more. And now Dumbledore's breathing was fading. His brain whirling in panic, Harry knew, instinctively, the only way left to get water, because Voldemort had planned it so …

He flung himself over to the edge of the rock and plunged the goblet into the lake, bringing it up full to the brim of icy water that did not vanish.

'Sir – here!' Harry yelled, and lunging forwards he tipped the water clumsily over Dumbledore's face.

It was the best he could do, for the icy feeling on his arm not holding the cup was not the lingering chill of the water. A slimy white hand had gripped his wrist, and the creature to whom it belonged was pulling him, slowly, backwards across the rock. The surface of the lake was no longer mirror-smooth; it was churning, and everywhere Harry looked, white heads and hands were emerging from the dark water, men and women and children with sunken, sightless eyes were moving towards the rock: an army of the dead rising from the black water.

'*Petrificus Totalus!*' yelled Harry, struggling to cling on to the smooth, soaked surface of the island as he pointed his wand at the Inferius that had his arm: it released him, falling backwards into the water with a splash. He scrambled to his feet; but many more Inferi were already climbing on to the rock, their bony hands clawing at its slippery surface, their blank, frosted eyes upon him, trailing waterlogged rags, sunken faces leering.

'*Petrificus Totalus!*' Harry bellowed again, backing away as he swiped his wand through the air; six or seven of them crumpled, but more were coming towards him. '*Impedimenta! Incarcerous!*'

A few of them stumbled, one or two of them bound in ropes, but those climbing on to the rock behind them merely stepped over or on the fallen

## 第26章 岩洞

"刚才还有的——等等——清水如泉！"哈利又用魔杖指着杯子说道。转眼间，杯里又是满满的清水，可是他刚把它端到邓布利多的嘴边，水又一次消失了。

"先生，我在想办法，我在想办法！"哈利焦急万分地说，但是他知道邓布利多不可能听见。邓布利多翻过去侧身躺着，嗓子里发出粗重的、呼噜呼噜的喘息声，听上去令人心痛欲绝。"清水如泉——清水如泉——**清水如泉**！"

杯子再一次变满又变空。邓布利多的呼吸已经很微弱了。哈利的大脑紧张地转动，他本能地知道只有一个办法能够弄到水，那是伏地魔早就计划好了的……

他奔过去扑倒在岩石边，把杯子伸进湖里，舀了满满一杯冰冷的湖水，这次水没有消失。

"先生——给！"哈利喊道，他向前一扑，笨手笨脚地把水倒在了邓布利多的脸上。

他只能做到这样了，因为，他那没拿杯子的胳膊上有一种冷飕飕的感觉，却并不是有冰冷的湖水溅在上面。一只黏糊糊、白森森的手抓住了他的手腕，那家伙正在慢慢地把他往岩石后面拖。湖面不再光滑如镜，而是在剧烈地搅动。哈利抬眼望去，到处都是白森森的脑袋和手从黑黑的水里冒出来，男人的，女人的，孩子的，都睁着凹陷的、没有视觉的眼睛，朝岩石这边漂浮过来：漆黑的湖水里浮现出一大片死尸。

"统统石化！"哈利大喊，他一边拼命抓住岛上光滑潮湿的岩石表面，一边用魔杖指着那个抓住他胳膊的阴尸。阴尸松开了他，扑通一声跌回水里。哈利挣扎着站起来。可是更多的阴尸已经爬上了岩石，用枯槁的手抓住滑溜溜的岩石，空洞洞、雾蒙蒙的眼睛盯着他，被水浸湿的破衣烂衫拖在身后，一张张凹陷的脸上带着邪恶的神情。

"统统石化！"哈利又大喊一声，一边后退一边使劲在空中挥舞魔杖。六七具阴尸被击倒了，但是更多的阴尸朝他逼来。"障碍重重！速速绑缚！"

几具阴尸踉踉跄跄地摔倒了，其中一两个被绳子捆了起来，然而，在它

## CHAPTER TWENTY-SIX    The Cave

bodies. Still slashing at the air with his wand, Harry yelled, '*Sectumsempra! SECTUMSEMPRA!*'

But though gashes appeared in their sodden rags and their icy skin, they had no blood to spill: they walked on, unfeeling, their shrunken hands outstretched towards him, and as he backed away still further he felt arms enclose him from behind, thin, fleshless arms cold as death, and his feet left the ground as they lifted him and began to carry him, slowly and surely, back to the water, and he knew there would be no release, that he would be drowned, and become one more dead guardian of a fragment of Voldemort's shattered soul ...

But then, through the darkness, fire erupted: crimson and gold, a ring of fire that surrounded the rock so that the Inferi holding Harry so tightly stumbled and faltered; they did not dare pass through the flames to get to the water. They dropped Harry; he hit the ground, slipped on the rock and fell, grazing his arms, but scrambled back up, raising his wand and staring around.

Dumbledore was on his feet again, pale as any of the surrounding Inferi, but taller than any, too, the fire dancing in his eyes; his wand was raised like a torch and from its tip emanated the flames, like a vast lasso, encircling them all with warmth.

The Inferi bumped into each other, attempting, blindly, to escape the fire in which they were enclosed ...

Dumbledore scooped the locket from the bottom of the stone basin and stowed it inside his robes. Wordlessly, he gestured to Harry to come to his side. Distracted by the flames, the Inferi seemed unaware that their quarry was leaving as Dumbledore led Harry back to the boat, the ring of fire moving with them, around them, the bewildered Inferi accompanying them to the water's edge, where they slipped gratefully back into their dark waters.

Harry, who was shaking all over, thought for a moment that Dumbledore might not be able to climb into the boat; he staggered a little as he attempted it; all his efforts seemed to be going into maintaining the ring of protective flame around them. Harry seized him and helped him back to his seat. Once they were both safely jammed inside again, the boat began to move back across the black water, away from the rock, still encircled by that ring of fire, and it seemed that the Inferi swarming below them did not dare resurface.

## 第26章 岩洞

们后面爬上岩石的那些阴尸只是跨过它们，或踩着它们倒下的身体又走了过来。哈利继续使劲挥舞着魔杖，大声喊道："神锋无影！**神锋无影！**"

阴尸们破烂的湿衣服和冰冷的皮肤上出现了深深的大口子，但没有一滴血流出来。它们无知无觉，继续一步步逼近，朝哈利伸出一双双干枯的手。哈利又往后退了几步，感觉有胳膊从后面搂住了他，那些像死亡一样冰冷、没有血肉的胳膊，把他从地面上举了起来，缓缓地、但毫不犹豫地走向黑湖。哈利知道他没有办法脱身，他肯定会被淹死，成为另一具守护伏地魔某个灵魂碎片的阴尸……

可是就在这时，黑暗中出现了腾腾的火焰：一个明亮的、金红色的火环环绕在岩石周围，那些紧紧抓住哈利的阴尸一具具变得脚步踉跄，身体摇晃。它们不敢穿过火焰进入湖水，只好扔下了哈利。哈利摔倒在地，脚滑在岩石上，擦破了胳膊，但是他赶紧挣扎着爬起来，举起魔杖警惕地望着四周。

邓布利多已经又站了起来，脸色像周围的阴尸一样惨白，但是个子比它们都高，火光在他的眼睛里跳动。他的魔杖像火把一样高高地举着，杖尖上蹿出一道道火焰，像一根巨大而温暖的套索，把阴尸们都围了起来。

阴尸们互相撞在一起，晕头转向地想逃避围住它们的火焰……

邓布利多从石盆底部捞起挂坠盒，塞进了他的长袍里面。他一言不发，示意哈利到他身边去。阴尸们被火焰弄昏了头脑，似乎没有意识到它们追捕的人正要离开小岛。邓布利多领着哈利向小船走去，那道火环围着他们，随着他们一起移动。不知所措的阴尸们簇拥着他们来到湖边，迫不及待地重新滑入黑暗的湖水中。

哈利浑身都在发抖，他以为邓布利多没有力气爬上小船了。邓布利多上船时脚步有些踉跄，他似乎在用全部的精力维持他们周围那道防护的火环。哈利扶他在小船里坐好。两人刚刚挤坐进去，小船就掠过漆黑的水面往回驶去，离开了仍然被火环包围的岩石。那些在水下漂浮的阴尸似乎再也不敢露面了。

## CHAPTER TWENTY-SIX    The Cave

'Sir,' panted Harry, 'sir, I forgot – about fire – they were coming at me and I panicked –'

'Quite understandable,' murmured Dumbledore. Harry was alarmed to hear how faint his voice was.

They reached the bank with a little bump and Harry leapt out, then turned quickly to help Dumbledore. The moment that Dumbledore reached the bank he let his wand hand fall; the ring of fire vanished, but the Inferi did not emerge again from the water. The little boat sank into the water once more; clanking and tinkling, its chain slithered back into the lake, too. Dumbledore gave a great sigh and leaned against the cavern wall.

'I am weak ...' he said.

'Don't worry, sir,' said Harry at once, anxious about Dumbledore's extreme pallor and his air of exhaustion. 'Don't worry, I'll get us back ... lean on me, sir ...'

And pulling Dumbledore's uninjured arm around his shoulders, Harry guided his headmaster back around the lake, bearing most of his weight.

'The protection was ... after all ... well designed,' said Dumbledore faintly. 'One alone could not have done it ... you did well, very well, Harry ...'

'Don't talk now,' said Harry, fearing how slurred Dumbledore's voice had become, how much his feet dragged, 'save your energy, sir ... we'll soon be out of here ...'

'The archway will have sealed again ... my knife ...'

'There's no need, I got cut on the rock,' said Harry firmly, 'just tell me where ...'

'Here ...'

Harry wiped his grazed forearm upon the stone: having received its tribute of blood the archway reopened instantly. They crossed the outer cave and Harry helped Dumbledore back into the icy sea water that filled the crevice in the cliff.

'It's going to be all right, sir,' Harry said over and over again, more worried by Dumbledore's silence than he had been by his weakened voice. 'We're nearly there ... I can Apparate us both back ... don't worry ...'

'I am not worried, Harry,' said Dumbledore, his voice a little stronger despite the freezing water. 'I am with you.'

## 第26章 岩 洞

"先生,"哈利喘着气说,"先生,我忘记了——忘记了火——它们突然朝我扑来,把我吓坏了——"

"可以理解。"邓布利多喃喃地说。哈利惊恐地听出他的声音十分虚弱。

随着砰的一声轻响,他们到了岸边,哈利抢先跳下小船,回身搀扶邓布利多。邓布利多刚一上岸,举着魔杖的手就垂了下去。火环消失了,但是阴尸没有再从湖里冒出来。小船又一次沉入水中,那根链条也叮叮当当地重新滑进湖水里。邓布利多重重地叹了一口气,身体靠在山洞的岩壁上。

"我很虚弱……"他说。

"别担心,先生,"哈利赶紧说道,他看到邓布利多极度苍白的脸色和精疲力竭的样子,心里非常不安,"别担心,我会把我们俩都带回去的……靠在我身上,先生……"

哈利把邓布利多那只没有受伤的手臂拉过来搭在自己的肩膀上,他承受着校长的大部分重量,沿着湖边往回走。

"那个保护机关……毕竟还是……设计得很巧妙的。"邓布利多有气无力地说,"一个人是不可能做到的……你干得不错,非常漂亮,哈利……"

"现在别说话了,"哈利说,邓布利多的声音变得这样含糊,脚步变得这样无力,真让他感到害怕,"节省些体力,先生……我们很快就会离开这里……"

"那道拱门肯定又封死了……我的刀子……"

"用不着了,我被岩石擦伤了,"哈利坚决地说,"你只要告诉我位置……"

"这儿……"

哈利把受伤的胳膊在石头上擦了擦,拱门收到这份血的礼物,立刻重新打开了。他们穿过外面的山洞,然后哈利搀扶着邓布利多,回到悬崖上那道裂缝里冰冷的海水中。

"一切都会顺利的,先生,"哈利一遍又一遍地说,刚才邓布利多虚弱的声音让他担忧,现在他的沉默更让他揪心,"差不多快要到了……我可以幻影显形,把我们俩都带回去……别担心……"

"我不担心,哈利,"邓布利多说,尽管海水寒冷刺骨,他的声音却多了一点儿气力,"我和你在一起呢。"

## CHAPTER TWENTY-SEVEN

# The Lightning-Struck Tower

Once back under the starry sky, Harry heaved Dumbledore on to the top of the nearest boulder and then to his feet. Sodden and shivering, Dumbledore's weight still upon him, Harry concentrated harder than he had ever done upon his destination: Hogsmeade. Closing his eyes, gripping Dumbledore's arm as tightly as he could, he stepped forwards into that feeling of horrible compression.

He knew it had worked before he opened his eyes: the smell of salt, the sea breeze had gone. He and Dumbledore were shivering and dripping in the middle of the dark High Street in Hogsmeade. For one horrible moment Harry's imagination showed him more Inferi creeping towards him around the sides of shops, but he blinked and saw that nothing was stirring; all was still, the darkness complete but for a few street lamps and lit upper windows.

'We did it, Professor!' Harry whispered with difficulty; he suddenly realised that he had a searing stitch in his chest. 'We did it! We got the Horcrux!'

Dumbledore staggered against him. For a moment, Harry thought that his inexpert Apparition had thrown Dumbledore off-balance; then he saw his face, paler and damper than ever in the distant light of a street lamp.

'Sir, are you all right?'

'I've been better,' said Dumbledore weakly, though the corners of his mouth twitched. 'That potion ... was no health drink ...'

And to Harry's horror, Dumbledore sank on to the ground.

'Sir – it's OK, sir, you're going to be all right, don't worry –'

He looked around desperately for help, but there was nobody to be seen and all he could think was that he must somehow get Dumbledore quickly to the hospital wing.

第 27 章

# 被闪电击中的塔楼

回到布满繁星的夜空下,哈利把邓布利多拖到离他们最近的那块巨型卵石顶上,扶他站了起来。邓布利多浑身透湿,瑟瑟发抖,全身的重量仍然压在哈利身上。哈利全神贯注,所有的意念都集中于他的目的地:霍格莫德村。他闭上眼睛,紧紧抓着邓布利多的胳膊,一下子跨进了那种恐怖的挤压感中。

没等睁开眼睛,他就知道成功了:海风和海腥味都消失了。他和邓布利多站在霍格莫德村漆黑的大街上,浑身发抖,衣服往下滴水。恍惚间,哈利似乎看见又有阴尸从一些商店旁边钻出来,朝他一步步紧逼过来,可是他眨眨眼睛,却发现什么动静也没有。四下里一片寂静,夜黑得很深,只看见几盏路灯和楼上几扇亮灯的窗户。

"我们成功了,教授!"哈利费了很大的力气低声说。他突然发现他的胸口火辣辣地痛。"我们成功了!我们拿到了魂器!"

邓布利多东倒西歪地撞在他身上。哈利起初还以为是他的幻影移形不够熟练,使邓布利多脚下失去了平衡,紧接着他看见了邓布利多的脸,在远处一盏路灯的映照下,这张脸比任何时候都苍白、没有生气。

"先生,你没事吧?"

"没有以前好了,"邓布利多虚弱地说,他的嘴角在抽搐,"那种药水……可不是什么健康饮料……"

令哈利大为惊恐的是,邓布利多一下子瘫倒在地上。

"先生——没事了,先生,你很快就会好的,别担心——"

他焦急地四处张望,想找人来帮忙,可是看不见一个人影,他只知道必须想办法赶紧把邓布利多送到校医院去。

## CHAPTER TWENTY-SEVEN    The Lightning-Struck Tower

'We need to get you up to the school, sir ... Madam Pomfrey ...'

'No,' said Dumbledore. 'It is ... Professor Snape whom I need ... but I do not think ... I can walk very far just yet ...'

'Right – sir, listen – I'm going to knock on a door, find a place you can stay – then I can run and get Madam –'

'Severus,' said Dumbledore clearly. 'I need Severus ...'

'All right then, Snape – but I'm going to have to leave you for a moment so I can –'

Before Harry could make a move, however, he heard running footsteps. His heart leapt: somebody had seen, somebody knew they needed help – and looking around he saw Madam Rosmerta scurrying down the dark street towards them on high-heeled, fluffy slippers, wearing a silk dressing-gown embroidered with dragons.

'I saw you Apparate as I was pulling my bedroom curtains! Thank goodness, thank goodness, I couldn't think what to – but what's wrong with Albus?'

She came to a halt, panting, and stared down, wide-eyed, at Dumbledore.

'He's hurt,' said Harry. 'Madam Rosmerta, can he come into the Three Broomsticks while I go up to the school and get help for him?'

'You can't go up there alone! Don't you realise – haven't you seen –?'

'If you help me support him,' said Harry, not listening to her, 'I think we can get him inside –'

'What has happened?' asked Dumbledore. 'Rosmerta, what's wrong?'

'The – the Dark Mark, Albus.'

And she pointed into the sky, in the direction of Hogwarts. Dread flooded Harry at the sound of the words ... he turned and looked.

There it was, hanging in the sky above the school: the blazing green skull with a serpent tongue, the mark Death Eaters left behind whenever they had entered a building ... wherever they had murdered ...

'When did it appear?' asked Dumbledore, and his hand clenched painfully upon Harry's shoulder as he struggled to his feet.

'Must have been minutes ago, it wasn't there when I put the cat out, but when I got upstairs –'

"我们需要把你送到学校,先生……庞弗雷女士……"

"不,"邓布利多说,"我需要的……是斯内普教授……不过我认为……我走不了多远……"

"好的——先生,听我说——我去敲一户人家的门,找一个地方让你待着——然后我就可以跑去找庞弗雷——"

"西弗勒斯,"邓布利多清清楚楚地说,"我需要西弗勒斯……"

"好吧,斯内普——但是我需要暂时离开你一会儿,好去——"

然而,哈利还没动身,就听见奔跑的脚步声。他的心欢跳起来:有人看见了,有人知道他们需要帮助了——他扭头一看,罗斯默塔女士顺着漆黑的街道朝他们跑来,脚上穿着毛绒高跟拖鞋,身上是一件绣着火龙的丝绸晨衣。

"我刚才拉上卧室窗帘时,看见你们幻影显形来着!谢天谢地,谢天谢地,我真不知道该——咦,阿不思这是怎么啦?"

她刹住脚步,气喘吁吁,瞪大眼睛低头望着邓布利多。

"他受伤了。"哈利说,"罗斯默塔女士,能不能让他到三把扫帚里待一会儿,我到学校里找人来帮忙?"

"你不能独自回去!你没有发现——你没有看见吗——?"

"麻烦你帮我扶他一下,"哈利没有听她说话,只管对她说道,"我想我们可以把他弄进去——"

"出什么事了?"邓布利多问,"罗斯默塔,怎么回事?"

"黑——黑魔标记,阿不思。"

她用手指着霍格沃茨方向的天空。哈利听见这几个字,内心顿时充满了恐惧……他转眼望去。

它果然在那儿,悬挂在学校上空:那个绿得耀眼的骷髅,嘴里吐出蛇芯子般的舌头,食死徒们无论什么时候闯入一座建筑物……无论在什么地方杀了人……都要留下这样的标记……

"它是什么时候出现的?"邓布利多问,他挣扎着站了起来,手把哈利的肩膀抓得生疼。

"一定是几分钟前,我把猫放出去的时候它还不在那儿,可是等我上了楼——"

## CHAPTER TWENTY-SEVEN    The Lightning-Struck Tower

'We need to return to the castle at once,' said Dumbledore. 'Rosmerta,' and though he staggered a little, he seemed wholly in command of the situation, 'we need transport – brooms –'

'I've got a couple behind the bar,' she said, looking very frightened. 'Shall I run and fetch –?'

'No, Harry can do it.'

Harry raised his wand at once.

'*Accio Rosmerta's brooms.*'

A second later they heard a loud bang as the front door of the pub burst open; two brooms had shot out into the street and were racing each other to Harry's side, where they stopped dead, quivering slightly, at waist height.

'Rosmerta, please send a message to the Ministry,' said Dumbledore, as he mounted the broom nearest him. 'It might be that nobody within Hogwarts has yet realised anything is wrong ... Harry, put on your Invisibility Cloak.'

Harry pulled his cloak out of his pocket and threw it over himself before mounting his broom; Madam Rosmerta was already tottering back towards her pub as Harry and Dumbledore kicked off from the ground and rose up into the air. As they sped towards the castle, Harry glanced sideways at Dumbledore, ready to grab him should he fall, but the sight of the Dark Mark seemed to have acted upon Dumbledore like a stimulant: he was bent low over his broom, his eyes fixed upon the Mark, his long silver hair and beard flying behind him in the night air. And Harry, too, looked ahead at the skull, and fear swelled inside him like a venomous bubble, compressing his lungs, driving all other discomfort from his mind ...

How long had they been away? Had Ron, Hermione and Ginny's luck run out by now? Was it one of them who had caused the Mark to be set over the school, or was it Neville, or Luna, or some other member of the DA? And if it was ... he was the one who had told them to patrol the corridors, he had asked them to leave the safety of their beds ... would he be responsible, again, for the death of a friend?

As they flew over the dark, twisting lane down which they had walked earlier, Harry heard, over the whistling of the night air in his ears, Dumbledore muttering in some strange language again. He thought he understood why as he felt his broom shudder for a moment when they flew

## 第27章 被闪电击中的塔楼

"我们需要立刻回城堡去。"邓布利多说,"罗斯默塔,"他虽然脚步还有些踉跄,但似乎已经完全控制住了局面,"我们需要交通工具——飞天扫帚——"

"我的酒吧后面有两把,"罗斯默塔说,神色非常惊恐,"要不要我跑去取来——?"

"不,哈利可以办到。"

哈利立刻举起魔杖。

"罗斯默塔的扫帚飞来!"

一秒钟后,他们就听见砰的一声巨响,酒吧的前门被撞开了。两把扫帚嗖地蹿到街上,你追我赶地冲到哈利身边,随后突然停在腰那么高的位置上,微微地颤动着。

"罗斯默塔,请给魔法部送一个情报。"邓布利多说着骑上了离他最近的那把扫帚,"也许霍格沃茨内部的人还不知道已经出事了……哈利,穿上你的隐形衣。"

哈利从口袋里掏出隐形衣披在身上,然后骑上了他的扫帚。当哈利和邓布利多一蹬地面,飞向空中时,罗斯默塔女士已经跌跌撞撞地朝她的酒吧跑去了。两把扫帚迅疾地朝城堡飞去,哈利侧眼看了看邓布利多,想在他万一摔落时拉他一把,没想到,黑魔标记的出现似乎给邓布利多注入了一针强心剂:他俯身在扫帚上,眼睛紧紧地盯着黑魔标记,银白色的长发和胡须在他身后的夜空中飘荡。哈利便也朝那个骷髅望去,恐惧像一个有毒的气泡一样膨胀,挤压着他的肺部,他已根本没有心思考虑其他不适……

他们离开了多久?罗恩、赫敏和金妮的好运气用完了没有?难道是他们中间的哪个人使得黑魔标记出现在学校上空?或者是纳威、卢娜,或D.A.的其他某个成员?如果真是那样……是他叫他们在走廊上巡逻的,是他叫他们离开安全的床铺的……难道他又要为一位朋友的死负责吗?

他们飞过先前走过的那些漆黑的、蜿蜒曲折的小巷,晚风在哈利耳边呼啸掠过,在这声音之外,他听见邓布利多又在用某种奇怪的语言低声说着什么。他们飞过围墙、进入场地时,哈利的扫帚颤抖了一

## CHAPTER TWENTY-SEVEN    The Lightning-Struck Tower

over the boundary wall into the grounds: Dumbledore was undoing the enchantments he himself had set around the castle, so that they could enter at speed. The Dark Mark was glittering directly above the Astronomy Tower, the highest of the castle. Did that mean the death had occurred there?

Dumbledore had already crossed the crenellated ramparts and was dismounting; Harry landed next to him seconds later and looked around.

The ramparts were deserted. The door to the spiral staircase that led back into the castle was closed. There was no sign of a struggle, of a fight to the death, of a body.

'What does it mean?' Harry asked Dumbledore, looking up at the green skull with its serpent's tongue glinting evilly above them. 'Is it the real Mark? Has someone definitely been – Professor?'

In the dim green glow from the Mark Harry saw Dumbledore clutching at his chest with his blackened hand.

'Go and wake Severus,' said Dumbledore faintly but clearly. 'Tell him what has happened and bring him to me. Do nothing else, speak to nobody else and do not remove your Cloak. I shall wait here.'

'But –'

'You swore to obey me, Harry – go!'

Harry hurried over to the door leading to the spiral staircase, but his hand had only just closed upon the iron ring of the door when he heard running footsteps on the other side. He looked round at Dumbledore, who gestured to him to retreat. Harry backed away, drawing his wand as he did so.

The door burst open and somebody erupted through it and shouted: '*Expelliarmus!*'

Harry's body became instantly rigid and immobile, and he felt himself fall back against the Tower wall, propped like an unsteady statue, unable to move or speak. He could not understand how it had happened – *Expelliarmus* was not a Freezing Charm –

Then, by the light of the Mark, he saw Dumbledore's wand flying in an arc over the edge of the ramparts and understood ... Dumbledore had wordlessly immobilised Harry, and the second he had taken to perform the spell had cost him the chance of defending himself.

Standing against the ramparts, very white in the face, Dumbledore still showed no sign of panic or distress. He merely looked across at his disarmer and said, 'Good evening, Draco.'

## 第27章 被闪电击中的塔楼

会儿，他知道这其中的原因：邓布利多正在解开他亲手设置在城堡周围的那些魔法，这样他们才能迅速进入学校。黑魔标记在城堡的制高点——天文塔的上空闪烁。难道这意味着那里已经有人死了？

邓布利多已经越过了钝锯齿形的城堡围墙，正从扫帚上下来。几秒钟后，哈利降落在他身边，朝四周张望着。

围墙里空无一人，通向城堡内旋转楼梯的门是关着的。四下里看不见搏斗、奋力抗争的迹象，也看不见一具尸体。

"这是什么意思？"哈利问邓布利多，他抬头望着空中的绿色骷髅，那蛇芯子般的舌头在他们头顶上闪烁着邪恶的光芒，"这个标记是真的吗？真的有人被——教授？"

就着黑魔标记发出的昏暗绿光，哈利看见邓布利多正用那只焦黑的手揪着自己的胸口。

"去把西弗勒斯叫醒，"邓布利多有气无力但十分清晰地说，"告诉他发生了什么事，叫他赶紧来见我。除此之外，什么也不要做，不要跟任何人说话，也不要脱掉你的隐形衣。我在这里等着。"

"可是——"

"你发誓要服从我的，哈利——快去！"

哈利匆匆跑向通往旋转楼梯的门，但他刚握住铁门环，就听见门的另一边传来奔跑的脚步声。他转脸看着邓布利多，邓布利多示意他往后退。哈利退后几步，一边拔出了自己的魔杖。

门突然被撞开，一个人闯了进来，同时喊道："除你武器！"

哈利的身体顿时变得十分僵硬，他感到自己倒向塔楼的围墙边，像一座雕像一样立在那里，浑身动弹不得，也说不出话来。他不明白这是怎么回事——除你武器并不是一个冰冻咒啊——

这时，就着黑魔标记的绿光，他看见邓布利多的魔杖在空中划出一道弧线，飞出了围墙外，他明白了……邓布利多用无声咒定住了哈利，他念这个咒语用去的一秒钟时间，使他失去了保护自己的机会。

邓布利多背靠围墙站在那里，脸色惨白，但仍然没有表现出丝毫的惊慌或忧虑。他只是望着那个除去他武器的人，说道："晚上好，德拉科。"

## CHAPTER TWENTY-SEVEN    The Lightning-Struck Tower

Malfoy stepped forwards, glancing around quickly to check that he and Dumbledore were alone. His eyes fell upon the second broom.

'Who else is here?'

'A question I might ask you. Or are you acting alone?'

Harry saw Malfoy's pale eyes shift back to Dumbledore in the greenish glare of the Mark.

'No,' he said. 'I've got back-up. There are Death Eaters here in your school tonight.'

'Well, well,' said Dumbledore, as though Malfoy was showing him an ambitious homework project. 'Very good indeed. You found a way to let them in, did you?'

'Yeah,' said Malfoy, who was panting. 'Right under your nose and you never realised!'

'Ingenious,' said Dumbledore. 'Yet ... forgive me ... where are they now? You seem unsupported.'

'They met some of your guard. They're having a fight down below. They won't be long ... I came on ahead. I – I've got a job to do.'

'Well, then, you must get on and do it, my dear boy,' said Dumbledore softly.

There was silence. Harry stood imprisoned within his own invisible, paralysed body, staring at the two of them, his ears straining to hear sounds of the Death Eaters' distant fight, and in front of him, Draco Malfoy did nothing but stare at Albus Dumbledore who, incredibly, smiled.

'Draco, Draco, you are not a killer.'

'How do you know?' said Malfoy at once.

He seemed to realise how childish the words had sounded; Harry saw him flush in the Mark's greenish light.

'You don't know what I'm capable of,' said Malfoy more forcefully, 'you don't know what I've done!'

'Oh, yes, I do,' said Dumbledore mildly. 'You almost killed Katie Bell and ronald Weasley. You have been trying, with increasing desperation, to kill me all year. Forgive me, Draco, but they have been feeble attempts ... so feeble, to be honest, that I wonder whether your heart has been really in it ...'

## 第27章 被闪电击中的塔楼

马尔福朝前逼近几步,迅速打量了一下四周,想看看除了他和邓布利多之外是否还有别人。他的目光落在第二把扫帚上。

"还有谁在这儿?"

"我正想问你这个问题呢。你是一个人单独行动吗?"

在黑魔标记的绿光下,哈利看见马尔福那双浅色的眼睛又盯住了邓布利多。

"不是,"他说,"有人支持我。今天晚上食死徒闯进了你的学校。"

"很好,很好,"邓布利多说,就好像马尔福给他看了一份雄心勃勃的作业计划,"确实不错。是你想办法把他们放进来的,是吗?"

"没错,"马尔福说,他的呼吸有些急促,"就在你的眼皮底下,你一直没有发现!"

"多么巧妙,"邓布利多说,"不过……冒昧问一句……他们此刻在哪儿呢?你好像孤立无援啊。"

"他们碰到了你的几个警卫,在下面搏斗呢。不会耽搁太久的……我自己先上来。我——我要完成一项工作。"

"好,那你就动手干吧,我亲爱的孩子。"邓布利多温和地说。

沉默。哈利被囚禁在他的隐形衣下,身体动弹不得。他眼睛望着面前的两个人,耳朵专心地听着远处食死徒们搏斗的声音。在他面前,德拉科·马尔福只是呆呆地盯着阿不思·邓布利多,而邓布利多竟然不可思议地笑了。

"德拉科啊德拉科,你不是一个杀人的人。"

"你怎么知道?"马尔福立刻问道。

他似乎也意识到这句话听上去多么幼稚。在黑魔标记的绿光下,哈利看到他的脸红了。

"你不知道我的能力,"马尔福说,语气变得凶狠,"你不知道我都做了什么!"

"噢,我当然知道。"邓布利多和蔼地说,"你差点杀死了凯蒂·贝尔和罗恩·韦斯莱。整个这一年你都在想办法杀死我,而且越来越迫不及待。原谅我这么说,德拉科,但是你的做法很蹩脚……说实在的,真是太蹩脚了,我简直怀疑你有没有用心去做……"

## CHAPTER TWENTY-SEVEN  The Lightning-Struck Tower

'It has been in it!' said Malfoy vehemently. 'I've been working on it all year, and tonight –'

Somewhere in the depths of the castle below Harry heard a muffled yell. Malfoy stiffened and glanced over his shoulder.

'Somebody is putting up a good fight,' said Dumbledore conversationally. 'But you were saying ... yes, you have managed to introduce Death Eaters into my school which, I admit, I thought impossible ... how did you do it?'

But Malfoy said nothing: he was still listening to whatever was happening below and seemed almost as paralysed as Harry was.

'Perhaps you ought to get on with the job alone,' suggested Dumbledore. 'What if your back-up has been thwarted by my guard? As you have perhaps realised, there are members of the Order of the Phoenix here tonight, too. And after all, you don't really need help ... I have no wand at the moment ... I cannot defend myself.'

Malfoy merely stared at him.

'I see,' said Dumbledore kindly, when Malfoy neither moved nor spoke. 'You are afraid to act until they join you.'

'I'm not afraid!' snarled Malfoy, though he still made no move to hurt Dumbledore. 'It's you who should be scared!'

'But why? I don't think you will kill me, Draco. Killing is not nearly as easy as the innocent believe ... so tell me, while we wait for your friends ... how did you smuggle them in here? It seems to have taken you a long time to work out how to do it.'

Malfoy looked as though he was fighting down the urge to shout, or to vomit. He gulped and took several deep breaths, glaring at Dumbledore, his wand pointing directly at the latter's heart. Then, as though he could not help himself, he said, 'I had to mend that broken Vanishing Cabinet that no one's used for years. The one Montague got lost in last year.'

'Aaaah.'

Dumbledore's sigh was half a groan. He closed his eyes for a moment.

'That was clever ... there is a pair, I take it?'

'The other's in Borgin and Burkes,' said Malfoy, 'and they make a kind of passage between them. Montague told me that when he was stuck in the Hogwarts one, he was trapped in limbo but sometimes he could hear what

## 第27章 被闪电击中的塔楼

"我当然用心了!"马尔福激动地说,"我整整一年都在忙这件事,今晚——"

哈利听见下面城堡内的什么地方传来一声沉闷的喊叫。马尔福僵住了,扭头往身后望去。

"有人正在奋力抵抗。"邓布利多态度随和地说,"你刚才说到……对了,你说你终于成功地让食死徒进了我的学校,我承认,我原来以为这是不可能的……你是怎么做到的?"

可是马尔福没有回答,他仍然在倾听下面的动静,似乎跟哈利一样被定住了,动弹不得。

"也许你应该一个人把活儿给干了。"邓布利多给他出主意道,"如果你的后援被我的警卫打败了呢?你恐怕也发现了,今晚这里还有凤凰社的成员。你反正并不需要帮助……我此刻没有魔杖……没有办法保护自己。"

马尔福只是呆呆地盯着他。

"我明白了,"邓布利多看到马尔福既不行动也不说话,就温和地对他说,"你很害怕,要等他们上来才敢动手。"

"我才不怕呢!"马尔福凶狠地吼道,但仍然没有动手伤害邓布利多,"感到害怕的应该是你!"

"可是为什么呢?我认为你不会杀死我的,德拉科。杀人并不像一般人以为的那么简单……好吧,就趁我们等候你的朋友们的这点工夫,你跟我说说……你是怎么把他们偷偷弄进来的?你似乎花了很长时间才想出这个办法。"

马尔福似乎在拼命克制,不让自己叫喊或呕吐出来。他咽了咽唾沫,深深吸了几口气,眼睛狠狠地瞪着邓布利多,魔杖直指邓布利多的胸膛。然后,他似乎不由自主地说道:"我不得不把那个多年没人使用的破消失柜修好。就是去年蒙太关在里面出不来的那个柜子。"

"啊——"

邓布利多的叹息像是一声呻吟。他闭了一会儿眼睛。

"很聪明的主意……我记得柜子有两个呢,是不是?"

"另一个在博金-博克商店里,"马尔福说,"两个柜子之间有一条通道。蒙太告诉我,他被关在霍格沃茨那个柜子里时,被困在了通道

## CHAPTER TWENTY-SEVEN    The Lightning-Struck Tower

was going on at school, and sometimes what was going on in the shop, as if the Cabinet was travelling between them, but he couldn't make anyone hear him ... in the end he managed to Apparate out, even though he'd never passed his test. He nearly died doing it. Everyone thought it was a really good story, but I was the only one who realised what it meant – even Borgin didn't know – I was the one who realised there could be a way into Hogwarts through the Cabinets if I fixed the broken one.'

'Very good,' murmured Dumbledore. 'So the Death Eaters were able to pass from Borgin and Burkes into the school to help you ... a clever plan, a very clever plan ... and, as you say, right under my nose ...'

'Yeah,' said Malfoy who, bizarrely, seemed to draw courage and comfort from Dumbledore's praise. 'Yeah, it was!'

'But there were times,' Dumbledore went on, 'weren't there, when you were not sure you would succeed in mending the Cabinet? And you resorted to crude and badly judged measures such as sending me a cursed necklace that was bound to reach the wrong hands ... poisoning mead there was only the slightest chance I might drink ...'

'Yeah, well, you still didn't realise who was behind that stuff, did you?' sneered Malfoy, as Dumbledore slid a little down the ramparts, the strength in his legs apparently fading, and Harry struggled fruitlessly, mutely, against the enchantment binding him.

'As a matter of fact, I did,' said Dumbledore. 'I was sure it was you.'

'Why didn't you stop me, then?' Malfoy demanded.

'I tried, Draco. Professor Snape has been keeping watch over you on my orders –'

'He hasn't been doing *your* orders, he promised my mother –'

'Of course that is what he would tell you, Draco, but –'

'He's a double-agent, you stupid old man, he isn't working for you, you just think he is!'

'We must agree to differ on that, Draco. It so happens that I trust Professor Snape –'

'Well, you're losing your grip, then!' sneered Malfoy. 'He's been offering me plenty of help – wanting all the glory for himself – wanting a bit of the action – "What are you doing? Did you do the necklace, that was stupid, it

## 第27章 被闪电击中的塔楼

里,但有时候能听见学校里的动静,有时候又能听见商店里发生的事情,就好像柜子在这两个地方跑来跑去似的,但是谁也听不见他的声音……最后,他总算通过幻影显形逃了出来,尽管他那项考试没有及格。他的幻影显形差点要了他的命。大家都以为这是一个很好玩的故事,只有我意识到了其中的含义——就连博金也不知道——只有我意识到,只要我把那个破柜子修好,就能通过两个消失柜进入霍格沃茨。"

"很好,"邓布利多喃喃地说,"这样食死徒就能从博金-博克商店进入学校来帮助你……一个巧妙的计划,一个十分巧妙的计划……而且,正如你说的,就在我的眼皮底下……"

"是啊,"马尔福说,奇怪的是他似乎从邓布利多的赞扬中获得了勇气和安慰,"没错,就是这样!"

"可是有些时候,"邓布利多继续说道,"你不能肯定是否能把柜子修好,对吗?于是你就采取了一些笨拙的、考虑不周的措施,比如捎给我一条中了魔法的项链,其实它肯定会落到别人手里……还有往蜂蜜酒里下毒,其实我喝那个酒的可能性微乎其微……"

"是啊,但你仍然不知道这些事情是谁策划的,是吧?"马尔福讥笑道,这时邓布利多的身体贴着墙壁往下出溜了一点儿,显然他的腿脚已经没有力气,哈利说不出话,拼命挣扎,想摆脱束缚他的魔咒,但毫无结果。

"实际上我早就知道了。"邓布利多说,"我相信是你干的。"

"那你为什么不阻止我呢?"马尔福问。

"我试过,德拉科。斯内普教授听从我的吩咐一直在监视你——"

"他才没有听从你的吩咐呢,他答应过我母亲——"

"他当然会跟你这么说,德拉科,可是——"

"他是个双重间谍,你这个愚蠢的老头儿,他根本就没有替你卖命,你还被蒙在鼓里呢!"

"就让我们彼此保留不同意见吧,德拉科。我碰巧很信任斯内普教授——"

"哼,你正在失去对他的控制!"马尔福讥笑道,"他一直提出要帮助我——想把功劳占为己有——想插手做点什么——'你在干什么?

## CHAPTER TWENTY-SEVEN    The Lightning-Struck Tower

could have blown everything —" But I haven't told him what I've been doing in the Room of Requirement, he's going to wake up tomorrow and it'll all be over and he won't be the Dark Lord's favourite any more, he'll be nothing compared to me, nothing!'

'Very gratifying,' said Dumbledore mildly. 'We all like appreciation for our own hard work, of course ... but you must have had an accomplice, all the same ... someone in Hogsmeade, someone who was able to slip Katie the — the — aaaah ...'

Dumbledore closed his eyes again and nodded, as though he was about to fall asleep.

'... of course ... Rosmerta. How long has she been under the Imperius Curse?'

'Got there at last, have you?' Malfoy taunted.

There was another yell from below, rather louder than the last. Malfoy looked nervously over his shoulder again, then back at Dumbledore, who went on, 'So poor Rosmerta was forced to lurk in her own bathroom and pass that necklace to any Hogwarts student who entered the room unaccompanied? And the poisoned mead ... well, naturally, Rosmerta was able to poison it for you before she sent the bottle to Slughorn, believing that it was to be my Christmas present ... yes, very neat ... very neat ... poor Mr Filch would not, of course, think to check a bottle of Rosmerta's ... tell me, how have you been communicating with Rosmerta? I thought we had all methods of communication in and out of the school monitored.'

'Enchanted coins,' said Malfoy, as though he was compelled to keep talking, though his wand hand was shaking badly. 'I had one and she had the other and I could send her messages —'

'Isn't that the secret method of communication the group that called themselves Dumbledore's Army used last year?' asked Dumbledore. His voice was light and conversational, but Harry saw him slip an inch lower down the wall as he said it.

'Yeah, I got the idea from them,' said Malfoy, with a twisted smile. 'I got the idea of poisoning the mead from the Mudblood Granger, as well, I heard her talking in the library about Filch not recognising potions ...'

'Please do not use that offensive word in front of me,' said Dumbledore.

Malfoy gave a harsh laugh.

## 第27章 被闪电击中的塔楼

那条项链是你弄的？太愚蠢了，会把事情都暴露出去的——'但是我没有告诉他我在那间有求必应屋里做什么，等他明天一早醒来，事情已经大功告成，他再也不会是黑魔王的宠儿了，他跟我一比什么都不是，什么都不是！"

"多么令人快慰。"邓布利多温和地说，"我们都希望自己的辛勤努力得到别人的赏识，这是不用说的……但你肯定有一个同伙……在霍格莫德有一个人，可以塞给凯蒂那条——那条——啊……"

邓布利多又闭上眼睛，微微点了点头，似乎快要睡着了。

"……不用说……是罗斯默塔。她中夺魂咒有多长时间了？"

"你终于想明白了，是吗？"马尔福嘲笑地说。

下面又传来一声喊叫，比刚才的那声更响。马尔福再次不安地扭过头去，然后又回过头来望着邓布利多。邓布利多继续说道："因此，可怜的罗斯默塔只好躲在她自己的厕所里，把那条项链塞给了任何一个独自上厕所的霍格沃茨学生？还有那瓶下过毒的蜂蜜酒……当然啦，罗斯默塔可以替你在那瓶酒里兑上毒药，再把它卖给斯拉格霍恩，以为它会作为圣诞礼物送给我……是啊，非常巧妙……非常巧妙……可怜的费尔奇怎么也想不到要检查罗斯默塔女士卖出的酒……那么你告诉我，你和罗斯默塔是怎么联系的呢？对于所有进出学校的通讯联络，我们都要严格监视的呀。"

"魔法硬币，"马尔福说，他似乎必须不停地往下说，他举着魔杖的那只手抖得很厉害，"我有一枚硬币，她也有一枚，我可以向她传递消息——"

"就是去年那个自称'邓布利多军'的小组采用的秘密联络方式？"邓布利多问。他的声音随和亲切，但哈利看见他说话时身子又往墙下滑了一英寸。

"对，我是跟他们学的。"马尔福狞笑着说，"给蜂蜜酒下毒的主意是从泥巴种格兰杰那里听来的，我听见她在图书馆里说费尔奇认不出药水……"

"请不要在我面前使用那个侮辱性的词。"邓布利多说。

马尔福发出一阵难听的大笑。

## CHAPTER TWENTY-SEVEN    The Lightning-Struck Tower

'You care about me saying "Mudblood" when I'm about to kill you?'

'Yes, I do,' said Dumbledore, and Harry saw his feet slide a little on the floor as he struggled to remain upright. 'But as for being about to kill me, Draco, you have had several long minutes now. We are quite alone. I am more defenceless than you can have dreamed of finding me, and still you have not acted ...'

Malfoy's mouth contorted involuntarily, as though he had tasted something very bitter.

'Now, about tonight,' Dumbledore went on, 'I am a little puzzled about how it happened ... you knew that I had left the school? But of course,' he answered his own question, 'Rosmerta saw me leaving, she tipped you off using your ingenious coins, I'm sure ...'

'That's right,' said Malfoy. 'But she said you were just going for a drink, you'd be back ...'

'Well, I certainly did have a drink ... and I came back ... after a fashion,' mumbled Dumbledore. 'So you decided to spring a trap for me?'

'We decided to put the Dark Mark over the Tower and get you to hurry up here, to see who'd been killed,' said Malfoy. 'And it worked!'

'Well ... yes and no ...' said Dumbledore. 'But am I to take it, then, that nobody has been murdered?'

'Someone's dead,' said Malfoy and his voice seemed to go up an octave as he said it. 'One of your people ... I don't know who, it was dark ... I stepped over the body ... I was supposed to be waiting up here when you got back, only your Phoenix lot got in the way ...'

'Yes, they do that,' said Dumbledore.

There was a bang and shouts from below, louder than ever; it sounded as though people were fighting on the actual spiral staircase that led to where Dumbledore, Malfoy and Harry stood, and Harry's heart thundered unheard in his invisible chest ... someone was dead ... Malfoy had stepped over the body ... but who was it?

'There is little time, one way or another,' said Dumbledore. 'So let us discuss your options, Draco.'

'My options!' said Malfoy loudly. 'I'm standing here with a wand – I'm about to kill you –'

'My dear boy, let us have no more pretence about that. If you were going

## 第27章 被闪电击中的塔楼

"眼看我就要取你的性命了，你还在意我说一句'泥巴种'？"

"是的，我很在意。"邓布利多说，这时哈利看见他双脚在地面打了个滑，使劲撑着不让自己瘫倒，"至于你要取我性命的事，德拉科，已经好几分钟过去了。周围没有别人，我现在手无寸铁，你做梦也不会想到有这样的好机会，可你还是没有动手……"

马尔福的嘴唇不由自主地扭曲，好像在品尝一种很苦的东西。

"再说说今晚的事，"邓布利多继续说道，"我还是有点儿不明白……你知道我离开学校了？当然啦，"邓布利多自己回答了这个问题，"罗斯默塔看见我离开的，我想，她一定用你们那种巧妙的硬币把消息告诉了你……"

"没错，"马尔福说，"但她说你只是去喝一杯，很快就会回来……"

"是啊，我确实是去喝了些东西……现在我回来了……勉强回来了，"邓布利多轻声嘟囔道，"所以你就决定给我设置一个陷阱？"

"我们决定在塔楼上空悬挂黑魔标记，逼你急忙赶回来看看谁遇害了。"马尔福说，"这个办法果然有效！"

"噢……也不一定……"邓布利多说，"那么，我是不是可以这样理解：目前还没有人遇害？"

"有一个人死了，"马尔福说，他的声音突然升高了一个八度，"一个你们的人……不知道是谁，天太黑了……我从尸体上跨过来的……我应该在这上面等你回来，都怪你们那些凤凰社的人出来挡道……"

"不错，这是他们的职责。"邓布利多说。

下面又传来碰撞声和人们的喊叫声，比刚才更响了，似乎有人就在通向邓布利多、马尔福和哈利这边的旋转楼梯上搏斗。哈利的心在他隐形的胸膛里狂跳，却没有人能够听见……死了一个人……马尔福从尸体上跨过来的……那会是谁呢？

"没有多少时间了，"邓布利多说，"何去何从，德拉科，我们讨论一下你的选择吧。"

"我的选择！"马尔福大声说，"我拿着魔杖站在这里——我要杀死你——"

"亲爱的孩子，我们别再演戏了。如果你真的要杀死我，刚才除去

## CHAPTER TWENTY-SEVEN    The Lightning-Struck Tower

to kill me, you would have done it when you first Disarmed me, you would not have stopped for this pleasant chat about ways and means.'

'I haven't got any options!' said Malfoy, and he was suddenly as white as Dumbledore. 'I've got to do it! He'll kill me! He'll kill my whole family!'

'I appreciate the difficulty of your position,' said Dumbledore. 'Why else do you think I have not confronted you before now? Because I knew that you would have been murdered if Lord Voldemort realised that I suspected you.'

Malfoy winced at the sound of the name.

'I did not dare speak to you of the mission with which I knew you had been entrusted, in case he used Legilimency against you,' continued Dumbledore. 'But now at last we can speak plainly to each other ... no harm has been done, you have hurt nobody, though you are very lucky that your unintentional victims survived ... I can help you, Draco.'

'No, you can't,' said Malfoy, his wand hand shaking very badly indeed. 'Nobody can. He told me to do it or he'll kill me. I've got no choice.'

'Come over to the right side, Draco, and we can hide you more completely than you can possibly imagine. What is more, I can send members of the Order to your mother tonight to hide her likewise. Your father is safe at the moment in Azkaban ... when the time comes we can protect him too ... come over to the right side, Draco ... you are not a killer ...'

Malfoy stared at Dumbledore.

'But I got this far, didn't I?' he said slowly. 'They thought I'd die in the attempt, but I'm here ... and you're in my power ... I'm the one with the wand ... you're at my mercy ...'

'No, Draco,' said Dumbledore quietly. 'It is my mercy, and not yours, that matters now.'

Malfoy did not speak. His mouth was open, his wand hand still trembling. Harry thought he saw it drop by a fraction –

But suddenly footsteps were thundering up the stairs and a second later Malfoy was buffeted out of the way as four people in black robes burst through the door on to the ramparts. Still paralysed, his eyes staring unblinkingly, Harry gazed in terror upon four strangers: it seemed the Death Eaters had won the fight below.

## 第27章 被闪电击中的塔楼

我的武器之后你就会动手了,而不会是停下来跟我愉快地谈论这些措施和方法。"

"我没有选择!"马尔福说,他的脸色突然变得和邓布利多一样惨白,"我非做不可!他会杀死我!他会杀死我的全家!"

"我理解你的处境,"邓布利多说,"不然我为什么在此之前一直没有跟你对质呢?我知道如果伏地魔发现我对你起了疑心,你就会被暗杀。"

马尔福听到那个名字,害怕地抽搐了一下。

"我知道你接受了那个任务,但我不敢跟你谈这件事,生怕他会对你使用摄神取念咒。"邓布利多继续说道,"现在我们终于可以开诚布公地说话了……你没有造成任何破坏,没有伤害任何人,你真是很幸运,被你误伤的那些人都活了下来……我可以帮助你,德拉科。"

"不,不可能,"马尔福说,他握着魔杖的那只手颤抖得非常厉害,"谁也不可能。他叫我做这件事,不然就会杀死我。我别无选择。"

"站到正确的道路上来吧,德拉科,我们可以把你藏在绝对安全的地方,比你所能想象的还要安全。而且,我今晚就可以派凤凰社的成员去把你母亲也藏起来。你父亲目前在阿兹卡班还不会有危险……到时候我们也会保护他的……站到正确的道路上来吧,德拉科……你不是一个杀人的人……"

马尔福呆呆地望着邓布利多。

"可是我已经有了这么多进展,不是吗?"他语速很慢地说,"他们以为我不等大功告成就会丧命,可是我还活着……而且你被我控制住了……现在拿魔杖的是我……你听我的摆布……"

"不,德拉科,"邓布利多平静地说,"现在是你听我摆布,而不是我听你摆布。"

德拉科没有说话。他的嘴巴张得大大的,握着魔杖的那只手仍在抖个不停。哈利仿佛觉得它往下降了一点儿——

突然,一阵脚步声噔噔噔地上了楼梯,一眨眼间,马尔福被拨拉到一边,四个穿黑袍子的人破门而出,拥到了围墙边。哈利仍然动弹不得,他怀着惊恐的心情,眼睛一眨不眨地盯着这四个陌生人:看来食死徒在下面的搏斗中占了上风。

## CHAPTER TWENTY-SEVEN  The Lightning-Struck Tower

A lumpy-looking man with an odd lopsided leer gave a wheezy giggle.

'Dumbledore cornered!' he said, and he turned to a stocky little woman who looked as though she could be his sister and who was grinning eagerly. 'Dumbledore wandless, Dumbledore alone! Well done, Draco, well done!'

'Good evening, Amycus,' said Dumbledore calmly, as though welcoming the man to a tea party. 'And you've brought Alecto too ... charming ...'

The woman gave an angry little titter.

'Think your little jokes'll help you on your death bed, then?' she jeered.

'Jokes? No, no, these are manners,' replied Dumbledore.

'Do it,' said the stranger standing nearest to Harry, a big, rangy man with matted grey hair and whiskers, whose black Death Eater's robes looked uncomfortably tight. He had a voice like none that Harry had ever heard: a rasping bark of a voice. Harry could smell a powerful mixture of dirt, sweat and, unmistakeably, of blood coming from him. His filthy hands had long yellowish nails.

'Is that you, Fenrir?' asked Dumbledore.

'That's right,' rasped the other. 'Pleased to see me, Dumbledore?'

'No, I cannot say that I am ...'

Fenrir Greyback grinned, showing pointed teeth. Blood trickled down his chin and he licked his lips slowly, obscenely.

'But you know how much I like kids, Dumbledore.'

'Am I to take it that you are attacking even without the full moon now? This is most unusual ... you have developed a taste for human flesh that cannot be satisfied once a month?'

'That's right,' said Greyback. 'Shocks you, that, does it, Dumbledore? Frightens you?'

'Well, I cannot pretend it does not disgust me a little,' said Dumbledore. 'And, yes, I am a little shocked that Draco here invited you, of all people, into the school where his friends live ...'

'I didn't,' breathed Malfoy. He was not looking at Greyback; he did not seem to want to even glance at him. 'I didn't know he was going to come –'

## 第 27 章 被闪电击中的塔楼

一个身材粗壮、脸上带着古怪狞笑的男人发出了呼哧带喘的笑声。

"邓布利多被逼到墙角了！"他说完便转向一个壮实的小个子女人，她看上去像是他的妹妹，脸上也带着迫不及待的笑容，"邓布利多没有魔杖，邓布利多孤立无援！干得漂亮，德拉科，干得漂亮！"

"晚上好，阿米库斯，"邓布利多语气十分平静，像在欢迎那人参加茶会，"你还带来了阿莱克托……太可爱了……"

那女人恼怒地假笑了一声。

"你都死到临头了，还以为这些小玩笑能救你的命？"她讥笑道。

"玩笑？不，不，这是礼貌。"邓布利多回答。

"动手吧。"站得离哈利最近的那个陌生人说，他身材高大，四肢修长，灰色的头发和络腮胡子都纠结在一起，那件食死徒的黑袍子很不舒服地紧紧勒在身上。他的声音很古怪，是哈利从来没听过的：一种嘶哑刺耳的咆哮。哈利还闻到他身上散发出一股冲鼻的怪味儿，混杂着泥土味、汗味，以及——毫无疑问——血腥味。他肮脏的手指上留着长长的黄指甲。

"是你吗，芬里尔？"邓布利多问。

"没错，"那人用刺耳的声音说，"见到我很高兴吧，邓布利多？"

"不，不能说很高兴……"

芬里尔·格雷伯克咧嘴一笑，露出尖尖的牙齿。鲜血滴到他的下巴上，他慢慢地、令人恶心地舔着嘴唇。

"但你知道我是多么喜欢孩子，邓布利多。"

"我是否可以这样理解：现在即使在月亮不圆的日子你也要咬人？这可真奇怪……你养成了这种吃人肉的癖好，一个月一次都不能满足吗？"

"说得对，"格雷伯克说，"让你震惊了，是不是，邓布利多？让你害怕了？"

"唉，坦白地说，确实让我感到有些恶心，"邓布利多说，"而且，我确实有点儿震惊：这位德拉科竟然偏偏把你请到他的朋友们居住的学校里来……"

"我没有。"马尔福喘着气说。他没有看格雷伯克，似乎连瞄都不愿瞄他一眼。"我不知道他要来——"

'I wouldn't want to miss a trip to Hogwarts, Dumbledore,' rasped Greyback. 'Not when there are throats to be ripped out … delicious, delicious …'

And he raised a yellow fingernail and picked at his front teeth, leering at Dumbledore.

'I could do you for afters, Dumbledore …'

'No,' said the fourth Death Eater sharply. He had a heavy, brutal-looking face. 'We've got orders. Draco's got to do it. Now, Draco, and quickly.'

Malfoy was showing less resolution than ever. He looked terrified as he stared into Dumbledore's face, which was even paler, and rather lower than usual, as he had slid so far down the rampart wall.

'He's not long for this world anyway, if you ask me!' said the lopsided man, to the accompaniment of his sister's wheezing giggles. 'Look at him – what's happened to you, then, Dumby?'

'Oh, weaker resistance, slower reflexes, Amycus,' said Dumbledore. 'Old age, in short … one day, perhaps, it will happen to you … if you are lucky …'

'What's that mean, then, what's that mean?' yelled the Death Eater, suddenly violent. 'Always the same, weren't yeh, Dumby, talking and doing nothing, nothing, I don't even know why the Dark Lord's bothering to kill yeh! come on, Draco, do it!'

But at that moment, there were renewed sounds of scuffling from below and a voice shouted, '*They've blocked the stairs – Reducto! REDUCTO!*'

Harry's heart leapt: so these four had not eliminated all opposition, but merely broken through the fight to the top of the Tower, and, by the sound of it, created a barrier behind them –

'Now, Draco, quickly!' said the brutal-faced man angrily.

But Malfoy's hand was shaking so badly that he could barely aim.

'I'll do it,' snarled Greyback, moving towards Dumbledore with his hands outstretched, his teeth bared.

'I said no!' shouted the brutal-faced man; there was a flash of light and the werewolf was blasted out of the way; he hit the ramparts and staggered, looking furious. Harry's heart was hammering so hard it seemed impossible that nobody could hear him standing there, imprisoned by Dumbledore's spell – if he could only move, he could aim a curse from under the Cloak –

## 第27章　被闪电击中的塔楼

"我可不愿意错过到霍格沃茨来的美差，邓布利多。"格雷伯克用刺耳的声音说，"有这么多的喉咙可以撕开……味道真好，味道真好啊……"

他举起一根黄黄的指甲剔起了大门牙，一边朝邓布利多狞笑着。

"我可以把你当成餐后的甜食，邓布利多……"

"不行。"第四个食死徒厉声说道。他满脸横肉，一副凶相。"我们有命令的。必须让德拉科动手。好了，德拉科，快行动吧。"

马尔福更加没有斗志了。他看上去很害怕，呆呆地瞪着邓布利多的脸。邓布利多的脸色越发苍白，个头也显得比平常矮了许多，因为他靠在墙上的身体一直在往下出溜。

"要我说，他在这个世界上的日子反正也不多了！"那个撇着嘴笑的男人说，他妹妹在一旁呼哧呼哧地笑着给他助阵，"你看看他——你这是怎么回事啊，邓老头儿？"

"唉，体力不支，反应迟钝啊，阿米库斯。"邓布利多说，"总之，年老不中用啦……总有一天，你也会落到这步田地……如果你幸运的话……"

"这话是什么意思？这话是什么意思？"食死徒喊道，突然变得凶狠起来，"你还是老样子，是不是，邓老头儿？满嘴空话，不干实事，我真弄不懂黑魔王为什么要费心把你干掉！好了，德拉科，快动手吧！"

就在这时，下面又传来许多人混战的声音，其中一个人喊道："他们把楼梯堵住了——**粉身碎骨**！**粉身碎骨**！"

哈利的心欢跳起来：这么说，这四个人并没有把对手完全消灭，他们只是突围出来跑到了塔楼顶上，而且，听下面的声音，他们好像在身后筑了一道路障——

"快，德拉科，快动手吧！"一脸凶相的男人恼怒地说。

可是马尔福抖得太厉害了，没有办法瞄准目标。

"我来吧。"格雷伯克恶狠狠地说着就朝邓布利多逼了过去，他张开两只手，露出了嘴里的尖牙。

"我说过不行！"一脸凶相的男人喊道。一道强光一闪，狼人被击到一边，撞在墙上，差点儿摔倒，脸上一副恼羞成怒的样子。哈利站在那儿，被邓布利多的魔咒束缚着，心咚咚跳得像打鼓一样，但竟然谁也听不见，这简直不可思议——只要他能够动弹，就可以从隐形衣下面射出魔咒——

## CHAPTER TWENTY-SEVEN    The Lightning-Struck Tower

'Draco, do it, or stand aside so one of us –' screeched the woman, but at that precise moment the door to the ramparts burst open once more and there stood Snape, his wand clutched in his hand as his black eyes swept the scene, from Dumbledore slumped against the wall, to the four Death Eaters, including the enraged werewolf, and Malfoy.

'We've got a problem, Snape,' said the lumpy Amycus, whose eyes and wand were fixed alike upon Dumbledore, 'the boy doesn't seem able –'

But somebody else had spoken Snape's name, quite softly.

'Severus …'

The sound frightened Harry beyond anything he had experienced all evening. For the first time, Dumbledore was pleading.

Snape said nothing, but walked forwards and pushed Malfoy roughly out of the way. The three Death Eaters fell back without a word. Even the werewolf seemed cowed.

Snape gazed for a moment at Dumbledore, and there was revulsion and hatred etched in the harsh lines of his face.

'Severus … please …'

Snape raised his wand and pointed it directly at Dumbledore.

'*Avada Kedavra!*'

A jet of green light shot from the end of Snape's wand and hit Dumbledore squarely in the chest. Harry's scream of horror never left him; silent and unmoving, he was forced to watch as Dumbledore was blasted into the air: for a split second he seemed to hang suspended beneath the shining skull, and then he fell slowly backwards, like a great rag doll, over the battlements and out of sight.

## 第27章 被闪电击中的塔楼

"德拉科,快动手,不然就闪开,让我们——"那女人尖声尖气地说。然而就在这时,通向围墙的门又一次被撞开了,斯内普攥着魔杖站在那里,一双黑眼睛迅速扫视着面前的场景,从瘫倒在墙上的邓布利多到那四个食死徒——其中包括气势汹汹的狼人,还有马尔福。

"我们遇到难题了,斯内普,"体格粗壮的阿米库斯说,他的目光和魔杖都牢牢地锁定邓布利多,"这小伙子好像不能——"

但是另外一个人念着斯内普的名字,声音很轻很轻。

"西弗勒斯……"

这声音比哈利整晚经历的任何事情都叫他害怕。邓布利多在哀求,这可是破天荒的第一次。

斯内普没有说话,他走上前,粗暴地把马尔福推到一边。三个食死徒一言不发地闪到后面,就连狼人似乎也被吓住了。

斯内普凝视了邓布利多片刻,他脸上粗犷的线条里刻着深深的厌恶和仇恨。

"西弗勒斯……请求你……"

斯内普举起魔杖,直指邓布利多。

"阿瓦达索命!"

斯内普的魔杖尖上射出一道绿光,不偏不倚地击中了邓布利多的胸膛。哈利惊恐的尖叫声被憋在了喉咙里,他发不出声音,也动弹不得,只能眼睁睁地望着邓布利多被击到空中。邓布利多似乎在那闪亮的骷髅下停留了一秒钟,然后像一个破烂的大玩偶似的,慢慢地仰面倒下去,从围墙的垛口栽下去不见了。

## CHAPTER TWENTY-EIGHT

# Flight of the Prince

Harry felt as though he, too, were hurtling through space; *it had not happened ... it could not have happened ...*

'Out of here, quickly,' said Snape.

He seized Malfoy by the scruff of the neck and forced him through the door ahead of the rest; Greyback and the squat brother and sister followed, the latter both panting excitedly. As they vanished through the door Harry realised he could move again; what was now holding him paralysed against the wall was not magic, but horror and shock. He threw the Invisibility Cloak aside as the brutal-faced Death Eater, last to leave the Tower top, was disappearing through the door.

'*Petrificus Totalus!*'

The Death Eater buckled as though hit in the back with something solid, and fell to the ground, rigid as a waxwork, but he had barely hit the floor when Harry was clambering over him and running down the darkened staircase.

Terror tore at Harry's heart ... he had to get to Dumbledore and he had to catch Snape ... somehow the two things were linked ... he could reverse what had happened if he had them both together ... Dumbledore could not have died ...

He leapt the last ten steps of the spiral staircase and stopped where he landed, his wand raised: the dimly lit corridor was full of dust; half the ceiling seemed to have fallen in and a battle was raging before him, but even as he attempted to make out who was fighting whom, he heard the hated voice shout, '*It's over, time to go!*' and saw Snape disappearing round the corner at the far end of the corridor; he and Malfoy seemed to have forced their way through the fight unscathed. As Harry plunged after them, one of the fighters detached themself from the fray and flew at him: it was the werewolf,

## 第28章

## 王子逃逸

哈利觉得自己好像也飞了出去;这没有发生……这不可能……

"离开这里,快点儿!"斯内普说。

他一把抓住马尔福的后脖颈,用力把他第一个推出了门外;格雷伯克和那身材短粗的食死徒兄妹紧跟其后,他们俩兴奋地喘着粗气。他们从门口消失后,哈利意识到自己又可以动了。现在让他木呆呆地瘫靠在墙上的不是魔法,而是恐惧和震惊。当那个一脸凶相的食死徒最后一个离开塔顶、正要从门口消失时,他一把掀开了隐形衣。

"统统石化!"

食死徒跟跄了一下,好像有什么硬东西砸到了他背上,然后就像尊蜡像一样倒了下去。但是他刚一着地,哈利就已经越过了他,朝着漆黑的楼梯跑了下去。

恐惧撕扯着哈利的心……他必须找到邓布利多,必须抓住斯内普……不知怎的这两件事联系在了一起……如果这两件事都做成了,他就可以使一切逆转……邓布利多就不会死去……

他纵身跃过最后十级螺旋形楼梯,落地后停住脚,举起魔杖。昏暗的灯光照着的走廊满是灰尘,好像半个屋顶都塌了。一场激烈的战斗正在他面前进行,他试图弄清是谁和谁在交战,忽然听到那个令他憎恶的声音叫道:"都结束了,该走了!"只见斯内普消失在走廊远处的拐角处,他和马尔福似乎是毫无损伤地突围了出去。哈利拔腿急追,忽有一人抽身朝他扑来,原来是狼人格雷伯克。哈利还没来得及举起魔杖,格雷伯克已经扑到他身上。哈利仰天倒了下去,感到又脏又乱

### CHAPTER TWENTY-EIGHT    Flight of the Prince

Greyback. He was on top of Harry before Harry could raise his wand: Harry fell backwards, with filthy matted hair in his face, the stench of sweat and blood filling his nose and mouth, hot greedy breath at his throat –

'*Petrificus Totalus!*'

Harry felt Greyback collapse against him; with a stupendous effort he pushed the werewolf off and on to the floor as a jet of green light came flying towards him; he ducked and ran, head first, into the fight. His feet met something squashy and slippery on the floor and he stumbled: there were two bodies lying there, lying face down in a pool of blood, but there was no time to investigate: Harry now saw red hair flying like flames in front of him: Ginny was locked in combat with the lumpy Death Eater, Amycus, who was throwing hex after hex at her while she dodged them: Amycus was giggling, enjoying the sport: '*Crucio – Crucio –* you can't dance for ever, pretty –'

'*Impedimenta!*' yelled Harry.

His jinx hit Amycus in the chest: he gave a piglike squeal of pain, was lifted off his feet and slammed into the opposite wall, slid down it and fell out of sight behind Ron, Professor McGonagall and Lupin, each of whom was battling a separate Death Eater: beyond them, Harry saw Tonks fighting an enormous blond wizard who was sending curses flying in all directions, so that they ricocheted off the walls around them, cracking stone, shattering the nearest window –

'Harry, where did you come from?' Ginny cried, but there was no time to answer her. He put his head down and sprinted forwards, narrowly avoiding a blast that erupted over his head, showering them all in bits of wall: Snape must not escape, he must catch up with Snape –

'Take *that*!' shouted Professor McGonagall, and Harry glimpsed the female Death Eater, Alecto, sprinting away down the corridor with her arms over her head, her brother right behind her. Harry launched himself after them, but his foot caught on something and next moment he was lying across someone's legs: looking around, he saw Neville's pale, round face flat against the floor.

'Neville, are you –?'

''M'all right,' muttered Neville, who was clutching his stomach, 'Harry ... Snape 'n' Malfoy ... ran past ...'

'I know, I'm on it!' said Harry, aiming a hex from the floor at the enormous blond Death Eater who was causing most of the chaos: the man

## 第28章 王子逃逸

的头发遮住了他的脸,汗臭和血腥味灌入他的口鼻之中,贪婪的热气喷到他的喉咙口……

"统统石化!"

哈利感到格雷伯克倒在他身上,赶忙使出九牛二虎之力推开狼人。这时一道绿光飞来,他赶忙躲开,然后不顾一切地向混战的人群冲去。脚下好像踩到了又软又滑的什么东西,他踉跄了一下,见是两具躯体脸朝下躺在血泊之中,但他来不及细看。哈利看到了火光般飞舞的红发,是金妮正在和粗壮的食死徒阿米库斯对战。阿米库斯朝金妮不停地施魔法,金妮左躲右闪,阿米库斯哈哈大笑,乐在其中:"钻心剜骨——钻心剜骨——你不可能永远跳来跳去,宝贝儿——"

"障碍重重!"哈利大喊道。

他的魔咒正中阿米库斯的胸口,随着一声杀猪似的号叫,阿米库斯的身子陡然飞起,撞到对面的墙上,然后滑了下去,被挡住看不见了,因为罗恩、麦格教授和卢平正在那边各自迎战一个食死徒。更远一点儿,唐克斯和一个身材庞大的金发巫师正战得不可开交,那巫师发的咒语四处乱飞,碰到墙壁反弹出去,石头震裂了,窗户玻璃震碎了……

"哈利,你从哪儿来?"金妮叫道,但哈利没有时间回答她。他低着头,向前急奔,惊险地躲过头顶上方的一个爆炸,瓦砾碎片如阵雨一般崩落。绝不能让斯内普逃掉,他必须抓住斯内普……

"接招!"麦格教授喊道,哈利瞥见女食死徒阿莱克托双手护头飞奔着从走廊上逃去,她哥哥紧随其后。哈利奋力追赶,可是脚被什么东西绊了一下,摔了一跤,他发现自己横躺在一个人的腿上,扭头一看,竟是脸色苍白的纳威趴在地上。

"纳威,你——?"

"我没事。"纳威嘟囔了一声,手紧紧地捂住肚子,"哈利……斯内普和马尔福……跑掉了……"

"我知道,我正在追他们!"哈利说道,在地上冲着那个正在制造最多混乱的大块头金发食死徒施了一个魔咒,正中他的脸部,他发

## CHAPTER TWENTY-EIGHT  Flight of the Prince

gave a howl of pain as the spell hit him in the face; he wheeled round, staggered and then pounded away after the brother and sister.

Harry scrambled up from the floor and began to sprint along the corridor, ignoring the bangs issuing from behind him, the yells of the others to come back, and the mute call of the figures on the ground, whose fate he did not yet know ...

He skidded round the corner, his trainers slippery with blood; Snape had an immense head-start – was it possible that he had already entered the Cabinet in the Room of Requirement, or had the Order made steps to secure it, to prevent the Death Eaters retreating that way? He could hear nothing but his own pounding feet, his own hammering heart as he sprinted along the next empty corridor, but then spotted a bloody footprint which showed that at least one of the fleeing Death Eaters was heading towards the front doors – perhaps the Room of Requirement was indeed blocked –

He skidded round another corner and a curse flew past him; he dived behind a suit of armour which exploded; he saw the brother and sister Death Eaters running down the marble staircase ahead and aimed jinxes at them, but merely hit several bewigged witches in a portrait on the landing, who ran screeching into neighbouring paintings; as he leapt over the wreckage of armour Harry heard more shouts and screams; other people within the castle seemed to have awoken ...

He pelted towards a short cut, hoping to overtake the brother and sister and close in on Snape and Malfoy, who must surely have reached the grounds by now; remembering to leap the vanishing step halfway down the concealed staircase he burst through a tapestry at the bottom and out into a corridor where a number of bewildered and pyjama-clad Hufflepuffs stood.

'Harry! We heard a noise and someone said something about the Dark Mark –' began Ernie Macmillan.

'Out of the way!' yelled Harry, knocking two boys aside as he sprinted towards the landing and down the remainder of the marble staircase. The oak front doors had been blasted open; there were smears of blood on the flagstones and several terrified students stood huddled against the walls, one or two still cowering with their arms over their faces; the giant Gryffindor hour-glass had been hit by a curse and the rubies within were still falling, with a loud rattle, on to the flagstones below ...

Harry flew across the Entrance Hall and out into the dark grounds: he

## 第28章 王子逃逸

出一声痛苦的怒吼,转过身晃了两下,吃力地跟在食死徒兄妹后面逃走了。

哈利从地上爬起来,顺着走廊向前飞奔,不顾身后乒乒乓乓的激战声、其他人叫他回去的大喊声,以及躺在地上、不知死活的人的无声的求助……

他在拐弯处刹住脚,运动鞋踩在血迹上直打滑,斯内普已经没有踪影。莫非他已经进入了有求必应屋的消失柜,还是凤凰社设了屏障,不让食死徒朝那边撤退?他飞奔着冲向下一条空空的走廊,只听见自己沉重的脚步声和咚咚的心跳声。幸好他突然看到一行带血的脚印,说明至少有一个食死徒正朝着前门的方向逃去——也许有求必应屋真的被堵上了——

他又在一个拐弯处刹住脚,正好一个咒语飞过,他连忙俯身躲到一副盔甲后面,盔甲被炸烂了。他突然看见食死徒兄妹正从大理石楼梯上奔逃下去,连忙向他们施了几个魔咒,但只击中了楼梯口肖像中几个戴假发的女巫,她们尖叫着跑进了旁边的相框。哈利从被炸烂的盔甲上跳过,听见越来越多的尖叫声和喊叫声,好像城堡里的其他人都被惊醒了……

他朝一个近道飞奔而去,希望超过食死徒兄妹并追上斯内普和马尔福,他们现在一定已经到达场地了。在那段隐蔽楼梯的中部,他没忘记跳过那级会消失的台阶,然后从底部一个挂毯后面冲了出去,看到走廊里站着一群穿着睡衣、不知所措的赫奇帕奇学生。

"哈利!我们听到一声响动,还有人提到了黑魔标记——"厄尼·麦克米兰说道。

"闪开!"哈利喊道,把两个男生撞到一边,奔下大理石楼梯。橡木大门被炸开了,门前的石板上沾有血痕,好几个吓呆了的学生在墙边挤成一团,其中一两个还用胳膊遮住了脸。巨大的格兰芬多沙漏被咒语击中,里面的红宝石仍在噼里啪啦地往石板上掉……

哈利飞奔过门厅,冲进外面漆黑的场地。他依稀看见三个人影正

## CHAPTER TWENTY-EIGHT — Flight of the Prince

could just make out three figures racing across the lawn, heading for the gates beyond which they could Disapparate – by the looks of them, the huge blond Death Eater and, some way ahead of him, Snape and Malfoy ...

The cold night air ripped at Harry's lungs as he tore after them; he saw a flash of light in the distance that momentarily silhouetted his quarry; he did not know what it was but continued to run, not yet near enough to get a good aim with a curse –

Another flash, shouts, retaliatory jets of light, and Harry understood: Hagrid had emerged from his cabin and was trying to stop the Death Eaters escaping, and though every breath seemed to shred his lungs and the stitch in his chest was like fire, Harry sped up as an unbidden voice in his head said: *not Hagrid ... not Hagrid too ...*

Something caught Harry hard in the small of the back and he fell forwards, his face smacking the ground, blood pouring out of both nostrils: he knew, even as he rolled over, his wand ready, that the brother and sister he had overtaken using his short cut were closing in behind him ...

'*Impedimenta!*' he yelled as he rolled over again, crouching close to the dark ground, and miraculously his jinx hit one of them, who stumbled and fell, tripping up the other; Harry leapt to his feet and sprinted on, after Snape ...

And now he saw the vast outline of Hagrid, illuminated by the light of the crescent moon revealed suddenly from behind clouds; the blond Death Eater was aiming curse after curse at the gamekeeper, but Hagrid's immense strength, and the toughened skin he had inherited from his giantess mother, seemed to be protecting him; Snape and Malfoy, however, were still running; they would soon be beyond the gates, able to Disapparate –

Harry tore past Hagrid and his opponent, took aim at Snape's back and yelled, '*Stupefy!*'

He missed; the jet of red light soared past Snape's head; Snape shouted, '*Run, Draco!*' and turned; twenty yards apart he and Harry looked at each other before raising their wands simultaneously.

'*Cruc–*'

But Snape parried the curse, knocking Harry backwards off his feet before he could complete it; Harry rolled over and scrambled back up again as the huge Death Eater behind him yelled, '*Incendio!*'; Harry heard an explosive bang and a dancing orange light spilled over all of them: Hagrid's house was on fire.

## 第28章 王子逃逸

在草坪上奔跑,从外形看是大块头金发食死徒,以及跑在前面的斯内普和马尔福。一旦出了校门,他们就可以使用幻影移形了……

哈利奋力急追,夜晚的凉风撕扯着他的肺。他突然看见前方一道闪光映出了那三人的轮廓,他不知道是哪里来的光亮,仍继续狂追,还够不着向他们瞄准发射咒语——

又是一道闪光,接着是叫喊声和还击的光束,哈利知道了,是海格从他的木屋里冲了出来,正在试图阻止食死徒逃跑。尽管每次呼吸都像要把肺撕裂,胸部的刺痛像火烧火燎一样,哈利还是加快了脚步,他脑海里响着一个声音:"别让海格……别让海格也……"

突然有个东西狠狠地砸在哈利的后腰上,他向前栽倒了,脸重重地磕在地面上,鼻孔流出了血。他翻过身,举起魔杖,知道自己走近道超过的那一对食死徒兄妹又追上来了……

"障碍重重!"他一边大叫,一边又翻过身,匍匐在漆黑的地面上,他的魔咒奇迹般地击中了一个,那人踉跄着倒在地上,又绊倒了另一个。哈利纵身跃起,向斯内普追去……

直到这时,他才透过突然钻出云层的月牙的微光,看见海格的巨大轮廓。金发食死徒正向这个猎场看守一个接一个地发射魔咒,但从巨人母亲那里继承来的强健体魄和粗厚皮肤似乎保护了海格。然而斯内普和马尔福仍在逃跑,很快就要跑出大门,然后就可以幻影移形了——

哈利狂奔着从海格和他的对手身边跑了过去,指着斯内普的后背大喊:"昏昏倒地!"

没有打中,红光飞过斯内普的头顶。斯内普大叫道:"德拉科,快跑!"然后他转过身,和哈利相距二十米开外,四目对视,几乎同时举起了魔杖。

"钻心剜——"

但是斯内普挡开了咒语,在哈利的咒语还未说完前就将他击倒了。哈利打了个滚又爬了起来,却听见身后的大块头食死徒大吼道:"火焰熊熊!"随着一声爆破般的巨响,一个飞舞着的橙色火球四蹿开来。海格的木屋着火了。

## CHAPTER TWENTY-EIGHT    Flight of the Prince

'Fang's in there, yeh evil –!' Hagrid bellowed.

'*Cruc–*' yelled Harry for the second time, aiming for the figure ahead illuminated in the dancing firelight, but Snape blocked the spell again; Harry could see him sneering.

'No Unforgivable Curses from you, Potter!' he shouted over the rushing of the flames, Hagrid's yells and the wild yelping of the trapped Fang. 'You haven't got the nerve or the ability –'

'*Incarc–*' Harry roared, but Snape deflected the spell with an almost lazy flick of his arm.

'Fight back!' Harry screamed at him. 'Fight back, you cowardly –'

'Coward, did you call me, Potter?' shouted Snape. 'Your father would never attack me unless it was four on one, what would you call him, I wonder?'

'*Stupe–*'

'Blocked again, and again, and again until you learn to keep your mouth shut and your mind closed, Potter!' sneered Snape, deflecting the curse once more. 'Now *come!*' he shouted at the huge Death Eater behind Harry. 'It is time to be gone, before the Ministry turns up –'

'*Impedi–*'

But before he could finish this jinx, excruciating pain hit Harry; he keeled over in the grass, someone was screaming, he would surely die of this agony, Snape was going to torture him to death or madness –

'No!' roared Snape's voice and the pain stopped as suddenly as it had started; Harry lay curled on the dark grass, clutching his wand and panting; somewhere above him Snape was shouting, 'Have you forgotten our orders? Potter belongs to the Dark Lord – we are to leave him! Go! Go!'

And Harry felt the ground shudder under his face as the brother and sister and the enormous Death Eater obeyed, running towards the gates. Harry uttered an inarticulate yell of rage: in that instant, he cared not whether he lived or died; pushing himself to his feet again, he staggered blindly towards Snape, the man he now hated as much as he hated Voldemort himself –

'*Sectum–*'

Snape flicked his wand and the curse was repelled yet again; but Harry was mere feet away now and he could see Snape's face clearly at last: he was

## 第28章 王子逃逸

"牙牙在里面,你这个恶魔——!"海格怒吼道。

"钻心剜——"哈利指着前面火光映照的身影再次高喊,但是斯内普又把他的魔咒挡掉了。哈利看到他在冷笑。

"你别用不可饶恕咒了,波特!"斯内普在熊熊的火焰、海格的怒吼和火屋里牙牙的狂吠声中喊道,"你还没有足够的胆量和能力——"

"速速绑——"哈利咆哮,但斯内普几乎是懒洋洋地轻轻拨开了他的魔咒。

"回击啊!"哈利冲他狂叫道,"回击啊,你这个懦夫——"

"懦夫,你是说我吗,波特?"斯内普吼道,"你父亲从来不敢攻击我,除非是四对一,我倒想知道你会叫他什么呢?"

"昏昏倒——"

"又被挡掉了,又被挡掉了,一直挡到你知道闭上嘴巴、闭上大脑为止,波特!"斯内普冷笑道,同时又一次拨开了魔咒,"快过来!"他冲着哈利身后的大块头食死徒喊道,"该走了,别让魔法部发现我们——"

"障碍重——"

但哈利还没来得及说完咒语,一阵无法忍受的剧痛突然袭来,他倒在了草地上。有人在尖叫,剧痛足以使他毙命,斯内普要把他折磨致死或者致疯——

"不!"斯内普咆哮道,剧痛消失得像来时一样迅速,哈利蜷曲着躺在漆黑的草地上,紧握魔杖,不停地喘着粗气,只听见头顶上的什么地方斯内普大叫着:"你们忘记命令了吗?波特属于黑魔王——我们别碰他!走!走!"

食死徒兄妹和大块头食死徒服从了命令,朝大门口跑去,哈利觉得自己脸下的大地都在颤抖。哈利使足力气,愤怒地呐喊一声,他不顾自己死活,再次站了起来,步履蹒跚地朝斯内普追去,他现在像憎恨伏地魔一样憎恨斯内普了——

"神锋无——"

斯内普轻挥魔杖,魔咒再次被击退。但这时哈利离斯内普只有几

889

no longer sneering or jeering; the blazing flames showed a face full of rage. Mustering all his powers of concentration, Harry thought, *Levi–*

'No, Potter!' screamed Snape. There was a loud BANG and Harry was soaring backwards, hitting the ground hard again, and this time his wand flew out of his hand. He could hear Hagrid yelling and Fang howling as Snape closed in and looked down on him where he lay, wandless and defenceless as Dumbledore had been. Snape's pale face, illuminated by the flaming cabin, was suffused with hatred just as it had been before he had cursed Dumbledore.

'You dare use my own spells against me, Potter? It was I who invented them – I, the Half-Blood Prince! And you'd turn my inventions on me, like your filthy father, would you? I don't think so … *no!*'

Harry had dived for his wand; Snape shot a hex at it and it flew feet away into the darkness and out of sight.

'Kill me, then,' panted Harry, who felt no fear at all, but only rage and contempt. 'Kill me like you killed him, you coward –'

'DON'T –' screamed Snape, and his face was suddenly demented, inhuman, as though he was in as much pain as the yelping, howling dog stuck in the burning house behind them, '– CALL ME COWARD!'

And he slashed at the air: Harry felt a white-hot, whiplike something hit him across the face and was slammed backwards into the ground. Spots of light burst in front of his eyes and for a moment all the breath seemed to have gone from his body, then he heard a rush of wings above him and something enormous obscured the stars: Buckbeak had flown at Snape, who staggered backwards as the razor-sharp claws slashed at him. As Harry raised himself into a sitting position, his head still swimming from its last contact with the ground, he saw Snape running as hard as he could, the enormous beast flapping behind him and screeching as Harry had never heard him screech –

Harry struggled to his feet, looking around groggily for his wand, hoping to give chase again, but even as his fingers fumbled in the grass, discarding twigs, he knew it would be too late, and sure enough, by the time he had located his wand he turned only to see the Hippogriff circling the gates: Snape had managed to Disapparate just beyond the school's boundaries.

'Hagrid,' muttered Harry, still dazed, looking around. 'HAGRID?'

## 第28章 王子逃逸

步远，终于可以看清斯内普的脸了。斯内普不再冷笑或讥笑，闪耀的火光映照着一张充满愤怒的脸。哈利集中全部意念想道："倒挂金——"

"不，波特！"斯内普尖叫道。随着一声巨响，哈利向后炸飞了，又一次重重地摔在地上，这次手中的魔杖飞了出去。他听见海格的大喊声和牙牙的狂吠声。斯内普走近哈利，低头瞪着他，此时的哈利同邓布利多一样手无魔杖，毫无反抗之力。燃烧的木屋映照出斯内普苍白的脸庞，脸上满是憎恨，同杀死邓布利多时一样。

"你竟敢用我的魔咒来攻击我，波特？是我发明了这些魔咒——我，混血王子！你要用我的发明来攻击我，像你那肮脏的父亲一样，是吗？我说不行……不行！"

哈利扑向自己的魔杖，但斯内普向魔杖施了个魔咒，魔杖飞入黑暗中不见了。

"那么你杀了我吧！"哈利喘息道，他一点儿都不害怕，只有愤怒和蔑视，"像杀他一样杀了我吧，懦夫——"

"**不许**——"斯内普尖叫道，脸突然变得无比疯狂，毫无人性，好像同他们身后火屋里厉声狂吠的那条狗一样痛苦，"**——叫我懦夫！**"

斯内普猛烈地抽打着空气。哈利感到有种白热的、像鞭子样的东西打在脸上。他满眼冒着金星，有一阵子好像停止了呼吸。就在这时，他听见一阵翅膀的扑棱声，巨大的影子遮住了天空的星星。巴克比克已经飞到了斯内普的头上，刀一样锋利的爪子抓得斯内普连连后退。哈利坐了起来，刚才撞到地上的脑袋还在发晕，他看见斯内普拼命奔跑，巨大的巴克比克拍着翅膀在后面紧追不放，发出一种哈利从未听过的尖厉吼叫——

哈利挣扎着站了起来，东倒西歪地寻找他的魔杖，希望能继续追击。但当他在草丛里拨开树枝摸索时，就知道已经太晚了。确实是太晚了，等他找到魔杖转过身，只看见鹰头马身有翼兽在大门口的空中盘旋，斯内普已经在魔法学校外幻影移形了。

"海格，"哈利喃喃道，他环顾四周，头还在发晕，"**海格？**"

## CHAPTER TWENTY-EIGHT — Flight of the Prince

He stumbled towards the burning house as an enormous figure emerged from out of the flames carrying Fang on his back. With a cry of thankfulness, Harry sank to his knees; he was shaking in every limb, his body ached all over and his breath came in painful stabs.

'Yeh all righ', Harry? Yeh all righ'? Speak ter me, Harry ...'

Hagrid's huge, hairy face was swimming above Harry, blocking out the stars. Harry could smell burnt wood and dog hair; he put out a hand and felt Fang's reassuringly warm and alive body quivering beside him.

'I'm all right,' panted Harry. 'Are you?'

'Course I am ... take more'n that ter finish me.'

Hagrid put his hands under Harry's arms and raised him up with such force that Harry's feet momentarily left the ground before Hagrid set him upright again. He could see blood trickling down Hagrid's cheek from a deep cut under one eye, which was swelling rapidly.

'We should put out your house,' said Harry, 'the charm's *Aguamenti* ...'

'Knew it was summat like that,' mumbled Hagrid, and he raised a smouldering, pink flowery umbrella and said, '*Aguamenti!*'

A jet of water flew out of the umbrella tip. Harry raised his wand arm, which felt like lead, and murmured '*Aguamenti*' too: together, he and Hagrid poured water on the house until the last flame was extinguished.

''S not too bad,' said Hagrid hopefully a few minutes later, looking at the smoking wreck. 'Nothin' Dumbledore won' be able to put righ' ...'

Harry felt a searing pain in his stomach at the sound of the name. In the silence and the stillness, horror rose inside him.

'Hagrid ...'

'I was bindin' up a couple o' Bowtruckle legs when I heard 'em comin',' said Hagrid sadly, still staring at his wrecked cabin. 'They'll've bin burnt ter twigs, poor little things ...'

'Hagrid ...'

'But what happened, Harry? I jus' saw them Death Eaters runnin' down from the castle, but what the ruddy hell was Snape doin' with 'em? Where's he gone — was he chasin' 'em?'

'He ...' Harry cleared his throat; it was dry from panic and the smoke.

## 第28章 王子逃逸

他跌跌撞撞地朝燃烧的房子走去,只见一个巨大的身影扛着牙牙从火焰中走了出来。哈利欣慰地叫了一声,跪了下去。他的四肢都在发抖,浑身疼痛,每吸一口气都是一阵刺痛。

"你没事吧,哈利?你没事吧?说话呀,哈利……"

海格毛发浓密的大脸在哈利脑袋上方晃来晃去,把星星都遮住了。哈利能闻到木头和狗毛烧焦的味道。他伸出手摸了摸旁边牙牙温热而颤抖的身体,知道它还活着。

"我没事,"哈利喘息着说,"你呢?"

"我当然……那还要不了我的命。"

海格双手钳住哈利的双臂把他扶起来,力气那么大,哈利的双脚都悬空了。海格把哈利放回地上,他看到海格的一只眼睛下面有个很深的伤口,血正顺着脸颊往下流,伤口在迅速肿胀。

"应该把你房子的火灭掉,"哈利说,"咒语是清水如泉……"

"我知道差不多是那样。"海格嘟囔道。他举起一把冒着烟的粉红色花伞,说道:"清水如泉!"

一道水柱从伞顶飞出。哈利也举起魔杖——此时他觉得胳膊像是铅做的,也念道:"清水如泉!"他和海格把水浇在房子上,直到浇灭了最后一点火星。

"还不算太糟,"几分钟后,海格望着冒烟的废墟,满怀希望地说,"没有什么邓布利多摆不平的……"

一听到邓布利多的名字,哈利的胃里一阵剧烈的灼痛。沉默和寂静中,恐惧感在体内增长。

"海格……"

"听到他们过来的时候,我正在给护树罗锅包扎伤腿,"海格悲伤地说,仍然盯着他那烧毁的木屋,"都烧成枯树枝了,可怜的小东西们……"

"海格……"

"到底发生什么事了,哈利?我看到那些食死徒从城堡里跑下来,斯内普怎么和他们在一起?他去哪儿了——他是在追他们吗?"

"他……"哈利清了一下嗓子,惊吓和烟雾使得他喉咙发干,"海格,

## CHAPTER TWENTY-EIGHT    Flight of the Prince

'Hagrid, he killed ...'

'Killed?' said Hagrid loudly, staring down at Harry. 'Snape killed? What're yeh on abou', Harry?'

'Dumbledore,' said Harry. 'Snape killed ... Dumbledore.'

Hagrid simply looked at him, the little of his face that could be seen completely blank, uncomprehending.

'Dumbledore wha', Harry?'

'He's dead. Snape killed him ...'

'Don' say that,' said Hagrid roughly. 'Snape kill Dumbledore – don' be stupid, Harry. Wha's made yeh say tha'?'

'I saw it happen.'

'Yeh couldn' have.'

'I saw it, Hagrid.'

Hagrid shook his head; his expression was disbelieving but sympathetic and Harry knew that Hagrid thought he had sustained a blow to the head, that he was confused, perhaps by the after-effects of a jinx ...

'What musta happened was, Dumbledore musta told Snape ter go with them Death Eaters,' Hagrid said confidently. 'I suppose he's gotta keep his cover. Look, let's get yeh back up ter the school. Come on, Harry ...'

Harry did not attempt to argue or explain. He was still shaking uncontrollably. Hagrid would find out soon enough, too soon ... As they directed their steps back towards the castle, Harry saw that many of its windows were lit now: he could imagine, clearly, the scenes inside as people moved from room to room, telling each other that Death Eaters had got in, that the Mark was shining over Hogwarts, that somebody must have been killed ...

The oak front doors stood open ahead of them, light flooding out on to the drive and the lawn. Slowly, uncertainly, dressing-gowned people were creeping down the steps, looking around nervously for some sign of the Death Eaters who had fled into the night. Harry's eyes, however, were fixed upon the ground at the foot of the tallest tower. He imagined that he could see a black, huddled mass lying in the grass there, though he was really too far away to see anything of the sort. even as he stared wordlessly at the place where he thought Dumbledore's body must lie, however, he saw people beginning to move towards it.

## 第28章 王子逃逸

他杀了……"

"杀了？"海格低头瞪着哈利大声说，"斯内普杀人了？你在说什么，哈利？"

"邓布利多，"哈利说，"斯内普杀了……邓布利多。"

海格呆呆地看着哈利，毛发间露出的那一小块脸庞一片茫然，困惑不解。

"邓布利多怎么了，哈利？"

"他死了。斯内普杀了他……"

"别这么说，"海格粗声说，"斯内普杀了邓布利多——别说傻话，哈利。你是怎么了？"

"我看到的。"

"不可能。"

"我看到了，海格。"

海格摇着头，表情混合着怀疑和同情。哈利知道海格以为他是刚才被魔咒击中了头，现在还眩晕着说胡话呢……

"事情一定是这样，邓布利多准是让斯内普跟着那些食死徒，"海格充满信心地说，"我猜他不能暴露身份。现在，把你送回学校去吧。快，哈利……"

哈利也不再试图争辩或解释了。他仍然不由自主地瑟瑟发抖。海格很快就会知道的……当他们朝城堡走去时，哈利见到许多窗子里的灯都亮了。他可以清楚地想象里面的情景，大家奔走相告，说食死徒刚刚闯入学校，黑魔标记闪耀在霍格沃茨魔法学校的上空，一定有人被杀了……

橡木大门敞开在他们面前，灯光照在车道和草坪上。慢慢地，穿着睡衣的人群疑惑地走下楼梯，紧张地向四周张望，寻找在夜幕中逃走的食死徒留下的痕迹。然而哈利的眼睛却紧盯着那座最高的塔楼下的空地，想象着会看到一团黑色的身影躺在草地上，尽管他离那里还很远，什么也看不见。就在他一言不发地盯着邓布利多尸体应该在的地方时，他看见人群开始往那里移动。

## CHAPTER TWENTY-EIGHT    Flight of the Prince

'What're they all lookin' at?' said Hagrid, as he and Harry approached the castle front, Fang keeping as close as he could to their ankles. 'Wha's tha', lyin' on the grass?' Hagrid added sharply, heading now towards the foot of the Astronomy Tower, where a small crowd was congregating. 'See it, Harry? Righ' at the foot o' the Tower? Under where the Mark ... blimey ... yeh don' think someone got thrown –?'

Hagrid fell silent, the thought apparently too horrible to express aloud. Harry walked alongside him, feeling the aches and pains in his face and his legs where the various hexes of the last half an hour had hit him, though in an oddly detached way, as though somebody near him was suffering them. What was real and inescapable was the awful pressing feeling in his chest ...

He and Hagrid moved, dreamlike, through the murmuring crowd to the very front, where the dumbstruck students and teachers had left a gap.

Harry heard Hagrid's moan of pain and shock, but he did not stop; he walked slowly forwards until he reached the place where Dumbledore lay, and crouched down beside him.

Harry had known there was no hope from the moment that the Body-Bind Curse Dumbledore had placed upon him lifted, known that it could have happened only because its caster was dead; but there was still no preparation for seeing him here, spread-eagled, broken: the greatest wizard Harry had ever, or would ever, meet.

Dumbledore's eyes were closed; but for the strange angle of his arms and legs, he might have been sleeping. Harry reached out, straightened the half-moon spectacles upon the crooked nose and wiped a trickle of blood from the mouth with his own sleeve. Then he gazed down at the wise old face and tried to absorb the enormous and incomprehensible truth: that never again would Dumbledore speak to him, never again could he help ...

The crowd murmured behind Harry. After what seemed like a long time he became aware that he was kneeling upon something hard and looked down.

The locket they had managed to steal so many hours before had fallen out of Dumbledore's pocket. It had opened, perhaps due to the force with which it had hit the ground. And although he could not feel more shock or horror or sadness than he felt already, Harry knew, as he picked it up, that there was something wrong ...

He turned the locket over in his hands. This was neither as large as the locket he remembered seeing in the Pensieve, nor were there any markings

## 第28章 王子逃逸

"他们在看什么?"走近城堡时,海格问。牙牙紧跟在他们脚后。"那是什么,躺在草地上?"海格又急切地问道,直奔天文楼的脚下,那里正聚集起一小群人,"看见了吗,哈利?就在塔楼下,在标记下面……哎呀……你不觉得有人被摔——?"

海格不说话了,那想法显然太恐怖,无法说出来。哈利和他并肩前行,感到半小时前被魔咒击中的脸和腿还在隐隐作痛,但有一种奇怪的超脱感,好像那是近旁别人身上的疼痛。他真切感到并难以摆脱的是胸口那种压得透不过气来的可怕感觉……

他和海格像做梦一样穿过低语的人群,来到最前面,吓呆了的师生们在那儿让出了一个缺口。

哈利听见了海格痛苦和震惊的呻吟声,但他没有停住脚步,继续慢慢地向前移动,最后走到邓布利多躺着的地方,蹲在他的身旁。

当邓布利多施在他身上的全身束缚咒解开后,哈利就知道没有希望了,如果施魔咒的人不死,魔咒是不会自然解开的。但是哈利仍没有心理准备见到眼前这一幕:他今生今世遇到的、也许以后再也遇不到的最好的巫师,四肢摊开,手脚折断,横躺在眼前。

邓布利多双眼紧闭,从他四肢摊开的角度看像是在熟睡。哈利伸手扶正那歪鼻子上的半月形眼镜,用自己的袖子擦了一下他嘴角的血痕,然后低头凝视那张充满智慧的苍老的脸庞,努力去面对这个难以接受的事实:邓布利多再也不会对他说什么了,再也不可能帮他什么了……

哈利身后的人群在低语。过了好一会儿,哈利才觉得自己好像是跪在什么硬东西上,他低头看了看。

他们许多个小时之前偷到的挂坠盒从邓布利多的口袋里掉了出来。盒盖开着,可能是掉在地上时弹开的。哈利捡起小盒,尽管此时他震惊、恐惧、悲伤得无以复加,但他知道,这里面肯定有问题……

他把挂坠盒翻了过来。同他在冥想盆里看到的那个相比,这个既没有那个大,也缺少花纹标志,也没有斯莱特林特有的华丽的"S"标

upon it, no sign of the ornate S that was supposed to be Slytherin's mark. Moreover, there was nothing inside but for a scrap of folded parchment wedged tightly into the place where a portrait should have been.

Automatically, without really thinking about what he was doing, Harry pulled out the fragment of parchment, opened it, and read by the light of the many wands that had now been lit behind him:

> To the Dark Lord
> I know I will be dead long before you read this but I want you to know that it was I who discovered your secret.
> I have stolen the real Horcrux and intend to destroy it as soon as I can.
> I face death in the hope that when you meet your match, you will be mortal once more.
> R.A.B.

Harry neither knew nor cared what the message meant. Only one thing mattered: this was not a Horcrux. Dumbledore had weakened himself by drinking that terrible potion for nothing. Harry crumpled the parchment in his hand and his eyes burned with tears as behind him Fang began to howl.

## 第28章 王子逃逸

记。另外，里面除了在放肖像的地方紧紧地塞了一张折叠的羊皮纸外，别无他物。

哈利机械地、不假思索地取出那片羊皮纸，借着身后许多魔杖的亮光，打开来读道：

致黑魔头

在你读到这之前我早就死了
但我要你知道，是我发现了你的秘密。
我偷走了真正的魂器，并打算尽快销毁。
我甘冒一死，是希望你在遇到对手时
能被杀死。
R. A. B.

哈利既不懂也不关心那上面说的是什么意思。重要的只有一点：这不是伏地魔的魂器。邓布利多喝了那可怕的药水自废功力，全都是白费。身后的牙牙开始嗥叫，哈利把那片羊皮纸在手心揉作一团，泪水模糊了他的眼睛。

## CHAPTER TWENTY-NINE

# The Phoenix Lament

'C'mere, Harry ...'

'No.'

'You can' stay here, Harry ... come on, now ...'

'No.'

He did not want to leave Dumbledore's side, he did not want to move anywhere. Hagrid's hand on his shoulder was trembling. Then another voice said, 'Harry, come on.'

A much smaller and warmer hand had enclosed his and was pulling him upwards. He obeyed its pressure without really thinking about it. Only as he walked blindly back through the crowd did he realise, from a trace of flowery scent on the air, that it was Ginny who was leading him back into the castle. Incomprehensible voices battered him, sobs and shouts and wails stabbed the night, but Harry and Ginny walked on, back up the steps into the Entrance Hall: faces swam on the edges of Harry's vision, people were peering at him, whispering, wondering, and Gryffindor rubies glistened on the floor like drops of blood as they made their way towards the marble staircase.

'We're going to the hospital wing,' said Ginny.

'I'm not hurt,' said Harry.

'It's McGonagall's orders,' said Ginny. 'Everyone's up there, Ron and Hermione and Lupin and everyone –'

Fear stirred in Harry's chest again: he had forgotten the inert figures he had left behind.

'Ginny, who else is dead?'

'Don't worry, none of us.'

# 第29章

# 凤凰挽歌

"**走**吧,哈利……"
"不。"
"你不能待在这儿,哈利……走吧……"
"不。"

哈利不想离开邓布利多,不想到任何地方去。海格扶着哈利肩膀的手在颤抖。这时另一个声音说道:"哈利,走吧。"

一只小了许多的、更加温暖的手握住了哈利的手,把他向上拉。哈利糊里糊涂地顺势站了起来,直到他茫然地穿过人群,从空气中飘来了一丝花香,这才意识到是金妮一直在拉着他往城堡里走。听不清楚的话语从四面传来,抽泣、叫喊和哀号划破了夜空,但哈利和金妮继续向前,走上台阶,进入门厅。一张张面孔在哈利视线的边缘晃动,人们盯着他,窃窃私语,惊愕迷茫。他们向大理石楼梯走去,格兰芬多的红宝石散落在地上,闪耀着血滴一样的红光。

"我们去校医院。"金妮说。

"我没受伤。"哈利说。

"是麦格的命令,"金妮说,"大家都在那里,罗恩、赫敏、卢平和所有的人——"

恐惧再次从哈利的心中升起。他刚才几乎忘记那些一动不动的躯体了。

"金妮,还有谁死了?"

"别害怕,我们之中没有人死。"

## CHAPTER TWENTY-NINE    The Phoenix Lament

'But the Dark Mark – Malfoy said he stepped over a body –'

'He stepped over Bill, but it's all right, he's alive.'

There was something in her voice, however, that Harry knew boded ill.

'Are you sure?'

'Of course I'm sure ... he's a – a bit of a mess, that's all. Greyback attacked him. Madam Pomfrey says he won't – won't look the same any more ...' Ginny's voice trembled a little. 'We don't really know what the after-effects will be – I mean, Greyback being a werewolf, but not transformed at the time.'

'But the others ... there were other bodies on the ground ...'

'Neville's in the hospital wing, but Madam Pomfrey thinks he'll make a full recovery, and Professor Flitwick was knocked out, but he's all right, just a bit shaky. He insisted on going off to look after the Ravenclaws. And a Death Eater's dead, he got hit by a Killing Curse the huge blond one was firing off everywhere – Harry, if we hadn't had your Felix potion, I think we'd all have been killed, but everything seemed to just miss us –'

They had reached the hospital wing: pushing open the doors, Harry saw Neville lying, apparently asleep, in a bed near the door. Ron, Hermione, Luna, Tonks and Lupin were gathered around another bed near the far end of the ward. At the sound of the doors opening, they all looked up. Hermione ran to Harry and hugged him; Lupin moved forwards too, looking anxious.

'Are you all right, Harry?'

'I'm fine ... how's Bill?'

Nobody answered. Harry looked over Hermione's shoulder and saw an unrecognisable face lying on Bill's pillow, so badly slashed and ripped that he looked grotesque. Madam Pomfrey was dabbing at his wounds with some harsh-smelling green ointment. Harry remembered how Snape had mended Malfoy's *Sectumsempra* wounds so easily with his wand.

'Can't you fix them with a charm or something?' he asked the matron.

'No charm will work on these,' said Madam Pomfrey. 'I've tried everything I know, but there is no cure for werewolf bites.'

'But he wasn't bitten at the full moon,' said Ron, who was gazing down into his brother's face as though he could somehow force him to mend just by

## 第29章 凤凰挽歌

"但是黑魔标记——马尔福说他踩到了一具尸体——"

"他踩到了比尔,但比尔没事,还活着。"

然而,她的嗓音有点异样,哈利心知不妙。

"你确定?"

"我当然确定……他只是——伤得很重。芬里尔·格雷伯克袭击了他。庞弗雷女士说,他不会——他看上去不会再像从前一样了……"金妮的声音有点发抖,"我们不知道会有什么样的后遗症——我是说,芬里尔·格雷伯克是狼人,但他当时没有变成狼形。"

"其他人呢……当时地上还有别人……"

"纳威也在医院里,庞弗雷女士认为他会完全康复的。弗立维教授也被打昏了,但他没事,只是有一点虚弱。他坚持要去照顾拉文克劳的学生。死了一个食死徒,是被那个大块头金发食死徒射出的四处乱飞的杀戮咒击中的——哈利,如果我们没有喝你给的福灵剂,我想我们肯定都阵亡了,那些咒语好像都刚好差一点点,就是击不中我们——"

他们到了校医院,推开门,哈利看见纳威躺在门口的一张床上,明显是睡着了。罗恩、赫敏、卢娜、唐克斯和卢平围在最里面的一张床边。听到开门声,他们都抬起头。赫敏跑了过来,一把抱住哈利。卢平也满脸忧虑地走了过来。

"你没事吧,哈利?"

"我没事……比尔怎么样?"

没有人回答。哈利越过赫敏的肩膀看到比尔的枕头上躺着一张皮开肉绽、奇形怪状、无法辨认的脸。庞弗雷女士正在用一种刺鼻的绿色药膏擦拭他的伤口。哈利想起斯内普轻挥魔杖,马尔福被神锋无影切开的伤口就抚平了。

"你不可以用一个魔咒或什么把他治好吗?"他问庞弗雷女士。

"没有魔咒可以治疗这些创伤,"庞弗雷女士说,"我已经试过我知道的所有魔法,没有一种可以治愈狼人咬的伤口。"

"但他不是在满月时被狼人咬的呀?"罗恩说,他低头凝视着他哥哥的脸,好像能用目光使他的伤口愈合似的,"芬里尔·格雷伯克没有

## CHAPTER TWENTY-NINE  The Phoenix Lament

staring. 'Greyback hadn't transformed, so surely Bill won't be a – a real –?'

He looked uncertainly at Lupin.

'No, I don't think that Bill will be a true werewolf,' said Lupin, 'but that does not mean that there won't be some contamination. Those are cursed wounds. They are unlikely ever to heal fully, and – and Bill might have some wolfish characteristics from now on.'

'Dumbledore might know something that'd work, though,' Ron said. 'Where is he? Bill fought those maniacs on Dumbledore's orders, Dumbledore owes him, he can't leave him in this state –'

'Ron – Dumbledore's dead,' said Ginny.

'No!' Lupin looked wildly from Ginny to Harry, as though hoping the latter might contradict her, but when Harry did not, Lupin collapsed into a chair beside Bill's bed, his hands over his face. Harry had never seen Lupin lose control before; he felt as though he was intruding upon something private, indecent; he turned away and caught Ron's eye instead, exchanging in silence a look that confirmed what Ginny had said.

'How did he die?' whispered Tonks. 'How did it happen?'

'Snape killed him,' said Harry. 'I was there, I saw it. We arrived back on the Astronomy Tower because that's where the Mark was ... Dumbledore was ill, he was weak, but I think he realised it was a trap when we heard footsteps running up the stairs. He immobilised me, I couldn't do anything, I was under the Invisibility Cloak – and then Malfoy came through the door and Disarmed him –'

Hermione clapped her hands to her mouth, and Ron groaned. Luna's mouth trembled.

'– more Death Eaters arrived – and then Snape – and Snape did it. The Avada Kedavra.' Harry couldn't go on.

Madam Pomfrey burst into tears. Nobody paid her any attention except Ginny, who whispered, 'Shh! Listen!'

Gulping, Madam Pomfrey pressed her fingers to her mouth, her eyes wide. Somewhere out in the darkness, a phoenix was singing in a way Harry had never heard before: a stricken lament of terrible beauty. And Harry felt, as he had felt about phoenix song before, that the music was inside him, not without: it was his own grief turned magically to song that echoed across the

## 第29章 凤凰挽歌

变成狼形，所以比尔肯定不会变成————一个真的——"

他有点不确定地看着卢平。

"对，我想比尔不会变成真正的狼人，"卢平说，"但并不是说一点变化都没有。这些是带魔咒的伤口。它们不可能彻底愈合，而且——而且比尔今后可能会有些狼人的特征。"

"邓布利多可能知道该怎么办，"罗恩说，"他在哪儿？比尔是听从他的命令迎战那些疯子的，邓布利多要对他负责，他不能就这样放手不管——"

"罗恩，邓布利多死了。"金妮说。

"不可能！"卢平狂乱地把目光从金妮转向了哈利，希望他能否认，但哈利没有，卢平瘫坐在比尔床边的椅子上，双手捂着脸。哈利从没见卢平失控过。哈利觉得自己好像看到了什么不体面的隐私，他转过身，却撞到了罗恩的目光。他们默默地交换眼神，证实了金妮所说的话。

"他是怎么死的？"唐克斯低声问，"是怎么发生的？"

"斯内普杀了他，"哈利说，"我当时在场，亲眼看到的。我们一起回到天文塔，因为黑魔标记就在那儿……邓布利多病了，他很虚弱，但我认为，当我们听到有人跑上楼来时，他已经意识到那是一个圈套。邓布利多用魔咒把我定住了，我什么都做不了，我穿着隐形衣——然后马尔福从门口进来，缴了他的武器——"

赫敏猛然捂住嘴巴，罗恩叹息着，卢娜的嘴唇在打战。

"——来了更多的食死徒——然后斯内普——斯内普下了手，阿瓦达索命咒。"哈利说不下去了。

庞弗雷女士突然泪如雨下。别人都没注意到她，只有金妮低声道："嘘——听！"

庞弗雷女士用手捂住嘴，倒吸一口气，眼睛睁得大大的。在外面黑暗中的某个地方，凤凰正在用哈利从未听过的方式唱着令人动容的凄婉挽歌。像以前听凤凰的歌声一样，哈利感觉到这首挽歌的曲子是在他的脑海里，而不是在现实中，仿佛是他自己的悲伤化作了挽歌，

## CHAPTER TWENTY-NINE    The Phoenix Lament

grounds and through the castle windows.

How long they all stood there, listening, he did not know, nor why it seemed to ease their pain a little to listen to the sound of their mourning, but it felt like a long time later that the hospital door opened again and Professor McGonagall entered the ward. Like all the rest, she bore marks of the recent battle: there were grazes on her face and her robes were ripped.

'Molly and Arthur are on their way,' she said, and the spell of the music was broken: everyone roused themselves as though coming out of trances, turning again to look at Bill, or else to rub their own eyes, shake their heads. 'Harry, what happened? According to Hagrid you were with Professor Dumbledore when he – when it happened. He says Professor Snape was involved in some –'

'Snape killed Dumbledore,' said Harry.

She stared at him for a moment, then swayed alarmingly; Madam Pomfrey, who seemed to have pulled herself together, ran forwards, conjuring a chair from thin air, which she pushed under McGonagall.

'Snape,' repeated McGonagall faintly, falling into the chair. 'We all wondered ... but he trusted ... always ... *Snape* ... I can't believe it ...'

'Snape was a highly accomplished Occlumens,' said Lupin, his voice uncharacteristically harsh. 'We always knew that.'

'But Dumbledore swore he was on our side!' whispered Tonks. 'I always thought Dumbledore must know something about Snape that we didn't ...'

'He always hinted that he had an iron-clad reason for trusting Snape,' muttered Professor McGonagall, now dabbing at the corners of her leaking eyes with a tartan-edged handkerchief. 'I mean ... with Snape's history ... of course people were bound to wonder ... but Dumbledore told me explicitly that Snape's repentance was absolutely genuine ... wouldn't hear a word against him!'

'I'd love to know what Snape told him to convince him,' said Tonks.

'I know,' said Harry, and they all turned to stare at him. 'Snape passed Voldemort the information that made Voldemort hunt down my mum and dad. Then Snape told Dumbledore he hadn't realised what he was doing, he was really sorry he'd done it, sorry that they were dead.'

## 第29章 凤凰挽歌

在校园和城堡的窗户间回荡。

哈利不知道他们站在那里听了多久，也不知道为什么他们听着这哀悼之歌会得到一丝安慰，只感觉过了很久，麦格教授才推门走进病房。同其他人一样，她身上也有战斗后的痕迹，脸上有些许擦伤，长袍也被撕破了。

"莫丽和亚瑟正向这边赶来。"她说，音乐的魔力被打断了，大家好像从恍惚中惊醒，都转过身去看着比尔，或是揉揉眼睛、摇摇头。"哈利，怎么回事？听海格说你当时是和邓布利多教授在一起的，当他——当那件事发生的时候。海格还说斯内普教授好像参与了什么——"

"斯内普杀了邓布利多。"哈利说。

麦格盯着他愣了一会儿，然后令人揪心地摇晃起来。庞弗雷女士已经冷静下来，她向前跑了几步，用魔法变出一把椅子，放在了麦格的身后。

"斯内普，"麦格虚弱地说，跌坐在椅子上，"我们都怀疑……但邓布利多相信……一直……斯内普……简直令人难以置信……"

"斯内普是很高超的大脑封闭大师，"卢平说，他的声音刺耳，与平时大不一样，"这是我们都知道的事实。"

"但是邓布利多发誓说他是我们这边的人！"唐克斯轻声道，"我一直认为邓布利多一定知道斯内普的一些情况，而我们都不知道……"

"他总是暗示他有牢不可破的理由信任斯内普，"麦格教授喃喃道，一边用格子花边的手帕擦着不断流泪的眼角，"我是说……考虑到斯内普的过去……大家当然会对他存有怀疑……但是邓布利多明确地告诉我，斯内普的忏悔绝对是发自内心的……他不想听到一句说斯内普的坏话！"

"我倒想知道斯内普是怎么说服他的。"唐克斯说。

"我知道，"哈利说，大家都转过身盯着他，"斯内普透露消息给伏地魔，导致伏地魔追杀我的父母。然后斯内普告诉邓布利多，他当时没有意识到自己那样做的后果，他十分抱歉走漏了消息，他对于他们的死感到遗憾。"

## CHAPTER TWENTY-NINE  The Phoenix Lament

'And Dumbledore believed that?' said Lupin incredulously. 'Dumbledore believed Snape was sorry James was dead? Snape *hated* James ...'

'And he didn't think my mother was worth a damn, either,' said Harry, 'because she was Muggle-born ... "Mudblood", he called her ...'

Nobody asked how Harry knew this. All of them seemed to be lost in horrified shock, trying to digest the monstrous truth of what had happened.

'This is all my fault,' said Professor McGonagall suddenly. She looked disorientated, twisting her wet handkerchief in her hands. 'My fault. I sent Filius to fetch Snape tonight, I actually sent for him to come and help us! If I hadn't alerted Snape to what was going on, he might never have joined forces with the Death Eaters. I don't think he knew they were there before Filius told him, I don't think he knew they were coming.'

'It isn't your fault, Minerva,' said Lupin firmly. 'We all wanted more help, we were glad to think Snape was on his way ...'

'So when he arrived at the fight, he joined in on the Death Eaters' side?' asked Harry, who wanted every detail of Snape's duplicity and infamy, feverishly collecting more reasons to hate him, to swear vengeance.

'I don't know exactly how it happened,' said Professor McGonagall distractedly. 'It's all so confusing ... Dumbledore had told us that he would be leaving the school for a few hours and that we were to patrol the corridors just in case ... Remus, Bill and Nymphadora were to join us ... and so we patrolled. All seemed quiet. Every secret passageway out of the school was covered. We knew nobody could fly in. There were powerful enchantments on every entrance into the castle. I still don't know how the Death Eaters can possibly have entered ...'

'I do,' said Harry, and he explained, briefly, about the pair of Vanishing Cabinets and the magical pathway they formed. 'So they got in through the Room of Requirement.'

Almost against his will he glanced from Ron to Hermione, both of whom looked devastated.

'I messed up, Harry,' said Ron bleakly. 'We did like you told us: we checked the Marauder's Map and we couldn't see Malfoy on it, so we thought he must be in the Room of Requirement, so me, Ginny and Neville went to keep watch on it ... but Malfoy got past us.'

## 第29章 凤凰挽歌

"邓布利多就相信他了?"卢平难以置信地问,"邓布利多就相信了斯内普对詹姆的死感到抱歉?斯内普一直憎恨詹姆……"

"而且他认为我妈妈也一钱不值,"哈利说,"因为她是麻瓜生的……他叫她'泥巴种'……"

没有人问哈利怎么会知道这些的,好像大家都迷失在恐怖和震惊之中,正试图接受这些已经发生的荒诞事实。

"这都是我的错,"麦格教授突然说道,她看上去不知所措,双手拧着湿乎乎的手帕,"是我的错,是我让弗立维晚上去叫斯内普的,我竟然还请斯内普来帮我们!如果我没有通知斯内普这里发生了什么事,他可能不会加入到食死徒那边。我认为在弗立维告诉他之前,斯内普并不知道食死徒在这里,不知道他们会来。"

"不是你的错,米勒娃,"卢平肯定地说,"当时我们都需要更多的帮助,知道斯内普会来我们挺高兴的……"

"那么他到了之后,是直接加入食死徒一边的吗?"哈利问道,他想知道斯内普奸诈和罪恶的每一个细节,拼命搜集更多仇恨他的理由,发誓要报仇。

"我不知道具体是怎么发生的,"麦格教授心烦意乱地说,"一切都令人迷惑……邓布利多说他要离开学校一会儿,让我们在走廊巡逻以备不测……莱姆斯、比尔和尼法朵拉都加入进来了……于是我们在一起巡视。一切似乎都很平静。所有通往校外的秘密通道都被堵住了,我们知道没有人可以飞进来,进入城堡的每一个入口都罩着强力的魔法。我仍然没有弄明白食死徒是怎么进来的……"

"我知道,"哈利说,他简单地说了那一对消失柜组成的魔法通道,"所以他们是从有求必应屋溜进来的。"

他不由自主地瞟了罗恩和赫敏一眼,他们俩都显得很狼狈。

"是我搞砸了,哈利,"罗恩沮丧地说,"我们照你说的做了,检查了活点地图,没有看到马尔福在上面,我们想他一定在有求必应屋,所以我、金妮和纳威就跑过去守在那里……但是却让马尔福给溜过去了。"

## CHAPTER TWENTY-NINE    The Phoenix Lament

'He came out of the Room about an hour after we started keeping watch,' said Ginny. 'He was on his own, clutching that awful shrivelled arm –'

'His Hand of Glory,' said Ron. 'Gives light only to the holder, remember?'

'Anyway,' Ginny went on, 'he must have been checking whether the coast was clear to let the Death Eaters out, because the moment he saw us he threw something into the air and it all went pitch black –'

'– Peruvian Instant Darkness Powder,' said Ron bitterly. 'Fred and George's. I'm going to be having a word with them about who they let buy their products.'

'We tried everything – *Lumos, Incendio,*' said Ginny. 'Nothing would penetrate the darkness; all we could do was grope our way out of the corridor again, and meanwhile we could hear people rushing past us. Obviously Malfoy could see because of that Hand thing and was guiding them, but we didn't dare use any curses or anything in case we hit each other, and by the time we'd reached a corridor that was light, they'd gone.'

'Luckily,' said Lupin hoarsely, 'Ron, Ginny and Neville ran into us almost immediately and told us what had happened. We found the Death Eaters minutes later, heading in the direction of the Astronomy Tower. Malfoy obviously hadn't expected more people to be on the watch; he seemed to have exhausted his supply of Darkness Powder, at any rate. A fight broke out, they scattered and we gave chase. One of them, Gibbon, broke away and headed up the Tower stairs –'

'To set off the Mark?' asked Harry.

'He must have done, yes, they must have arranged that before they left the Room of Requirement,' said Lupin. 'But I don't think Gibbon liked the idea of waiting up there alone for Dumbledore, because he came running back downstairs to rejoin the fight and was hit by a Killing Curse that just missed me.'

'So if Ron was watching the Room of Requirement with Ginny and Neville,' said Harry, turning to Hermione, 'were you –?'

'Outside Snape's office, yes,' whispered Hermione, her eyes sparkling with tears, 'with Luna. We hung around for ages outside it and nothing happened ... we didn't know what was going on upstairs, Ron had taken the Marauder's Map ... it was nearly midnight when Professor Flitwick came sprinting down into the dungeons. He was shouting about Death Eaters in

"我们守了大约一个钟头,他从那个屋里出来了,"金妮说,"独自一人,抓着那只恶心的枯手——"

"他的'光荣之手',"罗恩说,"只有拿着它的人才能看见亮光,记得吗?"

"不管怎样,"金妮接着说,"他一定是在检查食死徒溜进来是否安全,因为他一看到我们就向空中扔了个什么东西,顿时漆黑一团——"

"——从秘鲁进口的隐身烟幕弹,"罗恩痛苦地说,"是弗雷德和乔治的。我倒要问问他们都是在跟什么人做生意。"

"我们试了所有的办法——荧光闪烁,火焰熊熊,"金妮说,"没有东西能穿透那一片黑暗,我们只好从走廊里再摸索着出来,同时还听到有人从旁边冲了过去。很显然是因为马尔福有光荣之手,可以看见并引导他们,但我们不敢施任何魔法,怕误伤了自己人。当我们走到一个有灯光的走廊时,他们都跑光了。"

"幸运的是,"卢平嘶哑地说道,"罗恩、金妮和纳威几乎是马上就碰到了我们,并且告诉我们发生了什么事情。几分钟后我们发现那些食死徒正在奔向天文塔。马尔福显然没有料到有这么多人放哨,然而他似乎用完了他的隐身烟幕弹。战斗爆发了,他们分散开来,我们上去追击。一个叫吉本的食死徒却突围跑掉了,朝着塔楼的楼梯奔去——"

"去放出黑魔标记?"哈利问道。

"对,肯定是这样,他们准是在离开有求必应屋前就安排好的,"卢平说,"但我想吉本不愿意一个人待在那里等邓布利多,因为他又返回楼下加入了战斗,结果被一个没打到我的杀戮咒击中了。"

"罗恩在和金妮、纳威一起盯着有求必应屋,"哈利转向赫敏说,"那你在——?"

"在斯内普的办公室外面,是啊,"赫敏轻声道,眼眶里泪光闪耀,"和卢娜一起。我们在外面待了很久,什么也没有发生……我们不知道楼上发生了什么,活点地图在罗恩那儿……将近午夜的时候,弗立维教授闯进地下教室,大叫着城堡里有食死徒,他直接冲进斯内普的办公

## CHAPTER TWENTY-NINE  The Phoenix Lament

the castle, I don't think he really registered that Luna and I were there at all, he just burst his way into Snape's office and we heard him saying that Snape had to go back with him and help and then we heard a loud thump and Snape came hurtling out of his room and he saw us and – and –'

'What?' Harry urged her.

'I was so stupid, Harry!' said Hermione in a high-pitched whisper. 'He said Professor Flitwick had collapsed and that we should go and take care of him while he – while he went to help fight the Death Eaters –'

She covered her face in shame and continued to talk into her fingers, so that her voice was muffled.

'We went into his office to see if we could help Professor Flitwick and found him unconscious on the floor ... and, oh, it's so obvious now, Snape must have Stupefied Flitwick, but we didn't realise, Harry, we didn't realise, we just let Snape go!'

'It's not your fault,' said Lupin firmly. 'Hermione, had you not obeyed Snape and got out of the way, he would probably have killed you and Luna.'

'So then he came upstairs,' said Harry, who in his mind's eye was watching Snape running up the marble staircase, his black robes billowing behind him as ever, pulling his wand from under his cloak as he ascended, 'and he found the place where you were all fighting ...'

'We were in trouble, we were losing,' said Tonks in a low voice. 'Gibbon was down, but the rest of the Death Eaters seemed ready to fight to the death. Neville had been hurt, Bill had been savaged by Greyback ... it was all dark ... curses flying everywhere ... the Malfoy boy had vanished, he must have slipped past, up the stairs to the Tower ... then more of them ran after him, but one of them blocked the stairs behind them with some kind of curse ... Neville ran at it and got thrown up into the air –'

'None of us could break through,' said Ron, 'and that massive Death Eater was still firing off jinxes all over the place, they were bouncing off the walls and barely missing us ...'

'And then Snape was there,' said Tonks, 'and then he wasn't –'

'I saw him running towards us, but that huge Death Eater's jinx just missed me right afterwards and I ducked and lost track of things,' said Ginny.

'I saw him run straight through the cursed barrier as though it wasn't there,'

## 第29章 凤凰挽歌

室,我想他根本就没有注意到我和卢娜在那里。我们听到他说斯内普必须和他一起回去帮忙,然后听到一声响亮的重击声,斯内普奔了出来。他看到了我们,然后——然后——"

"什么?"哈利催促着她。

"我真是太蠢了,哈利!"赫敏用尖细的嗓音小声说,"他说弗立维教授瘫倒了,我们应该进去照看,他要去——他要去帮助迎战食死徒——"

她羞愧地捂着脸,从指缝里接着说下去,所以声音有点发闷。

"我们进了他的办公室,看能不能帮助弗立维教授,只见他昏迷在地板上……现在看来很明显,一定是斯内普对弗立维使了昏迷咒,但我们当时没有意识到,哈利。我们没有意识到,我们竟然让斯内普走了!"

"不是你们的错,"卢平肯定地说,"赫敏,如果你们没有听从斯内普的话闪开的话,他可能已经杀了你和卢娜。"

"那么他就上了楼,"哈利说,他仿佛看见斯内普顺着大理石楼梯往上跑,黑色的长袍像往常一样在身后飘动,边跑边从袍子里抽出魔杖,"然后他就找到了你们战斗的地方……"

"我们遇到了麻烦,我们正处于下风。"唐克斯小声地说,"吉本倒下了,但其他食死徒似乎要血战到底。纳威受了伤,比尔遭到了芬里尔·格雷伯克的猛烈攻击……当时漆黑一团……魔咒四处乱飞……那个叫马尔福的男孩不见了,他一定是溜了,顺着楼梯上了塔楼……然后更多的食死徒跟在他后面,其中有人施了一个魔咒封住了他们身后的楼梯……纳威直冲过去,被弹向了空中——"

"我们没有人能够突破魔障,"罗恩说,"那个大块头食死徒仍然朝四周乱施魔咒,从墙上反弹回来的魔咒都差一点儿击中了我们……"

"然后斯内普出现了,"唐克斯说,"然后他又不见了——"

"我看到他冲着我们跑过来,但是恰好大块头食死徒的一个魔咒打来,我躲开魔咒后,斯内普就不见了。"金妮说。

"我看到他直接跑过了那道魔障,好像魔障不存在似的。"卢平说,

## CHAPTER TWENTY-NINE    The Phoenix Lament

said Lupin. 'I tried to follow him but was thrown back just like Neville ...'

'He must have known a spell we didn't,' whispered McGonagall. 'After all – he was the Defence Against the Dark Arts teacher ... I just assumed that he was in a hurry to chase after the Death Eaters who'd escaped up to the Tower ...'

'He was,' said Harry savagely, 'but to help them, not to stop them ... and I'll bet you had to have a Dark Mark to get through that barrier – so what happened when he came back down?'

'Well, the big Death Eater had just fired off a hex that caused half the ceiling to fall in, and also broke the curse blocking the stairs,' said Lupin. 'We all ran forwards – those of us who were still standing, anyway – and then Snape and the boy emerged out of the dust – obviously, none of us attacked them –'

'We just let them pass,' said Tonks in a hollow voice, 'we thought they were being chased by the Death Eaters – and next thing, the other Death Eaters and Greyback were back and we were fighting again – I thought I heard Snape shout something, but I don't know what –'

'He shouted, "It's over,"' said Harry. 'He'd done what he'd meant to do.'

They all fell silent. Fawkes's lament was still echoing over the dark grounds outside. As the music reverberated upon the air, unbidden, unwelcome thoughts slunk into Harry's mind ... had they taken Dumbledore's body from the foot of the Tower yet? What would happen to it next? Where would it rest? He clenched his fists tightly in his pockets. He could feel the small cold lump of the fake Horcrux against the knuckles of his right hand.

The doors of the hospital wing burst open, making them all jump: Mr and Mrs Weasley were striding up the ward, Fleur just behind them, her beautiful face terrified.

'Molly – Arthur –' said Professor McGonagall, jumping up and hurrying to greet them. 'I am so sorry –'

'Bill,' whispered Mrs Weasley, darting past Professor McGonagall as she caught sight of Bill's mangled face. 'Oh, *Bill*!'

Lupin and Tonks had got up hastily and retreated so that Mr and Mrs Weasley could get nearer to the bed. Mrs Weasley bent over her son and pressed her lips to his bloody forehead.

'You said Greyback attacked him?' Mr Weasley asked Professor

## 第29章 凤凰挽歌

"我试图跟在他后面冲过去,结果和纳威一样被扔到了空中……"

"他肯定熟悉一个我们不知道的魔咒,"麦格轻声道,"毕竟——他是黑魔法防御术的教师……我当时想他是忙着去追赶逃上塔楼的食死徒……"

"他是,"哈利狂怒地说,"但是他是追过去帮助他们,而不是阻止他们……我敢打赌有黑魔标记才能通过那道魔障——那么,他从楼上下来之后又发生了什么?"

"嗯,当时大块头食死徒恰好施了一个魔咒,砸下来半个天花板,也把挡着楼梯口的魔障给破了,"卢平说,"我们——我们中间还没倒下的都冲上前去。这时斯内普和那男孩出现在灰尘中——显然,我们谁也没有攻击他们——"

"就让他们通过了,"唐克斯用空洞的声音说道,"我们以为他们正被食死徒追赶——接着,别的食死徒和芬里尔·格雷伯克回来了,我们又打了起来——我好像听到斯内普喊了一声,但不知道他喊的是什么——"

"他大叫道:'结束了。'"哈利说,"就是说,他完成了他要做的事。"

大家都沉默了。福克斯的挽歌仍在外面漆黑的场地上回荡。音乐声在空气里颤动着,一个突如其来的不舒服的想法涌进了哈利的脑海……他们已经把邓布利多的遗体从塔楼底下收走了吗?遗体要怎么处理呢?邓布利多会在哪里安息呢?他的拳头在口袋里攥得更紧了,他能感觉到那个小小的、冰凉的假魂器紧贴在他右手的关节上。

医院的门突然被撞开,大家都吓了一跳。韦斯莱夫妇大踏步走进来,芙蓉紧跟在后面,她美丽的脸庞上满是恐惧。

"莫丽——亚瑟——"麦格教授急忙跳起来跟他们打招呼,"我很抱歉——"

"比尔,"韦斯莱夫人轻声道,她看到比尔血肉模糊的脸后,疾步从麦格教授旁边走过,"哦,比尔!"

卢平和唐克斯迅速站起来,朝后退了几步,让韦斯莱夫妇走近床边。韦斯莱夫人弯下身,轻吻着儿子血染的额头。

"你是说芬里尔·格雷伯克攻击了他?"韦斯莱先生担忧地问麦格

## CHAPTER TWENTY-NINE    The Phoenix Lament

McGonagall distractedly. 'But he hadn't transformed? So what does that mean? What will happen to Bill?'

'We don't yet know,' said Professor McGonagall, looking helplessly at Lupin.

'There will probably be some contamination, Arthur,' said Lupin. 'It is an odd case, possibly unique ... we don't know what his behaviour might be like when he wakes up ...'

Mrs Weasley took the nasty-smelling ointment from Madam Pomfrey and began dabbing at Bill's wounds.

'And Dumbledore ...' said Mr Weasley. 'Minerva, is it true ... is he really ...?'

As Professor McGonagall nodded, Harry felt Ginny move beside him and looked at her. Her slightly narrowed eyes were fixed upon Fleur, who was gazing down at Bill with a frozen expression on her face.

'Dumbledore gone,' whispered Mr Weasley, but Mrs Weasley had eyes only for her eldest son; she began to sob, tears falling on to Bill's mutilated face.

'Of course, it doesn't matter how he looks ... it's not r – really important ... but he was a very handsome little b – boy ... always very handsome ... and he was g – going to be married!'

'And what do you mean by zat?' said Fleur suddenly and loudly. 'What do you mean, 'e was *going* to be married?'

Mrs Weasley raised her tear-stained face, looking startled.

'Well – only that –'

'You theenk Bill will not wish to marry me any more?' demanded Fleur. 'You theenk, because of these bites, he will not love me?'

'No, that's not what I –'

'Because 'e will!' said Fleur, drawing herself up to her full height and throwing back her long mane of silver hair. 'It would take more zan a werewolf to stop Bill loving me!'

'Well, yes, I'm sure,' said Mrs Weasley, 'but I thought perhaps – given how – how he –'

'You thought I would not weesh to marry him? Or per'aps, you 'oped?' said Fleur, her nostrils flaring. 'What do I care how 'e looks? I am good-looking enough for both of us, I theenk! All these scars show is zat my husband is brave! and I shall do zat!' she added fiercely, pushing Mrs Weasley

## 第29章 凤凰挽歌

教授,"'芬里尔·格雷伯克当时没有变成狼形'?这是什么意思?比尔会怎么样?"

"我们现在还不知道。"麦格教授回答道,一边无助地看着卢平。

"可能会有一些变化,亚瑟,"卢平说,"这种情况很少见,可能很特殊……我们还不知道他醒来后会变得怎样……"

韦斯莱夫人从庞弗雷女士手中拿过那个难闻的药膏,开始往比尔的伤口上涂抹。

"那么邓布利多……"韦斯莱先生问,"米勒娃,是真的吗……他真的……?"

麦格教授点头时,哈利察觉金妮走到了他身边,她眯起眼睛盯着芙蓉,后者正低头凝视比尔,脸上一副惊呆了的表情。

"邓布利多死了。"韦斯莱先生轻声道,但韦斯莱夫人眼睛一直盯着她的长子。她开始抽噎,眼泪滴在比尔满是伤痕的脸上。

"当然,长相并不重要……并不真——的重要……但他一直是个英俊的——孩子……一直很英俊……他本来打——算要结婚的!"

"什么意思?"芙蓉突然大声地说,"你是什么意思,他本来打算要结婚的?"

韦斯莱夫人抬起满是泪痕的面庞,很是惊讶。

"我——只是说——"

"你认为比尔不再想和我结婚了?"芙蓉质问道,"你认为,因为这些伤口,他就会不爱我了?"

"不,我不是那——"

"他不会的!"芙蓉说,同时挺直了腰,把银色的长发向后一甩,"一个狼人是阻止不了比尔爱我的!"

"嗯,对,我也相信,"韦斯莱夫人说,"但我想可能——考虑到他——他——"

"你认为我会不想和他结婚?或者你希望我不想和他结婚?"芙蓉说,鼻孔翕动,"我只是在乎他的长相吗?我认为我一个人的美貌对我们俩来说已经足够了!所有这些伤疤说明我的丈夫是勇敢的!我来!"

## CHAPTER TWENTY-NINE  The Phoenix Lament

aside and snatching the ointment from her.

Mrs Weasley fell back against her husband and watched Fleur mopping up Bill's wounds with a most curious expression upon her face. Nobody said anything; Harry did not dare move. Like everybody else, he was waiting for the explosion.

'Our Great auntie Muriel,' said Mrs Weasley after a long pause, 'has a very beautiful tiara – goblin-made – which I am sure I could persuade her to lend you for the wedding. She is very fond of Bill, you know, and it would look lovely with your hair.'

'Thank you,' said Fleur stiffly. 'I am sure zat will be lovely.'

And then – Harry did not quite see how it happened – both women were crying and hugging each other. Completely bewildered, wondering whether the world had gone mad, he turned round: Ron looked as stunned as Harry felt and Ginny and Hermione were exchanging startled looks.

'You see!' said a strained voice. Tonks was glaring at Lupin. 'She still wants to marry him, even though he's been bitten! She doesn't care!'

'It's different,' said Lupin, barely moving his lips and looking suddenly tense. 'Bill will not be a full werewolf. The cases are completely –'

'But I don't care either, I don't care!' said Tonks, seizing the front of Lupin's robes and shaking them. 'I've told you a million times ...'

And the meaning of Tonks's Patronus and her mouse-coloured hair, and the reason she had come running to find Dumbledore when she had heard a rumour someone had been attacked by Greyback, all suddenly became clear to Harry; it had not been Sirius that Tonks had fallen in love with after all ...

'And I've told *you* a million times,' said Lupin, refusing to meet her eyes, staring at the floor, 'that I am too old for you, too poor ... too dangerous ...'

'I've said all along you're taking a ridiculous line on this, Remus,' said Mrs Weasley over Fleur's shoulder as she patted her on the back.

'I am not being ridiculous,' said Lupin steadily. 'Tonks deserves somebody young and whole.'

'But she wants you,' said Mr Weasley, with a small smile. 'And after all, Remus, young and whole men do not necessarily remain so.' He gestured sadly at his son, lying between them.

## 第29章 凤凰挽歌

她气势汹汹地加了一句,一把推开韦斯莱夫人,从她手中抢过药膏。

韦斯莱夫人跌到了丈夫身上,看着芙蓉大把地给比尔抹药膏,脸上带着古怪的表情。没有人说话。哈利动都不敢动,像所有的人一样,他等待着一场火山爆发。

"我们的穆丽尔姨妈,"停了很久之后,韦斯莱夫人说,"有一个很漂亮的头冠——妖精做的——我相信我能说服她借给你在婚礼上用,她很喜欢比尔,你知道。那头冠戴在你头发上会很美丽的。"

"谢谢你,"芙蓉生硬地说,"我相信会很美丽的。"

突然——哈利还没有反应过来是怎么回事——两个女人抱头痛哭。哈利被彻底搞糊涂了,转过身去,怀疑这个世界是不是疯了。罗恩看起来和哈利一样惊讶。金妮和赫敏也在交换着惊讶的眼神。

"你看!"一个不自然的声音说道,唐克斯瞪着卢平,"她仍然想和他结婚,尽管他被咬过了!她不在乎!"

"这不一样。"卢平嘴唇几乎没动地说,他突然显得很紧张,"比尔不会变成一个完全的狼人。这件事完全——"

"但我也不在乎,我不在乎!"唐克斯说,抓住卢平的袍襟不停地摇着,"我告诉过你一百万次了……"

唐克斯守护神的意义和她灰褐色的头发,还有她听说有人被芬里尔·格雷伯克攻击后跑来找邓布利多,所有这一切哈利突然都明白了。唐克斯爱的不是小天狼星……

"我告诉过你一百万次了,"卢平躲避着唐克斯的目光,低头盯着地板说,"我年纪太大,不适合你,也太穷……太危险了……"

"我也是一直在说,你这个理由太荒谬了,莱姆斯。"韦斯莱夫人轻轻拍着芙蓉的背,从芙蓉的肩上冲着他说。

"我一点都不荒谬,"卢平坚定地说,"唐克斯应该有一个年轻而健全的人爱她。"

"但是她想要你,"韦斯莱先生说,同时轻轻地一笑,"再说,莱姆斯,年轻而健全的男人不一定能永远保持那样。"他悲伤地指了指他的儿子。

## CHAPTER TWENTY-NINE   The Phoenix Lament

'This is ... not the moment to discuss it,' said Lupin, avoiding everybody's eyes as he looked around distractedly. 'Dumbledore is dead ...'

'Dumbledore would have been happier than anybody to think that there was a little more love in the world,' said Professor McGonagall curtly, just as the hospital doors opened again and Hagrid walked in.

The little of his face that was not obscured by hair or beard was soaking and swollen; he was shaking with tears, a vast spotted handkerchief in his hand.

'I've ... I've done it, Professor,' he choked. 'M – moved him. Professor Sprout's got the kids back in bed. Professor Flitwick's lyin' down but he says he'll be all right in a jiffy, an' Professor Slughorn says the Ministry's bin informed.'

'Thank you, Hagrid,' said Professor McGonagall, standing up at once and turning to look at the group around Bill's bed. 'I shall have to see the Ministry when they get here. Hagrid, please tell the Heads of House – Slughorn can represent Slytherin – that I want to see them in my office forthwith. I would like you to join us, too.'

As Hagrid nodded, turned and shuffled out of the room again, she looked down at Harry.

'Before I meet them I would like a quick word with you, Harry. If you'll come with me ...'

Harry stood up, murmured, 'See you in a bit,' to Ron, Hermione and Ginny, and followed Professor McGonagall back down the ward. The corridors outside were deserted and the only sound was the distant phoenix song. It was several minutes before Harry became aware that they were not heading for Professor McGonagall's office, but for Dumbledore's, and another few seconds before he realised that, of course, she had been Deputy Headmistress ... apparently she was now Headmistress ... so the room behind the gargoyle was now hers ...

In silence they ascended the moving spiral staircase and entered the circular office. He did not know what he had expected: that the room would be draped in black, perhaps, or even that Dumbledore's body might be lying there. In fact, it looked almost exactly as it had done when he and Dumbledore had left it mere hours previously: the silver instruments whirring and puffing on their spindle-legged tables, Gryffindor's sword in its glass case gleaming in the moonlight, the Sorting Hat on a shelf behind the

## 第29章 凤凰挽歌

"现在……讨论这个不合适,"卢平说,他慌乱地环顾四周,回避着大家的目光,"邓布利多死了……"

"如果这个世界拥有更多的爱,邓布利多会比任何人都高兴。"麦格教授简短地说,这时门又开了,海格走了进来。

他脸上没有胡子和头发的那一小块地方被泪水浸透,而且肿了起来,他哭得身子发抖,手中攥着一块斑点图案的大手帕。

"我已经……我已经完成了,教授,"他哽噎着说,"把——把他搬走了。斯普劳特教授让孩子们都回床上睡觉了。弗立维教授还躺着,但他说过一会儿就会好的,斯拉格霍恩教授说已经通知魔法部了。"

"谢谢你,海格。"麦格教授马上站了起来,转过身看着围在比尔床边的人们,"魔法部的人来后,我可能得去见见他们。海格,请你告诉四个学院的院长——斯拉格霍恩可以代表斯莱特林——说我要马上在我的办公室会见他们,我希望你也来。"

海格点着头,转过身慢慢地走出了屋子。麦格教授低头看着哈利。

"在见他们之前,我想和你说几句话,哈利。你可以过来一下吗?"

哈利站了起来,喃喃地对罗恩、赫敏和金妮说:"一会儿见。"便跟在麦格教授后面走出了病房。外面的走廊显得空空荡荡的,唯一的声音是远处凤凰的歌声。过了好几分钟哈利才反应过来,他们不是朝麦格教授的办公室走去,而是去邓布利多的办公室。又过了好几秒钟,他才意识到,麦格教授曾是代理校长……所以她现在当然是校长……所以滴水嘴石兽后面的房间现在是她的了……

他们一声不响地登上螺旋形楼梯,走进了圆形的办公室。哈利不知道自己以为会看到什么:也许房间里挂着黑纱,甚至邓布利多的遗体也停放在那里。然而事实却是,办公室里的一切同他和邓布利多几个小时前离开时一模一样:银质仪器在细腿桌子上嗡嗡旋转,喷吐着烟雾,玻璃匣中格兰芬多的宝剑在月光下闪闪发光,分院帽仍在桌子

## CHAPTER TWENTY-NINE  The Phoenix Lament

desk. But Fawkes's perch stood empty; he was still crying his lament to the grounds. And a new portrait had joined the ranks of the dead headmasters and headmistresses of Hogwarts ... Dumbledore was slumbering in a golden frame over the desk, his half-moon spectacles perched upon his crooked nose, looking peaceful and untroubled.

After glancing once at this portrait, Professor McGonagall made an odd movement as though steeling herself, then rounded the desk to look at Harry, her face taut and lined.

'Harry,' she said, 'I would like to know what you and Professor Dumbledore were doing this evening when you left the school.'

'I can't tell you that, Professor,' said Harry. He had expected the question and had his answer ready. It had been here, in this very room, that Dumbledore had told him that he was to confide the contents of their lessons to nobody but Ron and Hermione.

'Harry, it might be important,' said Professor McGonagall.

'It is,' said Harry, 'very, but he didn't want me to tell anyone.'

Professor McGonagall glared at him.

'Potter' (Harry registered the renewed use of his surname) 'in the light of Professor Dumbledore's death, I think you must see that the situation has changed somewhat –'

'I don't think so,' said Harry, shrugging. 'Professor Dumbledore never told me to stop following his orders if he died.'

'But –'

'There's one thing you should know before the Ministry gets here, though. Madam Rosmerta's under the Imperius Curse, she was helping Malfoy and the Death Eaters, that's how the necklace and the poisoned mead –'

'Rosmerta?' said Professor McGonagall incredulously, but before she could go on, there was a knock on the door behind them and Professors Sprout, Flitwick and Slughorn traipsed into the room, followed by Hagrid, who was still weeping copiously, his huge frame trembling with grief.

'Snape!' ejaculated Slughorn, who looked the most shaken, pale and sweating. 'Snape! I taught him! I thought I knew him!'

But before any of them could respond to this, a sharp voice spoke from high on the wall: a sallow-faced wizard with a short black fringe had just

## 第29章 凤凰挽歌

后面的架子上。但是福克斯的栖木空了,那凤凰仍在场地上哀唱挽歌。一幅新的肖像已经加入霍格沃茨学院已故校长们的行列……邓布利多沉睡在桌子上方的一个金色相框里,半月形的眼镜架在歪鼻子上,他看上去安详而宁静。

麦格教授瞥了一眼他的肖像,然后做了一个奇怪的动作,似乎是让自己硬下心来,然后才绕到桌后。她看着哈利,紧绷的脸上满是皱纹。

"哈利,"她说,"我想知道你和邓布利多教授晚上离开学校后都做了些什么。"

"我不能告诉你,教授。"哈利说。他已经预料到了这个问题,他的答案也是早就想好了的。就是在这里,就是在这个房间,邓布利多对他说过,他只可以把他们经历的事情告诉罗恩和赫敏。

"哈利,这可能很重要。"麦格教授说。

"确实,"哈利说,"很重要,但是他不想让我告诉任何人。"

麦格教授生气地瞪着他。

"波特(哈利注意到麦格又用姓来称呼他了),邓布利多教授已经死了,我想你应该看到情况有些不同——"

"我不这么认为,"哈利耸耸肩说道,"邓布利多从没告诉过我,他死了就可以不继续执行他的命令。"

"但是——"

"但是在魔法部的人来之前,有一件事你应该知道。罗斯默塔女士中了夺魂咒,是她帮助了马尔福和食死徒,所以项链和下了毒的蜂蜜酒——"

"罗斯默塔?"麦格教授难以置信地问,但这时有人敲门,斯普劳特、弗立维和斯拉格霍恩教授跨进屋来,后面跟着仍在大哭的海格,他巨大的身躯随着悲伤而抖动。

"斯内普!"斯拉格霍恩迫不及待地说,他看上去最为震惊,脸色苍白,不停地出汗,"斯内普!我教过他!我以为我了解他!"

还没人来得及答话,一个尖尖的声音从墙上的高处传来,一位黑

## CHAPTER TWENTY-NINE    The Phoenix Lament

walked back into his empty canvas.

'Minerva, the Minister will be here within seconds, he has just Disapparated from the Ministry.'

'Thank you, Everard,' said Professor McGonagall, and she turned quickly to her teachers.

'I want to talk about what happens to Hogwarts before he gets here,' she said quickly. 'Personally, I am not convinced that the school should reopen next year. The death of the Headmaster at the hands of one of our colleagues is a terrible stain upon Hogwarts' history. It is horrible.'

'I am sure Dumbledore would have wanted the school to remain open,' said Professor Sprout. 'I feel that if a single pupil wants to come, then the school ought to remain open for that pupil.'

'But will we have a single pupil after this?' said Slughorn, now dabbing his sweating brow with a silken handkerchief. 'Parents will want to keep their children at home and I can't say I blame them. Personally, I don't think we're in more danger at Hogwarts than we are anywhere else, but you can't expect mothers to think like that. They'll want to keep their families together, it's only natural.'

'I agree,' said Professor McGonagall. 'And in any case, it is not true to say that Dumbledore never envisaged a situation in which Hogwarts might close. When the Chamber of Secrets reopened he considered the closure of the school – and I must say that Professor Dumbledore's murder is more disturbing to me than the idea of Slytherin's monster living undetected in the bowels of the castle …'

'We must consult the governors,' said Professor Flitwick in his squeaky little voice; he had a large bruise on his forehead but seemed otherwise unscathed by his collapse in Snape's office. 'We must follow the established procedures. A decision should not be made hastily.'

'Hagrid, you haven't said anything,' said Professor McGonagall. 'What are your views, ought Hogwarts to remain open?'

Hagrid, who had been weeping silently into his large spotted handkerchief throughout this conversation, now raised puffy red eyes and croaked, 'I dunno, Professor … that's fer the Heads of House an' the Headmistress ter decide …'

'Professor Dumbledore always valued your views,' said Professor McGonagall kindly, 'and so do I.'

'Well, I'm stayin',' said Hagrid, fat tears still leaking out of the corners of

头发、留着短刘海的黄脸巫师刚刚回到他的空画布上。

"米勒娃，部长几秒钟后就到，他刚从魔法部幻影移形。"

"谢谢你，埃弗拉。"麦格教授说，然后迅速转身看着教授们。

"在部长到来之前，我想谈谈霍格沃茨学校该何去何从，"她快速地说，"我个人认为我们学校明年不能继续办下去了。校长死在我们一个同事手里，这简直是对霍格沃茨校史的极大玷污，太恐怖了。"

"我相信邓布利多一定希望我们能继续办学，"斯普劳特教授说，"我觉得只要有一个学生想来上学，学校就应该开办。"

"但这之后我们还会有学生吗？"斯拉格霍恩说道，他正用丝绸手帕擦着额头，"父母们会让孩子待在家里，对此我不能指责他们。我个人认为，在霍格沃茨并不比在其他地方更危险，但你不能希望母亲们也这么想。她们会希望全家人在一起，这是很自然的事情。"

"我同意，"麦格教授说，"其实，要说邓布利多从未设想过霍格沃茨可能有一天会关门，那也是不对的。当初密室重新打开的时候，他就考虑过关闭学校——我必须说，与城堡深处藏有斯莱特林的怪兽相比，我认为邓布利多教授被谋杀更加令人不安……"

"我们必须找董事们商议，"弗立维教授用又尖又细的声音说道，他额头上有很大一块瘀斑，但除此之外，昏倒在斯内普办公室似乎并未给他造成损伤，"必须按章办事。不能这么草率地做决定。"

"海格，你一句话还没有说呢，"麦格教授说，"你的意见是什么，霍格沃茨要继续开办吗？"

在这场谈话中，海格一直用斑点图案的大手帕捂着脸，默默地抽噎着。他抬起红肿的双眼，用嘶哑的声音说道："我不知道，教授……这得由几位院长和校长您做决定……"

"邓布利多教授向来看重你的意见，"麦格教授和蔼地说，"我也一样。"

"嗯，我会留下，"海格说，硕大的泪珠从他的眼角滑落，流进凌

925

## CHAPTER TWENTY-NINE  The Phoenix Lament

his eyes and trickling down into his tangled beard. 'It's me home, it's bin me home since I was thirteen. An' if there's kids who wan' me ter teach 'em, I'll do it. But ... I dunno ... Hogwarts without Dumbledore ...'

He gulped and disappeared behind his handkerchief once more, and there was silence.

'Very well,' said Professor McGonagall, glancing out of the window at the grounds, checking to see whether the Minister was yet approaching, 'then I must agree with Filius that the right thing to do is to consult the governors, who will take the final decision.

'Now, as to getting students home ... there is an argument for doing it sooner rather than later. We could arrange for the Hogwarts Express to come tomorrow if necessary –'

'What about Dumbledore's funeral?' said Harry, speaking at last.

'Well ...' said Professor McGonagall, losing a little of her briskness as her voice shook, 'I – I know that it was Dumbledore's wish to be laid to rest here, at Hogwarts –'

'Then that's what'll happen, isn't it?' said Harry fiercely.

'If the Ministry thinks it appropriate,' said Professor McGonagall. 'No other headmaster or headmistress has ever been –'

'No other headmaster or headmistress ever gave more to this school,' growled Hagrid.

'Hogwarts should be Dumbledore's final resting place,' said Professor Flitwick.

'Absolutely,' said Professor Sprout.

'And in that case,' said Harry, 'you shouldn't send the students home until the funeral's over. They'll want to say –'

The last word caught in his throat, but Professor Sprout completed the sentence for him.

'Goodbye.'

'Well said,' squeaked Professor Flitwick. 'Well said indeed! Our students should pay tribute, it is fitting. We can arrange transport home afterwards.'

'Seconded,' barked Professor Sprout.

'I suppose ... yes ...' said Slughorn in a rather agitated voice, while Hagrid let out a strangled sob of assent.

'He's coming,' said Professor McGonagall suddenly, gazing down into the grounds. 'The Minister ... and by the looks of it, he's brought a delegation ...'

## 第29章 凤凰挽歌

乱的胡须里,"这是我的家,从我十三岁以来一直是。如果有小孩想要我教他们,我会教的。但是……我不知道……霍格沃茨没有了邓布利多……"

他抽噎了一下,脸又一次消失在手帕后面。一阵沉默。

"很好,"麦格教授说着朝窗外的场地上瞅了一眼,看部长是否已经来了,"这样的话,我必须赞成弗立维的意见,应当先找董事会商议一下,由他们来做最后的决定。"

"现在,怎么送学生回家……有一个意见是宜早不宜迟。必要的话,明天我们可以安排霍格沃茨特快过来——"

"邓布利多的葬礼怎么办?"哈利最后问道。

"嗯……"麦格教授说,声音颤抖,好像少了点儿原有的果断,"我——我知道邓布利多的愿望是长眠在这里,在霍格沃茨——"

"那么就这么办,是吗?"哈利急切地问。

"如果部里认为合适的话。"麦格教授说,"还没有一位校长——"

"还没有一位校长对学校做出过如此大的贡献。"海格咆哮道。

"霍格沃茨应该是邓布利多最后安息的地方。"弗立维教授说。

"绝对如此。"斯普劳特教授说。

"那样的话,"哈利说,"就该等到葬礼结束后再送学生回家。他们想跟校长——"

最后一个词卡在他的喉咙里,但是斯普劳特教授帮他把话说全了。

"告别。"

"说得好,"弗立维教授尖叫道,"说得很好!我们的学生应该感恩,理应如此。我们可以在这之后再安排他们回家。"

"同意。"斯普劳特教授吼道。

"我想……是的……"斯拉格霍恩声音很激动,海格闷闷地发出了一声赞同的抽噎。

"他来了,"麦格教授突然说,眼睛凝视着场地上,"部长……他好像带了个代表团……"

## CHAPTER TWENTY-NINE   The Phoenix Lament

'Can I leave, Professor?' said Harry at once.

He had no desire at all to see, or be interrogated by, Rufus Scrimgeour tonight.

'You may,' said Professor McGonagall, 'and quickly.'

She strode towards the door and held it open for him. He sped down the spiral staircase and off along the deserted corridor; he had left his Invisibility Cloak at the top of the Astronomy Tower, but it did not matter; there was nobody in the corridors to see him pass, not even Filch, Mrs Norris or Peeves. He did not meet another soul until he turned into the passage leading to the Gryffindor common room.

'Is it true?' whispered the Fat Lady as he approached her. 'Is it really true? Dumbledore – dead?'

'Yes,' said Harry.

She let out a wail and, without waiting for the password, swung forwards to admit him.

As Harry had suspected it would be, the common room was jam-packed. The room fell silent as he climbed through the portrait hole. He saw Dean and Seamus sitting in a group nearby: this meant that the dormitory must be empty, or nearly so. Without speaking to anybody, without making eye-contact at all, Harry walked straight across the room and through the door to the boys' dormitories.

As he had hoped, Ron was waiting for him, still fully dressed, sitting on his bed. Harry sat down on his own four-poster and, for a moment, they simply stared at each other.

'They're talking about closing the school,' said Harry.

'Lupin said they would,' said Ron.

There was a pause.

'So?' said Ron in a very low voice, as though he thought the furniture might be listening in. 'Did you find one? Did you get it? A – a Horcrux?'

Harry shook his head. All that had taken place around that black lake seemed like an old nightmare now; had it really happened, and only hours ago?

'You didn't get it?' said Ron, looking crestfallen. 'It wasn't there?'

'No,' said Harry. 'Someone had already taken it and left a fake in its place.'

'Already *taken* –?'

## 第29章 凤凰挽歌

"我可以离开吗，教授？"哈利马上问。

他今晚一点也不想看到鲁弗斯·斯克林杰，或者被他讯问。

"可以，"麦格教授说，"要快点儿。"

她大步走到门前，拉开门等着他。哈利迅速走下螺旋形楼梯，穿过空荡荡的走廊，他的隐形衣丢在了天文塔的顶上，但是没有关系，走廊里没人看到他，连费尔奇、洛丽丝或皮皮鬼都不在。在他拐入通往格兰芬多公共休息室的过道之前，一个人影都没有碰到。

"是真的吗？"他走近时胖夫人轻声地问，"确实是真的吗？邓布利多——死了？"

"是的。"哈利说。

她哀号一声，不等哈利说口令就向前旋开，让他进去了。

不出哈利所料，公共休息室里挤满了人。当他爬进肖像洞口时，公共休息室里变得鸦雀无声。他看到迪安和西莫坐在近旁的一堆人里，这说明宿舍里一定没人，或者几乎没人。哈利没同任何人说话，也没和任何人交换眼神，径直穿过房间，走进了通往男生宿舍的门。

正像他希望的那样，罗恩在等他，仍然穿得很整齐，坐在床上。哈利也坐到自己的床上，他们互相对视了一会儿。

"他们在讨论关闭学校。"哈利说。

"卢平说他们会的。"罗恩说。

停顿了片刻。

"这么说，"罗恩放低了声音，好像旁边的家具会听到似的，"你们找到一个？你们拿到了一个？一个——一个魂器？"

哈利摇了摇头。所有发生在黑湖周围的一切，现在都好像是一场可怕的噩梦。真的发生了吗，仅仅是在几小时之前？

"你们没拿到？"罗恩问，看上去大失所望，"不在那儿？"

"没拿到，"哈利说，"被人拿走了，放了一个假的在那儿。"

"被人拿走了——？"

## CHAPTER TWENTY-NINE    The Phoenix Lament

Wordlessly, Harry pulled the fake locket from his pocket, opened it and passed it to Ron. The full story could wait ... it did not matter tonight ... nothing mattered except the end, the end of their pointless adventure, the end of Dumbledore's life ...

'R.A.B.,' whispered Ron, 'but who was that?'

'Dunno,' said Harry, lying back on his bed fully clothed and staring blankly upwards. He felt no curiosity at all about R.A.B.: he doubted that he would ever feel curious again. As he lay there, he became aware suddenly that the grounds were silent. Fawkes had stopped singing.

And he knew, without knowing how he knew it, that the phoenix had gone, had left Hogwarts for good, just as Dumbledore had left the school, had left the world ... had left Harry.

## 第29章 凤凰挽歌

哈利默不作声地从口袋里掏出那个假挂坠盒,打开来递给了罗恩。整个故事以后再说吧……今晚这已经无关紧要……重要的是结束了,无意义的冒险结束了,邓布利多的生命结束了……

"R.A.B.,"罗恩低语道,"他又是谁呢?"

"不知道。"哈利说,一边和衣躺了下去,双目无神地看着上方。他对于R.A.B.一点都没有好奇心,他怀疑将来也不会再有任何好奇心。他躺在那里,突然觉得场地上异常寂静。福克斯已停止了歌唱。

他知道——虽然搞不清为什么会知道——凤凰已经走了,永远地离开了霍格沃茨,像邓布利多一样永远地离开了学校,离开了这个世界……离开了哈利。

## CHAPTER THIRTY

# The White Tomb

All lessons were suspended, all examinations postponed. Some students were hurried away from Hogwarts by their parents over the next couple of days – the Patil twins were gone before breakfast on the morning following Dumbledore's death and Zacharias Smith was escorted from the castle by his haughty-looking father. Seamus Finnigan, on the other hand, refused point-blank to accompany his mother home; they had a shouting match in the Entrance Hall which was resolved when she agreed that he could remain behind for the funeral. She had difficulty in finding a bed in Hogsmeade, Seamus told Harry and Ron, for wizards and witches were pouring into the village, preparing to pay their last respects to Dumbledore.

Some excitement was caused among the younger students, who had never seen it before, when a powder-blue carriage the size of a house, pulled by a dozen giant winged palominos, came soaring out of the sky in the late afternoon before the funeral and landed on the edge of the Forest. Harry watched from a window as a gigantic and handsome olive-skinned, black-haired woman descended the carriage steps and threw herself into the waiting Hagrid's arms. Meanwhile a delegation of Ministry officials, including the Minister for Magic himself, was being accommodated within the castle. Harry was diligently avoiding contact with any of them; he was sure that, sooner or later, he would be asked again to account for Dumbledore's last excursion from Hogwarts.

Harry, Ron, Hermione and Ginny were spending all of their time together. The beautiful weather seemed to mock them; Harry could imagine how it would have been if Dumbledore had not died, and they had had this time together at the very end of the year, Ginny's examinations finished, the pressure of homework lifted ... and hour by hour, he put off saying the thing that he knew he must say, doing what he knew it was right to do, because it was too hard to forgo his best source of comfort.

## 第30章

## 白色坟墓

所有的课程都暂停了,所有的考试都推迟了。在随后的几天里,有些学生被家长从霍格沃茨匆匆接走——邓布利多死后的第二天早晨,帕瓦蒂孪生姐妹没吃早饭就走了,扎卡赖斯·史密斯那趾高气扬的父亲护送着他离开了城堡。西莫·斐尼甘断然拒绝跟他母亲一起回家,他们在门厅里扯着嗓子吵了一架,最后他母亲同意他留下来参加葬礼,争吵才算结束。西莫后来告诉哈利和罗恩,他母亲在霍格莫德很难找到一张床位,因为有那么多男男女女的巫师拥到了村子里,来向邓布利多作最后的告别。

葬礼前一天的傍晚时分,一辆房子那么大的浅蓝色马车被十几匹巨大的、长着翅膀的银鬃马拉着,从天空中飞了过来,降落在禁林边缘。低年级的学生们十分兴奋,他们以前从没见过这种景象。哈利从窗口注视着一位人高马大、气宇轩昂,黑头发橄榄色皮肤的女人从马车里走下来,一头扑进了等在那里的海格的怀抱。与此同时,魔法部的一支代表团——其中包括部长本人——被安排在城堡里住了下来。哈利煞费苦心地避免跟他们中间的任何人碰面,他相信他们迟早会盘问他邓布利多最后一次离开霍格沃茨的来龙去脉。

哈利、罗恩、赫敏和金妮整天待在一起。阳光明媚的天气似乎在嘲弄他们。哈利不禁想象,如果邓布利多没死该有多好。现在到了期末,金妮的考试已经结束,作业的压力减轻了,他们整天泡在一起……他知道自己必须说什么和应该做什么,但他一小时一小时地往后拖延,因为实在舍不得放弃最能给他带来慰藉的东西。

## CHAPTER THIRTY    The White Tomb

They visited the hospital wing twice a day: Neville had been discharged, but Bill remained under Madam Pomfrey's care. His scars were as bad as ever; in truth, he now bore a distinct resemblance to Mad-Eye Moody, though thankfully with both eyes and legs, but in personality he seemed just the same as ever. All that appeared to have changed was that he now had a great liking for very rare steaks.

'... so eet ees lucky 'e is marrying me,' said Fleur happily, plumping up Bill's pillows, 'because ze British overcook their meat, I 'ave always said this.'

'I suppose I'm just going to have to accept that he really is going to marry her,' sighed Ginny later that evening, as she, Harry, Ron and Hermione sat beside the open window of the Gryffindor common room, looking out over the twilit grounds.

'She's not that bad,' said Harry. 'Ugly, though,' he added hastily, as Ginny raised her eyebrows, and she let out a reluctant giggle.

'Well, I suppose if Mum can stand it, I can.'

'Anyone else we know died?' Ron asked Hermione, who was perusing the *Evening Prophet*.

Hermione winced at the forced toughness in his voice.

'No,' she said reprovingly, folding up the newspaper. 'They're still looking for Snape, but no sign ...'

'Of course there isn't,' said Harry, who became angry every time this subject cropped up. 'They won't find Snape till they find Voldemort, and seeing as they've never managed to do that in all this time ...'

'I'm going to go to bed,' yawned Ginny. 'I haven't been sleeping that well since ... well ... I could do with some sleep.'

She kissed Harry (Ron looked away pointedly), waved at the other two and departed for the girls' dormitories. The moment the door had closed behind her, Hermione leaned forwards towards Harry with a most Hermione-ish look on her face.

'Harry, I found something out this morning, in the library ...'

'R.A.B.?' said Harry, sitting up straight.

He did not feel the way he had so often felt before, excited, curious, burning to get to the bottom of a mystery; he simply knew that the task of

## 第30章 白色坟墓

他们每天到校医院探望两次。纳威已经出院，比尔还在那里继续接受庞弗雷女士的照料。他的伤疤还是那么触目惊心。说实在的，他现在的模样跟疯眼汉穆迪有几分相似，幸好他的眼睛和双腿还完好无损，不过他的性格似乎一点儿没变。唯一有所改变的，是他现在突然酷爱吃煎得很嫩的牛排了。

"……幸亏他要跟我结婚，"芙蓉一边帮比尔把枕头拍得松软一些，一边高兴地说，"因为英国人总是把肉煎得太老，这话我说过好多遍了。"

"看来我只好面对现实，他是真的要娶她了。"金妮叹着气说，那天晚上她和哈利、罗恩、赫敏一起坐在格兰芬多公共休息室敞开的窗户旁边，望着外面暮色中的场地。

"她并没有那么糟糕。"哈利说，"虽说有点儿丑。"他看见金妮扬起了眉毛，赶紧找补了一句，金妮勉强笑了几声。

"唉，既然妈妈都能忍受，我想我也没问题。"

"有我们认识的人死了吗？"罗恩看到赫敏在细读《预言家晚报》，便问道。

赫敏对他故意装出来的男子汉声音皱了皱眉。

"没有，"她不满地说，一边把报纸叠了起来，"他们还在寻找斯内普，但没有线索……"

"当然不会有。"哈利说，每次提起这个话题，他都要发火，"他们要等找到伏地魔之后才能找到斯内普，既然这么长时间都没能办到那一点……"

"我要去睡觉了。"金妮打着哈欠说，"我最近一直睡得不好，自从……好吧……我需要好好地补补觉了。"

她亲了亲哈利（罗恩生硬地扭过头去），朝另外两个人挥了挥手，就去女生宿舍了。门刚在她身后关上，赫敏就朝哈利探过身来，脸上带着赫敏特有的那种表情。

"哈利，我今天上午有所发现，在图书馆……"

"R.A.B.？"哈利坐直了身子问道。

他不像以前那样容易激动、好奇，一心想弄个水落石出了。他只知

## CHAPTER THIRTY    The White Tomb

discovering the truth about the real Horcrux had to be completed before he could move a little further along the dark and winding path stretching ahead of him, the path that he and Dumbledore had set out upon together, and which he now knew he would have to journey alone. There might still be as many as four Horcruxes out there somewhere and each would need to be found and eliminated before there was even a possibility that Voldemort could be killed. He kept reciting their names to himself, as though by listing them he could bring them within reach: 'the locket ... the cup ... the snake ... something of Gryffindor's or Ravenclaw's ... the locket ... the cup ... the snake ... something of Gryffindor's or Ravenclaw's ...'

This mantra seemed to pulse through Harry's mind as he fell asleep at night, and his dreams were thick with cups, lockets and mysterious objects that he could not quite reach, though Dumbledore helpfully offered Harry a rope ladder that turned to snakes the moment he began to climb ...

He had shown Hermione the note inside the locket the morning after Dumbledore's death, and although she had not immediately recognised the initials as belonging to some obscure wizard about whom she had been reading, she had since been rushing off to the library a little more often than was strictly necessary for somebody who had no homework to do.

'No,' she said sadly, 'I've been trying, Harry, but I haven't found anything ... there are a couple of reasonably well-known wizards with those initials – Rosalind Antigone Bungs ... Rupert "Axebanger" Brookstanton ... but they don't seem to fit at all. Judging by that note, the person who stole the Horcrux knew Voldemort, and I can't find a shred of evidence that Bungs or Axebanger ever had anything to do with him ... no, actually, it's about ... well, Snape.'

She looked nervous even saying the name again.

'What about him?' asked Harry heavily, slumping back in his chair.

'Well, it's just that I was sort of right about the Half-Blood Prince business,' she said tentatively.

'D'you have to rub it in, Hermione? How d'you think I feel about that now?'

'No – no – Harry, I didn't mean that!' she said hastily, looking around to check that they were not being overheard. 'It's just that I was right about Eileen Prince once owning the book. You see ... she was Snape's mother!'

## 第30章 白色坟墓

道，他必须弄清那个魂器的真实去向，才能深入探索他面前那条黑暗而曲折的小路——当初他和邓布利多共同踏上了那条小路，而现在他知道他将一个人继续走下去。大概还有四个魂器藏在不知道什么地方，他需要把它们一个个找到、销毁，才有可能最终消灭伏地魔。他不停地暗暗背诵它们的名字，似乎这样就能把它们吸引过来："挂坠盒……杯子……蛇……格兰芬多或拉文克劳的什么东西……挂坠盒……杯子……蛇……格兰芬多或拉文克劳的什么东西……"

夜里睡着后，这段咒文似乎还在哈利的脑海里跳动，结果他的梦里充斥着杯子、挂坠盒和其他神秘的东西，看得见却够不着，尽管邓布利多热心地递给了他一架绳梯，可是他刚开始往上爬，绳梯就变成了蛇……

邓布利多死后的第二天早晨，他就把挂坠盒里的那张纸条拿给赫敏看了，赫敏当时没有认出那三个字母属于她在书里读到过的哪位无名巫师，但是从那以后，她就整天往图书馆跑，而对于一个不用做家庭作业的人来说是没必要这么用功的。

"没戏，"她悲哀地说，"我一直在努力，哈利，但什么也没有发现……倒是有两个比较出名的巫师，姓名的开头是这几个字母——罗萨琳·安提冈·班格斯……"旋风斧"鲁伯特·阿克斯班奇·布鲁克斯坦顿……但他们根本对不上号。从那张纸条上看，那个偷去魂器的人应该认识伏地魔，而我找不到丝毫线索证明班格斯或"旋风斧"跟伏地魔有什么关系……实际上我要说的是关于……嗯，关于斯内普的事。"

她再次提起这个名字时显得很紧张。

"他怎么啦？"哈利粗声粗气问，重新跌坐在椅子上。

"是这样，我原来说的关于'混血王子'的话并没有错。"她迟疑地说。

"你非得哪壶不开提哪壶吗，赫敏？你知道我现在的感受吗？"

"不——不——哈利，我不是那个意思！"她慌慌张张地说，一边左右张望，看有没有人在偷听，"我的意思是，我说那本书原来是艾琳·普林斯的没有错。知道吗？她是斯内普的母亲！"

## CHAPTER THIRTY    The White Tomb

'I thought she wasn't much of a looker,' said Ron. Hermione ignored him.

'I was going through the rest of the old *Prophets* and there was a tiny announcement about Eileen Prince marrying a man called Tobias Snape, and then later an announcement saying that she'd given birth to a –'

'– murderer,' spat Harry.

'Well ... yes,' said Hermione. 'So ... I was sort of right. Snape must have been proud of being "half a Prince", you see? Tobias Snape was a Muggle from what it said in the *Prophet*.'

'Yeah, that fits,' said Harry. 'He'd play up the pure-blood side so he could get in with Lucius Malfoy and the rest of them ... he's just like Voldemort. Pure-blood mother, Muggle father ... ashamed of his parentage, trying to make himself feared using the Dark Arts, gave himself an impressive new name – *Lord* Voldemort – the Half-Blood *Prince* – how could Dumbledore have missed –?'

He broke off, looking out of the window. He could not stop himself dwelling upon Dumbledore's inexcusable trust in Snape ... but as Hermione had just inadvertently reminded him, he, Harry, had been taken in just the same ... in spite of the increasing nastiness of those scribbled spells, he had refused to believe ill of the boy who had been so clever, who had helped him so much ...

*Helped him* ... it was an almost unendurable thought, now ...

'I still don't get why he didn't turn you in for using that book,' said Ron. 'He must've known where you were getting it all from.'

'He knew,' said Harry bitterly. 'He knew when I used *Sectumsempra*. He didn't really need Legilimency ... he might even have known before then, with Slughorn talking about how brilliant I was at Potions ... shouldn't have left his old book in the bottom of that cupboard, should he?'

'But why didn't he turn you in?'

'I don't think he wanted to associate himself with that book,' said Hermione. 'I don't think Dumbledore would have liked it very much if he'd known. And even if Snape pretended it hadn't been his, Slughorn would have recognised his writing at once. Anyway, the book was left in Snape's old classroom, and I'll bet Dumbledore knew his mother was called "Prince".'

## 第30章 白色坟墓

"我认为她不能算是个美女。"罗恩说,赫敏没理他。

"我把剩下来的旧《预言家日报》翻了一遍,发现了一条不起眼的告示,说艾琳·普林斯嫁给了一个名叫托比亚·斯内普的男人,后来又有一条告示,说她生下了一个——"

"——杀人犯。"哈利咬牙切齿地说。

"对……是这样。"赫敏说,"所以……我说得不错,斯内普肯定因为自己是'半个普林斯'而感到自豪,明白吗?从《预言家日报》看,托比亚·斯内普是个麻瓜。"

"是啊,这就对了,"哈利说,"他假装自己是纯血统,这样就能跟卢修斯·马尔福以及其他人攀上关系……他就像伏地魔。纯血统母亲,麻瓜父亲……为自己的出身感到羞愧,想利用黑魔法使别人畏惧他,给自己取了一个够威风的新名字——伏地魔——混血王子——邓布利多怎么就没有——?"

他顿住了,眼睛望着窗外。他忍不住老是去想邓布利多对斯内普的不可原谅的信任……可是就像赫敏刚才无意中指出的,他,哈利,也同样受了欺骗……尽管那些随意涂写的咒语越来越残忍,但他仍不肯相信那个曾经那么聪明、给了他那么多帮助的男孩是坏人……

给了他帮助……现在想起来,简直让人无法忍受……

"我还是不明白,他为什么没有揭穿你利用了那本书。"罗恩说,"他肯定知道你那些知识是从哪儿来的。"

"他早就知道,"哈利恨恨地说,"我使用神锋无影咒的时候他就知道了。他实际上并不需要摄神取念咒……他大概早在那之前就已知道,因为斯拉格霍恩总是念叨我在魔药学方面多么出色……他不应该把他的旧课本留在储藏柜底部的,是不是?"

"可是他为什么不揭穿你呢?"

"我认为他不想把自己跟那本书联系在一起。"赫敏说,"我想,要是让邓布利多知道了,他肯定会不高兴的。即使斯内普不承认那本书是他的,斯拉格霍恩也会一眼认出他的笔迹。不管怎么说,那本书是留在斯内普原来的教室里的,我敢肯定邓布利多知道斯内普的母亲叫'普林斯'。"

## CHAPTER THIRTY    The White Tomb

'I should've shown the book to Dumbledore,' said Harry. 'All that time he was showing me how Voldemort was evil even when he was at school, and I had proof Snape was, too –'

'"Evil" is a strong word,' said Hermione quietly.

'You were the one who kept telling me the book was dangerous!'

'I'm trying to say, Harry, that you're putting too much blame on yourself. I thought the Prince seemed to have a nasty sense of humour, but I would never have guessed he was a potential killer ...'

'None of us could've guessed Snape would ... you know,' said Ron.

Silence fell between them, each of them lost in their own thoughts, but Harry was sure that they, like him, were thinking about the following morning, when Dumbledore's body would be laid to rest. Harry had never attended a funeral before; there had been no body to bury when Sirius had died. He did not know what to expect and was a little worried about what he might see, about how he would feel. He wondered whether Dumbledore's death would be more real to him once the funeral was over. Though he had moments when the horrible fact of it threatened to overwhelm him, there were blank stretches of numbness where, despite the fact that nobody was talking about anything else in the whole castle, he still found it difficult to believe that Dumbledore had really gone. Admittedly he had not, as he had with Sirius, looked desperately for some kind of loophole, some way that Dumbledore would come back ... he felt in his pocket for the cold chain of the fake Horcrux, which he now carried with him everywhere, not as a talisman, but as a reminder of what it had cost and what remained still to do.

Harry rose early to pack the next day; the Hogwarts Express would be leaving an hour after the funeral. Downstairs he found the mood in the Great Hall subdued. Everybody was wearing their dress robes and no one seemed very hungry. Professor McGonagall had left the throne-like chair in the middle of the staff table empty. Hagrid's chair was deserted too: Harry thought that perhaps he had not been able to face breakfast; but Snape's place had been unceremoniously filled by Rufus Scrimgeour. Harry avoided his yellowish eyes as they scanned the Hall; Harry had the uncomfortable feeling that Scrimgeour was looking for him. Among Scrimgeour's entourage Harry spotted the red hair and horn-rimmed glasses of Percy Weasley. Ron gave no sign that he was aware of Percy, apart from stabbing pieces of kipper with unwonted venom.

## 第30章 白色坟墓

"我应该把书拿给邓布利多看看的。"哈利说,"他一直想让我认清伏地魔在学校时有多么邪恶,现在我可以证明斯内普也是——"

"'邪恶'这个词太重了。"赫敏轻声说道。

"不是你一直在对我说那本书很危险吗!"

"我是想说,哈利,你过于责怪自己了。我本来认为王子有一种很残忍的幽默感,但我怎么也猜想不到他日后会成为一个杀人犯……"

"我们谁也不可能猜到斯内普会……你知道。"罗恩说。

他们沉默下来,每个人都陷入了沉思,但是哈利相信另外两个人和他一样,都想到了第二天早上邓布利多遗体被安葬的事。哈利以前没有参加过葬礼,小天狼星死的时候,根本没有遗骨可埋。他不知道到时候会是怎样的情景。他会看到什么?会有什么感受?他隐约有些担忧。他不知道等葬礼结束后,邓布利多的死对他来说是不是会更加真实。那个可怕的事实有时几乎要将他袭倒,但更多的时候他内心是一片空白和麻木。尽管整个城堡里的人都在谈论这件事,他仍然很难相信邓布利多真的不在了。当然啦,他没有像小天狼星死后那样,绝望地寻找某些漏洞,眼巴巴地盼着邓布利多还能回来……他伸手到口袋里摸着那个假魂器的冰冷的链子,现在他走到哪儿都带着它,不是作为护身符,而是提醒自己得到它的代价,提醒自己还有多少事情要做。

第二天,哈利一早起来收拾行李。霍格沃茨特快列车将在葬礼结束一小时后出发。他来到楼下,发现礼堂里的气氛非常压抑。每个人都穿着礼服长袍,而且似乎谁也没有多少食欲。麦格教授让教工餐桌中间那个王位般的座位空着。海格的椅子也没有人坐。哈利猜想他也许没有心情来吃早饭。可是斯内普的座位上却坐着鲁弗斯·斯克林杰,看着十分扎眼。他那双黄眼睛扫视着礼堂,哈利避开了他的目光。哈利很不舒服地感觉到斯克林杰是在找他。在斯克林杰的随行人员中,哈利看见了红头发、戴着角质边眼镜的珀西·韦斯莱。罗恩丝毫没有表现出他知道珀西来了,只是格外狠劲儿地切着他的熏鱼。

### * CHAPTER THIRTY  The White Tomb *

Over at the Slytherin table Crabbe and Goyle were muttering together. Hulking boys though they were, they looked oddly lonely without the tall, pale figure of Malfoy between them, bossing them around. Harry had not spared Malfoy much thought. His animosity was all for Snape, but he had not forgotten the fear in Malfoy's voice on that Tower top, nor the fact that he had lowered his wand before the other Death Eaters arrived. Harry did not believe that Malfoy would have killed Dumbledore. He despised Malfoy still for his infatuation with the Dark Arts, but now the tiniest drop of pity mingled with his dislike. Where, Harry wondered, was Malfoy now, and what was Voldemort making him do under threat of killing him and his parents?

Harry's thoughts were interrupted by a nudge in the ribs from Ginny. Professor McGonagall had risen to her feet and the mournful hum in the Hall died away at once.

'It is nearly time,' she said. 'Please follow your Heads of House out into the grounds. Gryffindors, after me.'

They filed out from behind their benches in near silence. Harry glimpsed Slughorn at the head of the Slytherin column, wearing magnificent long emerald-green robes embroidered with silver. He had never seen Professor Sprout, Head of the Hufflepuffs, looking so clean; there was not a single patch on her hat, and when they reached the Entrance Hall, they found Madam Pince standing beside Filch, she in a thick black veil that fell to her knees, he in an ancient black suit and tie reeking of mothballs.

They were heading, as Harry saw when he stepped out on to the stone steps from the front doors, towards the lake. The warmth of the sun caressed his face as they followed Professor McGonagall in silence to the place where hundreds of chairs had been set out in rows. An aisle ran down the centre of them: there was a marble table standing at the front, all chairs facing it. It was the most beautiful summer's day.

An extraordinary assortment of people had already settled into half of the chairs: shabby and smart, old and young. Most Harry did not recognise, but there were a few that he did, including members of the Order of the Phoenix: Kingsley Shacklebolt, Mad-Eye Moody, Tonks, her hair miraculously returned to vividest pink, Remus Lupin, with whom she seemed to be holding hands, Mr and Mrs Weasley, Bill supported by Fleur and

## 第30章 白色坟墓

在那边斯莱特林的餐桌上,克拉布和高尔凑在一起窃窃私语。虽说两人都是身材粗笨的大小伙子,但是中间少了马尔福那苍白瘦长的身影,少了马尔福对他们发号施令,他们俩显得特别孤单。哈利没有更多地去想马尔福,他的仇恨全集中在斯内普身上。他没有忘记在塔楼顶上马尔福的声音里流露出的恐惧,也没有忘记在另外几个食死徒赶到之前,马尔福的魔杖已经垂落下去。哈利不相信马尔福会杀死邓布利多。他仍然因为马尔福醉心于黑魔法而鄙夷他,但现在这种厌恶里混杂着一点点同情。哈利琢磨着,马尔福此刻在什么地方呢?伏地魔以杀害马尔福和他的父母相威胁,命令他做的究竟是一件什么事情呢?

金妮捅了捅哈利,打断了他的思绪。麦格教授站起身,礼堂里悲哀的低语声立刻平静下来。

"时间差不多了,"她说,"请跟着你们的院长到场地去。格兰芬多的同学跟我来。"

他们排着队从板凳后面走出来,几乎没有发出一点声响。哈利瞥见斯拉格霍恩站在斯莱特林队伍的最前面,穿着一件华贵的、用银线刺绣的鲜绿色长袍。而且,他从来没有看见赫奇帕奇的院长斯普劳特教授这么整洁干净过,帽子上一块补丁也没有了。走到门厅时,他发现平斯女士站在费尔奇身边,戴着一块垂到膝盖上的厚厚的黑色面纱,费尔奇穿了一套老式黑色西服,打着领带,身上散发出一股樟脑球的味儿。

哈利出了大门,来到石阶上,发现他们正朝着湖的方向走去。温暖的阳光照在他的脸上,他们默默地跟着麦格教授走向排列着好几百把椅子的地方。椅子中间有一条过道,前面放着一张大理石桌子,所有的椅子都朝向它。这是夏季一个最最美丽宜人的日子。

一半椅子上已经坐了人,这些人各式各样,鱼龙混杂:有衣衫褴褛的,有整洁体面的;有老年人,也有年轻人。大多数人哈利都不认识,但有一些他是知道的,其中包括凤凰社的成员:金斯莱·沙克尔,疯眼汉穆迪,唐克斯——她的头发又奇迹般地变成了耀眼的粉红色,莱

### CHAPTER THIRTY    The White Tomb

followed by Fred and George, who were wearing jackets of black dragonskin. Then there was Madame Maxime, who took up two-and-a-half chairs on her own, Tom, the landlord of the Leaky Cauldron, Arabella Figg, Harry's Squib neighbour, the hairy bass player from the wizarding group the Weird Sisters, Ernie Prang, driver of the Knight Bus, Madam Malkin, of the robe shop in Diagon Alley, and some people whom Harry merely knew by sight, such as the barman of the Hog's Head and the witch who pushed the trolley on the Hogwarts Express. The castle ghosts were there too, barely visible in the bright sunlight, discernible only when they moved, shimmering insubstantially in the gleaming air.

Harry, Ron, Hermione and Ginny filed into seats at the end of a row beside the lake. People were whispering to each other; it sounded like a breeze in the grass, but the birdsong was louder by far. The crowd continued to swell; with a great rush of affection for both of them, Harry saw Neville being helped into a seat by Luna. They alone of all the DA had responded to Hermione's summons the night that Dumbledore had died, and Harry knew why: they were the ones who had missed the DA most ... probably the ones who had checked their coins regularly in the hope that there would be another meeting ...

Cornelius Fudge walked past them towards the front rows, his expression miserable, twirling his green bowler hat as usual; Harry next recognised Rita Skeeter, who, he was infuriated to see, had a notebook clutched in her red-taloned hand; and then, with a worse jolt of fury, Dolores Umbridge, an unconvincing expression of grief upon her toad-like face, a black velvet bow set atop her iron-coloured curls. At the sight of the centaur Firenze, who was standing like a sentinel near the water's edge, she gave a start and scurried hastily into a seat a good distance away.

The staff were seated at last. Harry could see Scrimgeour looking grave and dignified in the front row with Professor McGonagall. He wondered whether Scrimgeour or any of these important people were really sorry that Dumbledore was dead. But then he heard music, strange, otherworldly music, and he forgot his dislike of the Ministry in looking around for the source of it. He was not the only one: many heads were turning, searching, a little alarmed.

## 第30章 白色坟墓

姆斯·卢平——唐克斯跟他手拉着手,韦斯莱夫妇,还有芙蓉搀扶着比尔,后面跟着穿黑色火龙皮夹克衫的弗雷德和乔治。此外还有马克西姆女士——她一个人就占了两把半椅子,破釜酒吧的老板汤姆、哈利的哑炮邻居阿拉贝拉·费格、古怪姐妹演唱组里那位毛发粗重的贝斯手、骑士公共汽车驾驶员厄恩·普兰、对角巷长袍专卖店的摩金夫人,还有几个人哈利只是看着面熟,如猪头酒吧的那个服务员、霍格沃茨特快列车上推小车的女巫。城堡里的幽灵也来了,他们在阳光下几乎看不见,只有走动时才能辨认出来,在明亮的空气中闪烁着虚幻的光芒。

哈利、罗恩、赫敏和金妮依次坐到湖边那排椅子的最后几个座位上。人们在小声地互相交谈,声音像微风吹过草地,而鸟叫的声音显得格外响亮。人群还在不断拥来。哈利看见卢娜扶着纳威在椅子上坐下,不由得对他们俩产生了强烈的好感。在邓布利多去世的那天夜里,D.A.的所有成员中只有他们俩响应了赫敏的召唤,哈利知道这是为什么:他们俩最怀念D.A.……也许他们经常会把硬币拿出来看看,希望D.A.还会再组织活动……

康奈利·福吉经过他们身边朝前排的座位走去,他愁眉苦脸,像往常一样旋转着他那顶绿帽子。随后,哈利认出了丽塔·斯基特,并恼火地发现她那红爪子般的手里竟然攥着一个笔记本,接着他又认出了多洛雷斯·乌姆里奇,顿时火冒三丈。乌姆里奇那张癞蛤蟆般的脸上装出一副悲哀的表情,铁褐色的鬈发上顶着一只黑色天鹅绒蝴蝶结。她一看见像哨兵一样站在湖边的马人费伦泽,就吓得匆匆忙忙坐到远处一个座位上去了。

终于,全体教员也都已落座。哈利可以看见斯克林杰跟麦格教授一起坐在前排,显得神色庄重,很有气派。哈利不知道斯克林杰和其他大人物是不是真的为邓布利多的死感到悲伤。接着,他听见了音乐,宛如另一个世界飘来的仙乐,他忘记了对魔法部的反感,转脸寻找这音乐的来源。这样做的不止他一个人:许多脑袋都在转动、寻找,带着一点儿惊异。

# CHAPTER THIRTY    The White Tomb

'In there,' whispered Ginny in Harry's ear.

And he saw them in the clear green sunlit water, inches below the surface, reminding him horribly of the Inferi; a chorus of merpeople singing in a strange language he did not understand, their pallid faces rippling, their purplish hair flowing all around them. The music made the hair on Harry's neck stand up and yet it was not unpleasant. It spoke very clearly of loss and of despair. As he looked down into the wild faces of the singers he had the feeling that they, at least, were sorry for Dumbledore's passing. Then Ginny nudged him again and he looked round.

Hagrid was walking slowly up the aisle between the chairs. He was crying quite silently, his face gleaming with tears, and in his arms, wrapped in purple velvet spangled with golden stars, was what Harry knew to be Dumbledore's body. A sharp pain rose in Harry's throat at this sight: for a moment, the strange music and the knowledge that Dumbledore's body was so close seemed to take all warmth from the day. Ron looked white and shocked. Tears were falling thick and fast into both Ginny and Hermione's laps.

They could not see clearly what was happening at the front. Hagrid seemed to have placed the body carefully upon the table. Now he retreated down the aisle, blowing his nose with loud trumpeting noises that drew scandalised looks from some, including, Harry saw, Dolores Umbridge ... but Harry knew that Dumbledore would not have cared. He tried to make a friendly gesture to Hagrid as he passed, but Hagrid's eyes were so swollen it was a wonder he could see where he was going. Harry glanced at the back row to which Hagrid was heading and realised what was guiding him, for there, dressed in a jacket and trousers each the size of a small marquee, was the giant Grawp, his great ugly boulder-like head bowed, docile, almost human. Hagrid sat down next to his half-brother and Grawp patted Hagrid hard on the head, so that his chair legs sank into the ground. Harry had a wonderful momentary urge to laugh. But then the music stopped and he turned to face the front again.

A little tufty-haired man in plain black robes had got to his feet and stood now in front of Dumbledore's body. Harry could not hear what he was saying. Odd words floated back to them over the hundreds of heads. 'Nobility of spirit' ... 'intellectual contribution' ... 'greatness of heart' ... it did not

# 第30章 白色坟墓

"在那儿。"金妮贴着哈利的耳朵小声说。

于是，他看见了他们，就在阳光照耀下的清澈的绿色湖水中，就在湖面下几英寸的地方，这使他想起了那些阴尸，恐惧再次袭上心头。一支人鱼组成的合唱队用一种奇怪的、他听不懂的语言在婉转歌唱，他们苍白的面孔荡漾不定，紫色的头发在身体周围漂浮。这音乐听得哈利脖子后面的汗毛根根竖立，却并不刺耳难听。它明明白白地诉说着哀痛和绝望。哈利低头望着水里那些情绪激动的面孔，觉得至少他们是在为邓布利多的离去感到忧伤。这时，金妮又捅了捅他，他转过脸来。

海格沿着座位中间的过道慢慢往前走。他在无声地哭泣，脸上挂满亮晶晶的泪水，哈利知道，他怀里抱着的是邓布利多的遗体，用缀满金星的紫色天鹅绒包裹着。看到这一幕，一阵钻心的刺痛涌上哈利的喉咙：一时间，那奇特的音乐，还有离他如此之近的邓布利多的遗体，似乎带走了那一天所有的温暖。罗恩显得十分震惊，脸色煞白。大滴大滴的泪珠不断滚落在金妮和赫敏的腿上。

他们看不清前面的情况。海格似乎把遗体小心翼翼地放在了桌子上。他顺着过道往回走，一边使劲擤着鼻子，发出吹喇叭般的响声，有些人朝他投去不满的目光，哈利看到其中就有多洛雷斯·乌姆里奇……可是哈利知道邓布利多是不会介意的。海格经过时，哈利想对他友好地打个招呼，但是海格的眼睛肿成了一道缝，真奇怪他居然还能看清脚下的路。哈利看了看海格要去的后排，明白了是什么在给他指路。巨人格洛普就坐在那里，穿着像小帐篷那么大的夹克衫和长裤，那颗硕大无比、像巨型卵石一样丑陋的脑袋低垂着，显得很温顺，甚至善解人意。海格在他的同母异父弟弟旁边坐了下来，格洛普重重地拍了拍海格的头，使得椅子的四条腿都陷进了地里。哈利一时忍不住想笑。但就在这时，音乐停止了，他转过脸，重新望着前面。

一个头发浓密、穿一身朴素黑袍子的小个子男人从座位上站起身，站在邓布利多的遗体前。哈利听不清他在说些什么。偶尔有只言片语越过几百个脑袋飘到后面。"高贵的精神"……"学术成就"……"伟

CHAPTER THIRTY  The White Tomb

mean very much. It had little to do with Dumbledore as Harry had known him. He suddenly remembered Dumbledore's idea of a few words: 'nitwit', 'oddment', 'blubber' and 'tweak', and again, had to suppress a grin ... what was the matter with him?

There was a soft splashing noise to his left and he saw that the merpeople had broken the surface to listen, too. He remembered Dumbledore crouching at the water's edge two years ago, very close to where Harry now sat, and conversing in Mermish with the Merchieftainess. Harry wondered where Dumbledore had learned Mermish. There was so much he had never asked him, so much he should have said ...

And then, without warning, it swept over him, the dreadful truth, more completely and undeniably than it had until now. Dumbledore was dead, gone ... he clutched the cold locket in his hand so tightly that it hurt, but he could not prevent hot tears spilling from his eyes: he looked away from Ginny and the others and stared out over the lake, towards the Forest, as the little man in black droned on ... there was movement among the trees. The centaurs had come to pay their respects, too. They did not move into the open but Harry saw them standing quite still, half hidden in shadow, watching the wizards, their bows hanging at their sides. And Harry remembered his first nightmarish trip into the Forest, the first time he had ever encountered the thing that was then Voldemort, and how he had faced him, and how he and Dumbledore had discussed fighting a losing battle not long thereafter. It was important, Dumbledore said, to fight, and fight again, and keep fighting, for only then could evil be kept at bay, though never quite eradicated ...

And Harry saw very clearly as he sat there under the hot sun how people who cared about him had stood in front of him one by one, his mother, his father, his godfather, and finally Dumbledore, all determined to protect him; but now that was over. He could not let anybody else stand between him and Voldemort; he must abandon for ever the illusion he ought to have lost at the age of one: that the shelter of a parent's arms meant that nothing could hurt him. There was no waking from his nightmare, no comforting whisper in the dark that he was safe really, that it was all in his imagination; the last and greatest of his protectors had died and he was more alone than he had ever been before.

The little man in black had stopped speaking at last and resumed his seat.

## 第30章 白色坟墓

大的心灵"……这些都没有多大意义。这些都跟哈利认识的那个邓布利多没有多大关系。他突然想起邓布利多说过的那几个词:"笨蛋!""哭鼻子!""残渣"和"拧",又一次忍不住想笑……他这是怎么了?

左边传来了水花泼溅的声音,他扭头一看,那些人鱼都冒出了水面,也在仔细倾听。哈利想起两年前邓布利多蹲在水边,差不多就在此刻哈利所坐的这个位置,用人鱼的语言跟人鱼的首领交谈。哈利不知道邓布利多是在哪儿学会了人鱼的语言。他有那么多事情没有问他,他有那么多话应该对他讲……

于是,突如其来地,可怕的事实朝他袭来,比任何时候都更加毫不留情,不可否认。邓布利多死了,不在了……他紧紧地攥住手里那个冰冷的挂坠盒,攥得手心生疼,但仍然挡不住泪水涌出他的眼眶:他避开金妮和其他人的目光,望着远处湖那边的禁林,穿黑衣服的小个子男人还在发表单调沉闷的讲话……禁林里有动静。马人也来表示他们的哀悼。他们没有走到空地上来,哈利看见他们半隐半现地站在阴影里,一动不动地望着这边的巫师们,他们的弓悬挂在身体一侧。哈利想起了他第一次进入禁林的噩梦般的经历,他在那里第一次看见了那个曾是伏地魔的家伙,他还想起了当时面对伏地魔的情景,想起了不久之后他和邓布利多怎样商量着去打这场注定要输的战斗。邓布利多说,重要的是不断斗争、斗争、再斗争,只有那样才能把邪恶控制住,虽然永远不可能完全消灭……

哈利坐在热辣辣的太阳底下,清清楚楚地看见那些关心他的人一个个站在他的面前,他的妈妈、爸爸,他的教父,最后是邓布利多,他们都决心要保护他,然而现在一切都结束了。他不能再让任何人挡在他和伏地魔之间。他必须永远抛弃那个早在一岁时就应该丢开的幻想,不再以为某位长辈的怀抱会保护他不受任何伤害。现在没有人会把他从噩梦中唤醒,没有人会在黑暗中低声安慰他,说他实际上是安全的,一切都是他自己想象出来的。他的最后一位也是最了不起的一位保护者也死了,他比以前任何时候都更加孤独。

小个子男人终于说完,回到了座位上。哈利等着另外的人站起来,

## CHAPTER THIRTY   The White Tomb

Harry waited for somebody else to get to their feet; he expected speeches, probably from the Minister, but nobody moved.

Then several people screamed. Bright, white flames had erupted around Dumbledore's body and the table upon which it lay: higher and higher they rose, obscuring the body. White smoke spiralled into the air and made strange shapes: Harry thought, for one heart-stopping moment, that he saw a phoenix fly joyfully into the blue, but next second the fire had vanished. In its place was a white marble tomb, encasing Dumbledore's body and the table on which he had rested.

There were a few more cries of shock as a shower of arrows soared through the air, but they fell far short of the crowd. It was, Harry knew, the centaurs' tribute: he saw them turn tail and disappear back into the cool trees. Likewise the merpeople sank slowly back into the green water and were lost from view.

Harry looked at Ginny, Ron and Hermione: Ron's face was screwed up as though the sunlight was blinding him. Hermione's face was glazed with tears, but Ginny was no longer crying. She met Harry's gaze with the same hard, blazing look that he had seen when she had hugged him after winning the Quidditch Cup in his absence, and he knew that at that moment they understood each other perfectly, and that when he told her what he was going to do now, she would not say 'Be careful', or 'Don't do it', but accept his decision, because she would not have expected anything less of him. And so he steeled himself to say what he had known he must say ever since Dumbledore had died.

'Ginny, listen ...' he said very quietly, as the buzz of conversation grew louder around them and people began to get to their feet. 'I can't be involved with you any more. We've got to stop seeing each other. We can't be together.'

She said, with an oddly twisted smile, 'It's for some stupid, noble reason, isn't it?'

'It's been like ... like something out of someone else's life, these last few weeks with you,' said Harry. 'But I can't ... we can't ... I've got things to do alone now.'

She did not cry, she simply looked at him.

'Voldemort uses people his enemies are close to. He's already used you as

## 第30章 白色坟墓

他以为还会有人讲话，比如部长大人，但是谁也没有动弹。

突然，几个人尖叫起来。耀眼的白色火焰从邓布利多的遗体和那张桌子周围蹿了出来：火苗越蹿越高，遮挡住了遗体。白色的烟袅袅升向空中，呈现出各种奇怪的形状：一刹那间，哈利仿佛看见一只凤凰欢快地飞上了蓝天，但紧接着火焰就消失了，那里出现了一座白色的大理石坟墓，把邓布利多的遗体和安放遗体的那张桌子都包在了里面。

无数枚箭像阵雨一样射向空中，引起了几声惊叫，但它们在离人群很远的地方就坠落了。哈利知道，这是马人们在致哀。他看见马人掉转身体，消失在阴凉的树丛中。那些人鱼也慢慢沉入绿色的水底，再也看不见了。

哈利看着金妮、罗恩和赫敏。罗恩的脸缩成一团，似乎太阳刺得他睁不开眼睛。赫敏脸上满是亮晶晶的泪痕，但金妮已经不哭了。她迎着哈利的目光，神情刚毅而热烈，就像哈利缺席的那天球队赢得魁地奇杯后她拥抱哈利的时候那样。在那一刻，哈利知道他们彼此心心相印，知道当他把他要做的事情告诉她时，她不会说"你要小心"或"你别去做"，而是会欣然接受他的决定，因为她从心底里知道他就是那样一个人。于是，他咬咬牙，说出了自从邓布利多死后他就知道非说不可的话。

"金妮，你听我说……"他用很轻的声音说，这时周围的说话声越来越响，人们纷纷站了起来，"我不能再跟你保持这种关系了。我们不能再见面，不能再在一起。"

她脸上带着古怪的、扭曲的笑容，说道："是为了某个愚蠢而崇高的理由，是吗？"

"这几个星期和你在一起……就像是……就像是从别人那里偷来的日子，"哈利说，"但我不能……我们不能……现在有些事情必须我一个人去做。"

金妮没有哭，只是望着他。

"伏地魔总是利用与他敌人关系亲近的人。他已经有过一次把你当

## CHAPTER THIRTY  The White Tomb

bait once, and that was just because you're my best friend's sister. Think how much danger you'll be in if we keep this up. He'll know, he'll find out. He'll try and get to me through you.'

'What if I don't care?' said Ginny fiercely.

'I care,' said Harry. 'How do you think I'd feel if this was your funeral ... and it was my fault ...'

She looked away from him, over the lake.

'I never really gave up on you,' she said. 'Not really. I always hoped ... Hermione told me to get on with life, maybe go out with some other people, relax a bit around you, because I never used to be able to talk if you were in the room, remember? And she thought you might take a bit more notice if I was a bit more – myself.'

'Smart girl, that Hermione,' said Harry, trying to smile. 'I just wish I'd asked you sooner. We could've had ages ... months ... years maybe ...'

'But you've been too busy saving the wizarding world,' said Ginny, half laughing. 'Well ... I can't say I'm surprised. I knew this would happen in the end. I knew you wouldn't be happy unless you were hunting Voldemort. Maybe that's why I like you so much.'

Harry could not bear to hear these things, nor did he think his resolution would hold if he remained sitting beside her. Ron, he saw, was now holding Hermione and stroking her hair while she sobbed into his shoulder, tears dripping from the end of his own long nose. With a miserable gesture, Harry got up, turned his back on Ginny and on Dumbledore's tomb and walked away around the lake. Moving felt much more bearable than sitting still: just as setting out as soon as possible to track down the Horcruxes and kill Voldemort would feel better than waiting to do it ...

'Harry!'

He turned. Rufus Scrimgeour was limping rapidly towards him around the bank, leaning on his walking stick.

'I've been hoping to have a word ... do you mind if I walk a little way with you?'

'No,' said Harry indifferently, and set off again.

'Harry, this was a dreadful tragedy,' said Scrimgeour quietly, 'I cannot tell you how appalled I was to hear of it. Dumbledore was a very great wizard.

## 第30章 白色坟墓

作诱饵，那只是因为你是我最好朋友的妹妹。你想一想，如果我们保持这种关系，那会给你带来多大的危险。他会知道的，会弄清楚的。他会试图通过你来接近我。"

"如果我不在乎呢？"金妮感情激烈地说。

"我在乎。"哈利说，"如果这是你的葬礼……而一切都是我造成的……你认为我会有什么感受……"

金妮扭过脸去望着湖面。

"我其实一直没有放弃你，"她说，"没有真的放弃。我一直存着希望……赫敏叫我投入生活，试着跟别人相处，在你周围放松一些，因为，你还记得吗，以前只要你在屋里，我就连话也说不出来。赫敏认为，如果我拥有更多的——自我，你或许就会更加注意到我。"

"赫敏真是个鬼灵精，"哈利说着，想让自己笑一笑，"我特别后悔没有早一点问你。不然我们可以有很长时间……好几个月……也许好几年……"

"但是你一直忙着拯救巫师界呢。"金妮哽笑着说，"唉……其实我并不感到意外。我早就知道最后会是这样的结局。我早就知道你不去寻找伏地魔是不会甘心的。也许正因为这个我才这么喜欢你。"

听着这些话，哈利再也忍受不住了，他想，如果他继续坐在金妮身边，他的决心肯定会动摇。他看见罗恩此刻把赫敏搂在怀里，轻轻地抚摸她的头发，赫敏趴在罗恩的肩头伤心哭泣，大滴的眼泪也从罗恩的长鼻子尖上滚落下来。哈利狠狠地站起身，背对着金妮和邓布利多的坟墓，绕着湖边走去。走动一下比静静坐着好受多了：正如尽早动身去寻找魂器，消灭伏地魔，会比焦虑地等待好受得多……

"哈利！"

他一转身，看见鲁弗斯·斯克林杰拄着拐杖一瘸一拐地绕着湖岸快步朝他走来。

"我一直想跟你谈谈……我陪你走走，你不反对吧？"

"好吧。"哈利淡淡地说，抬脚又往前走去。

"哈利，真是一个可怕的悲剧。"斯克林杰轻声说道，"听到这个消息，我震惊得简直无法形容。邓布利多是一位非常了不起的巫师。我们之

## CHAPTER THIRTY  The White Tomb

We had our disagreements, as you know, but no one knows better than I –'

'What do you want?' asked Harry flatly.

Scrimgeour looked annoyed but, as before, hastily modified his expression to one of sorrowful understanding.

'You are, of course, devastated,' he said. 'I know that you were very close to Dumbledore. I think you may have been his favourite ever pupil. The bond between the two of you –'

'What do you want?' Harry repeated, coming to a halt.

Scrimgeour stopped too, leaned on his stick and stared at Harry, his expression shrewd now.

'The word is that you were with him when he left the school the night that he died.'

'Whose word?' said Harry.

'Somebody Stupefied a Death Eater on top of the Tower after Dumbledore died. There were also two broomsticks up there. The Ministry can add two and two, Harry.'

'Glad to hear it,' said Harry. 'Well, where I went with Dumbledore and what we did is my business. He didn't want people to know.'

'Such loyalty is admirable, of course,' said Scrimgeour, who seemed to be restraining his irritation with difficulty, 'but Dumbledore is gone, Harry. He's gone.'

'He will only be gone from the school when none here are loyal to him,' said Harry, smiling in spite of himself.

'My dear boy ... even Dumbledore cannot return from the –'

'I am not saying he can. You wouldn't understand. But I've got nothing to tell you.'

Scrimgeour hesitated, then said, in what was evidently supposed to be a tone of delicacy, 'The Ministry can offer you all sorts of protection, you know, Harry. I would be delighted to place a couple of my Aurors at your service –'

Harry laughed.

'Voldemort wants to kill me himself and Aurors won't stop him. So thanks for the offer, but no thanks.'

'So,' said Scrimgeour, his voice cold now, 'the request I made of you at Christmas –'

## 第30章 白色坟墓

间有些分歧,你也知道,但是谁也不如我更了解——"

"你想要什么?"哈利直截了当地问。

斯克林杰似乎有些恼火,但他像以前一样,迅速地把面部表情调整为忧伤和理解。

"是啊,你肯定万分痛苦,"他说,"我知道你跟邓布利多非常亲近。我想你大概是他这辈子最喜欢的学生了。你们俩之间的关系——"

"你想要什么?"哈利停下脚步,又问了一遍。

斯克林杰也站住了,身体倚在拐杖上,眼睛盯着哈利,表情变得严厉了。

"我听说,他去世那天夜里离开学校时,你跟他在一起。"

"听谁说的?"哈利问。

"邓布利多死后,在塔楼顶上有人对一个食死徒念了一句'统统石化!'而且那上面有两把扫帚。部里是会推断的,哈利。"

"我听了真高兴。"哈利说,"不过,我跟邓布利多去了哪里,我们做了什么,都是我的私事。他不想让人知道。"

"这样的忠诚实在令人敬佩。"斯克林杰说,他似乎在强压着内心的恼怒,"可是邓布利多已经不在了,哈利。他已经不在了。"

"只有当这里的人都不再忠实于他,他才会离开这所学校。"哈利说着,脸上不由得露出了微笑。

"我的好孩子……即使邓布利多也不可能起死回——"

"我并没有说他能复活。你不会理解。但我真的没有什么可以告诉你的。"

斯克林杰迟疑着,然后用故作矜持的口吻说:"部里可以给你提供各种保护,哈利。我很愿意安排我的两个傲罗为你服务——"

哈利笑了起来。

"伏地魔想要亲手杀死我,傲罗是阻挡不了他的。谢谢你这么说,但是不必了。"

"那么,"斯克林杰换了一种冷冰冰的口气说,"圣诞节时我向你提出的请求——"

## CHAPTER THIRTY    The White Tomb

'What request? Oh yeah ... the one where I tell the world what a great job you're doing in exchange for –'

'– for raising everyone's morale!' snapped Scrimgeour.

Harry considered him for a moment.

'Released Stan Shunpike yet?'

Scrimgeour turned a nasty purple colour highly reminiscent of Uncle Vernon.

'I see you are –'

'Dumbledore's man through and through,' said Harry. 'That's right.'

Scrimgeour glared at him for another moment, then turned and limped away without another word. Harry could see Percy and the rest of the Ministry delegation waiting for him, casting nervous glances at the sobbing Hagrid and Grawp, who were still in their seats. Ron and Hermione were hurrying towards Harry, passing Scrimgeour going in the opposite direction; Harry turned and walked slowly on, waiting for them to catch up, which they finally did in the shade of a beech tree under which they had sat in happier times.

'What did Scrimgeour want?' Hermione whispered.

'Same as he wanted at Christmas,' shrugged Harry. 'Wanted me to give him inside information on Dumbledore and be the Ministry's new poster boy.'

Ron seemed to struggle with himself for a moment, then he said loudly to Hermione, 'Look, let me go back and hit Percy!'

'No,' she said firmly, grabbing his arm.

'It'll make me feel better!'

Harry laughed. even Hermione grinned a little, though her smile faded as she looked up at the castle.

'I can't bear the idea that we might never come back,' she said softly. 'How can Hogwarts close?'

'Maybe it won't,' said Ron. 'We're not in any more danger here than we are at home, are we? Everywhere's the same now. I'd even say Hogwarts is safer, there are more wizards inside to defend the place. What d'you reckon, Harry?'

## 第30章 白色坟墓

"什么请求?噢,对了……叫我告诉全世界你们在从事多么了不起的工作,为了——"

"——为了提高大家的士气!"斯克林杰厉声说道。

哈利端详了他片刻。

"斯坦·桑帕克放出来了吗?"

斯克林杰的脸涨成了一种难看的酱紫色,哈利一下子想起了弗农姨父。

"看得出来,你——"

"彻头彻尾是邓布利多的人。"哈利说,"没错。"

斯克林杰又狠狠瞪了他几眼,然后一言不发地掉转身,一瘸一拐地走了。哈利看到珀西和魔法部代表团的其他成员都在等他,他们还不时担忧地望望仍然坐在座位上哭泣的海格和格洛普。罗恩和赫敏匆匆朝哈利走来,与迎面而去的斯克林杰擦肩而过。哈利转过身,慢慢地往前走,等着他们赶上来。最后,他们在一棵山毛榉树的绿荫下追上了哈利。在过去的好时光里,他们曾在这棵树下坐过。

"斯克林杰想干什么?"赫敏小声问。

"和圣诞节那次一样,"哈利耸了耸肩膀说,"希望我向他透露邓布利多的内部消息,并希望我充当魔法部新的形象大使。"

罗恩似乎在作激烈的思想斗争,然后他大声对赫敏说:"我决定了,我要回去把珀西揍一顿!"

"别。"赫敏一把抓住他的胳膊,坚决地说。

"那样我会好受一些!"

哈利笑出了声,就连赫敏也咧嘴笑了,不过她抬眼望望城堡,笑容隐去了。

"一想到我们也许再也不能回来,我就觉得受不了。"她轻声说,"霍格沃茨怎么可能关闭呢?"

"它也许不会关。"罗恩说,"我们在这里并不比在家里更危险,不是吗?现在到处都一样了。我倒认为霍格沃茨更安全些,有那么多巫师在里面保卫着这个地方。你说呢,哈利?"

## CHAPTER THIRTY  The White Tomb

'I'm not coming back even if it does reopen,' said Harry.

Ron gaped at him, but Hermione said sadly, 'I knew you were going to say that. But then what will you do?'

'I'm going back to the Dursleys' once more, because Dumbledore wanted me to,' said Harry. 'But it'll be a short visit, and then I'll be gone for good.'

'But where will you go if you don't come back to school?'

'I thought I might go back to Godric's Hollow,' Harry muttered. He had had the idea in his head ever since the night of Dumbledore's death. 'For me, it started there, all of it. I've just got a feeling I need to go there. And I can visit my parents' graves, I'd like that.'

'And then what?' said Ron.

'Then I've got to track down the rest of the Horcruxes, haven't I?' said Harry, his eyes upon Dumbledore's white tomb, reflected in the water on the other side of the lake. 'That's what he wanted me to do, that's why he told me all about them. If Dumbledore was right – and I'm sure he was – there are still four of them out there. I've got to find them and destroy them and then I've got to go after the seventh bit of Voldemort's soul, the bit that's still in his body, and I'm the one who's going to kill him. And if I meet Severus Snape along the way,' he added, 'so much the better for me, so much the worse for him.'

There was a long silence. The crowd had almost dispersed now, the stragglers giving the monumental figure of Grawp a wide berth as he cuddled Hagrid, whose howls of grief were still echoing across the water.

'We'll be there, Harry,' said Ron.

'What?'

'At your aunt and uncle's house,' said Ron. 'And then we'll go with you, wherever you're going.'

'No –' said Harry quickly; he had not counted on this, he had meant them to understand that he was undertaking this most dangerous journey alone.

'You said to us once before,' said Hermione quietly, 'that there was time to turn back if we wanted to. We've had time, haven't we?'

'We're with you whatever happens,' said Ron. 'But, mate, you're going to have to come round my mum and dad's house before we do anything else,

## 第30章 白色坟墓

"即使重新开学,我也不会回来了。"哈利说。

罗恩吃惊地瞪着他,赫敏悲哀地说:"我就知道你会这么说。可是你打算做什么呢?"

"我要再到德思礼家去一趟,因为邓布利多希望我这么做,"哈利说,"但时间不会很长,然后我就一去不回头了。"

"你不回来上学,准备去哪儿呢?"

"我想回一趟戈德里克山谷。"哈利低声说。从邓布利多去世的那个晚上起,他脑子里就盘算着这个念头。"对我来说,所有的一切都源于那里。我有一种感觉,我需要到那里去一趟。我还可以看看我父母的坟墓。"

"然后呢?"罗恩问。

"然后我就得去追查另外几个魂器的下落,不是吗?"哈利说,他望着邓布利多的白色坟墓在湖对岸水中投下的倒影,"他希望我这么做,为此才把这些都告诉了我。如果邓布利多是对的——我相信他是对的——现在还剩下四个魂器。我要把它们找到,一一销毁,然后我再去寻找伏地魔的第七个灵魂碎片,就是仍然存在于他身体里的那个,最后由我来结果他的性命。如果半路上碰到西弗勒斯·斯内普,"他又说道,"对我来说那再好不过,但他就要倒霉了。"

良久的沉默。人群差不多已经散光了,落在后面的人让出很大一块地方,让庞然大物般的格洛普搂抱着海格通过,海格的哀号声仍然在湖面上回荡。

"我们也去,哈利。"罗恩说。

"什么?"

"去你的姨妈姨父家,"罗恩说,"然后我们会一直陪着你,不管你去哪儿。"

"不行——"哈利赶紧说道。他没有料到这一点,他本来想让他们明白他准备一个人踏上这千难万险的旅途。

"你有一次对我们说过,"赫敏轻声说,"如果我们想后退,还来得及。我们曾经有时间考虑过这件事,是不是?"

"不管发生什么,我们都在你身边。"罗恩说,"可是,伙计,你必

CHAPTER THIRTY   The White Tomb

even Godric's Hollow.'

'Why?'

'Bill and Fleur's wedding, remember?'

Harry looked at him, startled; the idea that anything as normal as a wedding could still exist seemed incredible and yet wonderful.

'Yeah, we shouldn't miss that,' he said finally.

His hand closed automatically around the fake Horcrux, but in spite of everything, in spite of the dark and twisting path he saw stretching ahead for himself, in spite of the final meeting with Voldemort he knew must come, whether in a month, in a year, or in ten, he felt his heart lift at the thought that there was still one last golden day of peace left to enjoy with Ron and Hermione.

## 第30章 白色坟墓

须上我爸妈家来一趟，然后我们再开始做别的，包括去戈德里克山谷。"

"为什么？"

"比尔和芙蓉的婚礼啊，你忘记了？"

哈利不胜惊讶地望着他。世界上仍然存在婚礼这样平凡的事情，真是令人不可思议，同时也令人感到美妙无比。

"对啊，这是我们不应该错过的。"他最后说道。

他的手不由自主地握紧了那个假魂器，尽管种种的一切，尽管等待他的是一条漆黑而曲折的道路，尽管他知道最后——也许是一个月、一年或十年之后——他肯定要跟伏地魔面对面地较量，可是想到他仍然可以和罗恩、赫敏一起享受最后一个黄金般的平静日子，他就感到无比地愉快。

WIZARDING WORLD